PENGUIN  CLASSICS

FRENCH POETRY
1820–1950

William Rees grew up in Swansea and was educated at the Bishop Gore Grammar School. After a first degree at the University College of Wales, Aberystwyth, he continued his studies in modern French literature and theatre at the University of Exeter and at St Catherine's College, Oxford. Apart from a year spent at St Michael's University School in Canada, he has taught at Eton College, Windsor, since 1975 and is a housemaster there.

French Poetry

1820–1950

With prose translations

Selected, translated
and introduced by

WILLIAM REES

PENGUIN BOOKS

PENGUIN BOOKS

Published by the Penguin Group
27 Wrights Lane, London W8 5TZ, England
Viking Penguin Inc., 40 West 23rd Street, New York, New York 10010, USA
Penguin Books Australia Ltd, Ringwood, Victoria, Australia
Penguin Books Canada Ltd, 2801 John Street, Markham, Ontario, Canada L3R 1B4
Penguin Books (NZ) Ltd, 182–190 Wairau Road, Auckland 10, New Zealand

Penguin Books Ltd, Registered Offices: Harmondsworth, Middlesex, England

This selection first published 1990
1 3 5 7 9 10 8 6 4 2

The acknowledgements on pp. xxxvii–xli constitute an extension of this copyright page

Filmset in Bembo by
Morton Word Processing Ltd, Scarborough

Printed in England by Clays Ltd, St Ives plc

For Jane, Eleanor and Christopher

CONTENTS

ACKNOWLEDGEMENTS

I would like to thank, for their help and encouragement during this project: my colleague Jean-Paul Dubois, an invaluable linguistic sounding-board; the Librarians and their staff at the Taylor Institution, Oxford, and at the University of Victoria, British Columbia; Stuart John of UCW Aberystwyth, who kindled the spark long ago; Dr John Green of the University of Victoria, BC; Martin Hammond; Donald McFarlan; Paul Keegan; Nicholas Wetton, who cleared the permissions; Warren Brown of the Cirrus company, Victoria, BC; Dr Bernard McGuirk; the many friends and colleagues who have helped with references and obscurities of all kinds, including Dr Michael Atkinson, Philippe Delaveau, Dr Keith Gore, Christopher Robinson, Paul Quarrie, Dr Angela Slater, Dick Haddon, Anthony Ray, Dr Malcolm Smith-Walker, Dr Peter Cogman, John King, Dr Stephen Spurr, Fr Peter Knott SJ, Francis Dalvin and the late Revd Terence Davies; finally my wife Jane for her tireless proof-reading and support, and my children for their tolerance and their enthusiastic research assistance.

INTRODUCTION

France in the nineteenth and twentieth centuries offers an unusually rich and rewarding field for students and lovers of poetry. It is an intense battleground of diverse aesthetic ideas, and yet also presents fascinating lines of continuity and patterns of influence. Through Eliot and Pound above all, those influences have extended beyond the borders of France into the work of many modern poets writing in English. The immense reading assignment preceding the compilation of this book has been partly a labour of love, reopening all kinds of familiar and half-forgotten doors, but it has also revealed many new and unsuspected delights, and kindled many fresh enthusiasms.

This anthology of fifty-six poets writing in French between 1820 and 1950 departs a little from the Penguin tradition. Each set of poems is preceded by an introduction to their author, his life and his affinities, his aesthetics and his place in the evolution of poetry. Certain significant literary movements are also signalled and briefly characterized. The tendency of '-isms' to suck in individuals who deserve to be treated as individuals is well known, and I hope that patterns of adherence and independence are clear. If the book is read in chronological order, a pattern of development should emerge without the need for a lengthy historical preamble, and those who enter the world of French poetry at an arbitrary point should find enough signposts.

Before the challenge of translation can be met, the process of selection presents some stimulating – and sometimes agonizing – problems. Which poets, and why? Which poems, and why? Is it possible to determine universal and consistent criteria for choice, or must they be pragmatic? Should selection be on a 'greatest hits' basis, or should an editor consciously, even iconoclastically, seek less polished and less well-known works, juvenile and senile productions, and throw out the most prestigious items on the grounds that they can take care of themselves? Or is it important to represent all periods in a poet's career? Given both limited space and the awareness that such an anthology may have some influence in shaping literary perceptions, how is it possible to reconcile the claims of interesting 'minor' poets with the need to ensure an adequate and undistorted representation of the work of established giants? Should all literary movements be represented, however undistinguished or ephemeral? Should the maximum possible number of poets perhaps be included in a 'smorgasbord' approach that would provide no real landmarks, and no implicit evaluation? Where is the line to be drawn, if at all, in the incorporation of prose-poems?

There are many tightropes to be walked here. Experience has taught me that only the pragmatic approach works, for the conditions surrounding the editorial balancing act alter from poet to poet and period to period. Instinct and personal predilection must come into play, as well as an awareness of the judgements of posterity; enthusiasm and objectivity have to find a fresh working relationship in each individual case. To take as an example the question of representing all phases of a poet's career: only a masochist (or a dedicated researcher) would want to read now the verse which Lamartine or Musset trundled out long after the emotional traumas that produced their best work, or share Verlaine's descent into self-parodying mediocrity; it seems essential on the other hand to perceive the linear evolution of Laforgue or Rimbaud, and the imaginative breadth of Baudelaire or Apollinaire.

Many fine poets, of course, have had to be excluded. The names of a good number of them are mentioned in the chapters on Romanticism, on the Parnassians, on Symbolism, on Cubism, and on the Surrealists. Choices and compromises have to be made: Lautréamont, for example, must do duty for the whole satanic, self-destructive fringe of

Romanticism; Anna de Noailles and Catherine Pozzi, briefly, for the relative abundance of women poets in the early decades of this century; Cendrars for the cosmopolitan spirit of compulsive travelling (to the exclusion of Larbaud, a dilettante by comparison with Cendrars, whose work blazes like his name with love, anguish, irony, originality of perception and of technique). That dated and clumsy optimist of the age of technology, Jules Romains, is similarly eclipsed by the fire of Verhaeren's vision. And no doubt certain inclusions will be controversial, but sometimes it is important to include a poet scorned by some of his successors, yet whose work nevertheless is symptomatic of something interesting in his times.

In this comprehensive panorama of French poetry through a 130-year period, it has also been impossible to include some poets who had certainly established a reputation by 1950. This is the date at which I have drawn the line, allowing readers to see the emergence of Michaux, Ponge and Char as major and innovative post-war poets (1945, originally seen as an end-point, would have been less satisfactory, for it would have interrupted the linear development of poetry at a fairly low point in qualitative terms, however passionately felt much Resistance poetry undoubtedly is). There is, sadly, no room for Queneau, Follain, Tardieu, Guillevic, La Tour du Pin, Emmanuel, Albert-Birot, Bousquet, Mac Orlan, Daumal, Fombeure and others, in addition to those mentioned in my presentational chapters.

And of course this anthology has to stop short of an impressive list of fine contemporary poets who first captured major attention in the 1950s and '60s: Bonnefoy, Bosquet, Dadelsen, Deguy, du Bouchet, Dupin, Gaspar, Jabès, Jacottet, Mansour, Pleynet, Réda, Renard, Roubaud and others, whose work I hope readers will explore for themselves.[1]

[1]Valuable translations of some recent French poetry are to be found in anthologies by Paul Auster (*The Random House Book of Twentieth Century French Poetry*, published by Vintage Books) and by Graham Dunstan Martin (*Anthology of Contemporary French Poetry*, published by Edinburgh University Press and the University of Texas).

For some of them, poetry remains a means, an existential or spiritual quest; for others, it is an end in itself, a self-referential, Mallarmé-haunted, self-analytical play of language.

To avoid distorting the historical perception of the state of poetic composition, it also seemed logical to draw that 1950 line right across the board, even for those contemporary poets who have been included (the point is stretched only very slightly for Césaire's revised version of *Ode à la Guinée*, and for Char's *L'inoffensif* and *Front de la rose*).

Much has been written on the theory of translation, and I do not propose to add anything weighty to it. It is important, nevertheless, to comment on the practical strategy used here. The main purpose is to provide access to meaning by removing semantic barriers, and thus to accelerate the penetration of the poem itself by the non-French reader. My translations are, I hope, neither woodenly literal nor pretentiously literary. They seek neither to efface themselves nor to blur criteria by competing with the original for attention. Above all, they are intended as a service, and to excite interest in the original as a creative event.

The prose format implies a discipline in the rendering of sense which inhibits the verse-to-verse translator rather less, particularly if he is reshaping the original impulse into a new metrical and rhyming structure (reading of existing work in this field has convinced me that only a small number of gifted individuals can do this without producing distortion or bathos). Even so, if my translations are successful they are a step above the literal. They have decided rhythms and sound-patterns that please the ear, or at least do not displease it. They may occasionally even have a certain equivalent musicality. At times they interpret cautiously (Fargue's '*le trottoir tout gras de bouges*' is rendered as 'the pavement swilling with brothels'); and in places they modify syntax and grammar or translate one word by two (Baudelaire's smoking log sings 'in shrill discord' for '*en fausset*', with its falsetto and out-of-tune connotations), or two words by one. Every small liberty thus taken has emerged as the best solution after thorough componential analysis and consideration of more literal options, and I do not think any major liberties have been taken. I have tried at all times to balance my responsibilities to the reader with those I have to the poet, to find an intuitive blend of communicative and formal levels of equivalence, for a poem, as Claudel pointed out, is not just a bag of words.

As with selection policy, pragmatism dictates the outcome. Only with Mallarmé does a mainly literal approach often seem the most productive, and even there an occasional communicative adjustment is called for. In *Petit Air I*, for example, I have judged it right to add a word to clarify '*Au regard que j'abdiquai / Ici*' as 'in the gaze which I withdrew *Down* here'. In the same poem, despite the third-person endings of the verbs '*longe*' and '*plonge*', some translators have settled on '*toi*' as their subject. If, as I believe, '*ta jubilation nue*' is the subject, then '*devenue*' qualifies '*onde*'. Thus 'your naked jubilation' in English must come earlier in the sentence structure, and the waters subsequently mentioned '(have) become you' rather than any question of 'you having become your naked jubilation'.

It is of course much harder to take account of the semantic potential of rhythm and sound-patterns, but the effort must be made whenever possible. In Jammes' *Il va neiger*, for example, a subtle change of line-order at the end produces a soft, serene, feminine ending that contrasts with the clipped aggression in the opening quatrain, and in itself expresses the personal therapy that the poet has performed. It would be wrong to translate '*Qu'est-ce?*' by the crisp 't' sounds, for example, of 'What is it?' It may be possible to capture at least intermittently the railway-train rhythms of Cendrars or the kaleidoscopic effects of Apollinaire and Reverdy, and the supple rhythmic plasticity of the best Parnassian poetry, such as the movement of our eyes down the creepers or the progress of the animal through the jungle in Leconte de Lisle's *Le Rêve du Jaguar*. But when an experimental metre is itself part of the message, as it is in *Je ne sais pourquoi ...* by Verlaine or in Apollinaire's *La jolie rousse*, the translator is probably defeated – as he is, in a different way, by Hugo's *Demain, dès l'aube* ... In this beautifully understated poem, grief is projected concretely on to a lonely figure walking compulsively and rhythmically along a road. No close translation could do justice to the reinforcement of the dominant future tense by an insistent sound-pattern (the 'ai' sound, in various spellings, recurs fourteen times with further supportive assonance in a 12-line poem), and to the internal rhymes at rhythmically regular points. The sense that a destiny is operating here comes as much through musical versification as through images.

Ambiguities of sense have also been assessed individually: in some cases a happy equivalent can be found in English, in some I have expanded a word or phrase slightly to incorporate the ambiguity, in some I have resorted to an explanatory footnote, and in some I have simply decided to opt for one sense. Once again, the method here is pragmatic, and I hope renderings will be judged on their individual merits.

Except when absolutely necessary, I have not taken liberties with punctuation where the original poet has used it. For the translator into prose, however, a difficulty arises with the invention of free verse, and above all with the discovery by Cendrars, Apollinaire, Aragon and many others that a poem's spatial presence on the page can be enhanced and its resonance greatly expanded through the abolition of formal punctuation, and through a reliance on the internal dynamics of rhythm and pause to shape the phrases. It seems to me that translations which supply punctuation of their own for such material are intrusive, presumptuous and disrespectful of authorial intention. A partially satisfactory alternative is to use as a marker the capital letter with which many poets continue to begin each line, though of course proper names and 'I' cause a small degree of confusion that cannot be helped. Where the capital letter has also been abandoned, the oblique stroke has to serve as divider. These are, I hope, acceptable conventions.

Almost all drafts of translations could be reworked for

ever, unlike finished poems. Those privileged moments when the translator feels entirely satisfied with a piece of work are rare, and are more than counterbalanced by the usual awareness that, like Gautier, he is chipping away doggedly at a resistant marble block, gaining intermittent fulfilment in pursuit of something ideal. But decisions have to be made, final versions have to be typed to meet the deadline, though he would love to go on moulding them *ad infinitum*. As Ernest Hemingway pointed out, the typewriter sometimes fixes words before they're ready to be fixed, but if these translations are offered now as a vehicle to carry the reader into the marvellous domain of French poetry, I hope that the journey will not be an uncomfortable one.

W. H. Rees

TECHNICALITIES

Invented in the twelfth century and named after Alexandre de Bernay, one of its first exponents, the 12-syllable *Alexandrine* verse line came to dominate French poetry from the middle of the seventeenth century, and classically educated Frenchmen have it in their bloodstream still today. Indeed, despite the proliferation of other metrical forms and the breakdown of regular structure into *vers libres* and the Claudelian *verset* at the end of the nineteenth century, the Alexandrine has a remarkably tenacious hold on French poets. It often appears still, sometimes openly, sometimes in semi-disguise within the rhythms that give modern verse composition and prose-poetry their shape and dynamics.

In its classical form, the Alexandrine is end-stopped by punctuation, and divided in half by a *caesura*, which is a pause both formal and natural, whether punctuated or not. Each half is called a *hemistich*. This line is an ideal expression of intellectual balance, symmetry and wholeness, of thesis, antithesis and implied synthesis. In the hands of Racine, probably its greatest exponent, it is the perfect form for the expression of tragic dilemma. Established in his time as the prescriptive model, it became in the eighteenth century (a bleak period in the history of French poetry) a hollow shell, which the Romantics were to crack, if not break, in the post-Napoleonic period. They experimented with new positions for the caesura and were particularly successful with their more musical *Alexandrin trimètre*, or threefold division of the line, as in: '*Je marcherai les yeux fixés sur mes pensées*' (Hugo). Nevertheless, Hugo continued to make memorable use of the *Alexandrin classique* for balanced antithesis, often incorporating syntactic inversion or chiasmus: '*Ces murs maudits par Dieu, par Satan profanés*'.

There have always been lines of fewer syllables than 12, of course, but rarely more than 12 until Laforgue effectively invented free verse, and rarely an uneven number of syllables. The haunting, lyrical *Impair* line of 5, 7, 9 or 11 units, extolled and demonstrated beautifully by Verlaine above all, suggests to the French intellect and instinct even today a frustrating lack of shape, balance, precision and finality, and it is interesting that the most fastidious and self-conscious perfectionists among the poets, Mallarmé and Valéry, rarely used it.

Lamartine brings to the Alexandrine some fluidity and elegiac musicality, with soft consonants and mellow assonance, gently modifying old conventions. In line two of *Le Lac*, for example, he makes a very smooth *elision* immediately after the central caesura:

Dans la nuit éternelle emportés sans retour

This sliding of the last vowel of '*éternelle*' into the first vowel of '*emportés*' effectively dilutes the stress that would normally come at the sixth syllable, before the pause, and creates a mellifluous 12-syllable unit to be spoken in one breath. He follows it with an 18-syllable unit that brings added force and poignancy to his metaphor:

Ne pourrons-nous jamais sur l'océan des ages
  Jeter l'ancre un seul jour?

To create an effect of emotion welling up, he is using here the technique of *enjambement* ('striding over' or 'encroaching'). Hugo and the other Romantics, and then the Parnassians, were to find in this a major instrument of rhythmic and metrical flexibility. There are two types of *enjambement*, which is the overflowing of a phrase from one line to the next in a suppression of end-stopping punctuation. Its effect is often to delay or hasten stress, and to attenuate the force of rhyme.

(a) Enjambement with a *rejet*: where the extra element is in the line following the main bulk of the whole unit, as in:

En un creux du bois sombre interdit au soleil
Il s'affaisse, ...

(Leconte de Lisle)

Here the poet represents rhythmically the sinking down of a jaguar at the end of its journey back to its lair.

(b) Enjambement with a *contre-rejet*: where the extra element is in the line preceding the main bulk of the whole unit, as in:

Le jeune Cellini, sans rien voir, ciselait
Le combat des Titans au pommeau d'une dague.

(Heredia)

Or in:

Pour n'être pas changés en bêtes, ils s'enivrent
D'espace et de lumière et de cieux embrasés.

(Baudelaire)

Musset brings a more intimate and colloquial tone to the 12-syllable line, but Nerval constructs his evocative private mythology using *alexandrins classiques* almost exclusively. Hugo experiments with other metrical forms, but the Alexandrine reimposes itself continually on his work. *Fenêtres ouvertes* is an attempt by him at literary Impressionism but, despite the apparent fragmentation, it is revealed, when scanned, to be in Alexandrines. The same will apply, very much more powerfully, to Aragon's magnificent 1940 poem, *Les lilas et les roses*, which filters the poet's overwhelming emotion at the fall of France through a 'whirlwind' of surreal visual correlatives, in a superficially chaotic, unpunctuated, torrential stream of consciousness that ends arbitrarily. The rhythm breathes in and out as emotion surges in excitement or panic or subsides in unhappy peace. But not only does the poem rhyme, it is also written in Alexandrines and most of them are classical. Thus the poem *is* what it celebrates and pledges to continue: the spirit and historical continuity of French culture.

Baudelaire uses a variety of forms, but his finest talent probably lies in the sonnet in Alexandrines. In his hands it is a vibrant object, bursting with compressed imaginative and emotional energy, with which he works a sensuous magic and gives to the poem the status of an event. The best Parnassian poetry continues to operate within the Alexandrine, enhancing its three-dimensional concrete images with supple rhythms. In *Le Rêve du Jaguar*, again, Leconte de Lisle makes the jungle creepers hang, suspended on the isolated conjunction '*et*', before their 9-syllable spiralling plunge. The jaguar's motion is given majesty by the isolated two-stress phrase '*Il va*', before the powerfully rhythmical and internally rhyming 10-syllable unit, '*frottant ses reins musculeux qu'il bossue*', which is almost English in its stress pattern.

It is important for the inexperienced reader to grasp the essential facts that French scansion is a matter of syllable-counting, and that *stress* in the English sense is very intermittent and very much attenuated in French verse. There are points in the line where a syllable will certainly be *accented*: in the *Alexandrin classique* these are the 6th and 12th, in such a way that the final word of each hemistich is likely to be a key element in what is being communicated. In the *Alexandrin trimètre* the 4th, 8th and 12th syllables will be most heavily accented (in so far as stress in French verse could ever be described as 'heavy'), though the displaced caesuras are weaker than their classical counterparts.

It is in a sense more 'monotonous' than English poetry, lacking a thumping regular dynamic, but it achieves tonal variety through subtle action of sound-patterns (mainly assonance) and subtle interplay through pitch, tempo and syntactic position of the subordinate stresses that certainly do exist and do bring into relief other syllables in the line.

In the decasyllabic line (as used, for example, by Valéry in *Le Cimetière marin*), the caesura comes most often after the 4th syllable, though a 6/4 division also occurs, and there are a few poems with a 5/5 division. The octosyllable usually divides 4/4 if it divides at all, and in some of Mallarmé's most enigmatic verse the caesura could be at any one of several points in the line.

In the absence of a strong metrical pulse, it is perhaps not surprising that in the evolution of poetry the French have found it harder than the English to dispense with rhyme, a strong unifying factor.

It is also essential to know that a mute 'e' in an orthodox line of French verse is counted as a syllable, except:

(a) when it ends the line.

(b) when followed by a vowel (or silent *h*) which starts the next word, if there is no intervening '*-s*' or '*-nt*' ending. If we consider again the two Baudelaire lines already quoted:

> Pour n'être pas changés en bêtes, ils s'enivrent
> D'espace et de lumière et de cieux embrasés,

we can see that the second syllable of *être* and of *bêtes* is counted, and the 'e' at the end of *espace* and *lumière* is not. The *-ent* of *enivrent* is a mute 'e', and is not counted.

There are elaborately detailed classical rules governing the use of the mute 'e' with other vowels and in elisions, as there are on *hiatus* (the juxtaposition of sounded vowels belonging to different syllables). They need not detain us in an anthology beginning at 1820, though they were applied rigorously during the two previous centuries.

Gautier, the Parnassians, Mallarmé and, later, Valéry were attracted by *difficulty* as an essential part of the creative process, and resisted the liberation offered by the Verlainian *Impair* line and of modernist *vers libres*. They enjoyed the challenge of turning shackles into virtues and singing in their chains.

But the trustful and very French assumption that ordered, declamatory language could satisfactorily express ordered perceptions, feelings and concepts broke down around 1870. Through Verlaine and Corbière to an extent, Rimbaud and Laforgue much more powerfully, the Alexandrine began to receive body-blows. The surges and rests of rhythm became progressively more important than metre, as new free verse forms emerged. These are discussed in the chapters on Laforgue, Claudel, Apollinaire, Cendrars, Perse and others. As we have seen, however, the Alexandrine has certainly remained alive in spite of a great relaxation in the old rules of rhyme and scansion, and no more so than in the fascinating interplay between nostalgia for literary '*Ordre*' and the new spirit of '*Aventure*' in Apollinaire's *La jolie rousse*. Let us consider these five lines:

Vous dont la bouche est faite à l'image de celle de Dieu
Bouche qui est l'ordre même
Soyez indulgents quand vous nous comparez
A ceux qui furent la perfection de l'ordre
Nous qui quêtons partout l'aventure

The first line, technically 15 syllables, is virtually an Alexandrine if spoken with the antipedantic colloquial rhythm favoured by Apollinaire. Line two has 7 syllables, but 6 if it is spoken colloquially. Line three, referring to the modernists, clearly has 11 syllables. The scansion of line four is debatable, but it should I think be read as an Alexandrine, if not a classical one. The 9-syllable fifth line is emphatically, provocatively modern, even though its first 6 syllables form a classical hemistich. Lines one, two and four thus pay homage to Apollinaire's literary ancestors with their metre as much as with the ideas they contain, once we penetrate the surface appearance of metrical anarchy. Lines three and five are already grasping the expressive freedom Apollinaire is demanding to deal with the more unformed flux of modern sensory and intellectual experience.

Finally, some notes on *rhyme*. Though in recent times almost anything has become possible, the essential, traditional definitions of types and patterns of rhyme need to be presented here:

Masculine rhyme: a line not ending in a mute syllable. Redefined by Apollinaire as an oral or nasal vowel,˙ followed by an unpronounced consonant.

Feminine rhyme: a line ending in a mute syllable. Redefined by Apollinaire as a pronounced consonant, with or without a following mute 'e'.

Traditional principles dictate that two different masculine or two different feminine rhymes cannot succeed one another, and also that masculine and feminine endings cannot rhyme together. Apollinaire's modification, however, allows words traditionally incompatible to rhyme together, e.g. *ciel - querelles*, *sommeil - vermeille*.

Rime faible: vowel alone, not much more than assonance, e.g. *parlé - écouté*, *choisi - noirci*.

Rime suffisante: vowel plus consonant or vice versa, e.g. *attrapé - trompé*, *sure - aventure*.

Rime riche: three elements, comprising the rhyming syllable plus a supporting extra consonant (the *consonne d'appui*), e.g. *nombre - pénombre*, *verte - ouverte*, *rêne - arêne*, *hautaines - capitaines*.

This form of rhyming has been little used since the Symbolists rejected it as cloying and ostentatious.

Rimes croisées: ababcdcd.
Rimes plates: aabbccdd.
Rimes embrassées: abbacddc.
Rimes mêlées: no regular scheme.
Rimes redoublées: recurrence of the same rhyme in more than two lines.

For a valuable extended insight into the form of French verse, and an analysis of its organic relationship with emotion, image and idea, see *The Appreciation of Modern French Poetry* by P. Broome and G. Chesters (published by Cambridge University Press), a companion volume to their *Anthology of Modern French Poetry 1850–1950*. See also two highly illuminating books by Clive Scott: *French Verse Art: a study* and *A Question of Syllables* (both published by Cambridge University Press).

SOURCES AND ACKNOWLEDGEMENTS

The publishers would like to thank copyright holders for permission to reprint the following:

LOUIS ARAGON: to Editions Gallimard for 'Les lilas et les roses' from *Le Crève-Coeur*, copyright 1941 by Editions Gallimard and Louis Aragon; to Editions Robert Laffont for 'Elsa au miroir' and 'Ballade de celui qui chanta dans les supplices'.

ANDRE BRETON: to Editions Gallimard for 'L'Union libre', 'Tournesol', 'Vigilance' and 'Sur la route de San Romano' from *Clair de terre*, copyright © Editions Gallimard, 1966.

BLAISE CENDRARS: to Editions Denoël for 'Prose du Transsibérien et de la petite Jeanne de France', 'Contrastes', 'Construction', 'Orion', 'Mississippi' and 'Aube' from *Du monde entier*, copyright 1947 by Editions Denoël.

AIME CESAIRE: to Editions Gallimard for 'N'ayez point pitié', 'Soleil serpent', 'Perdition', 'Prophétie' and 'Tam-tam I' from *Les Armes miraculeuses,* copyright 1946 by Editions Gallimard.

RENE CHAR: to Editions Gallimard for 'Chant du refus' and 'Les premiers instants' from *Fureur et mystère* (1948), new edition 1967, copyright © Editions Gallimard, 1967; 'A***' from *Recherche de la base et du sommet* (1955), new and revised edition 1965, copyright © Editions Gallimard, 1965; 'L'inoffensif' and 'Front de la rose' from *La Parole en archipel* (1962), new edition 1986, copyright © Editions Gallimard, 1986; to Librairie José Corti for 'Artine', 'Migration' and 'Commune Présence' from *Le Marteau sans maître*, copyright 1934 by Librairie José Corti.

PAUL CLAUDEL: to Editions Gallimard for 'Ballade' from *Corona Benignitatis Anni Dei* copyright 1915 by Editions Gallimard; 'La Muse qui est la Grâce' and 'L'Esprit et l'Eau' from *Cinq grandes Odes*, copyright 1913 by Editions Gallimard.

ROBERT DESNOS: to Librairie Grund for 'Le Zèbre' from *Chantefables et chantefleurs*, Librairie Grund, Paris; to Editions Gallimard for 'J'ai tant rêvé de toi' (from 'A la Mystérieuse'), 'La Voix de Robert Desnos' and 'Desespoir du soleil' from *Corps et biens*, copyright 1930 by Editions Gallimard; 'Destinée arbitraire' from *Destinée arbitraire*, copyright © Editions Gallimard, 1975; 'Mi-Route' from *Fortunes*, copyright 1942 by Editions Gallimard; and 'Le Paysage' from *Calixto*, copyright © Editions Gallimard, 1962.

PAUL ELUARD: to Editions de Minuit for 'Faire vivre' from *Au rendez-vous allemand*; to Editions Robert Laffont for 'La Mort l'Amour la Vie' from *Le Phénix*; to Editions Gallimard for 'L'Amoureuse' (from *Mourir de ne pas mourir*), 'La courbe de tes yeux' (from *Capitale de la douleur*), 'Le front aux vitres' (from *l'Amour la poésie)*, 'A perte de vue dans le sens de mon corps' (from *La Vie immédiate*), 'Tu te lèves' (from *Facile*), 'La victoire de Guernica' (from *Cours naturel*), and 'La terre est bleue comme une orange ...' from *Oeuvres complètes*, vol. I, copyright © Editions Gallimard, 1968.

LEON-PAUL FARGUE: to Editions Gallimard for 'Sur le trottoir tout gras' and 'La rampe s'allume' from *Poésies*, copyright © Editions Gallimard, 1963; 'Postface' and 'La Gare' from *Sous la Lampe*, copyright 1929 by Editions Gallimard.

PAUL FORT: to Editions Flammarion for 'Complainte du Roi et de la Reine', 'La grande Ivresse', 'La Grenouille bleue' and 'L'Eçureuil'.

ANDRE FRENAUD: to Editions Gallimard for 'Naissance', 'Maison à vendre' and 'Les Rois Mages' from *Les Rois Mages (1938–1943)*, copyright © Editions Gallimard, 1977; 'Présence réelle' from *Il n'y a pas de paradis: Poèmes 1943–1960*, copyright © Editions Gallimard, 1962; 'Assèchement de la plaie' from *La Sainte Face*, copyright © Editions Gallimard, 1968.

MAX JACOB: to Editions Gallimard for 'La Guerre', 'Dans la forêt silencieuse', 'Ruses du Démon pour ravoir sa proie' and 'Août 39' from *Le cornet à dés*, vols. I (1945) and II (1955), copyright © Editions Gallimard, 1955; 'Etablissement d'une communauté au Brésil' from *Le Laboratoire central*, copyright © Editions Gallimard, 1960; 'Présence de Dieu' from *Derniers poèmes en vers et en prose*, copyright 1945 by Editions Gallimard.

FRANCIS JAMMES: to Mercure de France for 'J'aime dans les temps...', 'Prière pour aller au Paradis avec les ânes', 'Les cinq Mystères douloureux' and 'Il va neiger'.

PIERRE-JEAN JOUVE: to Editions Mercure de France for 'Vallée de larmes', 'Vrai Corps', 'L'Oeil et la chevelure', 'Lamentations au cerf', 'La Femme et la terre', 'Je suis succession furieuse', 'Angles' and 'A soi-même'.

HENRI MICHAUX: (in French) to Editions Gallimard for 'Mes Occupations' (from *Mes Propriétés*), 'Crier' (from *Mes Propriétés*), 'Emportez-moi' (from *Mes Propriétés*), 'Le grand Violon' (from *Lointain intérieur*), 'Clown' (from *Peintures*) and 'Dragon' (from *Peintures*) from *L'Espace du dedans (1927–1959)*, revised edition, copyright © Editions Gallimard, 1966; 'Portrait des Meidosems' from *La Vie dans les plis*, copyright 1949 by Editions Gallimard; and 'Après ma Mort' from *Epreuves, exorcismes*, copyright 1945 by Editions Gallimard; (in English) to New Directions Publishing Corporation for 'Mes Occupations', 'Le grand Violon', 'Clown' and 'Dragon' from *Selected Writings*, copyright © New Directions Publishing Corporation, 1968.

OSCAR VLADISLAS DE LUBICZ MILOSZ: to Editions André Silvaire for 'Quand elle viendra...' and 'Aux sons d'une musique ...' from *Les Sept Solitudes* (*Poésies* I and *Oeuvres complètes*); and 'Cantique de la connaissance' from *La Confession de Lemuel* (*Poésies* II and *Oeuvres complètes*).

SAINT-JOHN PERSE: to the Fondation Saint-John Perse and Editions Gallimard for 'Eloges II and XIV' from *Eloges*, copyright 1911 by Editions Gallimard; 'Anabase VII' from *Anabase*, copyright 1924 by Editions Gallimard; 'Exil II' from *Exil*, copyright 1945 by Editions Gallimard; 'Neiges IV' from *Neiges*, copyright 1945 by Editions Gallimard; and 'Vents: Chant II, i' from *Vents*, copyright 1946 by Editions Gallimard.

FRANCIS PONGE: to Editions Gallimard for 'Les Mûres', 'L'Orange' and 'Végétation' from *Le Parti pris des choses*, copyright 1942 by Editions Gallimard.

JACQUES PREVERT: to Editions Gallimard for 'Le Cancre', 'Familiale', 'Déjeuner du matin', 'L'Ordre nouveau' and 'Barbara' from *Paroles*, copyright 1949 by Editions Gallimard; 'Sanguine' from *Spectacle*, copyright 1951 by Editions Gallimard.

PIERRE REVERDY: to Editions Mercure de France for 'Couloir', 'Chauffage central', 'Drame', 'Les Mots qu'on échange', 'X' and 'Chair vive'; to Editions Flammarion for 'Après le Bal', 'Toujours là', 'Auberge' and 'Nomade' from *Plupart du temps*.

SAINT-POL ROUX: to Rougerie Editeur for 'Golgotha' from *Tablettes*, copyright © Rougerie, 1986; 'Alouettes' from *Les Reposoirs de la procession*, vol. I, copyright © Rougerie, 1980; 'La Carafe d'eau pure' from *Les Reposoirs de la procession*, vol. III, copyright © Rougerie, 1981.

LEOPOLD SEDAR SENGHOR: to Editions du Seuil for 'Femme noire' and 'Camp 1940' from *Poèmes*, copyright © Editions du Seuil, 1984.

PHILIPPE SOUPAULT: to the author for 'Dimanche', 'La grande Mélancolie d'une avenue', 'Say it with music' and 'Stumbling' from *Poèmes et poésies*.

JULES SUPERVIELLE: (in French) to Editions Gallimard for 'Montévidéo' and 'Haute mer' from *Gravitations*, copyright 1925 by Editions Gallimard; 'Tristesse de Dieu' and 'Nuit en moi, nuit au dehors' from *La Fable du monde*, copyright 1938 by Editions Gallimard; 'Plein Ciel' and '1940' from *Choix de poèmes*, copyright 1947 by Editions Gallimard; 'Les Poissons' from *Les Amis inconnus*, copyright 1934 by Editions Gallimard; 'Dans la forêt sans heures' from *Le Forcat innocent*, copyright 1930 by Editions Gallimard; (in English) to New Directions Publishing Corporation for 'Montévidéo', 'Tristesse de Dieu', 'Nuit en moi, nuit au dehors', 'Plein Ciel' and 'Dans la forêt sans heures' from *Selected Writings*, copyright © New Directions Publishing Corporation, 1967.

TRISTAN TZARA: to Editions Flammarion for 'La grande complainte de mon obscurité trois', 'La Mort de Guillaume Apollinaire', 'Sur une ride du soleil' and 'Volt'.

PAUL VALERY: (in French) to Editions Gallimard for 'La Fileuse' and 'Le Bois amical' from *Album de vers anciens*, copyright 1929 by Editions Gallimard; 'Au platane', 'L'Abeille', 'Les Pas', 'L'Insinuant', 'Les Grenades' and 'Le Cimetière marin' from *Charmes*, copyright 1922 by Editions Gallimard; (in English) to Routledge & Kegan Paul Ltd and Princeton University Press for 'Au platane', 'L'Abeille', 'Les pas', 'L'Insinuant', 'Les Grenades' and 'Le Cimetière marin' from *The Collected Works in English*, Bollingen Series 45, Vol. 1: *Poems*, translated by David Paul, copyright © Princeton University Press, 1971.

The publishers regret that their attempts to contact the copyright holders of poems by Louis Aragon ('Poème à crier dans les ruines'), Aimé Césaire ('Ode à la Guinée') and Maurice Maeterlinck have been unsuccessful. Due acknowledgement will gladly be made in later editions if the relevant information is forthcoming.

Romanticism in France

The Romantic movement brought a liberation of artistic creativity from universal standards and prescriptive constraints, so that artistic form became a more organic product of the intuitive and imaginative life of the artist. The new spirit encouraged a preoccupation with the self, its sensibilities, its sufferings and its dreams; with love, its ecstasies, its uncertainties and its torments; with time, death and eternity. It conceived the natural world as a double mirror reflecting both the will of God and the temperament of man, and thus the medium through which the two commune. It brought into the light again those cultural links with the medieval past that had remained buried through the neo-classical era. Its wilder exponents began to probe the irrational, the demonic, revealing an unhealthy morbidity in addition to a certain emotional masochism in the interests of art (an alternative tyranny for the liberated), and an increasingly unbridgeable gap developed between the artist and the 'philistine' middle classes. The paralysis that is the product of unrealizable dreams engendered nervous tension and mental disorder in some cases, and even a deliberate embracing of evil as the outcast's road to the infinite.

All of this, because of Revolution, Terror and war, came later to France than to England and Germany, and the first French Romantics were able to draw from those other literary springs. They read Heine and Hoffmann with enthusiasm, they imitated the renewal of contact in those other cultures with a native lyrical and epic tradition, they followed the Lake Poets in discovering a new pantheistic mysticism in solitary contemplation of Nature, and they identified Werther, Faust and Lord Byron as archetypal heroes.

The Romantics cracked the mould that had previously

constricted and refined the subject-matter of poetry. They learned how to reach a wide new audience through an enfranchised press and publishing industry, and poetry became a popular art form after perhaps two centuries as a plaything of the socio-intellectual élite. Individual spirituality, the natural world in its elemental being, the exotic, the occult, adolescent passions and frustrations, dreams and nightmares, the sublime and the grotesque of city life, all these now surged up as the currency of poetry, and the new young public was electrified.

Coupled necessarily with this liberation of subject-matter came an equally dynamic expansion of the verbal range open to the poet, and a relaxation of rhetoric. Later in the century Rimbaud and Laforgue would propel this revolution towards completion, but the Romantics certainly opened the way to modernism. A formerly rarefied sphere was invaded by both exotic and popular terminology, and by the realism of concrete nouns and adjectives. An invigorating verbosity reigned for a time until first Nerval and then Baudelaire demonstrated the rich connotative potential of dynamic concision.

In versification the long-established Alexandrine (12-syllable) line remained dominant, but the Romantics gave it some rhythmic suppleness by mobilizing and sometimes multiplying the *caesura*[1] and by frequent use of *enjambement*.[1] These techniques subverted the intellectual symmetry inherent in the classical Alexandrine line, with its strict mid-point caesura and its end-stopped wholeness, in favour of a more fluid reproduction of the ebb and flow of feelings and ideas. The new poets unveiled the musical potential of language, promoting assonance and internal rhyme to complement these more natural rhythms, and to draw the reader's sensibility more fully into the poem. Poetry became more intuitive in both creation and reception, as form and content found a more organic relationship, and a more sub-

[1]See Technicalities, page xxix and xxx.

liminal use of language was initiated that would be perfected by Verlaine in the late 1860s. Baudelaire, for his part, would develop the Romantic intimation that we live in a forest of mysterious and interconnected signs. He senses that their significance can be glimpsed as yet only intermittently by the artist's receptive soul, but their vast harmonious beauty is to be revealed progressively in the future.

As the Romantic movement developed in the 1830s and 1840s, there was a clear divergence in the ranks of what had always been in any case a loose-knit group of individuals rather than a cohesive school. Some, notably Hugo, Lamartine and Vigny, saw the poet as an integrated element in society, a responsible seer and spokesman for the people, with a role to play in socio-political progress. This reformist yet 'bourgeois' conception was rejected with increasing vehemence and contempt by those who were disillusioned with politics and for whom art had become a superior form of existence with no utilitarian application. A first generation of '*maudits*' (Musset, Nerval, Borel, Forneret, Bertrand) began to scandalize the middle classes by their appearance, their morals, their aesthetics and their despair. Many more visionary outcasts would later follow the anti-social path, compensating for their sense of exile by an increasingly 'occult' view of poetic creativity as a magical operation.

A third attitude, that of pure, sober, undemonstrative dedication to art as both craft and sublime activity, and as the only value worth considering in life, was to be struck by Gautier, by the Parnassians, and by Mallarmé and his disciples. These poets too would have regarded any political 'engagement' as a prostitution of their gifts.

Some poets of the Romantic period for whom there is no room in this anthology, but of interest to students of the movement: Casimir Delavigne, Auguste Barbier, Auguste Brizeux, Félix Arvers, Maurice de Guérin.

The following group might be called the 'wild bunch' of socially rebellious, even rather satanic poets. Their work is uneven, sometimes visionary and 'automatic', prompting the interest of the Surrealists nearly a century later: Aloysius Bertrand (a prose poet), Xavier Forneret, Pétrus Borel, Philothée O'Neddy (an anagram of Théophile Dondey), Alphonse Esquiros.

Alphonse de Lamartine
(1790–1869)

Lamartine was born into a Royalist and devout family. A solitary and sensitive youth whose health was poor, he read widely in English, German and classical literature, and was strongly influenced by the writings of Rousseau and Chateaubriand, together with the stimulus given to French Romanticism by the intellectual activity of Madame de Staël. He travelled to Italy (a *sine qua non* for Romantic poets) in 1811–12, and was an aide to Louis XVIII during the brief Bourbon restoration before Waterloo.

The major love affair of his life, which gave rise to his finest work, began in 1816 at Aix-les-Bains. His relationship with Madame Julie Charles was brief, idyllic and tragic. She died of tuberculosis in December 1817.

Finding some consolation in religion and in contemplation of Nature, he composed the *Méditations poétiques*. Published in 1820, this volume brought him rapid success, especially among young readers who responded to his new personal and spiritual note; but its quality was rarely matched in his later verse, which is more epic and philosophical in character. He moved via diplomacy into politics, and from the Catholic conservatism of his youth to a moderate and reformist Republican stance characterized by consistent idealism. He was a *député* from 1833, and headed the government briefly during the turbulent events of 1848, but lost popular support and ended his life in poverty, something of a literary hack.

His elegiac *Méditations*, with their aspiration to eternity and their atmosphere of muted grief, suggest a strong intuitive relationship with Nature and with God. While the poet-craftsman still works in an essentially classical mode of versification, the sensitive soul finds a new musical expression of its longings and its pain. Memory is associated evocatively with place, in the creation of a '*paysage intérieur*' through soft alliteration, mellow fluidity of vowel sounds, and gentle variations on a semi-soporific Alexandrine rhythm. Though it is possible to view him as a transitional figure, Lamartine's place as the first Romantic poet in France seems assured by a sustained tone of unaffected pathos, by harmony of form and content, and by his thematic emphases on love and loss and on the natural as a mirror of the divine. The influence of his musicality was later to be acknowledged by Verlaine and the Symbolists.

Le Lac

Ainsi, toujours poussés vers de nouveaux rivages,
Dans la nuit éternelle emportés sans retour,
Ne pourrons-nous jamais sur l'océan des âges
    Jeter l'ancre un seul jour?

O lac! l'année à peine a fini sa carrière,
Et près des flots chéris qu'elle devait revoir
Regarde! je viens seul m'asseoir sur cette pierre
    Où tu la vis s'asseoir!

The Lake

And so, driven on ceaselessly towards new shores, carried beyond return into eternal darkness, shall we never cast anchor for a single day in the ocean of time?

O lake! the year has scarce run its course, and by the cherished waves that she was meant to see again, see now! I come alone to sit upon this stone where you saw her sit!

Tu mugissais ainsi sous ces roches profondes;
Ainsi tu te brisais sur leurs flancs déchirés:
Ainsi le vent jetait l'écume de tes ondes
  Sur ses pieds adorés.

Un soir, t'en souvient-il? nous voguions en silence;
On n'entendait au loin, sur l'onde et sous les cieux,
Que le bruit des rameurs qui frappaient en cadence
  Tes flots harmonieux.

Tout à coup des accents inconnus à la terre
Du rivage charmé frappèrent les échos;
Le flot fut attentif, et la voix qui m'est chère
  Laissa tomber ces mots:

"O temps, suspends ton vol! et vous, heures propices,
  Suspendez votre cours!
Laissez-nous savourer les rapides délices
  Des plus beaux de nos jours!

Then as now you moaned beneath these plunging rocks; you broke against their jagged flanks; the wind sprayed the foam of your waves on her beloved feet.

One evening, do you remember? we were sailing in silence, hearing over the waters and beneath the heavens only the distant rhythmic beat of oarsmen on your harmonious waves.

Suddenly a voice, its strains unknown on earth, struck echoes from the enchanted shore; the waters listened, and that precious voice let fall these words:

'O time, suspend your flight! and you, fortunate hours, stay your journey! Let us savour the fleeting delights of the finest of our days!

"Assez de malheureux ici-bas vous implorent:
Coulez, coulez pour eux;
Prenez avec leurs jours les soins qui les dévorent;
Oubliez les heureux.

"Mais je demande en vain quelques moments encore,
Le temps m'échappe et fuit;
Je dis à cette nuit: "Sois plus lente"; et l'aurore
Va dissiper la nuit.

"Aimons donc, aimons donc! de l'heure fugitive,
Hâtons-nous, jouissons!
L'homme n'a point de port, le temps n'a point de rive;
Il coule, et nous passons!"

Temps jaloux, se peut-il que ces moments d'ivresse,
Où l'amour à longs flots nous verse le bonheur,
S'envolent loin de nous de la même vitesse
Que les jours de malheur?

Enough unhappy beings here below invoke you: flow on, flow on for them; remove their consuming cares as you take away their days; forget the happy ones.

But I ask in vain for a few moments more, time escapes me and slips away; I say to this night: "Pass more slowly"; and dawn will soon dissolve the night.

Let us love then, let us love! be quick to enjoy the fleeting hour! Mankind has no harbour, time has no shore; it flows, and we pass on!'

Jealous time, can it be that these intoxicating moments, when love pours happiness into us in long draughts, fly far from us as swiftly as days of misery?

Hé quoi! n'en pourrons-nous fixer au moins la trace?
Quoi! passés pour jamais? quoi! tout entiers perdus?
Ce temps qui les donna, ce temps qui les efface,
Ne nous les rendra plus?

Éternité, néant, passé, sombres abîmes,
Que faites-vous des jours que vous engloutissez?
Parlez: nous rendrez-vous ces extases sublimes
Que vous nous ravissez?

O lac! rochers muets! grottes! forêt obscure!
Vous que le temps épargne ou qu'il peut rajeunir,
Gardez de cette nuit, gardez, belle nature,
Au moins le souvenir!

Qu'il soit dans ton repos, qu'il soit dans tes orages,
Beau lac, et dans l'aspect de tes riants coteaux,
Et dans ces noirs sapins, et dans ces rocs sauvages
Qui pendent sur tes eaux!

What! can we not grasp and hold at least their impression? What! gone for ever? What! entirely lost? Will time that gave them, time that effaces them, never give them back to us?

Eternity, nothingness, past, dark chasms, what do you do with the days that you engulf? Speak: will you give back those sublime ecstasies that you steal from us?

O lake! wordless rocks! caves! dark forest! You who are untouched or made young again by time, cherish, fair nature, cherish at least the memory of that night!

Let it be in your calmness, let it be in your storms, lovely lake, and in the face of your laughing hillsides, and in these black pines, and in these wild rocks that overhang your waters!

Qu'il soit dans le zéphyr qui frémit et qui passe,
Dans les bruits de tes bords par tes bords répétés,
Dans l'astre au front d'argent qui blanchit ta surface
De ses molles clartés!

Que le vent qui gémit, le roseau qui soupire,
Que les parfums légers de ton air embaumé,
Que tout ce qu'on entend, l'on voit ou l'on respire,
Tout dise: "Ils ont aimé!"

Let it be in the zephyr which trembles and passes on, in the sounds of your shores which your shores re-echo, in the silver-browed star which whitens your surface with its soft glimmer!

Let the moaning wind, the sighing reed, the gentle scents of your fragrant air, let all that is heard, seen or breathed, let all say: 'They loved!'

Le Vallon

Mon cœur, lassé de tout, même de l'espérance,
N'ira plus de ses vœux importuner le sort;
Prêtez-moi seulement, vallon de mon enfance,
Un asile d'un jour pour attendre la mort.

Voici l'étroit sentier de l'obscure vallée:
Du flanc de ces coteaux pendent des bois épais,
Qui, courbant sur mon front leur ombre entremêlée,
Me couvrent tout entier de silence et de paix.

Là, deux ruisseaux cachés sous des ponts de verdure
Tracent en serpentant les contours du vallon;
Ils mêlent un moment leur onde et leur murmure,
Et non loin de leur source ils se perdent sans nom.

The Vale

My heart, weary of all things, even of hope, will trouble fate no more with its wishes; grant me only, vale of my childhood, refuge for one day to wait for death.

Here is the narrow path through the dark valley: from these hillsides hang dense woodlands which, bending over my brow their shade of blended colours, cloak me entirely in silence and peace.

There, two streams, hidden under bridges of greenery, wind as they trace the contours of the valley; they mingle for a moment their waters and their murmur, and not far from their source they are lost without name.

La source de mes jours comme eux s'est écoulée;
Elle a passé sans bruit, sans nom et sans retour:
Mais leur onde est limpide, et mon âme troublée
N'aura pas réfléchi les clartés d'un beau jour.

La fraîcheur de leurs lits, l'ombre qui les couronne,
M'enchaînent tout le jour sur les bords des ruisseaux;
Comme un enfant bercé par un chant monotone,
Mon âme s'assoupit au murmure des eaux.

Ah! c'est là qu'entouré d'un rempart de verdure,
D'un horizon borné qui suffit à mes yeux,
J'aime à fixer mes pas, et, seul dans la nature,
A n'entendre que l'onde, à ne voir que les cieux.

J'ai trop vu, trop senti, trop aimé dans ma vie;
Je viens chercher vivant le calme du Léthé.
Beaux lieux, soyez pour moi ces bords où l'on oublie:
L'oubli seul désormais est ma félicité.

The source of my days has passed away like them; it has passed without sound, without name, with no return: but their waters are limpid, and my clouded soul will never have reflected the clear light of a beautiful day.

The freshness of their beds, the shade which wreathes them, hold me all day long on the banks of the streams; like a child rocked by an unchanging song, my soul is lulled by the waters' murmur.

Ah! there, surrounded by a rampart of greenery, by a limited horizon, enough for my eyes, I love to direct my steps, and, alone in nature, to hear only the waters, to see only the skies.

I have seen too much, felt too much, loved too much in my life; I come to seek, still living, the calm of Lethe. Lovely place, be for me those banks of oblivion: to forget is my only happiness now.

Mon cœur est en repos, mon âme est en silence;
Le bruit lointain du monde expire en arrivant,
Comme un son éloigné qu'affaiblit la distance,
A l'oreille incertaine apporté par le vent.

D'ici je vois la vie, à travers un nuage,
S'évanouir pour moi dans l'ombre du passé;
L'amour seul est resté, comme une grande image
Survit seul au réveil dans un songe effacé.

Repose-toi, mon âme, en ce dernier asile,
Ainsi qu'un voyageur qui, le cœur plein d'espoir,
S'assied, avant d'entrer, aux portes de la ville,
Et respire un moment l'air embaumé du soir.

Comme lui, de nos pieds secouons la poussière;
L'homme par ce chemin ne repasse jamais:
Comme lui, respirons au bout de la carrière
Ce calme avant-coureur de l'éternelle paix.

My heart is at peace, my soul is quiet; the distant noise of the world dies away as it reaches me, like a faraway sound weakened by distance, carried by the wind to an uncertain ear.

From here I see life, through a cloud, fading into the shadows of the past; love alone remains, as one great image alone survives our waking from a vanished dream.

Rest, my soul, in this last refuge, as a traveller, his heart full of hope, sits before entering the gates of the city, and breathes for a moment the scented air of evening.

Like him, let us shake the dust from our feet; man never passes this way again: like him, let us breathe at the end of life's course this calm that heralds eternal peace.

Tes jours, sombres et courts comme les jours d'automne,
Déclinent comme l'ombre au penchant des coteaux;
L'amitié te trahit, la pitié t'abandonne,
Et, seule, tu descends le sentier des tombeaux.

Mais la nature est là qui t'invite et qui t'aime;
Plonge-toi dans son sein qu'elle t'ouvre toujours:
Quand tout change pour toi, la nature est la même,
Et le même soleil se lève sur tes jours.

De lumière et d'ombrage elle t'entoure encore:
Détache ton amour des faux biens que tu perds;
Adore ici l'écho qu'adorait Pythagore,
Prête avec lui l'oreille aux célestes concerts.

Suis le jour dans le ciel, suis l'ombre sur la terre;
Dans les plaines de l'air vole avec l'aquilon;
Avec le doux rayon de l'astre du mystère
Glisse à travers les bois dans l'ombre du vallon.

Your days, dark and brief like the days of autumn, are waning like the shadow on the hillsides; friendship betrays you, pity abandons you, and you descend alone the pathway to the graves.

But nature is there, inviting you, loving you; plunge into her ever-open bosom: when for you all is changing, nature stays the same, and the same sun rises on your days.

With light and shade she surrounds you still: unbind your love from the false possessions you are losing; worship here the echo that Pythagoras worshipped, give ear with him to the heavenly harmonies.

Follow the daylight in the sky, follow the darkness on the earth; fly with the north wind in the plains of the air; with the soft beam of the star of mystery slip through the woods in the shade of the valley.

Dieu, pour le concevoir, a fait l'intelligence:
Sous la nature enfin découvre son auteur!
Une voix à l'esprit parle dans son silence:
Qui n'a pas entendu cette voix dans son cœur?

God made intelligence to conceive it: discover at last within nature her creator! A voice in the silence speaks to the spirit: who has not heard this voice in his heart?

Marceline Desbordes-Valmore
(1786–1859)

From a life of emotional torment and financial struggle Marceline Desbordes-Valmore distilled a poetry of remarkable lyrical force. Disappointed in her marriage to a mediocre actor, she drew emotional nourishment from a secret affair (probably with Henri de Latouche, a minor poet).

Her poems of love, motherhood, friendship, faith and loss were admired by more famous contemporaries, and later by Verlaine and the Symbolists who valued in her verse a delicate musicality of sound and rhythm, a freshness of imagery and an absence of rhetoric. Not highly educated, she wrote with a compulsive spontaneity: 'The music revolved in my afflicted mind, and a steady beat structured my ideas independently of reflection.'

Major works: *Elégies et Poésies nouvelles* 1825, *Poésies* 1830, *Les Fleurs* 1833, *Pauvres Fleurs* 1839, *Bouquets et Prières* 1843, *Poésies posthumes* 1860.

Souvenir

Quand il pâlit un soir, et que sa voix tremblante
S'éteignit tout à coup dans un mot commencé;
Quand ses yeux, soulevant leur paupière brûlante,
Me blessèrent d'un mal dont je le crus blessé;
Quand ses traits plus touchants, éclairés d'une flamme
    Qui ne s'éteint jamais,
S'imprimèrent vivants dans le fond de mon âme,
    Il n'aimait pas, j'aimais!

Memory

When he grew pale one evening, and his trembling voice died suddenly on a half-formed word; when his eyes, raising their burning lids, pierced me with a wound with which I thought him pierced; when his more touching features, illumined with a fire that never dies, made their living imprint in the depth of my soul, he did not love, I loved!

Les Roses de Saadi

J'ai voulu ce matin te rapporter des roses;
Mais j'en avais tant pris dans mes ceintures closes
Que les nœuds trop serrés n'ont pu les contenir.

The Roses of Saadi[1]

I wanted to bring you roses this morning; but I had gathered so many in my tightly fastened sashes that the overstrained knots could not contain them.

[1]A thirteenth-century Persian poet. The poem's central image first appears in the preface to his work 'Gulistan'.

Les nœuds ont éclaté. Les roses envolées
Dans le vent, à la mer s'en sont toutes allées.
Elles ont suivi l'eau pour ne plus revenir;

La vague en a paru rouge et comme enflammée.
Ce soir, ma robe encore en est tout embaumée...
Respires-en sur moi l'odorant souvenir.

The knots burst open. The roses, borne on the wind, all flew away to the sea. They followed the water, never to return;

The waves seemed red with them, as if on fire. Tonight, my gown is still filled with their scent ... Breathe on me their fragrant memory.

La Couronne effeuillée

J'irai, j'irai porter ma couronne effeuillée
Au jardin de mon père où revit toute fleur;
J'y répandrai longtemps mon âme agenouillée:
Mon père a des secrets pour vaincre la douleur.

The Wreath stripped of petals

I will go, I will carry my wreath stripped of petals to my father's garden where all flowers live again; there on my knees I will pour out my soul's long confession: my father has secrets that triumph ovei grief.

J'irai, j'irai lui dire, au moins avec mes larmes:
"Regardez, j'ai souffert..." Il me regardera
Et sous mes jours changés, sous mes pâleurs sans charmes,
Parce qu'il est mon père il me reconnaîtra.

Il dira: "C'est donc vous, chère âme désolée!
La terre manque-t-elle à vos pas égarés?
Chère âme, je suis Dieu: ne soyez plus troublée;
Voici votre maison, voici mon cœur, entrez!"

O clémence! ô douceur! ô saint refuge! ô Père!
Votre enfant qui pleurait vous l'avez entendu!
Je vous obtiens déjà puisque je vous espère
Et que vous possédez tout ce que j'ai perdu.

Vous ne rejetez pas la fleur qui n'est plus belle,
Ce crime de la terre au ciel est pardonné.
Vous ne maudirez pas votre enfant infidèle,
Non d'avoir rien vendu, mais d'avoir tout donné.

I will go, I will say to him, at least with my tears: 'Look, I have suffered ...' He will look at me and beneath the changes wrought in me by time, beneath my unenchanting pallor, because he is my father he will recognize me.

He will say: 'So it is you, dear grieving soul! Does earth not support your erring steps? Dear soul, I am God: be no longer troubled; here is your home, here is my heart, come in!'

O mercy! O sweetness! O holy refuge! O Father! You have heard your weeping child! Already I secure you because I hope for you and because you possess all that I have lost.

You do not reject the flower whose beauty has faded, that earthly crime is forgiven in heaven. You will not curse your faithless child, not for having sold anything, but for having given all.

Alfred de Vigny
(1797–1863)

Vigny was born into an aristocratic and military family with a strong and increasingly inappropriate sense of rank, duty, honour and tradition. He served as an army officer in the post-Napoleonic period.

He nursed an invalid wife for thirty years, but also had a passionate, difficult and destructive affair with the actress Marie Dorval. An introspective and depressive character, with a sense of persecution both individual and cosmic, he nevertheless cultivated a stoical endurance of his personal and intellectual torments, transmuting emotion into thought and avoiding the cloying self-pity of some of his contemporaries.

Much of his best work is on Biblical themes. He projects his own doubts and sufferings on to grandiose figures whose vision, strength and pain give them a special relationship with God, but also mark them out for isolation and betrayal.

His style can be stiff, even pompous; but at its finest his verse has a monumental quality, and he shares to an extent Hugo's gift for the vivid visual communication of place, time, character and drama. A genuine religious and emotional anguish can still move us, despite the rhetoric and the absence of lyrical intimacy in his verse.

In later life Vigny developed a more optimistic confidence in human progress through the activity of '*L'Esprit pur*' – the human spirit, purified of material concerns and vested in an élite of philosophers and poets. He saw poetry as the supreme embodiment and expression of thought, as an austere and noble assertion of human dignity against the world and against death.

Major volumes: *Poèmes antiques et modernes* 1826, *Les Destinées* 1864.

La Colère de Samson

Le désert est muet, la tente est solitaire.
Quel pasteur courageux la dressa sur la terre
Du sable et des lions? – La nuit n'a pas calmé
La fournaise du jour dont l'air est enflammé.
Un vent léger s'élève à l'horizon et ride
Les flots de la poussière ainsi qu'un lac limpide.
Le lin blanc de la tente est bercé mollement;
L'œuf d'autruche allumé veille paisiblement,
Des voyageurs voilés intérieure étoile,
Et jette longuement deux ombres sur la toile.

The Wrath of Samson

The desert is silent, the tent is solitary. What brave shepherd placed it on the land of sand and lions? Night has not calmed the furnace of the day, its air is still fiery. A gentle wind rises on the horizon and ripples the ocean of dust like a limpid lake. The white linen of the tent rocks softly; the lighted ostrich egg keeps peaceful watch, inner star of the veiled travellers, and throws two elongated shadows on the cloth.

L'une est grande et superbe, et l'autre est à ses pieds:
C'est Dalila, l'esclave, et ses bras sont liés
Aux genoux réunis du maître jeune et grave
Dont la force divine obéit à l'esclave.
Comme un doux léopard elle est souple, et répand
Ses cheveux dénoués aux pieds de son amant.
Ses grands yeux, entr'ouverts comme s'ouvre l'amande,
Sont brûlants du plaisir que son regard demande
Et jettent, par éclats, leurs mobiles lueurs.
Ses bras fins tout mouillés de tièdes sueurs,
Ses pieds voluptueux qui sont croisés sous elle,
Ses flancs, plus élancés que ceux de la gazelle,
Pressés de bracelets, d'anneaux, de boucles d'or,
Sont bruns, et, comme il sied aux filles de Hatsor,
Ses deux seins, tout chargés d'amulettes anciennes,
Sont chastement pressés d'étoffes syriennes.

One is great and proud, the other is at his feet: it is the slave Delilah, and her arms enlace the knees of her grave young master whose divine strength obeys the slave. Like a gentle leopard she is lithe, and spreads her loosened hair over the feet of her lover. Her large eyes, half-open as an almond opens, are burning with the pleasure that her gaze seeks and flash as they cast their restless gleam. Her delicate arms, moist with warm sweat, her voluptuous feet crossed beneath her, her flanks more slender than a gazelle's, all hung with bracelets, rings and golden buckles, are brown, and, as befits the daughters of Hatsor, both her breasts, laden with ancient amulets, are chastely held in Syrian cloths.

Les genoux de Samson fortement sont unis
Comme les deux genoux du colosse Anubis.
Elle s'endort sans force et riante et bercée
Par la puissante main sous sa tête placée.
Lui, murmure ce chant funèbre et douloureux
Prononcé dans la gorge avec des mots hébreux.
Elle ne comprend pas la parole étrangère,
Mais le chant verse un somme en sa tête légère.

"Une lutte éternelle en tout temps, en tout lieu,
Se livre sur la terre, en présence de Dieu,
Entre la bonté d'Homme et la ruse de Femme,
Car la femme est un être impur de corps et d'âme.

Samson's knees are strongly pressed together like the knees of the colossus Anubis. She slumbers, powerless and laughing and cradled by the powerful hand beneath her head. He murmurs in his throat this sombre and sorrowful song with its Hebrew words. She does not understand the foreign tongue, but the song pours sleep into her capricious[1] head.

'An eternal struggle in every time and place is waged on earth, in the presence of God, between Man's goodness and the guile of Woman, for woman is a being impure in body and soul.

[1]The double meaning of 'léger' (light in physical terms, but also fickle, irresponsible) is not readily translatable.

"L'Homme a toujours besoin de caresse et d'amour,
Sa mère l'en abreuve alors qu'il vient au jour,
Et ce bras le premier l'engourdit, le balance
Et lui donne un désir d'amour et d'indolence.
Troublé dans l'action, troublé dans le dessein,
Il rêvera partout à la chaleur du sein,
Aux chansons de la nuit, aux baisers de l'aurore,
A la lèvre de feu que sa lèvre dévore,
Aux cheveux dénoués qui roulent sur son front,
Et les regrets du lit, en marchant, le suivront.
Il ira dans la ville, et là les vierges folles
Le prendront dans leurs lacs aux premières paroles.
Plus fort il sera né, mieux il sera vaincu,
Car plus le fleuve est grand et plus il est ému.
Quand le combat que Dieu fit pour la créature
Et contre son semblable et contre la Nature
Force l'Homme à chercher un sein où reposer,
Quand ses yeux sont en pleurs, il lui faut un baiser,

Man always needs caresses and love, his mother quenches his thirst for them when he comes to the light of day, and this arm is the first to benumb him, to rock him and give him a desire for love and languor. Anxious in his actions, anxious in his plans, he will dream wherever he goes of the warmth of the breast, of the songs of night and the kisses of dawn, of the fiery lips consumed by his lips, of the loosened hair cascading over his brow, and, as he goes, yearnings for the bed will follow him. He will go to the town, and there the foolish virgins will take him in their snares with the first words. The stronger he is born, the more readily he will be conquered, for the greater the river, the more turbulent it is. When the battle which God made for his creature both against his fellow and against Nature forces Man to seek a breast on which to rest, when his eyes are weeping, he needs a kiss, but he has not yet

Mais il n'a pas encor fini toute sa tâche:
Vient un autre combat plus secret, traître et lâche;
Sous son bras, sur son cœur se livre celui-là;
Et, plus ou moins, la Femme est toujours DALILA.

"Elle rit et triomphe; en sa froideur savante,
Au milieu de ses sœurs elle attend et se vante
De ne rien éprouver des atteintes du feu.
A sa plus belle amie elle en a fait l'aveu:
Elle se fait aimer sans aimer elle-même;
Un maître lui fait peur. C'est le plaisir qu'elle aime;
L'Homme est rude et le prend sans savoir le donner.
Un sacrifice illustre et fait pour étonner
Rehausse mieux que l'or, aux yeux de ses pareilles,
La beauté qui produit tant d'étranges merveilles
Et d'un sang précieux sait arroser ses pas.

fulfilled his task: there comes another conflict, more secret treacherous and cowardly; in his arms, on his heart this one is waged; and, more or less, the Woman is always DELILAH.

She laughs and triumphs; in her knowing coldness, among her sisters she waits and boasts of feeling nothing of the fire's pangs. To her fairest friend she has confessed it: she inspires love without herself loving. A master frightens her. It is pleasure that she loves; Man is rough and takes it without knowing how to give it. An illustrious sacrifice, done to astonish, enhances more than gold, in the eyes of her equals, the beauty that engenders so many strange marvels and knows how to sprinkle its steps with precious blood.

– Donc, ce que j'ai voulu, Seigneur, n'existe pas! –
Celle à qui va l'amour et de qui vient la vie,
Celle-là, par orgueil, se fait notre ennemie.
La Femme est à présent pire que dans ces temps
Où, voyant les humains, Dieu dit: "Je me repens!"
Bientôt, se retirant dans un hideux royaume,
La Femme aura Gomorrhe et l'Homme aura Sodome;
Et, se jetant de loin un regard irrité,
Les deux sexes mourront chacun de son côté.

– So what I have wished for, Lord, does not exist! – she to whom love goes and from whom life comes, she, through pride, makes herself our enemy. Woman is worse now than in those times when God, seeing mankind, said: "I repent!" Soon, withdrawing into a hideous kingdom, Woman will have Gomorrha and Man will have Sodom; and casting from a distance a gaze of mutual anger, the two sexes will die, each on its own side.

"Éternel! Dieu des forts! vous savez que mon âme
N'avait pour aliment que l'amour d'une femme,
Puisant dans l'amour seul plus de sainte vigueur
Que mes cheveux divins n'en donnaient à mon cœur.
– Jugez-nous. – La voilà sur mes pieds endormie.
Trois fois elle a vendu mes secrets et ma vie,
Et trois fois a versé des pleurs fallacieux
Qui n'ont pu me cacher la rage de ses yeux;
Honteuse qu'elle était plus encor qu'étonnée
De se voir découverte ensemble et pardonnée;
Car la bonté de l'Homme est forte, et sa douceur
Écrase, en l'absolvant, l'être faible et menteur.

Eternal! God of the strong! you know that my soul had no food but the love of a woman, drawing from love alone more holy strength than my divine hair gave to my heart. – Judge us. – There she is asleep at my feet. Three times she has sold my secrets and my life, and three times shed false tears which could not hide from me the fury in her eyes; ashamed as she was, even more than astonished, to see herself both discovered and forgiven; for Man's goodness is strong, and his gentleness crushes, by absolving it, the weak and deceitful creature.

"Mais enfin je suis las. J'ai l'âme si pesante
Que mon corps gigantesque et ma tête puissante
Qui soutiennent le poids des colonnes d'airain
Ne la peuvent porter avec tout son chagrin.
Toujours voir serpenter la vipère dorée
Qui se traîne en sa fange et s'y croit ignorée!
Toujours ce compagnon dont le cœur n'est pas sûr,
La Femme, enfant malade et douze fois impur!
Toujours mettre sa force à garder sa colère
Dans son cœur offensé, comme en un sanctuaire
D'où le feu s'échappant irait tout dévorer,
Interdire à ses yeux de voir ou de pleurer,
C'est trop! Dieu, s'il le veut, peut balayer ma cendre.
J'ai donné mon secret, Dalila va le vendre.
Qu'ils seront beaux les pieds de celui qui viendra
Pour m'annoncer la mort! – Ce qui sera, sera!"

But at long last I am weary. My soul is so heavy that my giant body and my powerful head which hold up the weight of columns of bronze cannot carry it with all its sorrow. Always to see the gilded viper slithering in its filth and thinking itself unseen! Always this companion whose heart is untrustworthy, Woman, a sick and twelve times impure child! Always to spend one's strength in keeping anger within the offended heart, as in a sanctuary; if the fire escaped from there it would consume everything; to forbid one's eyes to see or weep, it is too much! God, if he wishes, can sweep away my ashes. I have given my secret, Delilah will sell it. How beautiful will be the feet of the one who comes to announce my death to me! – What will be, will be.'

Il dit et s'endormit près d'elle jusqu'à l'heure
Où les guerriers, tremblant d'être dans sa demeure,
Payant au poids de l'or chacun de ses cheveux,
Attachèrent ses mains et brûlèrent ses yeux,
Le traînèrent sanglant et chargé d'une chaîne
Que douze grands taureaux ne tiraient qu'avec peine,
Le placèrent debout, silencieusement,
Devant Dagon, leur Dieu, qui gémit sourdement
Et deux fois, en tournant, recula sur sa base
Et fit pâlir deux fois ses prêtres en extase;
Allumèrent l'encens, dressèrent un festin
Dont le bruit s'entendait du mont le plus lointain;
Et près de la génisse aux pieds du Dieu tuée
Placèrent Dalila, pâle prostituée,
Couronnée, adorée et reine du repas,
Mais tremblante et disant: "IL NE ME VERRA PAS!"

He spoke and fell asleep beside her until the hour when the warriors, fearful to be within his dwelling, paying its weight in gold for each strand of his hair, bound his hands and burned his eyes, dragged him bleeding and laden with a chain that twelve great bulls could barely pull, placed him upright, silently, before Dagon their God, who with a hollow groan recoiled twice, turning on his plinth, and twice made his ecstatic priests turn pale; they lit the incense, prepared a banquet whose clamour was heard from the furthest mountain; and near the heifer killed at the feet of the God they placed Delilah, the pale whore, crowned, worshipped, and queen of the feast, but trembling and saying: 'HE WILL NOT SEE ME!'

Terre et Ciel! avez-vous tressailli d'allégresse
Lorsque vous avez vu la menteuse maîtresse
Suivre d'un œil hagard les yeux tachés de sang
Qui cherchaient le soleil d'un regard impuissant?
Et quand enfin Samson, secouant les colonnes
Qui faisaient le soutien des immenses Pylônes,
Écrasa d'un seul coup, sous les débris mortels,
Ses trois mille ennemis, leurs dieux et leurs autels?
Terre et Ciel! punissez par de telles justices
La trahison ourdie en des amours factices,
Et la délation du secret de nos cœurs
Arraché dans nos bras par des baisers menteurs!

Earth and Heaven! did you quiver with joy when you saw the deceitful mistress follow with a wild stare the bloodstained eyes that sought the sunlight with a helpless gaze? And when at last Samson, shaking the columns that held up the vast temple gateway, crushed with one blow under the fatal ruins his three thousand enemies, their gods and their altars? Earth and Heaven! punish by such acts of justice the treachery hatched within feigned love, and the betrayal of the secret of our hearts, torn away as we embrace by lying kisses!

Le Mont des Oliviers

I

Alors il était nuit, et Jésus marchait seul,
Vêtu de blanc ainsi qu'un mort de son linceul:
Les disciples dormaient au pied de la colline.
Parmi les oliviers, qu'un vent sinistre incline,
Jésus marche à grands pas en frissonnant comme eux,
Triste jusqu'à la mort, l'œil sombre et ténébreux,
Le front baissé, croisant les deux bras sur sa robe
Comme un voleur de nuit cachant ce qu'il dérobe;
Connaissant les rochers mieux qu'un sentier uni,
Il s'arrête en un lieu nommé Gethsémani.
Il se courbe à genoux, le front contre la terre;
Puis regarde le ciel en appelant: "Mon père!"
– Mais le ciel reste noir, et Dieu ne répond pas.
Il se lève étonné, marche encore à grands pas,
Froissant les oliviers qui tremblent. Froide et lente

The Mount of Olives

I

Then it was night, and Jesus walked alone, dressed in white like a dead man in his shroud: the disciples were sleeping at the foot of the hill. Among the olives, bent by an ominous wind, Jesus strides, shivering like them, sorrowful even unto death, his eye dark and sombre, his head lowered, crossing his arms over his robe like a thief of the night hiding his booty; knowing the rocks better than a level path, he stops at a place called Gethsemane. He bends low, on his knees, his brow against the earth; then looks at the sky and calls: 'My father!' – But the sky remains dark, and God does not answer. He rises in astonishment and strides on again, brushing the trembling

Découle de sa tête une sueur sanglante.
Il recule, il descend, il crie avec effroi:
"Ne pouviez-vous prier et veiller avec moi?"
Mais un sommeil de mort accable les apôtres.
Pierre à la voix du maître est sourd comme les autres.
Le Fils de l'Homme alors remonte lentement;
Comme un pasteur d'Égypte, il cherche au firmament
Si l'Ange ne luit pas au fond de quelque étoile.
Mais un nuage en deuil s'étend comme le voile
D'une veuve, et ses plis entourent le désert.
Jésus, se rappelant ce qu'il avait souffert
Depuis trente-trois ans, devint homme, et la crainte
Serra son cœur mortel d'une invincible étreinte.
Il eut froid. Vainement il appela trois fois:
"Mon Père!" Le vent seul répondit à sa voix.
Il tomba sur le sable assis, et, dans sa peine,
Eut sur le monde et l'homme une pensée humaine.
– Et la terre trembla, sentant la pesanteur
Du Sauveur qui tombait aux pieds du Créateur.

olives. Cold and slow, a bloody sweat flows down from his head. He draws back, he descends, he cries in terror: 'Could you not pray and watch with me?' But the apostles are deep within a deathlike sleep. Peter is deaf like the others to the voice of his master. So the Son of Man climbs slowly up again; like an Egyptian shepherd, he scans the firmament to see if the Angel is not shining deep in some star. But a cloud of mourning spreads like a widow's veil, and its folds enclose the desert. Jesus, remembering what he had suffered for thirty-three years, became a man, and fear gripped his mortal heart in an invincible embrace. He felt cold. In vain he called three times: 'My Father!' The wind alone answered his voice. He fell on the sand and sat, and, in his affliction, had a human thought on the world and on mankind. – And the earth trembled, feeling the weight of the Saviour falling at the Creator's feet.

II

Jésus disait: "O Père, encor laisse-moi vivre!
Avant le dernier mot ne ferme pas mon livre!
Ne sens-tu pas le monde et tout le genre humain
Qui souffre avec ma chair et frémit dans ta main?
C'est que la Terre a peur de rester seule et veuve,
Quand meurt celui qui dit une parole neuve,
Et que tu n'as laissé dans son sein desséché
Tomber qu'un mot du ciel par ma bouche épanché.
Mais ce mot est si pur, et sa douceur est telle,
Qu'il a comme enivré la famille mortelle
D'une goutte de vie et de divinité,
Lorsqu'en ouvrant les bras j'ai dit: "Fraternité."

II

Jesus said: 'O Father, let me live on! Do not close my book before the last word! Can you not feel the world and all the human race suffering with my flesh and trembling in your hand? For Earth is afraid to remain alone and widowed by the death of the man who has spoken a new word, and you have let fall on her withered breast only one word from heaven given through my mouth. But that word is so pure, its sweetness is such, that it almost intoxicated the human family with a drop of life and of divinity, when I opened my arms and said: "Brotherhood."

Père, oh! si j'ai rempli mon douloureux message:
Si j'ai caché le Dieu sous la face du sage,
Du sacrifice humain si j'ai changé le prix,
Pour l'offrande des corps recevant les esprits,
Substituant partout aux choses le symbole,
La parole au combat, comme au trésor l'obole,
Aux flots rouges du sang les flots vermeils du vin,
Aux membres de la chair le pain blanc sans levain:
Si j'ai coupé les temps en deux parts, l'une esclave
Et l'autre libre; – au nom du passé que je lave,
Par le sang de mon corps qui souffre et va finir,
Versons-en la moitié pour laver l'avenir!
Père libérateur! jette aujourd'hui, d'avance,
La moitié de ce sang d'amour et d'innocence
Sur la tête de ceux qui viendront en disant:
"Il est permis pour tous de tuer l'innocent."
Nous savons qu'il naîtra, dans le lointain des âges,
Des dominateurs durs escortés de faux sages
Qui troubleront l'esprit de chaque nation
En donnant un faux sens à ma rédemption.
– Hélas! je parle encor, que déjà ma parole

Father, oh! if I have fulfilled my painful mission: if I have hidden the God beneath the face of the sage, if I have changed the price of human sacrifice, receiving spirits for the offering of bodies, substituting everywhere the symbol for the thing, the word for the battle, like the farthing for the treasure, the ruby flow of wine for the red tides of blood, the white unleavened bread for the limbs of the flesh: if I have cut time into two, one part slave and the other free; – in the name of the past which I wash with the blood of my body which suffers and will end, let us pour half of it to wash the future! Liberating Father! Cast today half of this blood of love and innocence in advance upon the heads of those who will come saying: "It is lawful for all to kill the innocent." We know that in the distant future ages there will be born harsh oppressors with a retinue of false prophets who will disturb the spirit of every nation by giving a false meaning to my redemption. – Alas, I speak still,

Est tournée en poison dans chaque parabole;
Éloigne ce calice impur et plus amer
Que le fiel, ou l'absinthe, ou les eaux de la mer.
Les verges qui viendront, la couronne d'épine,
Les clous des mains, la lance au fond de ma poitrine,
Enfin toute la croix qui se dresse et m'attend,
N'ont rien, mon Père, oh! rien qui m'épouvante autant!
Quand les Dieux veulent bien s'abattre sur les mondes,
Ils n'y doivent laisser que des traces profondes;
Et, si j'ai mis le pied sur ce globe incomplet,
Dont le gémissement sans repos m'appelait,
C'était pour y laisser deux Anges à ma place
De qui la race humaine aurait baisé la trace,
La Certitude heureuse et l'Espoir confiant,
Qui, dans le paradis, marchent en souriant.
Mais je vais la quitter, cette indigente terre,
N'ayant que soulevé ce manteau de misère
Qui l'entoure à grands plis, drap lugubre et fatal,
Que d'un bout tient le Doute et de l'autre le Mal.

even though my words are already turned to poison in every parable; take away this impure cup, more bitter than gall, or wormwood, or the waters of the sea. The rods that will come, the crown of thorns, the nails through the hands, the lance deep in my breast, then at last the whole cross which stands awaiting me, have nothing, my Father, oh! nothing which frightens me as much! When Gods wish to swoop down on worlds, they must leave only deep imprints behind: and if I set foot on this imperfect globe, whose restless groaning called me, it was to leave two Angels in my place whose footsteps humanity would have kissed, happy Certainty and confident Hope, who walk smiling in Paradise. But I shall leave this needy earth, having merely lifted this mantle of misery which envelops it in great folds, a dismal and fatal cloth, held at one end by Doubt, at the other by Evil.

"Mal et Doute! En un mot je puis les mettre en poudre.
Vous les aviez prévus, laissez-moi vous absoudre
De les avoir permis. – C'est l'accusation
Qui pèse de partout sur la création! –
Dans son tombeau désert faisons monter Lazare.
Du grand secret des morts qu'il ne soit plus avare,
Et de ce qu'il a vu donnons-lui souvenir;
Qu'il parle. – Ce qui dure et ce qui doit finir,
Ce qu'a mis le Seigneur au cœur de la Nature,
Ce qu'elle prend et donne à toute créature,
Quels sont avec le ciel ses muets entretiens,
Son amour ineffable et ses chastes liens;
Comment tout s'y détruit et tout s'y renouvelle;
Pourquoi ce qui s'y cache et ce qui s'y révèle;
Si les astres des cieux tour à tour éprouvés
Sont comme celui-ci coupables et sauvés;
Si la terre est pour eux ou s'ils sont pour la terre;
Ce qu'a de vrai la fable et de clair le mystère,
D'ignorant le savoir et de faux la raison;
Pourquoi l'âme est liée en sa faible prison,
Et pourquoi nul sentier entre deux larges voies,

Evil and Doubt! With one word I can reduce them to dust. You had foreseen them, let me now absolve you from having allowed them. – This is the accusation that weighs everywhere on creation! – Let us make Lazarus climb on his lonely tomb. Let him no longer keep like a miser the great secret of the dead, and let us grant him memory of what he has seen; let him speak. – What endures and what must end, what the Lord has placed in the heart of Nature, what she takes and gives to every creature, what are her wordless dialogues with heaven, her ineffable love and her chaste affinities; how all in her is destroyed and in her renewed; the reason for what is hidden and what revealed in her; if the stars in the sky, each put to the test in turn, are like this one guilty and redeemed; if the earth is for them or they are for the earth; what is true in the fable and clear in the mystery, ignorant in knowledge and false in reason; why the soul is fettered in its feeble prison, and why

Entre l'ennui du calme et des paisibles joies
Et la rage sans fin des vagues passions,
Entre la léthargie et les convulsions;
Et pourquoi pend la Mort comme une sombre épée
Attristant la Nature à tout moment frappée;
Si le juste et le bien, si l'injuste et le mal
Sont de vils accidents en un cercle fatal,
Ou si de l'univers ils sont les deux grands pôles,
Soutenant terre et cieux sur leurs vastes épaules;
Et pourquoi les Esprits du mal sont triomphants
Des maux immérités, de la mort des enfants;
Et si les Nations sont des femmes guidées
Par les étoiles d'or des divines idées,
Ou de folles enfants sans lampes dans la nuit,
Se heurtant et pleurant, et que rien ne conduit;
Et si, lorsque des temps l'horloge périssable
Aura jusqu'au dernier versé ses grains de sable,
Un regard de vos yeux, un cri de votre voix,
Un soupir de mon cœur, un signe de ma croix,
Pourra faire ouvrir l'ongle aux Peines éternelles.
Lâcher leur proie humaine et reployer leurs ailes

there is no path between two broad roads, between the tedium of tranquillity and peaceful joys and the endless fury of shapeless passions, between lethargy and convulsions; and why Death hangs like a dark sword casting a sad shadow over Nature and striking it constantly; if justice and good, injustice and evil are base contingencies in a fatal circle, or if they are the two great poles of the universe, bearing earth and the heavens on their vast shoulders; and why malevolent Spirits triumph through undeserved evils, through the death of children; and if the Nations are women guided by the golden stars of divine ideas, or senseless children, lampless in the night, colliding and weeping and guided by nothing; and if, when the perishable clock of the ages has poured out to the last its grains of sand, a glance from your eyes, a cry of your voice, a sigh from my heart, a sign from my cross, will be able to make the eternal Torments open their claws, release their human prey

– Tout sera révélé dès que l'homme saura
De quels lieux il arrive et dans quels il ira."

III

Ainsi le divin Fils parlait au divin Père.
Il se prosterne encor, il attend, il espère,
Mais il renonce et dit: "Que votre volonté
Soit faite et non la mienne, et pour l'éternité."
Une terreur profonde, une angoisse infinie
Redoublent sa torture et sa lente agonie.
Il regarde longtemps, longtemps cherche sans voir.
Comme un marbre de deuil tout le ciel était noir;
La Terre, sans clartés, sans astre et sans aurore,
Et sans clartés de l'âme ainsi qu'elle est encore,
Frémissait. – Dans le bois il entendit des pas,
Et puis il vit rôder la torche de Judas.

and fold back their wings. – All will be revealed once man knows whence he comes and where he will go.'

III

Thus the divine Son spoke to the divine Father. He prostrates himself again, he waits, he hopes, but he gives up and says: 'Let your will be done and not mine, and for all eternity!' A profound terror, an infinite anguish redouble his torment and his slow agony. For a long time he gazes, searches without seeing. Like funereal marble the whole sky was black; the Earth, without light, without stars, without dawn, and with no light in the soul just as it still is now, shuddered. – In the wood he heard footsteps, then saw the prowling torch of Judas.

LE SILENCE

S'il est vrai qu'au Jardin sacré des Écritures,
Le Fils de l'homme ait dit ce qu'on voit rapporté;
Muet, aveugle et sourd au cri des créatures,
Si le Ciel nous laissa comme un monde avorté.
Le juste opposera le dédain à l'absence
Et ne répondra plus que par un froid silence
    Au silence éternel de la Divinité.

THE SILENCE

If it is true that in the holy Garden of the Scriptures the Son of man said what we see recounted; if, dumb, blind and deaf to the cry of created beings, Heaven abandoned us like an aborted world, the just man will confront absence with disdain and will reply only with cold silence to the eternal silence of the Divinity.

Victor Hugo
(1802–85)

An extravagant figure, a literary giant, Hugo worked in many genres in a career that spanned much of the nineteenth century. Novelist, dramatist and poet, he was the acknowledged leader of the Romantic movement. It is impossible to classify his poetry concisely, for his output ranges in tone and subject from understated and evocatively lyrical love poetry through powerfully dramatic religious experience to violent political invective, and from homely family scenes through grandiose epics to extended metaphysical meditations on the nature and works of mankind, God and the Devil.

From a modern point of view, it is tempting to look at Hugo with some scepticism and even amusement. His rhetoric is at times undeniably pompous, inflated and humourless. His conception of the poet's role as intermediary and interpreter between man and God, man and Nature, man and History, can seem to us the outrageous pretentiousness of an overdeveloped ego. But it is an acceptable hubris when viewed in its literary and historical context, and when set against the achievements of an innovative and authoritative artist of great vision, sensitivity and technical skill, justly admired for the scope and force of his visual imagination and for the strength of his ideas. He felt himself to be the authentic voice of the French people, and their response seemed to confirm it. Rarely can any poet have received such widespread popular acclaim, and at his funeral millions lined the streets of Paris.

His family suffered financial insecurity when his father, a general, was forced to retire in 1814; but in spite of considerable strife between his parents, a warm image of family life predominates in his lyrical poetry. After law studies, Hugo began to develop literary contacts, published his first volume in 1822, and, avoiding parental prohibition, married Adèle Foucher. The eventual failure of the marriage was perhaps inevitable from the wedding breakfast itself, when his brother Eugène broke down under the strain of his own love for Adèle. Hugo was to find other fulfilment in his love for Juliette Drouet, the subject of many of his tenderest verses.

His early work remained formally orthodox on the whole, but introduced new and typically Romantic subjects: medieval legend, for example, and a rather synthetic Oriental exoticism (inspired respectively by Walter Scott and the *Arabian Nights*, both enjoying a vogue in France at the time), and flirtations with the occult. The verse of this period is colourfully descriptive and dramatic; already his prime faculty, an accumulative visual imagination in love with antithesis, is very much in evidence. By 1830 Hugo was the focus of a dynamic group of young writers, artists and composers (the 'Cénacle', including Delacroix, David, Berlioz, Vigny and Musset), with an aggressive belief in their own talent and revolutionary importance.

In the 1830s his poetry became more personal and reflective, yet imbued with emotional universality. He developed too a strong vein of humanitarianism which would grow later into a sustained assertion of the human spirit against the repressive regime of Napoléon III, and against the betrayal of the people by their leaders in 1870–71.

A tendency to didacticism, rooted in his conception of the poet as seer and spokesman, was increased by political developments in the 1840s and 1850s, and the government of Napoléon III was so distasteful to him that he lived in voluntary exile in the Channel Islands from 1852 to 1870. Yet in addition to political satire and an energetic defence of human rights, he also wrote in those years a series of volumes of personal, religious and philosophical verse, including much of the immense historical project *La Légende des Siècles*, charting patterns of moral elevation and decline, achievement and suffering in human development. He also had to come to terms with personal tragedy: 'Demain, dès l'aube' and 'A Villequier' are contrasting responses to the accidental drowning of his newly married daughter.

Hugo is arguably at his best when moving with fluency

and imaginative vigour from image to image rather than idea to idea. His concrete, impassioned pictorial vision can compete even with that of Rimbaud, and at times a vibrant, atmospheric musicality matches that of the Symbolists who tended to underrate him. Hugo released the Alexandrine line to a considerable extent from its traditional inflexibility, but perhaps his greatest contribution to poetic development was his liberation of subject-matter and vocabulary from the old restraints and artificialities. After Hugo, anything and everything could be the stimulus, substance and style of poetry, in an expressive revolution that Baudelaire, Verlaine, Rimbaud, Corbière and Laforgue would push close to its limits even before the twentieth century: 'The modern Muse will sense that all creation is not humanly lovely, that the ugly exists alongside the beautiful, the deformed beside the graceful, the grotesque on the reverse of the sublime, evil with good, shadow with light' (from Hugo's preface to his play *Cromwell*).

Major volumes: *Odes et Poésies diverses* 1822, *Nouvelles Odes* 1824, *Odes et Ballades* 1826, *Les Orientales* 1829, *Les Feuilles d'automne* 1831, *Les Chants du crépuscule* 1835, *Les Voix intérieures* 1837, *Les Rayons et les ombres* 1840, *Les Châtiments* 1853, *Les Contemplations* 1856, *La Légende des siècles* 1859–1877–1883, *Les Chansons des rues et des bois* 1865, *L'Année terrible* 1872, *L'Art d'être grand-père* 1877, *La Pitié suprême* 1879, *Les Quatre Vents de l'esprit* 1881. Posthumous: *La Fin de Satan*, *Toute la Lyre*, *Dieu*, *L'Océan*, *La Gerbe*.

Extase

Et j'entendis une grande voix.
Apocalypse

J'étais seul près des flots, par une nuit d'étoiles.
Pas un nuage aux cieux, sur les mers pas de voiles.
Mes yeux plongeaient plus loin que le monde réel.
Et les bois, et les monts, et toute la nature,
Semblaient interroger dans un confus murmure
    Les flots des mers, les feux du ciel.

Et les étoiles d'or, légions infinies,
A voix haute, à voix basse, avec mille harmonies,
Disaient, en inclinant leurs couronnes de feu;
Et les flots bleus, que rien ne gouverne et n'arrête,
Disaient, en recourbant l'écume de leur crête:
  – C'est le Seigneur, le Seigneur Dieu!

Ecstasy

'And I heard a great voice'
Apocalypse

I was alone by the waters, on a starlit night. Not a cloud in the heavens, on the seas not a sail. My vision plunged deeper than the real world. And the woods, and the mountains, and all nature seemed to question in an indistinct murmur the waves of the oceans, the fires in the sky.

And the golden stars, infinite legions, with loud or hushed voices, with a thousand harmonies, said as they bowed their fiery crowns; and the blue waters, which nothing steers and nothing brings to rest, said as they bent low their foaming crests: – It is the Lord, the Lord God!

Puisque mai tout en fleur ...

Puisque mai tout en fleur dans les prés nous réclame,
Viens! ne te lasse pas de mêler à ton âme
La campagne, les bois, les ombrages charmants,
Les larges clairs de lune au bord des flots dormants,
Le sentier qui finit où le chemin commence,
Et l'air et le printemps et l'horizon immense,
L'horizon que ce monde attache humble et joyeux
Comme une lèvre au bas de la robe des cieux!
Viens! et que le regard des pudiques étoiles,
Qui tombe sur la terre à travers tant de voiles,
Que l'arbre pénétré de parfums et de chants,
Que le souffle embrasé de midi dans les champs,
Et l'ombre et le soleil, et l'onde et la verdure,
Et le rayonnement de toute la nature
Fasse épanouir, comme une double fleur,
La beauté sur ton front et l'amour dans ton cœur!

Since flowering May ...

Since flowering May calls us from the meadows, come! do not tire of mingling with your soul the countryside, the woods, the enchanting shade, the broad beams of moonlight beside the sleeping waters, the path which ends where the road begins, and the air and the spring and the vast horizon, the horizon, a lip with which this humble, joyous world kisses the hem of heaven's robe! Come, and let the gaze of the chaste stars which falls on the earth through so many veils, let the tree imbued with scents and songs, let the burning breath of midday in the fields, and the shade and the sunlight, the water and the greenery, and let the radiance of all nature bring out, like a double blossoming flower, the beauty on your brow and the love in your heart!

Souvenir de la nuit du 4

L'enfant avait reçu deux balles dans la tête.
Le logis était propre, humble, paisible, honnête;
On voyait un rameau bénit sur un portrait.
Une vieille grand-mère était là qui pleurait.
Nous le déshabillions en silence. Sa bouche,
Pâle, s'ouvrait; la mort noyait son œil farouche;
Ses bras pendants semblaient demander des appuis.
Il avait dans sa poche une toupie en buis.
On pouvait mettre un doigt dans les trous de ses plaies.
Avez-vous vu saigner la mûre dans les haies?
Son crâne était ouvert comme un bois qui se fend.
L'aïeule regarda déshabiller l'enfant,
Disant: – Comme il est blanc! approchez donc la lampe.
Dieu! ses pauvres cheveux sont collés sur sa tempe! –
Et quand ce fut fini, le prit sur ses genoux.
La nuit était lugubre; on entendait des coups
De fusil dans la rue où l'on en tuait d'autres.
– Il faut ensevelir l'enfant, dirent les nôtres.

Memory of the Night of the Fourth

The child had received two bullets in the head. The dwelling was clean, humble, peaceful, decent; we could see a holy palm above a portrait. An old grandmother was there, weeping. We undressed him in silence. His pale mouth hung open; death was drowning his eyes full of fear; his dangling arms seemed to seek support. He had in his pocket a boxwood top. You could put a finger in the holes of his wounds. Have you seen the blackberry bleeding in the hedgerows? His skull was open like a splitting log. The grandmother watched as the child was undressed, saying: – How white he is! Come, bring the lamp closer. God! his poor hair is stuck to his temples! And when it was over, she took him on her knees. The night was dark and dismal; you could hear gunshots in the streets where they were killing others. – We must wrap the child, our people said. And

Et l'on prit un drap blanc dans l'armoire en noyer.
L'aïeule cependant l'approchait du foyer
Comme pour réchauffer ses membres déjà roides.
Hélas! ce que la mort touche de ses mains froides
Ne se réchauffe plus aux foyers d'ici-bas!
Elle pencha la tête et lui tira ses bas,
Et dans ses vieilles mains prit les pieds du cadavre.
– Est-ce que ce n'est pas une chose qui navre!
Cria-t-elle! monsieur, il n'avait pas huit ans!
Ses maitres, il allait en classe, étaient contents.
Monsieur, quand il fallait que je fisse une lettre,
C'est lui qui l'écrivait. Est-ce qu'on va se mettre
A tuer les enfants maintenant? Ah! mon Dieu!
On est donc des brigands! Je vous demande un peu,
Il jouait ce matin, là, devant la fenêtre!
Dire qu'ils m'ont tué ce pauvre petit être!
Il passait dans la rue, ils ont tiré dessus.
Monsieur, il était bon et doux comme un Jésus.
Moi je suis vieille, il est tout simple que je parte;
Cela n'aurait rien fait à monsieur Bonaparte
De me tuer au lieu de tuer mon enfant! –

a white sheet was taken from the walnut cupboard. And yet the grandmother brought him close to the hearth as if to warm his already stiffened limbs. Alas! what is touched by the cold hands of death can no more be warmed at firesides here below! She bent her head and pulled off his stockings, and in her aged hands she took the corpse's feet. – Isn't it a heartbreaking thing! she cried! Sir, he wasn't even eight years old! His masters – he went to school – were pleased with him. Sir, when I had to send a letter, it was he who wrote it. Are they going to start killing children now? Ah! my God! They are just brigands now! I ask you, he was playing this morning, there, just by the window! To think they've killed him, this poor little creature of mine! He was walking in the street, they shot at him. Sir, he was as good and gentle as a Jesus. I'm old, it's natural I should go; it would have made no difference to Monsieur Bonaparte to kill me instead of killing my child! – She broke off, choked by

Elle s'interrompit, les sanglots l'étouffant,
Puis elle dit, et tous pleuraient près de l'aïeule:
– Que vais-je devenir à présent toute seule?
Expliquez-moi cela, vous autres, aujourd'hui.
Hélas! je n'avais plus de sa mère que lui.
Pourquoi l'a-t-on tué? je veux qu'on me l'explique.
L'enfant n'a pas crié vive la République. –
Nous nous taisons, debout et graves, chapeau bas,
Tremblant devant ce deuil qu'on ne console pas.

Vous ne compreniez point, mère, la politique.
Monsieur Napoléon, c'est son nom authentique,
Est pauvre et même prince; il aime les palais;
Il lui convient d'avoir des chevaux, des valets,
De l'argent pour son jeu, sa table, son alcôve,
Ses chasses: par la même occasion, il sauve
La famille, l'église et la société;
Il veut avoir Saint-Cloud, plein de roses l'été,
Où viendront l'adorer les préfets et les maires;
C'est pour cela qu'il faut que les vieilles grand-mères,
De leurs pauvres doigts gris que fait trembler le temps,
Cousent dans le linceul des enfants de sept ans.

her sobs, and then she said, with all in tears beside the grandmother: – What will become of me now, all alone? Tell me that, you people, here today. Alas! he was all I had left of his mother. Why did they kill him! I want someone to tell me. The child didn't shout Long Live the Republic. – We are silent, standing gravely, hats held low, trembling before this grief that cannot be consoled.

Mother, you didn't understand politics. Monsieur Napoléon, for that's his real name, is poor and yet a prince; he loves palaces; it suits him to have horses, valets, money for his gambling, his table, his secluded bedroom, his hunting; into the bargain, he is the saviour of family, church and society; he covets Saint-Cloud, filled with roses in summer, where prefects and mayors will come and worship him; that's why old grandmothers, with their poor grey fingers that tremble with age, must sew into winding-sheets seven-year-old children.

Stella

Je m'étais endormi la nuit près de la grève.
Un vent frais m'éveilla, je sortis de mon rêve,
J'ouvris les yeux, je vis l'étoile du matin.
Elle resplendissait au fond du ciel lointain
Dans une blancheur molle, infinie et charmante.
Aquilon s'enfuyait emportant la tourmente.
L'astre éclatant changeait la nuée en duvet.
C'était une clarté qui pensait, qui vivait;
Elle apaisait l'écueil où la vague déferle;
On croyait voir une âme à travers une perle.
Il faisait nuit encor, l'ombre régnait en vain,
Le ciel s'illuminait d'un sourire divin.
La lueur argentait le haut du mât qui penche;
Le navire était noir, mais la voile était blanche;
Des goélands debout sur un escarpement,
Attentifs, contemplaient l'étoile gravement
Comme un oiseau céleste et fait d'une étincelle.
L'océan, qui ressemble au peuple, allait vers elle.

Stella

I had fallen asleep in the darkness near the shore. A cool wind woke me, I emerged from my dream, I opened my eyes, I saw the morning star. It was shining brightly in the depths of a distant sky in a soft whiteness, infinite, bewitching. The north wind fled away, carrying the tempest with it. The brilliant star changed the stormclouds into down. It was a light that thought, that lived; it calmed the reef where the waves break; it was as if one saw a soul through a pearl. Though it was still night, the darkness reigned in vain, the sky was illumined by a divine smile. The gleam flashed silver on the tilting mast; the ship was dark, but the sail was white; seagulls perched upright on a cliff beheld the star with solemn, rapt attention as if it were a heavenly bird made from a spark. The ocean, which is like the people, moved towards it and, with its

Et, rugissant tout bas, la regardait briller,
Et semblait avoir peur de la faire envoler.
Un ineffable amour emplissait l'étendue.
L'herbe verte à mes pieds frissonnait éperdue.
Les oiseaux se parlaient dans les nids; une fleur
Qui s'éveillait me dit: c'est l'étoile ma sœur.
Et pendant qu'à longs plis l'ombre levait son voile,
J'entendis une voix qui venait de l'étoile
Et qui disait: – Je suis l'astre qui vient d'abord.
Je suis celle qu'on croit dans la tombe et qui sort.
J'ai lui sur le Sina, j'ai lui sur le Taygète;
Je suis le caillou d'or et de feu que Dieu jette,
Comme avec une fronde, au front noir de la nuit.
Je suis ce qui renaît quand un monde est détruit.
O nations! je suis la Poésie ardente.
J'ai brillé sur Moïse et j'ai brillé sur Dante.
Le lion océan est amoureux de moi.
J'arrive. Levez-vous, vertu, courage, foi!
Penseurs, esprits, montez sur la tour, sentinelles!
Paupières, ouvrez-vous! allumez-vous, prunelles!
Terre, émeus le sillon; vie, éveille le bruit;

muted roar, watched it shine, and seemed afraid of putting it to flight. An ineffable love filled the vast expanse. The green grass at my feet was quivering in wild rapture. The birds spoke together in their nests; a waking flower told me: it is my sister star. And as the darkness lifted the long folds of its veil, I heard a voice that came from the star, saying: – I am the star that comes before. I am the one believed to be in the tomb and who emerges. I shone on Sinai, I shone on Taygeta; I am the fiery golden pebble hurled by God, as from a catapult, into the black brow of night. I am what is reborn when a world is destroyed. O nations! I am the burning fire of Poetry. I shone upon Moses and I shone upon Dante. The lion ocean is in love with me. I come. Rise up, virtue, courage, faith! Thinkers, minds, climb upon the tower, sentinels! Eyelids, open! eyes, kindle your spark! Earth, stir your furrow; life, arouse your

Debout, vous qui dormez! – car celui qui me suit,
Car celui qui m'envoie en avant la première,
C'est l'ange Liberté, c'est le géant Lumière!

sound; rise up, you sleepers! – for he who follows me, for he who sends me ahead as herald, is the angel called Liberty, the giant called Light!

Mes deux filles

Dans le frais clair-obscur du soir charmant qui tombe,
L'une pareille au cygne et l'autre à la colombe,
Belles, et toutes deux joyeuses, ô douceur!
Voyez, la grande sœur et la petite sœur
Sont assises au seuil du jardin, et sur elles
Un bouquet d'œillets blancs aux longues tiges frêles,
Dans une urne de marbre agité par le vent,
Se penche, et les regarde, immobile et vivant,
Et frissonne dans l'ombre, et semble, au bord du vase,
Un vol de papillons arrêté dans l'extase.

My two daughters

In the cool half-light of the enchanting fall of evening, one like the swan and the other like the dove, beautiful, and both happy, O sweetness! See, the big sister and the little sister sitting on the threshold of the garden, and above them a cluster of white carnations with long fragile stems, stirred in their marble urn by the wind, bends forward, motionless and living, and looks at them, and quivers in the shade, at the lip of the vase, like a flight of butterflies suspended in rapture.

Demain, dès l'aube ...

Demain, dès l'aube, à l'heure où blanchit la campagne,
Je partirai. Vois-tu, je sais que tu m'attends.
J'irai par la forêt, j'irai par la montagne.
Je ne puis demeurer loin de toi plus longtemps.

Je marcherai les yeux fixés sur mes pensées,
Sans rien voir au dehors, sans entendre aucun bruit,
Seul, inconnu, le dos courbé, les mains croisées,
Triste, et le jour pour moi sera comme la nuit.

Je ne regarderai ni l'or du soir qui tombe,
Ni les voiles au loin descendant vers Harfleur,
Et quand j'arriverai, je mettrai sur ta tombe
Un bouquet de houx vert et de bruyère en fleur.

Tomorrow, as soon as day breaks ...

Tomorrow, as soon as day breaks, at the hour when the landscape whitens, I will set out. You see, I know you are waiting for me. I will go by the forest, I will go by the mountain. I can stay no longer far from you.

I will walk with my gaze fixed on my thoughts, seeing nothing outside, hearing no sound, alone, unknown, with bent back and crossed hands, sad, and the daylight for me will be like night.

I will not look at the golden fall of evening, nor at the distant sails going down towards Harfleur, and when I arrive I will place on your tomb a bouquet of green holly and of flowering heather.

A Villequier

Maintenant que Paris, ses pavés et ses marbres,
Et sa brume et ses toits sont bien loin de mes yeux;
Maintenant que je suis sous les branches des arbres,
Et que je puis songer à la beauté des cieux;

Maintenant que du deuil qui m'a fait l'âme obscure
    Je sors, pâle et vainqueur,
Et que je sens la paix de la grande nature
    Qui m'entre dans le cœur;

Maintenant que je puis, assis au bord des ondes,
Ému par ce superbe et tranquille horizon,
Examiner en moi les vérités profondes
Et regarder les fleurs qui sont dans le gazon;

At Villequier

Now that Paris, its pavements and its marbles and its mist and its roofs are far from my eyes; now that I am beneath the branches of the trees, and I can muse on the beauty of the heavens;

Now that I am emerging, pale and victorious, from the grief that darkened my soul, and feel great nature's peace entering my heart;

Now that, seated at the waters' edge, moved by this proud and calm horizon, I can examine the deep truths within myself and gaze at the flowers in the grass;

Maintenant, ô mon Dieu! que j'ai ce calme sombre
    De pouvoir désormais
Voir de mes yeux la pierre où je sais que dans l'ombre
    Elle dort pour jamais;

Maintenant qu'attendri par ces divins spectacles,
Plaines, forêts, rochers, vallons, fleuve argenté,
Voyant ma petitesse et voyant vos miracles,
Je reprends ma raison devant l'immensité;

Je viens à vous, Seigneur, père auquel il faut croire;
    Je vous porte, apaisé,
Les morceaux de ce cœur tout plein de votre gloire
    Que vous avez brisé;

Je viens à vous, Seigneur! confessant que vous êtes
Bon, clément, indulgent et doux, ô Dieu vivant!
Je conviens que vous seul savez ce que vous faites,
Et que l'homme n'est rien qu'un jonc qui tremble au vent;

Now, O God! that I have this dark tranquillity in which I can henceforward see with my eyes the stone where I know she sleeps for ever in the shadow;

Now that, touched by these heavenly sights, plains, forests, rocks, valleys, silvery river, seeing my own smallness and seeing your miracles, I recover my reason in the face of the immensity;

I come to you, Lord, father in whom we must believe; pacified, I bring you the fragments of this heart, full of your glory, which you have shattered;

I come to you, Lord, confessing that you are good, merciful, indulgent and gentle, O living God! I acknowledge that you alone know what you do, and that man is nothing but a reed trembling in the wind;

Je dis que le tombeau qui sur les morts se ferme
    Ouvre le firmament;
Et que ce qu'ici-bas nous prenons pour le terme
    Est le commencement;

Je conviens à genoux que vous seul, père auguste,
Possédez l'infini, le réel, l'absolu;
Je conviens qu'il est bon, je conviens qu'il est juste
Que mon cœur ait saigné, puisque Dieu l'a voulu!

Je ne résiste plus à tout ce qui m'arrive
    Par votre volonté.
L'âme de deuils en deuils, l'homme de rive en rive,
    Roule à l'éternité.

Nous ne voyons jamais qu'un seul côté des choses;
L'autre plonge en la nuit d'un mystère effrayant.
L'homme subit le joug sans connaître les causes.
Tout ce qu'il voit est court, inutile et fuyant.

I say that the tomb as it closes on the dead opens the firmament; and that what we take here below for the end is the beginning;

I acknowledge on my knees that you alone, majestic father, possess the infinite, the real, the absolute; I grant that it is good, I grant that it is just that my heart has bled, since God has wished it!

I resist no longer all that happens to me by your will. The soul from grief to grief, mankind from shore to shore, drifts onward to eternity.

We never see more than a single side of things; the other plunges into the darkness of a frightening mystery. Man endures the yoke without knowing the causes. All that he sees is brief, futile and ephemeral.

Vous faites revenir toujours la solitude
    Autour de tous ses pas.
Vous n'avez pas voulu qu'il eût la certitude
    Ni la joie ici-bas!

Dès qu'il possède un bien, le sort le lui retire.
Rien ne lui fut donné, dans ses rapides jours,
Pour qu'il s'en puisse faire une demeure, et dire:
C'est ici ma maison, mon champ et mes amours!

Il doit voir peu de temps tout ce que ses yeux voient;
    Il vieillit sans soutiens.
Puisque ces choses sont, c'est qu'il faut qu'elles soient;
    J'en conviens, j'en conviens!

Le monde est sombre, ô Dieu! l'immuable harmonie
Se compose des pleurs aussi bien que des chants;
L'homme n'est qu'un atome en cette ombre infinie,
Nuit où montent les bons, où tombent les méchants.

You always bring back solitude round every step he takes. You have not wished him to have certainty or joy here on earth!

As soon as he owns a treasure, fate takes it back from him. Nothing was given to him, in his fleeting days, with which to make a dwelling, saying: Here are my home, my field, my loves!

He must see only briefly all that his eyes can see; he grows old without support. Since these things are, then they must be; I acknowledge it, I acknowledge it!

The world is dark, O God! the unchanging harmony is written in tears as well as songs; man is merely an atom in this infinite shadow, this night in which the good ascend and the wicked fall.

Je sais que vous avez bien autre chose à faire
    Que de nous plaindre tous,
Et qu'un enfant qui meurt, désespoir de sa mère,
    Ne vous fait rien, à vous.

Je sais que le fruit tombe au vent qui le secoue,
Que l'oiseau perd sa plume et la fleur son parfum;
Que la création est une grande roue
Qui ne peut se mouvoir sans écraser quelqu'un;

Les mois, les jours, les flots des mers, les yeux qui pleurent,
    Passent sous le ciel bleu;
Il faut que l'herbe pousse et que les enfants meurent;
    Je le sais, ô mon Dieu!

Dans vos cieux, au delà de la sphère des nues,
Au fond de cet azur immobile et dormant,
Peut-être faites-vous des choses inconnues
Où la douleur de l'homme entre comme élément.

I know that you have other things to do than to pity us all, and that a dying child, the despair of its mother, means nothing to you.

I know that the fruit falls in the wind that shakes it, that the bird loses its feather and the flower its scent; that creation is a great wheel which cannot move on without crushing someone;

The months, the days, the waves of the seas, the weeping eyes, pass by beneath the blue sky; the grass must grow and children must die; I know it, O my God!

In your heavens, beyond the cloudy sphere, deep in that motionless, sleeping blue, perhaps you are creating unknown things in which man's suffering plays a part.

Peut-être est-il utile à vos desseins sans nombre
    Que des êtres charmants
S'en aillent, emportés par le tourbillon sombre
    Des noirs événements.

Nos destins ténébreux vont sous des lois immenses
Que rien ne déconcerte et que rien n'attendrit.
Vous ne pouvez avoir de subites clémences
Qui dérangent le monde, ô Dieu, tranquille esprit!

Je vous supplie, ô Dieu! de regarder mon âme,
    Et de considérer
Qu'humble comme un enfant et doux comme une femme
    Je viens vous adorer!

Considérez encor que j'avais, dès l'aurore,
Travaillé, combattu, pensé, marché, lutté,
Expliquant la nature à l'homme qui l'ignore,
Éclairant toute chose avec votre clarté;

Perhaps it serves your countless purposes that delightful creatures should vanish, carried away by the dark whirlwind of black events.

Our shadowy destinies move under vast laws which nothing throws off balance and nothing moves to pity. You cannot have sudden merciful urges that upset the world, O God, calm spirit!

I beseech you, O God! to look at my soul, and to consider that I come, humble as a child and gentle as a woman, to worship you!

Consider too that since the dawn I had worked, fought, thought, marched and struggled, explaining nature to man who does not know it, clarifying all things with your bright light;

Que j'avais, affrontant la haine et la colère,
  Fait ma tâche ici-bas,
Que je ne pouvais pas m'attendre à ce salaire,
  Que je ne pouvais pas

Prévoir que, vous aussi, sur ma tête qui ploie
Vous appesantiriez votre bras triomphant,
Et que, vous qui voyiez comme j'ai peu de joie,
Vous me reprendriez si vite mon enfant!

Qu'une âme ainsi frappée à se plaindre est sujette,
  Que j'ai pu blasphémer,
Et vous jeter mes cris comme un enfant qui jette
  Une pierre à la mer!

Considérez qu'on doute, ô mon Dieu! quand on souffre,
Que l'œil qui pleure trop finit par s'aveugler,
Qu'un être que son deuil plonge au plus noir du gouffre,
Quand il ne vous voit plus, ne peut vous contempler,

That I, braving hatred and anger, had performed my task here below, that I could not expect that recompense, that I could not

Foresee that you too, upon my sinking head, would bring down the weight of your triumphant arm, and that you, who saw what little joy I have, would take back my child from me so swiftly!

That a soul so stricken is likely to complain, that I may have blasphemed, and hurled my cries at you like a child throwing a stone into the sea!

Consider, O my God! that we doubt when we suffer, that the eye that weeps too much will in the end go blind, that a being plunged by his grief into the blackest chasm, when he sees you no more, cannot contemplate you,

Et qu'il ne se peut pas que l'homme, lorsqu'il sombre
    Dans les afflictions,
Ait présente à l'esprit la sérénité sombre
    Des constellations!

Aujourd'hui, moi qui fus faible comme une mère,
Je me courbe à vos pieds devant vos cieux ouverts.
Je me sens éclairé dans ma douleur amère
Par un meilleur regard jeté sur l'univers.

Seigneur, je reconnais que l'homme est en délire
    S'il ose murmurer;
Je cesse d'accuser, je cesse de maudire,
    Mais laissez-moi pleurer!

Hélas! laissez les pleurs couler de ma paupière,
Puisque vous avez fait les hommes pour cela!
Laissez-moi me pencher sur cette froide pierre
Et dire à mon enfant: Sens-tu je suis là?

And that it cannot be that man, when he sinks into affliction, can have present in his mind the melancholy serenity of the constellations!

Today, I who was as weak as a mother, bend low at your feet before your open heavens. I feel enlightened in my bitter sorrow by a more mellow gaze cast on the universe.

Lord, I recognize that mankind is insane if he dares to complain; I accuse no more, I curse no more, but let me weep!

Alas! let the tears flow from my eyelids, since you have made men for that! Let me bend low over this cold stone and say to my child: Do you sense that I am here?

Laissez-moi lui parler, incliné sur ses restes,
    Le soir, quand tout se tait,
Comme si, dans sa nuit rouvrant ses yeux célestes,
    Cet ange m'écoutait!

Hélas! vers le passé tournant un œil d'envie,
Sans que rien ici-bas puisse m'en consoler,
Je regarde toujours ce moment de ma vie
Où je l'ai vue ouvrir son aile et s'envoler.

Je verrai cet instant jusqu'à ce que je meure,
    L'instant, pleurs superflus!
Où je criai: L'enfant que j'avais tout à l'heure,
    Quoi donc! je ne l'ai plus!

Ne vous irritez pas que je sois de la sorte,
O mon Dieu! cette plaie a si longtemps saigné!
L'angoisse dans mon âme est toujours la plus forte,
Et mon cœur est soumis, mais n'est pas résigné.

Let me speak to her, bent over her remains, in the evening, when all is silent, as if, reopening her heavenly eyes in her darkness, that angel were listening to me!

Alas! turning an eye of longing towards the past, with no solace for me here on earth, I gaze still at that moment in my life when I saw her spread her wings and fly away.

I shall see that moment until I die, the moment, pointless tears! when I cried: The child I had just now, how can it be! I have her no more!

Do not be angry that I am like this, O my God! this wound has bled so long! Anguish still holds sway in my soul, and my heart is submissive, but not resigned.

Ne vous irritez pas! fronts que le deuil réclame,
    Mortels sujets aux pleurs,
Il nous est malaisé de retirer notre âme
    De ces grandes douleurs.

Voyez-vous, nos enfants nous sont bien nécessaires,
Seigneur; quand on a vu dans sa vie, un matin,
Au milieu des ennuis, des peines, des misères,
Et de l'ombre que fait sur nous notre destin,

Apparaître un enfant, tête chère et sacrée,
    Petit être joyeux,
Si beau, qu'on a cru voir s'ouvrir à son entrée
    Une porte des cieux;

Quand on a vu, seize ans, de cet autre soi-même
Croître la grâce aimable et la douce raison,
Lorsqu'on a reconnu que cet enfant qu'on aime
Fait le jour dans notre âme et dans notre maison;

Do not be angry! with our brows claimed by grief, mortals prone to tears, it is hard for us to recover our soul from these great sorrows.

You see, our children are indispensable to us, Lord; when we have seen in our life, one morning, in the midst of the burdens, the troubles, the sorrows and the shadow cast upon us by our fate,

A child appear, a precious sacred head, a joyous little creature, so beautiful, it was as if a gate of Heaven opened as she came in;

When we have seen through sixteen years the growth of delightful grace and sweet reason in this, our other self, aware that this child whom we love brings daylight into our soul and into our home;

Que c'est la seule joie ici-bas qui persiste
    De tout ce qu'on rêva,
Considérez que c'est une chose bien triste
    De le voir qui s'en va!

That of all we dreamed it is the only earthly joy that lasts, consider that it is a sad thing indeed to see it slip away!

Booz endormi

Booz s'était couché de fatigue accablé;
Il avait tout le jour travaillé dans son aire,
Puis avait fait son lit à sa place ordinaire;
Booz dormait auprès des boisseaux pleins de blé.

Ce vieillard possédait des champs de blés et d'orge;
Il était, quoique riche, à la justice enclin;
Il n'avait pas de fange en l'eau de son moulin,
Il n'avait pas d'enfer dans le feu de sa forge.

Boaz sleeping

Boaz had laid himself down, overwhelmed by fatigue; he had worked all day on his threshing floor, then had made his bed in its usual place; Boaz slept beside the bushels filled with corn.

This old man owned fields of corn and barley; though rich, he was inclined to justice; he had no dirt in the water of his mill, nor inferno in the fire of his forge.

Sa barbe était d'argent comme un ruisseau d'avril.
Sa gerbe n'était point avare ni haineuse;
Quand il voyait passer quelque pauvre glaneuse,
– Laissez tomber exprès des épis, disait-il.

Cet homme marchait pur loin des sentiers obliques,
Vêtu de probité candide et de lin blanc;
Et, toujours du côté des pauvres ruisselant,
Ses sacs de grains semblaient des fontaines publiques.

Booz était bon maître et fidèle parent;
Il était généreux, quoiqu'il fût économe;
Les femmes regardaient Booz plus qu'un jeune homme,
Car le jeune homme est beau, mais le vieillard est grand.

His beard was of silver like an April stream. His sheaf was not mean or grudging; when he saw some poor woman gleaning as she passed: – Let fall some ears of corn on purpose, he would say.

This man walked in purity far from devious ways, dressed in simple integrity and white linen; and, flowing always towards the poor, his sacks of grain seemed public fountains.

Boaz was a good master and a faithful kinsman; he was generous, although he was thrifty; the women looked at Boaz more than at a young man, for the young man is handsome, but the old man is great.

Le vieillard, qui revient vers la source première,
Entre aux jours éternels et sort des jours changeants;
Et l'on voit de la flamme aux yeux des jeunes gens,
Mais dans l'œil du vieillard on voit de la lumière.

★

Donc, Booz dans la nuit dormait parmi les siens;
Près des meules, qu'on eût prises pour des décombres,
Les moissonneurs couchés faisaient des groupes sombres;
Et ceci se passait dans des temps très anciens.

Les tribus d'Israël avaient pour chef un juge;
La terre, où l'homme errait sous la tente, inquiet
Des empreintes de pieds de géant qu'il voyait,
Était encor mouillée et molle du déluge.

★

The old man, moving back towards the fountain-head, is entering on eternal days and leaving the days of change; fire can be seen in young men's eyes, but in the old man's eyes there is light.

★

So Boaz in the night slept among his people; near the millstones which one might have thought were ruins, the sleeping harvesters formed shadowy groups; and this took place in very ancient times.

The tribes of Israel had as their leader a judge; the earth, where men wandered with their tents, troubled by the giant footprints which they saw, was still moist and soft from the flood.

★

Comme dormait Jacob, comme dormait Judith,
Booz, les yeux fermés, gisait sous la feuillée;
Or, la porte du ciel s'étant entre-bâillée
Au-dessus de sa tête, un songe en descendit.

Et ce songe était tel, que Booz vit un chêne
Qui, sorti de son ventre, allait jusqu'au ciel bleu;
Une race y montait comme une longue chaîne;
Un roi chantait en bas, en haut mourait un dieu.

Et Booz murmurait avec la voix de l'âme:
"Comment se pourrait-il que de moi ceci vînt?
Le chiffre de mes ans a passé quatre-vingt,
Et je n'ai pas de fils, et je n'ai plus de femme.

"Voilà longtemps que celle avec qui j'ai dormi,
O Seigneur! a quitté ma couche pour la vôtre;
Et nous sommes encore tout mêlés l'un à l'autre,
Elle à demi vivante et moi mort à demi.

As Jacob slept, as Judith slept, Boaz, his eyes closed, lay beneath the arbour. And now, the gate of heaven having half opened above his head, a dream came down from there.

And this dream was such that Boaz saw an oak which, issuing from his loins, went up to the blue sky; a people were climbing it like a long chain; a king sang at its foot, a god was dying at its peak.

And Boaz murmured with the voice of the soul: 'How could it be that this could come from me? The number of my years has passed eighty, and I have no son, nor now a wife.

It is a long time since she with whom I slept, O Lord, left my bed for yours; and we are still entwined together, she half living and I half dead.

"Une race naîtrait de moi! Comment le croire?
Comment se pourrait-il que j'eusse des enfants?
Quand on est jeune, on a des matins triomphants,
Le jour sort de la nuit comme d'une victoire;

"Mais, vieux, on tremble ainsi qu'à l'hiver le bouleau;
Je suis veuf, je suis seul, et sur moi le soir tombe,
Et je courbe, ô mon Dieu! mon âme vers la tombe,
Comme un bœuf ayant soif penche son front vers l'eau."

Ainsi parlait Booz dans le rêve et l'extase,
Tournant vers Dieu ses yeux par le sommeil noyés;
Le cèdre ne sent pas une rose à sa base,
Et lui ne sentait pas une femme à ses pieds.

★

Pendant qu'il sommeillait, Ruth, une moabite,
S'était couchée aux pieds de Booz, le sein nu,
Espérant on ne sait quel rayon inconnu,
Quand viendrait du réveil la lumière subite.

A people born of me! How could I believe it? How could I have children? When we are young, we have triumphant mornings, day comes out of night as from a victory;

But when we are old we tremble like a birch tree in winter; I am a widower, I am alone, the evening is falling on me, and, O God! I bow my soul towards the grave, as a thirsty ox lowers his brow towards the water.'

Thus spoke Boaz in dream and ecstasy, turning his sleep-drowned eyes towards God; the cedar does not sense a rose at its base, and he did not sense a woman at his feet.

★

While he slept Ruth, a Moabite, had laid herself bare-breasted at the feet of Boaz, hoping for we cannot guess what unknown gleam when suddenly should come the light of waking.

Booz ne savait point qu'une femme était là,
Et Ruth ne savait point ce que Dieu voulait d'elle.
Un frais parfum sortait des touffes d'asphodèle;
Les souffles de la nuit flottaient sur Galgala.

L'ombre était nuptiale, auguste et solennelle;
Les anges y volaient sans doute obscurément,
Car on voyait passer dans la nuit, par moment,
Quelque chose de bleu qui paraissait une aile.

La respiration de Booz qui dormait
Se mêlait au bruit sourd des ruisseaux sur la mousse.
On était dans le mois où la nature est douce,
Les collines ayant des lys sur leur sommet.

Ruth songeait et Booz dormait; l'herbe était noire;
Les grelots des troupeaux palpitaient vaguement;
Une immense bonté tombait du firmament;
C'était l'heure tranquille où les lions vont boire.

Boaz did not know that a woman was there, and Ruth did not know what God wanted of her. A cool scent drifted from the clusters of asphodel; the breath of night floated over Galgala.

The darkness was nuptial, majestic and solemn; no doubt angels flew unseen within it, for at moments, passing in the night, something blue was seen that seemed to be a wing.

The breathing of the sleeping Boaz mingled with the muted sound of the streams on the moss. It was the month when nature is gentle, and the hills had lilies on their summits.

Ruth mused and Boaz slept; the grass was dark; the bells of the flocks quivered indistinctly; an immense goodness was falling from the firmament; it was the peaceful hour when the lions go to drink.

Tout reposait dans Ur et dans Jérimadeth;
Les astres émaillaient le ciel profond et sombre;
Le croissant fin et clair parmi ces fleurs de l'ombre
Brillait à l'occident, et Ruth se demandait,

Immobile, ouvrant l'œil à moitié sous ses voiles,
Quel dieu, quel moissonneur de l'éternel été
Avait, en s'en allant, négligemment jeté
Cette faucille d'or dans le champ des étoiles.

All was at rest in Ur and Jerimadeth; the stars studded the deep dark sky; the bright and slender crescent moon, among those flowers of the darkness, shone in the west, and Ruth wondered,

Motionless, her eyes half open under her veils, what god, what harvester of the eternal summer had carelessly thrown, as he went by, that golden sickle into the field of stars.

Je suis fait d'ombre et de marbre ...

Je suis fait d'ombre et de marbre.
Comme les pieds noirs de l'arbre,
Je m'enfonce dans la nuit.
J'écoute; je suis sous terre;
D'en bas je dis au tonnerre:
Attends! ne fais pas de bruit.

I am made of shadow and marble ...

I am made of shadow and marble. Like the black feet of the tree I dig deep into darkness. I listen; I am underground; from below I say to the thunder: Wait! make no sound.

Moi qu'on nomme le poète,
Je suis dans la nuit muette
L'escalier mystérieux;
Je suis l'escalier Ténèbres;
Dans mes spirales funèbres
L'ombre ouvre ses vagues yeux.

Les flambeaux deviendront cierges.
Respectez mes degrés vierges,
Passez, les joyeux du jour!
Mes marches ne sont pas faites
Pour les pieds ailés des fêtes,
Pour les pieds nus de l'amour.

Devant ma profondeur blême
Tout tremble, les spectres même
Ont des gouttes de sueur.
Je viens de la tombe morte;
J'aboutis à cette porte
Par où passe une lueur.

I who am called the poet, I am the mysterious staircase in the wordless night; I am the staircase Darkness; in my deathly spirals the shadow opens its indistinct eyes.

The festive torches will become candles. Respect my virgin altar-steps; pass by, joyous people of the daylight! My steps are not made for the winged feet of celebration, for the bare feet of love.

Before my pallid depth all trembles, even the spectres have beads of sweat. I come from the dead tomb; my end is at this door through which a gleam of light passes.

Le banquet rit et flamboie.
Les maîtres sont dans la joie
Sur leur trône ensanglanté;
Tout les sert, tout les encense;
Et la femme à leur puissance
Mesure sa nudité

Laissez la clef et le pène.
Je suis l'escalier; la peine
Médite; l'heure viendra;
Quelqu'un qu'entourent les ombres
Montera mes marches sombres,
Et quelqu'un les descendra.

The banquet laughs and glows with light. The masters are in high spirits on their bloody throne; all serves them, all burns incense before them; and woman before their power measures her nakedness.

Leave alone the key and bolt. I am the staircase; suffering meditates; the hour will come; someone enveloped in shadows will climb my sombre steps, and someone will descend them.

Fenêtres ouvertes

Le matin. – En dormant

J'entends des voix. Lueurs à travers ma paupière.
Une cloche est en branle à l'église Saint-Pierre.
Cris des baigneurs. Plus près! plus loin! non, par ici!
Non, par là! Les oiseaux gazouillent, Jeanne aussi.
Georges l'appelle. Chant des coqs. Une truelle
Racle un toit. Des chevaux passent dans la ruelle.
Grincement d'une faulx qui coupe le gazon.
Chocs. Rumeurs. Des couvreurs marchent sur la maison.
Bruits du port. Sifflement des machines chauffées.
Musique militaire arrivant par bouffées.
Brouhaha sur le quai. Voix françaises. Merci.
Bonjour. Adieu. Sans doute il est tard, car voici
Que vient tout près de moi chanter mon rouge-gorge.
Vacarme de marteaux lointains dans une forge.
L'eau clapote. On entend haleter un steamer.
Une mouche entre. Souffle immense de la mer.

Open Windows

The morning – sleeping

I hear voices. Lights through my eyelid. A bell is in full swing at the Saint-Pierre church. Bathers' cries. Closer! further! no, this way! no, that way! The birds are twittering, Jeanne too. Georges calls her. Cocks crowing. A trowel scrapes a roof. Horses pass in the lane. Scratching of a scythe cutting grass. Thuds. Vague murmurings. Tilers walking on the house. Harbour noises. Whistling of stoked engines. Military music arriving in gusts. Hubbub on the quayside. French voices. Thank you. Good morning. Goodbye. It must be late, for here comes my robin singing right beside me. Din of distant hammers in a forge. The water laps. A steamer pants audibly. A fly comes in. Boundless breath of the sea.

Bêtise de la guerre

Ouvrière sans yeux, Pénélope imbécile,
Berceuse du chaos où le néant oscille,
Guerre, ô guerre occupée au choc des escadrons,
Toute pleine du bruit furieux des clairons,
O buveuse de sang, qui, farouche, flétrie,
Hideuse, entraînes l'homme en cette ivrognerie,
Nuée où le destin se déforme, où Dieu fuit,
Où flotte une clarté plus noire que la nuit,
Folle immense, de vent et de foudres armée,
A quoi sers-tu, géante, à quoi sers-tu, fumée,
Si tes écroulements reconstruisent le mal,
Si pour le bestial tu chasses l'animal,
Si tu ne sais, dans l'ombre où ton hasard se vautre,
Défaire un empereur que pour en faire un autre?

Mindlessness of War

Eyeless drudge, idiot Penelope, cradle-rocker of chaos where obliteration lurches, war, O war, engaging the clash of squadrons, filled with the passionate sound of bugles, O drinker of blood, savage, withered, hideous, dragging man into this drunken orgy, thundercloud distorting destiny, shunned by God, where hangs a gleaming darkness, blacker than the night, colossal madwoman, armed with wind and lightning bolts, what use are you, giantess, what use are you, smoke, if your crumbling debris rebuilds evil, if you drive out the animal in favour of the bestial, if, in the shadows where your randomness wallows, you can unmake an emperor only to make another?

Charles-Augustin Sainte-Beuve
(1804–69)

Later to become an influential literary critic, Sainte-Beuve as a young man was a Romantic poet of intimate lyricism and delicately understated melancholy. Artistically tentative, wounded by life and love, and in awe of Hugo, he nevertheless produced some memorably sensitive work of which one example is given here. His atmospheric musicality and the use of a concrete image as a 'landscape of the soul' prefigure Symbolist poetry.

Volumes: *Vie, poésie et pensées de Joseph Delorme* 1829, *Les Consolations* 1830, *Les Pensées d'août* 1837.

Mon âme est ce lac même ...

Mon âme est ce lac même où le soleil qui penche,
Par un beau soir d'automne, envoie un feu mourant:
Le flot frissonne à peine, et pas une aile blanche,
Pas une rame au loin n'y joue en l'effleurant.
    Tout dort, tout est tranquille, et le cristal limpide
En se refroidissant à l'air glacé des nuits,
Sans écho, sans soupir, sans un pli qui le ride,
Semble un miroir tout fait pour les pâles ennuis.
    Mais ne sentez-vous pas, Madame, à son silence,
A ses flots transparents de lui-même oubliés,
A sa calme étendue où rien ne se balance,
Le bonheur qu'il éprouve à se taire à vos pieds
    A réfléchir en paix le bien-aimé rivage,
A le peindre plus pur en ne s'y mêlant pas,
A ne rien perdre en soi de la divine image
De Celle dont sans bruit il recueille les pas?

My soul is this very lake ...

My soul is this very lake over which the setting sun, on a lovely autumn evening, sends a dying glow: the waters scarcely quiver and no white wing nor distant oar plays skimming on its surface.

All sleeps, all is calm, and the limpid crystal, cooling in the icy air of night, with no echo, no sigh, nor any ripple to crease it, seems a perfect mirror for pale melancholy.

But do you not sense, Madame, in its silence, in its transparent waters which it has itself forgotten, in its placid expanse where nothing rocks, the happiness it feels in its silence at your feet,

In reflecting peacefully the beloved shore, painting it more pure by not intruding itself, losing nothing in itself of the heavenly image of Her whose steps it soundlessly records?

Gérard de Nerval
(1808–55)

Nerval was a popular if unstable and tormented member of the Romantic group. His exotic behaviour (walking a lobster on a blue silk lead, for example, in the Palais Royal gardens) later deepened into insanity and culminated in his suicide, hanged from a Paris streetlamp. His replacement of his real surname, Labrunie, by the name of a country property he had known and loved in childhood was characteristic of a man who sought to give all his experience the value of myth.

His fame rests chiefly on a short but highly influential series of densely allusive sonnets, published in 1853 as *Les Chimères*. Before this volume, he had written more recognizably Romantic verse (represented by the first two examples here), and had translated Heine, Hoffmann and Goethe.

In *Les Chimères* this traveller and scholar of the occult, of pagan metaphysics, of mythology and anthropology, condensed his erudition into sonnets of unusually compressed emotional power. They are endowed with a subjective and mystical unity that escapes rational formulation, even though most of the individual allusions can be decoded (to do so here would require a vast number of footnotes, and exegeses of Nerval exist in plenty).

Obsessed with reincarnation and the Tarot pack, Nerval lived a life in which reality and dream were fused in a mythical world. The present is here inhabited by talismanic images from the past, many of them connected with an unrequited love. He stands on the threshold of an ancient Golden Age, awaiting its imminent rebirth.

The Alexandrine sonnet as Nerval exploits it produces a fascinating tension between classicism of form and visionary originality of content. Each poem, with its echoing musicality and its evocative proper names in combinations following dream-logic, is an infinite hallucination contained within a jewel. It is easy to understand why he is often seen as a source of Surrealism, a poet far ahead of his time. Some caution is needed here, however, for his composition was formal and lucid rather than 'automatic', and another school of thought places him firmly in his own time as a Romantic.

Major works: *Les Odelettes* 1852, *Les Chimères* 1853.

Fantaisie

Il est un air pour qui je donnerais
Tout Rossini, tout Mozart et tout Weber,
Un air très vieux, languissant et funèbre,
Qui pour moi seul a des charmes secrets.

Or, chaque fois que je viens à l'entendre,
De deux cents ans mon âme rajeunit:
C'est sous Louis-Treize... – et je crois voir s'étendre
Un coteau vert que le couchant jaunit;

Dream Memory

There is a melody for which I'd give all Rossini, all Mozart and all Weber, an ancient, listless and funereal tune, which for me alone holds secret charms.

Now, each time I chance to hear it, my soul grows younger by two hundred years: in the time of Louis the Thirteenth ... – and I seem to see the expanse of a green hillside tinged yellow by the sunset;

Puis un château de brique à coins de pierre,
Aux vitraux teints de rougeâtres couleurs,
Ceint de grands parcs, avec une rivière
Baignant ses pieds, qui coule entre des fleurs.

Puis une dame, à sa haute fenêtre,
Blonde aux yeux noirs, en ses habits anciens...
Que, dans une autre existence, peut-être,
J'ai déjà vue – et dont je me souviens!

Then a brick mansion with stone corners, with reddish-tinted stained glass windows, girded with broad parklands, with a river that bathes its feet and flows amidst flowers.

Then a lady, at her high window, with flaxen hair and dark eyes, in her ancient garments ... whom in another existence perhaps I have already seen – and I remember her!

Vers dorés

Eh quoi! tout est sensible!
PYTHAGORE

Homme, libre penseur! te crois-tu seul pensant
Dans ce monde où la vie éclate en toute chose?
Des forces que tu tiens ta liberté dispose,
Mais de tous tes conseils l'univers est absent.

Respecte dans la bête un esprit agissant:
Chaque fleur est une âme à la nature éclose;
Un mystère d'amour dans le métal repose;
'Tout est sensible!' Et tout sur ton être est puissant.

Gilded Verses

What! All is sentient!
Pythagoras[1]

Man, free thinker! do you imagine you think alone in this world where life bursts forth in all things? Your freedom has at its service the strength which you possess, but the universe is absent from all your councils.[2]

Respect in the animal an active spirit: each flower is a soul opened up to Nature; a mystery of love is at rest within metal; 'All is sentient!' And everything has power over your being.

[1]Probably derived from Delisle de Sales' *De la philosophie de la nature* (1777) rather than from Pythagoras himself.
[2]'Conseils' could also be translated as 'counsels'.

Crains, dans le mur aveugle, un regard qui t'épie:
A la matière même un verbe est attaché...
Ne la fais pas servir à quelque usage impie!

Souvent dans l'être obscur habite un Dieu caché;
Et comme un œil naissant couvert par ses paupières,
Un pur esprit s'accroît sous l'écorce des pierres!

Fear in the unseeing wall a watchful gaze: to matter itself a word is linked ... Do not make it serve some blasphemous purpose!

Often in the shadowy being there lies a hidden God; and, like a newborn eye covered by its lids, a pure spirit grows beneath the husk of stones!

El Desdichado

Je suis le ténébreux, – le veuf, – l'inconsolé,
Le prince d'Aquitaine à la tour abolie:
Ma seule *étoile* est morte, – et mon luth constellé
Porte le *Soleil noir* de la *Mélancolie*.

El Desdichado[1]

I am the shadow-man, the widower, the unconsoled, the Prince of Aquitaine dispossessed of his tower: my only *star* is dead, – and my star-decked lute bears the *black Sun* of *Melancholy*.

[1]The disinherited one.

Dans la nuit du tombeau, toi qui m'as consolé,
Rends-moi le Pausilippe et la mer d'Italie,
La *fleur* qui plaisait tant à mon cœur désolé,
Et la treille où la pampre à la rose s'allie.

Suis-je Amour ou Phébus?...Lusignan ou Biron?
Mon front est rouge encor du baiser de la reine;
J'ai rêvé dans la grotte où nage la syrène...

Et j'ai deux fois vainqueur traversé l'Achéron:
Modulant tour à tour sur la lyre d'Orphée
Les soupirs de la sainte et les cris de la fée.

In the darkness of the tomb, you who consoled me, restore to me Posilipo and the Italian sea, the *flower* that so pleased my stricken heart, and the arbour where the vine joins with the rose.

Am I Eros or Apollo? ... Lusignan or Biron? My forehead is still red from the kiss of the queen; I have dreamed in the cave where the siren swims ...

And twice victorious I have crossed Acheron: rendering in turn on Orpheus' lyre the sighs of the saint and the fairy's cries.

Myrtho

Je pense à toi, Myrtho, divine enchanteresse,
Au Pausilippe altier, de mille feux brillant,
A ton front inondé des clartés d'Orient,
Aux raisins noirs mêlés avec l'or de ta tresse.

C'est dans ta coupe aussi que j'avais bu l'ivresse,
Et dans l'éclair furtif de ton œil souriant,
Quand aux pieds d'Iacchus on me voyait priant,
Car la Muse m'a fait l'un des fils de la Grèce.

Je sais pourquoi là-bas le volcan s'est rouvert...
C'est qu'hier tu l'avais touché d'un pied agile,
Et de cendres soudain l'horizon s'est couvert.

Myrtho

I think of you, Myrtho, divine enchantress, of proud Posilipo shining with a thousand fires, of your brow flooded with the brightness of the East, of the black grapes mingled with the gold of your plait.

It was in your cup too that I had drunk intoxication, and in the surreptitious gleam of your smiling eye, when I was seen praying at the feet of Bacchus, for the Muse has made me one of the sons of Greece.

I know why yonder volcano opened once again ... for yesterday you had touched it with a nimble foot, and suddenly the horizon was enveloped in ashes.

Depuis qu'un duc normand brisa tes dieux d'argile,
Toujours, sous les rameaux du laurier de Virgile,
Le pâle Hortensia s'unit au Myrthe vert!

Since a Norman duke smashed your gods of clay, beneath the boughs of Virgil's laurel the pale Hydrangea has always entwined with the green Myrtle!

Antéros

Tu demandes pourquoi j'ai tant de rage au cœur
Et sur un col flexible une tête indomptée;
C'est que je suis issu de la race d'Antée,
Je retourne les dards contre le dieu vainqueur.

Oui, je suis de ceux-là qu'inspire le Vengeur,
Il m'a marqué le front de sa lèvre irritée,
Sous la pâleur d'Abel, hélas! ensanglantée,
J'ai parfois de Caïn l'implacable rougeur!

Anteros

You ask why I have so much fury in my heart and above a pliant neck an unconquered head; it is that I am descended from the race of Antaeus, I turn back the arrows against the victorious god.

Yes, I am of those whom the Avenger inspires, he has marked my brow with his angry lip, beneath Abel's pallor, alas! stained with blood, I have sometimes the implacable crimson of Cain!

Jéhovah! le dernier, vaincu par ton génie,
Qui, du fond des enfers, criait: "O tyrannie!"
C'est mon aïeul Bélus ou mon père Dagon ...

Ils m'ont plongé trois fois dans les eaux du Cocyte,
Et protégeant tout seul ma mère Amalécyte,
Je ressème à ses pieds les dents du vieux dragon.

Jehovah! the last one, conquered by your genius, who from the depths of hell cried 'O tyranny!' was my grandfather Baal or my father Dagon ...

They immersed me three times in the waters of Cocytus, and, sole protector of my Amalekite mother, I sow once more at her feet the old dragon's teeth.

Delfica

La connais-tu, Dafné, cette ancienne romance,
Au pied du sycomore, ou sous les lauriers blancs,
Sous l'olivier, le myrthe ou les saules tremblants,
Cette chanson d'amour...qui toujours recommence!

Delfica

Daphne, do you know this old ballad, at the foot of the sycamore or beneath the white laurels, under the olive tree, the myrtle or the quivering willows, this song of love ... which always begins anew!

Reconnais-tu le TEMPLE, au péristyle immense,
Et les citrons amers où s'imprimaient tes dents?
Et la grotte, fatale aux hôtes imprudents,
Où du dragon vaincu dort l'antique semence.

Ils reviendront ces dieux que tu pleures toujours!
Le temps va ramener l'ordre des anciens jours;
La terre a tressailli d'un souffle prophétique ...

Cependant la sibylle au visage latin
Est endormie encor sous l'arc de Constantin:
– Et rien n'a dérangé la sévère portique.

Do you recognize the TEMPLE with the vast peristyle, and the bitter lemons which bore the marks of your teeth? And the cave, fatal to rash visitors, where sleeps the ancient seed of the defeated dragon.

They will return, those gods for whom you still weep! Time will bring back the ancient order; the earth has shuddered with a prophetic breath ...

And yet the sibyl with the Latin face still sleeps beneath the arch of Constantine: – and nothing has disturbed the austere portico.

Artémis

La Treizième revient ... C'est encor la première;
Et c'est toujours la Seule, – ou c'est le seul moment:
Car es-tu Reine, ô toi! la première ou dernière?
Es-tu Roi, toi le seul ou le dernier amant?...

Aimez qui vous aima du berceau dans la bière;
Celle que j'aimai seul m'aime encor tendrement:
C'est la Mort – ou la Morte ... O délice! ô tourment!
La rose qu'elle tient, c'est la *Rose trémière.*

Sainte napolitaine aux mains pleines de feux,
Rose au cœur violet, fleur de sainte Gudule:
As-tu trouvé ta Croix dans le désert des cieux?

Artemis

The Thirteenth returns ... and yet also the first; and still the Only One, – or it is the only moment: for art thou Queen, o thou! the first or last? Art thou King, thou the only or the last lover? ...

Love the one who loved you from the cradle to the grave; she whom I alone loved still loves me tenderly: she is Death – or the Dead Woman ... O delight! O torment! the rose she holds is the *hollyhock*.

Neapolitan saint with your hands full of fires, rose with the violet heart, Saint Gudula's flower: have you found your Cross in the desert of the heavens?

Roses blanches, tombez! vous insultez nos dieux,
Tombez, fantômes blancs, de votre ciel qui brûle;
– La Sainte de l'abîme est plus sainte à mes yeux!

White roses, fall! you insult our gods; fall, white spectres, from your burning sky; the saint of the abyss, she is holier in my sight!

Alfred de Musset
(1810–57)

Seen in his time as a rather Byronic figure, Musset has perhaps lost status in recent critical evaluations (and indeed since he was execrated by Rimbaud), though his plays have enjoyed some resurgent interest. He remains, nevertheless, a significant if ambiguous poet of the Romantic era. His verse blends lyrical pathos with a relaxed colloquial touch and a strong vein of irony, within an essentially classical frame.

After abortive law and medical studies, he came under Hugo's influence at the 'Cénacle', and published *Contes d'Espagne et d'Italie* in 1830. The most emotionally turbulent and artistically productive period of his life, the mid-1830s, carried him first as great lover and then as misogynist through and beyond a stormy affair with the novelist George Sand (Aurore Dupin, Mme Dudevant), into a prolonged oscillation between bitterness and recognition of the personal and artistic value of the experience, in which love, if only crystallized as a memory, gives form and meaning to life. Always in fragile health aggravated by alcoholic and sexual excess, he died at the age of 47.

Like his life, Musset's work is a restless and perplexing blend of emotion and analysis, despair and wit, spontaneity and irony. Artistically insecure and wryly aware of his thematic limitations, masochistic in his need for emotional crisis, a self-indulgent dandy burning himself out in a remorseful search for purity, he has a schizoid quality which takes strikingly objectified form in the 'Nuits' poems. These are a series of dialogues between the poet and his Muse, set on a nerve-strand of precarious creativity.

His work was published in a piecemeal way, but a definitive version of his *Premières Poésies* and *Poésies Nouvelles* appeared in 1852. Later groupings included *Poésies Complémentaires* and *Poésies Posthumes*.

Une Soirée perdue

J'étais seul, l'autre soir, au Théâtre-Français,
Ou presque seul; l'auteur n'avait pas grand succès.
Ce n'était que Molière, et nous savons de reste
Que ce grand maladroit, qui fit un jour *Alceste*,
Ignora le bel art de chatouiller l'esprit
Et de servir à point un dénoûment bien cuit.
Grâce à Dieu, nos auteurs ont changé de méthode,
Et nous aimons bien mieux quelque drame à la mode
Où l'intrigue, enlacée et roulée en feston,
Tourne comme un rébus autour d'un mirliton.

A Wasted Evening

I was alone the other evening at the Comédie Française, or almost alone; the author wasn't having much success. It was only Molière, and we know only too well that that great bungler, who one day created *Alceste*, knew nothing of the fine art of titillating the mind and of serving up a well-cooked ending done to a turn. God be thanked, our authors have changed their methods, and we prefer by far some fashionable play whose plot, entwined and rolled up in festoons, spins like a punning conundrum around some doggerel verse.

J'écoutais cependant cette simple harmonie,
Et comme le bon sens fait parler le génie.
J'admirais quel amour pour l'âpre vérité
Eut cet homme si fier en sa naïveté,
Quel grand et vrai savoir des choses de ce monde,
Quelle mâle gaieté, si triste et si profonde
Que, lorsque'on vient d'en rire, on devrait en pleurer!
Et je me demandais: "Est-ce assez d'admirer?
Est-ce assez de venir un soir, par aventure,
D'entendre au fond de l'âme un cri da la nature,
D'essuyer une larme, et de partir ainsi,
Quoi qu'on fasse d'ailleurs, sans en prendre souci?"

Yet I listened to that simple harmony, and how good sense made genius speak. I admired the love of harsh truth in that man so proud in his ingenuousness, what great and true knowledge of the things of this world, what manly humour, so sad and so profound that, when one has just laughed at it, one should be weeping! And I wondered: 'Is it enough to admire? Is it enough to come by chance one evening, to hear nature's cry in the depths of the soul, to wipe away a tear, and so to leave, whatever else one does, without taking any heed?'

Enfoncé que j'étais dans cette rêverie,
Ça et là, toutefois, lorgnant la galerie,
Je vis que, devant moi, se balançait gaîment
Sous une tresse noire un cou svelte et charmant;
Et, voyant cet ébène enchâssé dans l'ivoire,
Un vers d'André Chénier chanta dans ma mémoire,
Un vers presque inconnu, refrain inachevé,
Frais comme le hasard, moins écrit que rêvé.
J'osai m'en souvenir, même devant Molière;
Sa grande ombre, à coup sûr, ne s'en offensa pas;
Et, tout en écoutant, je murmurais tout bas,
Regardant cette enfant, que ne s'en doutait guère:
"Sous votre aimable tête, un cou blanc, délicat,
Se plie, et de la neige effacerait l'éclat."

Immersed as I was in these musings, yet glancing here and there at the gallery, I saw before me, delightfully poised beneath a black plait, a slim and charming neck; and, seeing this ebony set in ivory, a line from André Chénier sang in my memory, an almost unknown line, an unfinished refrain, fresh as chance, less written than dreamed. I dared to remember it, even before Molière; his great shade, I'm sure, was not offended; and as I listened, I murmured gently, gazing at that child who could scarcely even guess at it: 'Beneath your lovely head, a white and delicate neck inclines, and would eclipse the brightness of snow.'

Puis je songeais encore (ainsi va la pensée)
Que l'antique franchise, à ce point délaissée,
Avec notre finesse et notre esprit moqueur,
Ferait croire, après tout, que nous manquons de cœur;
Que c'était une triste et honteuse misère
Que cette solitude à l'entour de Molière,
Et qu'il est *pourtant temps*, comme dit la chanson,
De sortir de ce siècle ou d'en avoir raison;
Car à quoi comparer cette scène embourbée,
Et l'effroyable honte où la muse est tombée?
La lâcheté nous bride, et les sots vont disant
Que, sous ce vieux soleil, tout est fait à présent;
Comme si les travers de la famille humaine
Ne rejeunissaient pas chaque an, chaque semaine.
Notre siècle a ses mœurs, partant, sa vérité;
Celui qui l'ose dire est toujours écouté.

Then I thought further (for so goes thought) that such an abandonment of the old frankness, along with our subtlety and our mocking wit, would make one believe, after all, that we lack heart; that this solitude around Molière was a sad and shameful disgrace, and that it is *high time*, as the song says, to quit this age or to get the better of it; for with what can we compare this muddy stage, and the frightful shame into which the muse has fallen? Cowardice bridles us, and the fools say that everything has now been done beneath this aged sun; as if the human family's foibles were not renewed each year, each week. Our century has its manners, and therefore its truth; he who dares to tell it always finds listeners.

Ah! j'oserais parler, si je croyais bien dire,
J'oserais ramasser le fouet de la satire,
Et l'habiller de noir, cet homme aux rubans verts,
Qui se fâchait jadis pour quelques mauvais vers.
S'il rentrait aujourd'hui dans Paris, la grand'ville,
Il y trouverait mieux pour émouvoir sa bile
Qu'une méchante femme et qu'un méchant sonnet;
Nous avons autre chose à mettre au cabinet.
O notre maître à tous! si ta tombe est fermée,
Laisse-moi, dans ta cendre un instant ranimée,
Trouver une étincelle, et je vais t'imiter!
Apprends-moi de quel ton, dans ta bouche hardie,
Parlait la vérité, ta seule passion,
Et, pour me faire entendre, à défaut du génie,
J'en aurai le courage et l'indignation!

Ah! I would dare to speak, if I thought I could speak well, I would dare to pick up satire's whip and dress in black that man in green ribbons who once was angered by a few bad lines of verse. If he came back to Paris now, the great city, he would find more to move him to anger than a mischievous woman and a wretched sonnet; we have other things to flush away. O master of us all, if your tomb is closed, let me find a spark in your briefly rekindled ashes, and I will follow your example! Teach me in what tone, in your fearless mouth, spoke truth, your only passion, and to make myself heard, in the absence of genius, I will have its courage and its indignation!

Ainsi je caressais une folle chimère.
Devant moi cependant, à côté de sa mère,
L'enfant restait toujours, et le cou svelte et blanc
Sous les longs cheveux noirs se berçait mollement.
Le spectacle fini, la charmante inconnue
Se leva. Le beau cou, l'épaule à demi nue,
Se voilèrent; la main glissa dans le manchon;
Et, lorsque je la vis au seuil de sa maison
S'enfuir, je m'aperçus que je l'avais suivie.
Hélas! mon cher ami, c'est là toute ma vie.
Pendant que mon esprit cherchait sa volonté,
Mon corps savait la sienne et suivait la beauté;
Et, quand je m'éveillai de cette rêverie,
Il ne m'en restait plus que l'image chérie:
"Sous votre aimable tête, un cou blanc, délicat,
Se plie, et de la neige effacerait l'éclat."

So I indulged a foolish fancy. Before me meanwhile, beside her mother, the child remained, and her slender white neck rocked softly beneath the long black hair. When the play was finished, the enchanting stranger rose. The beautiful neck, the half-naked shoulder were veiled; the hand slipped into the muff; and when I saw her melt away at the threshold of her home, I realized that I had followed her. Alas! my dear friend, there is my whole life. While my mind sought its will, my body knew its own, and followed beauty; and when I awoke from this dream, there remained for me only the precious image: 'Beneath your lovely head, a white and delicate neck inclines, and would eclipse the brightness of snow.'

A Julie

On me demande, par les rues,
Pourquoi je vais bayant aux grues,
Fumant mon cigare au soleil,
A quoi se passe ma jeunesse,
Et depuis trois ans de paresse
Ce qu'ont fait mes nuits sans sommeil.

Donne-moi tes lèvres, Julie;
Les folles nuits qui t'ont pâlie
Ont séché leur corail luisant.
Parfume-les de ton haleine;
Donne-les-moi, mon Africaine,
Tes belles lèvres de pur sang.

To Julie

They ask me in the streets why I go gaping at the tarts, smoking my cigar in the sun, how my youth is spent, and what my three lazy years' sleepless nights have produced.

Give me your lips, Julie; the wild nights that made you pale have dried their shining coral. Perfume them with your breath; give them to me, my African beauty, your lovely thoroughbred lips.

Mon imprimeur crie à tue-tête
Que sa machine est toujours prête,
Et que la mienne n'en peut mais.
D'honnêtes gens, qu'un club admire,
N'ont pas dédaigné de prédire
Que je n'en reviendrai jamais.

Julie, as-tu du vin d'Espagne?
Hier, nous battions la campagne;
Va donc voir s'il en reste encor.
Ta bouche est brûlante, Julie;
Inventons donc quelque folie
Qui nous perde l'âme et le corps.

On dit que ma gourme me rentre,
Que je n'ai plus rien dans le ventre,
Que je suis vide à faire peur;
Je crois, si j'en valais la peine,
Qu'on m'enverrait à Sainte-Hélène,
Avec un cancer dans le cœur.

My printer is shouting his head off that his machine is always ready, and that mine is at the end of its tether. Decent folk, admired by a club, have condescended to predict that I will never get over it.

Julie, have you Spanish wine? Yesterday, we were roving wild; just go and see if there is still some left. Your mouth is burning, Julie; let's conjure up some madness to destroy us body and soul.

They say I'm reaping my wild oats, that I have nothing more in my belly, that I am frighteningly empty; I think that if I were worth it they would send me to Saint Helena with a cancer in my heart.

Allons, Julie, il faut t'attendre
A me voir quelque jour en cendre,
Comme Hercule sur son rocher.
Puisque c'est par toi que j'expire,
Ouvre ta robe, Déjanire,
Que je monte sur mon bûcher.

Come, Julie, you must expect to see me in ashes some day, like Hercules on his rock. Since it is through you I breathe my last, open your dress, Deianira,[1] that I may climb upon my funeral pyre.

La Nuit de mai

LA MUSE

Poète, prends ton luth, et me donne un baiser;
La fleur de l'églantier sent ses bourgeons éclore.
Le printemps naît ce soir; les vents vont s'embraser;
Et la bergeronnette, en attendant l'aurore,
Aux premiers buissons verts commence à se poser.
Poète, prends ton luth, et me donne un baiser.

May Night

THE MUSE

Poet, take up your lute and kiss me; the flower of the wild rose senses its buds bursting forth. Spring is born tonight; the winds will catch fire; and the wagtail, waiting for the dawn, begins to settle on the first green bushes. Poet, take up your lute and kiss me.

[1]Deianira: the wife of Heracles. She poisoned him unintentionally, and his body was burned on a pyre.

LE POÈTE

Comme il fait noir dans la vallée!
J'ai cru qu'une forme voilée
Flottait là-bas sur la forêt.
Elle sortait de la prairie;
Son pied rasait l'herbe fleurie;
C'est une étrange rêverie;
Elle s'efface et disparaît.

LA MUSE

Poète, prends ton luth; la nuit, sur la pelouse,
Balance le zéphyr dans son voile odorant.
La rose, vierge encor, se referme jalouse
Sur le frelon nacré qu'elle enivre en mourant.
Écoute! tout se tait; songe à ta bien-aimée.
Ce soir, sous les tilleuls, à la sombre ramée
Le rayon du couchant laisse un adieu plus doux.
Ce soir, tout va fleurir: l'immortelle nature
Se remplit de parfums, d'amour et de murmure,
Comme le lit joyeux de deux jeunes époux.

THE POET

How dark it is in the valley! I thought I saw a veiled figure floating there above the forest. She came out of the meadow; her foot was skimming the flower-strewn grass; it is a strange dream; she fades and disappears.

THE MUSE

Poet, take up your lute; the night, above the lawn, rocks the gentle breeze in its fragrant veil. The rose, still virgin, closes jealously on the pearly hornet, intoxicated as it dies. Listen! all is silent; think of your beloved. This evening, under the lime trees, the glow of sunset leaves a sweeter farewell in the dark foliage. This evening, all will blossom; immortal nature is filled with scents, with love and murmuring, like the blissful bed of two young newlyweds.

LE POÈTE

Pourquoi mon cœur bat-il si vite?
Qu'ai-je donc en moi qui s'agite,
Dont je me sens épouvanté?
Ne frappe-t-on pas à ma porte?
Pourquoi ma lampe à demi morte
M'éblouit-elle de clarté?
Dieu puissant! tout mon corps frissonne.
Qui vient? qui m'appelle? – Personne.
Je suis seul; c'est l'heure qui sonne;
O solitude? ô pauvreté!

THE POET

Why does my heart beat so fast? What is it within me that stirs and alarms my senses? Isn't that a knock at my door? Why is my half-dead lamp dazzling me with brightness? Powerful God! my whole body shudders. Who comes? Who calls me? – No one. I am alone; it is the hour chiming; O solitude? O poverty!

LA MUSE

Poète, prends ton luth; le vin de la jeunesse
Fermente cette nuit dans les veines de Dieu.
Mon sein est inquiet; la volupté l'oppresse,
Et les vents altérés m'ont mis la lèvre en feu.
O paresseux enfant! regarde, je suis belle.
Notre premier baiser, ne t'en souviens-tu pas,
Quand je te vis si pâle au toucher de mon aile,
Et que, les yeux en pleurs, tu tombas dans mes bras?
Ah! je t'ai consolé d'une amère souffrance!
Hélas! bien jeune encor, tu te mourais d'amour.
Console-moi ce soir, je me meurs d'espérance;
J'ai besoin de prier pour vivre jusqu'au jour.

THE MUSE

Poet, take up your lute; the wine of youth ferments this night in the veins of God. My breast is restless; sensuality oppresses it, and the changing winds have set my lips on fire. O indolent child! look, I am beautiful. Our first kiss, do you not remember it, when I saw you so pale at the touch of my wing, and when, with tearful eyes, you fell into my arms? Ah, I consoled you for a bitter suffering! Alas! still very young, you were dying of love. Console me this evening, I am dying of hope; I need to pray to live until daybreak.

LE POÈTE

Est-ce toi dont la voix m'appelle,
O ma pauvre Muse, est-ce toi?
O ma fleur, ô mon immortelle!
Seul être pudique et fidèle
Où vive encor l'amour de moi!
Oui, te voilà, c'est toi, ma blonde,
C'est toi, ma maîtresse et ma sœur!
Et je sens, dans la nuit profonde,
De ta robe d'or qui m'inonde
Les rayons glisser dans mon cœur.

THE POET

Is it you whose voice calls me, O my poor Muse, is it you? O my flower, my everlasting flower! The only being, chaste and true, in whom lives still a love of me! Yes, there you are, my fair one, you, my mistress and my sister! And in the deep darkness I feel gliding into my heart the radiance of your golden robe which floods over me.

LA MUSE

Poète, prends ton luth; c'est moi, ton immortelle,
Qui t'ai vu cette nuit triste et silencieux,
Et qui, comme un oiseau que sa couvée appelle,
Pour pleurer avec toi descends du haut des cieux.
Viens, tu souffres, ami. Quelque ennui solitaire
Te ronge; quelque chose a gémi dans ton cœur;
Quelque amour t'est venu, comme on en voit sur terre,
Une ombre de plaisir, un semblant de bonheur.
Viens, chantons devant Dieu; chantons dans tes pensées,
Dans tes plaisirs perdus, dans tes peines passées;
Partons, dans un baiser, pour un monde inconnu.
Eveillons au hasard les échos de ta vie,
Parlons-nous de bonheur, de gloire et de folie,
Et que ce soit un rêve, et le premier venu.
Inventons quelque part des lieux où l'on oublie;
Partons, nous sommes seuls, l'univers est à nous.
Voici la verte Ecosse et la brune Italie,
Et la Grèce, ma mère, où le miel est si doux,
Argos, et Ptéléon, ville des hécatombes,

THE MUSE

Poet, take up your lute; it is I, your everlasting one, who saw you sad and silent this night, and who, like a bird called by its brood, come down to weep with you from high in the heavens. Come, you are suffering, friend. Some lonely distress torments you; something moaned in your heart; some love has come to you, of an earthly kind, the shadow of a pleasure, a semblance of happiness. Come, let us sing before God; let us sing in your thoughts, in your lost pleasures, in your bygone sorrows; let us leave, in a kiss, for an unknown world. Let us awake at random the echoes of your life, talk together of happiness, of glory and of madness, and let it be a dream, and the first that comes to mind. Let us conjure up somewhere places of forgetfulness; let us leave, we are alone, the universe is ours. Here is green Scotland and dusky Italy, and Greece, my mother, where the honey is so sweet, Argos, and Pteleos, city

Et Messa, la divine, agréable aux colombes,
Et le front chevelu du Pélion changeant,
Et le bleu Titarèse, et le golfe d'argent,
Qui montre dans ses eaux, où le cygne se mire,
La blanche Oloossone à la blanche Camyre.
Dis-moi, quel songe d'or nos chants vont-ils bercer?
D'où vont venir les pleurs que nous allons verser?
Ce matin, quand le jour a frappé ta paupière,
Quel séraphin pensif, courbé sur ton chevet,
Secouait des lilas dans sa robe légère,
Et te contait tous bas les amours qu'il rêvait?
Chanterons-nous l'espoir, la tristesse ou la joie?
Tremperons-nous de sang les bataillons d'acier?
Suspendrons-nous l'amant sur l'échelle de soie?
Jetterons-nous au vent l'écume du coursier?
Dirons-nous quelle main, dans les lampes sans nombre
De la maison céleste, allume nuit et jour
L'huile sainte de vie et d'éternel amour?

of hecatombs, and sacred Messa, favoured haunt of doves, and the hairy brow of fickle Pelion, and the blue Titaresios, and the silver bay that in its waters, where the swan admires its own reflection, shows white Oloosson to white Kameiros. Tell me, what golden dream will be cradled by our songs? From where will come the tears we shall shed? This morning, when daylight touched your eyelid, what pensive seraph, bending over your bedside, shook down lilacs from his airy robe, and told you in a whisper of the loves which he was dreaming? Shall we sing of hope, of sadness or of joy? Shall we soak in blood the steely battalions? Shall we suspend the lover on the silken ladder? Shall we throw to the wind the foam of the charger? Shall we say what hand, among the countless lamps of the celestial house, lights night and day the holy oil of life and of eternal

Crierons-nous à Tarquin: "Il est temps, voici l'ombre!"
Descendrons-nous cueillir la perle au fond des mers?
Mènerons-nous la chèvre aux ébéniers amers?
Montrerons-nous le ciel à la Mélancolie?
Suivrons-nous le chasseur sur les monts escarpés?
La biche le regarde; elle pleure et supplie;
Sa bruyère l'attend: ses faons sont nouveau-nés;
Il se baisse, il l'égorge, il jette à la curée
Sur les chiens en sueur son cœur encor vivant.
Peindrons-nous une vierge à la joue empourprée,
S'en allant à la messe, un page la suivant,
Et d'un regard distrait, à côté de sa mère,
Sur sa lèvre entr'ouverte oubliant sa prière?
Elle écoute en tremblant, dans l'écho du pilier,
Résonner l'éperon d'un hardi cavalier.
Dirons-nous aux héros des vieux temps de la France
De monter tout armés aux créneaux de leurs tours,
Et de ressusciter la naïve romance

love? Shall we cry to Tarquin: 'It is time, here is the darkness!'[1] Shall we go down to gather pearls in the depths of the seas? Shall we guide the goat to the bitter laburnum? Shall we show the sky to Melancholy? Shall we follow the hunter on the craggy mountains? The doe looks at him; she weeps and begs; her moorland awaits her; her fawns are newly born; he bends, he cuts her throat, he throws to the slaughter among his sweating hounds her still living heart. Shall we depict a virgin with a flushed face, on her way to mass, followed by a page, and with distracted gaze, beside her mother, forgetting the prayer on her half-open lips? She listens, trembling, to the resonance in the echoing pillars of the spur of a bold cavalier. Shall we tell the heroes of olden times in France to climb fully armed to the battlements of their towers, and to revive the

[1]Presumably a reference to *The Rape of Lucrece.* Shakespeare's line is: 'Now stole upon the time the dead of night.'

Que leur gloire oubliée apprit aux troubadours?
Vêtirons-nous de blanc une molle élégie?
L'homme de Waterloo nous dira-t-il sa vie,
Et ce qu'il a fauché du troupeau des humains
Avant que l'envoyé de la nuit éternelle
Vînt sur son tertre vert l'abattre d'un coup d'aile,
Et sur son cœur de fer lui croiser les deux mains?
Clouerons-nous au poteau d'une satire altière
Le nom sept fois vendu d'un pâle pamphlétaire,
Qui, poussé par la faim, du fond de son oubli
S'en vient, tout grelottant d'envie et d'impuissance,
Sur le front du génie insulter l'espérance
Et mordre le laurier que son souffle a sali?
Prends ton luth! prends ton luth! je ne peux plus me taire.
Mon aile me soulève au souffle du printemps.
Le vent va m'emporter; je vais quitter la terre.
Une larme de toi! Dieu m'écoute; il est temps.

innocent romance which their forgotten glory taught the troubadours? Shall we dress in white a soft elegy? Will the man of Waterloo tell us of his life, and how much he scythed down of the human flock before the messenger of eternal darkness came to his green hillock to strike him down with the blow of a wing, and to cross his hands on his iron heart? Shall we nail to the stake with an arrogant epigram the name seven times sold of a pallid critic who, driven by hunger from the depths of his oblivion, comes shivering with envy and helplessness to insult the hope on the brow of genius and to bite the laurel wreath that his breath has sullied? Take up your lute! take up your lute! I can no more be silent. My wing lifts me on the breath of spring. The wind will bear me away; I will leave the earth. A tear from you! God is listening to me; it is time.

LE POÈTE

S'il ne te faut, ma sœur chérie,
Qu'un baiser d'une lèvre amie
Et qu'une larme de mes yeux,
Je te les donnerai sans peine;
De nos amours qu'il te souvienne,
Si tu remontes dans les cieux.
Je ne chante ni l'espérance,
Ni la gloire, ni le bonheur,
Hélas! pas même la souffrance.
La bouche garde le silence
Pour écouter parler le cœur.

LA MUSE

Crois-tu donc que je sois comme le vent d'automne,
Qui se nourrit de pleurs jusque sur un tombeau,
Et pour qui la douleur n'est qu'une goutte d'eau?
O poète! un baiser, c'est moi qui te le donne.

THE POET

If you need, my beloved sister, only a kiss from friendly lips, only a tear from my eyes, I will give them to you without trouble; may you remember our loves, if you climb once more to the heavens. I sing neither hope nor glory nor happiness, alas! not even suffering. The mouth keeps silent to hear the heart speak.

THE MUSE

Do you believe then that I am like the autumn wind, which feeds on tears even upon a grave, and for whom suffering is merely a drop of water? O poet! a kiss, it is I who give it to

L'herbe que je voulais arracher de ce lieu,
C'est ton oisiveté; ta douleur est à Dieu.
Quel que soit le souci que ta jeunesse endure,
Laisse-la s'élargir, cette sainte blessure
Que les noirs séraphins t'ont faite au fond du cœur;
Rien ne nous rend si grands qu'une grande douleur.
Mais, pour en être atteint, ne crois pas, ô poète,
Que ta voix ici-bas doive rester muette.
Les plus désespérés sont les chants les plus beaux,
Et j'en sais d'immortels qui sont de purs sanglots.
Lorsque le pélican, lassé d'un long voyage,
Dans les brouillards du soir retourne à ses roseaux,
Ses petits affamés courent sur le rivage,
En le voyant au loin s'abattre sur les eaux.
Déjà, croyant saisir et partager leur proie,
Ils courent à leur père avec des cris de joie,

you. The weed which I wanted to tear up from this place is your indolence; your suffering belongs to God. Whatever cares your youth endures, let it open up, that sacred wound made deep in your heart by the black seraphs; nothing makes us so sublime as a sublime grief. But, in your stricken state, do not believe, O poet, that your voice here below must stay silent. The songs of deepest despair are the loveliest songs, and I know immortal songs that are pure sobs. When the pelican, weary after a long journey, returns to its reeds in the mists of evening, its hungry children run along the bank, seeing it in the distance swoop down upon the waters. Already, as if seizing and sharing their prey, they run to their father with cries of

En secouant leurs becs sur leurs goitres hideux.
Lui, gagnant à pas lents une roche élevée,
De son aile pendante abritant sa couvée,
Pêcheur mélancolique, il regarde les cieux.
Le sang coule à longs flots de sa poitrine ouverte;
En vain il a des mers fouillé la profondeur:
L'Océan était vide et la plage déserte;
Pour toute nourriture il apporte son cœur.
Sombre et silencieux, étendu sur la pierre,
Partageant à ses fils ses entrailles de père,
Dans son amour sublime il berce sa douleur,
Et, regardant couler sa sanglante mamelle,
Sur son festin de mort il s'affaisse et chancelle,
Ivre de volupté, de tendresse et d'horreur.

joy, shaking their beaks above their hideous pouches. Climbing slowly upon a high rock, sheltering his brood with his drooping wing, a melancholy fisherman, he surveys the heavens. Blood flows in great waves from his open breast; in vain he has searched the depths of the seas: the Ocean was empty and the beach deserted; he brings for their only food his heart. Dark and silent, stretched out on the stone, sharing out to his sons his paternal entrails, in his sublime love he cradles his pain and, watching the flow from his bleeding breast, upon his funeral banquet he sinks down and staggers, his senses drunk with pleasure, with tenderness and horror. But

Mais parfois, au milieu du divin sacrifice,
Fatigué de mourir dans un trop long supplice,
Il craint que ses enfants ne le laissent vivant;
Alors il se soulève, ouvre son aile au vent,
Et se frappant le cœur avec un cri sauvage,
Il pousse dans la nuit un si funèbre adieu,
Que les oiseaux des mers désertent le rivage,
Et que le voyageur attardé sur la plage,
Sentant passer la mort, se recommande à Dieu.
Poète, c'est ainsi que font les grands poètes.
Ils laissent s'égayer ceux qui vivent un temps;
Mais les festins humains qu'ils servent à leurs fêtes
Ressemblent la plupart à ceux des pélicans.
Quand ils parlent ainsi d'espérances trompées,
De tristesse et d'oubli, d'amour et de malheur,
Ce n'est pas un concert à dilater le cœur.
Leurs déclamations sont comme des épées:
Elles tracent dans l'air un cercle éblouissant,
Mais il y pend toujours quelque goutte de sang.

sometimes, in the midst of the holy sacrifice, weary of dying in a torture too prolonged, he fears that his children may leave him alive; so he rises, opening his wings to the wind, and, striking his heart with a wild cry, he utters into the night a farewell so deathly that the birds of the ocean desert the shore, and the lingering traveller on the beach, feeling death pass by, commends himself to God. Poet, thus it is with the great poets. They let those who live amuse themselves a while; but the human banquets that they serve at their feasts resemble for the most part those of the pelicans. When they speak in these terms of hopes deceived, of sadness and oblivion, of love and misfortune, it is not music to swell the heart. Their utterances are like swords: they trace a dazzling circle in the air, but there hangs on them always some drop of blood.

LA NUIT DE MAI

LE POÈTE

O Muse! spectre insatiable,
Ne m'en demande pas si long.
L'homme n'écrit rien sur le sable
A l'heure où passe l'aquilon.
J'ai vu le temps où ma jeunesse
Sur mes lèvres était sans cesse
Prête à chanter comme un oiseau;
Mais j'ai souffert un dur martyre,
Et le moins que j'en pourrais dire,
Si je l'essayais sur ma lyre,
La briserait comme un roseau.

THE POET

O Muse! insatiable spectre, do not ask so much of me. Man writes nothing on the sand at the hour when the north wind passes. I have seen the time when my youth was forever ready on my lips to sing like a bird; but I have suffered a harsh martyrdom, and the least that I could say of it, were I to venture it on my lyre, would break it like a reed.

Rappelle-toi

(VERGISS MEIN NICHT)

Paroles faites sur la musique de Mozart.

Rappelle-toi, quand l'Aurore craintive
Ouvre au soleil son palais enchanté;
Rappelle-toi, lorsque la Nuit pensive
Passe en rêvant sous son voile argenté;
A l'appel du plaisir lorsque ton sein palpite,
Aux doux songes du soir lorsque l'ombre t'invite,
Écoute au fond des bois
Murmurer une voix –
Rappelle-toi.

Remember

(VERGISS MEIN NICHT)

Words composed to the music of Mozart.

Remember, when timid Dawn opens to the sun its enchanted palace; remember, when pensive Night passes dreaming beneath its silvery veil; when your breast quivers at the call of pleasure, when the shadows beckon you to the sweet dreams of evening, listen to a murmuring voice deep in the woods – Remember.

Rappelle-toi, lorsque les destinées
M'auront de toi pour jamais séparé,
Quand le chagrin, l'exil et les années
Auront flétri ce cœur désespéré;
Songe à mon triste amour, songe à l'adieu suprême!
L'absence ni le temps ne sont rien quand on aime.
Tant que mon cœur battra,
Toujours il te dira:
Rappelle-toi.

Rappelle-toi, quand sous la froide terre
Mon cœur brisé pour toujours dormira;
Rappelle-toi, quand la fleur solitaire
Sur mon tombeau doucement s'ouvrira.
Je ne te verrai plus; mais mon âme immortelle
Reviendra près de toi comme une sœur fidèle.
Écoute, dans la nuit,
Une voix qui gémit –
Rappelle-toi.

Remember, when fortunes have parted me from you for ever, when grief, exile and the years have withered this despairing heart; think of my sorrowful love, think of the supreme farewell! Absence and time are nothing when we love. For as long as my heart shall beat, it will always say to you: Remember.

Remember, when beneath the cold earth my broken heart sleeps for ever; remember, when the solitary flower on my tomb gently opens. I shall see you no more; but my immortal soul will come back close to you like a faithful sister. Listen in the darkness to a voice that moans – Remember.

Théophile Gautier
(1811–72)

Gautier came to Paris from Tarbes in the Pyrenees. His poor eyesight cut short his intended career as a painter, but he found through his association with Hugo a taste and talent for poetry, and later wrote fiction, criticism and journalism. His early verse was elegiac and intimate, then macabre, but in time he found his true voice in a transposition of the spirit of the plastic artist into poetry.

Moving away in the late 1830s from Romantic emotionalism and morbidity, Gautier expounded the doctrine known as 'Art for Art's Sake' ('*L'Art pour l'Art*'). This separated beauty from utility, the aesthetic from the moral, the eternal from the contingent, the stylized creation from the shapeless banality of life. Though Gautier's own poetic achievements were perhaps limited, he set in motion one of the essential trains of thought in nineteenth-century aesthetics. The key is now to be found in a refined process of selection, and in a search, based on mastery of technique, for an impersonal mode of creation. The chisel of the sculptor-poet is to exclude transparent emotion from the 'marble block' that is the completed poem. Thus old distinctions between form and content, and between art and craft, are abolished in a superior and ritualistic kind of creativity that becomes a way of life. In Gautier's own words, 'Art for us is not the means, but the end.'

Major volume: *Emaux et Camées* 1852.
Other works: *Poésies* 1830, *Albertus* 1832, *La Comédie de la Mort* 1838, *España* 1845.

Chinoiserie

Ce n'est pas vous, non, madame, que j'aime,
Ni vous non plus, Juliette, ni vous,
Ophélia, ni Béatrix, ni même
Laure la blonde, avec ses grands yeux doux.

Celle que j'aime, à présent, est en Chine;
Elle demeure avec ses vieux parents,
Dans une tour de porcelaine fine,
Au fleuve Jaune, où sont les cormorans.

Elle a des yeux retroussés vers les tempes,
Un pied petit à tenir dans la main,
Le teint plus clair que le cuivre des lampes,
Les ongles longs et rougis de carmin.

Chinoiserie

No, it is not you, madame, that I love, nor you Juliet, nor you Ophelia, nor Beatrice, nor even the fair Laura, with her large and gentle eyes.

The one I love just now is in China; she dwells with her old parents, in a tower of delicate porcelain, by the Yellow River, where the cormorants are.

Her eyes are turned up towards her temples, her foot small enough to be held in the hand, her complexion brighter than the copper of the lamps, her nails long and reddened with carmine.

Par son treillis elle passe sa tête,
Que l'hirondelle, en volant, vient toucher,
Et, chaque soir, aussi bien qu'un poète,
Chante le saule et la fleur du pêcher.

Through her lattice screen her head looks out, touched by the swallow as it flies, and every evening, like a poet, she sings of the willow and the flower of the peach.

A une robe rose

Que tu me plais dans cette robe
Qui te déshabille si bien,
Faisant jaillir ta gorge en globe,
Montrant tout nu ton bras païen!

Frêle comme une aile d'abeille,
Frais comme un cœur de rose-thé,
Son tissu, caresse vermeille,
Voltige autour de ta beauté.

De l'épiderme sur la soie
Glissent des frissons argentés,
Et l'étoffe à la chair renvoie
Ses éclairs roses reflétés.

To a Pink Dress

How you delight me in that dress that undresses you so well, accentuating your rounded breasts, displaying quite naked your pagan arm!

As delicate as a bee's wing, cool as the heart of a tea-rose, its fabric, a rosy caress, flutters around your beauty.

From the skin to the silk steal silvery quiverings, and the tissue sends back to the flesh its reflected pink flickerings.

A UNE ROBE ROSE

D'où te vient cette robe étrange
Qui semble faite de ta chair,
Trame vivante qui mélange
Avec ta peau son rose clair?

Est-ce à la rougeur de l'aurore,
A la coquille de Vénus,
Au bouton de sein près d'éclore,
Que sont pris ces tons inconnus?

Ou bien l'étoffe est-elle teinte
Dans les roses de ta pudeur?
Non; vingt fois modelée et peinte,
Ta forme connaît sa splendeur.

Jetant le voile qui te pèse,
Réalité que l'art rêva,
Comme la princesse Borghèse
Tu poserais pour Canova.

Where have you found this strange dress that seems to be made from your flesh, a living web that blends its bright pink with your skin?

Is it from the dawn's red blush, from the shell of Venus, from the breast's nipple about to blossom, that these unknown tints are taken?

Or else is the fabric dyed in the roses of your modesty? No; twenty times modelled and painted, your figure knows its own magnificence.

Throwing off the veil that weighs on you, the reality now that art dreamt of, like the Princess Borghese you would pose for Canova.[1]

[1]The reference is to the portrait of Pauline, Napoléon's sister, sculpted by Canova in 1807.

Et ces plis roses sont les lèvres
De mes désirs inapaisés,
Mettant au corps dont tu les sèvres
Une tunique de baisers.

And these pink folds are the lips of my unsatisfied desires, dressing the body of which you deprive them in a tunic of kisses.

Symphonie en blanc majeur

De leur col blanc courbant les lignes
On voit dans les contes du Nord,
Sur le vieux Rhin, des femmes-cygnes
Nager en chantant près du bord;

Ou, suspendant à quelque branche
Le plumage qui les revêt,
Faire luire leur peau plus blanche
Que la neige de leur duvet.

Symphony in white major

Curving the lines of their white necks in tales of the North we see swan-maidens swimming on the old Rhine, singing near the bank.

Or, hanging on some branch the plumage that clothes them, they display their glossy skin, whiter than the snow of their down.

De ces femmes il en est une
Qui chez nous descend quelquefois,
Blanche comme le clair de lune
Sur les glaciers dans les cieux froids;

Conviant la vue enivrée
De sa boréale fraîcheur
A des régals de chair nacrée,
A des débauches de blancheur!

Son sein, neige montée en globe,
Contre les camélias blancs
Et le blanc satin de sa robe
Soutient des combats insolents.

Dans ces grandes batailles blanches,
Satins et fleurs ont le dessous,
Et, sans demander leurs revanches,
Jaunissent comme des jaloux.

Among these women there is one who comes down to us sometimes, as white as the moonlight on the glaciers in the cold skies;

Inviting our sense of sight, intoxicated by her boreal coolness, to banquets of pearly flesh, to orgies of whiteness!

Her breast, snow modelled into a sphere, against the white camellias and the white satin of her gown, keeps up a lively conflict.

In these great white battles satins and flowers have the worst of it, and, without seeking their revenge, turn yellow as if jealous.

Sur les blancheurs de son épaule,
Paros au grain éblouissant,
Comme dans une nuit du pôle,
Un givre invisible descend.

De quel mica de neige vierge,
De quelle moelle de roseau,
De quelle hostie et de quel cierge
A-t-on fait le blanc de sa peau?

A-t-on pris la goutte lactée
Tachant l'azur du ciel d'hiver,
Le lis à la pulpe argentée,
La blanche écume de la mer;

Le marbre blanc, chair froide et pâle
Où vivent les divinités;
L'argent mat, la laiteuse opale
Qu'irisent de vagues clartés;

On the pure white surfaces of her shoulder, Paros marble of dazzling texture, as in a polar night an invisible hoar-frost descends.

From what mica of virgin snow, from what reed's pith, from what communion host and what candle was the whiteness of her skin made?

Was it with the milky drop that stains the blue of the winter sky, the lily with its silvery flesh, the white foam of the sea;

White marble, cold pale flesh in which the deities live; matt silver, milky opal iridescent with hazy splendours;

L'ivoire, où ses mains ont des ailes,
Et, comme des papillons blancs,
Sur la pointe des notes frêles
Suspendent leurs baisers tremblants;

L'hermine vierge de souillure,
Qui, pour abriter leurs frissons,
Ouate de sa blanche fourrure
Les épaules et les blasons;

Le vif-argent, aux fleurs fantasques
Dont les vitraux sont ramagés;
Les blanches dentelles des vasques,
Pleurs de l'ondine en l'air figés;

L'aubépine de mai qui plie
Sous les blancs frimas de ses fleurs;
L'albâtre où la mélancolie
Aime à retrouver ses pâleurs;

Ivory, where her hands have wings, and, like white butterflies, on the tip of the fragile notes hang their quivering kisses;

Undefiled ermine, which, to protect their shivers, quilts in its white fur shoulders and escutcheons;

Quicksilver rime with its fantastical flowers that pattern leaded windows; the white lace of fountains, tears of the water-sprite crystallized in the air;

The May hawthorn which bends beneath the white frosts of its flowers; alabaster where melancholy likes to find its own pallor;

Le duvet blanc de la colombe,
Neigeant sur les toits du manoir,
Et la stalactite qui tombe,
Larme blanche, de l'antre noir?

Des Groenlands et des Norvèges
Vient-elle avec Séraphita?
Est-ce la Madone des neiges,
Un sphinx blanc que l'hiver sculpta;

Sphinx enterré par l'avalanche,
Gardien des glaciers étoilés,
Et qui, sous sa poitrine blanche,
Cache de blancs secrets gelés?

Sous la glace où calme il repose,
Oh! qui pourra fondre ce cœur!
Oh! qui pourra mettre un ton rose
Dans cette implacable blancheur!

The white down of the dove, snowing on the manor's roofs, and the stalactite, a white tear falling from the cavern's black vault?

From Greenlands and Norways does she come with Seraphita? Is she the Madonna of the snows, a white sphinx sculpted by winter;

A sphinx buried by the avalanche, guardian of the starlit glaciers, who, beneath her white breast, hides white frozen secrets?

Under the ice where it lies calmly at rest, oh! who can melt this heart! oh! who can touch with a pink tint this unrelenting whiteness!

L'Art

Oui, l'œuvre sort plus belle
D'une forme au travail
Rebelle,
Vers, marbre, onyx, émail.

Point de contraintes fausses!
Mais que pour marcher droit
Tu chausses,
Muse, un cothurne étroit.

Fi du rythme commode,
Comme un soulier trop grand,
Du mode
Que tout pied quitte et prend!

Statuaire, repousse
L'argile que pétrit
Le pouce,
Quand flotte ailleurs l'esprit;

Art

Yes, the work emerges more beautiful from a form that resists working, verse, marble, onyx, enamel.

No false shackles! But to walk straight, Muse, put on a slender cothurnus.[1]

Shame on facile rhythm, like an outsize shoe, a mode put on and off by every foot!

Sculptor, reject clay that yields to the thumb, while the mind drifts elsewhere;

[1]*cothurnus*: a thick-soled shoe (buskin) worn by actors of classical tragedy.

Lutte avec le carrare,
Avec le paros dur
    Et rare,
Gardiens du contour pur;

Emprunte à Syracuse
Son bronze où fermement
    S'accuse
Le trait fier et charmant;

D'une main délicate
Poursuis dans un filon
    D'agate
Le profil d'Apollon.

Peintre, fuis l'aquarelle
Et fixe la couleur
    Trop frêle
Au four de l'émailleur.

Fais les Sirènes bleues,
Tordant de cent façons
    Leurs queues,
Les monstres des blasons;

Struggle with Carrara, with the hard rare marble of Paros, guardians of the pure outline;

Borrow from Syracuse its bronze in which the proud bewitching feature is firmly accentuated;

With a delicate hand seek out in a vein of agate the profile of Apollo.

Painter, shun the water-colour, and in the enameller's oven set firm the colour that is too frail.

Form blue sirens, writhing their tails in a hundred ways, the monsters of heraldic arms;

Dans son nimbe trilobe
La Vierge et son Jésus,
    Le globe
Avec la croix dessus.

Tout passe. – L'art robuste
Seul a l'éternité;
    Le buste
Survit à la cité.

Et la médaille austère
Que trouve un laboureur
    Sous terre
Révèle un empereur.

Les dieux eux-mêmes meurent,
Mais les vers souverains
    Demeurent
Plus forts que les airains.

In her triple halo the Virgin and her Jesus, the globe with the cross above it.

Everything passes. – Only vigorous art is eternal; the bust outlives the city.

And the austere medallion found by a ploughman beneath the earth reveals an emperor.

The gods themselves die. But sovereign lines of verse remain stronger than bronzes.

Sculpte, lime, cisèle;
Que ton rêve flottant
    Se scelle
Dans le bloc résistant!

Carve, file, chisel; let your irresolute dream be sealed in the unyielding block!

Théodore de Banville
(1823–91)

De Banville tends to be viewed as an influence, as a signpost to Parnassianism and eventually to Symbolism, rather than as a talented poet in his own right. That judgement perhaps does less than justice to his lyricism, his humour, his imagination, and his linguistic and technical virtuosity. His qualities were acknowledged in his time by Baudelaire and Mallarmé; and this dedicated craftsman certainly forms an important bridge between on the one hand Romanticism and the pre-classical verse tradition (the ballad, the ode, the rondeau), and on the other the new mid-nineteenth-century urge towards a sublime aesthetic ideal, purified of vulgarity and embodied in a more supple but still classically inspired verse line. He published an influential *Petit Traité de Poésie française* in 1872.

Among his numerous volumes, perhaps the best are: *Stalactites* 1846, *Les Odelettes* 1856, *Odes funambulesques* 1857, *Les Améthystes* 1862, *Les Exilés* 1867.

Nous n'irons plus au bois...[1]

Nous n'irons plus au bois, les lauriers sont coupés.
Les Amours des bassins, Naïades en groupe
Voient reluire au soleil en cristaux découpés
Les flots silencieux qui coulaient de leur coupe.
Les lauriers sont coupés, et le cerf aux abois
Tressaille au son du cor; nous n'irons plus au bois,
Où des enfants charmants riait la folle troupe
Sous les regards des lys aux pleurs du ciel trempés,
Voici l'herbe qu'on fauche et les lauriers qu'on coupe.
Nous n'irons plus au bois, les lauriers sont coupés.

We'll go no more to the wood...

We'll go no more to the wood, the laurels are cut down. The Cupids amid the pools, the cluster of Naiads see, fragmented into crystals and shining in the sun, the silent waters that flowed from their cup. The laurels are cut down, and the stag at bay shudders at the sound of the horn; we'll go no more to the wood, where the wild troupe of bewitching children laughed under the gaze of the lilies moistened by the tears of heaven, here is the grass they are scything and the laurels they are chopping. We'll go no more to the wood, the laurels are cut down.

[1]The first line of this poem is taken from a traditional French folk song.

Sculpteur, cherche avec soin...

Sculpteur, cherche avec soin, en attendant l'extase,
Un marbre sans défaut pour en faire un beau vase;
Cherche longtemps sa forme et n'y retrace pas
D'amours mystérieux ni de divins combats.
Pas d'Héraklès vainqueur du monstre de Némée,
Ni de Cypris naissant sur la mer embaumée;
Pas de Titans vaincus dans leurs rébellions,
Ni de riant Bacchos attelant les lions
Avec un frein tressé de pampres et de vignes;
Pas de Léda jouant dans la troupe des cygnes
Sous l'ombre des lauriers en fleurs, ni d'Artémis
Surprise au sein des eaux dans sa blancheur de lys.
Qu'autour du vase pur, trop beau pour la Bacchante,
La vervcine mêlée à des feuilles d'acanthe
Fleurisse, et que plus bas des vierges lentement

Sculptor, seek with care...

Sculptor, seek with care, while awaiting inspiration, a flawless marble with which to make a lovely vase; seek for long hours its form and engrave in it no mysterious loves nor divine combats. No Heracles victorious over the monster of Nemea, nor birth of Cypris[1] on the scented sea; no Titans vanquished in their revolts, nor laughing Bacchus harnessing the lions with a bridle plaited with vine branches and stems; no Leda playing amid the flock of swans in the shade of the flowering laurels, nor Artemis surprised in the lap of the waters in her lily whiteness. Around the pure vase, too lovely for the priestess of Bacchus, let the vervain blossom as it mingles with acanthus leaves, and lower down let maidens advance slowly two by

[1]Cypris: one of the names of Aphrodite.

S'avancent deux à deux, d'un pas sûr et charmant,
Les bras pendant le long de leurs tuniques droites
Et les cheveux tressés sur leurs têtes étroites.

two, their step firm and charming, their arms dangling along their straight tunics and their hair plaited on their slender heads.

Le Saut du tremplin

Clown admirable, en vérité!
Je crois que la postérité,
Dont sans cesse l'horizon bouge,
Le reverra, sa plaie au flanc,
Il était barbouillé de blanc,
De jaune, de vert et de rouge.

Même jusqu'à Madagascar
Son nom était parvenu, car
C'était selon tous les principes
Qu'après les cercles de papier,
Sans jamais les estropier
Il traversait le rond des pipes.

The Springboard Leap

Admirable clown, truly! I believe posterity, with its incessantly shifting horizon, will see him again, with his wounded flank, he was daubed in white, yellow, green and red.

Even to Madagascar his name had spread, for it was according to all the rules that after the paper hoops, never distorting them, he would spring through the smoke-rings.

De la pesanteur affranchi,
Sans y voir clair il eût franchi
Les escaliers de Piranèse.
La lumière qui le frappait
Faisait resplendir son toupet
Comme un brasier dans la fournaise.

Il s'élevait à des hauteurs
Telles, que les autres sauteurs
Se consumaient en luttes vaines.
Ils le trouvaient décourageant,
Et murmuraient: "Quel vif-argent
Ce démon a-t-il dans les veines?"

Tout le peuple criait: "Bravo!"
Mais lui, par un effort nouveau,
Semblait roidir sa jambe nue,
Et, sans que l'on sût avec qui,
Cet émule de la Saqui
Parlait bas en langue inconnue.

Freed from weight, blind to their form he would have leapt up Piranesi's stairways. The light that struck him made his tuft of hair shine like a coal in a furnace.

He rose to such heights that the other tumblers burned up their strength in futile struggles. They found him disheartening, and murmured: 'What quicksilver has that demon got in his veins?'

The people all cried: 'Bravo!' But he, with renewed effort, seemed to stiffen his naked leg, and, with whom there was no knowing, this rival of La Saqui[1] spoke quietly in an unknown tongue.

[1]La Saqui: a famous dancer and tightrope walker.

C'était avec son cher tremplin.
Il lui disait: "Théâtre, plein
D'inspiration fantastique,
Tremplin qui tressailles d'émoi
Quand je prends un élan, fais-moi
Bondir plus haut, planche élastique!

"Frêle machine aux reins puissants,
Fais-moi bondir, moi qui me sens
Plus agile que les panthères,
Si haut que je ne puisse voir
Avec leur cruel habit noir
Ces épiciers et ces notaires!

"Par quelque prodige pompeux,
Fais-moi monter, si tu le peux,
Jusqu'à ces sommets, où, sans règles,
Embrouillant les cheveux vermeils
Des planètes et des soleils,
Se croisent la foudre et les aigles.

It was with his precious springboard. He said to it: 'Theatre, filled with uncanny inspiration, springboard quivering with emotion when I launch myself, make me leap higher, elastic board!

Slender machine with powerful loins, make me leap, sensing as I do that I am more nimble than the panthers, so high that I cannot see these grocers and these lawyers with their cruel black coats!

By some magnificent marvel, make me rise if you can to those peaks where, beyond all rules, entangling the rosy red hair of the planets and suns, lightning bolts and eagles cross paths.

"Jusqu'à ces éthers pleins de bruits,
Où, mêlant dans l'affreuse nuit
Leurs haleines exténuées,
Les autans ivres de courroux
Dorment, échevelés et fous,
Sur les seins pâles des nuées.

"Plus haut encor, jusqu'au ciel pur!
Jusqu'à ce lapis dont l'azur
Couvre notre prison mouvante!
Jusqu'à ces rouges Orients
Où marchent des Dieux flamboyants,
Fous de colère et d'épouvante.

"Plus loin! plus haut! je vois encor
Des boursiers à lunettes d'or,
Des critiques, des demoiselles
Et des réalistes en feu.
Plus haut! plus loin! de l'air, du bleu!
Des ailes! des ailes! des ailes!"

Up to those ethers filled with noise where, mingling in the dreadful night their exhausted breaths, the stormy blasts drunk on wrath sleep, dishevelled and wild, on the pale breasts of the clouds.

Higher still, up to the pure sky! Up to that lapis whose azure covers our prison in motion! Up to those red Easts where blazing Gods march, mad with anger and terror.

Further! higher! I can still see brokers with gold-rimmed glasses, critics, spinsters and realists with flushed faces. Higher! further! air! blue! wings! wings! wings!'

Enfin, de son vil échafaud,
Le clown sauta si haut, si haut,
Qu'il creva le plafond de toiles
Au son du cor et du tambour,
Et, le cœur dévoré d'amour,
Alla rouler dans les étoiles.

At last, from his base scaffold, the clown leaped so high, so high, that he burst the canvas ceiling to the sound of horn and drum, and, with his heart consumed by love, he went tumbling among the stars.

Charles Baudelaire
(1821–67)

Baudelaire has a pivotal place in the history of French poetry, and his influence extends far beyond the borders of France, particularly into modern British and American verse. Though he wrote some interesting prose-poems, his importance rests principally on a single volume of verse entitled *Les Fleurs du Mal*. This constitutes a remarkable distillation of an artist's entire moral, emotional and intellectual experience; it is a work, in the words of Arthur Symons, 'made out of his whole intellect and all his nerves'.

As an adolescent, Baudelaire acted in ways guaranteed to enrage his stepfather, a diplomat and military man, and was expelled from his Paris school after a homosexual incident. By eighteen he had already contracted the recurrent venereal disease that would eventually combine with a stroke to kill him. His parents sent him to India, but he 'jumped ship' at Réunion and returned to Paris. He began to write, and lived as a bohemian dandy, with a half-caste mistress, Jeanne Duval, to answer his strong sexual drive, and a succession of society ladies who played more idealized roles in his aesthetic drama. Later in his life there was a more integrated if still ambiguous relationship with Marie Daubrun, the subject of 'L'Invitation au Voyage'. Surviving on a low parental allowance administered by trustees, and on fees for his excellent art criticism, Baudelaire lived a nocturnal life of physical indulgence, including experimentation with opium. He identified quite strongly with the personality of Edgar Allan Poe, though Poe's literary influence on him is slight.

Les Fleurs du Mal, a carefully planned volume with a thematic rather than chronological arrangement of poems, appeared in 1857. Baudelaire and his publisher were prosecuted, and several poems were banned as an offence to public morality. These appeared as an appendix in 1868, but the volume was not fully integrated until the middle of this century.

His last years were lived in squalor and illness, with only posterity to acknowledge the achievement of a supremely honest, Promethean and life-changing poet who confronts his 'hypocrite reader' with an extreme form of moral truth.

In Baudelaire, essentially a city-dweller, French poetry takes a new direction. With the reader's participation a key element, the poem becomes now an experience in itself rather than a vehicle for feeling or thought. Carefully worked despite an appearance of spontaneity, it takes on an autonomous, ritualized quality as the product of the Imagination, an idealizing faculty that uses a stimulus in the real world to give it flight. The starting point may be a scent, a sound, a taste, the feel and fragrance of the hair of Jeanne, or the sight of a grotesque maggot-ridden carcass. As with the Parnassians, Beauty is the goal, and (except in early pieces like 'L'Albatros') moral content is implicit in the image if it is there at all. The conscious Self, however, remains entirely present and active during the experience, whereas in the work of Verlaine and the Symbolists consciousness will be little more than a passive receiver of experience.

Sordid reality with its '*ennui*', its banal and purposeless tedium, is transcended by art. Out of evil and suffering and even failure come artistic profits ('*les fleurs du mal*'), created by the poet-alchemist whose receptive and creative spirit is in excited contact with a mysterious harmony of symbols beyond reality, an enigmatic mental dimension linked with our perception by synaesthetic '*Correspondances*' between our different senses. Experience is transferred intuitively between different planes of our awareness and across different art-forms, as we take with Baudelaire the first tentative steps into that 'temple of Nature', that 'forest of symbols' in which Rimbaud, a more dispassionate explorer, will later lose himself.

Baudelaire's poetry is full of fluctuations and dualities which produce a range of creative tensions: love and hatred, desire and disgust, the attractiveness of sin and the indulgence of remorse, sensuality and asceticism, oblivion and lucidity, idealism and baseness. Every experience engenders an awareness of its opposite, and 'Le Voyage' dramatizes the compulsion to continue despite the failures of desire and knowledge and the hostility of society. The major oscillation is between '*Idéal*', a heightened state of perception and fertile creative energy, an artistic salvation, and '*Spleen*', a condition of claustrophobic nervous tension, angry restlessness and uncreative self-disgust (out of which, paradoxically, he creates poems as memorable as those recording the '*Ideal*' state, by projecting himself and his nausea on to his physical surroundings). Sometimes the germ of one experience can be seen in the other: in 'La Chevelure', for example, there is a confident succession of future tenses and even a temporary withdrawal from the ecstatic experience in mid-poem in the certain knowledge that it will be repeated. But the closing lines with their exclamation marks, their subjunctive, and the final question which earlier in the poem would have been a statement, all imply an awareness of imminent disintegration. 'Harmonie du Soir', on the other hand, dramatizes the ritualistic creation of something out of nothing, luminous memory out of void, in a remarkable and explicit parallel with the incantatory process of the Mass.

In terms of versification Baudelaire is not revolutionary. Like Mallarmé and the best of the Parnassians, he makes a virtue of the Alexandrine and finds in it sufficient flexibility for most of his purposes, though he also uses the octosyllable and experiments occasionally with the '*impair*' line (an uneven number of syllables, particularly associated with Verlaine), as in 'La Musique' and 'L'Invitation au voyage'. Within this mainly orthodox frame he creates sensuous rhythms and sound patterns that draw us hypnotically into the '*magie suggestive*' he foresaw as the nature of poetry after him: '*... une magie suggestive contenant à la fois l'objet et le sujet, le monde extérieur à l'artiste et l'artiste lui-même*' (a suggestive magic containing both object and subject, the world outside the artist and the artist himself).

Correspondances

La Nature est un temple où de vivants piliers
Laissent parfois sortir de confuses paroles;
L'homme y passe à travers des forêts de symboles
Qui l'observent avec des regards familiers.

Comme de longs échos qui de loin se confondent
Dans une ténébreuse et profonde unité,
Vaste comme la nuit et comme la clarté,
Les parfums, les couleurs et les sons se répondent.

Il est des parfums frais comme des chairs d'enfants,
Doux comme les hautbois, verts comme les prairies,
– Et d'autres, corrompus, riches et triomphants,

Ayant l'expansion des choses infinies,
Comme l'ambre, le musc, le benjoin et l'encens,
Qui chantent les transports de l'esprit et des sens.

Connections

Nature is a temple where living pillars sometimes release indistinct words; man passes there through forests of symbols that observe him with intimate glances.

Like prolonged echoes mingling from afar into a deep and shadowy unity, as vast as darkness and as light, scents, colours and sounds answer one another.

There are scents as fresh as the flesh of children, sweet as oboes, green as meadows, – and others, corrupt, rich and triumphant,

having the expansiveness of infinite things, like amber, musk, benzoin and incense, which sing the raptures of the mind and the senses.

L'Albatros

Souvent, pour s'amuser, les hommes d'équipage
Prennent des albatros, vastes oiseaux des mers,
Qui suivent, indolents compagnons de voyage,
Le navire glissant sur les gouffres amers.

A peine les ont-ils déposés sur les planches,
Que ces rois de l'azur, maladroits et honteux,
Laissent piteusement leurs grandes ailes blanches
Comme des avirons traîner à côté d'eux.

Ce voyageur ailé, comme il est gauche et veule!
Lui, naguère si beau, qu'il est comique et laid!
L'un agace son bec avec un brûle-gueule,
L'autre mime, en boitant, l'infirme qui volait!

The Albatross

Often, for entertainment, crewmen capture albatrosses, great birds of the oceans, languid travelling companions that follow the ship as it glides over the bitter depths.

Scarcely have they downed them on the planks, than these kings of the azure, clumsy and shameful, droop their great white wings pitifully like trailing oars beside them.

This winged traveller, how awkward and feeble he is! Not long ago so fine, how grotesque and ugly! One torments his beak with a clay pipe, another mimics, limping, the cripple who could fly!

Le Poëte est semblable au prince des nuées
Qui hante la tempête et se rit de l'archer;
Exilé sur le sol au milieu des huées,
Ses ailes de géant l'empêchent de marcher.

The Poet is like the prince of the clouds, haunting the storm and mocking the archer; in exile on the ground, amidst the jeers, his giant wings prevent him from walking.

La Beauté

Je suis belle, ô mortels! comme un rêve de pierre,
Et mon sein, où chacun s'est meurtri tour à tour,
Est fait pour inspirer au poëte un amour
Éternel et muet ainsi que la matière.

Je trône dans l'azur comme un sphinx incompris;
J'unis un cœur de neige à la blancheur des cygnes;
Je hais le mouvement qui déplace les lignes,
Et jamais je ne pleure et jamais je ne ris.

Beauty

I am beautiful, o mortals, like a dream in stone, and my breast, where all have bruised themselves in turn, is destined to inspire in the poet a love that is eternal and wordless, like matter.

I am enthroned in the azure like an unfathomed sphinx; to the whiteness of swans I join a heart of snow; I hate motion which displaces the lines, and I never weep and never laugh.

Les poëtes, devant mes grandes attitudes,
Que j'ai l'air d'emprunter aux plus fiers monuments,
Consumeront leurs jours en d'austères études;

Car j'ai, pour fasciner ces dociles amants,
De purs miroirs qui font toutes choses plus belles:
Mes yeux, mes larges yeux aux clartés éternelles!

The poets, before my lofty attitudes, which I seem to borrow from the proudest monuments, will burn away their days in austere studies;

For I have, to fascinate these docile lovers, pure mirrors which make all things more beautiful: my eyes, my wide eyes with their eternal brightness!

La Chevelure

O toison, moutonnant jusque sur l'encolure!
O boucles! O parfum chargé de nonchaloir!
Extase! Pour peupler ce soir l'alcôve obscure
Des souvenirs dormant dans cette chevelure,
Je la veux agiter dans l'air comme un mouchoir!

The Hair

O fleece, foaming down like wool over neck and throat! O curls! O perfume heavy with nonchalance! Ecstasy! This evening to people the dark bedchamber with the memories sleeping in this mane of hair, I want to wave it in the air like a handkerchief!

La langoureuse Asie et la brûlante Afrique,
Tout un monde lointain, absent, presque défunt.
Vit dans tes profondeurs, forêt aromatique!
Comme d'autres esprits voguent sur la musique,
Le mien, ô mon amour! nage sur ton parfum.

J'irai là-bas où l'arbre et l'homme, pleins de sève,
Se pâment longuement sous l'ardeur des climats;
Fortes tresses, soyez la houle qui m'enlève!
Tu contiens, mer d'ébène, un éblouissant rêve
De voiles, de rameurs, de flammes et de mâts:

Un port retentissant où mon âme peut boire
A grands flots le parfum, le son et la couleur;
Où les vaisseaux, glissant dans l'or et dans la moire,
Ouvrent leurs vastes bras pour embrasser la gloire
D'un ciel pur où frémit l'éternelle chaleur.

Languorous Asia and burning Africa, an entire distant world, absent, almost extinct, lives in your depths, aromatic forest! As other spirits sail on music, mine, O my love, swims on your perfume.

I will go there, where trees and men, full of sap, swoon in a long slow trance in the burning heat of the climate; strong tresses, be the sea swell that carries me away! You enfold, ebony ocean, a dazzling dream of sails, of rowers, of pennants and of masts:

A reverberating harbour where my soul can drink scent, sound and colour in great draughts; where the vessels, gliding through gold and watered silk, open their great arms to receive the glory of a pure sky quivering with eternal heat.

Je plongerai ma tête amoureuse d'ivresse
Dans ce noir océan où l'autre est enfermé;
Et mon esprit subtil que le roulis caresse
Saura vous retrouver, ô féconde paresse!
Infinis bercements du loisir embaumé!

Cheveux bleus, pavillon de ténèbres tendues,
Vous me rendez l'azur du ciel immense et rond;
Sur les bords duvetés de vos mèches tordues
Je m'enivre ardemment des senteurs confondues
De l'huile de coco, du musc et du goudron.

Longtemps! toujours! ma main dans ta crinière lourde
Sèmera le rubis, la perle et le saphir,
Afin qu'à mon désir tu ne sois jamais sourde!
N'es-tu pas l'oasis où je rêve, et la gourde
Où je hume à longs traits le vin du souvenir?

I will plunge my head, in love with intoxication, into this black ocean where the other is enclosed; and my refined spirit, caressed by the swell, will surely find you once more, O fertile indolence! Infinite rockings of perfumed leisure!

Blue hair, canopy of stretched shadows, you yield to me the azure of the vast round sky; on the downy shores of your entwined locks I drink to passionate intoxication the mingled scents of coconut oil, musk and tar.

Let it go on! For ever! my hand will sow in your heavy mane ruby, pearl and sapphire, so that you may never be deaf to my desire! Are you not the oasis where I dream, and the gourd where I drink in long draughts the wine of memory?

Avec ses vêtements ...

Avec ses vêtements ondoyants et nacrés,
Même quand elle marche, on croirait qu'elle danse,
Comme ces longs serpents que les jongleurs sacrés
Au bout de leurs bâtons agitent en cadence.

Comme le sable morne et l'azur des déserts,
Insensibles tous deux à l'humaine souffrance,
Comme les longs réseaux de la houle des mers,
Elle se développe avec indifférence.

Ses yeux polis sont faits de minéraux charmants,
Et dans cette nature étrange et symbolique
Où l'ange inviolé se mêle au sphinx antique,

Où tout n'est qu'or, acier, lumière et diamants,
Resplendit à jamais, comme un astre inutile,
La froide majesté de la femme stérile.

With her undulating, lustrous clothes ...

With her undulating, lustrous clothes, even when she walks it is as if she's dancing, like those long snakes that the sacred jugglers wave rhythmically, at the ends of their sticks.

Like the desolate sand and the blue sky of the deserts, both insensitive to human suffering, like the long networks of the ocean's swell, she unfolds with indifference.

Her polished eyes are made of bewitching minerals, and in this strange and symbolic nature where the inviolate angel blends with the sphinx of antiquity,

Where all is merely gold, steel, light and diamonds, there shines for ever, like a useless star, the cold majesty of the sterile woman.

Une Charogne

Rappelez-vous l'objet que nous vîmes, mon âme,
  Ce beau matin d'été si doux:
Au détour d'un sentier une charogne infâme
  Sur un lit semé de cailloux,

Les jambes en l'air, comme une femme lubrique,
  Brûlante et suant les poisons,
Ouvrait d'une façon nonchalante et cynique
  Son ventre plein d'exhalaisons.

Le soleil rayonnait sur cette pourriture,
  Comme afin de la cuire à point,
Et de rendre au centuple à la grande Nature
  Tout ce qu'ensemble elle avait joint;

Carrion

Remember the object that we saw, love of my soul, that fine sweet summer morning: at the turn of a path a vile carcass on a bed strewn with pebbles,

Legs in the air, like a lascivious woman, burning and oozing out poisons, opened in casual, brazen fashion its fuming belly.

The sun was shining on this putrefaction, as if to cook it to a turn, and to yield a hundredfold back to great Nature all that it had joined together;

Et le ciel regardait la carcasse superbe
   Comme une fleur s'épanouir.
La puanteur était si forte, que sur l'herbe
   Vous crûtes vous évanouir.

Les mouches bourdonnaient sur ce ventre putride,
   D'où sortaient de noirs bataillons
De larves, qui coulaient comme un épais liquide
   Le long de ces vivants haillons.

Tout cela descendait, montait comme une vague,
   Ou s'élançait en pétillant;
On eût dit que le corps, enflé d'un souffle vague,
   Vivait en se multipliant.

Et ce monde rendait une étrange musique,
   Comme l'eau courante et le vent,
Ou le grain qu'un vanneur d'un mouvement rythmique
   Agite et tourne dans son van.

And the sky watched the proud carcass expanding like a flower. The stench was so strong that you thought you would faint on the grass.

The flies buzzed over that rotting belly, from which came black battalions of larvae, flowing like a viscous liquid along those living rags.

It all rose and fell like a wave, or darted, bubbling; it was as if the body, swollen by an undefined breath, lived by multiplying.

And this world gave off strange music, like running water and wind, or the grain that a winnower rhythmically shakes and spins in his basket.

Les formes s'effaçaient et n'étaient plus qu'un rêve,
    Une ébauche lente à venir,
Sur la toile oubliée, et que l'artiste achève
    Seulement par le souvenir.

Derrière les rochers une chienne inquiète
    Nous regardait d'un œil fâché,
Épiant le moment de reprendre au squelette
    Le morceau qu'elle avait lâché.

– Et pourtant vous serez semblable à cette ordure,
    A cette horrible infection,
Étoile de mes yeux, soleil de ma nature,
    Vous, mon ange et ma passion!

Oui! telle vous serez, ô la reine des grâces,
    Après les derniers sacrements,
Quand vous irez, sous l'herbe et les floraisons grasses,
    Moisir parmi les ossements.

The shapes vanished and were no more than a dream, a slowly forming sketch forgotten on the canvas, and completed by the artist only from memory.

Behind the rocks an anxious bitch gazed at us with an angry eye, watching for the moment to take back from the skeleton the piece that it had left.

– And yet you will be like this filth, this horrible contamination, star of my eyes, sun of my temperament, you, my angel and my passion!

Yes! thus you will be, O queen of graces, after the final sacrament, when you will go, beneath the grass and the thick floral abundance, to moulder among the bones.

Alors, ô ma beauté! dites à la vermine
    Qui vous mangera de baisers,
Que j'ai gardé la forme et l'essence divine
    De mes amours décomposés!

Well then, O my beauty! tell the vermin who will devour you with kisses, that I have kept the form and the divine essence of my decomposed loves!

Harmonie du soir

Voici venir les temps où vibrant sur sa tige
Chaque fleur s'évapore ainsi qu'un encensoir;
Les sons et les parfums tournent dans l'air du soir;
Valse mélancolique et langoureux vertige!

Chaque fleur s'évapore ainsi qu'un encensoir;
Le violon frémit comme un cœur qu'on afflige;
Valse mélancolique et langoureux vertige!
Le ciel est triste et beau comme un grand reposoir.

Harmony of Evening

Now is the time when, vibrating on its stem, each flower exhales itself in vapour like a censer; sounds and scents wheel around in the evening air; melancholy waltz and languorous vertigo!

Each flower exhales itself in vapour like a censer; the violin shudders like an afflicted heart; melancholy waltz and languorous vertigo! The sky is sad and beautiful like a great processional altar.

Le violon frémit comme un cœur qu'on afflige,
Un cœur tendre, qui hait le néant vaste et noir!
Le ciel est triste et beau comme un grand reposoir;
Le soleil s'est noyé dans son sang qui se fige.

Un cœur tendre, qui hait le néant vaste et noir,
Du passé lumineux recueille tout vestige!
Le soleil s'est noyé dans son sang qui se fige ...
Ton souvenir en moi luit comme un ostensoir!

The violin shudders like an afflicted heart, a tender heart, that loathes the great black void! The sky is sad and beautiful like a great processional altar; the sun has drowned in its own congealing blood.

A tender heart, that loathes the great black void, recovers every trace of the luminous past! The sun has drowned in its own congealing blood ... your memory within me shines like a monstrance!

L'Invitation au voyage

Mon enfant, ma sœur,
Songe à la douceur
D'aller là-bas vivre ensemble!
Aimer à loisir,
Aimer et mourir
Au pays qui te ressemble!
Les soleils mouillés
De ces ciels brouillés
Pour mon esprit ont les charmes
Si mystérieux
De tes traîtres yeux,
Brillant à travers leurs larmes.

Là, tout n'est qu'ordre et beauté,
Luxe, calme et volupté.

Invitation to a Journey

My child, my sister, think how sweet to go there and live together! To love as we please, to love and to die, in the land that is like you! The watery suns of those opaque skies hold for my spirit the mysterious charms of your treacherous eyes, shining through their tears.

There, all is simply order and beauty, abundance, calm, and pleasure for the senses.

Des meubles luisants,
Polis par les ans,
Décoreraient notre chambre;
Les plus rares fleurs
Mêlant leurs odeurs
Aux vagues senteurs de l'ambre
Les riches plafonds,
Les miroirs profonds,
La splendeur orientale,
Tout y parlerait
A l'âme en secret
Sa douce langue natale.

Là, tout n'est qu'ordre et beauté,
Luxc, calme et volupté.

Shining furniture, polished by the years, would adorn our room; the rarest flowers mingling their perfumes with the hazy scents of amber, the rich ceilings, the deep mirrors, the oriental splendour, all would speak there to the soul in secret in its soft and native tongue.

There, all is simply order and beauty, abundance, calm, and pleasure for the senses.

Vois sur ces canaux
Dormir ces vaisseaux
Dont l'humeur est vagabonde;
C'est pour assouvir
Ton moindre désir
Qu'ils viennent du bout du monde.
– Les soleils couchants
Revêtent les champs,
Les canaux, la ville entière,
D'hyacinthe et d'or;
Le monde s'endort
Dans une chaude lumière.

Là, tout n'est qu'ordre et beauté,
Luxe, calme et volupté.

See on the canals those sleeping ships with the vagabond temperament; it is to fulfil your least desire that they come from the end of the earth. – The sunsets clothe the fields, the canals, the whole city in hyacinth and gold; the world sinks into sleep in a warm light.

There, all is simply order and beauty, abundance, calm, and pleasure for the senses.

La Musique

La musique souvent me prend comme une mer!
Vers ma pâle étoile,
Sous un plafond de brume ou dans un vaste éther,
Je mets à la voile;

La poitrine en avant et les poumons gonflés
Comme de la toile,
J'escalade le dos des flots amoncelés
Que la nuit me voile;

Je sens vibrer en moi toutes les passions
D'un vaisseau qui souffre;
Le bon vent, la tempête et ses convulsions

Sur l'immense gouffre
Me bercent. D'autres fois, calme plat, grand miroir
De mon désespoir!

Music

Music often takes me like a sea! Towards my pale star, beneath a misty ceiling or in a vast ether I set sail;

Chest thrust forward and lungs inflated like sailcloth, I scale the backs of the mountainous waves veiled from me by the darkness;

I feel vibrating within me all the passions of a suffering ship; the fair wind, the storm and its convulsions

above the great abyss rock me. At other times, flat calm, broad mirror of my despair!

Spleen

Pluviôse, irrité contre la ville entière,
De son urne à grands flots verse un froid ténébreux
Aux pâles habitants du voisin cimetière
Et la mortalité sur les faubourgs brumeux.

Mon chat sur le carreau cherchant une litière
Agite sans repos son corps maigre et galeux;
L'âme d'un vieux poëte erre dans la gouttière
Avec la triste voix d'un fantôme frileux.

Le bourdon se lamente, et la bûche enfumée
Accompagne en fausset la pendule enrhumée,
Cependant qu'en un jeu plein de sales parfums,

Héritage fatal d'une vieille hydropique,
Le beau valet de cœur et la dame de pique
Causent sinistrement de leurs amours défunts.

Spleen (I)

Pluviose,[1] incensed with the whole city, pours from his urn in great cascades a murky cold for the inhabitants of the neighbouring cemetery and mortality over the misty suburbs.

My cat, seeking a resting place on the tiles, shifts incessantly its thin and mangy body; the soul of an old poet wanders in the guttering with the sad voice of a chilled spectre.

The tolling bell laments, and the smoking log accompanies in shrill discord the wheezing clock, while in a foul-smelling pack of cards,

the baleful legacy of a dropsical old woman, the handsome knave of hearts and the queen of spades converse darkly of their extinct passions.

[1]In the Revolutionary calendar, the name given to the period from 21 January to 21 February.

Spleen

Je suis comme le roi d'un pays pluvieux,
Riche, mais impuissant, jeune et pourtant très vieux,
Qui, de ses précepteurs méprisant les courbettes,
S'ennuie avec ses chiens comme avec d'autres bêtes.
Rien ne peut l'égayer, ni gibier, ni faucon,
Ni son peuple mourant en face du balcon.
Du bouffon favori la grotesque ballade
Ne distrait plus le front de ce cruel malade;
Son lit fleurdelisé se transforme en tombeau,
Et les dames d'atour, pour qui tout prince est beau,
Ne savent plus trouver d'impudique toilette
Pour tirer un souris de ce jeune squelette.
Le savant qui lui fait de l'or n'a jamais pu
De son être extirper l'élément corrompu,

Spleen (III)

I am like the king of a rainy country, rich yet impotent, young and yet age-old, who, contemptuous of the bowings of his tutors, spends his time in boredom with his dogs as with other animals. Nothing can raise his spirits, neither game nor falcon, nor his people dying in sight of his balcony. The comic ballad of his favourite fool no longer entertains the countenance of this cruel invalid; his bed, adorned with fleurs-de-lis, is changed into a tomb, and the ladies of the bedchamber, for whom any prince is handsome, can no longer find a shameless dress to draw a smile from this young skeleton. The scholar who makes gold for him has never been able to root out the corrupt element from his being, and in those baths of blood

Et dans ces bains de sang qui des Romains nous viennent,
Et dont sur leurs vieux jours les puissants se souviennent,
Il n'a su réchauffer ce cadavre hébété
Où coule au lieu de sang l'eau verte du Léthé.

which come down to us from the Romans and which the powerful recall in their old age, he has failed to warm this dull-eyed corpse through which in place of blood the green water of Lethe flows.

Les Aveugles

Contemple-les, mon âme; ils sont vraiment affreux!
Pareils aux mannequins; vaguement ridicules;
Terribles, singuliers comme les somnambules;
Dardant on ne sait où leurs globes ténébreux.

Leurs yeux, d'où la divine étincelle est partie,
Comme s'ils regardaient au loin, restent levés
Au ciel; on ne les voit jamais vers les pavés
Pencher rêveusement leur tête appesantie.

The Blind

Behold them, my soul; truly they are hideous! Like dummies; vaguely ludicrous; dreadful, bizarre like sleepwalkers; darting who knows where their murky globes.

Their eyes, abandoned by the divine spark, as if they were gazing afar, remain lifted to the sky; you never see them lower their burdensome head dreamily towards the cobbles.

Ils traversent ainsi le noir illimité,
Ce frère du silence éternel. O cité!
Pendant qu'autour de nous tu chantes, ris et beugles,

Éprise du plaisir jusqu'à l'atrocité,
Vois! je me traîne aussi! mais, plus qu'eux hébété,
Je dis: Que cherchent-ils au Ciel, tous ces aveugles?

Thus they traverse the boundless blackness, that brother of eternal silence. O city! while around us you sing, laugh and bellow,

In love with pleasure to the point of atrocity, see! I too drag myself along! but, more bewildered even than them, I say: What are they seeking in Heaven, all these blind men?

A une Passante

La rue assourdissante autour de moi hurlait.
Longue, mince, en grand deuil, douleur majestueuse,
Une femme passa, d'une main fastueuse
Soulevant, balançant le feston et l'ourlet;

To a passing woman

The deafening street howled around me. Tall, slender, deep in mourning, a majestic grief, a woman passed, one hand ostentatiously lifting and swinging scallop and hem;

Agile et noble, avec sa jambe de statue.
Moi, je buvais, crispé comme un extravagant,
Dans son œil, ciel livide où germe l'ouragan,
La douceur qui fascine et le plaisir qui tue.

Un éclair...puis la nuit! – Fugitive beauté
Dont le regard m'a fait soudainement renaître,
Ne te verrai-je plus que dans l'éternité?

Ailleurs, bien loin d'ici! trop tard! *jamais* peut-être!
Car j'ignore où tu fuis, tu ne sais où je vais,
O toi que j'eusse aimée, ô toi qui le savais!

Supple and stately, with her statuesque leg. And me, I was drinking, hunched up like a freak, in her eye, a pallid sky where the hurricane is born, the softness that fascinates and the pleasure that kills.

A lightning flash ... then darkness! Transient beauty whose glance has brought me sudden rebirth, will I see you no more save in eternity?

Elsewhere, far away from here! too late! perhaps *never*! For I know not where you are gliding, you know not where I am going, O you whom I would have loved, O you who knew it!

La Destruction

Sans cesse à mes côtés s'agite le Démon;
Il nage autour de moi comme un air impalpable;
Je l'avale et le sens qui brûle mon poumon
Et l'emplit d'un désir éternel et coupable.

Parfois il prend, sachant mon grand amour de l'Art,
La forme de la plus séduisante des femmes,
Et, sous de spécieux prétextes de cafard,
Accoutume ma lèvre à des philtres infâmes.

Il me conduit ainsi, loin du regard de Dieu,
Haletant et brisé de fatigue, au milieu
Des plaines de l'Ennui, profondes et désertes,

Et jette dans mes yeux pleins de confusion
Des vêtements souillés, des blessures ouvertes,
Et l'appareil sanglant de la Destruction!

Destruction

Ceaselessly the Demon writhes beside me; he swims around me like an intangible vapour; I swallow him and feel him burn my lung and fill it with eternal, guilty desire.

Sometimes, knowing my passion for Art, he takes the form of the most captivating of women, and, on the specious pretext of depression, accustoms my lips to vile potions.

Thus he leads me, far from the sight of God, breathless and racked with fatigue, to the middle of the plains of Tedium, deep and forsaken,

And throws into my disordered eyes soiled clothes, open wounds, and the blood-soaked apparatus of Destruction!

Le Voyage

à Maxime du Camp

i

Pour l'enfant, amoureux de cartes et d'estampes,
L'univers est égal à son vaste appétit.
Ah! que le monde est grand à la clarté des lampes!
Aux yeux du souvenir que le monde est petit!

Un matin nous partons, le cerveau plein de flamme,
Le cœur gros de rancune et de désirs amers,
Et nous allons, suivant le rythme de la lame,
Berçant notre infini sur le fini des mers:

The Voyage

for Maxime du Camp

I

For the child, in love with maps and engravings, the universe is equal to his vast appetite. Ah! how great the world is by lamplight! How small the world is in the eyes of memory!

One morning we set off, our brains full of passion, hearts swollen with rancour and with bitter desires, and we go, following the rhythm of the waves, rocking our infinity on the finite seas:

Les uns, joyeux de fuir une patrie infâme;
D'autres, l'horreur de leurs berceaux, et quelques-uns,
Astrologues noyés dans les yeux d'une femme,
La Circé tyrannique aux dangereux parfums.

Pour n'être pas changés en bêtes, ils s'enivrent
D'espace et de lumière et de cieux embrasés;
La glace qui les mord, les soleils qui les cuivrent,
Effacent lentement la marque des baisers.

Mais les vrais voyageurs sont ceux-là seuls qui partent
Pour partir; cœurs légers, semblables aux ballons,
De leur fatalité jamais ils ne s'écartent,
Et, sans savoir pourquoi, disent toujours: Allons!

Ceux-là dont les désirs ont la forme des nues,
Et qui rêvent, ainsi qu'un conscrit le canon,
De vastes voluptés, changeantes, inconnues,
Et dont l'esprit humain n'a jamais su le nom!

Some, glad to leave an abhorrent homeland; others, the horror of their cradles, and some, astrologers drowned in the eyes of a woman, tyrannical Circe with the dangerous perfumes.

To avoid being changed into beasts, they get drunk on space and light and fiery skies; the ice that bites them, the suns that bronze them, slowly efface the traces of kisses.

But the only true travellers are those who leave for the sake of leaving; with hearts light as balloons, they never deviate from their destiny and, not knowing why, they always say: Let's go!

Those whose desires have the form of clouds, and who dream, as a conscript dreams of cannon, of vast, shifting, unknown pleasures, whose name the human mind has never known!

ii

Nous imitons, horreur! la toupie et la boule
Dans leur valse et leurs bonds; même dans nos sommeils
La Curiosité nous tourmente et nous roule,
Comme un Ange cruel qui fouette des soleils.

Singulière fortune où le but se déplace,
Et, n'étant nulle part, peut être n'importe où!
Où l'Homme, dont jamais l'espérance n'est lasse,
Pour trouver le repos court toujours comme un fou!

Notre âme est un trois-mâts cherchant son Icarie;
Une voix retentit sur le pont: "Ouvre l'œil!"
Une voix de la hune, ardente et folle, crie:
"Amour...gloire...bonheur!" Enfer! c'est un écueil!

Chaque îlot signalé par l'homme de vigie
Est un Eldorado promis par le Destin;
L'Imagination qui dresse son orgie
Ne trouve qu'un récif aux clartés du matin.

II

We imitate, O horror! the spinning top and ball in their waltzing and their leaping; even in our sleep Curiosity torments us and rolls us on like a cruel Angel whipping suns.

Strange destiny in which the goal moves, and being nowhere may be anywhere! And in which Man, whose hope is never wearied, runs for ever like a madman in search of rest!

Our soul is a three-master seeking its Icaria; a voice resounds on deck: 'Alert!' A voice from the crow's nest, passionate and wild, cries: 'Love ... renown ... happiness!' Hell! it is a rock!

Each islet signalled by the lookout is an Eldorado promised by Destiny; the Imagination, preparing its orgy, finds only a reef in the morning light.

O le pauvre amoureux des pays chimériques!
Faut-il le mettre aux fers, le jeter à la mer,
Ce matelot ivrogne, inventeur d'Amériques
Dont le mirage rend le gouffre plus amer?

Tel le vieux vagabond, piétinant dans la boue,
Rêve, le nez en l'air, de brillants paradis;
Son œil ensorcelé découvre une Capoue
Partout où la chandelle illumine un taudis.

iii

Étonnants voyageurs! quelles nobles histoires
Nous lisons dans vos yeux profonds comme les mers!
Montrez-nous les écrins de vos riches mémoires,
Ces bijoux merveilleux, faits d'astres et d'éthers.

Nous voulons voyager sans vapeur et sans voile!
Faites, pour égayer l'ennui de nos prisons,
Passer sur nos esprits, tendus comme une toile,
Vos souvenirs avec leurs cadres d'horizons.

O the poor lover of illusory countries! Should we put him in irons or throw him in the sea, this drunken sailor, this inventor of Americas of which the mirage makes the abyss more bitter?

In the same way the old vagabond, tramping in the mud, dreams with nose in air of shining Edens; his bewitched eye discovers a Capua wherever a candle lights a hovel.

III

Astonishing travellers! what noble stories we read in your eyes as deep as the seas! Show us the coffers of your rich memories, those marvellous jewels made of stars and ether.

We want to travel without steam, without sail! To enliven the tedium of our prisons, set sailing over our minds, stretched out like canvas, your memories with the horizon for their frame.

Dites, qu'avez-vous vu?

iv

"Nous avons vu des astres
Et des flots; nous avons vu des sables aussi;
Et, malgré bien des chocs et d'imprévus désastres,
Nous nous sommes souvent ennuyés, comme ici.

La gloire du soleil sur la mer violette,
La gloire des cités dans le soleil couchant,
Allumaient dans nos cœurs une ardeur inquiète
De plonger dans un ciel au reflet alléchant.

Les plus riches cités, les plus grands paysages,
Jamais ne contenaient l'attrait mystérieux
De ceux que le hasard fait avec les nuages.
Et toujours le désir nous rendait soucieux!

Tell us, what have you seen?

IV

'We have seen stars and waves; we saw sand dunes too; and in spite of many shocks and unforeseen disasters we were often bored as we were here.

The glory of the sun on the violet sea, the glory of cities in the sunset, kindled in our hearts a restless urge to plunge into a sky whose reflection was so alluring.

The richest cities, the broadest landscapes never held the mysterious attraction of those that chance forms with the clouds. And always desire made us anxious!

– La jouissance ajoute au désir de la force.
Désir, vieil arbre à qui le plaisir sert d'engrais,
Cependant que grossit et durcit ton écorce,
Tes branches veulent voir le soleil de plus près!

Grandiras-tu toujours, grand arbre plus vivace
Que le cyprès? – Pourtant nous avons, avec soin,
Cueilli quelques croquis pour votre album vorace,
Frères qui trouvez beau tout ce qui vient de loin!

Nous avons salué des idoles à trompe;
Des trônes constellés de joyaux lumineux;
Des palais ouvragés dont la féerique pompe
Serait pour vos banquiers un rêve ruineux;

Des costumes qui sont pour les yeux une ivresse;
Des femmes dont les dents et les ongles sont teints,
Et des jongleurs savants que le serpent caresse."

Gratification adds strength to desire. Desire, that old tree that pleasure serves to fertilize, while your bark thickens and hardens, your branches want a closer view of the sun!

Will you always go on growing, great tree, longer-lived than the cypress? – And yet with care we have gathered some sketches for your voracious album, you brothers who find everything beautiful that comes from afar!

We have bowed before idols with elephants' trunks; thrones studded with luminous gems; carved palaces whose fairytale splendour would be a ruinous dream for your bankers;

Costumes that intoxicate the eyes; women whose teeth and nails are dyed, and skilful jugglers caressed by snakes.'

v

Et puis, et puis encore?

vi

"O cerveaux enfantins!

Pour ne pas oublier la chose capitale,
Nous avons vu partout, et sans l'avoir cherché,
Du haut jusques en bas de l'échelle fatale,
Le spectacle ennuyeux de l'immortel péché:

La femme, esclave vile, orgueilleuse et stupide,
Sans rire s'adorant et s'aimant sans dégoût;
L'homme, tyran goulu, paillard, dur et cupide,
Esclave de l'esclave et ruisseau dans l'égoût;

V

And then, and then what next?

VI

'O infantile brains! Not to forget the essential thing, we saw everywhere, without having sought it, from top to bottom of the fatal ladder, the tedious spectacle of immortal sin:

Woman, a base slave, arrogant and stupid, worshipping herself without laughter and loving herself without disgust; man, a gluttonous dissolute tyrant, hard and grasping, slave of the slave and a drain into the sewer;

Le bourreau qui jouit, le martyr qui sanglote;
La fête qu'assaisonne et parfume le sang;
Le poison du pouvoir énervant le despote,
Et le peuple amoureux du fouet abrutissant;

Plusieurs religions semblables à la nôtre,
Toutes escaladant le ciel; la Sainteté,
Comme en un lit de plume un délicat se vautre,
Dans les clous et le crin cherchant la volupté;

L'Humanité bavarde, ivre de son génie,
Et, folle maintenant comme elle était jadis,
Criant à Dieu, dans sa furibonde agonie:
"O mon semblable, ô mon maître, je te maudis!"

Et les moins sots, hardis amants de la Démence,
Fuyant le grand troupeau parqué par le Destin,
Et se réfugiant dans l'opium immense!
– Tel est du globe entier l'éternel bulletin."

The gratified torturer, the sobbing martyr; the feast flavoured and scented with blood; the poison of power that debilitates the despot, and the people in love with the brutalizing whip;

Several religions similar to ours, all scaling the walls of heaven; sanctity, like an aesthete wallowing in a feather bed, seeks pleasure in nails and hair-shirts;

Babbling humanity, drunk with its own genius, and, mad now as it was before, crying out to God in its frantic death-throes: "O my fellow creature, O my master, I curse thee!"

And the less foolish, bold lovers of Lunacy, shunning the great herd penned in by Fate, and taking refuge in the immensity of opium! – Such is the eternal report on the whole globe.'

vii

Amer savoir, celui qu'on tire du voyage!
Le monde, monotone et petit, aujourd'hui,
Hier, demain, toujours, nous fait voir notre image:
Une oasis d'horreur dans un désert d'ennui!

Faut-il partir? rester? Si tu peux rester, reste;
Pars, s'il le faut. L'un court, et l'autre se tapit
Pour tromper l'ennemi vigilant et funeste,
Le Temps! Il est, hélas, des coureurs sans répit,

Comme le Juif errant et comme les apôtres,
A qui rien ne suffit, ni wagon ni vaisseau,
Pour fuir ce rétiaire infâme; il en est d'autres
Qui savent le tuer sans quitter leur berceau.

VII

What bitter knowledge we gain from travelling! The world, monotonous and small, today, yesterday, tomorrow, always, shows us our own image: an oasis of horror in a desert of tedium!

Should we go? stay? If you can stay, stay; leave, if you must. One man runs, the other cowers to deceive the watchful, baleful enemy, Time! There are, alas, runners who have no respite,

Like the wandering Jew and like the apostles, for whom nothing suffices, neither carriage nor ship, to flee this vile gladiator with his net; there are others who can kill him without leaving their cradle.

Lorsque enfin il mettra le pied sur notre échine,
Nous pourrons espérer et crier: En avant!
De même qu'autrefois nous partions pour la Chine,
Les yeux fixés au large et les cheveux au vent,

Nous nous embarquerons sur la mer des Ténèbres
Avec le cœur joyeux d'un jeune passager.
Entendez-vous ces voix, charmantes et funèbres,
Qui chantent: "Par ici! vous qui voulez manger

Le Lotus parfumé! c'est ici qu'on vendange
Les fruits miraculeux dont votre cœur a faim;
Venez vous enivrer de la douceur étrange
De cette après-midi qui n'a jamais de fin!"

When at last he places his foot on our spine, we will be able to hope and cry out: Forward! Just as once we set out for China, our eyes fixed on the horizon and our hair in the wind,

We will embark upon the sea of Darkness with the joyful heart of a young voyager. Do you hear those enchanting and funereal voices singing: 'This way! you who wish to eat

The scented Lotus! here are harvested the wondrous fruits for which your heart hungers; come and get drunk on the strange sweetness of this afternoon that has no end!'

A l'accent familier nous devinons le spectre;
Nos Pylades là-bas tendent leurs bras vers nous.
"Pour rafraîchir ton cœur nage vers ton Électre!"
Dit celle dont jadis nous baisions les genoux.

viii

O Mort, vieux capitaine, il est temps! levons l'ancre!
Ce pays nous ennuie, ô Mort! Appareillons!
Si le ciel et la mer sont noirs comme de l'encre,
Nos cœurs que tu connais sont remplis de rayons!

Verse-nous ton poison pour qu'il nous réconforte!
Nous voulons, tant ce feu nous brûle le cerveau,
Plonger au fond du gouffre, Enfer ou Ciel, qu'importe?
Au fond de l'Inconnu pour trouver du *nouveau!*

We guess the name of the spectre from the familiar tone of voice; our Pylades yonder stretch out their arms to us. 'To refresh your heart swim towards your Electra!' says she whose knees we once kissed.

VIII

O Death, old Captain, it's time! let's raise anchor! This land bores us, O Death! Let's get under way! If the sky and sea are as black as ink, our hearts, which you know, are filled with rays of light!

Pour into us your poison that it may comfort us! This fire blazes so hot in our brains that we want to plunge to the bottom of the chasm, Hell or Heaven, what does it matter? to the depths of the Unknown to find something *new*.

Recueillement

Sois sage, ô ma Douleur, et tiens-toi plus tranquille.
Tu réclamais le Soir; il descend; le voici:
Une atmosphère obscure enveloppe la ville,
Aux uns portant la paix, aux autres le souci.

Pendant que des mortels la multitude vile,
Sous le fouet du Plaisir, ce bourreau sans merci,
Va cueillir des remords dans la fête servile,
Ma Douleur, donne-moi la main; viens par ici,

Loin d'eux. Vois se pencher les défuntes Années,
Sur les balcons du ciel, en robes surannées;
Surgir du fond des eaux le Regret souriant;

Le Soleil moribond s'endormir sous une arche,
Et, comme un long linceul traînant à l'Orient,
Entends, ma chère, entends la douce Nuit qui marche.

Meditation

Be discreet, O my Suffering, and be more placid. You craved the Evening; it comes down; here it is: a dusky atmosphere cloaks the city, bringing peace to some, anxiety to others.

While the vile multitude of mortals, under the whip of Pleasure, that pitiless torturer, goes gathering remorse in servile celebration, my Suffering, give me your hand; come this way,

Far from them. See the departed years leaning over the balconies of the sky, in old-fashioned gowns; smiling Regret welling up from the waters' depths;

The moribund sun going to sleep beneath an arch, and, like a long shroud trailing away into the East, hear, my beloved, hear the tread of gentle Night.

The Parnassian Movement

The name chosen by this group of poets derives from the 1867 verse anthology *Le Parnasse Contemporain*, and reflects their aspiration to a noble form of poetry, cleansed of emotionalism and the vulgar effusions of the Self. Their ideas constitute, in modern terms, a 'backlash' against Romanticism, and have much in common with those of Gautier, who published poems in that anthology along with Baudelaire, Mallarmé, Verlaine, Cros, de Banville and many others. This very diversity counsels caution in applying the term 'movement' to the new spirit, but an identifiable group (including none of the above) did subsequently emerge and continue regular gatherings around the abrasive, patrician figure of Leconte de Lisle. The group would have preferred leadership by Gautier (which would have been appropriate) or by Baudelaire (certainly inappropriate), but both refused the role.

'Passion is not an excuse for writing bad verse ...' they argue, in their quest for formal perfection of metre and rhyme. Wilfully and consciously elitist, despising the rabble, Parnassianism brings the spirit and patience of the sculptor and the precision of the scientist to verse composition, with a meticulous pursuit of objectivity and ennoblement of the subject as its aesthetic imperatives. Descriptive imagery emerges as their *forte*, enhanced by expressive sound patterns and by complementary rhythms that reinforce a sense of concrete three-dimensionality. Still working principally with the Alexandrine, they give it further internal flexibility with *enjambements* and mobile *caesurae*, exploiting ground prepared by Hugo, whom they continued to venerate in his exile.

Among their favourite subjects are impressive animals and scenes from classical antiquity. Often the subjects are placed in exotic environments and demonstrate physical power and speed, elemental violence, and superiority to ordinary human beings. Often there are morally uplifting implications in the images, which in the best poetry of this type are constructed very consciously and with great descriptive flair, plasticity and dynamism.

Art itself is elevated by this group to the top of the scale of values, withdrawn from the broad public courted so successfully by the Romantics, and removed from its temporal and social context into the rarefied sphere of Art for Art's Sake. But apart from Leconte de Lisle, possibly Dierx and Prudhomme, and certainly Heredia, they have not stood the test of time. Their limitations have been exposed by the achievements of their more expansive contemporaries, but the movement deserves consideration as a significant element in the literary climate in which those greater poets flourished.

Parnassians not featured here but of interest to students of the movement include Louis Bouilhet, Louis Ménard, Sully Prudhomme, Léon Dierx, Catulle Mendès, François Coppée, Albert Glatigny, Pierre Louys.

Leconte de Lisle
(1818–94)

An idealistic republican in his youth, Leconte de Lisle turned away from politics and the people after the disillusionment of 1848, and devoted himself to poetry and philosophy. Rejecting contemporary society and personal lyricism (*'une vanité et une profanation gratuites'*) as unfit and decadent subjects for art, he sought in the scientific study of past and distant civilizations models of less debased, materialistic and philistine societies, particularly societies in which art was a sacred activity and where artists were granted élite status. He also studied evolutionary science, and like Vigny cultivated a stoical and self-sufficient response to suffering and to man's apparent abandonment by God. As he grew older he grew increasingly pessimistic and disillusioned even with science, bitter about public rejection of his work, and confused by public hostility to his acceptance of an imperial pension.

Despite his Parnassian goal of impersonality, his frustration and arrogance are visible in his poetry, together with nostalgia for his childhood on the island of Réunion. Nevertheless, his verse exemplifies Parnassian principles such as rigorous perfection in versification, logical coherence of content and structure, clarity and plasticity of image, admiration for classical models, and the avoidance of both sentimental intimacy and overt moralizing (though there are exceptions) through concentration on the object of perception and on the intelligent creation of Beauty as an end in itself. He is at his best as a vividly descriptive poet, rather than as a pessimistic philosopher of humanity's decline and necessary extinction.

Major works: *Poèmes antiques* 1852, *Poèmes barbares* 1862, *Poèmes tragiques* 1884, *Derniers Poèmes* (posthumous).

Les Montreurs

Tel qu'un morne animal, meurtri, plein de poussière,
La chaîne au cou, hurlant au chaud soleil d'été,
Promène qui voudra son cœur ensanglanté
Sur ton pavé cynique, ô plèbe carnassière!

Pour mettre un feu stérile en ton œil hébété,
Pour mendier ton rire ou ta pitié grossière,
Déchire qui voudra la robe de lumière
De la pudeur divine et de la volupté.

Dans mon orgueil muet, dans ma tombe sans gloire,
Dussé-je m'engloutir pour l'éternité noire,
Je ne te vendrai pas mon ivresse ou mon mal,

Je ne livrerai pas ma vie à tes huées,
Je ne danserai pas sur ton tréteau banal
Avec tes histrions et tes prostituées.

Exhibitionists

Like a wretched animal, bruised and dusty, chained at the neck, howling at the hot summer sun, let him who wishes parade his bleeding heart on your shameless streets, O carnivorous rabble!

To kindle a sterile light in your vacant eye, to beg for your laughter or your vulgar pity, let him who wishes tear the robe of light of divine modesty and the pleasure of the senses.

In my silent pride, in my grave without renown, even if compelled to live entombed for black eternity, I will not sell you my rapture or my pain,

I will not surrender my life to your jeering, I will not dance on your commonplace stage with your mountebanks and whores.

Midi

Midi, roi des étés, épandu sur la plaine,
Tombe en nappes d'argent des hauteurs du ciel bleu.
Tout se tait. L'air flamboie et brûle sans haleine;
La terre est assoupie en sa robe de feu.

L'étendue est immense, et les champs n'ont point d'ombre,
Et la source est tarie où buvaient les troupeaux;
La lointaine forêt, dont la lisière est sombre,
Dort là-bas, immobile, en un pesant repos.

Seuls, les grands blés mûris, tels qu'une mer dorée,
Se déroulent au loin, dédaigneux du sommeil;
Pacifiques enfants de la terre sacrée,
Ils épuisent sans peur la coupe du soleil.

Parfois, comme un soupir de leur âme brûlante,
Du sein des épis lourds qui murmurent entre eux,
Une ondulation majestueuse et lente
S'éveille, et va mourir à l'horizon poudreux.

Noon

Noon, king of summers, radiating over the plain, falls in silver sheets from the heights of the blue sky. All is silent. The air flames and burns breathlessly; the earth lies drowsy in its fiery robe.

The expanse is vast, and the fields have no shade, and the spring where the herds drank has run dry; the distant dark-edged forest sleeps yonder, motionless, in a heavy torpor.

Only the great ripe cornfields, like a gilded sea, unfold into the distance, disdaining sleep; peaceful children of the holy earth, they drain without fear the cup of sunlight.

Sometimes, like a sigh from their burning soul, from the heart of the heavy murmuring ears of corn, a slow majestic undulation awakes, and rolls away to die on the dusty horizon.

Non loin, quelques bœufs blancs, couchés parmi les herbes,
Bavent avec lenteur sur leurs fanons épais,
Et suivent de leurs yeux languissants et superbes
Le songe intérieur qu'ils n'achèvent jamais.

Homme, si, le cœur plein de joie ou d'amertume,
Tu passais vers midi dans les champs radieux,
Fuis! la nature est vide et le soleil consume:
Rien n'est vivant ici, rien n'est triste ou joyeux.

Mais si, désabusé des larmes et du rire,
Altéré de l'oubli de ce monde agité,
Tu veux, ne sachant plus pardonner ou maudire,
Goûter une suprême et morne volupté,

Viens! Le soleil te parle en paroles sublimes;
Dans sa flamme implacable absorbe-toi sans fin;
Et retourne à pas lents vers les cités infimes,
Le cœur trempé sept fois dans le néant divin.

Not far away a few white oxen, lying in the grass, dribble slowly on their weighty dewlaps, and follow with their proud and languid eyes the inner dream they never finish.

Man, if, with your heart full of joy or bitterness, you were moving towards noon into the radiant fields, flee! nature is empty and the sun devours: nothing is living here, nothing is sad or joyful.

But if, disillusioned with tears or with laughter, thirsting for forgetfulness of this restless world, no longer able to pardon or to curse, you wish to taste an ultimate and bleak pleasure,

Come! The sun speaks to you in sublime words: be absorbed without end in its relentless flame; and return with slow steps towards the abject cities, your heart steeped seven times in the divine void.

Le Cœur de Hialmar

Une nuit claire, un vent glacé. La neige est rouge.
    Mille braves sont là qui dorment sans tombeaux,
L'épée au poing, les yeux hagards. Pas un ne bouge.
    Au-dessus tourne et crie un vol de noirs corbeaux.

La lune froide verse au loin sa pâle flamme.
    Hialmar se soulève entre les morts sanglants,
Appuyé des deux mains au tronçon de sa lame;
    La pourpre du combat ruisselle de ses flancs.

– "Holà! Quelqu'un a-t-il encore un peu d'haleine,
    Parmi tant de joyeux et robustes garçons
Qui, ce matin, riaient et chantaient à voix pleine
    Comme des merles dans l'épaisseur des buissons!

The Heart of Hialmar

A clear night, an icy wind. The snow is red. A thousand brave men are there, sleeping without tombs, sword in hand, wild-eyed. Not one moves. A flight of black crows wheels and shrieks above.

In the distance the cold moon sheds its pallid gleam. Hialmar raises himself amongst the bleeding dead, leaning with both hands on the stump of his sword. The crimson of battle runs dripping from his sides.

'Ho there! Has anyone still a little breath among so many merry, sturdy lads who this morning laughed and sang with full voice like blackbirds in the heart of the bushes?

"Tous sont muets. Mon casque est rompu, mon armure
Est trouée, et la hache a fait sauter ses clous.
Mes yeux saignent. J'entends un immense murmure
Pareil aux hurlements de la mer ou des loups.

"Viens par ici, corbeau, mon brave mangeur d'hommes;
Ouvre-moi la poitrine avec ton bec de fer.
Tu nous retrouveras demain tels que nous sommes.
Porte mon cœur tout chaud à la fille d'Ylmer.

"Dans Upsal, où les Jarls boivent la bonne bière,
Et chantent, en heurtant les cruches d'or, en chœur,
A tire-d'aile vole, ô rôdeur de bruyère!
Cherche ma fiancée et porte-lui mon cœur.

"Au sommet de la tour que hantent les corneilles
Tu la verras debout, blanche, aux longs cheveux noirs;
Deux anneaux d'argent fin lui pendent aux oreilles,
Et ses yeux sont plus clairs que l'astre des beaux soirs.

All are dumb. My helmet is smashed, my armour pierced, and the axe has burst its nails. My eyes are bleeding. I hear a vast murmuring like the howling of the sea or the wolves.

Come this way, Crow, my fine eater of men, open up my breast with your iron beak. Tomorrow you will find us again just as we are. Carry my heart, still warm, to the daughter of Ylmer.

In Uppsala, where the Jarls drink good beer and sing in chorus, clinking golden pitchers, fly at your fastest, O heathland prowler! Seek out my betrothed and take her my heart.

At the top of the rook-haunted tower you will see her standing, white, with long black hair. Two rings of fine silver hang from her ears, and her eyes are brighter than the fair evening star.

"Va, sombre messager, dis-lui bien que je l'aime,
    Et que voici mon cœur. Elle reconnaîtra
Qu'il est rouge et solide, et non tremblant et blême,
    Et la fille d'Ylmer, corbeau, te sourira!

"Moi, je meurs. Mon esprit coule par vingt blessures.
    J'ai fait mon temps. Buvez, ô loups, mon sang vermeil.
Jeune, brave, riant, libre et sans flétrissures,
    Ja vais m'asseoir parmi les Dieux, dans le soleil."

Go, dark messenger, be sure to tell her that I love her, and that here is my heart. She will acknowledge that it is red and firm, not trembling and pale; and the daughter of Ylmer, crow, will smile on you!

As for me, I am dying. My spirit flows away through twenty wounds. I have had my time. Drink, O wolves, my rose-red blood. Young, brave, laughing, free and untarnished, I go to sit among the Gods, in the sun!'

Le Rêve du jaguar

Sous les noirs acajous, les lianes en fleur,
Dans l'air lourd, immobile et saturé de mouches,
Pendent, et, s'enroulant en bas parmi les souches,
Bercent le perroquet splendide et querelleur,
L'araignée au dos jaune et les singes farouches.
C'est là que le tueur de bœufs et de chevaux,
Le long des vieux troncs morts à l'écorce moussue,
Sinistre et fatigué, revient à pas égaux.
Il va, frottant ses reins musculeux qu'il bossue;
Et, du mufle béant par la soif alourdi,
Un souffle rauque et bref, d'une brusque secousse,
Trouble les grands lézards, chauds des feux de midi,
Dont la fuite étincelle à travers l'herbe rousse.
En un creux du bois sombre interdit au soleil
Il s'affaisse, allongé sur quelque roche plate;
D'un large coup de langue il se lustre la patte;

The Jaguar's Dream

Beneath the black mahogany trees, the flowering creepers hang in the heavy, motionless, fly-soaked air, and, coiling downwards among the tree stumps, they cradle the gorgeous bickering parrot, the yellow-backed spider and the wild and timid monkeys.[1] It is there that the killer of oxen and horses, sinister and weary, returns with measured steps along the old dead trunks with their mossy bark. He goes, rubbing and hunching his muscular loins; and from his gaping muzzle, heavy with thirst, a short rasping breath abruptly stirs and disturbs the great lizards, hot from the fires of noon, whose flight glitters through the russet grass. In a hollow of the dark wood forbidden to the sun he sinks down, stretched out on some flat rock; with a broad stroke of his tongue he polishes

[1]No single English word can do justice to 'farouche'.

Il cligne ses yeux d'or hébetés de sommeil;
Et, dans l'illusion de ses forces inertes,
Faisant mouvoir sa queue et frissonner ses flancs,
Il rêve qu'au milieu des plantations vertes,
Il enfonce d'un bond ses ongles ruisselants
Dans la chair des taureaux effarés et beuglants.

his paw; he blinks his golden, sleep-dulled eyes; and, in the illusion of his dormant power, moving his tail, with quivering flanks, he dreams that in the heart of green groves with one bound he is plunging his dripping claws into the flesh of startled, bellowing bulls.

José-Maria de Heredia
(1842–1905)

Born in Cuba of a French mother and Spanish father, Heredia was educated in France, and trained as an archaeologist. He shared Leconte de Lisle's fascination with ancient and exotic civilizations, but not the older poet's chilling pessimism about humanity. A pleasing warmth, enthusiasm, colour and even eroticism characterize the work of this otherwise most Parnassian of poets, whose 118 collected sonnets were not published until 1893, in a volume called *Les Trophées*.

Critical evaluations of Heredia vary considerably. For some he is an ingenious, rich-rhyming and eventually tedious fabricator of tableaux full of erudition and visual richness. For others he comes close to Gautier's ideal of the pure artist, the serene and dedicated Cellini depicted in 'Sur le Pont Vieux', engraving with consummate skill the combat of the Titans on the pommel of a dagger. His rating in this anthology is unashamedly strong, for Heredia is a rarity, a positively enjoyable Parnassian poet in whose apparently static, luminous pictures beats a pulse of real drama.

Soir de bataille

Le choc avait été très rude. Les tribuns
Et les centurions, ralliant les cohortes,
Humaient encor dans l'air où vibraient leurs voix fortes
La chaleur du carnage et ses âcres parfums.

D'un œil morne, comptant leurs compagnons défunts,
Les soldats regardaient, comme des feuilles mortes,
Au loin, tourbillonner les archers de Phraortes;
Et la sueur coulait de leurs visages bruns.

C'est alors qu'apparut, tout hérissé de flèches,
Rouge du flux vermeil de ses blessures fraîches,
Sous la pourpre flottante et l'airain rutilant,

Au fracas des buccins qui sonnaient leur fanfare,
Superbe, maîtrisant son cheval qui s'effare,
Sur le ciel enflammé, l'Imperator sanglant.

Evening after Battle

The conflict had been very harsh. The tribunes and centurions, rallying the cohorts, in the air resonant with their strong voices still breathed in the heat of the slaughter and its acrid scents.

With dulled eyes, counting their dead comrades, the soldiers watched the bowmen of Phraates[1] swirling in the distance like dead leaves; and the sweat poured down their brown faces.

At that moment appeared, all bristling with arrows, red with the vermilion flow of his newly gathered wounds, beneath the undulating purple and the fiery reddened bronze,

In the din of fanfare-sounding trumpets, magnificent, master of his frightened horse, against the blazing sky, the bloodstained Imperator.

[1]Phraates IV of Parthia. His opponent, the 'Imperator', is Anthony.

Ariane

Au choc clair et vibrant des cymbales d'airain,
Nue, allongée au dos d'un grand tigre, la Reine
Regarde, avec l'Orgie immense qu'il entraîne,
Iacchos s'avancer sur le sable marin.

Et le monstre royal, ployant son large rein,
Sous le poids adoré foule la blonde arène,
Et, frôlé par la main d'où pend l'errante rêne,
En rugissant d'amour mord les fleurs de son frein.

Laissant sa chevelure à son flanc qui se cambre
Parmi les noirs raisins rouler ses grappes d'ambre,
L'Épouse n'entend pas le sourd rugissement;

Et sa bouche éperdue, ivre enfin d'ambroisie,
Oubliant ses longs cris vers l'infidèle amant,
Rit au baiser prochain du Dompteur de l'Asie.

Ariadne

As shining, vibrant, brazen cymbals clash, naked, stretched on the back of a great tiger, the Queen watches as Bacchus, bringing vast Orgy in his wake, advances along the seashore.

And the kingly monster, flexing its broad loins, beneath that beloved burden paws at the sandy arena, and, brushed by the hand that trails the rein at random, roars with love as it bites the flowers of its bit.

Letting her hair cascade down the arching flank, amber clusters amid the black grapes, the Bride does not hear the muted bellow;

And her ecstatic mouth, drunk at last with ambrosia, forgetting its prolonged cries to the faithless lover,[1] welcomes, laughing, the imminent kiss of the Conqueror of Asia.

[1]Theseus, who abandoned Ariadne on the island of Naxos.

Sur le Pont-Vieux

Antonio di Sandro orefice

Le vaillant Maître Orfèvre, à l'œuvre dès matines,
Faisait, de ses pinceaux d'où s'égouttait l'émail,
Sur la paix niellée ou sur l'or du fermail
Epanouir la fleur des devises latines.

Sur le Pont, au son clair des cloches argentines,
La cape coudoyait le froc et le camail;
Et le soleil montant en un ciel de vitrail
Mettait un nimbe au front des belles Florentines.

On the Ponte Vecchio

Antonio di Sandro orefice

The stout-hearted Master Goldsmith, at his work since Matins, with his brushes dripping with enamel, brought forth on the inlaid niello paten or on the golden clasp the flower of Latin inscriptions.

On the bridge, to the limpid sound of the silver-toned bells, cloak rubbed shoulders with cowl and capuchin; and the sun rising in a stained-glass sky cast a halo on the brow of the fair Florentine women.

Et prompts au rêve ardent qui les savait charmer,
Les apprentis, pensifs, oubliaient de fermer
Les mains des fiancés au chaton de la bague;

Tandis que d'un burin trempé comme un stylet,
Le jeune Cellini, sans rien voir, ciselait
Le combat des Titans au pommeau d'une dague.

And, responsive to the passionate dream that bewitched them so well, the apprentices, lost in thought, forgot to join the hands of betrothal on the stone of the ring;

While with an engraving needle tempered like a stiletto, the young Cellini, seeing nothing, was carving the struggle of the Titans on the pommel of a dagger.

Les Conquérants

Comme un vol de gerfauts hors du charnier natal,
Fatigués de porter leurs misères hautaines,
De Palos de Moguer, routiers et capitaines
Partaient, ivres d'un rêve héroïque et brutal.

Ils allaient conquérir le fabuleux métal
Que Cipango mûrit dans ses mines lointaines,
Et les vents alizés inclinaient leurs antennes
Aux bords mystérieux du monde Occidental.

Chaque soir, espérant des lendemains épiques,
L'azur phosphorescent de la mer des Tropiques
Enchantait leur sommeil d'un mirage doré;

The Conquistadores

Like a flight of gerfalcons from the eyrie of their birth, weary of bearing their haughty destitution, from Palos de Moguer soldiers of fortune and captains set out, drunk with a heroic, brutal dream.

They were going to conquer the fabulous metal matured by Cipangu[1] in its distant mines, and the trade winds tilted their yards towards the mysterious shores of the Western world.

Each evening, in hope of epic morrows, the phosphorescent blue of the Tropical sea bewitched their sleep with a gilded mirage;

[1] Marco Polo's name for Japan.

Ou penchés à l'avant des blanches caravelles,
Ils regardaient monter en un ciel ignoré
Du fond de l'Océan des étoiles nouvelles.

Or leaning over the bow of white caravels, they watched as in an unknown sky from the depths of the Ocean there rose new stars.

La Sieste

Pas un seul bruit d'insecte ou d'abeille en maraude.
Tout dort sous les grands bois accablés de soleil
Où le feuillage épais tamise un jour pareil
Au velours sombre et doux des mousses d'émeraude.

Criblant le dôme obscur, Midi splendide y rôde
Et, sur mes cils mi-clos alanguis de sommeil,
De mille éclairs furtifs forme un réseau vermeil
Qui s'allonge et se croise à travers l'ombre chaude.

The Siesta

Not a single sound of insect or plundering bee. Under the overpowering sun all sleeps in the forest where the dense foliage filters a light with the texture of[1] the dark soft velvet of the emerald mosses.

Sifting through the dark dome, resplendent Noon prowls up there and, above my half-closed sleep-languid lashes, with a thousand furtive flashes forms a rose-red web stretching and interlacing across the warm shade.

[1]Though I believe my translation here captures Heredia's idea, it is just possible that 'pareil' could be an adjective suggesting a steady, consistent light.

Vers la gaze de feu que trament les rayons,
Vole le frêle essaim des riches papillons
Qu'enivrent la lumière et le parfum des sèves;

Alors mes doigts tremblants saisissent chaque fil,
Et dans les mailles d'or de ce filet subtil,
Chasseur harmonieux, j'emprisonne mes rêves.

Towards the fiery gauze woven by the rays flies the delicate swarm of rich butterflies intoxicated by light and the scent of sap;

Then my trembling fingers grasp each thread, and in the golden mesh of this tenuous net, a harmonious hunter, I imprison my dreams.

Soleil couchant

Les ajoncs éclatants, parure du granit,
Dorent l'âpre sommet que le couchant allume;
Au loin, brillante encor par sa barre d'écume,
La mer sans fin commence où la terre finit.

Sunset

The vivid gorse, the adornment of granite, gilds the harsh hilltop fired by the sunset; in the distance, still shining through its band of foaming surf, the endless sea begins where the land comes to an end.

A mes pieds, c'est la nuit, le silence. Le nid
Se tait, l'homme est rentré sous le chaume qui fume;
Seul, l'Angélus du soir, ébranlé dans la brume,
A la vaste rumeur de l'Océan s'unit.

Alors, comme du fond d'un abîme, des traînes,
Des landes, des ravins, montent des voix lointaines
De pâtres attardés ramenant le bétail.

L'horizon tout entier s'enveloppe dans l'ombre,
Et le soleil mourant, sur un ciel riche et sombre,
Ferme les branches d'or de son rouge éventail.

At my feet there is darkness, silence. The nest falls silent, man has gone back beneath his smoking thatch; only the evening Angelus, ringing in the mist, is joined with the vast murmur of the Ocean.

Then, as if from deep in a chasm, from the sunken roads, from the moors, from the gullies, rise distant voices of lingering herdsmen bringing in the cattle.

The whole horizon is wrapped in shadow, and the dying sun, against a rich dark sky, closes the golden branches of its red fan.

Stéphane Mallarmé
(1842–98)

Rejecting suggestions that he should follow family tradition by entering government service after his education, Mallarmé taught English in several provincial towns before returning to his native Paris in 1871. A remarkable degree of stability characterized his life, despite chronic financial difficulties, and his marriage to Marie Gerhard survived his affair with Méry Laurent. He suffered two painful bereavements, losing a sister in his youth and his eight-year-old son in 1879. The poet's bedside notes on the latter experience reveal an extraordinary capacity for analytical thought within or alongside emotional anguish.

In 1866–7 he had undergone a profound existential, metaphysical and artistic crisis. He 'overthrew God', only to be faced with a vertiginous awareness, both enthralling and terrifying, of a void into which all reality seemed inexorably to be sucked. He accepted this 'abolition' of the world, envisaging a resurrection of his intellect through the conscious creation of a supreme and indestructible fiction, radiant with light, and truly poetic. 'Poetry is the expression, through human language restored to its essential rhythm, of the mysterious meaning of existence: it thus grants authenticity to our time on earth and constitutes the unique spiritual task.' It may be unattainable except literally in death, but the struggle to produce this creative rebirth, this presence within absence, is at the centre of Mallarmé's artistic life. It is dramatized in a number of poems, notably 'Le vierge, le vivace et le bel aujourd'hui', 'Ses purs ongles très haut dédiant leur onyx' and 'L'Après-midi d'un Faune'. Understandably, unfinished works are another Mallarméan characteristic, the most significant being the verse tragedy *Hérodiade* and the prose poem *Igitur*, and he never progressed beyond notes for 'The Book', a monumental projected work which was to be the sum of all books, a universal statement: 'The world exists to end up in a book'.

Though his cryptic musicality can appeal to the uninitiated, the serious reader of Mallarmé needs to arm himself with exegeses. Malcolm Bowie's title, 'Mallarmé and the Art of being difficult', is humorously appropriate, but also pays homage to one of the French language's most refined exponents, a perfectionist whose exemplary commitment to an uncompromising aesthetic ideal is breathtaking. Mallarmé is not difficult for the sake of being difficult. His hermeticism has a purpose.

Poetry alone, for Mallarmé, has reality, permanence and value. The surface of life is a contingent, uninteresting flux. The artist is in contact with a superior world of analogies, affinities or '*correspondances*' (to use the Baudelairean term) forming an ineffable harmony. He is, paradoxically, obliged to use words in seeking its expression. Now the creations of Poetry are to be holy, necessarily veiled in secrecy, necessarily elliptical and ambiguous, to prevent Beauty from contamination by vulgar thought and its medium, commonplace language: 'All that is sacred and wishes to remain sacred wraps itself in mystery'. Mallarmé's own highly selective language is therefore syntactically convoluted, inward-turned, self-protecting in order to 'give a purer meaning to the words of the tribe'. He seeks an immaculate expression of an idea or perception in the most compressed, concrete terms imaginable, often suppressing conjunctions, articles and prepositions, and re-inventing grammatical relationships. Yet all this takes place within lines of verse that are for the most part firmly Alexandrine or octosyllabic in structure.

This is an entirely unspontaneous poetry, detached by patient artistry from the reality which may have been its initial stimulus: 'Do not paint the thing, but the effect which it produces'. In his terms, the poem is the completed dice-throw that is beyond the reach of Chance, even if it does not in itself abolish Chance. Once initiated, the reader will find that he can share in this creative process as fully as he can with Baudelaire or Verlaine, and discover an intensity of emotion within the perfectionism of style.

An uncompromising cult figure, surrounded by disciples

at his regular Tuesday gatherings, and a true verbal alchemist, Mallarmé inaugurates *Symbolism* in French verse. His refined language is entirely distinct from prose, and its music has stronger resonances than the essentially atmospheric tone-poems of Verlaine, effectively the co-founder of that movement. It is beyond doubt that those resonances are still being felt in French poetry today, much of which is still haunted by the problem of presence within absence, of expressing the inexpressible.

Major works: *L'Après-Midi d'un Faune* 1876, *Les Poésies* 1887, *Poèmes en prose* 1891, *Divagations* 1897, *Un coup de dés jamais n'abolira le hasard* 1897.

Les Fenêtres

Las du triste hôpital, et de l'encens fétide
Qui monte en la blancheur banale des rideaux
Vers le grand crucifix ennuyé du mur vide,
Le moribond sournois y redresse un vieux dos,

The Windows

Weary of the sad infirmary, and of the foetid incense that rises within the banal whiteness of the curtains towards the great bored crucifix on the empty wall, the dying man artfully straightens an old back,

Se traîne et va, moins pour chauffer sa pourriture
Que pour voir du soleil sur les pierres, coller
Les poils blancs et les os de la maigre figure
Aux fenêtres qu'un beau rayon clair veut hâler.

Et la bouche, fiévreuse et d'azur bleu vorace,
Telle, jeune, elle alla respirer son trésor,
Une peau virginale et de jadis! encrasse
D'un long baiser amer les tièdes carreaux d'or.

Ivre, il vit, oubliant l'horreur des saintes huiles,
Les tisanes, l'horloge et le lit infligé,
La toux; et quand le soir saigne parmi les tuiles,
Son œil, à l'horizon de lumière gorgé,

Voit des galères d'or, belles comme des cygnes,
Sur un fleuve de pourpre et de parfums dormir
En berçant l'éclair fauve et riche de leurs lignes
Dans un grand nonchaloir chargé de souvenir!

Drags himself and goes, less to warm his decaying flesh than to see sunlight on the stones, to press the white stubble and the bones of the scrawny face against the windows that a beautiful limpid sunbeam wants to burnish.

And the mouth, feverish and craving the blue azure, just as in childhood it sought and breathed in its treasure, a virginal skin of time past! fouls with a long bitter kiss the warm golden panes.

Intoxicated, he is alive, forgetting the horror of the holy oils, the infusions, the clock and the confinement to bed, the cough; and when evening bleeds among the tiles, his eye, on the horizon gorged with light,

Sees golden galleys, beautiful as swans, sleeping on a river of purple and perfumes cradling the rich and tawny brilliance of their form in a great warm indolence heavy with memory!

Ainsi, pris du dégoût de l'homme à l'âme dure
Vautré dans le bonheur, où ses seuls appétits
Mangent, et qui s'entête à chercher cette ordure
Pour l'offrir à la femme allaitant ses petits,

Je fuis et je m'accroche à toutes les croisées
D'où l'on tourne l'épaule à la vie, et, béni,
Dans leur verre, lavé d'éternelles rosées,
Que dore le matin chaste de l'Infini

Je me mire et me vois ange! et je meurs, et j'aime
– Que la vitre soit l'art, soit la mysticité –
A renaître, portant mon rêve en diadème,
Au ciel antérieur où fleurit la Beauté!

Mais, hélas! Ici-bas est maître: sa hantise
Vient m'écœurer parfois jusqu'en cet abri sûr,
Et le vomissement impur de la Bêtise
Me force à me boucher le nez devant l'azur.

Thus, seized with loathing for man with his hardened soul wallowing in contentment where his appetites alone eat, and who persistently seeks that filth to offer it to the woman giving milk to her children,

I escape and cling to all the windows from which one turns one's shoulder on life, and, blessed, in their glass, cleansed by eternal dews, gilded by the chaste morning of the Infinite

I see myself mirrored and see myself angel! and I am dying, and I love – let the glass pane be art, and be mysticism – to be reborn, bearing my dream as a diadem, in that antecedent heaven where Beauty flourishes!

But alas! the here-below is master: its haunting presence comes to nauseate me sometimes even in this safe refuge, and the tainted vomit of Stupidity makes me hold my nose in the face of the azure.

Est-il moyen, ô Moi qui connais l'amertume,
D'enfoncer le cristal par le monstre insulté
Et de m'enfuir, avec mes deux ailes sans plume
– Au risque de tomber pendant l'éternité?

Is there a way, O Self familiar with bitterness, of breaking through the crystal insulted by the monstrous and escaping with my two featherless wings – at the risk of falling for all eternity?

Brise marine

La chair est triste, hélas! et j'ai lu tous les livres.
Fuir! là-bas fuir! Je sens que des oiseaux sont ivres
D'être parmi l'écume inconnue et les cieux!
Rien, ni les vieux jardins reflétés par les yeux
Ne retiendra ce cœur qui dans la mer se trempe
O nuits! ni la clarté déserte de ma lampe
Sur le vide papier que la blancheur défend
Et ni la jeune femme allaitant son enfant.
Je partirai! Steamer balançant ta mâture,
Lève l'ancre pour une exotique nature!

Sea Wind

The flesh is sad, alas! and I've read all the books. To escape! escape out there! I sense that birds are drunk to be amidst the unknown foam and the skies! Nothing, not old gardens reflected in eyes will hold back this heart which immerses itself in the sea O nights! nor the desolate brightness of my lamp on the empty paper defended by its whiteness nor even the young wife with her child at the breast. I will leave! Steamer swaying your masts, hoist anchor for exotic climes!

Un Ennui, désolé par les cruels espoirs,
Croit encore à l'adieu suprême des mouchoirs!
Et, peut-être, les mâts, invitant les orages
Sont-ils de ceux qu'un vent penche sur les naufrages
Perdus, sans mâts, sans mâts, ni fertiles îlots ...
Mais, ô mon cœur, entends le chant des matelots!

A Tedium, ravaged by cruel hopes, still believes in the supreme farewell of handkerchiefs! And, perhaps, the masts, inviting storms, are of the kind that a wind tilts over shipwrecks lost without masts, without masts or fertile isles ... But, O my heart, hear the sailors' song!

L'Après-midi d'un faune

Églogue

LE FAUNE

Ces nymphes, je les veux perpétuer.

Si clair,

Leur incarnat léger, qu'il voltige dans l'air
Assoupi de sommeils touffus.

The Afternoon of a Faun

Eclogue

THE FAUN

I want to perpetuate these nymphs.

So bright, their light incarnadine, that it flutters in the air drowsy with tufted slumbers.

Aimai-je un rêve?
Mon doute, amas de nuit ancienne, s'achève
En maint rameau subtil, qui, demeuré les vrais
Bois mêmes, prouve, hélas! que bien seul je m'offrais
Pour triomphe la faute idéale de roses.
Réfléchissons ...

Did I love a dream? My doubt, accumulation of old darkness, ends in many a tenuous bough which, remaining the true woods themselves, proves, alas! that I offered myself alone for triumph the ideal sin of roses. Let us reflect ...

ou si les femmes dont tu gloses
Figurent un souhait de tes sens fabuleux!
Faune, l'illusion s'échappe des yeux bleus
Et froids, comme une source en pleurs, de la plus chaste
Mais, l'autre tout soupirs, dis-tu qu'elle contraste
Comme brise du jour chaude dans ta toison?
Que non! par l'immobile et lasse pâmoison
Suffoquant de chaleurs le matin frais s'il lutte,
Ne murmure point d'eau que ne verse ma flûte
Au bosquet arrosé d'accords; et le seul vent
Hors des deux tuyaux prompt à s'exhaler avant
Qu'il disperse le son dans une pluie aride,
C'est, à l'horizon pas remué d'une ride,
Le visible et serein souffle artificiel
De l'inspiration, qui regagne le ciel.

Or suppose the women that you expound represent a desire of your fable-rich senses! Faun, illusion escapes like a weeping spring from the blue and cold eyes of the most chaste: but the other, all sighs, do you say she contrasts like a day breeze warm in your fleece! No! through the motionless and torpid swoon suffocating the cool morning with heat if it struggles, there murmurs no water but that poured by my flute on the grove sprinkled with chords; and the only wind quick to exhale itself from the two pipes before it disperses the sound in an arid rain, is, on the horizon unstirred by any wrinkle, the visible, serene and artificial breath of inspiration, returning to the sky.

O bords siciliens d'un calme marécage
Qu'à l'envi de soleils ma vanité saccage,
Tacite sous les fleurs d'étincelles, CONTEZ
"*Que je coupais ici les creux roseaux domptés*
Par le talent; quand, sur l'or glauque de lointaines
Verdures dédiant leur vigne à des fontaines,
Ondoie une blancheur animale au repos:
Et qu'au prélude lent où naissant les pipeaux
Ce vol de cygnes, non! de naïades se sauve
Ou plonge ..."

Inerte, tout brûle dans l'heure fauve
Sans marquer par quel art ensemble détala
Trop d'hymen souhaité de qui cherche le *la:*
Alors m'éveillerai-je à la ferveur première,
Droit et seul, sous un flot antique de lumière,
Lys! et l'un de vous tous pour l'ingénuité.

O Sicilian shores of a calm marsh that my vanity plunders, rivalling suns, tacit beneath the flowers of the sparks, TELL '*That I was cutting here the hollow reeds tamed by talent; when, on the glaucous gold of distant verdures inscribing their vine on springs, an animal whiteness undulates to rest: and that at the slow prelude in which the pipes are born this flight of swans, no! of naiads flees or dives ...*'

Inert, all burns in the tawny hour without showing by what art ran off together an excess of hymen desired by him who seeks the *A*-note: then I shall awaken to the primary fervour, erect and alone, under an ancient flood of light, lilies! and one of you all in ingenuousness.

Autre que ce doux rien par leur lèvre ébruité,
Le baiser, qui tout bas des perfides assure,
Mon sein, vierge de preuve, atteste une morsure
Mystérieuse, due à quelque auguste dent;
Mais, bast! arcane tel élut pour confident
Le jonc vaste et jumeau dont sous l'azur on joue:
Qui, détournant à soi le trouble de la joue,
Rêve, dans un solo long, que nous amusions
La beauté d'alentour par des confusions
Fausses entre elle-même et notre chant crédule;
Et de faire aussi haut que l'amour se module
Évanouir du songe ordinaire de dos
Ou de flanc pur suivis avec mes regards clos,
Une sonore, vaine et monotone ligne.

Other than this sweet nothing rumoured by their lip, the kiss, which quietly gives assurance of the treacherous, my breast, virgin of proof, bears witness to a mysterious bite, due to some august tooth; but enough of that! such a mystery chose for confidant the immense twin reed on which we play beneath the azure: which, turning to itself the cheek's emotion, dreams in a long solo that we were entertaining the beauty around us by false confusions between itself and our credulous song; and, as high as love can be modulated, of making vanish, from the ordinary dream of back or pure flank followed through my closed eyes, a resonant, vain and monotonous line.

Tâche donc, instrument des fuites, ô maligne
Syrinx, de refleurir aux lacs où tu m'attends!
Moi, de ma rumeur fier, je vais parler longtemps
Des déesses; et par d'idolâtres peintures,
A leur ombre enlever encore des ceintures:
Ainsi, quand des raisins j'ai sucé la clarté,
Pour bannir un regret par ma feinte écarté,
Rieur, j'élève au ciel d'été la grappe vide
Et, soufflant dans ses peaux lumineuses, avide
D'ivresse, jusqu'au soir je regarde au travers.

Try then, instrument of escapes, O wicked Syrinx, to flower once more on the lakes where you await me. I, proud of my murmur, shall speak at length of the goddesses; and by idolatrous paintings from their shadow lift still more girdles: thus, when I have sucked the grapes' brightness to banish a regret moved aside by my pretence, laughing, I raise the empty cluster to the summer sky and, blowing in its luminous skins, greedy for drunkenness, until evening I gaze through it.

O nymphes, regonflons des SOUVENIRS divers.
"Mon œil, trouant les joncs, dardait chaque encolure
Immortelle, qui noie en l'onde sa brûlure
Avec un cri de rage au ciel de la forêt;
Et le splendide bain de cheveux disparaît
Dans les clartés et les frissons, ô pierreries!
J'accours; quand, à mes pieds, s'entrejoignent (meurtries
De la langueur goûtée à ce mal d'être deux)
Des dormeuses parmi leurs seuls bras hasardeux;
Je les ravis, sans les désenlacer, et vole
A ce massif, haï par l'ombrage frivole,
De roses tarissant tout parfum au soleil,
Où notre ébat au jour consumé soit pareil."
Je t'adore, courroux des vierges, ô délice
Farouche du sacré fardeau nu qui se glisse
Pour fuir ma lèvre en feu buvant, comme un éclair
Tressaille! la frayeur secrète de la chair:
Des pieds de l'inhumaine au cœur de la timide
Que délaisse à la fois une innocence, humide
De larmes folles ou de moins tristes vapeurs.
"Mon crime, c'est d'avoir, gai de vaincre ces peurs

O nymphs, let us inflate once more some diverse MEMORIES. '*My eye, piercing the reeds, darted on each immortal neck, that drowns its burning in the waters with a cry of rage to the forest sky; and the splendid bath of hair disappears in the pools of light and in the quiverings, O precious stones! I come running; when, at my feet, are clasped together (bruised by the languor tasted in this evil of being two) sleeping women amid their mere, daring arms; I carry them off, without disentangling them, and fly to this thicket, shunned by the frivolous shade, of roses drying up every perfume in the sunlight, where may our sport be like the consumed day.*' I adore you, wrath of virgins, O wild and timorous delight of the holy naked burden which slides away to escape my burning lip drinking, as lightning quivers! the secret terror of the flesh: from the feet of the heartless one to the heart of the timid one, abandoned at the same time by an innocence wet with wild tears or less sad vapours. '*My crime is to have divided, happy at the conquest of these*

Traîtresses, divisé la touffe échevelée
De baisers que les dieux gardaient si bien mêlée:
Car, à peine j'allais cacher un rire ardent
Sous les replis heureux d'une seule (gardant
Par un doigt simple, afin que sa candeur de plume
Se teignît à l'émoi de sa sœur qui s'allume,
La petite, naïve et ne rougissant pas:)
Que de mes bras, défaits par de vagues trépas,
Cette proie, à jamais ingrate se délivre
Sans pitié du sanglot dont j'étais encore ivre."

Tant pis! vers le bonheur d'autres m'entraîneront
Par leur tresse nouée aux cornes de mon front:

treacherous fears, the dishevelled tuft of kisses that the gods kept so well mingled: for scarcely was I going to hide a passionate laugh under the blissful coils of one alone (holding by a mere finger, so that her feather-like innocence might be tinted by her sister's emotion taking fire, the little one, naive, not blushing:) when from my arms, loosened by vague deaths, that ever ungrateful prey frees herself with no pity for the sob with which I was still drunk.'

No matter! towards happiness others will pull me by their tresses knotted to the horns on my brow: you know, my

Tu sais, ma passion, que, pourpre et déjà mûre,
Chaque grenade éclate et d'abeilles murmure;
Et notre sang, épris de qui le va saisir,
Coule pour tout l'essaim éternel du désir.
A l'heure où ce bois d'or et de cendres se teinte
Une fête s'exalte en la feuillée éteinte:
Etna! c'est parmi toi visité de Vénus
Sur ta lave posant ses talons ingénus,
Quand tonne un somme triste ou s'épuise la flamme.
Je tiens la reine!

O sûr châtiment ...

Non, mais l'âme
De paroles vacante et ce corps alourdi
Tard succombent au fier silence de midi:
Sans plus il faut dormir en l'oubli du blasphème,
Sur le sable altéré gisant et comme j'aime
Ouvrir ma bouche à l'astre efficace des vins!

Couple, adieu; je vais voir l'ombre que tu devins.

passion, that, purple and ripe already, every pomegranate bursts and murmurs with bees; and our blood, in love with whoever will seize it, flows for all the eternal swarm of desire. At the hour when this wood is tinted with gold and ashes, a festival flares up in the darkened foliage: Etna! it is upon you visited by Venus placing her ingenuous heels upon your lava, when a sad slumber thunders or the flame exhausts itself. I hold the queen!

O certain punishment ...

No, but the soul empty of words and this weighted body succumb late to the proud silence of noon: with no more ado we must sleep in forgetfulness of blasphemy, lying on the thirsty sand and how I love to open my mouth to the wine-making star!

Couple, farewell: I'm going to see the shadow you became.

Sainte

A la fenêtre recelant
Le santal vieux qui se dédore
De sa viole étincelant
Jadis avec flûte ou mandore,

Est la Sainte pâle, étalant
Le livre vieux qui se déplie
Du Magnificat ruisselant
Jadis selon vêpre et complie:

A ce vitrage d'ostensoir
Que frôle une harpe par l'Ange
Formée avec son vol du soir
Pour la délicate phalange

Du doigt que, sans le vieux santal
Ni le vieux livre, elle balance
Sur le plumage instrumental,
Musicienne du silence.

Saint

In the window concealing the old sandalwood that is losing its gilt of her viol once sparkling with flute or mandola,

Is the pale saint; she displays the old unfolding book of the Magnificat flowing in ages past according to vespers and compline:

Within this monstrance glass brushed by a harp formed by the Angel with his evening flight for the delicate tip

Of the finger which, without the old sandalwood or the old book, she holds poised on the instrumental plumage, musician of silence.

Petit Air I

Quelconque une solitude
Sans le cygne ni le quai
Mire sa désuétude
Au regard que j'abdiquai

Ici de la gloriole
Haute à ne la pas toucher
Dont maint ciel se bariole
Avec les ors de coucher

Mais langoureusement longe
Comme de blanc linge ôté
Tel fugace oiseau si plonge
Exultatrice à côté

Dans l'onde toi devenue
Ta jubilation nue.

Little Melody I

Some commonplace solitude without swan or quay reflects its desuetude in the gaze which I withdrew

Down here from the vainglory too high to touch in which many a sky paints itself gaudy with the golds of sunset

But languorously moves along like white linen discarded some fleeting bird if exultant alongside your naked jubilation

Plunges into the waters become you.

Quand l'ombre menaça …

Quand l'ombre menaça de la fatale loi
Tel vieux Rêve, désir et mal de mes vertèbres,
Affligé de périr sous les plafonds funèbres
Il a ployé son aile indubitable en moi.

Luxe, ô salle d'ébène où, pour séduire un roi
Se tordent dans leur mort des guirlandes célèbres,
Vous n'êtes qu'un orgueil menti par les ténèbres
Aux yeux du solitaire ébloui de sa foi.

Oui, je sais qu'au lointain de cette nuit, la Terre
Jette d'un grand éclat l'insolite mystère,
Sous les siècles hideux qui l'obscurcissent moins.

L'espace à soi pareil qu'il s'accroisse ou se nie
Roule dans cet ennui des feux vils pour témoins
Que s'est d'un astre en fête allumé le génie.

When the Shadow threatened …

When the shadow threatened with the fatal law a certain old Dream, desire and suffering of my vertebrae, grieved at dying beneath the funereal ceilings it folded its unquestionable wing within me.

Funeral splendour, O ebony hall where, to seduce a king renowned garlands writhe in their death, you are only a pride denied by the shadows in the eyes of the hermit dazzled by his faith.

Yes, I know that far off in this night, the Earth radiates the singular mystery of a great burst of light, beneath the hideous centuries that obscure it less.

Space like unto itself whether it grows or denies itself revolves in this tedium vile fires for witnesses that the genius of a festive star has been ignited.

Le vierge, le vivace et le bel aujourd'hui ...

Le vierge, le vivace et le bel aujourd'hui
Va-t-il nous déchirer avec un coup d'aile ivre
Ce lac dur oublié que hante sous le givre
Le transparent glacier des vols qui n'ont pas fui!

Un cygne d'autrefois se souvient que c'est lui
Magnifique mais qui sans espoir se délivre
Pour n'avoir pas chanté la région où vivre
Quand du stérile hiver a resplendi l'ennui.

Tout son col secouera cette blanche agonie
Par l'espace infligé à l'oiseau qui le nie,
Mais non l'horreur du sol où le plumage est pris.

Fantôme qu'à ce lieu son pur éclat assigne,
Il s'immobilise au songe froid de mépris
Que vêt parmi l'exil inutile le Cygne.

The Virgin, the vigorous and the beauteous today ...

The virgin, the vigorous and the beauteous today, will it cleave for us with an intoxicated wing-beat this hard forgotten lake haunted beneath the frost by the transparent glacier of flights that have not taken flight!

A swan of time past remembers that it is he, magnificent but who without hope frees himself for not having sung of the region where life is when sterile winter's tedium shone.

His whole neck will shake off this white agony inflicted by space on the bird which denies it, but not the horror of the ground where the plumage is caught.

A phantom appointed to this place by his pure brilliance, he becomes motionless in the cold dream of contempt worn in purposeless exile by the Swan.

Autre éventail

de Mademoiselle Mallarmé

O rêveuse, pour que je plonge
Au pur délice sans chemin,
Sache, par un subtil mensonge,
Garder mon aile dans ta main.

Une fraîcheur de crépuscule
Te vient à chaque battement
Dont le coup prisonnier recule
L'horizon délicatement.

Vertige! voici que frissonne
L'espace comme un grand baiser
Qui, fou de naître pour personne,
Ne peut jaillir ni s'apaiser.

Another Fan

of Mademoiselle Mallarmé

O dreaming girl, that I may plunge into pure pathless delight, be skilful in keeping, through a subtle lie, my wing in your hand.

A twilight freshness comes to you at every beat whose imprisoned movement wafts back the horizon delicately.

Vertigo! and now space shivers like a great kiss which, frantic at being born for no one, can neither surge up nor subside.

Sens-tu le paradis farouche
Ainsi qu'un rire enseveli
Se couler du coin de ta bouche
Au fond de l'unanime pli!

Le sceptre des rivages roses
Stagnants sur les soirs d'or, ce l'est,
Ce blanc vol fermé que tu poses
Contre le feu d'un bracelet.

Do you sense the innocently wild paradise like a buried laugh gliding from the corner of your mouth deep into the unanimous fold!

The sceptre of pink lagoon shores over golden evenings, this it is, this closed white flight which you place against a bracelet's fire.

Le Tombeau d'Edgar Poe

Tel qu'en Lui-même enfin l'éternité le change,
Le Poëte suscite avec un glaive nu
Son siècle épouvanté de n'avoir pas connu
Que la mort triomphait dans cette voix étrange!

Eux, comme un vil sursaut d'hydre oyant jadis l'ange
Donner un sens plus pur aux mots de la tribu
Proclamèrent très haut le sortilège bu
Dans le flot sans honneur de quelque noir mélange.

Du sol et de la nue hostiles, ô grief!
Si notre idée avec ne sculpte un bas-relief
Dont la tombe de Poe éblouissante s'orne,

Calme bloc ici-bas chu d'un désastre obscur,
Que ce granit du moins montre à jamais sa borne
Aux noirs vols du Blasphème épars dans le futur.

The Tomb of Edgar Poe

Such as into Himself at last eternity changes him, the Poet arouses with a naked sword his century terrified at not having recognized that death triumphed in that strange voice!

They, like the vile convulsion of a hydra hearing in olden days the angel give a purer sense to the words of the tribe, proclaimed aloud the spell drunk in the flow without honour of some black mixture.

Out of the hostile soil and cloud, O grievance! if with them our idea carve no bas-relief to adorn the dazzling tomb of Poe,

Calm block fallen here below from a mysterious disaster, may this granite at least present for ever its frontier to the black flights of Blasphemy scattered in the future.

Ses purs ongles très haut dédiant leur onyx

Ses purs ongles très haut dédiant leur onyx,
L'Angoisse, ce minuit, soutient, lampadophore,
Maint rêve vespéral brûlé par le Phénix
Que ne recueille pas de cinéraire amphore.

Sur les crédences, au salon vide: nul ptyx,
Aboli bibelot d'inanité sonore,
(Car le Maître est allé puiser des pleurs au Styx
Avec ce seul objet dont le Néant s'honore).

Mais proche la croisée au nord vacante, un or
Agonise selon peut-être le décor
Des licornes ruant du feu contre une nixe,

Elle, défunte nue en le miroir, encor
Que, dans l'oubli fermé par le cadre, se fixe
De scintillations sitôt le septuor.

Her pure nails …

Her pure nails raised high dedicating their onyx, Anguish, this midnight, sustains, torch-bearing, many an evening dream burned by the Phoenix that no cinerary amphora gathers.

On the sideboards, in the empty parlour: no ptyx, abolished trinket of sonorous vacuity (for the Master has gone to draw tears from the Styx with this sole object with which the Void honours itself).

But near the empty north window, a golden light is dying in accordance perhaps with the scene of unicorns lashing fire against a water nymph,

She, dead and naked in the mirror, and yet in the oblivion enclosed by the frame, is fixed instantaneously the septet of scintillations.

Le Démon de l'analogie

Des paroles inconnues chantèrent-elles sur vos lèvres, lambeaux maudits d'une phrase absurde?

Je sortis de mon appartement avec la sensation propre d'une aile glissant sur les cordes d'un instrument, traînante et légère, que remplaça une voix prononçant les mots sur un ton descendant: "La Pénultième est morte", de façon que

La Pénultième

finit le vers et

Est morte

se détacha de la suspension fatidique plus inutilement en le vide de signification. Je fis des pas dans la rue et reconnus en le son *nul* la corde tendue de l'instrument de musique, qui était oublié et que le glorieux Souvenir certainement venait de visiter de son aile ou d'une palme et, le doigt sur l'artifice du mystère, je souris et implorai de vœux intellectuels une spéculation différente. La phrase revint, virtuelle, dégagée

The Demon of Analogy

Did unknown words sing upon your lips, accursed shreds of an absurd sentence?

I left my apartment with the clear sensation of a wing gliding over the strings of an instrument, lingering and light, replaced by a voice uttering with a falling intonation the words: 'The Penultimate is dead', in such a way that *The Penultimate* ended the line and *Is dead* stood out from the fateful suspension more uselessly within the void of meaning. I took some steps in the street and recognized in the *nul* sound the taut string of the musical instrument, which was forgotten and which glorious Memory had certainly just visited with its wing or with a palm and, with my finger on the contrivance of the mystery, I smiled and with intellectual desires begged for a different subject for conjecture. The phrase came back, virtual, dislodged

d'une chute antérieure de plume ou de rameau, dorénavant à travers la voix entendue, jusqu'à ce qu'enfin elle s'articula seule, vivant de sa personnalité. J'allais (ne me contentant plus d'une perception) la lisant en fin de vers, et, une fois, comme un essai, l'adaptant à mon parler; bientôt la prononçant avec un silence après "Pénultième" dans lequel je trouvais une pénible jouissance: "La Pénultième" puis la corde de l'instrument, si tendue en l'oubli sur le son *nul*, cassait sans doute et j'ajoutais en manière d'oraison: "Est morte". Je ne discontinuai pas de tenter un retour à des pensées de prédilection, alléguant, pour me calmer, que, certes, pénultième est le terme du lexique qui signifie l'avant-dernière syllabe des vocables, et son apparition, le reste mal abjuré d'un labeur de linguistique par lequel quotidiennement sanglote de s'interrompre ma noble faculté poétique: la sonorité même et l'air de mensonge assumé par la hâte de la facile affirmation étaient une cause de tourment. Harcelé, je résolus de laisser les mots de triste nature errer eux-mêmes sur ma bouche, et j'allai murmurant avec

from a previous fall of feather or twig, heard henceforward through the voice, until at last it articulated itself all alone, living and with its personality. I walked on (no longer content with a perception) reading it as a line-ending, and, once, as a test, adapting it to my speech; soon uttering it with a silence after 'Penultimate' in which I found a laboured pleasure: 'The Penultimate' then the string of the instrument, so taut in forgetfulness on the *nul* sound, no doubt snapped and I added as a kind of prayer: 'Is dead'. I did not cease my attempt to return to preferred thoughts, asserting, to calm myself, that, surely, penultimate is the lexical term that signifies the last syllable but one of the vocables, and its appearance is the imperfectly renounced remnant of a labour of linguistics; my noble poetic faculty sobs daily as it is interrupted by this: the very sonority and the air of falsehood assumed by the eagerness of facile assertion were a cause of torment. Harassed, I resolved to let the sad-natured words themselves wander over my mouth, and I walked on murmuring with an intonation

l'intonation susceptible de condoléance: "La Pénultième est morte, elle est morte, bien morte, la désespérée Pénultième", croyant par là satisfaire l'inquiétude, et non sans le secret espoir de l'ensevelir en l'amplification de la psalmodie quand, effroi! – d'une magie aisément déductible et nerveuse – je sentis que j'avais, ma main réfléchie par un vitrage de boutique y faisant le geste d'une caresse qui descend sur quelque chose, la voix même (la première, qui indubitablement avait été l'unique).

potentially of sympathy: 'The Penultimate is dead, she is dead, quite dead, the despairing Penultimate', thinking thereby that I would answer my anxiety, and not without the secret hope of burying it in the swelling of the chant when, terror! – by a readily deducible and nervous magic – I sensed that I had, as my hand reflected by a shop window made the gesture of a downward caress on something, the voice itself (the first, which beyond doubt had been the only one).

Mais où s'installe l'irrécusable intervention du surnaturel, et le commencement de l'angoisse sous laquelle agonise mon esprit naguère seigneur c'est quand je vis, levant les yeux, dans la rue des antiquaires instinctivement suivie, que j'étais devant la boutique d'un luthier vendeur de vieux instruments pendus au mur, et, à terre, des palmes jaunes et les ailes enfouies en l'ombre, d'oiseaux anciens. Je m'enfuis, bizarre, personne condamnée à porter probablement de deuil de l'inexplicable Pénultième.

But when the unimpeachable intervention of the supernatural takes its place, and the beginning of the anguish beneath which my once lordly spirit lies in its agony, that is when I saw, raising my eyes, in the street of antique dealers which I had instinctively followed, that I was in front of a lute-maker's shop selling old instruments that hung on the wall, and, on the ground, yellow palms and, hidden in the shadow, the wings of ancient birds. I fled, freakish, an individual probably condemned to wear mourning for the inexplicable Penultimate.

Charles Cros
(1842–88)

Charles Cros was a brilliant scientist and inventor as well as poet, a pioneering researcher in electricity, colour photography, acoustics and telegraphy, and even envisaged interplanetary communication. But he was no 'boffin', preferring the bohemian existence of the Parisian artistic world, his friendships with Nouveau, Mendès and Huysmans, and the 'green enlightenment' of absinth.

Rather overshadowed in his own time by Baudelaire, Verlaine, Rimbaud and Mallarmé, Cros has been acknowledged more recently as a significant poet, whose rather *fin-de-siècle* blend of emotion and self-mocking, suspicious irony prefigures Corbière and especially Laforgue, who recognized the influence.

Passionate and analytical, self-dramatizing and sardonic, this philologist has a taste for crisp, laconic, unpretentious lines of verse where lyricism interacts with wit. He experiments with a wide range of metres and stanza forms, and is adept at coining original and delightful combinations of noun and adjective, often drawing together the naïve and the refined. His sound associations and rhythmic control show a dynamic mastery of technique that parallels a tight intellectual mastery of his feelings, leaving us often with a mixed sense of exhilaration and anti-climax.

Major works: *Le Coffret de santal* 1873, *Le Collier de griffes* (posthumous)

Lendemain

À Henri Mercier

Avec les fleurs, avec les femmes,
Avec l'absinthe, avec le feu,
On peut se divertir un peu,
Jouer son rôle en quelque drame.

L'absinthe bue un soir d'hiver
Éclaire en vert l'âme enfumée,
Et les fleurs, sur la bien-aimée
Embaument devant le feu clair.

Puis les baisers perdent leurs charmes,
Ayant duré quelques saisons.
Les réciproques trahisons
Font qu'on se quitte un jour, sans larmes.

Morrow

for Henri Mercier

With flowers, with women, with absinth, with fire, one can have a little entertainment, play one's role in some drama.

Absinth drunk on a winter evening enlightens in green the smoky soul, and flowers on the loved one give off scents before the shining fire.

Then kisses lose their charms, having lasted a few seasons. Mutual betrayals one day bring separation, without tears.

On brûle lettres et bouquets
Et le feu se met à l'alcôve,
Et, si la triste vie est sauve,
Restent l'absinthe et ses hoquets.

Les portraits sont mangés des flammes;
Les doigts crispés sont tremblotants ...
On meurt d'avoir dormi longtemps
Avec les fleurs, avec les femmes.

Letters and bouquets are burned and fire sets the bedchamber ablaze, and, if melancholy life is spared, absinth and its hiccoughs remain.

Portraits are consumed by flames; taut fingers are quivering ... one dies of having slept too long with flowers and with women.

Hiéroglyphe

J'ai trois fenêtres à ma chambre:
    L'amour, la mer, la mort,
Sang vif, vert calme, violet.

O femme, doux et lourd trésor!

Froids vitraux, cloches, odeurs d'ambre.
    La mer, la mort, l'amour,
Ne sentir que ce qui me plaît ...

Femme, plus claire que le jour!

Par ce soir doré de septembre,
    La mort, l'amour, la mer,
Me noyer dans l'oubli complet.

Femme! femme! cercueil de chair!

Hieroglyph

I have three windows in my room: love, sea, death, living blood, calm green, violet.

O woman, sweet and heavy treasure!

Cold stained glass, bells, scents of amber. Sea, death, love, to feel only what gives me pleasure ...

Woman, brighter than daylight!

On this gilded September evening, death, love, sea, to drown myself in entire oblivion.

Woman! woman! coffin of flesh!

Sonnet

A travers la forêt des spontanéités,
Écartant les taillis, courant par les clairières,
Et cherchant dans l'émoi des soifs aventurières
L'oubli des paradis pour un instant quittés,

Inquiète, cheveux flottants, yeux agités,
Vous allez et cueillez des plantes singulières,
Pour parfumer l'air fade et pour cacher les pierres
De la prison terrestre où nous sommes jetés.

Et puis, quand vous avez groupé les fleurs coupées,
Vous vous ressouvenez de l'idéal lointain,
Et leur éclat, devant ce souvenir, s'éteint.

Alors l'ennui vous prend. Vos mains inoccupées
Brisent les pâles fleurs et les jettent au vent.
Et vous recommencez ainsi, le jour suivant.

Sonnet

Through the forest of spontaneities, thrusting aside the undergrowth, running through the glades, and seeking in the ferment of adventurous thirsts forgetfulness of paradises momentarily abandoned,

Anxious, with hair flying and restless eyes, you go along gathering peculiar plants, to scent the insipid air and to hide the stones of the earthly prison into which we are thrown.

And then, when you have arranged the cut flowers, you remember once more the distant ideal, and their lustre is eclipsed before that memory.

Then tedium takes hold of you. Your idle hands break the pale flowers and cast them to the wind. And so you begin again, the following day.

Phantasma

J'ai rêvé l'archipel parfumé, montagneux,
Perdu dans une mer inconnue et profonde
Où le naufrage nous a jetés tous les deux
Oubliés loin des lois qui régissent le monde.

Sur le sable étendue en l'or de tes cheveux,
Des cheveux qui te font comme une tombe blonde,
Je te ranime au son nouveau de mes aveux
Que ne répéteront ni la plage ni l'onde.

C'est un rêve. Ton âme est un oiseau qui fuit
Vers les horizons clairs de rubis, d'émeraudes,
Et mon âme abattue est un oiseau de nuit.

Pour te soumettre, proie exquise, à mon ennui
Et pour te dompter, blanche, en mes étreintes chaudes,
Tous les pays sont trop habités aujourd'hui.

Phantasm

I have dreamed of the scented, mountainous archipelago, lost in a deep and unknown sea where shipwreck has cast us both, forgotten, far from the laws that govern the world.

On the sand where you are stretched out in the gold of your hair, hair which makes for you a kind of flaxen tomb, I bring you back to life with the renewed sound of my vows which neither beach nor waves will repeat.

It is a dream. Your soul is a bird that flies away towards shining ruby and emerald horizons, and my afflicted soul is a bird of night.

To subject you, exquisite prey, to my anxious tedium and to tame you, white being, in my warm embraces, all countries today are too densely peopled.

Sonnet

J'ai bâti dans ma fantaisie
Un théâtre aux décors divers:
– Magiques palais, grands bois verts –
Pour y jouer ma poésie.

Un peu trop au hasard choisie,
La jeune-première à l'envers
Récite quelquefois mes vers.
Faute de mieux je m'extasie.

Et je déclame avec tant d'art
Qu'on me croirait pris à son fard,
Au fard que je lui mets moi-même.

Non. Sous le faux air virginal
Je vois l'être inepte et vénal.
Mais c'est le rôle seul que j'aime.

Sonnet

I have built in my imagination a theatre with different settings: – magical palaces, great green forests – in which to play out my poetry.

Cast a little too haphazardly, the leading lady sometimes recites my lines inside-out. For want of anything better I go into raptures.

And I declaim with so much artistry that you'd think me the dupe of her make-up, the make-up I put on her myself.

No. Beneath that fake air of maidenly modesty I see the foolish, mercenary creature, but it's only the role I love.

Paul Verlaine
(1844–96)

A legendary '*maudit*' who rather lacked the courage of his convictions, Verlaine followed an indulged, mother-dominated childhood with an interesting but unsavoury adult life in which one part of him watched in fascinated, impotent, bourgeois horror as the other slipped into degradation.

His early literary contacts were with Baudelaire and the Parnassians, and the publication of *Poèmes Saturniens* (1866) and *Fêtes Galantes* (1869) brought him considerable success. But he became dependent on alcohol, and made a curious, inevitably disastrous marriage in 1870 to a girl of seventeen, Mathilde Mauté de Fleurville. They lived in illusory domestic bliss (*La Bonne Chanson*) until the arrival of the young prodigy Arthur Rimbaud from Charleville. Verlaine guided Rimbaud into Parisian literary circles, excusing the scruffy iconoclast's outrageous behaviour by asserting his genius, and became infatuated with him. He left Mathilde and began an unstable homosexual relationship with Rimbaud that took them on well-documented wanderings through northern France, Belgium and England in the period of *Romances sans Paroles* (published in 1874).

Periodic bouts of remorse and attempts at reconciliation with Mathilde were invariably followed by a return to Rimbaud, but the relationship between the two poets, briefly productive in terms of mutual artistic stimulation, was intense and stormy. In 1873 Verlaine, always the more dependent and desperate partner, shot Rimbaud in the wrist during a quarrel and was imprisoned for two years. Sheltered in prison from his emotional problems, Verlaine experienced a religious conversion, and in a new mood of repentance and discipline began the volume *Sagesse* (published in 1881). These good intentions were no doubt as sincere at the time as anything Verlaine ever felt or believed, but they were typically superficial and short-lived, and with hindsight can even appear a little nauseating.

A distasteful later life of alcoholism and difficult relationships, financial problems and mediocre poetry was relieved only by his influential 1883 articles entitled *Les Poètes maudits*, in which he surveyed the current poetic climate and helped to establish a number of reputations, notably those of Corbière, Mallarmé, Rimbaud and Cros. He tried teaching, farming, even a period in a Trappist monastery, but could not halt the decline into illness and degradation. His literary fame was considerable, but it was based on his earlier work rather than the late volumes *Jadis et Naguère* (1884), *Amour* (1888), *Parallèlement* (1889) and *Bonheur* (1891).

At its best, his poetry contains no ideas, no rhetoric, and explores neither social reality nor metaphysics. It avoids both sentimental effusion and Parnassian detachment. It is a brilliant, original art of extreme musicality '*sur le mode mineur*', a subtle transmission of intimate nuances of mood and feeling through sound patterns, rhythms and images arranged in an incantatory tone-poem. It has no finality, but lingers as a dream-like '*paysage intérieur*', the objective yet deliberately blurred expression of an inner state. The style is unemphatic, fluid, deceptively naïve, an evocative mixture of light and shade. Sense is subordinated to sound, or rather the two are inseparable, in a discreet, filtered kind of lyricism and allusive mystery not far removed from Impressionist painting or some of the music of Debussy and Ravel. Feelings and images are captured as they fade, and there is a sense that time is suspended, the poet's melancholy sensibility entranced with it in a somnolent, dangerously amorphous state. Consciousness is an attenuated, passive entity, unlike the powerfully present and active ego of Baudelaire, Rimbaud or Laforgue. Our identification with this music is intuitive and subtle, and its features will combine with Mallarméan aesthetics to form the basis of Symbolism.

In terms of versification, Verlaine is revolutionary and highly influential. He weakens the dominance of rhyme and guides it towards assonance, further relaxes the restraints on poetic vocabulary, and breaks the hold on French verse not only of the Alexandrine, whose qualities of intellectual symmetry and finality obviously do not suit such a poetic mode, but also of the decasyllable and octosyllable. He pioneers the '*impair*' line of 5, 7, 9, 11 (or even on occasion 13) syllables, so dislocating and incomplete to the ear of a classically educated Frenchman, for his half-secret, associative, open-ended music, bringing to French verse a new rhythmic flexibility and opening the way for the Symbolists to '*reprendre à la musique leur bien*'.

Mon Rêve familier

Je fais souvent ce rêve étrange et pénétrant
D'une femme inconnue, et que j'aime, et qui m'aime,
Et qui n'est, chaque fois, ni tout à fait la même
Ni tout à fait une autre, et m'aime et me comprend.

Car elle me comprend, et mon cœur, transparent
Pour elle seule, hélas! cesse d'être un problème
Pour elle seule, et les moiteurs de mon front blême,
Elle seule les sait rafraîchir, en pleurant.

Est-elle brune, blonde ou rousse? – Je l'ignore.
Son nom? Je me souviens qu'il est doux et sonore,
Comme ceux des aimés que la Vie exila.

Son regard est pareil au regard des statues,
Et, pour sa voix, lointaine, et calme, et grave, elle a
L'inflexion des voix chères qui se sont tues.

My Intimate Dream

I often dream this strange and penetrating dream of an unknown woman, whom I love and who loves me, and who is, each time, not quite the same nor yet quite different, and loves and understands me.

For she understands me, and my heart, open to her eyes alone, alas! presents for her alone no further problem, and she alone knows how to cool with her tears the clammy heat of my brow.

Is she brown-haired, blonde or russet! – I know not. Her name? I remember that it is sweet and resonant like those of the loved ones banished by Life.

Her gaze is like the gaze of statues, and as for her voice, distant, composed, and solemn, it has the inflexion of the precious voices that have fallen silent.

Effet de nuit

La nuit. La pluie. Un ciel blafard que déchiquette
De flèches et de tours à jour la silhouette
D'une ville gothique éteinte au lointain gris.
La plaine. Un gibet plein de pendus rabougris
Secoués par le bec avide des corneilles
Et dansant dans l'air noir des gigues nonpareilles,
Tandis que leurs pieds sont la pâture des loups.
Quelques buissons d'épine épars, et quelques houx
Dressant l'horreur de leur feuillage à droite, à gauche,
Sur le fuligineux fouillis d'un fond d'ébauche.
Et puis, autour de trois livides prisonniers
Qui vont pieds nus, un gros de hauts pertuisaniers
En marche, et leurs fers droits, comme des fers de herse,
Luisent à contre-sens des lances de l'averse.

Night Impression

Darkness. Rain. A pallid sky serrated with spires and open towers by the silhouette of a Gothic city without light in the grey distance. The plain. A gibbet full of shrivelled corpses convulsed by the greedy beaks of crows and dancing inimitable jigs in the black air, while their feet are food for wolves. A few straggling thorn-bushes and holly trees stand bristling to right and left in their abhorrent foliage, against a murky tangle like the background of a sketch. And then, around three ghastly barefoot prisoners, a body of towering halberdiers on the march, and their straight shafts like harrow rods gleam at an angle against the lances of the downpour.

Soleils couchants

Une aube affaiblie
Verse par les champs
La mélancolie
Des soleils couchants.
La mélancolie
Berce de doux chants
Mon cœur qui s'oublie
Aux soleils couchants.
Et d'étranges rêves,
Comme des soleils
Couchants sur les grèves,
Fantômes vermeils,
Défilent sans trêves,
Défilent, pareils
A des grands soleils
Couchants sur les grèves.

Setting Suns

A diluted dawn sheds over the fields the melancholy of setting suns. Melancholy with sweet songs cradles my heart in oblivion amid setting suns. And strange dreams, like suns setting on shores, vermilion spectres, a ceaseless procession, pass by, like great suns setting on shores.

Clair de lune

Votre âme est un paysage choisi
Que vont charmant masques et bergamasques
Jouant du luth et dansant et quasi
Tristes sous leurs déguisements fantasques.

Tout en chantant sur le mode mineur
L'amour vainqueur et la vie opportune,
Ils n'ont pas l'air de croire à leur bonheur
Et leur chanson se mêle au clair de lune,

Au calme clair de lune triste et beau,
Qui fait rêver les oiseaux dans les arbres
Et sangloter d'extase les jets d'eau,
Les grands jets d'eau sveltes parmi les marbres.

Moonlight

Your soul is a select landscape bewitched by masques and bergamasques playing the lute as they go and dancing and almost sad beneath their fanciful disguises.

Singing as they go in the minor key of conquering love and the favours of life, they don't seem quite to believe in their happiness and their song mingles with the moonlight,

With the clear moonlight, sad and beautiful, that sets the birds dreaming in the trees and the fountains sobbing in ecstasy, the tall slender fountains amid the marble statues.

En sourdine

Calmes dans le demi-jour
Que les branches hautes font,
Pénétrons bien notre amour
De ce silence profond.

Fondons nos âmes, nos cœurs
Et nos sens extasiés,
Parmi les vagues langueurs
Des pins et des arbousiers.

Ferme tes yeux à demi,
Croise tes bras sur ton sein.
Et de ton cœur endormi
Chasse à jamais tout dessein.

Laissons-nous persuader
Au souffle berceur et doux
Qui vient à tes pieds rider
Les ondes de gazon roux.

Muted

Tranquil in the half-light cast by the high branches, let us imbue our love with this deep silence.

Let us merge our souls, our hearts and our enraptured senses, amid the hazy listlessness of the pines and the arbutus trees.

Half close your eyes, cross your arms on your breast, and from your dormant heart chase out for ever all purpose.

Let us offer no resistance to the gentle rocking breeze that comes and ruffles at your feet the waves of russet grass.

Et quand, solennel, le soir
Des chênes noirs tombera,
Voix de notre désespoir,
Le rossignol chantera.

And when night falls, solemnly, from the black oak trees, the voice of our despair, the nightingale will sing.

Colloque sentimental

Dans le vieux parc solitaire et glacé,
Deux formes ont tout à l'heure passé.

Leurs yeux sont morts et leurs lèvres sont molles,
Et l'on entend à peine leurs paroles.

Dans le vieux parc solitaire et glacé,
Deux spectres ont évoqué le passé.

– Te souvient-il de notre extase ancienne?
– Pourquoi voulez-vous donc qu'il m'en souvienne?

Sentimental Dialogue

In the lonely, frozen old park, two figures passed by just now.

Their eyes are dead and their lips are limp, and their words can hardly be heard.

In the lonely, frozen old park, two spectres evoked the past.

– Do you remember our old rapture?
– Why on earth should I remember that?

–Ton cœur bat-il toujours à mon seul nom?
Toujours vois-tu mon âme en rêve? – Non.

– Ah! les beaux jours de bonheur indicible
Où nous joignions nos bouches! – C'est possible.

– Qu'il était bleu, le ciel, et grand, l'espoir!
– L'espoir a fui, vaincu, vers le ciel noir.

Tels ils marchaient dans les avoines folles,
Et la nuit seule entendit leurs paroles.

– Does your heart still beat at my very name? Do you still see my soul in dreams? – No.

– Ah! those fine days of ineffable bliss when our lips were joined! – It may have been so.

– How blue the sky was, how great was hope!
– Hope has fled, defeated, towards the black sky.

Thus they walked among the wild oats, and the darkness alone heard their words.

Il pleure dans mon cœur …

Il pleut doucement sur la ville.

(ARTHUR RIMBAUD)

Il pleure dans mon cœur
Comme il pleut sur la ville:
Quelle est cette langueur
Qui pénètre mon cœur?

O bruit doux de la pluie
Par terre et sur les toits!
Pour un cœur qui s'ennuie
O le chant de la pluie!

Il pleure sans raison
Dans ce cœur qui s'écœure.
Quoi! nulle trahison? …
Ce deuil est sans raison.

There is weeping in my heart …

It is raining gently on the city

(Arthur Rimbaud)

There is weeping in my heart like the rain on the city: what is this listlessness that penetrates my heart?

O sweet sound of the rain on the ground and the roofs! For a heart full of tedium O the song of the rain!

There is weeping without reason in this heart full of nausea. What! no betrayal? … This grief is without cause.

C'est bien la pire peine
De ne savoir pourquoi
Sans amour et sans haine
Mon cœur a tant de peine!

It's really the worst suffering not to know why with no love and no hate my heart has so much pain!

Dans l'interminable ...

Dans l'interminable
Ennui de la plaine
La neige incertaine
Luit comme du sable.

Le ciel est de cuivre
Sans lueur aucune.
On croirait voir vivre
Et mourir la lune.

Comme des nuées
Flottent gris les chênes
Des forêts prochaines
Parmi les buées.

In the interminable ...

In the interminable tedium of the plain the unstable snow shines like sand.

The sky is of copper without any light. It's like seeing the life and death of the moon.

Like storm-clouds the oaks of nearby forests float grey amidst the vapours.

Le ciel est de cuivre
Sans lueur aucune.
On croirait voir vivre
Et mourir la lune.

Corneille poussive
Et vous, les loups maigres,
Par ces bises aigres
Quoi donc vous arrive?

Dans l'interminable
Ennui de la plaine
La neige incertaine
Luit comme du sable.

The sky is of copper without any light. It's like seeing the life and death of the moon.

Wheezing crow and you, lean wolves, in these bitter blasts, what's coming over you?

In the interminable tedium of the plain the unstable snow shines like sand.

Les chères mains qui furent miennes ...

Les chères mains qui furent miennes,
Toutes petites, toutes belles,
Après les méprises mortelles
Et toutes ces choses païennes,

Après les rades et les grèves,
Et les pays et les provinces,
Royales mieux qu'au temps des princes,
Les chères mains m'ouvrent les rêves.

Mains en songe, mains sur mon âme,
Sais-je, moi, ce que vous daignâtes,
Parmi ces rumeurs scélérates,
Dire à cette âme qui se pâme?

Ment-elle, ma vision chaste
D'affinité spirituelle,
De complicité maternelle,
D'affection étroite et vaste?

The precious hands that were mine ...

The precious hands that were mine, minute, quite beautiful, after all the mortal misunderstandings and all those heathen things,

After the roadsteads and the sandbanks, and the countries and the provinces, more splendidly royal than in the age of princes, those precious hands open dreams to me.

Hands in a dream, hands on my soul, can I know what you deigned to say, amid that criminal uproar, to this fainting soul?

Is it a lie, my chaste vision of spiritual affinity, of maternal understanding, of close and vast affection?

Remords si cher, peine très bonne,
Rêves bénis, mains consacrées,
O ces mains, ces mains vénérées,
Faites le geste qui pardonne!

Remorse so dear, suffering most kind, blessed dreams, hallowed hands, O these hands, these revered hands, make the gesture of forgiveness!

Le ciel est, par-dessus le toit ...

Le ciel est, par-dessus le toit,
    Si bleu, si calme!
Un arbre, par-dessus le toit,
    Berce sa palme.

La cloche, dans le ciel qu'on voit,
    Doucement tinte.
Un oiseau sur l'arbre qu'on voit
    Chante sa plainte.

Mon Dieu, mon Dieu, la vie est là,
    Simple et tranquille.
Cette paisible rumeur-là
    Vient de la ville.

The sky, above the roof ...

The sky, above the roof, is so blue, so calm! A tree, above the roof, rocks its palm.

The bell, in the sky over there, gently rings. A bird on the tree over there plaintively sings.

My God, my God, life is there, simple and placid. That peaceful murmur comes from the town.

– Qu'as-tu fait, ô toi que voila
Pleurant sans cesse,
Dis, qu'as-tu fait, toi que voilà,
De ta jeunesse?

– What have you done, O you there weeping endlessly, say, what have you done, you there, with your youth?

Je ne sais pourquoi ...

Je ne sais pourquoi
Mon esprit amer
D'une aile inquiète et folle vole sur la mer.
Tout ce qui m'est cher,
D'une aile d'effroi
Mon amour le couve au ras des flots. Pourquoi, pourquoi?

Mouette à l'essor mélancolique,
Elle suit la vague, ma pensée,
A tous les vents du ciel balancée,
Et biaisant quand la marée oblique,
Mouette à l'essor mélancolique.

I know not why ...

I know not why my bitter spirit flies on a wild and restless wing over the sea. All that is dear to me, with a wing of terror my love broods over it as it skims the waves. Why? Why?

Melancholy soaring seagull, it follows the wave, my thought, buffeted by all the winds in the sky, and tilting with the slanting tide, melancholy soaring seagull.

Ivre de soleil
Et de liberté,
Un instinct la guide à travers cette immensité.
La brise d'été
Sur le flot vermeil
Doucement la porte en un tiède demi-sommeil.

Parfois si tristement elle crie
Qu'elle alarme au lointain le pilote,
Puis au gré du vent se livre et flotte
Et plonge, et l'aile toute meurtrie
Revole, et puis si tristement crie!

Je ne sais pourquoi
Mon esprit amer
D'une aile inquiète et folle vole sur la mer.
Tout ce qui m'est cher,
D'une aile d'effroi
Mon amour le couve au ras des flots. Pourquoi, pourquoi?

Drunk with sunlight and with freedom, an instinct guides it across this vastness. The summer breeze on the vermilion waters bears it gently in a warm half-sleep.

Sometimes it cries so plaintively that it startles the distant pilot, then to the whim of the wind it surrenders and hovers and dives, and the battered wing flies up once more, then cries so plaintively!

I know not why my bitter spirit flies on a wild and restless wing over the sea. All that is dear to me, with a wing of terror my love broods over it as it skims the waves. Why? Why?

Art poétique

A Charles Morice

De la musique avant toute chose,
Et pour cela préfère l'Impair
Plus vague et plus soluble dans l'air,
Sans rien en lui qui pèse ou qui pose.

Il faut aussi que tu n'ailles point
Choisir tes mots sans quelque méprise:
Rien de plus cher que la chanson grise
Où l'Indécis au Précis se joint.

C'est des beaux yeux derrière des voiles,
C'est le grand jour tremblant de midi,
C'est, par un ciel d'automne attiédi,
Le bleu fouillis des claires étoiles!

The Art of Poetry

for Charles Morice

Music above all else, and for that choose the Uneven metre, hazier and more soluble in the air, with nothing in it that is heavy or fixed.

Nor should you on any account choose your words without a certain obscurity: nothing is more precious than the grey song where the Indistinct meets the Precise.

It is lovely eyes behind veils, it is the shimmering light of noon, it is, in a cooling autumn sky, the blue disorder of the shining stars!

Car nous voulons la Nuance encore,
Pas la Couleur, rien que la nuance!
Oh! la nuance seule fiance
Le rêve au rêve et la flûte au cor!

Fuis du plus loin la Pointe assassine,
L'Esprit cruel et le Rire impur,
Qui font pleurer les yeux de l'Azur,
Et tout cet ail de basse cuisine!

Prends l'éloquence et tords-lui son cou!
Tu feras bien, en train d'énergie,
De rendre un peu la Rime assagie.
Si l'on n'y veille, elle ira jusqu'où?

O qui dira les torts de la Rime?
Quel enfant sourd ou quel nègre fou
Nous a forgé ce bijou d'un sou
Qui sonne creux et faux sous la lime?

For we still want the Nuance, not the Colour, nothing but the nuance! Oh! the nuance alone betrothes dream to dream and flute to horn!

Give a wide berth to the murderous Epigram, cruel Wit and base Laughter, that bring tears to the eyes of the Azure, and all that vulgar kitchen garlic!

Take eloquence and wring its neck! While you're about it, you'll do well to bring Rhyme to its senses a little. If we don't watch it, what lengths will it go to?

O who will tell of the crimes of Rhyme? What deaf infant or crazy negro forged for us this twopenny jewel that rings hollow and fake beneath the file?

De la musique encore et toujours!
Que ton vers soit la chose envolée
Qu'on sent qui fuit d'une âme en allée
Vers d'autres cieux à d'autres amours.

Que ton vers soit la bonne aventure
Éparse au vent crispé du matin
Qui va fleurant la menthe et le thym ...
Et tout le reste est littérature.

Music once more and for ever! Let your line of verse be a thing that takes wing that we sense as it flies from a soul on its way towards other skies to other loves.

Let your line of verse be fortune's wanderer scattered in the taut morning wind that goes scented with mint and with thyme ... And all the rest is literature.

Tristan Corbière
(1845–75)

Corbière lived his short life in Brittany; and the Breton landscape, culture, seafaring tradition and folk mythology are significant ingredients in his work. A self-conscious, unhealthy, abrasive figure, and yet also strangely moving, he caricatures himself cruelly as 'the toad'. He hides his insecurities and his failures in love behind a mask of irony and punning black humour, but it is a mask that does not fully conceal either the pain within or the potential for lyricism.

His discordant, dislocated verse, almost modernist at times in its clashing of registers and broken rhythms, has a raw energy that seems to explode literary conventions. On close examination, it can be quite surprising to find that he remains on the whole within orthodox metrical patterns, even if he is straining them to the limit. The Surrealists found in his 'Litanie du Sommeil' an early example of 'automatic writing', an associative avalanche of words, though once again careful study reveals consciously worked effects.

Corbière's uneven, patchily brilliant 1873 volume, *Les Amours jaunes* ('*jaunes*' here used as in '*un rire jaune*', a sickly laugh disguising other feelings) met with little immediate success. It gained more attention a decade after his death, through its promotion by Verlaine and through the critical but very real interest of Laforgue, whose own breakthrough into 'stream of consciousness' free verse would be based on more sophisticated mastery of technique.

Le Crapaud

Un chant dans une nuit sans air ...
– La lune plaque en métal clair
Les découpures du vert sombre.

... Un chant; comme un écho, tout vif
Enterré, là, sous le massif ...
– Ça se tait: Viens, c'est là, dans l'ombre ...

– Un crapaud! – Pourquoi cette peur,
Près de moi, ton soldat fidèle?
Vois-le, poète tondu, sans aile,
Rossignol de la boue ... – Horreur! –

... Il chante – Horreur!! – Horreur pourquoi?
Vois-tu pas son œil de lumière ...
Non: il s'en va, froid, sous sa pierre.

Bonsoir – ce crapaud-là, c'est moi.

The Toad

A song in an airless night ... – The moon coats with a metal sheen the cut-out patches of dark green.

... A song; like an echo, buried alive, there, under the clump of bushes ... – It's gone silent: come, it's there, in the shadow ...

– A toad! – Why this fear, beside me, your faithful soldier? See it, the shaven-headed poet, wingless, the nightingale of the mire ... – Horror! –

... He sings – Horror!! – Why horror? Can't you see his gleaming eye ... No: He's going away, cold, beneath his stone.

Goodnight – that toad over there, it's me.

A une Camarade

Que me veux-tu donc, femme trois fois fille? ...
Moi qui te croyais un si bon enfant!
– De l'amour? ... – Allons: cherche, apporte, pille!
M'aimer aussi, toi! ... moi qui t'aimais tant.

Oh! je t'aimais comme ... un lézard qui pèle
Aime le rayon qui cuit son sommeil ...
L'Amour entre nous vient battre de l'aile:
– Eh! qu'il s'ôte de devant mon soleil!

Mon amour, à moi, n'aime pas qu'on l'aime;
Mendiant, il a peur d'être écouté ...
C'est un lazzarone enfin, un bohème,
Déjeunant de jeûne et de liberté.

To a Friend

What do you want of me then, woman three times whore-child? I who thought you such a good infant! – Love? ... – Come on: seek, bring, plunder! To love me too, you? ... I who loved you so.

Oh! I loved you as ... a peeling lizard loves the ray of sunshine that bakes its sleep ... Love comes between us and flutters its wings: – Hey! I want it out of my sunlight!

My love, my own, doesn't like to be loved; a beggar, he's afraid of being listened to ... He's a good-for-nothing, after all, a wandering gypsy, breakfasting on fasting and on freedom.

– Curiosité, bibelot, bricole? ...
C'est possible: il est rare – et c'est son bien –
Mais un bibelot cassé se recolle;
Et lui, décollé, ne vaudra plus rien! ...

Va, n'enfonçons pas la porte entr'ouverte
Sur un paradis déjà trop rendu!
Et gardons à la pomme, jadis verte,
Sa peau, sous son fard de fruit défendu.

Que nous sommes-nous donc fait l'un à l'autre? ...
– Rien ... – Peut-être alors que c'est pour cela;
– Quel a commencé? – Pas moi, bon apôtre!
Après, quel dira: c'est donc tout – voilà!

– Tous les deux, sans doute ... – Et toi, sois bien sûre
Que c'est encor moi le plus attrapé:
Car si, par erreur, ou par aventure,
Tu ne me trompais ... je serais trompé!

– A curiosity, a trinket, a knick-knack? ... It's possible: he is rare – and that's his strong suit – but a broken trinket can be pasted; and he, unstuck, will have no more value at all! ...

No, let's not thrust open the door that's ajar on a paradise that's already yielded too much! And let's preserve on the apple that once was green its skin, made up to resemble forbidden fruit.

So what have we done to each other? ... – Nothing ... – Perhaps that's why it is; – Which of us began? – Not I, I play the honest man! Afterwards, which will say: that's it then – it's all over!

– Both, I dare say ... – And you, take good note that I'm still the more ensnared: for if, by mistake or by chance, you were not to deceive me ... I would be deceived!

Appelons cela: *l'amitié calmée*;
Puisque l'amour veut mettre son holà.
N'y croyons pas trop, chère mal-aimée …
– C'est toujours trop vrai ces mensonges-là! –

Nous pourrons, au moins, ne pas nous maudire
– Si ça t'est égal – le quart-d'heure après.
Si nous en mourons – ce sera de rire …
Moi qui l'aimais tant ton rire si frais!

Let's call it: *friendship in tranquillity*; since love wants to call a halt. Let's not be dupes of it, my dear unbeloved … – those lies are always too true! –

At least we'll be able not to curse each other – if it's all the same to you – a quarter of an hour afterwards. If we die of it – it'll be for laughing … I who so loved your laugh that was so fresh!

Sonnet de nuit

O croisée ensommeillée,
Dure à mes trente-six morts!
Vitre en diamant, éraillée
Par mes atroces accords!

Herse hérissant rouillée
Tes crocs où je pends et mords!
Oubliette verrouillée
Qui me renferme … dehors!

Pour Toi, Bourreau que j'encense,
L'amour n'est donc que vengeance? …
Ton balcon: gril à braiser? …

Ton col: collier de garotte?…
Eh bien! ouvre, Iscariote,
Ton judas pour un baiser!

Night Sonnet

O sleeping casement, hardened to my umpteen deaths! Diamond pane, scratched by my atrocious chords!

Spiky rusting portcullis your hooks where I hang and gnaw! Bolted dungeon which shuts me … out!

For you, Torturer before whom I burn incense, is love nothing then but vengeance? … Your balcony: a braising grill? …

Your necklace: a garrotte? … Well come on! Iscariot, open up your Judas spyhole for a kiss!

Paysage mauvais

Sables de vieux os – Le flot râle
Des glas: crevant bruit sur bruit ...
– Palud pâle, où la lune avale
De gros vers, pour passer la nuit.

– Calme de peste, où la fièvre
Cuit ... Le follet damné languit.
– Herbe puante où le lièvre
Est un sorcier poltron qui fuit ...

– La Lavandière blanche étale
Des trépassés le linge sale,
Au *soleil des loups* ... – Les crapauds,

Petits chantres mélancoliques
Empoisonnent de leurs coliques,
Les champignons, leurs escabeaux.

Evil landscape

Old bone sands – The waters rattle out death knells: bursting sound upon sound ... – Pallid marshland, where the moon swallows fat worms, to pass the night.

– A plague silence, where fever simmers ... the damned will-o'-the-wisp lies pining. – Stinking weeds where the hare is a cowardly fleeting wizard ...

The White Washerwoman spreads the dirty linen of all departed souls in the *sunlight of the wolves* ... – The toads,

Melancholy little choristers poison with their colic the mushrooms, their stools.

Litanie du Sommeil

"J'ai scié le sommeil" (*Macbeth*)[1]

Vous qui ronflez au coin d'une épouse endormie,
RUMINANT! Savez-vous ce soupir: L'INSOMNIE?
– Avez-vous vu la Nuit, et le Sommeil ailé,
Papillon de minuit dans la nuit envolé,
Sans un coup d'aile ami, vous laissant sur le seuil,
Seul, dans le pot-au-noir au couvercle sans œil?
– Avez-vous navigué? … La pensée est la houle
Ressassant le galet: ma tête … votre boule.
– Vous êtes-vous laissé voyager en ballon?
– Non? – bien, c'est l'insomnie. – Un grand coup de talon
Là! – Vous voyez cligner des chandelles étranges:
Une femme, une Gloire en soleil, des archanges …
Et, la nuit s'éteignant dans le jour à demi,
Vous vous réveillez coi, sans vous être endormi.

★

Sleep Litany

You snoring at your sleeping wifeside, CUD-CHEWER! do you know this sigh: INSOMNIA! – have you seen the Night, and winged Sleep, that midnight moth flown away in the darkness, with no friendly wing-beat, leaving you on the threshold, alone, in the pitch-pot with its eyeless lid? Have you sailed the sea? … Thought is the swell sifting the shingle: my head … your bonce. – Have you been taken up in a balloon? – No? – Well, that's insomnia. – A rough landing, there! – You see strange candles flickering: a woman, a sunlit Halo, archangels … And, as night fades into the semi-daylight, you wake in stillness, without having been to sleep.

★

[1]Corbière seems somehow to have distorted the words "Macbeth does murder sleep" in Act II sc.ii of Shakespeare's play.

SOMMEIL! écoute-moi: je parlerai bien bas:
Sommeil. – Ciel-de-lit de ceux qui n'en ont pas!

TOI qui planes avec l'Albatros des tempêtes,
Et qui t'assieds sur les casques-à-mèche honnêtes!
SOMMEIL! – Oreiller blanc des vierges assez bêtes!
Et Soupape à secret des vierges assez faites!
– Moelleux Matelas de l'échine en arête!
Sac noir où les chassés s'en vont cacher leur tête!
Rôdeur de boulevard extérieur! Proxénète!
Pays où le muet se réveille prophète!
Césure du vers long, et Rime du poète!

SOMMEIL – Loup-Garou gris! Sommeil! Noir de fumée!
SOMMEIL! – Loup de velours, de dentelle embaumée!
Baiser de l'Inconnue, et Baiser de l'Aimée!
– SOMMEIL! Voleur de nuit! Folle-brise pâmée!
Parfum qui monte au ciel des tombes parfumées!
Carrosse à Cendrillon ramassant *les Traînées!*
Obscène Confesseur des dévotes mort-nées!

SLEEP! listen to me: I'll speak in hushed tones: sleep. – Bed-canopy for those who don't have one!

YOU who soar with the Albatross of storms, and who sit on the honourable nightcaps! SLEEP! – White pillow of sufficiently foolish virgins! And secret Safety-valve of sufficiently developed virgins! – Mellow Mattress for the ridged spine! Black sack where the hunted go to hide their heads! Prowler of the outer rampart! Pimp! Land where the dumb man awakes as a prophet! Caesura of long verse line, and poet's Rhyme!

SLEEP! Grey Werewolf! Sleep! Black with smoke! SLEEP! Velvet night-mask, scented with lace! Kiss of the Unknown Woman, and Kiss of the Beloved! – SLEEP! Thief of night! Fainting elf-breeze! Fragrance rising to heaven from the perfumed tombs! *Cinderella's carriage* gathering up the *Street-walkers*! Obscene Confessor of still-born sanctimonious women!

TOI qui viens, comme un chien, lécher la vieille plaie
Du martyr que la mort tiraille sur sa claie!
O sourire forcé de la crise tuée!
SOMMEIL! Brise alizée! Aurorale buée!

TROP-PLEIN de l'existence, et Torchon neuf qu'on passe,
Au CAFÉ DE LA VIE, à chaque assiette grasse!
Grain d'ennui qui nous pleut de l'ennui des espaces!
Chose qui court encore, sans sillage et sans traces!
Pont-levis des fossés! Passage des impasses!

SOMMEIL! – Caméléon tout pailleté d'étoiles!
Vaisseau-fantôme errant tout seul à pleines voiles!
Femme du rendez-vous, s'enveloppant d'un voile!
SOMMEIL! – Triste Araignée, étends sur moi ta toile!

YOU who come, like a dog, to lick the old wound of the martyr dragged about by death on its hurdle! O forced smile of the crisis slain! SLEEP! Soft trade wind! Auroral vapour!

OVERFLOW of existence, and clean Cloth passed in the CAFÉ OF LIFE over each greasy plate! Squall of tedium raining on us from the tedium of space! Thing running still, without wake or track! Drawbridge of moats! Corridor of dead-ends!

SLEEP! – Star-spangled chameleon! Ghost ship wandering alone under full sail! Assignation-woman, wrapping herself in a veil! SLEEP! – Sad Spider, spread your web over me!

SOMMEIL auréolé! féerique Apothéose,
Exaltant le grabat du déclassé qui pose!
Patient Auditeur de l'incompris qui cause!
Refuge du pécheur, de l'innocent qui n'ose!
Domino! Diables-bleus! Ange-gardien rose!

VOIX mortelle qui vibre aux immortelles ondes!
Réveil des échos morts et des choses profondes,
– Journal du soir: TEMPS, SIÈCLE et REVUE DES DEUX MONDES!

FONTAINE de Jouvence et Borne de l'envie!
– Toi qui viens assouvir la faim inassouvie!
Toi qui viens délier la pauvre âme ravie,
Pour la noyer d'air pur au large de la vie!

TOI qui, le rideau bas, viens lâcher la ficelle
Du Chat, du Commissaire et de Polichinelle.
Du violoncelliste et de son violoncelle,
Et la lyre de ceux dont la Muse est pucelle!

Haloed SLEEP! magical Apotheosis, exalting the litter of the prostrate down-and-out! Patient Listener to the chattering misunderstood! Refuge of the sinner, of the innocent who doesn't dare! Domino! Alpine infantry![1] Pink guardian-angel!

Mortal VOICE vibrant in the immortal waves! Awakening of dead echoes and of profound things, – Evening paper: TEMPS, SIÈCLE and REVUE DES DEUX MONDES!

FOUNTAIN of Youth and Frontier of longing! – You who come to satiate the unsatiated hunger! You who come to unfetter the poor captivated soul, to drown it in pure air on the high seas of life!

YOU who, with the curtain down, come to release the string of the Cat, of the Policeman and of Punch, of the cellist and his cello, and the lyre of those whose Muse is chaste!

[1] "*Diables-bleus*": military slang for *chasseurs alpins*.

GRAND Dieu, Maître de tout! Maître de ma Maîtresse
Qui me trompe avec toi – l'amoureuse Paresse –
O Bain de voluptés! Éventail de caresse!

SOMMEIL! Honnêteté des voleurs! Clair de lune
Des yeux crevés! – SOMMEIL! Roulette de fortune
De tout infortuné! Balayeur de rancune!

O corde de pendu de la Planète lourde!
Accord éolien hantant l'oreille sourde!
– Beau Conteur à dormir debout: conte ta bourde! ...
SOMMEIL! – Foyer de ceux dont morte est la falourde!

GREAT God, Master of all things! Master of my Mistress who is deceiving me with you – love-smitten Indolence – O Bath of sensualities! Caressing Fan!

SLEEP! Honesty of thieves! Moonlight for punctured eyes! – SLEEP! Wheel of fortune for every unfortunate! Scavenger of spite!

O hangman's noose[1] of the heavy Planet! Aeolian chord haunting the deaf ear! – Fine Teller of tall stories: spin your yarn! SLEEP! – Hearth of those whose firewood is dead!

[1]*Avoir de la corde-de-pendu*: to have the Devil's own luck.

SOMMEIL – Foyer de ceux dont la falourde est morte!
Passe-partout de ceux qui sont mis à la porte!
Face-de-bois pour les créanciers et leur sorte!
Paravent du mari contre la femme forte!

SURFACE des profonds! Profondeur des jocrisses!
Nourrice du soldat et Soldat des nourrices!
Paix des juges de paix! Police des polices!
SOMMEIL! – Belle-de-nuit entr'ouvrant son calice!
Larve, Ver-luisant et nocturne Cilice!
Puits de vérité de monsieur La Palisse!

SOUPIRAIL d'en haut! Rais de poussière impalpable,
Qui viens rayer du jour la lanterne implacable!

*

SLEEP! – Hearth of those whose firewood is dead! Master-key for those turned out of doors! Blank face for creditors and their kind! Screen for the husband against the virago!

SURFACE of the deep! Depth of the simpletons! Wet-nurse of the soldier and Soldier of the wet-nurses! Peace of justices of the peace! Police of the police! SLEEP! – Marvel-of-Peru[1] half opening its chalice! Larva, Glow-worm and nocturnal Hair-Shirt! Well of truth of Mister Platitude!

AIR-HOLE from on high! Impalpable ray of dust, coming to erase the relentless lamp of day!

*

[1] *Belle-de-nuit*: a flower, sometimes called "pretty-by-night"; also a prostitute.

SOMMEIL – Ecoute-moi, je parlerai bien bas;
Crépuscule flottant de l'*Être ou n'Être pas!* ...

SOMBRE lucidité! Clair-obscur! Souvenir
De l'Inouï! Marée! Horizon! Avenir!
Conte des *Mille-et-une-nuits* doux à ouïr!
Lampiste d'*Aladin* qui sais nous éblouir!
Eunuque noir! muet blanc! Derviche! Djinn! Fakir!
Conte de Fée où *le Roi* se laisse assoupir!
Forêt vierge où *Peau-d'Ane* en pleurs va s'accroupir!
Garde-manger où l'*Ogre* encor va s'assouvir!
Tourelle où *ma sœur Anne* allait voir rien venir!
Tour où *dame Malbrouck* voyait page courir ...
Où *Femme Barbe-Bleue* oyait l'heure mourir! ...
Où *Belle-au-Bois-Dormant* dormait dans un soupir!

SLEEP. – Listen to me, I'll speak in hushed tones: Floating twilight of *Being or not Being*! ...

DARK lucidity! Chiaroscuro! Memory of the Unprecedented! Tide! Horizon! Future! Tale from the *Arabian Nights* sweet on the ear! Lamp-maker of *Aladdin*, you know how to dazzle us! Black eunuch! white mute! Dervish! Genie! Fakir! Fairy Tale where *the King* grows drowsy! Virgin-forest where weeping *Donkey-Skin*[1] goes cowering! Larder where the *Ogre* goes once more for gluttony! Turret where *my sister Anne*[1] would go to see nothing coming! Tower where *Lady Marlborough*[2] saw a page running ... Where *Bluebeard's Wife* hearkened to the dying hour! ... Where *Sleeping Beauty* slept within a sigh!

[1]*'Peau-d'Ane'* and *'Ma sœur Anne'*: characters in stories by Perrault.
[2]Dame Malbrouck: Sarah Jennings, the wife of John Churchill, first Duke of Marlborough. She is the subject of a French children's traditional song.

CUIRASSE du petit! Camisole du fort!
Lampion des éteints! Eteignoir du remord!
Conscience du juste, et du pochard qui dort!
Contre-poids des poids faux de l'épicier du Sort!
Portrait enluminé de la livide Mort!

GRAND fleuve où Cupidon va retremper ses dards!
SOMMEIL! – Corne de Diane, et corne du cornard!
Couveur de magistrats et Couveur de lézards!
Marmite d'*Arlequin!* – bout de cuir, lard, homard –
SOMMEIL! – Noce de ceux qui sont dans les beaux-arts.

BREASTPLATE of the small! straitjacket of the strong! Lantern of the snuffed-out! Snuffer of remorse! Conscience of the just, and of the sleeping drunkard! Counterweight for the false weights of the grocer of Fate! Coloured portrait of livid Death!

GREAT river where Cupid goes to dip his darts once more! SLEEP! – Diana's horn, and horn of the cuckold! Hatcher of magistrates and Hatcher of lizards! *Harlequin*'s cooking-pot! – scrap of leather, back-fat, lobster – SLEEP! – nuptial feast of those in the fine arts!

BOULET des forcenés, Liberté des captifs!
Sabbat du somnambule et Relai des poussifs! –

SOMME! Actif du passif et Passif de l'actif!
Pavillon de *la Folle* et *Folle* du poncif! …
– O viens changer de patte au cormoran pensif!

O brun Amant de l'Ombre! Amant honteux du jour!
Bal de nuit où Psyché veut démasquer l'Amour!
Grosse Nudité du chanoine en jupon court!
Panier-à-salade idéal! Banal four!
Omnibus où, dans l'Orbe, on fait pour rien un tour!

BALL AND CHAIN of the passionate, Liberty of captives! Sabbath of the sleepwalker and Relief for the broken-winded! –

SLUMBER![1] Active of the passive and Passive of the active! Villa[2] of the *Madwoman*[3] and *Madwoman* of triteness! … O come and change the claw of the pensive cormorant!

O dusky Lover of the Shadow! Lover ashamed of the day! Night ball where Psyche wants to unmask Eros! Gross Nudity of the petticoated canon! Ideal Black Maria! Banal bakehouse![4] Omnibus for a free tour in Orbit!

[1]*Somme*: also a nap or short sleep; a pack-saddle; a sum or total.
[2]*Pavillon*: also a bed-canopy, or a flag, or an exhibition-hall, or a tent.
[3]*La Folle*: also "the Imagination", as in '*la folle du logis*' (Malebranche); *une folle* is also a kind of net.
[4]'*Un four*': also a flop, a wash-out.

SOMMEIL! Drame hagard! Sommeil, molle Langueur!
Bouche d'or du silence et Bâillon du blagueur!
Berceuse des vaincus! Perchoir des coqs vainqueurs!
Alinéa du livre où dorment les longueurs!

DU jeune homme rêveur Singulier Féminin!
De la femme rêvant pluriel masculin!

SLEEP! Wild-eyed drama! Sleep, flabby Languor! Golden mouth of silence and Muzzle for the joker! Cradle of the vanquished! Roost for conquering cocks! The book's indention where the tedious passages sleep!

Feminine Singular of the dreamy young man! Masculine plural of the dreaming woman!

SOMMEIL! – Râtelier du Pégase fringant!
SOMMEIL! – Petite pluie abattant l'ouragan!
SOMMEIL! – Dédale vague où vient le revenant!
SOMMEIL! – Long corridor où plangore le vent!

NÉANT du fainéant! Lazzarone infini
Aurore boréale au sein du jour terni!

SOMMEIL! – Autant de pris sur notre éternité!
Tour du cadran *à blanc!* Clou du Mont-de-Piété!
Héritage en Espagne à tout déshérité!
Coup de rapière dans l'eau du fleuve Léthé!
Génie au nimbe d'or des grands hallucinés!
Nid des petits hiboux! Aile des déplumés!

SLEEP! – Feeding-rack of nimble Pegasus! SLEEP! – Gentle rain beating down the hurricane! SLEEP! – Hazy Labyrinth where the ghost appears! SLEEP! – long corridor where the wind howls plaintively!

NOTHINGNESS of the good-for-nothing! Infinite beggar![1] Aurora Borealis in the heart of the tarnished day!

SLEEP! – So much snatched from our eternity! *Blank*[2] circuit of the clock-face! Pawnshop! Legacy in Spain for all the disinherited! Rapier thrust into the water of the river Lethe! Guiding spirit with the golden halo of the great hallucinators! Nest of little owls! Wing of the plucked!

[1] *Lazzarone*: a Naples street-beggar.

[2] *'A blanc'* suggests also 'white heat', and perhaps there is a link with *'une nuit blanche'* (a sleepless night).

IMMENSE Vache à lait dont nous sommes les veaux!
Arche où le hère et le boa changent de peaux!
Arc-en-ciel miroitant! Faux du vrai! Vrai du faux!
Ivresse que la brute appelle le repos!
Sorcière de Bohême à sayon d'oripeaux!
Tityre sous l'ombrage essayant des pipeaux!
Temps qui porte un chibouck à la place de faux!
Parque qui met un peu d'huile à ses ciseaux!
Parque qui met un peu de chanvre à ses fuseaux!
Chat qui joue avec le peloton d'Atropos!

SOMMEIL! – Manne de grâce au cœur disgracié!
....
LE SOMMEIL S'ÉVEILLANT ME DIT : TU M'AS SCIÉ.
....

⋆

IMMENSE Milk-cow whose calves we are! Ark where the stag and the boa change skins! Reflecting rainbow! False of true! True of false! Drunkenness called rest by the brutish! Bohemian sorceress with your tawdry tinsel tunic! Tityrus[1] testing reed-pipes in the shade! Time carrying a chibouk[2] in place of scythe! Fate putting a little oil on her scissors! Fate putting a little hemp on her spindles! Cat playing with Atropos' ball of thread!

SLEEP! Manna of grace for the heart disgraced!
....
SLEEP WAKING SAYS TO ME: YOU HAVE SAWN ME THROUGH.
....

⋆

[1]Tityrus: a herdsman in Virgil's eclogues.
[2]Chibouk: a long-stemmed Turkish pipe.

TOI qui souffles dessus une épouse enrayée,
RUMINANT! dilatant ta pupille éraillée.
Sais-tu? ... Ne sais-tu pas ce soupir – LE RÉVEIL! –
Qui bâille au ciel, parmi les crins d'or du soleil
Et les crins fous de ta Déesse ardente et blonde? ...
– Non!... – Sais-tu réveil du philosophe immonde
– Le Porc – rognonnant sa prière du matin;
Ou le réveil, extrait-d'âge de la catin?...
As-tu jamais sonné le réveil de la meute;
As-tu jamais senti l'éveil sourd de l'émeute,
Ou le réveil de plomb du malade fini?...
As-tu vu s'étirer l'œil des Lazzaroni?...
Sais-tu?... ne sais-tu pas le chant de l'alouette?
– Non – Gluants sont tes cils, pâteuse est ta luette,
Ruminant! Tu n'as pas L'INSOMNIE, éveillé;
Tu n'as pas LE SOMMEIL, ô Sac ensommeillé!

YOU puffing on top of a spouse jammed under, CUD-CHEWER! dilating your bloodshot pupil; Do you know! ... Don't you know this sigh – WAKING! – that yawns in the sky, among the golden fibres of the sun and the wild mane of your fiery flaxen Goddess? ... – No! ... – Do you know the waking of the foul philosopher – the Pig – muttering his morning prayer; or the waking, old-age-pension certificate of the whore! ... Have you ever sounded the reveille for the pack; have you ever felt the muffled stirring of riot, or the leaden waking of the sick man at his end? ... Have you seen the stretching eye of the beggars of Naples? ... Do you know? ... don't you know the song of the lark? – No – Sticky are your eyelashes, clammy is your uvula, cud-chewer! Awake, you do not possess INSOMNIA; you do not have SLEEP, O torpid Sack!

Petite Mort pour rire

Va vite, léger peigneur de comètes!
Les herbes au vent seront tes cheveux;
De ton œil béant jailliront les feux
Follets, prisonniers dans les pauvres têtes ...

Les fleurs de tombeau qu'on nomme Amourettes
Foisonneront plein ton rire terreux ...
Et les myosotis, ces fleurs d'oubliettes ...
Ne fais pas le lourd: cercueils de poètes

Pour les croque-morts sont de simples jeux,
Boîtes à violon qui sonnent le creux ...
Ils te croiront mort! – Les bourgeois sont bêtes –
Va vite, léger peigneur de comètes!

A Killing little Joke

Go swiftly, fleet-footed comber of comets! The grass in the wind will be your hair; from your gaping eye will spurt will-o'-the-wisps, which lie imprisoned in wretched heads ...

The funeral flowers they call lilies-of-the-valley will people in abundance your earthy laugh ... and the forget-me-nots, those dungeon-flowers ... Don't make heavy weather of it: coffins of poets

Are child's play for undertakers' mutes, violin cases with a hollow ring ... They'll think you are dead – The bourgeois are such fools – Go swiftly, fleet-footed comber of comets!

Épitaphe

pour
Tristan Joachim-Édouard Corbière, Philosophe, Épave, Mort-né

Mélange adultère de tout:
De la fortune et pas le sou,
De l'énergie et pas de force,
La Liberté, mais une entorse.
Du cœur, du cœur! de l'âme, non –
Des amis, pas un compagnon,
De l'idée et pas une idée,
De l'amour et pas une aimée,
La paresse et pas le repos.
Vertus chez lui furent défauts,
Ame blasée inassouvie.
Mort, mais pas guéri de la vie,
Gâcheur de vie hors de propos
Le corps à sec et la tête ivre,
Espérant, niant l'avenir,
Il mourut en s'attendant vivre
Et vécut s'attendant mourir.

Epitaph

for
Tristan-Joachim-Édouard Corbière, Philosopher, Waif, Still-born Child

Adulterous mixture of all things: riches yet not a penny, energy and no strength, Freedom, but a sprained ankle. Heart, lots of heart! soul, no – friends, but no companion, a mind but not an idea, love and no one to love, laziness and no rest. Virtues in him were defects,[1] that surfeited unsatisfied soul. Dead, but not cured of living, an irrelevant bungler of life with body dried up and drunken head, hoping, denying the future, he died expecting to live and lived expecting to die.

[1]Some editions have '*firent défaut*' here. *Faire défaut* means 'to be lacking' or 'to default', ideas that the poem could incorporate, but I have taken the Pléiade edition's '*furent défauts*' as definitive.

Comte de Lautréamont
(1846–70)

This is the pen-name of Isidore-Lucien Ducasse, a mysterious and extreme Romantic born in Montevideo of French parents. He became known superficially in Parisian literary circles around 1867, and wrote nocturnally, accompanying his phrases with crashing piano chords. He could find no publisher in his lifetime for his complete *Chants de Maldoror*, a series of hallucinatory and disturbing prose-poems in which the Surrealists were to acknowledge an early and influential example of unconscious creation. The *Chants* were eventually published in Belgium in 1874, but despite the interest of Huysmans and Maeterlinck widespread attention to Lautréamont's work was delayed until well into this century.

Little is known of him. He was an intense, violent adolescent with a wild imagination, an insomniac who read voraciously in classical and English literature as well as French. Paranoid schizophrenia is a conceivable diagnosis for his condition, which included severe headaches, and the many bizarre and unverifiable stories about him include his supposed killing by secret police.

His hero (or anti-hero) Maldoror is one of the great rebels of literature. Satanic, sadistic and Promethean, he plunges his whole being resolutely into evil and monstrosity, breaking taboos in search of transcendence. The Chants are a sequence of apocalyptic transformations in which Lauréamont, alternately '*Je*' within Maldoror and an external narrator, gives free rein to his subconscious. But there is also a cold and disconcerting controlling mechanism within the diseased vision, the operation of a clearly defined will, and a lucid irony that treats the reader as a cretin.

Maldoror turns away from loathsome, hypocritical humanity and takes on the form of various animals. He is both primitive and advanced, bestial and sophisticated, capable of all metamorphoses and blasphemies. It is not pleasant reading, but it has a strange inverted beauty, and clearly prefigures Surrealism in its oneiric content and its frenetic yet lucid style.

Chants de Maldoror

Chant deuxième, strophe 13 (extrait)

... Que m'importe le jugement dernier! Ma raison ne s'envole jamais, comme je le disais pour vous tromper. Et, quand je commets un crime, je sais ce que je fais: je ne voulais pas faire autre chose! Debout sur le rocher, pendant que l'ouragan fouettait mes cheveux et mon manteau, j'épiais dans l'extase cette force de la tempête, s'acharnant sur un navire, sous un ciel sans étoiles. Je suivis, dans une attitude triomphante, toutes les péripéties de ce drame, depuis l'instant où le vaisseau jeta ses ancres, jusqu'au moment où il s'engloutit, habit fatal qui entraîna, dans les boyaux de la mer, ceux qui s'en étaient revêtus comme d'un manteau. Mais, l'instant s'approchait, où j'allais, moi-même, me mêler comme acteur à ces scènes de la nature bouleversée. Quand la place où le vaisseau avait soutenu le combat montra

The Hymns of Maldoror

Second Hymn, strophe 13 (extract)

... What does the last judgement matter to me! My reason never takes flight, as I said earlier to deceive you. And when I commit a crime, I know what I am doing: I did not wish to do otherwise! Standing on the rock, while the tempest lashed my hair and my cloak, I watched in ecstasy that force of the storm beating implacably against a ship, beneath a starless sky. I followed, my posture triumphant, all the vicissitudes of that drama, from the moment when the vessel cast its anchors to the moment when it was engulfed, a fatal garment that dragged down into the bowels of the sea all those who had wrapped themselves in it like a cloak. But the moment was approaching when I myself was to be involved as an actor in these scenes of natural convulsion. When the place where the vessel had waged

clairement que celui-ci avait été passer le reste de ses jours au rez-de-chaussée de la mer, alors, ceux qui avaient été emportés avec les flots reparurent en partie à la surface. Ils se prirent à bras-le-corps, deux par deux, trois par trois; c'était le moyen de ne pas sauver leur vie; car, leurs mouvements devenaient embarrassés, et ils coulaient bas comme des cruches percées ... Quelle est cette armée de monstres marins qui fend les flots avec vitesse? Ils sont six; leurs nageoires sont vigoureuses, et s'ouvrent un passage, à travers les vagues soulevées. De tous ces êtres humains, qui remuent les quatre membres dans ce continent peu ferme, les requins ne font bientôt qu'une omelette sans œufs, et se la partagent d'après la loi du plus fort. Le sang se mêle aux eaux, et les eaux se mêlent au sang. Leurs yeux féroces éclairent suffisamment la scène du carnage ... Mais, quel est encore ce tumulte des eaux, là-bas, à l'horizon? On dirait une trombe qui s'approche. Quels coups de rame! J'aperçois ce que c'est. Une énorme femelle de requin vient prendre part au pâté de foie de canard, et manger du bouilli froid. Elle est furieuse;

its combat showed clearly that it had gone to spend the rest of its days on the ground floor of the sea, then those who had been carried away on the waters reappeared in part on the surface. They grasped each other round the waist, two by two, three by three; it was the way not to save their lives; for their movements were hampered, and they sank like broken jugs ... What is this army of sea monsters cleaving the waters at high speed? There are six of them; their fins are vigorous and open a passage through the rising waves. Of all those human beings, moving their four limbs in that unstable continent, the sharks soon make just an omelette without eggs, and distribute it according to the law of the strongest. Blood mingles with the waters, and the waters mingle with blood. Their ferocious eyes are sufficient light for the scene of carnage ... But what is this new turmoil in the waters, there, on the horizon? It looks like an approaching waterspout. What oar strokes! I perceive what it is. A huge female shark comes to share in the duck's liver pâté, and to eat cold beef broth. She is enraged, for she arrives

car, elle arrive affamée. Une lutte s'engage entre elle et les requins, pour se disputer les quelques membres palpitants qui flottent par-ci, par-là, sans rien dire, sur la surface de la crème rouge. A droite, à gauche, elle lance des coups de dent qui engendrent des blessures mortelles. Mais, trois requins vivants l'entourent encore, et elle est obligée de tourner en tous sens, pour déjouer leurs manœuvres. Avec une émotion croissante, inconnue jusqu'alors, le spectateur, placé sur le rivage, suit cette bataille navale d'un nouveau genre. Il a les yeux fixés sur cette courageuse femelle de requin, aux dents si fortes. Il n'hésite plus, il épaule son fusil, et, avec son adresse habituelle, il loge sa deuxième balle dans l'ouïe d'un des requins, au moment où il se montrait au-dessus d'une vague. Restent deux requins qui n'en témoignent qu'un acharnement plus grand. Du haut du rocher, l'homme à la salive saumâtre, se jette à la mer, et nage vers le tapis agréablement coloré, en tenant à la main ce couteau d'acier qui ne l'abandonne jamais. Désormais, chaque requin a affaire à un ennemi. Il s'avance vers son adversaire fatigué, et, prenant son temps, lui enfonce dans le

hungry. A combat begins between her and the sharks over the few palpitating limbs floating here and there, with nothing to say, on the surface of the red cream. To right and left she hurls bites that beget mortal wounds. But three living sharks still surround her, and she must turn in all directions to foil their manoeuvres. With a growing emotion until then unknown, the spectator standing on the shore follows this new form of naval battle. His eyes are fixed on this brave female shark with such strong teeth. With no more hesitation he shoulders his gun, and, with his habitual skill, he lodges his second bullet in the gills of one of the sharks, at the instant when it showed itself above a wave. There remain two sharks who demonstrate only greater fury. From high on his rock, the man with brackish saliva hurls himself into the sea and swims towards the pleasantly coloured carpet, holding in his hand that steel knife that never leaves him. Henceforward each shark must deal with an enemy. He advances towards his weary adversary and,

ventre sa lame aiguë. La citadelle mobile se débarrasse facilement du dernier adversaire ... Se trouvent en présence le nageur et la femelle de requin, sauvée par lui. Ils se regardèrent entre les yeux pendant quelques minutes; et chacun s'étonna de trouver tant de férocité dans les regards de l'autre. Ils tournent en rond en nageant, ne se perdent pas de vue, et se disent à part soi: "Je me suis trompé jusqu'ici; en voilà un qui est plus méchant." Alors, d'un commun accord, entre deux eaux, ils glissèrent l'un vers l'autre, avec une admiration mutuelle, la femelle de requin écartant l'eau de ses nageoires, Maldoror battant l'onde avec ses bras; et retirent leur souffle, dans une vénération profonde, chacun désireux de contempler, pour la première fois, son portrait vivant. Arrivés à trois mètres de distance, sans faire aucun effort, ils tombèrent brusquement l'un contre l'autre, comme deux aimants, et s'embrassèrent avec dignité et reconnaissance, dans une étreinte aussi tendre que celle d'un frère ou d'une sœur. Les désirs charnels suivirent de près cette démonstration d'amitié. Deux cuisses nerveuses se

taking his time, plunges his sharp blade into its belly. The fortress in motion easily disposes of the last opponent ... The swimmer and the female shark saved by him find themselves facing one another. They looked each other in the eyes for some minutes; and each was astounded to find so much ferocity in the gaze of the other. They swim in a circle, not losing sight of each other, each saying aside: 'I have been wrong until now; here is one who is more wicked.' Then, with common accord, just beneath the surface, they glided towards each other in mutual admiration, the female shark casting aside the water with her fins, Maldoror beating the waves with his arms; and held their breath in deep veneration, each wanting to contemplate for the first time his living image. Reaching a distance of three metres, without any effort, they fell abruptly one against the other like two magnets, clasped in an embrace of dignity and gratitude as tenderly as brother or sister. Carnal desires followed close on this demonstration of friendship. Two

collèrent étroitement à la peau visqueuse du monstre, comme deux sangsues; et, les bras et les nageoires entrelacés autour du corps de l'objet aimé qu'ils entouraient avec amour, tandis que leurs gorges et leurs poitrines ne faisaient bientôt plus qu'une masse glauque aux exhalaisons de goëmon; au milieu de la tempête qui continuait de sévir; à la lueur des éclairs; ayant pour lit d'hyménée la vague écumeuse, emportés par un courant sous-marin comme dans un berceau, et roulant, sur eux-mêmes, vers les profondeurs inconnues de l'abîme, ils se réunirent dans un accouplement long, chaste et hideux! ... Enfin, je venais de trouver quelqu'un qui me ressemblât ... Désormais, je n'étais plus seul dans la vie! ... Elle avait les mêmes idées que moi! ... J'étais en face de mon premier amour!

muscular loins clung tightly to the monster's viscous skin, like two leeches; and, arms and fins entwined around the body of the beloved object, surrounding it with love, while their throats and chests were soon no more than a glaucous mass exhaling the odour of seaweed; in the midst of the storm that continued to rage; by the light of lightning; having for marriage bed the foaming wave, borne away by an underwater current as if in a cradle, and rolling over one another, towards the unknown depths of the abyss, they were joined in a long, chaste and hideous coupling! ... At last I had found someone who resembled me! ... Henceforward I was no longer alone in life! ... She was of the same mind as I! ... I was in the presence of my first love!

Chant quatrième, strophe 6 (extrait)

Je rêvais que j'étais entré dans le corps d'un pourceau, qu'il ne m'était pas facile d'en sortir, et que je vautrais mes poils dans les marécages les plus fangeux. Était-ce comme une récompense? Objet de mes vœux, je n'appartenais plus à l'humanité! Pour moi, j'entendis l'interprétation ainsi, et j'en éprouvai une joie plus que profonde. Cependant, je recherchais activement quel acte de vertu j'avais accompli pour mériter, de la part de la Providence, cette insigne faveur. Maintenant que j'ai repassé dans ma mémoire les diverses phases de cet aplatissement épouvantable contre le ventre du granit, pendant lequel la marée, sans que je m'en aperçusse, passa, deux fois, sur ce mélange irréductible de matière morte et de chair vivante, il n'est peut-être pas sans utilité de proclamer que cette dégradation n'était probablement qu'une punition, réalisée sur moi par la justice divine. Mais, qui connaît ses besoins intimes ou la cause de

Fourth Hymn, strophe 6 (extract)

I was dreaming that I had entered into the body of a hog, that I could not easily get out, and that I was wallowing my hair in the foulest of swamps. Was this as a reward? Object of my desires, I no longer belonged to humanity! For myself, so I understood the interpretation, and I experienced a more than profound joy. And yet, I searched actively to know what virtuous deed I had accomplished to deserve, from the hands of Providence, this distinguished favour. Now that I have reviewed in my memory the different phases of that dreadful prostration against the granite belly, during which the tide, unseen by me, passed twice over that irreducible mixture of dead matter and living flesh, it is perhaps not without value to proclaim that that degradation was probably only a punishment executed on me by divine justice. But who can know his intimate needs or the cause of his pestilential joys! The

ses joies pestilentielles! La métamorphose ne parut jamais à mes yeux que comme le haut et magnanime retentissement d'un bonheur parfait, que j'attendais depuis longtemps. Il était enfin venu, le jour où je fus un pourceau! J'essayai mes dents sur l'écorce des arbres; mon groin, je le contemplais avec délice. Il ne restait plus la moindre parcelle de divinité: je sus élever mon âme jusqu'à l'excessive hauteur de cette volupté ineffable. Écoutez-moi donc, et ne rougissez pas, inépuisables caricatures du beau, qui prenez au sérieux le braiement risible de votre âme, souverainement méprisable; et qui ne comprenez pas pourquoi le Tout-puissant, dans un rare moment de bouffonnerie excellente, qui, certainement, ne dépasse pas les grandes lois générales du grotesque, prit, un jour, le mirifique plaisir de faire habiter une planète par des êtres singuliers et microscopiques, qu'on appelle *humains*, et dont la matière ressemble à celle du corail vermeil. Certes, vous avez raison de rougir, os et graisse, mais écoutez-moi. Je n'invoque pas votre intelligence; vous la feriez rejeter du

metamorphosis never appeared in my eyes as anything but the lofty and magnanimous reverberation of a perfect happiness that I had long awaited. It had come at last, the day when I was a hog! I tested my teeth on the bark of the trees; I contemplated my snout with delight. There remained not the slightest particle of divinity: I was able to elevate my soul to the exorbitant height of this ineffable voluptuousness. Now listen to me, and do not blush, you inexhaustible caricatures of beauty, who take seriously the ridiculous braying of your superlatively contemptible soul; and you who do not understand why the All-powerful, in a rare moment of exquisite buffoonery that certainly does not surpass the great general laws of the grotesque, indulged himself one day in the admirable pleasure of peopling a planet with odd microscopic beings called *humans*, whose substance resembles that of rosy coral. True, you have reason to blush, bones and fat, but listen to me. I am not invoking your intelligence; you would make it spit blood by the

sang par l'horreur qu'elle vous témoigne: oubliez-là, et soyez conséquents avec vous-mêmes ... Là, plus de contrainte. Quand je voulais tuer, je tuais; cela, même, m'arrivait souvent, et personne ne m'en empêchait. Les lois humaines me poursuivaient encore de leur vengeance, quoique je n'attaquasse pas la race que j'avais abandonnée si tranquillement; mais ma conscience ne me faisait aucun reproche. Pendant la journée, je me battais avec mes nouveaux semblables, et le sol était parsemé de nombreuses couches de sang caillé. J'étais le plus fort, et je remportais toutes les victoires. Des blessures cuisantes couvraient mon corps; je faisais semblant de ne pas m'en apercevoir. Les animaux terrestres s'éloignaient de moi, et je restais seul dans ma resplendissante grandeur. Quel ne fut pas mon étonnement, quand, après avoir traversé un fleuve à la nage, pour m'éloigner des contrées que ma rage avait dépeuplées, et gagner d'autres campagnes pour y planter mes coutumes de meurtre et de carnage, j'essayai de marcher sur cette rive

horror to which it testifies: forget it, and be consistent with yourselves ... In this form, no more constraints. When I wanted to kill, I killed; that even happened to me often, and no one stood in my way. Human laws pursued me still with their vengeance, though I did not attack the race which I had abandoned so calmly; but my conscience gave me no reproach. During the day I fought with my new peers, and the soil was spattered with many layers of coagulated blood. I was the strongest, and all victories were mine. Piercing wounds covered my body; I pretended not to notice them. The animals of the earth shunned me, and I remained alone in my resplendent greatness. Imagine my astonishment when, after swimming across a river to journey away from the lands that my fury had depopulated, and to reach other countries to implant there my customs of murder and slaughter, I tried to walk upon that

fleurie. Mes pieds étaient paralysés; aucun mouvement ne venait trahir la vérité de cette immobilité forcée. Au milieu d'efforts surnaturels, pour continuer mon chemin, ce fut alors que je me réveillai, et que je sentis que je redevenais homme. La Providence me faisait ainsi comprendre, d'une manière qui n'est pas inexplicable, qu'elle ne voulait pas que, même en rêve, mes projets sublimes s'accomplissent. Revenir à ma forme primitive fut pour moi une douleur si grande, que, pendant les nuits, j'en pleure encore. Mes draps sont constamment mouillés, comme s'ils avaient été passés dans l'eau, et, chaque jour, je les fais changer. Si vous ne le croyez pas, venez me voir; vous contrôlerez, par votre propre expérience, non pas las vraisemblance, mais, en outre, la vérité même de mon assertion. Combien de fois, depuis cette nuit passée à la belle étoile, sur une falaise, ne me suis-je pas mêlé à des troupeaux de pourceaux, pour reprendre, comme un droit, ma métamorphose détruit! Il est temps de quitter ces souvenirs glorieux, qui ne laissent, après leur suite, que la pâle voie lactée des regrets éternels.

flowering bank. My feet were paralysed, no movement came that might betray the truth of that forced immobility. Amid preternatural efforts to continue on my way, it was then that I awoke, and sensed that I was becoming a man once more. Thus Providence gave me to understand, in an inexplicable way, that it did not wish my sublime projects to be realized even in dreams. The return to my primitive form was so painful to me that I still weep over it at night. My sheets are constantly wet as if they had been steeped in water, and each day I have them changed. If you do not believe it, come to see me; you will verify through your own experience not the verisimilitude but, beyond that, the very truth of my assertion. How many times, since that night passed under the stars, on a clifftop, have I not mingled with herds of hogs, to recapture as a right my destroyed metamorphosis! It is time to abandon these glorious memories, which leave behind after their effect only the pale milky way of eternal yearnings.

Germain Nouveau
(1851–1920)

A friend of Cros, Mallarmé, Verlaine and Rimbaud (he travelled to England with Rimbaud during Verlaine's imprisonment), Nouveau was an enigmatic and restless poet who used a variety of pseudonyms and took no interest in the publication of his work, at times even opposing it actively.

Born at Pourrières (Var), he went to Paris in 1872 after brilliant studies at Aix-en-Provence, and made some impact on the literary scene, but left the city and drifted through a succession of provincial teaching jobs. Towards the end of his life he became an ascetic wandering beggar, disowning possessions and living on charity, back in his native region. He received periodic treatment for mental disorders (including mystical delirium) and alcoholic debilitation, and died in his home village.

His religious conversion had led him to envisage a rather Hugolian multiple hymn to existence called '*La Doctrine de l'Amour*'. He made some progress in its composition, expressing in a mosaic of poems an ecstatic, sensual response to both profane and divine beauty. His work, often based on traditional ballad and madrigal forms, is uneven in quality, but his best pieces have been highly praised by modern poets including Breton, Eluard and Aragon. He blends musical delicacy and verbal inventiveness with irony and Gallic bluntness in a style that can resemble at different times that of Verlaine, of Corbière and of Rimbaud, and the influences may well have been mutual.

Nouveau's poetry was published in a piecemeal way, but there are five identifiable groupings: *Premiers Poèmes*, *Dixains réalistes*, *La Doctrine de l'Amour*, *Valentines* and *Ave Maris Stella*. They were gathered finally into a Pléiade edition of his *Oeuvres Complètes* in 1970 (combined with Lautréamont).

Poison perdu

Des nuits du blond et de la brune
Rien dans la chambre n'est resté;
Pas une dentelle d'été,
Pas une cravate commune.

Rien sur le balcon où le thé
Se prend aux heures de la lune.
Ils n'ont laissé de trace aucune,
Aucun souvenir n'est resté.

Au bord d'un rideau bleu piquée
Luit une épingle à tête d'or,
Comme un gros insecte qui dort.

Pointe d'un fin poison trempée,
Je te prends: sois-moi préparée
Aux heures des désirs de mort.

Poison lost

Of the nights of the fair man and the dark-haired woman nothing has remained in the room; not a summer lace, not a commonplace tie.

Nothing on the balcony where tea is taken in the moonlit hours. They have left not a trace, no memory has remained.

Caught on the hem of a blue curtain gleams a pin with a golden head, like a great sleeping insect.

Tip steeped in a refined poison, I'll take you: be ready for me when death is desired.

Mendiants

Pendant qu'hésite encor ton pas sur la prairie,
Le pays s'est de ciel houleux enveloppé.
Tu cèdes, l'œil levé vers la nuagerie,
A ce doux midi blême et plein d'osier coupé.

Nous avons tant suivi le mur de mousse grise
Qu'à la fin, à nos flancs qu'une douleur emplit,
Non moins bon que ton sein, tiède comme l'église,
Ce fossé s'est ouvert aussi sûr que le lit.

Dédoublement sans fin d'un typique fantôme,
Que l'or de ta prunelle était peuplé de rois!
Est-ce moi qui riais à travers ce royaume?
Je tenais la martyre, ayant ses bras en croix.

Beggars

While your step still hesitates on the meadow, the land has been shrouded by a turbulent sky. You surrender, eyes raised towards the cloud formations, to this sweet sallow noon full of cut willow.

We followed so long the wall of grey moss that at last, for our flanks filled with pain, no less kind than your breast, as warm as the church, this ditch opened, as secure as the bed.

Endless doubling of a symbolical chimera, how the gold of your pupil was thronged with kings! Was that me laughing through that kingdom? I was holding the martyr, her arms forming a cross.

Le fleuve au loin, le ciel en deuil, l'eau de tes lèvres,
Immense trilogie amère aux cœurs noyés,
Un goût m'est revenu de nos plus forts genièvres,
Lorsque ta joue a lui, près des yeux dévoyés!

Et pourtant, oh! pourtant, des seins de l'innocente
Et de nos doigts, sonnant, vers notre rêve éclos
Sur le ventre gentil comme un tambour qui chante,
Dianes aux désirs, et charger aux sanglots,

De ton attifement de boucles et de ganses,
Vieux Bébé, de tes cils essuyés simplement,
Et de vos piétés, et de vos manigances
Qui m'auraient bien pu rendre aussi chien que l'amant,

Il ne devait rester qu'une ironie immonde,
Une langueur des yeux détournés sans effort.
Quel bras, impitoyable aux Échappés du monde,
Te pousse à l'Est, pendant que je me sauve au Nord!

The distant river, the sky in mourning, the water of your lips, vast bitter trilogy for drowned hearts, a taste came back to me of our strongest junipers, when your cheek shone, close by the errant eyes!

And yet, oh! yet, of the breasts of the innocent girl and of our fingers, ringing, towards our dream made manifest on the graceful stomach like a singing drum, sounding reveilles to desires and the charge to sobs,

Of your adornment of buckles and braids, old Baby, of your lashes naïvely wiped dry, and of your pieties, and of your schemings, which could well have made me as doglike as the lover,

Nothing was to remain but a foul irony, a listlessness in the eyes turned aside without effort. What arm, relentless towards the Fugitives of the world, drives you to the East, while I escape to the North!

Pourrières

Un vieux clocher coiffé de fer sur la colline.
Des fenêtres sans cris, sous des toits sans oiseaux.
D'un barbaresque Azur la paix du Ciel s'incline.
Soleil dur! Mort de l'ombre! Et Silence des Eaux.

Marius! son fantôme à travers les roseaux,
Par la plaine! Un son lent de l'Horloge féline.
Quatre enfants sur la place où l'ormeau perd ses os,
Autour d'un Pauvre, étrange, avec sa mandoline.

Un banc de pierre chaud comme un pain dans le four,
Où trois Vieux, dans ce coin de la Gloire du Jour,
Sentent au rayon vif cuire leur vieillesse.

Pourrières

An old steeple topped with iron on the hill. Windows without shouts, under roofs without birds. From a Barbary Blue sky the peace of heaven bows low. Unyielding sun! Death of shadow! And Silence of the Waters.

Marius![1] his ghost through the reeds, across the plain! A slow tone from the feline Clock. Four children on the market square where the young elm is losing its bones, around a Pauper, a strange man, with his mandolin.

A warm stone bench like a loaf in the oven, where three Old Men, in this corner of the Halo of the Day,[2] feel their old age baking in the ardent ray.

[1]Marius defeated the Teutons in 102 B.C. The field is near Pourrières.
[2]The stone bench is at the entrance to the village bistrot, the Cercle Saint-Hubert.

Babet revient du bois, tenant sa mule en laisse.
Noir, le Vicaire au loin voit, d'une ombre au ton bleu,
Le Village au soleil fumer vers le Bon Dieu.

Babet comes back from the wood, with his mule on a string. Black in the distance, the Curate sees, from a blue-toned shadow, the Village rising in smoke in the sunlight towards the Good Lord.

Arthur Rimbaud
(1854–91)

An uncompromising, anti-social adolescent genius, Rimbaud occupies a unique place in world literature. His poetic development was alarmingly accelerated, and came to an equally startling and definitive end.

At sixteen he could parody the style of most known poets, and his home town of Charleville became, along with his repressive home and educational background, the first butt of his own iconoclastic talent. Only his literature teacher, Georges Izambard, was exempt. Rimbaud set off in the turbulent summer of 1870 for Paris, on foot. Removal home after his arrest for 'vagabondage' was ineffective. He set out again for Douai, Charleroi and Brussels, then eventually back to Paris at the end of February 1871, where a profound personal and artistic crisis coincided with the days of the Commune. The *Lettre du Voyant*, a key document in the history of poetry, was written from Charleville in May.

Later that year he became the flea-ridden sensation of the Paris avant-garde, the protégé of Verlaine and the destroyer of his domestic harmony. After a period of depression at Charleville early in 1872 he returned to Paris, before starting the erratic odyssey with Verlaine that ended with the shooting incident in Brussels (see page 224).

It is known that Rimbaud finished the prose-poem collection *Une Saison en Enfer*, an artistic whole culminating in his farewell to poetry, in 1873. The problem of dating *Les Illuminations* has vexed researchers for over a century, and these visionary but disjointed prose-poems may well originate in several different phases of his experience, some perhaps even post-dating *Une Saison en Enfer*. Verlaine was responsible for their eventual publication as an integrated volume in 1886.

Rimbaud's response to the artistic impasse he reached was to abandon literature. He left Europe for a nomadic life of soldiering (and desertion), trading in Cyprus and Aden, and even illegal arms-trafficking in Abyssinia. He returned to France in 1891 with a gangrenous tumour on his knee, and died shortly afterwards.

In 1871 Rimbaud had seen in poetry the potential to change life where political revolution had failed, and what had been in him a generalized and anarchic revolt took a more specific and conscious artistic direction. This revolutionary project, involving a total commitment of the poet to experience, is set out in the *Lettre du Voyant*. In this exuberant, arrogant manifesto he dismisses a great body of poetry, including some of his own, as lacking in Vision ('*Voyance*'). The genius of many poets, where it has existed, has been an accidental, unconscious gift. His genius will have conscious control over its creative powers in their journey through '*Correspondances*', destroying the old rhetoric that enslaved even his predecessor Baudelaire, and searching dynamically for radically original forms of expression. He will pursue self-knowledge to an extreme degree to discover and communicate his deepest impulses, however irrational, discontinuous and disturbing both the process and its expression may be, and even if calculated self-destruction and degradation are to be the price of that knowledge. Penetrating far beyond Baudelaire's experience, it will be a 'long, immense and reasoned disordering of all the senses ...' in which the artist becomes 'the great sick man, the great criminal, the great outcast ...' but most importantly 'the Supreme Sage ... for he arrives at the unknown'. In this ineffable torture, he 'consumes all the poisons within him, keeping only their quintessences'. Disruption of the normal workings of the mind (through sleep deprivation, alcohol, drugs, solitude, sickness, unorthodox sexual experience ...) will be carried out with lucid control, and the personality that emerges out of euphoria and horror will be the prototype of a new human being. Thus the purpose is moral and social as well as aesthetic, and the poet is to be a 'multiplier of progress'. His language will be new, it will be 'of the soul, for the soul, encompassing everything, scents, sounds, colours, thought hooking on to thought and pulling'.

In practice, '*Voyance*' becomes a plunge into subjectivity, illuminating and inspirational but fragmented and ultimately uncommunicable. Though each poem justifies itself independently of 'meaning' in the conventional sense, he recognizes finally that his Alchemy of the Word is for him only: 'I alone have the key to this savage Parade'. He had indeed foreseen this in the *Lettre*. But his Promethean effort multiplies infinitely the potential of poetry as a vehicle for the inflamed imagination, for the spontaneous, discontinuous yet lucid activity of the revealed Unconscious. He throws off the shackles of versification, via some experimentation with free-verse forms, to produce vivid, rhythmic prose-poems of great associative power. Though subjectivity limits our ability to follow him, we need not share his mockery of his own hubris, and the subsequent history of poetry has fulfilled his prophecy that 'more horrible workers will come; they will begin at the horizons where the other has collapsed!'

A la Musique

Place de la Gare, à Charleville

Sur la place taillée en mesquines pelouses,
Square où tout est correct, les arbres et les fleurs,
Tous les bourgeois poussifs qu'étranglent les chaleurs
Portent, les jeudis soirs, leurs bêtises jalouses.

– L'orchestre militaire, au milieu du jardin,
Balance ses schakos dans la *Valse des fifres:*
– Autour, aux premiers rangs, parade le gandin;
Le notaire pend à ses breloques à chiffres.

Des rentiers à lorgnons soulignent tous les couacs:
Les gros bureaux bouffis traînent leurs grosses dames
Auprès desquelles vont, officieux cornacs,
Celles dont les volants ont des airs de réclames;

To Music

Station Square, Charleville

On the square chopped squarely into mean little lawns, an all-correct square with trees and flowers, all the wheezy well-to-do, stifled by the heat, bring each Thursday evening their envious stupidity.

– The military band, in the middle of the garden, nod their shakos in the *Waltz of the Fifes*: – Around them in the front rows the town dandy struts; the notary hangs from his own trinketed watch-chain.

Men of independent means in pince-nez point out all the wrong notes: great bloated bureaucrats dragging their fat ladies flanked by an officious female retinue of elephant-keepers, whose flounces look like advertisements.

Sur les bancs verts, des clubs d'épiciers retraités
Qui tisonnent le sable avec leur canne à pomme,
Fort sérieusement discutent les traités,
Puis prisent en argent, et reprennent: "En somme! ..."

Épatant sur son banc les rondeurs de ses reins,
Un bourgeois à boutons clairs, bedaine flamande,
Savoure son onnaing d'où le tabac par brins
Déborde – vous savez, c'est de la contrebande; –

Le long des gazons verts ricanent les voyous;
Et, rendus amoureux par le chant des trombones,
Très naïfs, et fumant des roses, les pioupious
Caressent les bébés pour enjôler les bonnes ...

On the green benches, clubs of retired grocers, poking the gravel with their pommelled sticks, discuss trade agreements with gravity, then take snuff from silver boxes, and resume: 'In short! ...'

Spreading over his bench the whole roundness of his rump, a burgher with bright buttons, a Flemish paunch, savours his Onnaing pipe overflowing with tobacco — it's contraband, you realize; –

Along the green lawns the yobs go sniggering; and, their thoughts turned to love by the song of the trombones, very naïve, and smoking pinks,[1] the little red soldiers fondle the babies to seduce the nursemaids ...

[1]A type of cigarette.

– Moi, je suis, débraillé comme un étudiant,
Sous les marronniers verts les alertes fillettes:
Elles le savent bien; et tournent en riant,
Vers moi, leurs yeux tout pleins de choses indiscrètes.

Je ne dis pas un mot: je regarde toujours
La chair de leurs cous blancs brodés de mèches folles:
Je suis, sous le corsage et les frêles atours,
Le dos divin après la courbe des épaules.

J'ai bientôt déniché la bottine, le bas ...
– Je reconstruis les corps, brûlé de belles fièvres.
Elles me trouvent drôle et se parlent tout bas ...
– Et mes désirs brutaux s'accrochent à leurs lèvres ...

– As for me, I follow, dishevelled like a student, the lively little girls under the green chestnut trees: they know it very well; and turn towards me, laughing, their eyes full of indiscreet things.

I say not a word: I keep on looking at the flesh of their white necks embroidered with stray curls: I follow, beneath the bodice and the flimsy finery, the heavenly back below the curve of the shoulders.

Soon I've hunted out the ankle-boot, the stocking ... – I reconstruct their bodies, burning with fine fevers. They find me peculiar and whisper to each other ... – And my brutal desires clutch at their lips ...

Ma Bohème

(Fantaisie)

Je m'en allais, les poings dans mes poches crevées;
Mon paletot aussi devenait idéal;
J'allais sous le ciel, Muse! et j'étais ton féal;
Oh! là là! que d'amours splendides j'ai rêvées!

Mon unique culotte avait un large trou.
– Petit-Poucet rêveur, j'égrenais dans ma course
Des rimes. Mon auberge était à la Grande-Ourse.
– Mes étoiles au ciel avaient un doux frou-frou

Et je les écoutais, assis au bord des routes,
Ces bons soirs de septembre où je sentais des gouttes
De rosée à mon front, comme un vin de vigueur;

My Bohemian Life

(Caprice)

Off I went with my fists in my punctured pockets; my greatcoat too was becoming ideal; on I went beneath the sky, Muse! and I was your trusty vassal; oh my word! what splendid loves I dreamed!

My only pair of breeches had a big hole. – A dreamy Tom Thumb, shelling out rhymes on my path. My inn was at the sign of the Great Bear. – My stars in the sky made gentle rustling noises.

And I listened to them, sitting on the roadsides, on those good September evenings when I felt drops of dew on my forehead like invigorating wine;

Où, rimant au milieu des ombres fantastiques,
Comme des lyres, je tirais les élastiques
De mes souliers blessés, un pied près de mon cœur!

When, rhyming amid fantastical shadows, I plucked like lyre-strings the elastics of my afflicted boots, one foot close to my heart!

Oraison du soir

Je vis assis, tel qu'un ange aux mains d'un barbier,
Empoignant une chope à fortes cannelures,
L'hypogastre et le col cambrés, une Gambier
Aux dents, sous l'air gonflé d'impalpables voilures.

Tels que les excréments chauds d'un vieux colombier,
Mille Rêves en moi font de douces brûlures:
Puis par instants mon cœur triste est comme un aubier
Qu'ensanglante l'or jeune et sombre des coulures.

Evening Prayer

I spend my life sitting, like an angel in the hands of a barber, gripping a deeply fluted tankard in my fist, abdomen and neck arched, a Gambier pipe between my teeth, beneath the air distended with impalpable sails.

Just like the warm excrements of an old dovecote, a thousand Dreams burn softly inside me: then at moments my sad heart is like sap-wood bled upon by the dark yellow gold of its secretions.

Puis, quand j'ai ravalé mes Rêves avec soin,
Je me tourne, ayant bu trente ou quarante chopes,
Et me recueille, pour lâcher l'âcre besoin:

Doux comme le Seigneur du cèdre et des hysopes,
Je pisse vers les cieux bruns, très haut et très loin,
Avec l'assentiment des grands héliotropes.

Then, when I have carefully swallowed my Dreams, I turn around, having drunk thirty or forty tankards, and collect myself, to relieve pungent need:

As sweetly as the Lord of cedar and hyssops I piss towards the dusky heavens, very high and very far, with the scented acquiescence of the great heliotropes.

Le Cœur volé

Mon triste cœur bave à la poupe,
Mon cœur couvert de caporal:
Ils y lancent des jets de soupe,
Mon triste cœur bave à la poupe:
Sous les quolibets de la troupe
Qui pousse un rire général,
Mon triste cœur bave à la poupe,
Mon cœur couvert de caporal!

The Stolen Heart

My sad heart is dribbling at the stern, my heart strewn with rough tobacco: they're squirting jets of soup over it, my sad heart is dribbling at the stern: under the jibes of the crew, laughing in chorus, my sad heart is dribbling at the stern, my heart strewn with rough tobacco.

Ithyphalliques et pioupiesques,
Leurs quolibets l'ont dépravé!
Au gouvernail on voit des fresques
Ithyphalliques et pioupiesques.
O flots abracadabrantesques,
Prenez mon cœur, qu'il soit lavé!
Ithyphalliques et pioupiesques,
Leurs quolibets l'ont dépravé!

Quand ils auront tari leurs chiques,
Comment agir, ô cœur volé?
Ce seront des hoquets bachiques:
Quand ils auront tari leurs chiques:
J'aurai des sursauts stomachiques,
Moi, si mon cœur est ravalé:
Quand ils auront tari leurs chiques
Comment agir, ô cœur volé?

Ithyphallic and barrack-room, their jibes have corrupted it! On the helm there are ithyphallic and barrack-room frescoes. O abracadabrantic waves, take my heart, that it may be cleansed! Ithyphallic and barrack-room, their jibes have corrupted it!

When they have chewed their quids dry, what shall we do, O stolen heart? There will be Bacchic hiccups then: when they have chewed their quids dry: I shall have stomach-heavings, if my heart is degraded again: when they have chewed their quids dry what shall we do, O stolen heart?

Les Chercheuses de poux

Quand le front de l'enfant, plein de rouges tourmentes,
Implore l'essaim blanc des rêves indistincts,
Il vient près de son lit deux grandes sœurs charmantes
Avec de frêles doigts aux ongles argentins.

Elles assoient l'enfant devant une croisée
Grande ouverte où l'air bleu baigne un fouillis de fleurs,
Et dans ses lourds cheveux où tombe la rosée
Promènent leurs doigts fins, terribles et charmeurs.

Il écoute chanter leurs haleines craintives
Qui fleurent de longs miels végétaux et rosés,
Et qu'interrompt parfois un sifflement, salives
Reprises sur la lèvre ou désirs de baisers.

The Lice Seekers

When the child's brow, full of red torments, craves the white swarm of hazy dreams, there come near his bed two tall enchanting sisters with slender fingers and silvery nails.

They sit the child in front of a wide open casement where the blue air bathes a tangle of flowers, and into his dense hair, moistened by falling dew, they send their delicate, terrible, spellbinding fingers.

He listens to the song of their apprehensive breath, fragrant of thin roseate plant-honeys, interrupted now and then by a sibilant sound, saliva caught on the lip or desires for kisses.

Il entend leurs cils noirs battant sous les silences
Parfumés; et leurs doigts électriques et doux
Font crépiter parmi ses grises indolences
Sous leurs ongles royaux la mort des petits poux.

Voilà que monte en lui le vin de la Paresse,
Soupir d'harmonica qui pourrait délirer;
L'enfant se sent, selon la lenteur des caresses,
Sourdre et mourir sans cesse un désir de pleurer.

He hears their dark lashes beating in the scented silences; and their gentle electric fingers in his grey indolence bring beneath their queenly nails a crackling death to the little lice.

Now rises in him the wine of Lethargy, a harmonica sigh that could lead to delirium; the child senses within him, according to the slowness of the caresses, the ceaseless welling and dying of a desire to weep.

Voyelles

A noir, E blanc, I rouge, U vert, O bleu: voyelles,
Je dirai quelque jour vos naissances latentes:
A, noir corset velu des mouches éclatantes
Qui bombinent autour des puanteurs cruelles,

Vowels

A black, E white, I red, U green, O blue: vowels, one day I shall disclose your secret births: A, hairy black corset of dazzling flies buzzing around cruel smells,

Golfes d'ombre; E, candeurs des vapeurs et des tentes,
Lances des glaciers fiers, rois blancs, frissons d'ombelles;
I, pourpres, sang craché, rire des lèvres belles
Dans la colère ou les ivresses pénitentes;

U, cycles, vibrements divins des mers virides,
Paix des pâtis semés d'animaux, paix des rides
Que l'alchimie imprime aux grands fronts studieux;

O, suprême Clairon plein des strideurs étranges,
Silences traversés des Mondes et des Anges:
– O l'Oméga, rayon violet de Ses Yeux!

Gulfs of shadow; E, whiteness of vapours and of tents, lances of proud glaciers, white kings, the quiverings of umbels; I, crimsons, blood spat out, laughter of beautiful lips in anger or the intoxication of repentance;

U, cycles, divine vibration of viridescent seas, the peace of pastures dotted with animals, the peace of the furrows imprinted by alchemy on great studious brows;

O, supreme Clarion full of strange stridencies, silences traversed by Worlds and Angels: – O the Omega, the violet ray of Her Eyes![1]

[1]The ambiguity of '*Ses Yeux*' (are they the eyes of a man or woman, a human being or God?) is of course impossible to translate.

Le Bateau ivre

Comme je descendais des Fleuves impassibles,
Je ne me sentis plus guidé par les haleurs:
Des Peaux-Rouges criards les avaient pris pour cibles,
Les ayant cloués nus aux poteaux de couleurs.

J'étais insoucieux de tous les équipages,
Porteur de blés flamands ou de cotons anglais.
Quand avec mes haleurs ont fini ces tapages,
Les Fleuves m'ont laissé descendre où je voulais.

Dans les clapotements furieux des marées,
Moi, l'autre hiver, plus sourd que les cerveaux d'enfants,
Je courus! Et les Péninsules démarrées
N'ont pas subi tohu-bohus plus triomphants.

The Drunken Boat

As I was floating down impassive Rivers, I no longer felt myself guided by haulers: shrieking Redskins had taken them as targets, having nailed them naked to coloured stakes.

Carrying Flemish wheat or English cotton, I was heedless of all ships' crews. When that uproar was finished along with my haulers, the Rivers let me float down where I pleased.

In the ferocious chopping tidal pulls, last winter, more insensible than the minds of children, I ran! And the unmoored Peninsulas never underwent more triumphant chaos.

La tempête a béni mes éveils maritimes.
Plus léger qu'un bouchon j'ai dansé sur les flots
Qu'on appelle rouleurs éternels de victimes,
Dix nuits, sans regretter l'œil niais des falots!

Plus douce qu'aux enfants la chair des pommes sures,
L'eau verte pénétra ma coque de sapin
Et des taches de vins bleus et des vomissures
Me lava, dispersant gouvernail et grappin.

Et dès lors, je me suis baigné dans le Poème
De la Mer, infusé d'astres, et lactescent,
Dévorant les azurs verts; où, flottaison blême
Et ravie, un noyé pensif parfois descend;

Où, teignant tout à coup les bleuités, délires
Et rythmes lents sous les rutilements du jour,
Plus fortes que l'alcool, plus vastes que nos lyres,
Fermentent les rousseurs amères de l'amour!

The storm blessed my sea-borne awakenings. Lighter than a cork I danced on the waves which men call eternal rollers of victims, for ten nights, without missing the stupid eye of the harbour lights!

Sweeter than the flesh of sour apples for children, the green water penetrated my pinewood hull and washed me clean of blue wine stains and vomit, carrying away both rudder and anchor.

And since then I have bathed in the Poem of the Sea, infused with stars, lactescent, devouring the green azures; where, pallid and spellbound flotsam, a dreaming drowned man sometimes goes down;

Where, suddenly dyeing the bluenesses, deliriums and slow rhythms under the red glow of daylight, stronger than alcohol, more expansive than our lyres, ferment the bitter rednesses of love!

Je sais les cieux crevant en éclairs, et les trombes
Et les ressacs et les courants: je sais le soir,
L'Aube exaltée ainsi qu'un peuple de colombes,
Et j'ai vu quelquefois ce que l'homme a cru voir!

J'ai vu le soleil bas, taché d'horreurs mystiques,
Illuminant de longs figements violets,
Pareils à des acteurs de drames très-antiques
Les flots roulant au loin leurs frissons de volets!

J'ai rêvé la nuit verte aux neiges éblouies,
Baiser montant aux yeux des mers avec lenteurs,
La circulation des sèves inouïes,
Et l'éveil jaune et bleu des phosphores chanteurs!

J'ai suivi, des mois pleins, pareille aux vacheries
Hystériques, la houle à l'assaut des récifs,
Sans songer que les pieds lumineux des Maries
Pussent forcer le mufle aux Océans poussifs!

I know the skies that burst with lightning, and the waterspouts and the undertows and currents: I know the evening, the Dawn lifted up like a nation of doves, and I have seen sometimes what man has imagined he saw!

I have seen the low sun, stained with mystic horrors, casting long violet coagulations of light, like actors in most ancient dramas the waves shuddering into the distance like shutters!

I have dreamed of the green night with dazzled snows, a kiss rising slowly to the eyes of the seas, the circulation of unimagined sap, and the blue and yellow awakening of singing phosphorus!

I have followed for months on end, like hysterical cattle in their pen, the swell storming the reefs, never dreaming that the shining feet of the Marys could wrench around the muzzle of the wheezing Oceans!

J'ai heurté, savez-vous, d'incroyables Florides
Mêlant aux fleurs des yeux de panthères à peaux
D'hommes! Des arcs-en-ciel tendus comme des brides
Sous l'horizon des mers, à de glauques troupeaux!

J'ai vu fermenter les marais énormes, nasses
Où pourrit dans les joncs tout un Léviathan!
Des écroulements d'eaux au milieu des bonaces,
Et les lointains vers les gouffres cataractant!

Glaciers, soleils d'argent, flots nacreux, cieux de braises!
Echouages hideux au fond des golfes bruns
Où les serpents géants dévorés des punaises
Choient, des arbres tordus, avec de noirs parfums!

J'aurais voulu montrer aux enfants ces dorades
Du flot bleu, ces poissons d'or, ces poissons chantants.
– Des écumes de fleurs ont bercé mes dérades
Et d'ineffables vents m'ont ailé par instants.

I have collided, you know, with incredible Floridas where mingle with flowers the eyes of panthers in the skins of men! Rainbows stretched like bridles under the seas' horizon, around glaucous herds!

I have seen vast seething marshes, traps where a whole Leviathan lies rotting in the reeds! Water collapsing amidst perfect calm, and distances cataracting down towards the abyss!

Glaciers, silver suns, pearly waters, skies of glowing embers! Hideous strandings deep in dusky gulfs where giant snakes consumed by insect vermin fall, from the twisted trees, giving off black odours!

I would have liked to show to children those dolphins of the blue waves, those golden fish, those singing fish. – Foam of flowers cradled my wanderings and ineffable winds gave me wings now and then.

Parfois, martyr lassé des pôles et des zones,
La mer dont le sanglot faisait mon roulis doux
Montait vers moi ses fleurs d'ombre aux ventouses jaunes
Et je restais, ainsi qu'une femme à genoux ...

Presque île, ballottant sur mes bords les querelles
Et les fientes d'oiseaux clabaudeurs aux yeux blonds.
Et je voguais, lorsqu'à travers mes liens frêles
Des noyés descendaient dormir, à reculons!

Or moi, bateau perdu sous les cheveux des anses,
Jeté par l'ouragan dans l'éther sans oiseau,
Moi dont les Monitors et les voiliers des Hanses
N'auraient pas repêché la carcasse ivre d'eau;

Libre, fumant, monté de brumes violettes,
Moi qui trouais le ciel rougeoyant comme un mur
Qui porte, confiture exquise aux bons poètes,
Des lichens de soleil et des morves d'azur;

Sometimes, a martyr weary of poles and zones, the sea whose sobs softened my rolling lifted towards me its shadow-flowers with their yellow suckers and I remained suspended there, like a kneeling woman ...

Almost an island, tossing on my shores the squabbles and droppings of pale-eyed babbling birds. And I was sailing along, when across my frail ropes drowned men sank backwards into sleep! ...

Now I, a ship lost under the hair of coves, hurled by the hurricane into the birdless ether, I whose water-drunken carcass neither Monitors nor Hanseatic sailing ships would have fished up;

Free, smoking, risen from violet fogs, I who pierced the lurid red sky like a wall which bears, exquisite sweetmeats for good poets, lichens of sunlight and azure mucus;

Qui courais, taché de lunules électriques,
Planche folle, escorté des hippocampes noirs,
Quand les juillets faisaient crouler à coups de triques
Les cieux ultramarins aux ardents entonnoirs;

Moi qui tremblais, sentant geindre à cinquante lieues
Le rut des Béhémots et les Maelstroms épais,
Fileur éternel des immobilités bleues,
Je regrette l'Europe aux anciens parapets!

J'ai vu des archipels sidéraux! et des îles
Dont les cieux délirants sont ouverts au vogueur:
– Est-ce en ces nuits sans fonds que tu dors et t'exiles,
Million d'oiseaux d'or, ô future Vigueur?

Mais, vrai, j'ai trop pleuré! Les Aubes sont navrantes.
Toute lune est atroce et tout soleil amer:
L'âcre amour m'a gonflé de torpeurs enivrantes.
O que ma quille éclate! O que j'aille à la mer!

I who ran on, speckled with lunula of electricity, a crazy plank escorted by black sea-horses, when under cudgel blows Julys were crushing the ultramarine skies into burning funnels;

I who trembled as I felt at fifty leagues' distance the whine of rutting Behemoths and the dense Maelstroms, an eternal spinner of the blue immobilities, I yearn for Europe with its ancient parapets!

I have seen astral archipelagos! and islands whose delirious skies are open to the sailor: – Is it in those unfathomable nights that you are sleeping and in exile, you million golden birds, O Life Force of the future? –

But truly, I have wept too much! The Dawns are heartbreaking. Every moon is cruel and every sun is bitter: acrid love has distended me with intoxicating torpors. O let my keel split! O let me sink into the sea!

Si je désire une eau d'Europe, c'est la flache
Noire et froide où vers le crépuscule embaumé
Un enfant accroupi plein de tristesses, lâche
Un bateau frêle comme un papillon de mai.

Je ne puis plus, baigné de vos langueurs, ô lames,
Enlever leur sillage aux porteurs de cotons,
Ni traverser l'orgueil des drapeaux et des flammes,
Ni nager sous les yeux horribles des pontons.

If I long for European water, it is for the black cold puddle where towards the scented twilight a squatting child, full of sadness, launches a boat as fragile as a May butterfly.

No longer can I, bathed in your languors, O waves, follow in the wake of the carriers of cotton, nor cross the pride of flags and pennants, nor swim beneath the horrible eyes of prison hulks.

Mémoire

I

L'eau claire; comme le sel des larmes d'enfance,
L'assaut au soleil des blancheurs des corps de femme;
la soie, en foule et de lys pur, des oriflammes
sous les murs dont quelque pucelle eut la défense;

Memory

I

Clear water; like the salt of childhood tears, the assault on the sunlight of the whiteness of women's bodies; silk, a profusion of pure lily, banners beneath walls defended by some maiden;

l'ébat des anges; – Non ... le courant d'or en marche,
meut ses bras, noirs et lourds, et frais surtout, d'herbe. Elle
sombre, ayant le Ciel bleu pour ciel-de-lit, appelle
pour rideaux l'ombre de la colline et de l'arche.

II

Eh l'humide carreau tend ses bouillons limpides!
L'eau meuble d'or pâle et sans fond les couches prêtes;
Les robes vertes et déteintes des fillettes
font les saules, d'où sautent les oiseaux sans brides.

Plus pure qu'un louis, jaune et chaude paupière
le souci d'eau – ta foi conjugale, ô l'Épouse! –
au midi prompt, de son terne miroir, jalouse
au ciel gris de chaleur la Sphère rose et chère.

angels at play; – No ... the current of gold in motion moves its arms, dark and heavy, and above all cool, of grass. She sinks down, with the blue Heavens for canopy, summons for curtains the shadow of the hill and of the arch.

II

Oh the wet glassy surface is taut with its limpid bubbles! The water furnishes the waiting beds in pale and unfathomable gold; the faded green dresses of the little girls form the willows, from which leap the unbridled birds.

Purer than a gold sovereign, a warm yellow eyelid the marsh marigold – O Wife, thy marriage vow! – at noon sharp, from its matt mirror, envies the pink and precious Sphere in the sky grey with heat.

III

Madame se tient trop debout dans la prairie
prochaine où neigent les fils du travail; l'ombrelle
aux doigts; foulant l'ombelle; trop fière pour elle;
des enfants lisant dans la verdure fleurie

leur livre de maroquin rouge! Hélas, Lui, comme
mille anges blancs qui se séparent sur la route,
s'éloigne par delà la montagne! Elle, toute
froide, et noire, court! après le départ de l'homme!

IV

Regret des bras épais et jeunes d'herbe pure!
Or des lunes d'avril au cœur du saint lit! Joie
des chantiers riverains à l'abandon, en proie
aux soirs d'août qui faisaient germer ces pourritures!

III

My Lady stands too upright in the nearby meadow where the threads of toil are snowing down; her parasol in her fingers; treading on umbels; too proud for her; children reading in the flower-strewn greenery

their book bound in red morocco! Alas, He, like a thousand white angels dispersing on the road, journeys away beyond the mountain! She, quite cold, and dark, runs! after the man's departing!

IV

Yearning for the thick young arms of pure grass! Gold of April moons in the heart of the holy bed! Joy of abandoned riverside boatyards, a prey to August evenings which brought to life these rottings!

Qu'elle pleure à présent sous les remparts! l'haleine
des peupliers d'en haut est pour la seule brise.
Puis, c'est la nappe, sans reflets, sans source, grise:
un vieux, dragueur, dans sa barque immobile, peine.

V

Jouet de cet œil d'eau morne, je n'y puis prendre,
ô canot immobile! oh! bras trop courts! ni l'une
ni l'autre fleur: ni la jaune qui m'importune,
là; ni la bleue, amie à l'eau couleur de cendre.

Ah! la poudre des saules qu'une aile secoue!
Les roses des roseaux dès longtemps dévorées!
Mon canot, toujours fixe; et sa chaîne tirée
Au fond de cet œil d'eau sans bords, – à quelle boue?

Let her weep[1] now under the ramparts! the breath of the poplars above is all the breeze there is. Then, it is still water, without reflections, without a spring, grey: an old man, dredging, toils in his motionless boat.

V

A plaything of this eye of dismal water, I cannot pick there, O motionless boat! oh! arms too short! either this flower or the other: neither the yellow I find intrusive, there; nor the blue, intimate with the ashen water.

Ah! the dust of the willows shaken by a wing! The reed-roses long since devoured! My boat, still immobile; and its chain pulled tight towards the bottom of this limitless eye of water, – to what mud?

[1]Alternative translation: 'How she weeps ...'

O saisons, ô châteaux ...

O saisons, ô châteaux,
Quelle âme est sans défauts!

O saisons, ô châteaux,

J'ai fait la magique étude
Du Bonheur, que nul n'élude.

O vive lui, chaque fois
Que chante son coq gaulois.

Mais! je n'aurai plus d'envie,
Il s'est chargé de ma vie.

Ce Charme! il prit âme et corps,
Et dispersa tous efforts.

O seasons, O mansions ...

O seasons, O mansions, what soul is without blemish?

O seasons, O mansions,

I practised the magical science of Happiness, which no one evades.

O may it live, each time the Gallic cock crows.

But I shall feel no more longing, it has taken my life on its shoulders.

That Spell! it took hold of body and soul, and dissipated every effort.

Que comprendre à ma parole?
Il fait qu'elle fuie et vole!

O saisons, ô châteaux!

What can be understood from my words? It makes them flee and fly away!

O seasons, O mansions!

Après le Déluge

Aussitôt que l'idée du Déluge se fut rassise,

Un lièvre s'arrêta dans les sainfoins et les clochettes mouvantes et dit sa prière à l'arc-en-ciel à travers la toile de l'araignée.

Oh! les pierres précieuses qui se cachaient, – les fleurs qui regardaient déjà.

Dans la grande rue sale les étals se dressèrent, et l'on tira les barques vers la mer étagée là-haut comme sur les gravures.

After the Flood

As soon as the idea of the Flood had abated,

A hare paused among the clover and the swaying bell-flowers and said his prayer to the rainbow through the spider's web.

Oh! the precious stones that were hiding, – the flowers already looking about them.

In the squalid main street the stalls sprang up, and boats were hauled towards the sea which rose up there in strata as in old engravings.

Le sang coula, chez Barbe-Bleue, – aux abattoirs, – dans les cirques, où le sceau de Dieu blêmit les fenêtres. Le sang et le lait coulèrent.

Les castors bâtirent. Les "mazagrans" fumèrent dans les estaminets.

Dans la grande maison de vitres encore ruisselante les enfants en deuil regardèrent les merveilleuses images.

Une porte claqua, – et sur la place du hameau, l'enfant tourna ses bras, compris des girouettes et des coqs des clochers de partout, sous l'éclatante giboulée.

Madame*** établit un piano dans les Alpes. La messe et les premières communions se célébrèrent aux cent mille autels de la cathédrale.

Les caravanes partirent. Et le Splendide-Hôtel fut bâti dans le chaos de glaces et de nuit du pôle.

Blood flowed, at Blue-Beard's house, – in the slaughterhouses, – in the circuses, where God's seal turned the windows pale. Blood and milk flowed.

Beavers built. Tall-stemmed coffee-glasses steamed in the taverns.

In the great house of glass still streaming with water, the children in mourning clothes looked at the marvellous pictures.

A door slammed, and on the hamlet square the child swung his arms, understood by weather-vanes and steeple-cocks everywhere, under the glittering shower of hail.

Madame*** set up a piano in the Alps. Mass and first communions were celebrated at the hundred thousand altars of the cathedral.

Caravans set out. And the Hotel Splendide was built in the chaos of polar ice and darkness.

Depuis lors, la Lune entendit les chacals piaulant par les déserts de thym, – et les églogues en sabots grognant dans le verger. Puis, dans la futaie violette, bourgeonnante, Eucharis me dit que c'était le printemps.

Sourds, étang, – Ecume, roule sur le pont et par-dessus les bois; – draps noirs et orgues, – éclairs et tonnerre, – montez et roulez; – Eaux et tristesses, montez et relevez les Déluges.

Car depuis qu'ils se sont dissipés, – oh les pierres précieuses s'enfouissant, et les fleurs ouvertes! – c'est un ennui! et la Reine, la Sorcière qui allume sa braise dans le pot de terre, ne voudra jamais nous raconter ce qu'elle sait, et que nous ignorons.

Ever after, the Moon heard the jackals whining across the deserts of thyme – and the eclogues in clogs grumbling in the orchard. Then, in the tall violet burgeoning forest, Eucharis told me that it was spring.

Well up, pool; – Foam, roll over the bridge and the woods; – black shrouds and organs, – lightning and thunder, – rise and roll; – Waters and sorrows, rise and refloat the Floods.

For since they dispersed, – oh! the precious stones seeking secret cover, and the opened flowers! – it's so tedious! and the Queen, the Witch who lights her embers in an earthen pot, will never consent to tell us what she knows, and what we do not know.

Matinée d'ivresse

O *mon* Bien! O *mon* Beau! Fanfare atroce où je ne trébuche point! Chevalet féerique! Hourra pour l'œuvre inouïe et pour le corps merveilleux, pour la première fois! Cela commença sous les rires des enfants, cela finira par eux. Ce poison va rester dans toutes nos veines même quand, la fanfare tournant, nous serons rendus à l'ancienne inharmonie. O maintenant nous si dignes de ces tortures! rassemblons fervemment cette promesse surhumaine faite à notre corps et à notre âme créés: cette promesse, cette démence! L'élégance, la science, la violence! On nous a promis d'enterrer dans l'ombre l'arbre du bien et du mal, de déporter les honnêtetés tyranniques, afin que nous amenions notre très pur amour. Cela commença par quelques dégoûts et cela finit, – ne pouvant nous saisir sur-le-champ de cette éternité, – cela finit par une débandade de parfums.

Morning of Intoxication

O *my* Good! O *my* Beautiful! Excruciating fanfare in which I do not stumble! Enchanted rack! Hurrah for the unprecedented work and for the marvellous substance, for the first time! It began in the laughter of children, it will end with it. This poison will remain in all our veins even when, with a turn of the fanfare, we are restored to the old disharmony. O now so worthy of these tortures! let us gather up fervently this superhuman promise made to our created bodies and souls: this promise, this madness! Elegance, science, violence! We have been promised the burial in darkness of the tree of good and evil, the deportation of tyrannical proprieties, so that we may bring in our most pure love. It began with a few aversions and it ends – since we cannot grasp this eternity at once – it ends with a riot of fragrances.

Rire des enfants, discrétion des esclaves, austérité des vierges, horreur des figures et des objets d'ici, sacrés soyez-vous par le souvenir de cette veille. Cela commençait par toute la rustrerie, voici que cela finit par des anges de flamme et de glace.

Petite veille d'ivresse, sainte! quand ce ne serait que pour le masque dont tu nous as gratifié. Nous t'affirmons, méthode! Nous n'oublions pas que tu as glorifié hier chacun de nos âges. Nous avons foi au poison. Nous savons donner notre vie tout entière tous les jours.

Voici le temps des *Assassins*.

Children's laughter, discretion of slaves, austerity of virgins, horror of the faces and the objects in this place, hallowed be you by the memory of this vigil. It began in total boorishness, and here it is ending with angels of flame and ice.

Little vigil of drunkenness, you are saintly! even if only for the mask with which you have graced us. We are your champions, method! We do not forget that yesterday you glorified our every age. We have faith in the poison. We know how to give our whole life every day.

Now is the time of the *Assassins*.

Ville

Je suis un éphémère et point trop mécontent citoyen d'une métropole crue moderne parce que tout goût connu a été éludé dans les ameublements et l'extérieur des maisons aussi bien que dans le plan de la ville. Ici vous ne signaleriez les traces d'aucun monument de superstition. La morale et la langue sont réduites à leur plus simple expression, enfin! Ces millions de gens qui n'ont pas besoin de se connaître amènent si pareillement l'éducation, le métier et la vieillesse, que ce cours de vie doit être plusieurs fois moins long que ce qu'une statistique folle trouve pour les peuples du continent. Aussi comme, de ma fenêtre, je vois des spectres nouveaux roulant à travers l'épaisse et éternelle fumée de charbon, – notre ombre des bois, notre nuit d'été! – des

City

I am an ephemeral and not too discontented citizen of a metropolis believed to be modern because all known taste has been avoided in the furnishing and the exterior of the houses as well as in the layout of the city. Here you could not point out the trace of a single monument to superstition. Morality and language are at last reduced to their simplest expression! These millions of people who have no need to know each other carry on their education, work and old age so similarly, that the course of this life must be several times shorter than the findings of senseless statistics for the peoples of the continent. Thus from my window I see new spectres wandering through the dense and eternal coal-smoke – our woodland shade, our summer's night! – new Erinnyes, before my cottage which is

Érinnyes nouvelles, devant mon cottage qui est ma patrie et tout mon cœur puisque tout ici ressemble à ceci, – la Mort sans pleurs, notre active fille et servante, un Amour désespéré, et un joli Crime piaulant dans la boue de la rue.

my homeland and my whole heart since everything here is like this, – Death without tears, our assiduous daughter and servant, a hopeless Love and a pretty Crime whining in the mud of the street.

Aube

J'ai embrassé l'aube d'été.

Rien ne bougeait encore au front des palais. L'eau était morte. Les camps d'ombres ne quittaient pas la route du bois. J'ai marché, réveillant les haleines vives et tièdes, et les pierreries regardèrent, et les ailes se levèrent sans bruit.

La première entreprise fut, dans le sentier déjà empli de frais et blêmes éclats, une fleur qui me dit son nom.

Dawn

I embraced the summer dawn.

Nothing yet stirred on the façades of the palaces. The water was dead. The camps of shadows had not been struck on the woodland road. I walked, awakening warm living breaths, and the precious stones watched, and the wings rose without a sound.

The first venture was, in the pathway already filled with cool, pale radiance, a flower which told me its name.

Je ris au wasserfall blond qui s'échevela à travers les sapins: à la cime argentée je reconnus la déesse.

Alors je levai un à un les voiles. Dans l'allée, en agitant les bras. Par la plaine, où je l'ai dénoncée au coq. A la grand'ville elle fuyait parmi les clochers et les dômes, et courant comme un mendiant sur les quais de marbre, je la chassais.

En haut de la route, près d'un bois de lauriers, je l'ai entourée avec ses voiles amassés, et j'ai senti un peu son immense corps. L'aube et l'enfant tombèrent au bas du bois.

Au réveil il était midi.

I laughed beside the flaxen waterfall, wildly loosening its hair through the fir trees: at the silvery summit I recognized the goddess.

Then I lifted the veils one by one. In the avenue, waving my arms. Across the plain, where I denounced her to the cock. In the city, she fled among the steeples and domes, and, running like a beggar on the marble quays, I chased after her.

At the road's highest point, near a laurel wood, I surrounded her with her gathered veils, and felt slightly her vast body. The dawn and the child fell to the foot of the wood.

At my awakening it was noon.

Marine

Les chars d'argent et de cuivre –
Les proues d'acier et d'argent –
Battent l'écume, –
Soulèvent les souches des ronces.
Les courants de la lande,
Et les ornières immenses du reflux,
Filent circulairement vers l'est,
Vers les piliers de la forêt, –
Vers les fûts de la jetée,
Dont l'angle est heurté par des tourbillons de lumière.

Seascape

Chariots of silver and copper – prows of steel and silver – thrash the foam, – uproot the stumps of the thorns. The currents of the heath, and the vast ruts of the ebbing tide, flow away in a circle towards the east, towards the pillars of the forest, – towards the shafts of the jetty, its angle struck by whirlpools of light.

Nuit de l'Enfer

J'ai avalé une fameuse gorgée de poison. – Trois fois béni soit le conseil qui m'est arrivé! – Les entrailles me brûlent. La violence du venin tord mes membres, me rend difforme, me terrasse. Je meurs de soif, j'étouffe, je ne puis crier. C'est l'enfer, l'éternelle peine! Voyez comme le feu se relève! Je brûle comme il faut. Va, démon!

J'avais entrevu la conversion au bien at au bonheur, le salut. Puis-je décrire la vision, l'air de l'enfer ne souffre pas les hymnes! C'était des millions de créatures charmantes, un suave concert spirituel, la force et la paix, les nobles ambitions, que sais-je?

Les nobles ambitions!

Night in Hell

I have swallowed a tremendous gulp of poison. – Thrice blessed be the counsel that came to me! – My entrails are burning. The violence of the venom contorts my limbs, deforms me, prostrates me on the ground. I am dying of thirst, I am choking, I cannot cry out. It is hell, the eternal torment! See how the fire rises up again! I am burning according to the rules. Go to it, demon!

I had glimpsed conversion to goodness and happiness, salvation. Let me describe the vision, the air of hell suffers no hymns! There were millions of enchanting creatures, a sweet spiritual harmony, strength and peace, noble ambitions, how should I know?

Noble ambitions!

Et c'est encore la vie! – Si la damnation est éternelle! Un homme qui veut se mutiler est bien damné, n'est-ce pas? Je me crois en enfer, donc j'y suis. C'est l'exécution du catéchisme. Je suis esclave de mon baptême. Parents, vous avez fait mon malheur et vous avez fait le vôtre. Pauvre innocent! – L'enfer ne peut attaquer les païens. – C'est la vie encore! Plus tard, les délices de la damnation seront plus profondes. Un crime, vite, que je tombe au néant, de par la loi humaine.

And still this is life! – Suppose damnation is eternal! A man who wishes to mutilate himself is truly damned, is he not? I think I am in hell, therefore I am there. It is the accomplishment of the catechism. I am the slave of my baptism. Parents, you have caused my misfortune and you have caused your own. Poor innocent! – Hell cannot attack the heathen! – Still this is life! Later, the delights of damnation will be deeper. A crime, quickly, that I may fall into the void in the name of human law.

Tais-toi, mais tais-toi! ... C'est la honte, le reproche, ici: Satan qui dit que le feu est ignoble, que ma colère est affreusement sotte. — Assez! ... Des erreurs qu'on me souffle, magies, parfums faux, musiques puériles. — Et dire que je tiens la vérité, que je vois la justice: j'ai un jugement sain et arrêté, je suis prêt pour la perfection ... Orgueil. – La peau de ma tête se dessèche. Pitié! Seigneur, j'ai peur. J'ai soif, si soif! Ah! l'enfance, l'herbe, la pluie, le lac sur les pierres, *le clair de lune quand le clocher sonnait douze* ... le diable est au clocher, à cette heure. Marie! Saint Vierge! ... – Horreur de ma bêtise.

Là-bas, ne sont-ce pas des âmes honnêtes, qui me veulent du bien? ... Venez ... J'ai un oreiller sur la bouche, elles ne m'entendent pas, ce sont des fantômes. Puis, jamais personne ne pense à autrui. Qu'on n'approche pas. Je sens le roussi, c'est certain.

Be silent, just be silent! ... here is shame, reproach: Satan who says that the fire is ignoble, that my anger is horribly foolish. – Enough! ... Of the errors whispered to me, magic arts, false perfumes, puerile music. – And to say that I hold the truth, that I see justice: I have sane and settled judgement, I am ready for perfection ... Pride. – My scalp is drying up. Pity! Lord, I am afraid. I am thirsty, so thirsty! Ah! childhood, grass, rain, lake over stones, *moonlight as the church clock was striking twelve* ... the devil is in the belfry, at this hour. Mary! Holy Virgin! ... The horror of my absurdity.

Over there, are they not honest souls, who wish me well? ... Come ... I have a pillow over my mouth, they cannot hear me, they are ghosts. And then, no one ever thinks of others. Let no one approach. I smell of burning, that's for sure.

Les hallucinations sont innombrables. C'est bien ce que j'ai toujours eu: plus de foi en l'histoire, l'oubli des principes. Je m'en tairai: poëtes et visionnaires seraient jaloux. Je suis mille fois le plus riche, soyons avare comme la mer.

Ah çà! l'horloge de la vie s'est arrêtée tout à l'heure. Je ne suis plus au monde. – La théologie est sérieuse, l'enfer est certainement *en bas* – et le ciel en haut. – Extase, cauchemar, sommeil dans un nid de flammes.

Que de malices dans l'attention dans la campagne ... Satan, Ferdinand, court avec les graines sauvages ... Jésus marche sur les ronces purpurines, sans les courber ... Jésus marchait sur les eaux irritées. La lanterne nous le montra debout, blanc et des tresses brunes, au flanc d'une vague d'émeraude ...

The hallucinations are innumerable. That has always been my problem: no more faith in history, principles forgotten. I shall say no more about it: poets and visionaries would be jealous. I am a thousand times the richest, let's be as miserly as the sea.

Ah there now! the clock of life stopped just now. I am no longer of the world. – Theology is in earnest, hell is certainly *down below* – and heaven above. – Ecstasy, nightmare, sleep in a nest of flames.

So many malicious tricks lurking in the countryside ... Satan, Ferdinand, runs with the wild seeds ... Jesus walks on the purplish brambles, without bending them ... Jesus was walking on the troubled waters. The lantern showed him to us standing white and with brown tresses, on the flank of a wave of emerald ...

Je vais dévoiler tous les mystères: mystères religieux ou naturels, mort, naissance, avenir, passé, cosmogonie, néant. Je suis maître en fantasmagories.

Écoutez! ...

J'ai tous les talents! – Il n'y a personne ici et il y a quelqu'un: je ne voudrais pas répandre mon trésor. – Veut-on des chants nègres, des danses de houris? Veut-on que je disparaisse, que je plonge à la recherche de l'*anneau*? Veut-on? Je ferai de l'or, des remèdes.

Fiez-vous donc à moi, la foi soulage, guide, guérit. Tous, venez, – même les petits enfants, – que je vous console, qu'on répande pour vous son cœur, – le cœur merveilleux! – Pauvres hommes, travailleurs! Je ne demande pas de prières; avec votre confiance seulement, je serai heureux.

I am about to unveil all mysteries: mysteries religious or natural, death, birth, future, past, cosmogony, void. I am the lord of phantasmagoria.

Listen! ...

I have all the talents! – There is no one here and there is someone: I do not wish to pour out my treasure. – Do they want negro songs, houri dances? Do they want me to disappear, to dive in search of the *ring*? Is that what they want? I shall make gold, and cures.

Trust in me then, faith comforts, guides, cures. Come all, – even the little children – that I may comfort you, that a heart may be opened to you, – the marvellous heart! – Poor men, workers! I ask for no prayers; with your trust alone I will be happy.

– Et pensons à moi. Ceci me fait peu regretter le monde. J'ai de la chance de ne pas souffrir plus. Ma vie ne fut quc folies douces, c'est regrettable.

Bah! faisons toutes les grimaces imaginables.

Décidément, nous sommes hors du monde. Plus aucun son. Mon tact a disparu. Ah! mon château, ma Saxe, mon bois de saules. Les soirs, les matins, les nuits, les jours ... Suis-je las!

Je devrais avoir mon enfer pour la colère, mon enfer pour l'orgueil, – et l'enfer de la caresse; un concert d'enfers.

Je meurs de lassitude. C'est le tombeau, je m'en vais aux vers, horreur de l'horreur! Satan, farceur, tu veux me dissoudre, avec tes charmes. Je réclame. Je réclame! un coup de fourche, une goutte de feu.

– And let us think on me. This gives me little nostalgia for the world. I am lucky not to suffer any more. My life was nothing but sweet extravagances, it's unfortunate.

Rubbish! let's make every grimace imaginable.

Decidedly, we are outside the world. Not a single sound now. My sense of touch has vanished. Ah! my castle, my Saxony, my willow wood. Evenings, mornings, nights, days ... How tired I am!

I should have my hell for anger, my hell for pride, – and the hell of caresses; a harmony of hells.

I am dying of weariness. This is the tomb, I'm on my way to the worms, horror of horrors! Satan, you joker, you want to dissolve me with your enchantments. I appeal. I appeal! a prod with the fork, a drop of fire.

Ah! remonter à la vie! Jeter les yeux sur nos difformités. Et ce poison, ce baiser mille fois maudit! Ma faiblesse, la cruauté du monde! Mon Dieu, pitié, cachez-moi, je me tiens trop mal! – Je suis caché et je ne le suis pas.

C'est le feu qui se relève avec son damné.

Ah! to rise once more to life! Cast eyes on our deformities. And this poison, this kiss a thousand times cursed! My weakness, the world's cruelty! My God, have pity, hide me, I cannot hold fast! – I am hidden and I am not hidden.

The fire is rising again with its damned soul.

Adieu

L'automne déjà! – Mais pourquoi regretter un éternel soleil, si nous sommes engagés à la découverte de la clarté divine, – loin des gens qui meurent sur les saisons.

Farewell

Autumn already! – But why look back with yearning at an eternal sun, if we are committed to the discovery of divine light, – far from people who die according to the seasons.

L'automne. Notre barque élevée dans les brumes immobiles tourne vers le port de la misèrc, la cité énorme au ciel taché de feu et de boue. Ah! les haillons pourris, le pain trempé de pluie, l'ivresse, les mille amours qui m'ont crucifié! Elle ne finira donc point cette goule reine de millions d'âmes et de corps morts *et qui seront jugés*! Je me revois la peau rongée par la boue et la peste, des vers plein les cheveux et les aisselles et encore de plus gros vers dans le cœur, étendu parmi les inconnus sans âge, sans sentiment ... J'aurais pu y mourir ... L'affreuse évocation! J'exècre la misère.

Et je redoute l'hiver parce que c'est la saison du confort!

Autumn. Our ship raised up in the motionless mists turns towards the port of wretchedness, the vast city, its sky stained with fire and mud. Ah! the rotten rags, the rain-soaked bread, the drunkenness, the thousand loves that have crucified me! Will she never then have done, this ghoul queen of millions of souls and dead bodies *which will be judged*! I see myself once more, my skin eaten by mud and plague, my hair and armpits full of worms and still larger worms in my heart, lying stretched out among strangers without age, without feeling ... I could have died there ... Dreadful evocation! I loathe poverty.

And I fear winter because it is the season of comfort!

– Quelquefois je vois au ciel des plages sans fin couvertes de blanches nations en joie. Un grand vaisseau d'or, au-dessus de moi, agite ses pavillons multicolores sous les brises du matin. J'ai créé toutes les fêtes, tous les triomphes, tous les drames. J'ai essayé d'inventer de nouvelles fleurs, de nouveaux astres, de nouvelles chairs, de nouvelles langues. J'ai cru acquérir des pouvoirs surnaturels. Eh bien! je dois enterrer mon imagination et mes souvenirs! Une belle gloire d'artiste et de conteur emportée!

Moi! moi qui me suis dit mage ou ange, dispensé de toute morale, je suis rendu au sol, avec un devoir à chercher, et la réalité rugueuse à étreindre! Paysan!

Suis-je trompé? la charité serait-elle sœur de la mort, pour moi?

Enfin, je demanderai pardon pour m'être nourri de mensonge. Et allons.

– Sometimes I see in the sky beaches without end covered with white nations in joyfulness. Above me a great golden vessel waves its multicoloured pennants in the morning breezes. I created all festivals, all triumphs, all dramas. I tried to invent new flowers, new stars, new flesh, new tongues. I thought I was acquiring supernatural powers. Well! I must bury my imagination and my memories! An artist and storyteller's fine fame swept away!

I! I who called myself mage or angel, exempt from all morality, I am returned to the earth, with a task to discover, and wrinkled reality to embrace! Peasant!

Am I deceived? could charity be, for me, the sister of death?

To round things off, I shall ask pardon for having fed on lies. And let's go.

Mais pas une main amie! et où puiser le secours?

★

Oui, l'heure nouvelle est au moins très-sévère.

Car je puis dire que la victoire m'est acquise: les grincements de dents, les sifflements de feu, les soupirs empestés se modèrent. Tous les souvenirs immondes s'effacent. Mes derniers regrets détalent, – des jalousies pour les mendiants, les brigands, les amis de la mort, les arriérés de toutes sortes. – Damnés, si je me vengeais!

Il faut être absolument moderne.

Point de cantiques: tenir le pas gagné. Dure nuit! le sang séché fume sur ma face, et je n'ai rien derrière moi, que cet horrible arbrisseau! ... Le combat spirituel est aussi brutal que la bataille d'hommes; mais la vision de la justice est le plaisir de Dieu seul.

But no friendly hand! and where shall I draw succour?

★

Yes, the new hour is to say the least very rigorous.

For I can say that victory is mine: the gnashing of teeth, the hissing of flame, the pestilent sighings diminish. All the foul memories are fading away. My last regrets take to their heels, – envy of beggars, brigands, the friends of death, all kinds of stunted creatures. – Damned souls, if I took my revenge!

One must be absolutely modern.

No canticles: keep the foothold gained. A harsh night! the dried blood smokes on my face, and I have nothing behind me but that horrible bush! ... Spiritual combat is as brutal as the battle of men; but the vision of justice is God's pleasure alone.

Cependant c'est la veille. Recevons tous les influx de vigueur et de tendresse réelle. Et à l'aurore, armés d'une ardente patience, nous entrerons aux splendides villes.

Que parlais-je de main amie! Un bel avantage, c'est que je puis rire des vieilles amours mensongères, et frapper de honte ces couples menteurs, – j'ai vu l'enfer des femmes là-bas; – et il me sera loisible de *posséder la vérité dans une âme et un corps*.

And yet this is the eve. Let us receive every influx of vigour and of real tenderness. And at dawn, armed with a passionate patience, we shall enter the glorious cities.

Why talk of a friendly hand! A great advantage is that I can laugh at old illusory loves, and strike shame into those deceitful couples, – I saw the hell of women down in that place; – and it will be lawful for me now to *possess truth in one soul and one body*.

Jules Laforgue
(1860–87)

It is only recently that Laforgue's importance in the evolution of poetry, not only within France but beyond its borders, has been fully appreciated. He is one of the originators of modern free verse, a strong influence on T. S. Eliot and Ezra Pound among many other poets, especially in the United States, and a man whose ironic temperament and conscious literary iconoclasm (from an established base of technical expertise that distinguishes him from the anarchic Corbière) make him a bridge between the nineteenth and twentieth centuries. Potentially a very great modern poet, Laforgue died of tuberculosis at the age of 27, after an accelerated artistic development which almost rivals that of Rimbaud, and without seeing his revolutionary *Derniers Vers* published in book form.

He was born (like Lautréamont and Supervielle) in Montevideo, Uruguay, but lived from 1876 in France and for a time in Germany, where he worked as French Reader to the Empress Augusta. He studied art, and formed an important friendship with Gustave Kahn, a minor Symbolist poet whose influential theories on free verse have more weight than his practical output. Reading widely in philosophy and drawn especially to Schopenhauer, Laforgue developed a Nihilist view of life and art, strongly coloured too by Hartmann's theories of the Unconscious. The replacement of ethics by aesthetics appealed to a young poet already rootless, alienated, cynical about contemporary values, and highly sensitive both to his own insecurities and to his perception of 'normal' life as deterministic and sterile. The new knowledge of psychology and neurology expanded his interest in the Unconscious and its relationship with sensory perception, and he located Art's future role in that area, while striking a superior attitude of Decadent '*ennui*' towards the vulgarity and materialism of society.

His work nevertheless contains strange dualities: taut emotion and destructive irony; lyricism and detachment; a jaundiced view of love and sex, yet a longing for success in both; a nausea induced by the bourgeoisie yet also the artistic exile's nostalgia for order. Most importantly, his immobilizing nineteenth-century sensitivity to the banality of external life is overridden by a dynamic twentieth-century urge to live through active exploration of his inner responses.

His first important volume, *Les Complaintes*, published in 1885 after his repudiation of his earlier work, is intermittently brilliant. In each 'lament' he projects his own state of mind ironically into another voice or voices, sometimes identified and sometimes not. But the poet's voice is powerfully present too; Laforgue could never have been a Symbolist, for the Ego is too urgently active and too articulate to disappear within the marble block or melt into the music. Transposed into images of striking originality, Nihilist ideas abound in *Les Complaintes*: behaviour is biologically determined; personality is multiple and infinitely complex; morality is a fraud and religion a fantasy; only Art has reality and permanence; only the study of our sensations is of interest; language must disintegrate and re-form to express the fractured yet vibrant experience of mind and senses. Laforgue orchestrates clashing registers of language and exploits latent verbal ambiguities with wit and virtuosity in this volume, in Alexandrine and octosyllabic verse that is highly flexible and in fact straining at its metrical seams, but still precariously intact.

After this his second volume, *L'Imitation de Notre-Dame la Lune* (1886), is perhaps surprisingly polished and even precious, cleanly articulated within metrical forms of exquisite and musical regularity. While the characteristics of style and tone exemplified in *Les Complaintes* are strongly present here too, it is almost as if Laforgue wanted to demonstrate his complete mastery of established technique, in this volume that concentrates thematically on the Pierrot clown figure, before his radical change of course towards modern '*vers libres*' in his *Derniers Vers*, published in 1890.

This move was stimulated by Laforgue's own translation of Walt Whitman which introduced the American poet to French readers, and by the encouragement of Kahn. 'L'Hiver qui vient', which opens this final volume, is probably the first genuine and successful free verse poem of any length in the French language, and the first of twelve such revolutionary works composed by Laforgue in the last full year of his life. These poems frequently rhyme, but in a semi-anarchic way; and the rhymes are part of a liberated, semi-unconscious pattern of verbal association in which recurring motifs provide landmarks. Metre and rhythm now follow very freely the impulse behind the expression, and each line has an 'inner law' dictated by what Rémy de Gourmont was to call its 'emotive idea'. The number of syllables in the line corresponds flexibly to an inhalation and exhalation, as Claudel would later conceive it, of image, feeling and idea. The stanza is now the sentence, or vice versa, its natural dynamics indicated by punctuation, syntactic shape on the page, '*points de suspension*' and blank spaces.

The whole is a taut equilibrium of *élan* and control, anarchy and form. Rich in associative resonance, it has a psychological rather than rhetorical unity that can be perceived only intuitively, and poetry is now conceived, in Laforgue's own words, as 'the visible tips of disconnected dreams'. Laforgue's last volume establishes him as one of the originators of modernism, for here we can see Baudelaire's dream of poetry as a 'subjective magic containing both object and subject' starting to become a reality.

Complainte des Pianos qu'on entend dans les quartiers aisés

Menez l'âme que les Lettres ont bien nourrie,
Les pianos, les pianos, dans les quartiers aisés!
Premiers soirs, sans pardessus, chaste flânerie,
Aux complaintes des nerfs incompris ou brisés.

Ces enfants, à quoi rêvent-elles,
Dans les ennuis des ritournelles?

– "Préaux des soirs,
Christs des dortoirs!

"Tu t'en vas et tu nous laisses,
Tu nous laiss's et tu t'en vas,
Défaire et refaire ses tresses,
Broder d'éternels canevas."

Lament of the Pianos heard in the Prosperous Districts

Conduct the soul well versed in Literature, pianos, pianos in the prosperous districts! First coatless evenings, chaste strolling, to the laments of misunderstood or fractured nerves.

What do they dream of, those girls, in the tedium of ritornellos?

– 'Evening schoolyards, Christs in the dormitories!

You go away and leave us, you leave us and you go away, to unbind our tresses and bind them once more, to embroider everlasting canvases.'

Jolie ou vague? triste ou sage? encore pure?
O jours, tout m'est égal? ou, monde, moi je veux?
Et si vierge, du moins, de la bonne blessure
Sachant quels gras couchants ont les plus blancs aveux?

Mon Dieu, à quoi donc rêvent-elles?
A des Roland, à des dentelles?

– "Cœurs en prison,
Lentes saisons!

"Tu t'en vas et tu nous quittes,
Tu nous quitt's et tu t'en vas!
Couvents gris, chœurs de Sulamites,
Sur nos seins nuls croisons nos bras."

Fatales clés de l'être un beau jour apparues;
Psitt! aux hérédités en ponctuels ferments,
Dans le bal incessant de nos étranges rues;
Ah! pensionnats, théâtres, journaux, romans!

Pretty or nondescript? sad or wise? still pure? O days, is it all the same to me? or, world, what I want is ...? And if virgin, at least, of the good wound knowing what plump sunsets have the whitest confessions?

My God, what then do they dream of? Of Rolands, of lace?

'Hearts imprisoned, slow seasons!

You go away and leave us, you leave us and you go away! Grey convents, choirs of Shulamites, let us fold our arms across our non-existent breasts.'

Fatal keys of being who appeared one fine day; psst! over here! to heredities in seasonal ferment, in the unceasing ball of our strange streets; ah! boarding schools, theatres, newspapers, novels!

Allez, stériles ritournelles,
La vie est vraie et criminelle.

– "Rideaux tirés,
Peut-on entrer?

"Tu t'en vas et tu nous laisses,
Tu nous laiss's et tu t'en vas,
La source des frais rosiers baisse,
Vraiment! Et lui qui ne vient pas..."

Il viendra! Vous serez les pauvres cœurs en faute,
Fiancés au remords comme aux essais sans fond,
Et les suffisants cœurs cossus, n'ayant d'autre hôte
Qu'un train-train pavoisé d'estime et de chiffons.

Mourir? peut-être brodent-elles,
Pour un oncle à dot, des bretelles?

– "Jamais! Jamais!
Si tu savais!

Come on, sterile ritornellos, life is real and criminal.

'Drawn curtains, may one enter?

You go away and leave us, you leave us and you go away, the spring amid fresh rose trees runs dry, truly! And he who does not come ...'

He will come! You'll be the wretched souls at fault, betrothed to remorse as to bottomless tests, and the bumptious affluent souls, having no other inhabitant but a daily round decked out with prestige and ribbons.

To die? perhaps they are embroidering braces for an endowed uncle?

'Never! Never! If only you knew!

"Tu t'en vas et tu nous quittes,
Tu nous quitt's et tu t'en vas,
Mais tu nous reviendras bien vite
Guérir mon beau mal, n'est-ce pas?"

Et c'est vrai! l'Idéal les fait divaguer toutes,
Vigne bohême, même en ces quartiers aisés.
La vie est là; le pur flacon des vives gouttes
Sera, *comme il convient*, d'eau propre baptisé.

Aussi, bientôt, se joueront-elles
De plus exactes ritournelles.

" – Seul oreiller!
Mur familier!

"Tu t'en vas et tu nous laisses,
Tu nous laiss's et tu t'en vas,
Que ne suis-je morte à la messe!
O mois, ô linges, ô repas!"

You go away and leave us, you leave us and you go away, but you'll come back quickly, won't you, to cure my sweet suffering?'

And it's true! The Ideal sets all their minds wandering, that bohemian vine, even in these prosperous districts. Life is there; the pure flask with its living drops will be baptized, *according to the form*, in clean water.

And so, before long, they'll make child's play of more rigorous ritornellos.

'Solo pillow! Familiar wall!

You go away and leave us, you leave us and you go away, would to God I'd died at mass! O months, O laundry, O meals!'

Complainte des Nostalgies préhistoriques

La nuit bruine sur les villes.
Mal repu des gains machinals,
On dîne; et gonflé d'idéal,
Chacun sirote son idylle,
  Ou furtive, ou facile.

Echos des grands soirs primitifs!
Couchants aux flambantes usines,
Rude paix des sols en gésine,
Cri jailli là-bas d'un massif,
  Violuptés à vif!

Dégringolant une vallée,
Heurter, dans des coquelicots,
Une enfant bestiale et brûlée,
Qui suce, en blaguant les échos,
  De juteux abricots.

Lament of Atavistic Hankerings

Darkness drizzles on the cities. Unsatiated by mechanical wages, we dine; and puffed up with an ideal, each of us sips at his idyll, be it furtive or facile.

Echoes of great primitive evenings! Sunsets over the flaming factories, rough peace of ground lying fallow,[1] a cry bursts out from the shrubs over there, vibrant voluptuous violations!

Tumbling down a valley, stumbling amid the poppies against a bestial scorched child; she sucks, bantering with the echoes, at juice-filled apricots.

[1]'*Gésine*': also a place for giving birth.

Livrer aux langueurs des soirées
Sa toison où du cristal luit,
Pourlécher ses lèvres sucrées,
Nous barbouiller le corps de fruits
  Et lutter comme essui!

Un moment, béer, sans rien dire,
Inquiets d'une étoile là-haut;
Puis, sans but, bien gentils satyres,
Nous prendre aux premiers sanglots
  Fraternels des crapauds.

Et, nous délèvrant de l'extase,
Oh! devant la lune en son plein,
Là-bas, comme un bloc de topaze,
Fous, nous renverser sur les reins,
  Riant, battant des mains!

La nuit bruine sur les villes:
Se raser le masque, s'orner
D'un frac deuil, avec art dîner,
Puis, parmi des vierges débiles,
  Prendre un air imbécile.

To surrender to the languid evenings our fleece where crystal gleams, lick sugared lips, daub our bodies with fruits and wrestle like sponges!

Gape for a moment, without words, apprehensive about a star up there; then, to no purpose, gracious satyrs, take each other to the first accompanying fraternal sobs of the toads.

And, delippering ourselves of ecstasy, oh! before the moon at the full, there, like a block of topaz, crazy, tip each other on our backsides, laughing, clapping hands!

Darkness drizzles on the cities: shave the mask, adorn oneself with a mourning coat, dine with artistry, then, among sickly virgins, take on an imbecilic air.

Complainte du Roi de Thulé

Il était un roi de Thulé,
Immaculé,
Qui, loin des jupes et des choses,
Pleurait sur la métempsychose
Des lys en roses,
Et quel palais!

Ses fleurs dormant, il s'en allait,
Traînant des clés,
Broder aux seuls yeux des étoiles,
Sur une tour, un certain Voile
De vive toile,
Aux nuits de lait!

Quand le voile fut bien ourlé
Loin de Thulé,
Il rama fort sur les mers grises,
Vers le soleil qui s'agonise,
Féerique Eglise!
Il ululait:

Lament of the King of Thule

There was a king of Thule, immaculate, who, remote from petticoats and things, wept over the metempsychosis of lilies into roses, and such a palace!

As his flowers slept, he would go, bearing keys, to embroider, on a tower, watched only by the stars, a certain Shroud of living cloth, in the milky nights!

When the shroud was stitched and hemmed, far from Thule he rowed with strength over the grey seas, towards the sun in its death throes, enchanted Church! He ululated:

"Soleil-crevant, encore un jour,
Vous avez tendu votre phare
Aux holocaustes vivipares,
Du culte qu'ils nomment l'Amour.

"Et comme, devant la nuit fauve,
Vous vous sentez défaillir,
D'un dernier flot d'un sang martyr
Vous lavez le seuil de l'Alcôve!

"Soleil! Soleil! moi je descends
Vers vos navrants palais polaires,
Dorloter dans ce Saint-Suaire
    Votre cœur bien en sang,
        En le berçant!"

Il dit, et, le Voile étendu,
    Tout éperdu,
Vers les coraux et les naufrages,
Le roi raillé des doux corsages,
    Beau comme un Mage
    Est descendu!

'Dying sun, for another day you have held out your beacon to the viviparous orgies of the cult called Love.

And as, before the savage night, you feel yourself grow faint, with a last wave of martyred blood you cleanse the threshold of the Bedchamber!

Sun! Sun! I am coming down towards your heartbreaking polar palaces, to comfort and to cradle in this Holy Shroud your blood-soaked heart!'

He spoke, and with the Shroud outstretched, distraught, towards corals and shipwrecks, the king, mocked by soft bodices, went down, beautiful as a Mage!

Braves amants! aux nuits de lait,
Tournez vos clés!
Une ombre, d'amour pur transie,
Viendrait vous gémir cette scie:
"Il était un roi de Thulé
Immaculé..."

Bold lovers! in the milky night, turn your keys! A shadow, transfixed with pure love, would come and moan to you this old refrain: 'There was a king of Thule, immaculate ...'

Complainte sur certains Temps déplacés

Le couchant de sang est taché
Comme un tablier de boucher;
Oh! qui veut aussi m'écorcher!

– Maintenant c'est comme une rade!
Ça vous fait le cœur tout nomade,
A cingler vers mille Lusiades!

Lament on certain displaced Times[1]

The sunset is stained with blood like a butcher's apron; oh! who wants to skin me too!

– Now it's like a roadstead! It makes your heart nomadic, scudding along towards a thousand Lusiads![2]

[1]'Tempos' may be suggested, or even 'tenses'.
[2]Reference to *Os Lusiadas* (1572), a long lyrical and epic poem by the Portuguese writer Luis de Camões.

Passez, ô nuptials appels,
Vers les comptoirs, les Archipels
Où l'on mastique le bétel!

Je n'aurai jamais d'aventures;
Qu'il est petit, dans la Nature,
Le chemin d'fer Paris-Ceinture!

– V'là la fontainier! il siffle l'air
(Connu) du bon roi Dagobert;
Oh! ces matins d'avril en mer!

– Le vent galope ventre à terre,
En vain voudrait-on le fair'taire!
Ah! nom de Dieu quelle misère!

– Le Soleil est mirobolant
Comme un poitrail de chambellan,
J'en demeure les bras ballants;

Pass on, O nuptial summonses, towards the godowns,[1] the Archipelagos where they chew betel!

I'll never have adventures; how small it is, in Nature, the Paris-Circle railway!

– There's the water engineer! he's whistling the (familiar) tune of good king Dagobert;[2] oh! those April mornings at sea!

– The wind gallops flat out, to silence it would be a futile wish! Ah! in God's name what wretchedness!

– The Sun is too good to be true like a chamberlain's breastplate, it roots me to the spot, my arms dangling;

[1]Godown: a dockside warehouse, in India and the Far East.
[2]*Le roi Dagobert*: one of the Merovingian dynasty of kings, rulers of Gaul from about A.D. 500 to 751.

Mais jugez si ça m'importune,
Je rêvais en plein de lagunes
De Venise au clair de la lune!

– Vrai! la vie est pour les badauds;
Quand on a du dieu sous la peau,
On cuve ça sans dire mot.

L'obélisque quadrangulaire,
De mon spleen monte; j'y digère,
En stylite, ce gros Mystère.

But you're joking if you think that bothers me, I was dreaming deep among the lagoons of Venice by moonlight!

– It's true! life is for the idlers; when you have divinity under your skin, you ferment it, saying nothing.

The quadrangular obelisk of my spleen rises; upon it I digest, like a Stylite, this bulky Mystery.

Pierrots

C'est, sur un cou qui, raide, émerge
D'une fraise empesée *idem*,
Une face imberbe au cold-cream,
Un air d'hydrocéphale asperge.

Pierrots

Above a neck that emerges stiffly from a ruff starched likewise, it is a beardless cold-creamed face, with the air of a hydrocephalic asparagus.

Les yeux sont noyés de l'opium
De l'indulgence universelle,
La bouche clownesque ensorcèle
Comme un singulier géranium.

Bouche qui va du trou sans bonde
Glacialement désopilé,
Au transcendental en-allé
Du souris vain de la Joconde.

Campant leur cône enfariné
Sur le noir serre-tête en soie,
Ils font rire leur patte d'oie
Et froncent en trèfle leur nez.

Ils ont comme chaton de bague
Le scarabée égyptien,
A leur boutonnière fait bien
Le pissenlit des terrains vagues.

The eyes are drowned in the opium of universal indulgence, the clown's mouth bewitches like a peculiar geranium.

Mouth which goes from the unbunged hole, glacially hilarious,[1] to the transcendental elusiveness of the Mona Lisa's empty smile.

Planting their floury conical hat above the black silk headband, they make their crow's-feet laugh and wrinkle their nose like clover.[2]

As stone-setting on their ring they have the Egyptian scarab, in their buttonhole the wasteland dandelion sits well.

[1]'*Désopilé*', a very unusual past participle, suggests hilarity, but also has the archaic sense of 'unbunged', the removal of an obstruction.
[2]'*Le trèfle*' is also 'Clubs' in a pack of cards.

Ils vont, se sustentant d'azur!
Et parfois aussi de légumes,
De riz plus blanc que leur costume,
De mandarines et d'œufs durs.

Ils sont de la secte du Blême,
Ils n'ont rien à voir avec Dieu,
Et sifflent: "Tout est pour le mieux,
Dans la meilleur' des mi-carême!"

They make their way, nourished on blue sky! and occasionally on vegetables too, on rice whiter than their costume, on mandarins and hard-boiled eggs.

They are of the Pallid sect, having nothing to do with God, and they whistle: 'All is for the best in the best of mid-Lent masquerades!'[1]

Locutions des Pierrots

I

Les mares de vos yeux aux joncs de cils,
O vaillante oisive femme,
Quand donc me renverront-ils
La Lune-levante de ma belle âme?

Pierrot Phrases

I

The pools of your eyes with lashes for rushes, O splendid slothful woman, when will they reflect back to me the Orient Moon of my exquisite soul?

[1]The emphasis here may be on abstinence, but mid-Lent is also associated with festivals, masquerades, a break from abstinence. The ambiguity is typically Laforguian.

Voilà tantôt une heure qu'en langueur
    Mon cœur si simple s'abreuve
    De vos vilaines rigueurs,
Avec le regard bon d'un terre-neuve.

Ah! madame, ce n'est vraiment pas bien,
    Quand on n'est pas la Joconde,
    D'en adopter le maintien
Pour induire en spleens tout bleus le pauv' monde!

II

Ah! le divin attachement
Que je nourris pour Cydalise,
Maintenant qu'elle échappe aux prises
De mon lunaire entendement!

Vrai, je me ronge en des détresses,
Parmi les fleurs de son terroir
A seule fin de bien savoir
Quelle est sa faculté-maîtresse!

For nearly an hour now in pining languor my heart, so unpretentious, has drunk to the dregs your sordid austerities, with the bland gaze of a Newfoundland dog.

Ah! madame, it really isn't right, when one isn't the Gioconda, to take on her manner to beguile poor men into deep blue depressions!

II

Ah! the divine affection that I nurse for Cydalise, now that she eludes the grasp of my lunar intellect!

True, I fret in anguish among the flowers of her native soil to the sole end of knowing which is her dominant faculty!

– C'est d'être la mienne, dis-tu?
Hélas! tu sais bien que j'oppose
Un démenti formel aux poses
Qui sentent par trop l'impromptu.

XII

Encore un livre; ô nostalgies
Loin de ces très-goujates gens,
Loin des saluts et des argents,
Loin de nos phraséologies!

Encore un de mes pierrots mort;
Mort d'un chronique orphelinisme;
C'était un cœur plein de dandysme
Lunaire, en un drôle de corps.

Les dieux s'en vont; plus que des hures;
Ah! ça devient tous les jours pis;
J'ai fait mon temps, je déguerpis
Vers l'Inclusive Sinécure!

– It is to be mine, you say? Alas! you know well that I present a formal resistance to poses that smack too much of spontaneity.

XII

Yet another book; O yearnings far from these highly boorish people, far from bowings and currencies, far from our phraseologies!

Yet another of my pierrots dead; dead of chronic orphanage; a heart full of lunar dandy manners, in a funny sort of body.

The gods are leaving; only severed heads left now; ah! it's getting worse every day; I've done my time, I'm clearing off towards the all-encompassing Sinecure!

XVI

Je ne suis qu'un viveur lunaire
Qui fait des ronds dans les bassins,
Et cela, sans autre dessein
Que devenir un légendaire.

Retroussant d'un air de défi
Mes manches de mandarin pâle,
J'arrondis ma bouche et – j'exhale
Des conseils doux de Crucifix.

Ah! oui, devenir légendaire,
Au seuil des siècles charlatans!
Mais où sont les Lunes d'antan?
Et que Dieu n'est-il à refaire?

XVI

I'm just a lunar reveller making rings in pools, and with no other purpose than to become legendary.

Tucking up with an air of defiance my pale mandarin's sleeves, I round my mouth and – I exhale soft words of Crucifix advice.

Ah! yes, to become a legend on the threshold of charlatan centuries! But where are the Moons of yesteryear? And why isn't God to be reinvented?

L'Hiver qui vient

Blocus sentimental! Messageries du Levant!...
Oh, tombée de la pluie! Oh! tombée de la nuit,
Oh! le vent!...
La Toussaint, la Noël et la Nouvelle Année,
Oh, dans les bruines, toutes mes cheminées!...
D'usines...

On ne peut plus s'asseoir, tous les bancs sont mouillés;
Crois-moi, c'est bien fini jusqu'à l'année prochaine,
Tant les bancs sont mouillés, tant les bois sont rouillés,
Et tant les cors ont fait ton ton, ont fait ton taine!...

Ah, nuées accourues des côtes de la Manche,
Vous nous avez gâté notre dernier dimanche.

Il bruine;
Dans la forêt mouillée, les toiles d'araignées
Ploient sous les gouttes d'eau, et c'est leur ruine.

The Coming Winter

Sentimental blockade! Levantine shipping-lines! ... Oh! falling of the rain! Oh! falling of the night, oh! the wind ... All Saints' Day, Christmas and New Year, oh, in the drizzle, all my chimneys! ... of factories ...

We can't sit down any more, all the benches are soaked; believe me, it's all over until next year, all the benches are so wet, so mildewed are the woods, and so often the horns have sounded ta-ran, ta-ra! ...

Ah, clouds pressing in from the Channel coast, you've ruined our last Sunday for us.

It's drizzling; in the damp forest, the spiders' webs give way beneath the drops of water, and that's the end of them.

Soleils plénipotentiaires des travaux en blonds Pactoles
Des spectacles agricoles,
Où êtes-vous ensevelis?
Ce soir un soleil fichu gît au haut du coteau
Gît sur le flanc, dans les genêts, sur son manteau,
Un soleil blanc comme un crachat d'estaminet
Sur une litière de jaunes genêts
De jaunes genêts d'automne.
Et les cors lui sonnent!
Qu'il revienne...
Qu'il revienne à lui!
Taïaut! Taïaut! et hallali!
O triste antienne, as-tu fini!...
Et font les fous!...
Et il gît là, comme une glande arrachée dans un cou,
Et il frissonne, sans personne!...

Suns plenipotentiary over the labours, gold-bearing like the Pactolus,[1] of agricultural shows, where are you buried? This evening a sun is lying, done for, on the hilltop it lies on its side, in the broom, on its cloak, a sun white like bar-room spittle on a litter of yellow broom, of yellow autumn broom. And the horns are sounding for him! May he return ... may he return to his senses! Tally-ho! Tally-ho! and on to the kill! O sad antiphon, have you finished! ... and they're playing the fool! ... and he lies there, like a gland ripped from a neck, and he shudders, left all alone! ...

[1]A river in Lydia in which Midas was said to have washed away his golden touch.

Allons, allons, et hallali!
C'est l'Hiver bien connu qui s'amène;
Oh! les tournants des grandes routes,
Et sans petit Chaperon Rouge qui chemine!...
Oh! leurs ornières des chars de l'autre mois,
Montant en don quichottesques rails
Vers les patrouilles des nuées en déroute
Que le vent malmène vers les transatlantiques bercails!...
Accélérons, accélérons, c'est la saison bien connue, cette fois.

Et le vent, cette nuit, il en a fait de belles!
O dégâts, ô nids, ô modestes jardinets!
Mon cœur et mon sommeil: ô échos des cognées!...

Forward, forward, and on to the kill! Old friend winter's just turned up; oh! the turnings of the highways, and no Little Red Riding Hood trudging along! ... oh! their ruts left by carts the other month, climbing in don-quixotic rails towards the routed cloud patrols in flight driven by the wind towards the transatlantic folds! ... Hurry faster, hurry on, it's the season we know so well, this time.

And the wind tonight has been up to some fine tricks! O havoc, O nests, O unassuming little gardens! My heart and my sleep: O echoes of axe-blows! ...

Tous ces rameaux avaient encor leurs feuilles vertes,
Les sous-bois ne sont plus qu'un fumier de feuilles mortes;
Feuilles, folioles, qu'un bon vent vous emporte
Vers les étangs par ribambelles,
Ou pour le feu du garde-chasse,
Ou les sommiers des ambulances
Pour les soldats loin de la France.

C'est la saison, c'est la saison, la rouille envahit les masses,
La rouille ronge en leurs spleens kilométriques
Les fils télégraphiques des grandes routes où nul ne passe.

Les cors, les cors, les cors – mélancoliques!...
Mélancoliques!...
S'en vont, changeant de ton,
Changeant de ton et de musique,
Ton ton, ton taine, ton ton!...
Les cors, les cors, les cors!...
S'en sont allés au vent du Nord.

All these boughs still had their green leaves, now the undergrowth is just a dunghill of dead leaves; leaves and leaflets, may a fair wind carry you off towards the ponds in trailing swarms, either for the gamekeeper's fire, or for the ambulance mattresses for the soldiers far from France.

It's the season, it's the season, rust attacks the sledgehammers, mildew eats away in their kilometric spleen at the telegraph poles on the highways where no one passes.

The horns, the horns, the horns – melancholy! ... melancholy! ... away they go, changing their tone and their music, ta-ran, ta-ra, ta-ran! ... the horns, the horns, the horns! ... have gone away on the North wind.

Je ne puis quitter ce ton: que d'échos!...
C'est la saison, c'est la saison, adieu vendanges!...
Voici venir les pluies d'une patience d'ange,
Adieu vendanges, et adieu tous les paniers,
Tous les paniers Watteau des bourrées sous les marronniers,
C'est la toux dans les dortoirs du lycée qui rentre,
C'est la tisane sans le foyer,
La phtisie pulmonaire attristant le quartier,
Et toute la misère des grands centres.

I cannot abandon this tone:[1] so many echoes! ... It's the season, it's the season, farewell wine-harvests! ... Here come the rains with their angelic patience, farewell wine-harvests, and farewell all the baskets, all the Watteau pannier-skirts of folk-dances beneath the chestnut trees, it's the coughing in the dormitories of the first night back at school, it's herb-tea away from hearth and home, pulmonary consumption bringing sadness to the neighbourhood, and all the wretchedness of the cities.

[1]'Pitch', 'key' and 'tune' are alternative possibilities here.

Mais, lainages, caoutchoucs, pharmacie, rêve,
Rideaux écartés du haut des balcons des grèves
Devant l'océan de toitures des faubourgs,
Lampes, estampes, thé, petits-fours,
Serez-vous pas mes seules amours!...
(Oh! et puis, est-ce que tu connais, outre les pianos,
Le sobre et vespéral mystère hebdomadaire
Des statistiques sanitaires
Dans les journaux?)

Non, non! c'est la saison et la planète falote!
Que l'autan, que l'autan
Effiloche les savates que le Temps se tricote!
C'est la saison, oh déchirements! c'est la saison!
Tous les ans, tous les ans,
J'essaierai en chœur d'en donner la note.

But, woollens, waterproofs, chemist's shop, dreaming, curtains drawn back high on balconies like shores facing the ocean of suburban rooftops, lamps, engravings, tea and petits-fours, will you not be my only loves! (Oh, and then, do you know, not to mention the pianos, the sober, vespertine weekly mystery of the health statistics in the newspapers?)

No, no! It's the season and the blood-sapped planet! Let the south wind, the south wind unravel the slippers that Time knits herself! It's the season, oh heartrendings! it's the season! Every year, every year, I'll strive to sound its note in chorus.

Dimanches

Bref, j'allais me donner d'un "Je vous aime"
Quand je m'avisaï non sans peine
Que d'abord je ne me possédais pas bien moi-même.

Sundays

To get to the point, I was about to give myself with an 'I love you' when it occurred to me by no means painlessly that I really didn't possess myself to start with.

(Mon Moi, c'est Galathée aveuglant Pygmalion!
Impossible de modifier cette situation.)

Ainsi donc, pauvre, pâle et piètre individu
Qui ne croit à son Moi qu'à ses moments perdus,
Je vis s'effacer ma fiancée
Emportée par le cours des choses,
Telle l'épine voit s'effeuiller,
Sous prétexte de soir sa meilleure rose.

Or, cette nuit anniversaire, toutes les Walkyries du vent
Sont revenues beugler par les fentes de ma porte:
Vae soli!
Mais, ah! qu'importe!
Il fallait m'en étourdir avant!
Trop tard! ma petite folie est morte!
Qu'importe *Vae soli!*
Je ne retrouverai plus ma petite folie.

(My Self, it's Galathea blinding Pygmalion! No way of altering this situation.)

So then, a poor, pale and paltry individual who believes in his Self only in absent-minded moments, I saw my fiancée fade away, carried off by the course of things, just as the briar sees its finest rose shed its petals on the pretext that it's evening.

Now, on this anniversary night, all the Valkyries of the wind have come back to bellow through the cracks in my door: *Vae soli*![1] But, ah! what does it matter? They should have sent my head reeling with it earlier! Too late! my little aberration is dead! What does *vae soli* matter! I'll not see my little aberration any more.

[1] *Vae soli*: 'Woe to the lonely man.'

Le grand vent bâillonné,
S'endimanche enfin le ciel du matin.
Et alors, eh! allez donc, carillonnez,
Toutes cloches des bons dimanches!
Et passez layettes et collerettes et robes blanches
Dans un frou-frou de lavande et de thym
Vers l'encens et les brioches!
Tout pour la famille, quoi! *Vae soli!* C'est certain.

La jeune demoiselle à l'ivoirin paroissien
Modestement rentre au logis.
On le voit, son petit corps bien reblanchi
Sait qu'il appartient
A un tout autre passé que le mien!

Mon corps, ô ma sœur, a bien mal à sa belle âme ...

With the gale gagged, at last the morning sky puts on its Sunday best. And then, hey! come on, ring out, all you good Sunday bells! And put on newborn linen and collarettes and white dresses in a swishing of lavender and thyme towards incense and brioches! Nothing spared for the family, eh? *Vae soli*! That's certain.

The young lady with the ivory prayer-book returns modestly to her home. It's obvious, her little freshly whitened body knows that it belongs to quite another past than mine!

My body, O my sister, has an ache in its beautiful soul ...

Oh! voilà que ton piano
Me recommence, si natal maintenant!
Et ton cœur qui s'ignore s'y ânonne
En ritournelles de bastringues à tout venant,
Et ta pauvre chair s'y fait mal! …
A moi, Walkyries!
Walkyries des hypocondries et des tueries!

Ah! que je te les tordrais avec plaisir,
Ce corps bijou, ce cœur à ténor,
Et te dirais leur fait, et puis encore
La manière de s'en servir
De s'en servir à deux,
Si tu voulais seulement m'approfondir ensuite un peu!

Non, non! C'est sucer la chair d'un cœur élu,
Adorer d'incurables organes
S'entrevoir avant que les tissus se fanent
En monomanes, en reclus!

Oh! how your piano renews me, so like a birth now! And your heart, unaware of itself, stumbles along through dance-hall ritornellos for all and sundry, and your poor flesh wounds itself on them! … Help me, Valkyries! Valkyries of hypochondria and slaughter!

Ah! how I would take pleasure in twisting them for you, that jewel body, that tenor heart, and tell you the straight truth about them, and then the way to use them, to use them together, if only you would gaze deeply into me for a while afterwards!

No, no! That would be to suck the flesh of a select heart, to worship incurable organs, to glimpse each other before the tissues wither into monomaniacs, into hermits!

Et ce n'est pas sa chair qui me serait tout,
Et je ne serais pas qu'un grand cœur pour elle,
Mais quoi s'en aller faire les fous
Dans des histoires fraternelles!
L'âme et la chair, la chair et l'âme,
C'est l'Esprit édénique et fier
D'être un peu l'Homme avec la Femme.

En attendant, oh! garde-toi des coups de tête,
Oh! file ton rouet et prie et reste honnête.

– Allons, dernier des poètes,
Toujours enfermé tu te rendras malade!
Vois, il fait beau temps tout le monde est dehors,
Va donc acheter deux sous d'ellébore,
Ça te fera une petite promenade.

And it's not her flesh that would be all to me, and I wouldn't be just a noble heart for her, but what's the point of playing the fool in Platonic affairs! The soul and the flesh, the flesh and the soul, it is the proud Spirit of Eden to be Man with Woman a while.

Meanwhile, oh! beware of rash impulses, oh! spin your wheel and pray and remain well-bred.

– Come on, lowest of poets, you'll make yourself ill, always shut in! See, the weather is fine everyone is out of doors, go and buy a ha'p'orth of hellebore, it'll be a nice little stroll for you.

Solo de lune

Je fume, étalé face au ciel,
Sur l'impériale de la diligence,
Ma carcasse est cahotée, mon âme danse
Comme un Ariel;
Sans miel, sans fiel, ma belle âme danse,
O routes, coteaux, ô fumées, ô vallons,
Ma belle âme, ah! récapitulons.

Nous nous aimions comme deux fous,
On s'est quitté sans en parler,
Un spleen me tenait exilé,
Et ce spleen me venait de tout. Bon.

Ses yeux disaient: "Comprenez-vous?
Pourquoi ne comprenez-vous pas?"
Mais nul n'a voulu faire le premier pas,
Voulant trop tomber *ensemble* à genoux.
(Comprenez-vous?)

Moonlight Solo

I smoke, splayed out facing the sky, on the top deck of the stagecoach, my carcass jolting, my soul dancing like an Ariel; without honey, without gall, my exquisite soul dances. O roads, hillsides! O smoke, O valleys, my exquisite soul, ah! let's recapitulate.

We loved each other like two mad creatures, we left each other without a word about it, a deep depression held me in exile, and that spleen came to me from everything. All right.

Her eyes said: 'Do you understand? Why don't you understand?' But neither would make the first move, wanting too much to fall to our knees *together*. (Do you understand?)

Où est-elle à cette heure?
Peut-être qu'elle pleure …
Où est-elle à cette heure?
Oh! du moins, soigne-toi, je t'en conjure!

O fraîcheur des bois le long de la route,
O châle de mélancolie, toute âme est un peu aux écoutes,
Que ma vie
Fait envie!
Cette impériale de diligence tient de la magie.

Accumulons l'irréparable!
Renchérissons sur notre sort!
Les étoiles sont plus nombreuses que le sable
Des mers ou d'autres ont vu se baigner son corps;
Tout n'en va pas moins à la Mort,
Y a pas de port.

Where is she at this hour? Perhaps she's weeping … where is she at this hour? Oh! at least take care of yourself, I beg you!

O coolness of the woods along the road, O shawl of melancholy, every soul is eavesdropping a little, how enviable my life is! This stagecoach rooftop has magical properties.

Let's accumulate the irreparable! Outdo our fate! The stars are more numerous than the sands of the seas where others have seen her body bathe; everything leads no less to Death, there's no haven.

Des ans vont passer là-dessus,
On s'endurcira chacun pour soi,
Et bien souvent et déjà je m'y vois,
On se dira: "Si j'avais su ..."
Mais mariés de même, ne se fût-on pas dit:
"Si j'avais su, si j'avais su! ..."?
Ah! rendez-vous maudit!
Ah! mon cœur sans issue! ...
Je me suis mal conduit.

Maniaques de bonheur,
Donc, que ferons-nous? Moi de mon âme,
Elle de sa faillible jeunesse?
O vieillissante pécheresse,
Oh! que de soirs je vais me rendre infâme
En ton honneur!

Ses yeux clignaient: "Comprenez-vous?
Pourquoi ne comprenez-vous pas?"
Mais nul n'a fait le premier pas
Pour tomber ensemble à genoux. Ah! ...

La Lune se lève,
O route en grand rêve! ...

Years will pass over it, we'll grow hardened each for himself, and very often and I can see myself already, we'll say: 'If I had known ...' But married even, wouldn't we have said: 'If I had known, if I had known ...'? Ah! cursed rendez-vous! ah! my dead-end heart! ... I've behaved badly.

Happiness maniacs, what shall we do then? Me with my soul, she with her fallible youth? O ageing sinner-woman, oh! how many evenings will I debase myself in your honour?

Her eyes flickered: 'Do you understand? Why don't you understand?' But neither would make the first move to fall together to our knees. Ah! ...

The Moon is rising, O road in a great dream! ...

On a dépassé les filatures, les scieries,
Plus que les bornes kilométriques,
De petits nuages d'un rose de confiserie,
Cependant qu'un fin croissant de lune se lève,
O route de rêve, ô nulle musique ...

Dans ces bois de pins où depuis
Le commencement du monde
Il fait toujours nuit,
Que de chambres propres et profondes!
Oh! pour un soir d'enlèvement!
Et je les peuple et je m'y vois,
Et c'est un beau couple d'amants,
Qui gesticulent hors la loi.

Et je passe et les abandonne,
Et me recouche face au ciel,
La route tourne, je suis Ariel,
Nul ne m'attend, je ne vais chez personne,
Je n'ai que l'amitié des chambres d'hôtel.

We've gone beyond the woollen mills, the sawmills, nothing now but milestones, little clouds in confectionery pink, while a delicate croissant moon rises, O dream road, O absence of music ...

In these pine woods where since the beginning of the world there has always been darkness, how many clean, dark bedrooms! Oh! for an evening of abduction! And I people them and see myself in there, and what a fine pair of lovers, gesturing outside the law.

And I pass and abandon them, and lie back facing the sky, the road turns, I am Ariel, no one expects me, I'm going to no one's house, for friendship I have only hotel rooms.

La lune se lève,
O route en grand rêve!
O route sans terme,
Voici le relais,
Où l'on allume les lanternes,
Où l'on boit un verre de lait,
Et fouette postillon
Dans le chant des grillons,
Sous les étoiles de juillet.

O clair de Lune,
Noce de feux de Bengale noyant mon infortune,
Les ombres des peupliers sur la route, ...
Le gave qui s'écoute, ...
Qui s'écoute chanter, ...
Dans ces inondations du fleuve du Léthé, ...

The moon is rising, O road in a dream! O road without end, here's the post-house, where they light the lanterns, where we drink a glass of milk, and gee-up we're away, in the song of the crickets, under the July stars.

O moonlight, wedding feast of Bengal lights drowning my distress, the shadows of the poplars on the road, ... the mountain torrent listening to itself, ... listening to itself singing, ... in these floods of the river of Lethe, ...

O Solo de lune,
Vous défiez ma plume,
Oh! cette nuit sur la route;
O Etoiles, vous êtes à faire peur,
Vous y êtes toutes! toutes!
O fugacité de cette heure ...
Oh! qu'il y eût moyen
De m'en garder l'âme pour l'automne qui vient! ...

Voici qu'il fait très très-frais,
Oh! si à la même heure,
Elle va de même le long des forêts,
Noyer son infortune
Dans les noces du clair de lune! ...
(Elle aime tant errer tard!)
Elle aura oublié son foulard,
Elle va prendre mal, vu la beauté de l'heure!
Oh! soigne-toi je t'en conjure!
Oh! je ne veux plus entendre cette toux!

O moonlight Solo, you challenge my pen, oh! this night on the road; O Stars, you are frightening, you're all there, all! O the transience of this hour ... oh! that there were a way to preserve the soul of it for the coming autumn! ...

And now it's very very cool, oh! if at the same hour she is moving like me along the forests, to drown her distress in the wedding-feast of moonlight! ... (She so loves her late-night wanderings!) She'll have forgotten her scarf, she'll catch her death, given the beauty of the hour! Oh! take care of yourself I beg you! Oh! I can't bear that cough any more!

Ah! que ne suis-je tombé à tes genoux!
Ah! que n'as-tu défailli à mes genoux!
J'eusse été le modèle des époux!
Comme le frou-frou de ta robe est le modèle des frou-frou.

Ah! why didn't I fall at your knees! Ah! why didn't you faint at my knees! I would have been an exemplary husband! as the rustling of your gown is an exemplary rustling.

The Symbolist Movement

In 1883–4 Verlaine's articles entitled *Les Poètes maudits* provided a focus and stimulus for a new surge of creative escapism, decadent revolt and aesthetic research. The atmosphere was intensified by the appearance of Jean Moréas' volume *Les Syrtes* in 1884, and by the publication that same year of Huysmans' novel *A Rebours*. Its hero, Des Esseintes, became the literary prototype of the over-sensitive, exquisitely bored, perverse *fin-de-siècle* dandy more interested in aesthetics than morality.

Simultaneously, Laforgue was composing his *Complaintes*, and feeling his way towards both free verse and the modernistic fusion of the unconscious with perceived reality, and the first signs were emerging of a major Belgian contribution to French literature, a Symbolist movement based in Gand and Louvain. This new source would produce two fine poets, Verhaeren and Maeterlinck, among an abundance of less innovative figures such as Elskamp, Rodenbach and Van Lerberghe. A number of the Belgians gravitated to Paris and specifically to Mallarmé's Tuesday gatherings, where they also met the young Claudel and Valéry.

Decadence was short-lived, though it featured some interesting extremist dandies like Laurent Tailhade and Comte Robert de Montesquiou-Fezensac (the latter a model for Des Esseintes and for Proust's Baron de Charlus), and its neurotic atmosphere imbues the work of Laforgue. But *Symbolism* (initially called Idealism) made a much more substantial impact, for in its various forms it dominated French verse to the turn of the century, and lived on beyond that time in the work of Paul Valéry, who brought it to perfection in an era when a fresh generation of modernist poets had already rejected it.

For the Symbolists, unlike the materialist and objective Parnassians, a landscape or scene or object is an '*état d'âme*', a projected state of sensibility or condition of the soul. Developing and synthesizing Baudelaire's theory of latent imaginative '*correspondances*', Rimbaud's '*Voyance*', Verlaine's musicality and Mallarmé's hermeticism, the poet seeks the inner meaning of things. He seeks a heightened state of awareness by concentration on the suggestive Symbol, the analogy that reveals progressively, by allusion, and does not name directly. In Mallarmé's words: 'To name an object is to suppress three-quarters of the delight of the poem, which consists in the pleasure of guessing little by little; to suggest it, that is the dream. It is the perfect use of this mystery that constitutes the symbol: to evoke an object gradually in order to reveal a state of the soul, or, inversely, to choose an object and from it identify a state of the soul, by a series of deciphering operations ... There must always be enigma in poetry.'

The poem is to be a resonant yet understated symphony composed of images, sound-patterns and rhythms that prolong and multiply to infinity impression, sensation and dream. Rodenbach offered this characteristically nebulous definition: 'The poetry of symbols is dream, nuance, art on a journey with the clouds, art capturing reflections, art for which reality is merely a point of departure, and the paper itself is a slender white certainty from which one is launched into chasms of mystery that are above us and draw us up.'

For the pure Symbolist, language is to be wilfully elliptical, complex, precious and melodic, excluding social reference and popular taste. Such is the spiritual power of the active, autonomously creative Word in poetic reverie, an energy described by Maeterlinck as a '*force occulte*', that a mystical and ideal network of affinities can be woven on the basis of semi-conscious verbal correspondences alone. This density of perception, at the opposite pole to Mallarmé's aesthetic of Absence, is effectively religious and is sometimes called 'ultra-symbolism'. Its major exponent is Saint-Pol Roux, but its influence is discernible in Claudel.

On the other hand, Verhaeren leads the Belgians into a marriage between Symbolism and realism, committing poetic vision to contemporary industrial reality, and moving on a path parallel to Laforgue's in seeking a blend of the unconscious and the material in the recording of perceptions.

Much Symbolist poetry now seems insipid, technical and imitative, and space cannot be found here even for the free-verse attempts of Vielé-Griffin and Merrill (both of American origin) and of Gustave Kahn (see the introduction to Laforgue, page 326). Another exclusion is Albert Samain, much admired in his time but rarely read now. Samain is perhaps typical of the empty mystique and gutlessness of Symbolism. His sensibility is dreamy, elegant, nostalgic, his versification languidly musical and atmospheric. But his verse is thematically conventional and devoid of vigour, lacking in stimulating irony or originality of imagery.

Some mention should also be made of Alfred Jarry, best known today for his remarkable pre-Absurdist *Ubu* plays. A flamboyant fringe Symbolist, a subversive apostle of esoteric counter-culture, his life was itself an iconoclastic work of art prefiguring Dadaism. Jarry wrote poems and prose-poems full of subtle word-play and technical virtuosity, few of which would be readily translatable.

Emile Verhaeren
(1855–1916)

Verhaeren is one of the most talented, most concrete and thematically wide-ranging of the Belgian Symbolists. His identity is firmly, even aggressively, rooted in his French-speaking Flemish background. He is a melancholy poet of Flemish mists and rural stagnation, but also a vibrant, passionate observer of the glories and horrors of industrial urbanization.

His early work on rural themes is marked by profound pessimism and psychological anguish, in which potentially suicidal depression is objectified into hallucinatory and even apocalyptic forms. Later he awakens to the exciting multiplicity of modern city life, and his own personality blends dynamically with it. Though he never loses his capacity for horrific perception, Verhaeren becomes increasingly an apostle of progress through the power of the human mind, and develops a prophetic, socialistic vision of a new society of joyful work and universal solidarity. As with Walt Whitman, whom Verhaeren admired, the poet is part of history in the making, intoxicated by the process.

A pioneer of free verse as the organic, flexible instrument of visionary thought, he writes often in a feverish, incantatory, uneven style given unity by leitmotifs and emotional force, but like all good free-verse poets he can also show mastery of orthodox technique.

Major volumes (his output was prolific): *Les Flamandes* 1883, *Les Moines* 1886, *Les Soirs* 1887, *Les Débâcles* 1888, *Les Flambeaux noirs* 1890, *Les Apparus dans mes chemins* 1891, *Les Campagnes hallucinées* 1893, *Les Villages illusoires* 1895, *Les Villes tentaculaires* 1895, *Les Heures claires* 1896, *Les Visages de la vie* 1899, *Les Forces tumultueuses* 1902, *La Multiple Splendeur* 1906, *Les Rythmes sourverains* 1910, etc.

Le Moulin[1]

Le moulin tourne au fond du soir, très lentement,
Sur un ciel de tristesse et de mélancolie,
Il tourne et tourne, et sa voile, couleur de lie,
Est triste et faible et lourde et lasse, infiniment.

Depuis l'aube, ses bras, comme des bras de plainte,
Se sont tendus et sont tombés; et les voici
Qui retombent encor, là-bas, dans l'air noirci
Et le silence entier de la nature éteinte.

The Mill

The mill turns in the deep of the evening, very slowly, against a sad and melancholy sky; it turns and turns, and its sail, the colour of dregs, is sad and weak and heavy and weary, to infinity.

Since dawn, its arms, like arms of lamentation, have stretched up and fallen; and now they fall again, there, in the blackened air and the all-encompassing silence of extinct nature.

[1]There is a later version of this poem, in which the emotional elements have been replaced by more objective description of the '*huttes*'. The resulting loss of poetic force leads me to prefer this original version.

Un jour souffrant d'hiver sur les hameaux s'endort,
Les nuages sont las de leurs voyages sombres,
Et le long des taillis qui ramassent leurs ombres
Les ornières s'en vont vers un horizon mort.

Sous un ourlet de sol, quelques huttes de hêtre
Très misérablement sont assises en rond;
Une lampe de cuivre est pendue au plafond
Et patine de feu le mur et la fenêtre.

Et dans la plaine immense et le vide dormeur
Elles fixent – les très souffreteuses bicoques! –
Avec les pauvres yeux de leurs carreaux en loques,
Le vieux moulin qui tourne et, las, qui tourne et meurt.

An ailing winter day sinks into sleep over the hamlets, the clouds are weary of their dark journeys, and along the copsewoods gathering up their shadows, the ruts run on towards a dead horizon.

Beneath a rim of soil, some beechwood huts sit most wretchedly in a circle; a copper lamp hangs from the ceiling and casts a patina of firelight on wall and window.

And in the vast plain and the sleeping void they stare – those impoverished hovels! – with the poor eyes of their tattered panes, at the old mill which turns and, weary, turns and dies.

Chanson de fou

Vous aurez beau crier contre la terre,
La bouche dans le fossé,
Jamais aucun des trépassés
Ne répondra à vos clameurs amères.

Ils sont bien morts, les morts,
Ceux qui firent jadis la campagne féconde;
Ils font l'immense entassement de morts
Qui pourrissent, aux quatre coins du monde,
Les morts.

Alors
Les champs étaient maîtres des villes,
Le même esprit servile
Ployait partout les fronts et les échines,
Et nul encor ne pouvait voir
Dressés, au fond du soir,
Les bras hagards et formidables des machines.

Madman's Song

You'll howl in vain at the earth, with your mouth in the pit, not one among the departed souls will ever answer your bitter clamour.

They are truly dead, the dead, those who once made the countryside fertile; they form the immense mass of the dead who rot, in the four corners of the world, the dead.

Then, the fields were masters of the cities, the same cringing spirit bent brows and backbones everywhere, and none could yet see raised, in the depths of evening, the gaunt and fearful arms of the machines.

Vous aurez beau crier contre la terre,
La bouche dans le fossé:
Ceux qui jadis étaient les trépassés
Sont aujourd'hui, jusqu'au fond de la terre,
Les morts.

You'll howl in vain at the earth, with your mouth in the pit: those who once were the departed souls are now, unto the depths of the earth, the dead.

Les Usines

Se regardant avec les yeux cassés de leurs fenêtres
Et se mirant dans l'eau de poix et de salpêtre
D'un canal droit, marquant sa barre à l'infini,
Face à face, le long des quais d'ombre et de nuit,
Par à travers les faubourgs lourds
Et la misère en pleurs de ces faubourgs,
Ronflent terriblement usines et fabriques.

The Factories

Gazing at each other with the shattered eyes of their windows and at their reflection in the pitch and saltpetre water of a straight canal, its line inscribed to infinity, face to face, along the wharves of shadow and darkness, all through the oppressive suburbs and the weeping poverty of those suburbs, factories and mills roar with terrible voice.

Rectangles de granit et monuments de briques,
Et longs murs noirs durant des lieues,
Immensément, par les banlieues;
Et sur les toits, dans le brouillard, aiguillonnées
De fers et de paratonnerres,
Les cheminées.

Se regardant de leurs yeux noirs et symétriques,
Par la banlieue, à l'infini,
Ronflent le jour, la nuit,
Les usines et les fabriques.

Oh les quartiers rouillés de pluie et leurs grand'rues!
Et les femmes et leurs guenilles apparues
Et les squares, où s'ouvre, en des caries
De plâtras blanc et de scories,
Une flore pâle et pourrie.

Granite rectangles and brick monuments, and long black walls that run for leagues, immeasurably, through the suburbs; and on the roofs, in the fog, needled with wires and lightning conductors, the chimneys.

Gazing at each other with their black symmetrical eyes, across the suburbs, to infinity, factories and mills roar day and night.

Oh! districts mildewed by rain and their main streets! And the women and their manifest ragged bodies and the squares where among rotting white plaster-work and slag a pale and putrid flora opens.

Aux carrefours, porte ouverte, les bars:
Étains, cuivres, miroirs hagards,
Dressoirs d'ébène et flacons fols
D'où luit l'alcool
Et sa lueur vers les trottoirs.
Et des pintes qui tout à coup rayonnent,
Sur le comptoir, en pyramides de couronnes;
Et des gens soûls, debout,
Dont les larges langues lapent, sans phrases,
Les ales d'or et le whisky, couleur topaze.

At the crossroads, with open doors, the bars: pewter, brasses, gaunt mirrors, ebony dressers and prodigious flagons whose alcohol shines its light towards the pavements. And pint-pots suddenly radiant, on the bar-top, in pyramids of diadems; and drunken people, standing there, their broad and wordless tongues lapping golden ales and topaz-coloured whisky.

Par à travers les faubourgs lourds
Et la misère en pleurs de ces faubourgs,
Et les troubles et mornes voisinages,
Et les haines s'entrecroisant de gens à gens
Et de ménages à ménages,
Et le vol même entre indigents,
Grondent, au fond des cours, toujours,
Les haletants battements sourds
Des usines et des fabriques symétriques.

Ici, sous de grands toits où scintille le verre,
La vapeur se condense en force prisonnière:
Des mâchoires d'acier mordent et fument;
De grands marteaux monumentaux
Broient des blocs d'or sur des enclumes,
Et, dans un coin, s'illuminent les fontes
En brasiers tors et effrénés qu'on dompte.

All through the oppressive suburbs and the weeping poverty of those suburbs, and the turmoils and the dismal proximity, and the hatreds criss-crossing from people to people and from household to household, and the theft even among the poverty-stricken, deep in the yards, never ceasing, sound the dull, rumbling, panting throbs of the symmetrical factories and mills.

Here, under great roofs where glass shimmers, steam condenses in captive power: steel jaws bite and smoke; great monumental hammers pound golden blocks on anvils, and in a corner glows the smelting iron in contorted, unbridled yet tamed furnaces.

Là-bas, les doigts méticuleux des métiers prestes,
A bruits menus, à petits gestes,
Tissent des draps, avec des fils qui vibrent
Légers et fins comme des fibres.
Des bandes de cuir transversales
Courent de l'un à l'autre bout des salles
Et les volants larges et violents
Tournent, pareils aux ailes dans le vent
Des moulins fous, sous les rafales.
Un jour de cour avare et ras
Frôle, par à travers les carreaux gras
Et humides d'un soupirail,
Chaque travail.
Automatiques et minutieux,
Des ouvriers silencieux
Règlent le mouvement
D'universel tictaquement
Qui fermente de fièvre et de folie
Et déchiquette, avec ses dents d'entêtement,
La parole humaine abolie.

And there, the meticulous fingers of the nimble crafts, with minute sounds, with spare gestures, weave sheets, with vibrating threads as light and delicate as fibres. Transversal leather bands run through the rooms from end to end and the broad violent flywheels turn like the sails of demented windmills in stormy blasts. A miserly, shorn daylight from the yard, through moist and oily ventilator panes, grazes each operation. Mechanical and meticulous, silent workers regulate the universal ticktacking movement that ferments in fever and madness and hacks to pieces, with the teeth of its obsession, abolished human speech.

Plus loin, un vacarme tonnant de chocs
Monte de l'ombre et s'érige par blocs;
Et, tout à coup, cassant l'élan des violences,
Des murs de bruit semblent tomber
Et se taire, dans une mare de silence,
Tandis que les appels exacerbés
Des sifflets crus et des signaux
Hurlent soudain vers les fanaux,
Dressant leurs feux sauvages,
En buissons d'or, vers les nuages.

Et tout autour, ainsi qu'une ceinture,
Là-bas, de nocturnes architectures,
Voici les docks, les ports, les ponts, les phares
Et les gares folles de tintamarres;
Et plus lointains encor des toits d'autres usines
Et des cuves et des forges et des cuisines
Formidables de naphte et de résines
Dont les meutes de feu et de lueurs grandies
Mordent parfois le ciel, à coups d'abois et d'incendies.

Further on, a clamour thundering with impacts rises from the shadow and forms itself in blocks; and suddenly, breaking the momentum of violent forces, walls of noise seem to fall and be stilled in a pool of silence, while the embittered cries of harsh whistles and sirens suddenly howl at the lanterns that raise their savage glow in golden bushes towards the clouds.

And all around, there like a girdle of nocturnal architectures, are the warehouses, the wharves, the bridges, the beacons and the insane hubbub of the railway depôts; and still further on, roofs of other factories and vats and forges and tremendous cooking-pots of naphtha and resins whose hounds of fire and magnified light sometimes bite at the sky, baying as their fire strikes.

Au long du vieux canal à l'infini,
Par à travers l'immensité de la misère
Des chemins noirs et des routes de pierre,
Les nuits, les jours, toujours,
Ronflent les continus battements sourds,
Dans les faubourgs,
Des fabriques et des usines symétriques.

L'aube s'essuie
A leurs carrés de suie;
Midi et son soleil hagard
Comme un aveugle, errent par leurs brouillards;
Seul, quand au bout de la semaine, au soir,
La nuit se laisse en ses ténèbres choir,
L'âpre effort s'interrompt, mais demeure en arrêt,
Comme un marteau sur une enclume,
Et l'ombre, au loin, parmi les carrefours, paraît
De la brume d'or qui s'allume.

Along the old canal to infinity, all through the vastness of the poverty of black pathways and roads of stone, night and day, for ever, the dull unbroken throbbing of the symmetrical factories and mills roars in the suburbs.

Dawn wipes itself on their squares of soot; noon and its sun, gaunt like a blind man, wander through the fogs; only when, at the end of the week, in the evening, night sinks down into its gloom, the harsh effort is interrupted, but remains suspended, like a hammer above an anvil, and the distant shadow, among the crossroads, seems to catch fire like golden mist.

Les Horloges

La nuit, dans le silence en noir de nos demeures,
Béquilles et bâtons qui se cognent, là-bas;
Montant et dévalant les escaliers des heures,
Les horloges, avec leurs pas;

Émaux naïfs derrière un verre, emblèmes
Et fleurs d'antan, chiffres maigres et vieux;
Lunes des corridors vides et blêmes
Les horloges, avec leurs yeux;

Sons morts, notes de plomb, marteaux et limes,
Boutique en bois de mots sournois
Et le babil des secondes minimes,
Les horloges, avec leurs voix;

The Clocks

In the darkness, in the black silence of our dwellings, crutches and canes clacking, there; climbing and tumbling down the staircases of the hours, the clocks, with their footsteps;

Artless enamels behind glass, symbols and flowers of yesteryear, scrawny old numbers; moons of the corridors, vacant and pallid, the clocks, with their eyes;

Dead sounds, notes of lead, hammers and files, wooden workshop of artful words and the babbling of the minuscule seconds, the clocks, with their voices;

Gaines de chêne et bornes d'ombre,
Cercueils scellés dans le mur froid,
Vieux os du temps que grignote le nombre,
Les horloges et leur effroi;

Les horloges
Volontaires et vigilantes,
Pareilles aux vieilles servantes
Boîtant de leurs sabots ou glissant sur leurs bas,
Les horloges que j'interroge
Serrent ma peur en leur compas.

Sheaths of oak and milestones of shadow, coffins encased in the cold wall, old bones of time gnawed away by mathematics, the clocks and their terror;

The clocks, wilful[1] and watchful, like old serving women limping in their clogs or gliding on their stockings, the clocks that I question compress my fear within their compass.

Les Heures claires

Le beau jardin fleuri de flammes
Qui nous semblait le double ou le miroir
Du jardin clair que nous portions dans l'âme,
S'immobilise en un gel d'or, ce soir.

Shining hours

The beautiful garden flowering with flames which seemed to us the double or the mirror of the luminous garden that we carried in our souls, becomes still this evening in a golden frost.

[1]'*Volontaires*' has a double meaning: 'willing' as well as 'wilful'.

Un grand silence blanc est descendu s'asseoir
Là-bas, aux horizons de marbre,
Vers où s'en vont, par défilés, les arbres
Avec leur ombre immense et bleue
Et régulière, à côté d'eux.

Aucun souffle de vent, aucune haleine,
Les grands voiles du froid
Se déplient seuls, de plaine en plaine,
Sur des marais d'argent ou des routes en croix.

Les étoiles paraissent vivre.
Comme l'acier, brille le givre
A travers l'air translucide et glacé.
De clairs métaux, pulvérisés
A l'infini, semblent neiger
De la pâleur d'une lune de cuivre.
Tout est scintillement dans l'immobilité.

Et c'est l'heure divine, où l'esprit est hanté
Par ces mille regards que projette sur terre,
Vers les hasards de l'humaine misère,
La bonne et pure et inchangeable éternité.

A great white silence has come down to settle there, on the marble horizons; towards them the trees stretch away in ranks with their vast, blue, precise shadow beside them.

No wind blows, not a breath, the great veils of cold unfold alone, from plain to plain, over silvery fens or intersecting roads.

The stars seem alive. Like steel, the hoar-frost shines through the translucid glacial air. Bright metals, atomized to infinity, seem to snow from the pallor of a copper moon. All scintillates in immobility.

It is the holy hour, when the spirit is haunted by those thousand gazes cast upon the earth, towards the contingencies of human wretchedness, by benign and pure and immutable eternity.

Un Soir

Celui qui me lira dans les siècles, un soir,
Troublant mes vers, dans leur sommeil et sous leur cendre,
Et ranimant leur sens lointain pour mieux comprendre
Comment ceux d'aujourd'hui s'étaient armés d'espoir,

Qu'il sache, avec quel violent élan, ma joie
S'est, à travers les cris, les révoltes, les pleurs,
Ruée au combat fier et mâle des douleurs,
Pour en tirer l'amour, comme on conquiert sa proie.

J'aime mes yeux fiévreux, ma cervelle, mes nerfs,
Le sang dont vit mon cœur, le cœur dont vit mon torse;
J'aime l'homme et le monde et j'adore la force
Que donne et prend ma force à l'homme et l'univers.

One Evening

He who will read me in centuries' time, one evening, disturbing my verses, in their slumber beneath their ashes, and rekindling their distant meaning to conceive more fully how those of today had armed themselves with hope,

May he know with what dynamic impetus my joy, through cries, rebellion and tears, hurled itself into the proud and virile combat of pain and sorrow, to draw out love, as a prey is conquered.

I love my restless eyes, my brain, my nerves, the blood that gives life to my heart, the heart that gives life to my torso; I love mankind and the world and I worship the power that my power gives to man and the universe and takes from them.

Car vivre, c'est prendre et donner avec liesse.
Mes pairs, ce sont ceux-là qui s'exaltent autant
Que je me sens moi-même avide et haletant
Devant la vie intense et sa rouge sagesse.

Heures de chute ou de grandeur! – tout se confond
Et se transforme en ce brasier qu'est l'existence;
Seul importe que le désir reste en partance
Jusqu'à la mort, devant l'éveil des horizons.

Celui qui trouve est un cerveau qui communie
Avec la fourmillante et large humanité.
L'esprit plonge et s'enivre en pleine immensité:
Il faut aimer, pour découvrir avec génie.

Une tendresse énorme emplit l'âpre savoir,
Il exalte la force et la beauté des mondes,
Il devine les liens et les causes profondes;
O vous qui me lirez, dans les siècles, un soir,

For living is taking and giving with joyful abandon. My peers are those who are as inflamed as I am aware of myself, eager and breathless before the intensity of life and its red-hot knowledge.

Times of ruin or of greatness! – all is merged and transformed in this furnace that is existence; the imperative is only that desire be outward bound until death, facing the awakening horizons.

He who discovers is an intellect in communion with broad teeming humanity. The spirit plunges, intoxicating itself in the heart of boundlessness: one must love, to discover with genius.

A vast tenderness imbues raw knowledge, which exalts the power and the beauty of worlds, and fathoms the links and profound causes; O you who will read me in centuries' time, one evening,

Comprenez-vous pourquoi mon vers vous interpelle?
C'est qu'en vos temps quelqu'un d'ardent aura tiré
Du cœur de la nécessité même, le vrai,
Bloc clair, pour y dresser l'entente universelle.

Do you understand why my poetry challenges you with its call? It is because in your time some passionate soul will have hauled out of the heart of necessity itself the truth, a shining block, to place erect upon it universal understanding.

Maurice Maeterlinck
(1862–1949)

Maeterlinck grew up and studied at Gand in Belgium, then moved to Paris in 1885. Influenced initially by Verlaine, Mallarmé and Huysmans, he became one of Symbolism's most interesting and durable exponents. Seeking to express the inexpressible, to render abstraction concrete, his poems have the visionary coherence and the mysterious associative power of dream-notations, yet their anguished moral and religious content also gives them a 'bite' often lacking in the more insipid, insubstantial Symbolist delicacies of Samain and the rest.

Much of his best work is to be found in *Serres Chaudes* (1896). Here the soul is enclosed claustrophobically within a symbolic hot-house full of plants and animals. The somnambulistic poet gazes through the semi-opaque glass at this sickly, stifling, slow-motion world of decadence, corruption and lassitude that is part of himself, and seeks a moral and metaphysical liberation from it.

Despite his more private symbolic repertoire, Maeterlinck plays, like Verhaeren, a significant role in the development of free verse in French literature after the pioneering work of Laforgue. With the concrete, hallucinatory, superficially discontinuous imagery of 'Hôpital', for example, he strikes another blow at the French rhetorical tradition, yet he can still produce works of compact, haunting musicality like 'Trois princesses m'ont embrassé'.

Further volumes include: *Quinze Chansons* 1900, *Neuf Chansons de la Trentaine*,[1] and *Treize Chansons de l'Age mûr.*[1] He also became known as a philosophical writer, and above all as an important contributor to the Symbolist movement in the theatre.

[1]These titles are given by Joseph Hanse to groups of poems in his 1965 edition of Maeterlinck's *Poésies complètes*.

Tentations

O les glauques tentations
Au milieu des ombres mentales,
Avec leurs flammes végétales
Et leurs éjaculations

Obscures de tiges obscures,
Dans le clair de lune du mal,
Eployant l'ombrage automnal
De leurs luxurieux augures!

Elles ont tristement couvert,
Sous leurs muqueuses enlacées
Et leurs fièvres réalisées,
La lune de leur givre vert.

Et leur croissance sacrilège,
Entr'ouvrant ses désirs secrets,
Est morne comme les regrets
Des malades sur de la neige.

Temptations

O the glaucous temptations among the shadows of the mind, with their vegetal fires and their mysterious

Discharges from obscure stems, in the moonlight of evil, unfolding the autumnal shade of their lascivious omens!

Mournfully they have covered the moon, beneath their entwined mucous membranes and their manifest fevers, with their green rime.

And their sacrilegious growth, opening its secret desires, is dismal like the yearnings of sick men on snow.

Sous les ténèbres de leur deuil,
Je vois s'emmêler les blessures
Des glaives bleus de mes luxures
Dans les chairs rouges de l'orgueil.

Seigneur, les rêves de la terre
Mourront-ils enfin dans mon cœur!
Laissez votre gloire, Seigneur,
Eclairer la mauvaise serre,

Et l'oubli vainement cherché!
Les feuilles mortes de leurs fièvres,
Les étoiles entre leurs lèvres,
Et les entrailles du péché!

Beneath the shadows of their mourning, I see intermingling the wounds of the blue swords of my lusts in the red fleshly bodies of pride.

Lord, will earthly dreams die once and for all in my heart! Let your glory, Lord, illumine the evil hot-house,

And vainly sought oblivion! The dead leaves of their fevers, the stars between their lips, and the entrails of sin!

Hôpital

Hôpital! hôpital au bord du canal!
Hôpital au mois de Juillet!
On y fait du feu dans la salle!
Tandis que les transatlantiques sifflent sur le canal!

Hospital

Hospital! hospital on the canal bank! Hospital in the month of July! They're making up a fire in the room! While the liners are whistling on the canal!

(Oh! n'approchez pas des fenêtres!)
Des émigrants traversent un palais!
Je vois un yacht sous la tempête!
Je vois des troupeaux sur tous les navires!
(Il vaut mieux que les fenêtres restent closes,
On est presque à l'abri du dehors.)
On a l'idée d'une serre sur la neige,
On croit célébrer des relevailles un jour d'orage,
On entrevoit des plantes éparses sur une couverture de laine,
Il y a un incendie un jour de soleil,
Et je traverse une forêt pleine de blessés.

Oh! voici enfin le clair de lune!

Un jet d'eau s'élève au milieu de la salle!
Une troupe de petites filles entr'ouvre la porte!
J'entrevois des agneaux dans une île de prairies!
Et de belles plantes sur un glacier!
Et des lys dans un vestibule de marbre!
Il y a un festin dans une forêt vierge!
Et une végétation orientale dans une grotte de glace!

(Oh! don't go near the windows!) Emigrants are passing through a palace! I see a yacht beneath the tempest! I see herds on all the ships! (It's better that the windows stay closed, we're almost sheltered from the outside world.) You have the notion of a hot-house on the snow, that you're celebrating a woman's churching on a stormy day, that you glimpse plants scattered on a woollen counterpane, there is a fire on a sunlit day, and I am passing through a forest filled with wounded.

Oh! here at last is the moonlight!

A fountain rises in the middle of the room! A troupe of little girls opens the door tentatively! I glimpse lambs on an island of meadows! And beautiful plants on a glacier! And lilies in a marble hall! There is a banquet in a virgin forest! And oriental vegetation in a cavern of ice!

Ecoutez! on ouvre les écluses!
Et les transatlantiques agitent l'eau du canal!

Oh! mais la sœur de charité attisant le feu!

Tous les beaux roseaux verts des berges sont en flamme!
Un bateau de blessés ballotte au clair de lune!
Toutes les filles du roi sont dans une barque sous l'orage!
Et les princesses vont mourir en un champ de ciguës!

Oh! n'entr'ouvrez pas les fenêtres!
Ecoutez: les transatlantiques sifflent encore à l'horizon!

On empoisonne quelqu'un dans un jardin!
Ils célèbrent une grande fête chez les ennemis!
Il y a des cerfs dans une ville assiégée!
Et une ménagerie au milieu des lys!
Il y a une végétation tropicale au fond d'une houillère!
Un troupeau de brebis traverse un pont de fer!
Et les agneaux de la prairie entrent tristement dans la salle!

Listen! the flood-gates are opening! And the liners stir the water of the canal!

Oh! but the sister of mercy stirring the fire!

All the beautiful green reeds on the embankments are aflame! A boatload of wounded tosses in the moonlight! All the king's daughters are in a boat beneath the storm! And the princesses are about to die in a field of hemlock!

Oh! don't even open the windows a little! Listen: the liners are still whistling on the horizon!

Someone is being poisoned in a garden! They're celebrating a great festival among the enemy! There are stags in a besieged city! And a menagerie among the lilies! There is tropical vegetation in the depths of a coal-mine! A flock of ewes is crossing an iron bridge! And the meadow lambs sadly enter the room!

Maintenant la sœur de charité allume les lampes,
Elle apporte le repas des malades,
Elle a clos les fenêtres sur le canal,
Et toutes les portes au clair de lune.

Now the sister of mercy is lighting the lamps, she is bringing the patients' meals, she has closed the windows on the canal, and all the doors to the moonlight.

Trois princesses m'ont embrassé

Trois princesses m'ont embrassé.
La première dans les souterrains.
J'ai vu tomber des pierreries
Sur mes lèvres et sur mes mains.

Trois princesses m'ont embrassé.
La seconde dans les corridors.
Le soleil mangeait nos baisers.
J'ai vu qu'il faisait beau dehors.

Trois princesses m'ont embrassé.
La troisième au haut de la tour.
J'ai vu la fuite de l'amour,
Et l'espace l'emporter sans retour.

Three Princesses kissed me

Three princesses kissed me. The first in the vaulted caverns. I saw precious stones falling on my lips and on my hands.

Three princesses kissed me. The second in the galleries. The sun ate our kisses. I saw that the day was beautiful outside.

Three princesses kissed me. The third at the top of the tower. I saw the escape of love, and space carry it beyond return.

Two synthesizing poets: Moréas and de Régnier

In their parallel evolution these two poets, often dismissed as insipid and bourgeois, can perhaps be seen more positively as model, undemonstrative professionals, blending their awareness of tradition and of new influences into a concise if transparent synthesis of nineteenth-century tendencies in poetry. They deserve some measure of recall from the oblivion into which most Symbolists have fallen.

Jean Moréas
(1856–1910)

Of Greek origin but French education and inclinations, Moréas' real name was Papadiamantopoulos. One of the initiators of the Symbolist movement in the 1880s and a prominent early theorist, he turned away from Symbolism's blurred vision at the end of that decade, favouring a return to Graeco-Latin inspiration and disciplined, lucid techniques. He founded a group known as the *Ecole Romane* which included Charles Maurras, Raymond de la Tailhède and Maurice du Plessys.

Les Stances are generally considered to be his most mature and valuable work. A sequence of highly compressed yet unhermetic poems, they are a refined blend of Romantic sentiment, classical clarity of image and Symbolist musicality, producing a haunting lyricism in which his technical virtuosity is less obviously contrived than in his early work.

Major volumes: *Les Syrtes* 1884, *Les Cantilènes* 1886, *Le Pèlerin passionné* 1891, *Enone au clair visage* 1893, *Eriphyle et quatre Sylves* 1894, *Les Stances* 1899–1901–1920.

Stances

Livre I, xii

Les morts m'écoutent seuls, j'habite les tombeaux;
Jusqu'au bout je serai l'ennemi de moi-même.
Ma gloire est aux ingrats, mon grain est aux corbeaux;
Sans récolter jamais je laboure et je sème.

Je ne me plaindrai pas: qu'importe l'Aquilon,
L'opprobre et le mépris, la face de l'injure!
Puisque quand je te touche, ô lyre d'Apollon,
Tu sonnes chaque fois plus savante et plus pure?

Stanzas

Book I, xii

The dead alone are my listeners, I am an inhabitant of tombs; until the end I will be my own enemy. The ungrateful have my halo, the ravens have my berries; never a harvester, I plough and I sow.

I will not complain: what matters the North Wind, disgrace and contempt, the countenance of slander! For at my touch, O lyre of Apollo, you sound each time more refined and more pure?

Livre III, vi

Relève-toi, mon âme, et redeviens la cible
De mille flèches d'or:
Il faut qu'avec ma main cette Minerve horrible
Frappe la lyre encor.

L'arbre portant ses fruits, le vent qui le renverse,
Sur le front d'un ami
La pâle mort déjà, la trahison qui berce
Le soupçon endormi,

L'étoile à l'horizon, le phare sur le môle,
La coupe au cristal fin
Que j'ai jetée ainsi par-dessus mon épaule,
Toute pleine de vin,

Et chacun de mes jours, tels qu'une fleur qui passe
Sur l'onde et disparaît:
Dans mon destin comment sauraient-ils trouver place,
Cet espoir, ce regret?

Book III, vi

Rise up, my soul, and become once more the target of a thousand golden arrows: with my hand this hideous Minerva must strike the lyre once more.

The tree bearing its fruits, the wind that uproots it, pale death already on the brow of a friend, treachery that cradles dormant suspicion,

The star on the horizon, the beacon on the breakwater, the goblet of fine crystal that I threw thus over my shoulder, brimming with wine,

And each of my days, like a flower drifting by to oblivion on the waters: how could they find a place in my destiny, this hope, this yearning?

Livre IV, iv

Sunium, Sunium, sublime promontoire
Sous le ciel le plus beau,
De l'âme et de l'esprit, de toute humaine gloire
Le berceau, le tombeau!

Jadis, bien jeune encore, lorsque le jour splendide
Sort de l'ombre vainqueur,
Ton image a blessé, comme d'un trait rapide,
Les forces de mon cœur.

Ah! qu'il saigne, ce cœur! et toi, mortelle vue,
Garde toujours doublé,
Au-dessus d'une mer azurée et chenue,
Un temple mutilé.

Book IV, iv

Sunium, Sunium, sublime promontory beneath the fairest of skies, of soul and spirit, of all human glory the cradle and the grave!

Once long ago, still very young, when resplendent day emerges from conquering shadows, your image has wounded, like a speeding dart, the strength of my heart.

Ah! how it bleeds, this heart! and you, mortal sight, keep for ever doubled, above an azure-coloured and foam-white sea, a mutilated temple.

Livre VI, viii

L'insidieuse nuit m'a grisé trop longtemps!
　Pensif à ma fenêtre,
O suave matin, je veille et je t'attends;
　Hâte-toi de paraître.

Viens! au dedans de moi s'épandra ta clarté
　En élément tranquille:
Ainsi l'eau te reçoit, ainsi l'obscurité
　Des feuilles te distille.

O jour, ô frais rayons, immobilisez-vous,
　Mirés dans mes yeux sombres,
Maintenant que mon cœur à chacun de ses coups
　Se rapproche des ombres.

Book VI, viii

The insidious night has intoxicated me too long! Thoughtful at my window, O sweet morning, I keep vigil and await you; come swiftly into sight.

Come! within me your brightness will spread as a placid element: thus water welcomes you, thus the darkness of leaves distils you.

O daylight, O fresh rays, be still, reflected in my lustreless eyes, now that my heart with each of its beats grows closer to the shadows.

Livre VII, iv

J'allais dans la campagne avec le vent d'orage,
Sous le pâle matin, sous les nuages bas;
Un corbeau ténébreux escortait mon voyage,
Et dans les flaques d'eau retentissaient mes pas.

La foudre à l'horizon faisait courir sa flamme
Et l'Aquilon doublait ses longs gémissements;
Mais la tempête était trop faible pour mon âme,
Qui couvrait le tonnerre avec ses battements.

De la dépouille d'or du frêne et de l'érable
L'Automne composait son éclatant butin,
Et le corbeau toujours d'un vol inexorable
M'accompagnait sans rien changer à mon destin.

Book VII, iv

Through the countryside I went with the stormy wind, in the pale morning light, beneath the low clouds; a shadowy raven accompanied my journey, and my steps reverberated in the pools of water.

Lightning launched its flame along the horizon and the North Wind redoubled its prolonged moaning; but the tempest was too weak for my soul, which drowned the thunder with its throbbing.

With the golden plunder of ash and maple Autumn gathered its resplendent booty, and the raven still with relentless flight travelled with me, changing nothing in my destiny.

Henri de Régnier
(1864–1936)

A versatile lyric poet who achieved in his work a harmonious blend of Romantic, Parnassian and Symbolist influences, de Régnier wrote both metrically orthodox and freer verse characterized by delicate musicality. Its Verlainian and Symbolist features never clouded entirely his capacity for sentiment and eroticism. His taste for plastic imagery and his admiration for Heredia led him firmly into a neo-classical Parnassianism at the turn of the century, but the emotional element never disappeared entirely from his work.

Major volumes: *Poèmes anciens et romanesques* 1890, *Tel qu'en songe* 1892, *Jeux rustiques et divins* 1897, *Les Médailles d'argile* 1900, *La Cité des Eaux* 1902, *La Sandale ailée* 1906, *Le Miroir des Heures* 1910.

Le Socle

L'Amour qui souriait en son bronze d'or clair
Au centre du bassin qu'enfeuille, soir à soir,
L'automne, a chancelé en se penchant pour voir
En l'onde son reflet lui rire, inverse et vert.

Le prestige mystérieux s'est entr'ouvert;
Sa chute, par sa ride, a brisé le miroïr,
Et dans la transparence en paix du cristal noir
On l'aperçoit qui dort sous l'eau qui l'a couvert.

Le lieu est triste; l'if est dur; le cyprès nu.
L'allée au loin s'enfonce où nul n'est revenu,
Dont le pas à jamais vibre au fond de l'écho;

Et, de l'Amour tombé du socle qu'il dénude,
Il reste un bloc égal qui semble le tombeau
Du songe, du silence et de la solitude.

The Plinth

The Cupid who smiled in his bright gilded bronze, at the centre of the pool strewn with leaves by autumn as evenings pass, toppled as he leaned to see in the waters his laughing reflection, inverted and green.

The mysterious illusion broke open; his fall through its ripple broke the mirror, and in the transparency at peace of the dark crystal he can be seen sleeping beneath the water that covered him.

The place is sad; the yew is hard; the cypress bare. The avenue penetrates the distance; no one has returned there whose step might resonate for ever in the depths of the echo;

And, of the Cupid fallen from the plinth he has denuded, there remains a uniform block which seems the tomb of dreaming, of silence and solitude.

La Prisonnière

Tu m'as fui; mais j'ai vu tes yeux quand tu m'as fui;
Je sais ce qu'à la main pèse ta gorge dure
Et le goût, la couleur, la ligne et la courbure
De ton corps disparu que mon désir poursuit.

Tu mets entre nous deux la forêt et la nuit;
Mais, malgré toi, fidèle à ta beauté parjure,
J'ai médité ta forme éparse en l'ombre obscure
Et je te referai la même. L'aube luit;

J'y dresserai le bloc debout de ta statue
Pour en remplir l'espace exact où tu fus nue.
Captive en la matière inerte, désormais,

Tu t'y tordras muette et encor furieuse
D'être prise, vivante et morte pour jamais,
Dans la pierre marbrée ou la terre argileuse.

The Prisoner

You have slipped away from me; but I saw your eyes when you slipped away from me; I know the weight of your firm breasts in the hand and the taste, the colour, the line and the curve of your vanished body pursued by my desire.

You put between us the forest and the night; but in spite of you, faithful to your false-swearing beauty, I have contemplated your figure diffused in the dark shadow and I will remake you identically. Dawn is breaking;

I will raise within it the upright block of your statue to fill with it the precise space where you were naked. A captive henceforth in inert matter,

You will writhe mute and yet enraged at being caught, alive and dead for ever, in marbled stone or clayish earth.

Julie aux yeux d'enfant

Lorsque Julie est nue et s'apprête au plaisir,
Ayant jeté la rose où s'amusait sa bouche,
On ne voit dans ses yeux ni honte ni désir;
L'attente ne la rend ni tendre ni farouche.

Sur son lit où le drap mêle sa fraîche odeur
Au parfum doux et chaud de sa chair savoureuse,
En silence, elle étend sa patiente ardeur
Et son oisive main couvre sa toison creuse.

Elle prépare ainsi sans curiosité
Pour l'instant du baiser sa gorge et son visage,
Car, fleur trop tôt cueillie et fruit trop tôt goûté,
Julie aux yeux d'enfant est jeune et n'est plus sage!

Julie with the Childlike Eyes

When Julie is naked and preparing herself for pleasure, having cast away the rose on which her mouth was playing, her eyes show neither shame nor desire; expectation makes her neither tender nor wild.

On her bed where the sheet mingles its fresh fragrance with the soft and warm perfume of her delicious flesh, in silence she displays her patient passion, and her indolent hand covers her hollowed fleece.

And so she makes ready without curiosity her breasts and her face for the moment of the kiss, for, a flower plucked too soon and a fruit tasted too early, Julie with the childlike eyes is young and no longer good!

Sa chambre aux murs savants lui montre en ses miroirs
Elle-même partout répétée autour d'elle
Ainsi qu'en d'autres lits, elle s'est, d'autres soirs,
Offerte, indifférente, en sa grâce infidèle.

Mais lorsqu'entre ses bras on la serre et l'étreint,
La caresse importune en son esprit n'éveille
Que l'écho monotone, ennuyeux et lointain
De quelque autre caresse, à celle-là pareille;

C'est pourquoi, sans tendresse, hélas! et sans désir,
Sur ce lit insipide où sa beauté la couche
Elle songe à la mort et s'apprête au plaisir,
Lasse d'être ce corps, ces membres, cette bouche ...

Et pourquoi, ô Julie, ayant goûté ta chair,
De ta jeunesse vaine et stérile on emporte
Un morne souvenir de ton baiser amer,
Julie aux yeux d'enfant, qui voudrais être morte.

Her room with the knowing walls shows to her in its mirrors herself repeated everywhere around her just as in other beds, on other evenings, she has offered herself, indifferent, in her faithless grace.

But when within arms she is clasped and embraced, the intrusive caress awakens in her mind only the monotonous, tiresome and distant echo of some other caress, resembling this one;

That is why, without affection, alas! and without desire, on this tasteless bed where her beauty lays her she muses on death and prepares herself for pleasure, weary of being this body, these limbs, this mouth ...

And that is why, O Julie, when one has tasted of your flesh, from your empty sterile youth is borne away a mournful memory of your bitter kiss, Julie with the childlike eyes, who would rather be dead.

Saint-Pol Roux
(1861–1940)

Pierre-Paul Roux adopted the name Saint-Pol Roux, and was also known by friends and admirers as '*le Magnifique*' and '*le Divin*'. Much of his verse and his rhythmic, highly assonanced prose-poetry has a religious impulse, and he represents one culmination of Symbolism: an emotional, intensely visionary power of language to generate an Image of the beauty of God's created universe. Metaphors abound, as the poet in his turn creates a world of essential signs, recognizing no barrier between conscious and subconscious orders. The revelatory nature of this poetry was much admired by the Surrealists, and he has also been likened to the German mystic Novalis.

Saint-Pol Roux conceived poetry as an '*esprit de participation*', a perception of abstract and concrete, of divine idea and physical matter, that is shared by children, mystics and primitive societies. He gave the name '*Idéoréalisme*' to this synthesis.

Born in Marseille, he later settled in Brittany, and died there shortly after he and his family had been brutally attacked by German soldiers in 1940.

Major volumes: *Les Reposoirs de la Procession* 1893, *La Rose et les épines du chemin* 1901, *Anciennetés* 1903, *De la Colombe au corbeau par le paon* 1904, *Les Féeries intérieures* 1907.

Golgotha

Le ciel enténébré de ses plus tristes hardes
S'accroupit sur le drame universel du pic.
Le violent triangle de l'arme des gardes
A l'air au bout du bois d'une langue d'aspic.

Parmi des clous, entre deux loups à face humaine,
Pantelant ainsi qu'un quartier de venaison
Agonise l'Agneau déchiré par la haine,
Celui-là qui donnait son âme et sa maison.

Jésus bêle un pardon suprême en la tempête
Où ses os tracassés crissent comme un essieu,
Cependant que le sang qui pleure de sa tête
Emperle de corail sa souffrance de Dieu.

Golgotha

The sky wrapped in the darkness of its saddest apparel crouches low over the universal drama of the peak. The violent triangle of the guards' weapon at the end of its wooden shaft looks like a viper's tongue.

Among nails, between two wolves with human faces, quivering like a haunch of venison the Lamb is in his agony lacerated by hatred, the one who gave his soul and his house.

Jesus bleats out an ultimate word of forgiveness into the storm in which his bones in turmoil grate like an axle, while the blood that weeps from his head crowns with coral pearls his Divine suffering.

Dans le ravin, Judas, crapaud drapé de toiles,
Balance ses remords sous un arbre indulgent,
– Et l'on dit que là-haut sont mortes les étoiles
Pour ne plus ressembler à des pièces d'argent.

In the gully, Judas, a toad draped in linen, rocks his remorse beneath an indulgent tree – And it is said that the stars above died to resemble pieces of silver no longer.

Alouettes

Les coups de ciseaux gravissent l'air.

Déjà le crêpe de mystère que jetèrent les fantômes du vêpre sur la chair fraîche de la vie, déjà le crêpe de ténèbres est entamé sur la campagne et sur la ville.

Les coups de ciseaux gravissent l'air.

Ouïs-tu pas la cloche tendre du bon Dieu courtiser de son tisonnier de bruit les yeux, ces belles-de-jour, les yeux blottis dessous les cendres de la nuit?

Larks

Scissor cuts ascend the air.

Already the mourning veil of mystery cast by the vesper spectres over the fresh flesh of life, already the mourning veil of darkness is pierced above the country and the town.

Scissor cuts ascend the air.

Do you not hear the tender bell of the good Lord wooing the eyes with its poker of sound, those convolvuli, the eyes huddled under the ashes of the night?

Les coups de ciseaux gravissent l'air.

Surgis donc du somme où comme morts nous sommes, ô Mienne, et pavoise ta fenêtre avec les lis, la pêche et les framboises de ton être.

Les coups de ciseaux gravissent l'air.

Viens-t'en sur la colline où les moulins nolisent leurs ailes de lin, viens-t'en sur la colline de laquelle on voit jaillir des houilles éternelles le diamant divin de la vaste alliance du ciel.

Les coups de ciseaux gravissent l'air.

Du faîte emparfumé de thym, lavande, romarin, nous assisterons, moi la caresse, toi la fleur, à la claire et sombre fête des heures sur l'horloge où loge le destin, et nous regarderons là-bas passer le sourire du monde avec son ombre longue de douleur.

Les coups de ciseaux gravissent l'air.

Scissor cuts ascend the air.

Rise up then from the slumber where we are as if dead, O my Love, and deck your window with the lilies, the peach and the raspberries of your being.

Scissor cuts ascend the air.

Come away to the hillside where the mills are freighting their flaxen sails, come away to the hillside whose eternal coals spurt forth before our eyes the divine diamond of the vast wedding-ring of the sky.

Scissor cuts ascend the air.

From the summit scented with thyme, with lavender, with rosemary, we will be present, I the caress, you the flower, at the bright and dark festival of the hours on the clock where destiny lives, and there we will watch as the smile of the world passes with its long shadow of grief.

Scissor cuts ascend the air.

La Carafe d'eau pure

A Jules Renard

Sur la table d'un bouge noir où l'on va boire du vin rouge.

Tout est sombre et turpitude entre ces quatre murs.
La mamelle de cristal, seule, affirme la merveille de son eau candide.
A-t-elle absorbé la lumière plénière de céans qu'elle brille ainsi, comme tombée de l'annulaire d'un archange?

The Carafe of pure water

for Jules Renard

On the table of a black den where men go to drink red wine.

All is dark and depravity between those four walls. The crystal breast, alone, asserts the marvel of its innocent water. Has it absorbed the entire light within this place for it to shine as it does, as if fallen from the ring-finger of an archangel?

Dès le seuil de la sentine sa vue m'a suggéré le sac d'argent sage que lègue à sa louche filleule une ingénue marraine ayant cousu toute la vie.
Voici que s'évoque une Phryné d'innocence, jaillie d'un puits afin d'aveugler les Buveurs de sa franchise.
En effet j'observe que la crapule appréhende la vierge ...
Il se fait comme une crainte d'elle ...
Les ronces des prunelles glissent en tangentes sournoises sur sa panse ...
Le crabe des mains, soucieuses d'amender leur gêne, va cueillir les flacons couleurs de sang ...

Mais la Carafe, aucun ne la butine.

Quelle est donc sa farouche vertu?

From the threshold of the place of iniquity the sight of it suggested to me the prudent bag of silver bequeathed to her degenerate goddaughter by an artless godmother after a lifetime of sewing. And now a Phryne[1] of innocence is evoked, springing forth from a well to blind the Drinkers with her candour. Indeed I observe that the vile rabble are fearful of the virgin ... A certain dread of her arises ... The brambles of eyeballs insinuate themselves slyly and tangentially over her stomach ... The hand crab, anxious to correct their discomfort, goes gathering blood-coloured flasks ...

But no one plunders the Carafe.

What then is its reticent virtue?

[1]A beautiful Greek courtesan.

Viendrait-elle, cette eau, des yeux de vos victimes, Buveurs, et redoutez-vous que s'y reflètent vos remords, ou bien ne voulez-vous que soient éteints les brasiers vils de vos tempes canailles?

Et je crus voir leur Conscience sur la table du bouge noir où l'on va boire du vin rouge!

Could it come, this water, from the eyes of your victims, Drinkers, and do you fear in it the reflection of your remorse, or is it that you do not want the foul burning coals of your riff-raff temples to be extinguished?

And I seemed to see their Conscience on the table of the black den where men go to drink red wine!

A Renewal of Lyricism

French poetry at the turn of the century reacted in a number of ways against the aesthetic refinements of Symbolism. The most radical and far-reaching changes were initiated by the poets of the city-based Cubist and Modernist movements (see page 511), but another tendency also deserves some recognition. The works which follow by Toulet, Jammes and Fort are part of a widespread desire to restore to French verse an element of spontaneous and unaffected lyricism. This involves a renewal of contact with the organic world, a sensitivity to the natural rhythms of human life, an awareness of the experience, culture and traditional wisdom of ordinary people. In Parisian circles such poets were often belittled for their alleged provincialism and unsophistication, but they struck a chord with a substantial section of the reading public, and indeed the work of that most Parisian of ladies, Anna de Noailles, shares many of their characteristics.

Paul-Jean Toulet
(1867–1920)

Toulet was probably the most talented and durable member of a group known as the *Fantaisistes*, that included Francis Carco, Franc-Nohain, Jehan Rictus, Tristan Derème and Jean Pellerin. These poets, whose influence is discernible in Jacob and Apollinaire, were determined (as was Jammes) to re-introduce simple popular lyricism into French verse. They renewed the traditions of ballad, fable, humour, satire, sentiment, eroticism, and the witty use of the vernacular. Tending towards an understated and elegiac tone, they diluted rhyme in favour of assonance.

Toulet himself was a rather self-destructive dandy. His origins were in south-western France, but after travelling in Africa and the Far East he became known in Parisian literary circles, and 'burned himself out' rapidly on alcohol, drugs and nocturnal living, chronicling this existence in novels and journalism. He was a poet of great if slightly precious technical skill, and a lively blend of traditional lyricism and modern irony characterizes his work. His principal work is contained in *Contrerimes*, published after his death. The '*contrerime*' is an original form, composed of two or three quatrains with lines of 8 and 6 syllables (or occasionally 6 and 4) in rhyming combination. This economical structure has both strength and nonchalance, and Toulet has the capacity to expand a fleeting experience into a complexity and depth that satisfy both intuition and intellect. Other poems are classified as '*chansons*' and '*coples*'.

Contrerimes

XL

L'immortelle et l'œillet de mer
    Qui pousse dans le sable,
La pervenche trop périssable,
    Ou ce fenouil amer

Qui craquait sous la dent des chèvres,
    Ne vous en souvient-il,
Ni de la brise au sel subtil
    Qui nous brûlait aux lèvres?

Counter-Rhymes

XL

The immortelle and the sea pink that grows in the sand, the all too fragile periwinkle, or that bitter fennel

Crackling between the goats' teeth, have you no memory of them, nor of the keen salt breeze that burned our lips?

XLV

Molle rive dont le dessin
  Est d'un bras qui se plie,
Colline de brume embellie
  Comme se voile un sein,

Filaos au chantant ramage –
  Que je meure et, demain,
Vous ne serez plus, si ma main
  N'a fixé votre image.

LXIII

Toute allégresse a son défaut
  Et se brise elle-même.
Si vous voulez que je vous aime,
  Ne riez pas trop haut.

C'est à voix basse qu'on enchante
  Sous la cendre d'hiver
Ce cœur, pareil au feu couvert,
  Qui se consume et chante.

XLV

Soft shore whose contour is that of a bending arm, hillside adorned with haze as a breast is veiled,

Casuarina trees with your singing boughs – I may die and, tomorrow, you will be no more, if my hand has not made fast your image.

LXIII

Every surge of joy has its flaw and shatters of its own accord. If you would have me love you, do not laugh too loudly.

It is in hushed tones beneath the winter ashes that this heart is captivated, this heart like a blanketed fire which smoulders and sings.

LXX

La vie est plus vaine une image
    Que l'ombre sur le mur.
Pourtant l'hiéroglyphe obscur
    Qu'y trace ton passage

M'enchante, et ton rire pareil
    Au vif éclat des armes;
Et jusqu'à ces menteuses larmes
    Qui miraient le soleil.

Mourir non plus n'est ombre vaine.
    La nuit, quand tu as peur,
N'écoute pas battre ton cœur:
    C'est une étrange peine.

LXX

Life is an image hollower than the shadow on the wall. Yct the mysterious hieroglyph inscribed there as you pass

Enthralls me, and your laughter like the vivid lustre of weapons; and even those deceitful tears that mirrored the sun.

Nor is dying a hollow shadow. At night, when you are afraid, do not listen to your beating heart: it is a strange affliction.

Chanson: Le Temps d'Adonis

Dans la saison qu'Adonis fut blessé,
Mon cœur aussi de l'atteinte soudaine
    D'un regard lancé.

Hors de l'abyme où le temps nous entraîne,
T'évoquerai-je, ô belle, en vain – ô vaines
    Ombres, souvenirs.

Ah! dans mes bras qui pleurais demi-nue,
Certe serais encore, à revenir,
    Ah! la bienvenue.

Song: The Time of Adonis

In the season when Adonis was wounded, my heart likewise by the sudden assault of a projected glance.

Out of the abyss into which time drags us, shall I recall you, O my beauty, in vain – O empty shadows, memories.

Ah! who wept half-naked in my arms, would surely still be, returning, ah! so welcome.

Cople CVII

C'est Dimanche aujourd'hui. L'air est couleur du miel.
Le rire d'un enfant perce la cour aride:
On dirait un glaïeul élancé vers le ciel.
Un orgue au loin se tait. L'heure est plate et sans ride.

Copla[1] *CVII*

It is Sunday today. The air is honey-coloured, a child's laughter pierces the sterile courtyard: as if it were a gladiolus launched towards the sky. A distant organ ceases. The hour is smooth, with no ripple.

[1]Toulet has Gallicized the word 'copla', which refers to a traditional Spanish verse-form.

Francis Jammes
(1868–1938)

Jammes was essentially a pastoral poet of the Pyrenees region, and received inadequate recognition in Paris. With his intimate Catholicism, his love of familiar natural things and contempt for artifice and intellectualism, and his direct, strong and supple style, he brought a breath of fresh air and popular appeal into French poetry after the elitist, esoteric and stylized experiments of Symbolism. This impulse was known at the time as '*le Jammisme*'.

Receptive to all natural stimuli, perceiving God in plants and animals without the verbosity of the Romantic pantheists, he is sincere to a disconcerting degree. But his unpretentiousness should not be confused with naïvety, for there is wit and refinement in his apparent primitivism, something of Chagall and Douanier Rousseau, a charming '*gaucherie*' that is at least partly deliberate.

It is sometimes argued that he courts bathos too closely, but that is a matter of taste.

Perhaps the best volumes in a prolific output are: *Vers* 1892–93–94, *La Naissance du poète* 1897, *De l'Angélus de l'aube à l'Angélus du soir* 1898, *Le Deuil des primevères* 1901, *Tristesses* 1905, *Clairières dans le Ciel* 1906, *Poèmes mesurés* 1908, *Rayons de miel* 1908, *La Vierge et les sonnets* 1919, *Livres des quatrains* 1922–23–24–25, *Diane* 1928, *Alouette* 1935, etc.

J'aime dans les temps ...

J'aime dans les temps Clara d'Ellébeuse,
l'écolière des anciens pensionnats,
qui allait, les soirs chauds, sous les tilleuls
lire les *magazines* d'autrefois.

Je n'aime qu'elle, et je sens sur mon cœur
la lumière bleue de sa gorge blanche.
Où est-elle! Où était donc ce bonheur?
Dans sa chambre claire il entrait des branches.

Elle n'est peut-être pas encore morte
– ou peut-être que nous l'étions tous deux.
La grande cour avait des feuilles mortes
dans le vent froid des fins d'Étés très vieux.

I love in times gone by ...

I love in times gone by Clara d'Ellébeuse, the girl at old private boarding schools, who used to walk beneath the linden trees, on warm evenings, to read the *magazines* of bygone days.

I love only her, and I feel on my heart the blue light of her white breasts. Where is she? So where was that happiness? Into her bright room branches came.

Perhaps she is not yet dead – or perhaps we both were dead. The big yard had dead leaves in the cold wind of Summers' endings long ago.

Te souviens-tu de ces plumes de paon,
dans un grand vase, auprès de coquillages? ...
on apprenait qu'on avait fait naufrage,
on appelait Terre-Neuve: *le Banc.*

Viens, viens, ma chère Clara d'Ellébeuse:
aimons-nous encore si tu existes.
Le vieux jardin a de vieilles tulipes.
Viens toute nue, ô Clara d'Ellébeuse.

Do you remember those peacock feathers, in a tall vase, beside shells? ... we learned that there had been a shipwreck, we called Newfoundland: *the Banks.*

Come, come, my precious Clara d'Ellébeuse: let us love still if you exist. The old garden has old tulips. Come quite naked, O Clara d'Ellébeuse.

Prière pour aller au Paradis avec les ânes

Lorsqu'il faudra aller vers vous, ô mon Dieu, faites
que ce soit par un jour où la campagne en fête
poudroiera. Je désire, ainsi que je fis ici-bas,
choisir un chemin pour aller, comme il me plaira,
au Paradis, où sont en plein jour les étoiles.
Je prendrai mon bâton et sur la grande route
j'irai, et je dirai aux ânes, mes amis:
Je suis Francis Jammes et je vais au Paradis,
car il n'y a pas d'enfer au pays du Bon Dieu.
Je leur dirai: Venez, doux amis du ciel bleu,
pauvres bêtes chéries qui, d'un brusque mouvement d'oreille,
chassez les mouches plates, les coups et les abeilles ...

Prayer to go to Paradise with the Donkeys

When I have to go to you, O God, grant that it may be on a day when the country is dusty with celebration. I wish to choose, just as I did here below, a road just as it suits me, to make my way to Paradise, where the stars shine in daylight. I'll take my stick and I'll go along the highway, and I'll say to my friends the donkeys: I'm Francis Jammes and I'm on my way to Paradise, for there is no hell in the land of the good Lord. I'll say to them: Come, gentle friends of the blue sky, poor precious beasts who with an abrupt movement of the ear chase away the dull flies, the blows and the bees ...

Que je vous apparaisse au milieu de ces bêtes
que j'aime tant parce qu'elles baissent la tête
doucement, et s'arrêtent en joignant leurs petits pieds
d'une façon bien douce et qui vous fait pitié.
J'arriverai suivi de leurs milliers d'oreilles,
suivi de ceux qui portèrent au flanc des corbeilles,
de ceux traînant des voitures de saltimbanques
ou des voitures de plumeaux et de fer-blanc,
de ceux qui ont au dos des bidons bossués,
des ânesses pleines comme des outres, aux pas cassés,
de ceux à qui l'on met de petits pantalons
à cause des plaies bleues et suintantes que font
les mouches entêtées qui s'y groupent en ronds.
Mon Dieu, faites qu'avec ces ânes je vous vienne.
Faites que dans la paix, des anges nous conduisent
vers des ruisseaux touffus où tremblent des cerises
lisses comme la chair qui rit des jeunes filles,
et faites que, penché dans ce séjour des âmes,
sur vos divines eaux, je sois pareil aux ânes
qui mireront leur humble et douce pauvreté
à la limpidité de l'amour éternel.

Let me appear to you amid these animals that I love so much because they lower their heads softly and stop, putting their little feet together in a gentle way that stirs your compassion. I'll arrive followed by their thousands of ears, followed by those who carried baskets on their flanks, by those who hauled wagons for travelling showmen or carts of feather dusters and tinware, by those who have battered churns on their backs, she-asses as rounded as goatskin flasks, with broken gait, by those dressed in little trousers because of the oozing blue wounds made by the stubborn flies that gather there in circles. God, grant that I come to you with these donkeys. Grant that angels guide us in peace towards leafy streams where cherries quiver, as smooth as the laughing flesh of girls, and grant that I, leaning in this resting place of souls over your divine waters, may resemble the donkeys who will find their humble, gentle poverty mirrored in the limpidity of eternal love.

Les cinq Mystères douloureux

Agonie

Par le petit garçon qui meurt près de sa mère
tandis que des enfants s'amusent au parterre;
et par l'oiseau blessé qui ne sait pas comment
son aile tout à coup s'ensanglante et descend;
par la soif et la faim et le délire ardent:
    Je vous salue, Marie.

Flagellation

Par les gosses battus par l'ivrogne qui rentre,
par l'âne qui reçoit des coups de pied au ventre,
par l'humiliation de l'innocent châtié,
par la vierge vendue qu'on a déshabillée,
par le fils dont la mère a été insultée:
    Je vous salue, Marie.

The Five Painful Mysteries

Agony

Through the little boy dying beside his mother while children are playing below; and through the wounded bird which does not know how its wing becomes suddenly bloody and falls; through thirst and hunger and burning delirium: Hail Mary.

Scourging

Through the youngsters beaten by the homecoming drunkard, through the donkey kicked in the belly, through the humiliation of the mortified innocent, through the sold virgin stripped of her clothes, through the son whose mother has been insulted: Hail Mary.

Couronnement d'épines

Par le mendiant qui n'eut jamais d'autre couronne
que le vol des frelons, amis des vergers jaunes,
et d'autre sceptre qu'un bâton contre les chiens;
par le poète dont saigne le front qui est ceint
des ronces des désirs que jamais il n'atteint:
Je vous salue, Marie.

Portement de Croix

Par la vieille qui, trébuchant sous trop de poids,
s'écrie "Mon Dieu!" Par le malheureux dont les bras
ne purent s'appuyer sur une amour humaine
comme la Croix du Fils sur Simon de Cyrène;
par le cheval tombé sous le chariot qu'il traîne:
Je vous salue, Marie.

Crowning with Thorns

Through the beggar who never had any other crown than the flight of hornets, those friends of yellow orchards, and no other sceptre but a stick to ward off dogs; through the poet whose brow bleeds, wreathed with the brambles of desires he can never attain: Hail Mary.

Bearing of the Cross

Through the old woman who, stumbling under too much weight, cries out: 'My God!' Through the poor wretch whose arms could not lean on a human love as did the Cross of the Son on Simon of Cyrene; through the horse fallen beneath the waggon he hauls: Hail Mary.

Crucifiement

Par les quatre horizons qui crucifient le Monde,
par tous ceux dont la chair se déchire ou succombe,
par ceux qui sont sans pieds, par ceux qui sont sans mains,
par le malade que l'on opère et qui geint
et par le juste mis au rang des assassins:
Je vous salue, Marie.

Crucifixion

Through the four horizons that crucify the World, through all those whose flesh is torn or perishes, through those who have no feet, through those who have no hands, through the sick man moaning in the operating room and through the just man placed among the murderers: Hail Mary.

Il va neiger ...

Il va neiger dans quelques jours. Je me souviens
de l'an dernier. Je me souviens de mes tristesses
au coin du feu. Si l'on m'avait demandé: qu'est-ce?
J'aurais dit: laissez-moi tranquille. Ce n'est rien.

It will snow ...

It will snow in a few days. I remember last year. I remember my sorrows at the fireside. If someone had asked me: is something wrong? I would have said: let me be. It's nothing.

J'ai bien réfléchi, l'année avant, dans ma chambre,
pendant que la neige lourde tombait dehors.
J'ai réfléchi pour rien. A présent comme alors
je fume une pipe en bois avec un bout d'ambre.

Ma vieille commode en chêne sent toujours bon.
Mais moi j'étais bête parce que tant de choses
ne pouvaient pas changer et que c'est une pose
de vouloir chasser les choses que nous savons.

Pourquoi donc pensons-nous et parlons-nous? C'est drôle,
nos larmes et nos baisers, eux, ne parlent pas
et cependant nous les comprenons, et les pas
d'un ami sont plus doux que de douces paroles.

On a baptisé les étoiles sans penser
qu'elles n'avaient pas besoin de nom, et les nombres
qui prouvent que les belles comètes dans l'ombre
passeront, ne les forceront pas à passer.

I thought long and hard, last year, in my room, while the heavy snow fell outside. All that thought was for nothing. At present just as then I am smoking a wooden pipe with an amber tip.

My old oak chest still smells good. But I was such a fool because so many things couldn't change and it's a pretence to want to drive away the things we know.

Why then do we think and speak? It's odd, our tears and kisses, they don't speak and yet we understand them, and the footsteps of a friend are sweeter than sweet words.

We have baptized the stars without thinking that they had no need of names, and the numbers which prove that beautiful comets will pass in the darkness will not force them to pass.

Et maintenant même, où sont mes vieilles tristesses
de l'an dernier? A peine si je m'en souviens.
Je dirais: Laissez-moi tranquille, ce n'est rien,
si dans ma chambre on venait me demander: qu'est-ce?

And now even, where are my old sorrows of last year? I can scarcely remember them. I would say: Let me be, it's nothing, if someone came into my room to ask me: is something wrong?

Paul Fort
(1872–1960)

Remaining outside 'movements', Paul Fort occupies a unique place as a modern exponent of the French ballad and folk tradition. His strong patriotism and simple religious faith are essentially rural, popular, apparently artless, and filled with a deep and unproblematic love for all regions and peoples of France and its colonies.

He reinvigorated old folk-songs and added numerous inventions of his own in a lifelong output of verse disguised as prose, with strong and spontaneous rhythms and musical assonance, but also firm and orthodox rhyming. Poetic eloquence blends with colloquial simplicity in an easy fluency: '*Je suis un arbre à poèmes: un poémier*'. His long sequence of *Ballades Françaises* appeared in a single volume under that title in 1963.

Complainte du Roi et de la Reine

Tout vêtus de noir, la reine et le roi s'en vont dans le soir, s'en vont par les bois.

Elle a le collier et lui, l'agneau d'or. – "Reprends le collier, notre amour est mort."

Lament of the King and Queen

Dressed all in black, the queen and the king fade away in the evening, fade away through the woods.

She has the necklace, he has the golden lamb. – 'Take back the necklace, our love has died.'

– "Tu m'as aimé, reine, puis-je l'oublier? Prends cet agneau d'or, garde le collier.

"Taisons, taisons-nous sous la lune blanche. Adieu pour adieu sous les voix des branches."

Une ombre au château, seule, repassa. Une ombre, un peu d'or fuyaient sous les bois. –

Que dirais-je encore qui n'ait été dit sur les amours morts dans les belles nuits?

Dire que jamais le ciel ne s'accorde avec notre vie et ses fantaisies?

Aimez, c'est l'orage qui vient en décor. Souffrez, sur nos rages la lune sourit.

Sur nos amours morts, c'est le ciel en or: bel exemple, oh! oui, d'amours infinis.

– 'You loved me, queen, can I forget it? Take this golden lamb, keep the necklace.

'Be still, let us be still beneath the white moon. Farewell requites farewell beneath the voices of the branches.'

One shade returned, alone, to the castle. One shade with a hint of gold slipped away beneath the woods.

What more could I say that has not been said on loves that have died in the beautiful nights?

Say that heaven is never in harmony with our life and its imaginings?

Love, and it's the storm that comes to form a setting. Suffer, and the moon smiles on our passions.

Above our dead loves, there is a sky of gold: a fine model, oh! yes, of infinite loves.

La complainte, ici, se meurt de tristesse. – "Une reine, un roi s'aimaient de tendresse."

La complainte, ici, se meurt de paresse. – "Mais qu'ils sont petits, nos amours terrestres ..."

Here the lament is dying of sadness. – 'A queen, a king loved tenderly.'

Here the lament is dying of indolence. – 'But how paltry they are, our earthly loves ...'

La grande Ivresse

Par les nuits d'été bleues où chantent les cigales, Dieu verse sur la France une coupe d'étoiles. Le vent porte à ma lèvre un goût du ciel d'été! Je veux boire à l'espace fraîchement argenté.

L'air du soir est pour moi le bord de la coupe froide où, les yeux mi-fermés et la bouche goulue, je bois, comme le jus pressé d'une grenade, la fraîcheur étoilée qui se répand des nues.

The Great Intoxication

Through the blue summer nights when the cicadas sing, God pours over France a chalice full of stars. The wind brings to my lips a taste of the summer sky! I want to drink from the freshly silvered firmament.

The evening air for me is the rim of the cold chalice where, with eyes half closed and greedy mouth, I drink, as if it were the expressed juice of a pomegranate, the starry coolness diffused from the skies.

Couché sur un gazon dont l'herbe est encor chaude de s'être prélassée sous l'haleine du jour, oh! que je viderais, ce soir, avec amour, la coupe immense et bleue où le firmament rôde!

Suis-je Bacchus ou Pan? je m'enivre d'espace, et j'apaise ma fièvre à la fraîcheur des nuits. La bouche ouverte au ciel où grelottent les astres, que le ciel coule en moi! que je me fonde en lui!

Enivrés par l'espace et les cieux étoilés, Byron et Lamartine, Hugo, Shelley sont morts. L'espace est toujours là; il coule illimité; à peine ivre il m'emporte, et j'avais soif encore!

Lying on turf, its grass still warm from basking beneath the breath of the day, oh! how I could drain tonight, with love, the vast blue chalice where the firmament wheels!

Am I Bacchus or Pan? I am intoxicated with space, and I soothe my fever in the coolness of the nights. Mouth open to the sky where the stars are shivering, how the sky flows within me! how I melt into the sky!

Intoxicated by space and the starry heavens, Byron and Lamartine, Hugo and Shelley have died. Space is still there; its flow is boundless; scarcely drunk it transports me, and I was still thirsty!

La Grenouille bleue

I

PRIERE AU BON FORESTIER

Nous vous en prions à genoux, bon forestier, dites-nous-le! à quoi reconnaît-on *chez vous* la fameuse grenouille bleue?

à ce que les autres sont vertes? à ce qu'elle est pesante? alerte? ce qu'elle fuit les canards? ou se balance aux nénuphars?

à ce que sa voix est perlée? à ce qu'elle porte une houppe? à ce qu'elle rêve par troupe? en ménage? ou bien isolée?

Ayant réfléchi très longtemps et reluquant un vague étang, le bonhomme nous dit: eh mais, à ce qu'on ne la voit jamais.

The Blue Frog

I

PRAYER TO THE GOOD FORESTER

We beg you on our knees, good forester, tell us! how *in your land* the famous blue frog is recognized.

because the others are green? because it is sluggish? vigilant? it flees from ducks? or sways on the water-lilies?

because its voice glistens with pearls? because it has a crest? because it dreams collectively? in couples? or all alone?

After long reflection, his eye on a hazy pond, the fellow said to us: well now, because you never see it.

II

REPONSE AU FORESTIER

Tu mentais, forestier. Aussi ma joie éclate! Ce matin je l'ai vue: un vrai saphir à pattes. Complice du beau temps, amante du ciel pur, elle était verte, mais réfléchissait l'azur.

III

LE REMORDS

Eh bien! non, elle existe et son petit cœur bouge, ou plutôt elle est morte: elle meurt dans nos mains. Nous nous la repassons. Un enfant, ce matin, nous l'a pêchée avec une épingle et du rouge.

Pardon, ma petite âme, ô douce chanterelle, qui chante quand la lune a ses parasélènes, morte ainsi dans nos mains, que tu me fais de peine! et bleue, oui, tu es bleue, du plus haut bleu du ciel!

II

ANSWER TO THE FORESTER

You were lying, forester. And so my joy bursts forth! This morning I saw it: a true sapphire on legs. In league with fine weather, lover of the pure sky, it was green, but reflected the azure.

III

REMORSE

Ah well! no, it exists and its little heart stirs, or rather it has died: it is dying in our hands. We pass it one to another. A child, this morning, fished it out for us with a pin and a red rag.

Forgive me, my little soul, O sweet luring-bird, singing when the moon has its paraselenae, dead like this in our hands, how you grieve me! and blue, yes, you are blue, the loftiest blue of the sky!

Faut-il que le zéphyr disperse tes atomes! Légère fée des bois, tu n'es plus qu'un fantôme. Bleue, je te pleure; verte, hélas! qu'eussé-je fait? je t'aurais rejetée. Le cœur n'est point parfait.

Must the zephyr scatter your atoms! nimble fairy of the woodlands, you are just a ghost now. Blue, I weep for you; green, alas, what would I have done? I would have thrown you back. The heart is far from perfect.

L'Ecureuil

Ecureuil du printemps, écureuil de l'été, qui domines la terre avec vivacité, que penses-tu, là-haut, de notre humanité?

– Les hommes sont des fous qui manquent de gaieté.

Ecureuil, queue touffue, doré trésor des bois, ornement de la vie et fleur de la nature, juché sur ton pin vert, dis-nous ce que tu vois?

The Squirrel

Spring squirrel, summer squirrel, lively at your vantage-point above the earth, what do you think, up there, of our human race?

– Men are humourless buffoons.

Squirrel, bushy tail, gilded gem of the woods, embellishment of life and flower of nature, perched on your green pine, will you tell us what you see?

– La terre qui poudroie sous des pas qui murmurent.

Ecureuil voltigeant, frère du pic bavard, cousin du rossignol, ami de la corneille, dis-nous ce que tu vois par-delà nos brouillards?

– Des lances, des fusils menacer le soleil.

Ecureuil, cul à l'air, cursif et curieux, ébouriffant ton col et gloussant un fin rire, dis-nous ce que tu vois sous la rougeur des cieux?

– Des soldats, des drapeaux qui traversent l'empire.

Ecureuil aux yeux vifs, pétillants, noirs et beaux, humant la sève d'or, la pomme entre tes pattes, que vois-tu sur la plaine autour de nos hameaux?

– Monter le lac de sang des hommes qui se battent.

– The earth dusty beneath murmuring footsteps.

Aerobatic squirrel, brother of the chattering woodpecker, cousin of the nightingale, friend of the crow, will you tell us what you see beyond our fogs?

– Lances, guns threatening the sun.

Squirrel, backside in the air, cursive and inquisitive, ruffling your neck and clucking out a slender laugh, will you tell us what you see beneath the redness of the skies?

– Soldiers, flags traversing the nation.

Squirrel with your eyes that are keen, sparkling, dark and beautiful, inhaling the golden sap, oak-apple in your paws, what do you see on the plain around our hamlets?

– The rising lake of blood of fighting men.

Ecureuil de l'automne, écureuil de l'hiver, qui lances vers l'azur, avec tant de gaieté, ces pommes ... que vois-tu? – Demain tout comme Hier

Les hommes sont des fous et pour éternité.

Autumn squirrel, winter squirrel, hurling those oak-apples so cheerfully towards the blue ... what do you see? – Tomorrow just as Yesterday

Men are buffoons and for all eternity.

Anna, Comtesse de Noailles
(1876–1933)

Anna de Noailles was an aristocrat, beautiful and gifted, and a central figure in Parisian artistic life, admired and cultivated by Proust, Valéry, Rostand, Cocteau and others.

She was a woman of strong passions and unapologetic sensuality, expressed concretely in a neo-Romantic and technically orthodox verse that renews from the feminine point of view the century-old themes of love and loss, God in Nature, solitude and the passage of time.

With Renée Vivien and others, she makes the inner life of women a new factor in poetry at the turn of the century, and her volume *Le Cœur Innombrable* met with considerable success on its publication in 1901.

There is a pagan intensity in her response to life and anticipation of death, and her commitment of her entire self to poetry excuses a certain verbosity.

Other volumes: *L'Ombre des Jours* 1902, *Les Eblouissements* 1907, *Les Vivants et les Morts* 1913, *Les Forces éternelles* 1921, *Anthologie* 1922, *Poème de l'Amour* 1924, *L'Honneur de souffrir* 1927, *Derniers Vers* 1933.

L'Empreinte

Je m'appuierai si bien et si fort à la vie,
D'une si rude étreinte et d'un tel serrement,
Qu'avant que la douceur du jour me soit ravie
Elle s'échauffera de mon enlacement.

La mer, abondamment sur le monde étalée,
Gardera, dans la route errante de son eau,
Le goût de ma douleur qui est âcre et salée
Et sur les jours mouvants roule comme un bateau.

Je laisserai de moi dans le pli des collines
La chaleur de mes yeux qui les ont vu fleurir,
Et la cigale assise aux branches de l'épine
Fera vibrer le cri strident de mon désir.

Imprint

I will press myself with such force against life, with an embrace so fierce and a grip so tight, that before the sweetness of the day is stolen away from me it will be warmed by my entwining arms.

The sea, spread abundantly over the world, will hold, in the wandering journey of its waters, the taste of my pain which is sour and salt and rolls like a ship on the shifting days.

I will leave of myself in the fold of the hills the warmth of my eyes which have seen them in blossom, and the cicada perched on the branches of the thornbush will be resonant with the piercing cry of my longing.

Dans les champs printaniers la verdure nouvelle
Et le gazon touffu sur le bord des fossés
Sentiront palpiter et fuir comme des ailes
Les ombres de mes mains qui les ont tant pressés.

La nature qui fut ma joie et mon domaine
Respirera dans l'air ma persistante ardeur,
Et sur l'abattement de la tristesse humaine
Je laisserai la forme unique de mon cœur ...

In the spring fields the fresh greenery and the tufted grass at the ditches' edge will feel, throbbing and elusive like wings, the ghosts of my hands which pressed them down so strongly.

Nature which was my joy and my domain will breathe in the air my unceasing fervour, and on the prostration of human sadness I will leave the unique configuration of my heart.

C'est après les moments...

C'est après les moments les plus bouleversés
De l'étroite union acharnée et barbare,
Que, gisant côte à côte, et le front renversé
Je ressens ce qui nous sépare!

It is after ...

It is after the most convulsive moments of close union, passionate and barbarous, that lying side by side, head thrown back, I feel what divides us!

Tous deux nous nous taisons, ne sachant pas comment,
Après cette fureur souhaitée, et suprême,
Chacun de nous a pu, soudain et simplement,
    Hélas! redevenir soi-même.

Vous êtes près de moi, je ne reconnais pas
Vos yeux qui me semblaient brûler sous mes paupières;
Comme un faible animal gorgé de son repas,
    Comme un mort sculpté sur sa pierre,

Vous rêvez immobile, et je ne puis savoir
Quel songe satisfait votre esprit vaste et calme,
Et moi je sens encore un indicible espoir
    Bercer sur moi ses jeunes palmes!

Je ne puis pas cesser de vivre, mon amour!
Ma guerrière folie, avec son masque sage,
Même dans le repos veut par mille détours
    Se frayer encore un passage!

We are both silent, not knowing how, after that desired and supreme frenzy, each of us suddenly and simply, alas! can have become a self again.

You are beside me, I do not recognize your eyes that seemed to burn me beneath my eyelids; like a puny animal gorged on its meal, like a dead man sculpted on his stone,

You dream without moving, and I cannot know what vision satisfies your vast and placid spirit, yet I still feel an ineffable hope wafting its young palms over me!

I cannot cease to live, my love! My warrior madness, with its sober mask, even at rest wants to cleave itself a passage along a thousand winding paths!

Et je vous vois content! Ma force nostalgique
Ne surprend pas en vous ce muet désarroi
Dans lequel se débat ma tristesse extatique.
– Que peut-il y avoir, ô mon amour unique,
  De commun entre vous et moi!

And I see you contented! My yearning power cannot detect within you that mute confusion in which my ecstatic sadness struggles. – What can there be, O my peerless love, in common between you and me!

Paul Claudel
(1868–1955)

A playwright, essayist, and a much-travelled and distinguished diplomat, Claudel also made a significant contribution to French poetry. His finest work is probably his *Cinq Grandes Odes*, composed between 1900 and 1908, from which two extracts are included here.

His early literary contacts were with Mallarmé and the Symbolists, and he was a scholar of classical literature, Shakespeare, Dostoevsky and the Bible. His reading of Rimbaud in 1886 influenced him as profoundly as a religious revelation in Notre-Dame on Christmas Day of that same year, and he embarked on a spiritual quest for a lyrical poetry that would express a virile, ecstatic hymn to Creation. This would be a hymn to the known world as opposed to Rimbaud's Unknown, a hymn to certainty as opposed to Mallarmé's Void. Reality for Claudel is sacred in itself, not an obstacle or springboard to transcendence. The physical is the spiritual, and language is the pulse of the universe in this poetry. Its resonance is still felt in the work of Jean-Claude Renard and like-minded poets of our own time.

Poetry is faith. Poetry is the organic voice of faith in Creation, and it reproduces the rhythms of existence, of the elements, of living human respiration. Vibration, dilation, heartbeats and breathing are the dramatic keys to Claudel's rhythm in his *versets*. These are poetic sentences that swell and subside, surge and rest like music, their shape corresponding to the breath, which corresponds in its turn to the underlying emotional impulse. 'Thought beats like the brain and the heart. Our thinking apparatus in a state of flux does not give forth an uninterrupted line. It yields up in flashes, convulsions, a disjointed mass of ideas, images, memories, notions, concepts, then relaxes before the spirit is realized into the conscious state in a new act ... it is impossible to give an exact image of the pace of thought if one takes no account of blankness and intermittence ...

expressive sound unfolds in time and is thus subject to the control of a measuring instrument … the inner metronome we carry within our breast … the fundamental iambus … and the substance of sound is given to us by the living air absorbed by our lungs and returned by our speaking apparatus that forms it into an utterance of intelligible words … the essential creative act is the emission of a sound-wave.'

Major volumes: *Cinq Grandes Odes* 1910, *La Cantate à trois voix* 1913, *Corona Benignitatis Anni Dei* 1915, *Poèmes de Guerre* 1922, *Feuilles de Saints* 1925, *Cent Phrases pour éventails* 1927, *Poèmes et paroles durant la Guerre de Trente Ans* 1945, *Le Livre de Job* 1946, *Visages radieux* 1947.

Deuxième Ode: L'Esprit et l'Eau (extrait)

Où que je tourne la tête
J'envisage l'immense octave de la Création!
Le monde s'ouvre et, si large qu'en soit l'empan, mon regard le traverse d'un bout à l'autre.
J'ai pesé le soleil ainsi qu'un gros mouton que deux hommes forts suspendent à une perche entre leurs épaules.
J'ai recensé l'armée des Cieux et j'en ai dressé état,
Depuis les grandes Figures qui se penchent sur le vieillard Océan
Jusqu'au feu le plus rare englouti dans le plus profond abîme,
Ainsi que le Pacifique bleu-sombre où le baleinier épie l'évent d'un souffleur comme un duvet blanc.
Vous êtes pris et d'un bout du monde jusqu'à l'autre autour de Vous
J'ai tendu l'immense rets de ma connaissance.

Second Ode: The Spirit and the Water (extract)

Wherever I turn my head I look upon the vast octave of Creation! The world opens, and, broad as the span is, my gaze traverses it from end to end. I have weighed the sun like a fat sheep hung by two men from a rod between their shoulders. I have enumerated the army of Heaven and drawn up the muster, from the great Forms who bend over the old man Ocean to the rarest light engulfed in the deepest abyss, like the dark-blue Pacific where the whaler watches for the dolphin's blowhole, white as down. You are caught and from one end to the other around You I have stretched the huge net of my

Comme la phrase qui prend aux cuivres
Gagne les bois et progressivement envahit les profondeurs de l'orchestre,
Et comme les éruptions du soleil
Se répercutent sur la terre en crises d'eau et en raz de marée,
Ainsi du plus grand Ange qui vous voit jusqu'au caillou de la route et d'un bout de votre création jusqu'à l'autre,
Il ne cesse point continuité, non plus que de l'âme au corps;
Le mouvement ineffable des Séraphins se propage aux Neuf ordres des Esprits,
Et voici le vent qui se lève à son tour sur la terre, le Semeur, le Moissonneur!
Ainsi l'eau continue l'esprit, et le supporte, et l'alimente,
Et entre
Toutes vos créatures jusqu'à vous il y a comme un lien liquide.

awareness. As the theme that begins in the brass is taken up by the woodwinds and progressively flows through the depths of the orchestra, and as the sun's eruptions reverberate on earth in paroxysms of the waters and in tidal waves, and similarly from the greatest Angel who gazes upon you to the pebble on the roadway and from one end of your creation to the other, there is unceasing continuity, no less than from body to soul; the ineffable movement of the Seraphim spreads to the Nine orders of Spirits, and here in turn the wind rises on earth, the Sower, the Reaper! Water is thus the extension of spirit, and upholds it, and feeds it, and between all your creatures and unto you there is a liquid bond.

Je vous salue, ô monde libéral à mes yeux!
Je comprends par quoi vous êtes présent,
C'est que l'Eternel est avec vous, et qu'où est la Créature, le Créateur ne l'a point quittée.
Je suis en vous et vous êtes à moi et votre possession est la mienne.
Et maintenant en nous à la fin
Eclate le commencement,
Eclate le jour nouveau, éclate dans la possession de la source je ne sais quelle jeunesse angélique!
Mon cœur ne bat plus le temps, c'est l'instrument de ma perdurance,
Et l'impérissable esprit envisage les choses passantes.
Mais ai-je dit passantes? voici qu'elles recommencent.
Et mortelles? il n'y a plus de mort avec moi.
Tout être, comme il est un
Ouvrage de l'Eternité, c'est ainsi qu'il en est l'expression.

I greet you, world liberal in my sight! I understand by what means you are present, it is that the Eternal is with you, and that wherever the Creature is, the Creator has not abandoned it. I am within you and you are mine and your possession is mine. And now within us at the end the beginning blazes, the new day blazes, an angelic youthfulness I cannot name shines out in the possession of the source! My heart no longer beats time, it is the instrument of my durability, and the imperishable spirit looks upon transient things. But did I say transient? see, they are renewed. And mortal? with me there is no more death. Every being, as it is a work of Eternity, is also thus its

Elle est présente et toutes choses présentes se passent en elle.
Ce n'est point le texte nu de la lumière: voyez, tout est écrit d'un bout à l'autre:
On peut recourir au détail le plus drôle: pas une syllabe qui manque.
La terre, le ciel bleu, le fleuve avec ses bateaux et trois arbres soigneusement sur la rive,
La feuille et l'insecte sur la feuille, cette pierre que je soupèse dans ma main,
Le village avec tous ces gens à deux yeux à la fois qui parlent, tissent, marchandent, font du feu, portent des fardeaux, complet comme un orchestre qui joue,
Tout cela est l'éternité et la liberté de ne pas être lui est retirée,
Je les vois avec les yeux du corps, je les produis dans mon cœur!

expression. It is present and all present things happen within it. This is not the naked text of the light: see, all is written from end to end: you can turn to the strangest of details: not a syllable is missing. The earth, the blue sky, the river with its boats and three trees carefully set on the bank, the leaf and the insect on the leaf, this stone that I weigh in my hand, the village with all these people each with two eyes who simultaneously speak, weave, bargain, light fires, carry burdens, entire like an orchestra playing, all that is eternity and the freedom not to exist is withdrawn from it, I see them with the eyes of the body, I bring them forth in my heart! With the eyes

Avec les yeux du corps, dans le paradis je ne me servirai pas d'autres yeux que ceux-ci mêmes!
Est-ce qu'on dit que la mer a péri parce que l'autre vague déjà, et la troisième, et la décumane, succède
A celle-ci qui se résout triomphalement dans l'écume?
Elle est contenue dans ses rivages et le
Monde dans ses limites, rien ne se perd en ce lieu qui est fermé,
Et la liberté est contenue dans l'amour,
Ebat
En toutes choses d'inventer l'approximation la plus exquise, toute beauté dans son insuffisance.
Je ne vous vois pas, mais je suis continu avec ces êtres qui vous voient.
On ne rend que ce que l'on a reçu.
Et comme toutes choses de vous
Ont reçu l'être, dans le temps elles restituent l'éternel.

of the body, in paradise I will use no other than these very eyes! Is it said that the sea has perished because another wave already, and the third, and the great tenth wave, follow this one triumphantly dissolving itself in foam? It is contained within its shores and the world within its limits, nothing is lost within this closed space, and freedom is contained within love, a free play to invent within all things the most exquisite approximation, all beauty in its insufficiency. I do not see you, but I am continuous with those beings who see you. What is given back is only what is received. And as all things from you have received their being, in time they restore what is eternal.

Et moi aussi
J'ai une voix, et j'écoute, et j'entends le bruit qu'elle fait.
Et je fais l'eau avec ma voix, telle l'eau qui est l'eau pure, et parce qu'elle nourrit toutes choses, toutes choses se peignent en elle.
Ainsi la voix avec qui de vous je fais des mots éternels! je ne puis rien nommer que d'éternel.
La feuille jaunit et le fruit tombe, mais la feuille dans mes vers ne périt pas,
Ni le fruit mûr, ni la rose entre les roses!
Elle périt, mais son nom dans l'esprit qui est mon esprit ne périt plus. La voici qui échappe au temps.
Et moi qui fais les choses éternelles avec ma voix, faites que je sois tout entier
Cette voix, une parole totalement intelligible!
Libérez-moi de l'esclavage et du poids de cette matière inerte!

And I too have a voice, and I listen, and I hear the sound it makes. And I create the water with my voice, like the water that is the pure water in which, since it nourishes all things, all things are depicted. Thus speaks the voice with which I make eternal words of you! I can name only what is eternal. The leaf yellows and the fruit falls, but the leaf in my lines does not perish, nor the ripe fruit, nor the rose among roses! It perishes, but its name no longer perishes in the spirit which is my spirit. Here it is, escaping from time. And I who make eternal things with my voice, grant that I may be wholly this voice, a totally intelligible form of words! Free me from slavery and the weight

Clarifiez-moi donc! dépouillez-moi de ces ténèbres exécrables et faites que je sois enfin
Toute cette chose en moi obscurément désirée.
Vivifiez-moi, selon que l'air aspiré par notre machine fait briller notre intelligence comme une braise!
Dieu qui avez soufflé sur le chaos, séparant le sec de l'humide,
Sur la Mer Rouge, et elle s'est divisée devant Moïse et Aaron,
Sur la terre mouillée, et voici l'homme,
Vous commandez de même à mes eaux, vous avez mis dans mes narines le même esprit de création et de figure.
Ce n'est point l'impur qui fermente, c'est le pur qui est semence de la vie.

of this inert matter! Purify me now! strip these abominable shadows from me and grant that I may be at last all that which within me is obscurely desired. Quicken me, according as the air breathed in by our machine makes our intellect shine like live coals! God who breathed over chaos, dividing the dry from the wet, over the Red Sea, and it parted before Moses and Aaron, over the wet earth, and man was made, equally you command the waters within me, you have put into my nostrils the same spirit of creation and form. It is not the impure that ferments, it is the pure that is the seed of life. What is water

Qu'est-ce que l'eau que le besoin d'être liquide
Et parfaitement clair dans le soleil de Dieu comme une goutte translucide?
Que me parlez-vous de ce bleu de l'air que vous liquéfiez? O que l'âme humaine est un plus précieux élixir!
Si la rosée rutile dans le soleil,
Combien plus l'escarboucle humaine et l'âme substantielle dans le rayon intelligible!
Dieu qui avez baptisé avec votre esprit le chaos
Et qui la veille de Pâques exorcisez par la bouche de votre prêtre la font païenne avec la lettre psi,
Vous ensemencez avec l'eau baptismale notre eau humaine
Agile, glorieuse, impassible, impérissable!
L'eau qui est claire voit par notre œil et sonore entend par notre oreille et goûte
Par la bouche vermeille abreuvée de la sextuple source,
Et colore notre chair et façonne notre corps plastique.

but the need to be liquid and perfectly clear in the sunlight of God like a translucid drop? What do you say to me of this blue of air that you liquefy? O how the human soul is a more precious elixir! If the dew glows in the sun, how much more brightly the human carbuncle and the substantial soul in the light of understanding! God who baptized chaos with your spirit and who on Easter eve exorcize the pagan fount with the letter psi in the mouth of your priest, you seed with the water of baptism our human water, Nimble, glorious, impassive, imperishable! The water that is clear sees through our eyes and, sonorous, it hears through our ears and tastes through the vermilion mouth quenched by the sextuple source, and colours our flesh and moulds our malleable body. And as the seminal

Et comme la goutte séminale féconde la figure mathématique, départissant
L'amorce foisonnante des éléments de son théorème,
Ainsi le corps de gloire désire sous le corps de boue, et la nuit
D'être dissoute dans la visibilité!

Mon Dieu, ayez pitié de ces eaux désirantes!
Mon Dieu, vous voyez que je ne suis pas seulement esprit, mais eau! ayez pitié de ces eaux en moi qui meurent de soif!
Et l'esprit est désirant, mais l'eau est la chose désirée.
O mon Dieu, vous m'avez donné cette minute de lumière à voir,
Comme l'homme jeune pensant dans son jardin au mois d'août qui voit par intervalles tout le ciel et la terre d'un seul coup,
Le monde d'un seul coup tout rempli par un grand coup de foudre doré!

drop fertilizes the mathematical form, distributing the abundant catalyst of the elements of its theorem, thus the body of glory yearns within the body of clay, and the darkness of being dissolves into visibility!

My God, have pity on these yearning waters! My God, you see that I am not only spirit but water! have pity on these waters within me that are dying of thirst! And the spirit yearns, but water is the thing it yearns for. O my God, you have given me this moment of light to see, like the young man meditating in his August garden who at moments sees all heaven and earth in a single flash, the world in one flash filled with a great

O fortes étoiles sublimes et quel fruit entr'aperçu dans le noir abîme! ô flexion sacrée du long rameau de la Petite-Ourse!
Je ne mourrai pas.
Je ne mourrai pas, mais je suis immortel!
Et tout meurt, mais je croîs comme une lumière plus pure!
Et, comme ils font mort de la mort, de son extermination je fais mon immortalité.
Que je cesse entièrement d'être obscur! Utilisez-moi!
Exprimez-moi dans votre main paternelle!
Sortez enfin
Tout le soleil qu'il y a en moi et capacité de votre lumière, que je vous voie
Non plus avec les yeux seulement, mais avec tout mon corps et ma substance et la somme de ma quantité resplendissante et sonore!

gilded thunderbolt! O strong and sublime stars and what fruit glimpsed in the black chasm! o holy curvature of the long bough of the Little Bear! I shall not die. I shall not die, but I am immortal! And all dies, but I grow like a purer light! And as they put death to death, so from its annihilation I create my immortality. May I cease wholly to be dark! Make use of me! Express me in your fatherly hand! Bring out at last all the sunlight within me and capacity for your light, that I may see you not with my eyes only now, but with all my body and my substance and the sum of my, resplendent and sonorous

L'eau divisible qui fait la mesure de l'homme
Ne perd pas sa nature qui est d'être liquide
Et parfaitement pure par quoi toutes choses se reflètent en elle.
Comme ces eaux qui portèrent Dieu au commencement,
Ainsi ces eaux hypostatiques en nous
Ne cessent de le désirer, il n'est désir que de lui seul!
Mais ce qu'il y a en moi de désirable n'est pas mûr.
Que la nuit soit donc en attendant mon partage où lentement se compose de mon âme
La goutte prête à tomber dans sa plus grande lourdeur.

abundance! The separable water which holds the measure of man does not lose its nature which is to be liquid and perfectly pure so that all things are mirrored in it. Like those waters which bore God in the beginning, so these hypostatic waters within us do not cease to desire him, there is no desire but for him alone! But that which is desirable in me is not yet mature. Then let there be darkness as I await my portion in which will be created from my soul the drop ready to fall in its greatest

Laissez-moi vous faire une libation dans les ténèbres,
Comme la source montagnarde qui donne à boire à l'Océan avec sa petite coquille!

heaviness. Let me offer a libation to you in the shadows, like the mountain spring that offers drink to the Ocean in its little shell!

Quatrième Ode: La Muse qui est la Grâce (première partie)

Encore! encore la mer qui revient me rechercher comme une barque,
La mer encore qui retourne vers moi à la marée de syzygie et qui me lève et remue de mon ber comme une galère allégée,
Comme une barque qui ne tient plus qu'à sa corde, et qui danse furieusement, et qui tape, et qui saque, et qui fonce, et qui encense, et qui culbute, le nez à son piquet,
Comme le grand pur sang que l'on tient aux naseaux et qui tangue sous le poids de l'amazone qui bondit sur lui de côté et qui saisit brutalement les rênes avec un rire éclatant!
Encore la nuit qui revient me rechercher,
Comme la mer qui atteint sa plénitude en silence à cette heure qui joint à l'Océan les ports humains pleins de navires attendants et qui décolle la porte et le batardeau!
Encore le départ, encore la communication établie, encore la porte qui s'ouvre!
Ah, je suis las de ce personnage que je fais entre les

Fourth Ode: The Muse who is Grace (opening section)

Once more! once more the sea coming back to seek me as if I were a boat, the sea once more coming back to me in the tide of syzygy and lifting me and moving me from my cradle like an unburdened galley, like a boat held now only by its hawser, dancing furiously, slapping, jerking, driving forward, tossing its head and stumbling, nose to the hitching-post, like the great thoroughbred held by the nostrils and pitching under the weight of the amazon who leaps on him from the side and brutally seizes the reins with a burst of laughter! Once more the night coming back to seek me, like the sea silently reaching its fullness at this hour which joins to the Ocean the human ports filled with waiting ships, unfastening the gate and the coffer-dam! Once more the departure, once more the contact made, once more the opening gate! Ah, I am weary of this figure I

hommes! Voici la nuit! Encore la fenêtre qui s'ouvre!
Et je suis comme la jeune fillc à la fenêtre du beau château blanc, dans le clair de lune,
Qui entend, le cœur bondissant, ce bienheureux sifflement sous les arbres et le bruit de deux chevaux qui s'agitent,
Et elle ne regrette point la maison, mais elle est comme un petit tigre qui se ramasse, et tout son cœur est soulevé par l'amour de la vie et par la grande force comique!
Hors de moi la nuit, et en moi la fusée de la force nocturne, et le vin de la Gloire, et le mal de ce cœur trop plein!
Si le vigneron n'entre pas impunément dans la cuve,
Croirez-vous que je sois puissant à fouler ma grande vendange de paroles,
Sans que les fumées m'en montent au cerveau!
Ah, ce soir est à moi! ah, cette grande nuit est à moi! tout le gouffre de la nuit comme la salle illuminée pour la jeune fille à son premier bal!
Elle ne fait que de commencer! il sera temps de dormir dans autre jour!

cut among men! Here is the night! Once more the opening window! And I am like the girl at the window of the beautiful white castle, in the moonlight, who hears, with a leaping heart, that blessed whistling under the trees and the sound of two restless horses, and feels no regret for home, but she is like a little tiger gathering itself to spring, and her whole heart is uplifted by love of life and by the great force of laughter! Outside of me the night, and within me the fuse of night's power, and the wine of Glory, and the ache of this overflowing heart! If the wine-grower does not go with impunity into the vat, will you believe that I have the power to tread my great harvest of words, without the fumes going to my head! Ah, this evening is mine! ah, this great night is mine! the entire chasm of night like the hall lit for the girl at her first ball! She is just beginning! there will be time to sleep another day! Ah, I

Ah, je suis ivre! ah, je suis livré au dieu! j'entends une voix en moi et la mesure qui s'accélère, le mouvement de la joie,
L'ébranlement de la cohorte Olympique, la marche divinement tempérée!
Que m'importent tous les hommes à présent! Ce n'est pas pour eux que je suis fait, mais pour le
Transport de cette mesure sacrée!
O le cri de la trompette bouchée! ô le coup sourd sur la tonne orgiaque!
Que m'importe aucun d'eux? Ce rythme seul! Qu'ils me suivent ou non? Que m'importe qu'ils m'entendent ou pas?
Voici le dépliement de la grande Aile poétique!
Que me parlez-vous de la musique? laissez-moi seulement mettre mes sandales d'or!
Je n'ai pas besoin de tout cet attirail qu'il lui faut. Je ne demande pas que vous vous bouchiez les yeux.
Les mots que j'emploie,
Ce sont les mots de tous les jours, et ce ne sont point les mêmes!

am drunk! ah, I am delivered to the god! I hear a voice within me and a tempo that gathers speed, the movement of joy, the coming to life of the Olympic cohort, their progress divinely tempered! What do all men matter to me now! It is not for them that I am made, but for the ecstasy of this holy metre! O the cry of the muted trumpet! O muffled drumming on the cask of orgy! What do any of them matter to me? This rhythm alone! Whether or not they follow me? What does it matter if they hear me or not? And now the great Wing of poetry unfolds! What speak you to me of music? let me simply put on my golden sandals! I have no need for all its paraphernalia. I do not ask you to blindfold your eyes. The words which I use, they are everyday words, and yet they are not the same! You

Vous ne trouverez point de rimes dans mes vers ni aucun sortilège. Ce sont vos phrases mêmes. Pas aucune de vos phrases que je ne sache reprendre!
Ces fleurs sont vos fleurs et vous dites que vous ne les reconnaissez pas.
Et ces pieds sont vos pieds, mais voici que je marche sur la mer et que je foule les eaux de la mer en triomphe!...

will find no rhymes in my verses nor any sorcery. They are your very phrases. Not one of your phrases that I cannot take up once more! These flowers are your flowers and you say you do not recognize them. And these feet are your feet, but see now how I walk on the sea and tread the waters of the sea in triumph!...

Ballade

Les négociateurs de Tyr et ceux-là qui vont à leurs affaires aujourd'hui sur l'eau dans de grandes imaginations mécaniques,
Ceux que le mouchoir par les ailes de cette mouette encore accompagne quand le bras qui l'agitait a disparu,
Ceux à qui leur vigne et leur champ ne suffisaient pas, mais Monsieur avait son idée personnelle sur l'Amérique,
Ceux qui sont partis pour toujours et qui n'arriveront pas non plus,
Tous ces dévoreurs de la distance, c'est la mer elle-même à présent qu'on leur sert, penses-tu qu'ils en auront assez?
Qui une fois y a mis les lèvres ne lâche point facilement la coupe:
Ce sera long d'en venir à bout, mais on peut tout de même essayer:

Il n'y a que la première gorgée qui coûte.

Ballad

The traders of Tyre and those who go about their business on the water today in great mechanical imaginings, those still accompanied by the handkerchief in the form of that seagull's wings when the waving arm has disappeared, those for whom their vine and field were not enough, but Sir had his own ideas about America, those who have left for ever and will not arrive either, all those consumers of distance, it's the sea itself that's served up to them now, do you think they'll have enough of it? He who once has put his lips to it does not easily give up the cup: it will take a long time to be done with it, but one can try all the same:

It's only the first mouthful that's hard to swallow.

Equipages des bâtiments torpillés dont on voit les noms dans les statistiques,
Garnisons des cuirassés tout à coup qui s'en vont par le plus court à la terre,
Patrouilleurs de chalutiers poitrinaires, pensionnaires de sous-marins ataxiques,
Et tout ce que décharge un grand transport pêle-mêle quand il se met la quille en l'air,
Pour eux tous voici le devoir autour d'eux à la mesure de cet horizon circulaire.
C'est la mer qui se met en mouvement vers eux, plus besoin d'y chercher sa route.
Il n'y a qu'à ouvrir la bouche toute grande et à se laisser faire:

Ce n'est que la première gorgée qui coûte.

Crews of torpedoed vessels, their names in the statistics, garrisons of ironclads gone suddenly to ground by the shortest route, consumptive patrollers on trawlers, ataxic lodgers in submarines, and all that is discharged pell-mell by a great transport ship when it turns its keel in the air, for them all here is duty around them on the scale of this circular horizon. It is the sea that starts to move towards them, no need now to seek one's course. All that's needed is to open the mouth wide and offer no resistance:

It's only the first mouthful that's hard to swallow.

Qu'est-ce qu'ils disaient, la dernière nuit, les passagers des grands transatlantiques,
La nuit même avant le dernier jour où le sans-fil a dit: "Nous sombrons!"
Pendant que les émigrants de troisième classe là-bas faisaient timidement un peu de musique
Et que la mer inlassablement montait et redescendait à chaque coupée du salon?
"Les choses qu'on a une fois quittées, à quoi bon leur garder son cœur?
"Qui voudrait que la vie recommence quand il sait qu'elle est finie toute?
"Retrouver ceux qu'on aime serait bon, mais l'oubli est encore meilleur:

Il n'y a que la première gorgée qui coûte."

What were they saying on the last night, the passengers on the great liners, the very night before the last day when the wireless said: 'We're sinking!' While the emigrants down there in third class made a little timid music and the sea rose untiringly and fell again at each port of the saloon? 'The things we once have left, what good is it to keep our hearts in them? Who would want life to start again when he knows it is quite ended? To find again those we love would be good, but oblivion is better:

It's only the first mouthful that's hard to swallow.'

Envoi

Rien que la mer à chaque côté de nous, rien que cela qui monte et qui descend!
Assez de cette épine continuelle dans le cœur, assez de ces journées goutte à goutte!
Rien que la mer éternelle pour toujours, et tout à la fois d'un seul coup! la mer et nous sommes dedans!

Il n'y a que la première gorgée qui coûte.

Envoy

Nothing but the sea on every side of us, nothing but that, rising and falling! Enough of this perpetual thorn in the heart, enough of these drop by drop days! Nothing but the eternal sea for ever, and all at once in a single blow! the sea and we are in it!

It's only the first mouthful that's hard to swallow.

Charles Péguy
(1873–1914)

Born at Orléans into a working-class family, Péguy excelled at school and at the Ecole Normale Supérieure. He founded the *Cahiers de la Quinzaine* in 1900, to promote the work of young writers. Religious yet anticlerical, and a patriotic socialist, he championed the people with moral idealism, always drawing inspiration from the figure of Jeanne d'Arc. He was killed in action at the Marne in 1914.

His best poems, of which one substantial extract is given here, resemble long, slowly evolving litanies or incantations, repetitive and hypnotic, in which the Hugolian rhetorical spirit is still at work within the free verse. Péguy celebrates both the simple virtuous life and the divine order, the harmony of the physical and the metaphysical, exploiting for his own purposes the spiritual elevation of language initiated by the Symbolists.

Major works: *Jeanne d'Arc* 1897, *Le Mystère de la Charité de Jeanne d'Arc* 1910, *Le Porche du Mystère de la deuxième Vertu* 1911, *Le Mystère des Saints innocents* 1912, *La Tapisserie de Sainte Geneviève et de Jeanne d'Arc* 1912, *La Tapisserie de Notre-Dame* 1913, *Eve* 1913.

La Nuit (extrait)

O ma Nuit étoilée je t'ai créée la première.
Toi qui endors, toi qui ensevelis déjà dans une Ombre éternelle
Toutes mes créatures
Les plus inquiètes, le cheval fougueux, la fourmi laborieuse,
Et l'homme ce monstre d'inquiétude.
Nuit qui réussis à endormir l'homme
Ce puits d'inquiétude.
A lui seul plus inquiet que toute la création ensemble.
L'homme, ce puits d'inquiétude.
Comme tu endors l'eau du puits.
O ma nuit à la grande robe
Qui prends les enfants et la jeune Espérance
Dans le pli de ta robe
Mais les hommes ne se laissent pas faire.
O ma belle nuit je t'ai créée la première.
Et presque avant la première
Silencieuse aux longs voiles
Toi par qui descend sur terre un avant goût

Night (extract)

O my starry night I created you first. You who bring sleep, you who bury already in an eternal shadow all my most restless creatures, the spirited horse, the toiling ant, and man that monster of anxiety. Night, you succeed in bringing sleep to man that well of anxiety. More restless in himself than all creation put together. Man, that well of anxiety. Just as you bring sleep to the water in the well. O my night with the great robe who gather children and young hope in the fold of your robe but men put up resistance. O my beautiful night I created you first. And almost before the first Silent one with the long veils You through whom there descends on earth a foretaste

Toi qui répands de tes mains, toi qui verses sur terre
Une première paix
    Avant-coureur de la paix éternelle.
Un premier repos
    Avant-coureur du repos éternel.
Un premier baume, si frais, une première béatitude
    Avant-coureur de la béatitude éternelle.
Toi qui apaises, toi qui embaumes, toi qui consoles
Toi qui bandes les blessures et les membres meurtris.
Toi qui endors les cœurs, toi qui endors les corps
Les cœurs endoloris, les corps endoloris,
Courbaturés,
Les membres rompus, les reins brisés
De fatigue, de soucis, des inquiétudes
Mortelles,
Des peines,
Toi qui verses le baume aux gorges déchirées d'amertume
Si frais
O ma fille au grand cœur je t'ai créée la première
Presque avant la première, ma fille au sein immense
Et je savais bien ce que je faisais.
Je savais peut-être ce que je faisais.

You who spread with your hands, you who shed on the earth a first peace the forerunner of eternal peace. A first rest the forerunner of eternal rest. A first balm, so cool, a first beatitude the forerunner of eternal beatitude. You who soothe, you who embalm, you who console, you who bandage wounds and bruised limbs. You who bring sleep to hearts, you who bring sleep to bodies, aching hearts, aching bodies, stiffened, exhausted limbs, backs broken with fatigue, with cares, with mortal anxieties, with afflictions, you who shed balm on breasts rent by bitterness, so cool O my daughter with the great heart I created you first almost before the first, my daughter whose bosom is boundless and I knew well what I was doing. I knew perhaps what I was doing. You who lay the child in his

Toi qui couches l'enfant au bras de sa mère
L'enfant tout éclairé d'une ombre de sommeil
Tout riant en dedans, tout riant secret d'une confiance en sa mère.
Et en moi,
Tout riant secret d'un pli des lèvres sérieux
Toi qui couches l'enfant tout en dedans gonflé, débordant d'innocence
Et de confiance
Au bras de sa mère.
Toi qui couchais l'enfant Jésus tous les soirs
Au bras de la Très Sainte et de l'Immaculée.
Toi qui es la sœur tourière de l'espérance.
O ma fille entre toutes première. Toi qui réussis même, Toi qui réussis quelquefois
Toi qui couches l'homme au bras de ma Providence
Maternelle
O ma fille *étincelante et sombre* je te salue
Toi qui répares, toi qui nourris, toi qui reposes
O silence de l'ombre
Un tel silence régnait avant la création de l'inquiétude.
Avant le commencement du règne de l'inquiétude.
Un tel silence régnera, mais un silence de lumière

mother's arms The child illumined by a shadow of sleep all laughter within himself, all secret laughter in his trust in his mother. And in me, all secret laughter with a serious wrinkling of lips You who lay the child inwardly filled, overflowing with innocence and trust in his mother's arms. You who laid the child Jesus every evening in the arms of the Most Holy and Immaculate One. You who are the extern sister of hope. O my daughter first among all. You who succeed even, you who succeed sometimes You who lay man in the arms of my maternal Providence O my *glittering and dark* daughter I greet you who restore, you who nourish, you who bring rest O *silence of the shadows* Such a silence reigned before the creation of unrest. Before the beginning of the reign of unrest. Such a

Quand toute cette inquiétude sera consommée,
Quand toute cette inquiétude sera épuisée.
Quand ils auront tiré toute l'eau du puits.
Après la consommation, après l'épuisement de toute cette inquiétude
D'homme.
Ainsi ma fille tu es ancienne et tu es en retard
Car dans ce règne d'inquiétude tu rappelles, tu commémores, tu rétablis presque,
Tu fais presque recommencer la Quiétude antérieure
Quand mon esprit planait sur les eaux.
Mais aussi ma fille étoilée, ma fille au manteau sombre, tu es très en avance, tu es très précoce.
Car tu annonces, car tu représentes, car tu fais presque commencer d'avance tous les soirs
Ma grande Quiétude de lumière
Eternelle.
Nuit tu es sainte, Nuit tu es grande, Nuit tu es belle.
Nuit au grand manteau.
Nuit je t'aime et je te salue et je te glorifie et tu es ma grande fille et ma créature.

silence will reign, but a silence of light when all that unrest is consumed, when all that unrest is exhausted. When they have drawn all the water from the well. After the consummation, after the exhaustion of all that anxiety of man. Thus my daughter you are ancient and you are tardy for in this reign of unrest you evoke, you commemorate, you almost establish anew, you almost bring the rebirth of the former Quietude when my spirit looked down upon the waters. But also my starry daughter, my daughter with the dark mantle, you are well ahead of time, you are very precocious. For you herald, for you represent, for you almost bring the rebirth each evening, ahead of time, of my great Quietude of eternal light. Night you are holy, Night you are great, Night you are beautiful. Night with the great mantle. Night I love you and I greet you and I glorify you and you are my great daughter and my creature. O beautiful night, night with the great mantle,

O belle nuit, nuit au grand manteau, ma fille au manteau étoilé
Tu me rappelles, à moi-même tu me rappelles ce grand silence qu'il y avait
Avant que j'eusse ouvert les écluses d'ingratitude.
Et tu m'annonces, à moi-même tu m'annonces ce grand silence qu'il y aura
Quand je les aurai fermées.
O douce, ô grande, ô sainte, ô belle nuit, peut-être la plus sainte de mes filles, nuit à la grande robe, à la robe étoilée
Tu me rappelles ce grand silence qu'il y avait dans le monde
Avant le commencement du règne de l'homme.
Tu m'annonces ce grand silence qu'il y aura
Après la fin du règne de l'homme, quand j'aurai repris mon sceptre.
Et j'y pense quelquefois d'avance, car cet homme fait vraiment beaucoup de bruit.
Mais surtout, Nuit, tu me rappelles cette nuit.
Et je me la rappellerai éternellement.
La neuvième heure avait sonné. C'était dans le pays de mon peuple d'Israël.
Tout était consommé. Cette énorme aventure.

my daughter with the starry mantle You remind me, you remind even me of that great silence that there was before I had opened the floodgates of ingratitude. And you foretell, even to me you foretell that great silence that there will be when I have closed them. O sweet, O great, O holy, O beautiful night, perhaps the holiest of my daughters, night with the great robe, with the starry robe you remind me of that great silence that there was in the world before the beginning of the reign of man. You foretell to me that great silence that there will be after the end of the reign of man, when I shall have taken up my sceptre once more. And I think of it sometimes ahead of time, for truly this man makes a great deal of noise. But above all, Night, you remind me of that night. And I shall remember it eternally. The ninth hour had struck. It was in the land of my people Israel. All was fulfilled. That vast adventure. Since

Depuis la sixième heure il y avait eu des ténèbres sur tout le pays, jusqu'à la neuvième heure.
Tout était consommé. Ne parlons plus de cela. Ça me fait mal.
Cette incroyable descente de mon fils parmi les hommes.
Chez les hommes.
Pour ce qu'ils en ont fait.
Ces trente ans qu'il fut charpentier chez les hommes.
Ces trois ans qu'il fut une sorte de prédicateur chez les hommes.
Un prêtre.
Ces trois jours où il fut une victime chez les hommes.
Parmi les hommes.
Ces trois nuits où il fut un mort chez les hommes.
Parmi les hommes morts.
Ces siècles et ces siècles où il est une hostie chez les hommes.
Tout était consommé, cette incroyable aventure
Par laquelle, moi, Dieu, j'ai les bras liés pour mon éternité.
Cette aventure par laquelle mon Fils m'a lié les bras.
Pour éternellement liant les bras de ma justice, pour éternellement déliant les bras de ma miséricorde.

the sixth hour there had been darkness over all the land, until the ninth hour. All was fulfilled. Let us speak no more of it. It gives me pain. That unbelievable descent of my son among men. Into the home of men. For what they made of it. Those thirty years when he was a carpenter among men. Those three years when he was a kind of preacher among men. A priest. Those three days when he was a victim in the home of men. Among men. Those three nights when he was a dead man in the home of men. Among the dead men. Those centuries and centuries when he has been a sacrificial offering among men. All was fulfilled, that unbelievable adventure by which I, God, have my arms tied for my eternity. That adventure through which my Son bound my arms. Binding the arms of my justice for eternity, unbinding the arms of my mercy for eternity. And

Et contre ma justice inventant une justice même.
Une justice d'amour. Une justice d'Espérance. Tout était consommé.
Ce qu'il fallait. Comme il avait fallu. Comme mes prophètes l'avaient annoncé. Le voile du temple s'était déchiré en deux, depuis le haut jusqu'en bas.
La terre avait tremblé; des rochers s'étaient fendus.
Des sépulcres s'étaient ouverts, et plusieurs corps des saints qui étaient morts étaient ressuscités.
Et environ la neuvième heure mon Fils avait poussé
Le cri qui ne s'effacera point. Tout était consommé. Les soldats s'en étaient retournés dans leurs casernes.
Riant et plaisantant parce que c'était un service de fini.
Un tour de garde qu'ils ne prendraient plus.
Seul un centenier demeurait, et quelques hommes.
Un tout petit poste pour garder ce gibet sans importance.
La potence où mon Fils pendait.
Seules quelques femmes étaient demeurées.
La Mère était là.
Et peut-être aussi quelques disciples, et encore on n'en est pas bien sûr.

in the face of my justice even inventing a justice. A justice of love. A justice of Hope. All was fulfilled. That which was necessary. In the way that had been necessary. As my prophets had foretold it. The veil of the temple had been rent in twain from top to bottom. The earth had trembled; rocks had cracked. Sepulchres had opened, and the bodies of several dead saints were brought back to life. And about the ninth hour my Son had uttered the cry that will never be effaced. All was fulfilled. The soldiers had gone away back to their barracks. Laughing and joking because that duty was over. A guard duty they would not have to do again. Only one centurion remained, and a few men. A very small outpost to guard that unimportant gibbet. The gallows on which my Son was hanging. Only a few women had remained. The Mother was there. And perhaps also a few disciples, and even of that one

Or tout homme a le droit d'ensevelir son fils.
Tout homme sur terre, s'il a ce grand malheur
De ne pas être mort avant son fils. Et moi seul, moi Dieu,
Les bras liés par cette aventure,
Moi seul à cette minute père après tant de pères,
Moi seul je ne pouvais pas ensevelir mon fils.
C'est alors, ô nuit, que tu vins.
O ma fille chère entre toutes et je le vois encore et je verrai cela dans mon éternité
C'est alors ô Nuit que tu vins et dans un grand linceul tu ensevelis
Le Centenier et ses hommes romains,
La Vierge et les saintes femmes,
Et cette montagne, et cette vallée, sur qui le soir descendait,
Et mon peuple d'Israël et les pécheurs et ensemble celui qui mourait, qui était mort pour eux

Et les hommes de Joseph d'Arimathée qui déjà s'approchaient

Portant le linceul blanc.

cannot be sure. Now every man has the right to bury his son. Every man on earth, if he has that great misfortune not to have died before his son. And I alone, I God, my arms tied by that adventure, I alone at that moment father after so many fathers, I alone could not bury my son. It was then, O night, that you came. O my daughter beloved among all and I still see it and shall see it in my eternity It was then O night that you came and in a great shroud you buried the centurion and his Roman men, the Virgin and the saintly women, and that mountain, and that valley, on which evening was descending, and my people Israel and the sinners and together he who was dying, who had died for them

And the men of Joseph of Arimathea who already were approaching

Bearing the white winding-sheet.

Oscar Vladislas de Lubicz Milocz
(1877–1939)

This aristocrat of Lithuanian descent and diplomatic background was a French speaker by choice, and took French citizenship in 1930. Views on the status of Milocz vary widely among critics and poets, and a tentative selection is offered here.

His early work was in a Symbolist mode, sometimes lyrical and nostalgic but often with a strong vein of decadent nihilism. Increasing metaphysical anguish and disillusionment with the 'intermediate world' of Symbolism led him into an intense mysticism that fused emotion, senses and intellect into a search for knowledge of archetypal truths. He adopted the Claudelian '*verset*' (sub-Claudelian for some critics) for this later work, represented here by the 'Cantique des Connaissances' from *La Confession de Lémuel* (1922).

Other volumes: *Le Poème des Décadences* 1899, *Les Sept Solitudes* 1906, *Les Eléments* 1911, *Symphonies* 1915, *Ars Magna* 1924, *Arcanes* 1927.

Quand elle viendra ...

Quand elle viendra – fera-t-il gris ou vert dans ses yeux,
Vert ou gris dans le fleuve?
L'heure sera nouvelle dans cet avenir si vieux,
Nouvelle, mais si peu neuve ...
Vieilles heures où l'on a tout dit, tout vu, tout rêvé!
Je vous plains si vous le savez ...

Il y aura de l'aujourd'hui et des bruits de la ville
Tout comme aujourd'hui et toujours – dures épreuves! –
Et des odeurs, – selon la saison – de septembre ou d'avril
Et du ciel faux et des nuages dans le fleuve;

Et des mots – selon le moment – gais ou sanglotants
Sous des cieux qui se réjouissent ou qui pleuvent,
Car nous aurons vécu et simulé, ah! tant et tant,
Quand elle viendra avec ses yeux de pluie sur le fleuve.

When she comes ...

When she comes – will it be grey or green in her eyes, green or grey in the river? The hour will be new in that future so old, new, but so scarcely new ... Old hours when we said everything, saw everything, dreamed everything! I pity you if you know it ...

There will be a today and city noises just like today and for ever – severe ordeals! – and smells – according to the season – of September or of April and deceptive sky and clouds in the river;

And spirited or sobbing words – according to the moment – beneath skies that rejoice or weep, for we will have lived and counterfeited, ah! so many times over, when she comes with her eyes like rain on the river.

Il y aura (voix de l'ennui, rire de l'impuissance)
Le vieux, le stérile, le sec moment présent,
Pulsation d'une éternité sœur du silence;
Le moment présent, tout comme à présent.

Hier, il y a dix ans, aujourd'hui, dans un mois,
Horribles mots, pensées mortes, mais qu'importe.
Bois, dors, meurs, – il faut bien qu'on se sauve de soi
De telle ou d'autre sorte ...

There will be (voice of apathy, laughter of impotence) the old, the sterile, the arid present moment, the pulse-beat of an eternity the sister of silence; the present moment, just as at present.

Yesterday, ten years ago, today, in a month, horrible words, dead thoughts, but what does it matter. Drink, sleep, die – you have to escape from yourself one way or another ...

Aux sons d'une musique ...

Aux sons d'une musique endormie et molle
Comme le glouglou des marais de la lune,
Enfant au sang d'été, à la bouche de prune
Mûre;
Aux sons de miel de tes chevrotantes paroles
Ici, dans l'ombre humide et chaude du vieux mur
Que s'endorme la bête paresseuse Infortune.
Aux sons de ta chanson de harpe rouillée,
Tiède fille qui luis comme une pomme mouillée,
– (Ma tête est si lourde d'éternité vide,
Les mouches d'or font un bruit doux et stupide
Qui prennent tes grands yeux de vache pour des fenêtres),
Aux sons de ta dormante et rousse voix d'été
Fais que je rêve à ce qui aurait pu être
Et n'a pas été ...

To the sounds ...

To the sounds of soft sluggish music like the gurgling of the marshes of the moon, child with the blood of summer, with your ripe plum mouth; to the honeyed sounds of your tremulous words, here, in the damp warm shadow of the old wall let stupid idle Misfortune fall asleep.

To the sound of your song like a rusty harp, tepid girl shining like a wet apple – (My head is so heavy with vacant eternity, the golden flies make a sweet foolish sound as they mistake your great cowlike eyes for windows), to the sounds of your dormant, russet summer voice make me dream of what might have been and has not been ...

Cantique de la Connaissance (2 extraits)

L'enseignement de l'heure ensoleillée des nuits du Divin.
A ceux, qui, ayant demandé, ont reçu et savent déjà.
A ceux que la prière a conduits à la méditation sur l'origine du langage.
Les autres, les voleurs de douleur et de joie, de science et d'amour, n'entendront rien à ces choses.
Pour les entendre, il est nécessaire de connaître les objets désignés par certains mots essentiels
Tels que pain, sel, sang, soleil, terre, eau, lumière, ténèbres, ainsi que par tous les noms de métaux.
Car ces noms ne sont ni les frères, ni les fils, mais bien les pères des objets sensibles.
Avec ces objets et le prince de leur substance, ils ont été précipités du monde immobile des archétypes dans l'abîme de tourmente du temps.
L'esprit seul des choses a un nom. Leur substance est innomée.

Hymn of Knowledge (opening and closing sections)

The teaching of the sunlit hour of the nights of the Divine. For those who, having asked, have received and know already. For those whom prayer has brought to meditation on the origin of language. The others, the thieves of pain and joy, of science and love, will comprehend nothing of these things. To comprehend them, it is necessary to know the objects designated by certain essential words such as bread, salt, blood, sun, earth, water, light, darkness, and similarly by all the names of metals. For these names are neither the brothers nor the sons, but truly the fathers of perceptible objects. With these objects and the prince of their substance, they have been hurled from the motionless world of archetypes into time's chasm of torment. Only the spirit of things has a name. Their substance

Le pouvoir de nommer des objets sensibles absolument impénétrables à l'être spirituel
nous vient de la connaissance des archétypes qui, étant de la nature de notre esprit, sont comme lui situés dans la conscience de l'œuf solaire.
Tout ce qui se décrit par le moyen des antiques métaphores existe en un lieu situé; de tous les lieux de l'infini le seul situé.
Ces métaphores que le langage aujourd'hui encore nous impose dès que nous interrogeons le mystère de notre esprit, sont des vestiges du langage pur des temps de fidélité et de connaissance.
Les poètes de Dieu voyaient le monde des archétypes et le décrivaient pieusement par le moyen des termes précis et lumineux du langage de la connaissance.
Le déclin de la foi se manifeste dans le monde de la science et de l'art par un obscurcissement du langage.
Les poètes de la nature chantent la beauté imparfaite du monde sensible selon l'ancien mode sacré.
Toutefois, frappés de la discordance secrète entre le mode

is unnamed. The power to name perceptible objects absolutely impenetrable to the spiritual being comes to us from knowledge of the archetypes which, being of the nature of our spirit, dwell like it in the consciousness of the solar egg. All that is described by means of the ancient metaphors exists in an assigned place; of all places in infinity the only one assigned. Those metaphors imposed upon us still today by language as soon as we question the mystery of our spirit, are vestiges of the pure language of the eras of fidelity and of knowledge. The poets of God saw the world of archetypes and depicted them piously by means of the exact and luminous terms of the language of knowledge. The decline of faith is manifest in the world of science and of art through an obfuscation of language. The poets of nature sing of the imperfect beauty of the perceptible world according to the former sacred mode. And yet, struck by the hidden dissonance between mode of

d'expression et le sujet,
et impuissants à s'élever jusqu'au lieu seul situé, j'entends Pathmos, terre de la vision des archétypes,
ils ont imaginé, dans la nuit de leur ignorance, un monde intermédiaire, flottant et stérile, le monde des symboles ...

⋆ ⋆ ⋆ ⋆ ⋆ ⋆

... L'esprit et le corps luttent quarante ans: c'est là le fameux âge critique dont parle leur pauvre science, la femme stérile.
Le mal a-t-il ouvert une porte dans ton visage? le messager de paix, Melchisedech entrera par cette porte et elle se refermera sur lui et sur son beau manteau de larmes. Mais répète après moi: *Pater noster.*
Vois-tu, le Père des Anciens, de ceux qui parlaient le langage pur, a joué avec moi comme un père avec son enfant. Nous, nous seuls, qui sommes ses petits enfants nous connaissons ce jeu sacré, cette danse sainte, ce flottement heureux entre la pire obscurité et la meilleure lumière.

expression and subject, and powerless to raise themselves up to the sole assigned place, I mean Patmos,[1] land of the vision of archetypes, they imagined, in the night of their ignorance, an intermediate world, floating and sterile, the world of symbols ...

⋆ ⋆ ⋆ ⋆ ⋆ ⋆

... The spirit and the body struggle for forty years: that is the renowned critical age spoken of by their wretched science, that barren woman. Has evil opened a door in your face? the messenger of peace, Melchizedek[2] will enter by that door and it will close on him and on his beautiful cloak of tears. But repeat after me: *Pater noster.* You see, the Father of the Ancients, of those who spoke the pure tongue, has played with me like a father with his child. We, alone, who are his little children know this hallowed game, this holy dance, this happy floating between the worst darkness and the best light. You must

[1]The island where St John the Divine is said to have written the Book of Revelation.
[2]The King of Salem and high priest who blessed Abraham.

Il faut se prosterner plein de doutes, et prier. Je me plaignais de ne le point connaître; une pierre où il était tout entier m'est descendue dans la main et j'ai reçu au même instant la couronne de lumière.
Et regarde-moi! environné d'embûches je ne redoute plus rien.
Des ténèbres de la conception à celles de la mort, un fil de catacombes court entre mes doigts dans la vie obscure.
Et pourtant, qu'étais-je! Un ver de cloaque, aveugle et gras, à queue aiguë, voilà ce que j'étais. Un homme créé par Dieu et révolté contre son créateur.
"Quelles qu'en soient l'excellence et la beauté, aucun avenir n'égalera jamais en perfection le non-être." Telle était ma certitude unique, telle était ma pensée secrète: une pauvre, pauvre pensée de femme stérile.
Comme tous les poètes de la nature, j'étais plongé dans une profonde ignorance. Car je croyais aimer les belles fleurs, les beaux lointains et même les beaux visages pour leur seule beauté.
J'interrogeais les yeux et le visage des aveugles: comme tous

prostrate yourself full of doubts, and pray. I used to lament my ignorance of that; a stone in which he was wholly contained dropped into my hand and at the same instant I received the crown of light. And look at me! surrounded by snares I fear nothing now. From the dark shadows of conception to those of death, a catacomb thread runs through my fingers into mysterious life. And yet what was I? A cesspool worm, blind and bloated, with a pointed tail, that is what I was. A man created by God and in revolt against his creator. 'Whatever may be its excellence and its beauty, no future will ever equal non-being in perfection.' Such was my unique certainty, such was my secret thought: poor, wretched, a barren woman's thought. Like all poets of nature, I was immersed in a profound ignorance. For I believed I loved the beautiful flowers, the beautiful backgrounds and even the beautiful faces for their beauty alone. I questioned the eyes and the faces of the blind:

les courtisans de la sensualité, j'étais menacé de cécité physique. Ceci est encore un enseignement de l'heure ensoleillée des nuits du Divin.

Jusqu'au jour où, m'apercevant que j'étais arrêté devant un miroir, je regardai derrière moi. La source des lumières et des formes était là, le monde des profonds, sages, chastes archétypes.

Alors cette femme qui était en moi mourut. Je lui donnai pour tombeau tout son royaume, la nature. Je l'ensevelis au plus secret du jardin décevant, là où le regard de la lune, de la prometteuse éternelle se divise dans le feuillage et descend sur les endormies par les mille degrés de la suavité.

C'est ainsi que j'appris que le corps de l'homme renferme dans ses profondeurs un remède à tous les maux et que la connaissance de l'or est aussi celle de la lumière et du sang.

O Unique! ne m'ôte pas le souvenir de ces souffrances, le jour où tu me laveras de mon mal et aussi de mon bien et me feras habiller de soleil par les tiens, par les souriants.

Amen

like all courtiers of sensuality, I was threatened by physical blindness. This is one more teaching of the sunlit hour of the nights of the Divine. Until the day when, noticing that I had paused before a mirror, I looked behind me. The source of enlightenment and of forms was there, the world of the profound, wise, chaste archetypes. Then that woman who was within me died. For a tomb I gave her all her kingdom, nature. I buried her in the most secret place in the deceptive garden, where the gaze of the moon, eternally full of promise, diverges amid the leaves and sinks down on the sleepers through a thousand degrees of bland sweetness. Thus I learned that the body of man contains in its depths a cure for all ills and that the knowledge of gold is also that of light and blood. O One and Only! do not remove from me the memory of those sufferings, on the day when you will cleanse me of my evil and also of my goodness and will have me dressed in sunlight by your followers, by the smiling ones. *Amen.*

Paul Valéry
(1871–1945)

As a young Symbolist writer attending Mallarmé's gatherings, Valéry was strongly influenced not only by the style of the older poet's verse but also by the example Mallarmé provided of dedication to an artistic goal. Valéry gave up poetry after an emotional and intellectual crisis in 1892, to spend twenty years in scientific and mathematical studies, and in philosophical meditation centred on the nature of his own being. This period did produce some important prose works, notably *Introduction à la Méthode de Léonard de Vinci* (1895) and *La Soirée avec M. Teste* (1896). In 1912 he was persuaded by André Gide to return to poetry, and emerged as perhaps the most intellectually profound and spiritually elevated of modern poets. An intelligent, elegant magician of language, he is beyond doubt a major figure in modern literature.

Valéry continues the Mallarméan quest, yet with an intense emotional strength and an often erotic warmth that can make Mallarmé seem clinical by comparison. Poetry for Valéry is an instrument of self-knowledge and self-possession through a pure creative operation of language, an initially narcissistic but ultimately expansive exercise combining spiritual energy and formal skill. The outcome is a lucid intensity of Being, and Mallarmé's Void is filled.

His creativity is a parallel experience for intellect and senses, in which the dynamic process leading to the completion of a poetic event brings satisfaction to both. There is a highly stimulating ambiguity here for the reader, and few poets offer as many renewed rewards on multiple rereadings. Valéry writes mainly in Alexandrines, octosyllables and the decasyllabic line of 'Le Cimetière marin', rejecting in his rigorous pursuit of purity the free verse being developed by his contemporaries, and preserving the sacred mystery and unique harmony of formally structured poetic language.

His musicality is rich and satisfying, and is never at odds with his chosen verse form.

His limited but very influential verse output ended in 1922, and subsequently he wrote criticism, essays and philosophical reflections. At his death in 1945 he was buried at the '*cimetière marin*' of the Mediterranean town of Sète, his birthplace.

Volumes of poetry: *La Jeune Parque* 1917, *Odes* 1920, *Le Cimetière marin* 1920, *Album de Vers anciens* 1920, *Charmes* 1922.

La Fileuse

Assise, la fileuse au bleu de la croisée
Où le jardin mélodieux se dodeline;
Le rouet ancien qui ronfle l'a grisée.

Lasse, ayant bu l'azur, de filer la câline
Chevelure, à ses doigts si faibles évasive,
Elle songe, et sa tête petite s'incline.

The Spinner

Sitting, the spinner in the blue of the casement where the melodious garden softly sways; the ancient whirring wheel has numbed her senses.

Weary, having drunk the azure, of threading the wheedling hairs that evade her weakened fingers, she dreams, and her little head tilts forward.

LA FILEUSE

Un arbuste et l'air pur font une source vive
Qui suspendue au jour, délicieuse arrose
De ses pertes de fleurs le jardin de l'oisive.

Une tige, où le vent vagabond se repose,
Courbe le salut vain de sa grâce étoilée,
Dédiant magnifique, au vieux rouet, sa rose.

Mais la dormeuse file une laine isolée:
Mystérieusement l'ombre frêle se tresse
Au fil de ses doigts longs et qui dorment, filée.

Le songe se dévide avec une paresse
Angélique, et sans cesse, au doux fuseau crédule,
La chevelure ondule au gré de la caresse ...

Derrière tant de fleurs, l'azur se dissimule,
Fileuse de feuillage et de lumière ceinte:
Tout le ciel vert se meurt. Le dernier arbre brûle.

A shrub and the pure air form a living spring which, suspended in the daylight, delightfully sprinkles with its falling petals the idle dreamer's garden.

A stem, where the vagabond wind comes to rest, bows down in the vain salute of its starry grace, magnificent, dedicating its rose to the aged wheel.

But the sleeping lady spins a lonely thread: mysteriously the tenuous shadow threads itself, divided, along her slender sleeping fingers.

The dream unwinds with an angelic indolence, and ceaselessly, trusting in the gentle spindle, the hair undulates, obedient to the caress ...

Behind so many flowers, the azure discreetly hides itself, spinner girdled with foliage and with light; the whole green sky is dying. The last tree blazes.

Ta sœur, la grande rose où sourit une sainte,
Parfume ton front vague au vent de son haleine
Innocente, et tu crois languir ... Tu es éteinte

Au bleu de la croisée où tu filais la laine.

Your sister, the great rose with the smile of a saint, perfumes your hazy brow with the wind of her innocent breath, and you feel you are pining away ... You have faded out

In the blue of the casement where you were spinning wool.

Le Bois amical

Nous avons pensé des choses pures
Côte à côte, le long des chemins,
Nous nous sommes tenus par les mains
Sans dire ... parmi les fleurs obscures;

Nous marchions comme des fiancés
Seuls, dans la nuit verte des prairies;
Nous partagions ce fruit de féeries
La lune amicale aux insensés

The Friendly Wood

We thought pure things side by side, along the paths, we held each other by the hands, wordless ... among the indistinct flowers;

We walked like a betrothed couple alone in the green meadow night; sharing that fairy fruit the moon, a friend to the mad

Et puis, nous sommes morts sur la mousse,
Très loin, tout seuls parmi l'ombre douce
De ce bois intime et murmurant;

Et là-haut, dans la lumière immense,
Nous nous sommes trouvés en pleurant
O mon cher compagnon de silence!

And then, we died on the moss, far away, all alone amid the soft shadows of that intimate murmuring wood;

And up there in the immense light we found each other, weeping, O my dear companion of silence!

Au platane

A André Fontainas

Tu penches, grand Platane, et te proposes nu,
    Blanc comme un jeune Scythe,
Mais ta candeur est prise, et ton pied retenu
    Par la force du site.

To the Plane Tree

for Anare Fontainas

You lean, great Plane tree, and offer yourself naked, white as a young Scythian, but your candour is trapped, and your foot held by the strength of its site.

Ombre retentissante en qui le même azur
    Qui t'emporte, s'apaise,
La noire mère astreint ce pied natal et pur
    A qui la fange pèse.

De ton front voyageur les vents ne veulent pas;
    La terre tendre et sombre,
O Platane, jamais ne laissera d'un pas
    S'émerveiller ton ombre!

Ce front n'aura d'accès qu'aux degrés lumineux
    Où la sève l'exalte;
Tu peux grandir, candeur, mais non rompre les nœuds
    De l'éternelle halte!

Pressens autour de toi d'autres vivants liés
    Par l'hydre vénérable;
Tes pareils sont nombreux, des pins aux peupliers,
    De l'yeuse à l'érable,

Reverberating shadow in which the same blue that transports you now grows calm, the dark mother constrains that pure and native foot weighed down by mud.

The winds want nothing of your journeying brow; the dark and tender earth, O Plane, will never let your shadow marvel at a single step!

That brow will accede only to the luminous heights to which the sap exalts it; grow you may, candid one, but never burst the knots of the eternal pause.

Sense around you other living creatures bound by the venerable hydra; your fellows are many, from the pines to the poplars, from the holm oak to the maple,

Qui, par les morts saisis, les pieds échevelés
    Dans la confuse cendre,
Sentent les fuir les fleurs, et leurs spermes ailés
    Le cours léger descendre.

Le tremble pur, le charme, et ce hêtre formé
    De quatre jeunes femmes,
Ne cessent point de battre un ciel toujours fermé,
    Vêtus en vain de rames.

Ils vivent séparés, ils pleurent confondus
    Dans une seule absence,
Et leurs membres d'argent sont vainement fendus
    A leur douce naissance.

Quand l'âme lentement qu'ils expirent le soir
    Vers l'Aphrodite monte,
La vierge doit dans l'ombre, en silence, s'asseoir,
    Toute chaude de honte.

Who, grasped tight by the dead, their feet dishevelled in the chaos of ashes, feel the flowers slip away from them and their winged sperms glide down the gentle way.

The pure aspen, the hornbeam, and that beech formed of four young women, beat unceasingly at a sky forever closed, dressed vainly with oars.[1]

They live separated, they weep mingled in a single absence, and their silver limbs are cleft in vain at their gentle birth.

When slowly the essence they breathe out in the evening rises towards Aphrodite, the virgin must sit silently in the shadow, all hot with shame.

[1]*rames*: both oars and boughs.

Elle se sent surprendre, et pâle, appartenir
A ce tendre présage
Qu'une présente chair tourne vers l'avenir
Par un jeune visage...

Mais toi, de bras plus purs que les bras animaux
Toi qui dans l'or les plonges,
Toi qui formes au jour le fantôme des maux
Que le sommeil fait songes,

Haute profusion de feuilles, trouble fier
Quand l'âpre tramontane
Sonne, au comble de l'or, l'azur du jeune hiver
Sur tes harpes, Platane,

Ose gémir!...Il faut, ô souple chair du bois,
Te tordre, te détordre,
Te plaindre sans te rompre, et rendre aux vents la voix
Qu'ils cherchent en désordre!

Taken by surprise, and pale, she feels herself a part of that tender premonition that a present flesh turns towards the future through a youthful face ...

But you, with arms purer than animal arms You who plunge them into gold, you who form by day the phantoms of the sufferings that sleep turns into dreams,

Lofty abundance of leaves, proud agitation when the harsh tramontane rings out, at the gold's highest point, the young winter's azure on your harps, Plane,

Dare to groan ! ... O lithe wooden flesh, you must twist and contort, complain without breaking, and give back to the winds the voice they seek in disorder!

Flagelle-toi!...Parais l'impatient martyr
    Qui soi-même s'écorche,
Et dispute à la flamme impuissante à partir
    Ses retours vers la torche!

Afin que l'hymne monte aux oiseaux qui naîtront,
    Et que le pur de l'âme
Fasse frémir d'espoir les feuillages d'un tronc
    Qui rêve de la flamme,

Je t'ai choisi, puissant personnage d'un parc,
    Ivre de ton tangage,
Puisque le ciel t'exerce, et te presse, ô grand arc.
    De lui rendre un langage!

O qu'amoureusement des Dryades rival,
    Le seul poète puisse
Flatter ton corps poli comme il fait du Cheval
    L'ambitieuse cuisse!...

Scourge yourself! ... Appear the impatient martyr flaying his own flesh, and contend with the flame, powerless to escape, in its returns towards the torch!

So that the hymn may rise to birds yet to be born, and that purity of the soul may set hope trembling in the foliage of a trunk that dreams of the flame,

I have chosen you, powerful figure in a park, drunk with your pitching, since the sky exerts you and forces you, O great bow, to give it back a tongue!

O that lovingly, the rival of the Dryads, the poet alone may caress your polished body as he does the ambitious thigh of the Horse! ...

– Non, dit l'arbre. Il dit: *Non!* par l'étincellement
De sa tête superbe,
Que la tempête traite universellement
Comme elle fait une herbe!

— No, says the tree. He says: *No*! by the glittering of his magnificent head, which the storm treats universally as it would a blade of grass!

L'Abeille

A Francis de Miomandre

Quelle, et si fine, et si mortelle,
Que soit ta pointe, blonde abeille
Je n'ai, sur ma tendre corbeille,
Jeté qu'un songe de dentelle.

Pique du sein la gourde belle,
Sur qui l'Amour meurt ou sommeille,
Qu'un peu de moi-même vermeille
Vienne à la chair ronde et rebelle!

The Bee

for Francis de Miomandre

Whatever, and however delicate, and lethal, may be your sting, golden bee, over my tender basket I have thrown only a mere dream of lace.

Prick the lovely gourd of the breast, where Love[1] lies dead or sleeping, so that a little of myself may rise rosy-red in the round, rebellious flesh!

[1] '*Amour*', in Valéry's terminology, is an awakened, creative state of the intellect, and the poem's eroticism is thus not its only level of meaning.

J'ai grand besoin d'un prompt tourment:
Un mal vif et bien terminé
Vaut mieux qu'un supplice dormant!

Soit donc mon sens illuminé
Par cette infime alerte d'or
Sans qui l'Amour meurt ou s'endort!

I greatly need an urgent pang: a keen and clear-cut pain is better than a sleeping torture!

So let my sense be illumined by that tiny golden alarm for lack of which Love dies or falls asleep!

Les Pas

Tes pas, enfants de mon silence,
Saintement, lentement placés,
Vers le lit de ma vigilance
Procèdent muets et glacés.

Personne pure, ombre divine,
Qu'ils sont doux, tes pas retenus!
Dieux!... tous les dons que je devine
Viennent à moi sur ces pieds nus!

The Footsteps

Your footsteps, the children of my silence, with slow and saintly pace, proceed mute and frozen towards the bed of my wakefulness.

Pure being, divine shadow, how soft are your discreet steps! Gods! ... all the gifts I can imagine come to me on those naked feet!

Si, de tes lèvres avancées,
Tu prépares pour l'apaiser,
A l'habitant de mes pensées
La nourriture d'un baiser,

Ne hâte pas cet acte tendre,
Douceur d'être et de n'être pas,
Car j'ai vécu de vous attendre,
Et mon cœur n'était que vos pas.

If, with your advancing lips you are preparing to appease the inhabitant of my thoughts with the sustenance of a kiss,

Do not hasten that tender act, sweet peace of being and not being, for I have lived in expectation of you, and my heartbeat was your footsteps alone.

L'Insinuant

O Courbes, méandre,
Secrets du menteur,
Est-il art plus tendre
Que cette lenteur?

Je sais où je vais,
Je t'y veux conduire,
Mon dessein mauvais
N'est pas de te nuire ...

The Sly One

O Windings, meandering, secrets of the deceiver, what art is more tender than this slowness?

I know where I'm going, I want to guide you there, my wicked design will do you no harm ...

(Quoique souriante
En pleine fierté
Tant de liberté
La désoriente!)

O Courbes, méandre,
Secrets du menteur,
Je veux faire attendre
Le mot le plus tendre.

(Smile though she may in the fullness of pride, so much freedom is leading her astray!)

O Windings, meandering, secrets of the deceiver, I will keep in suspense the most tender word.

Les Grenades

Dures grenades entr'ouvertes
Cédant à l'excès de vos grains,
Je crois voir des fronts souverains
Eclatés de leurs découvertes!

Pomegranates

Hard half-opened pomegranates yielding to your immoderate seeds, I seem to see sovereign brows bursting with their discoveries!

Si les soleils par vous subis,
O grenades entre-bâillées,
Vous ont fait d'orgueil travaillées
Craquer les cloisons de rubis,

Et que si l'or sec de l'écorce
A la demande d'une force
Crève en gemmes rouges de jus,

Cette lumineuse rupture
Fait rêver une âme que j'eus
De sa secrète architecture.

If the suns you have endured, O gaping pomegranates, fashioned by pride, have made you crack open the rubied bulkheads,

And if the dry gold of the rind responding to a force explodes in gems red with juice,

That luminous rupture sets a soul[1] I once had dreaming of its secret architecture.

[1]i.e. a *condition* of the soul, one of an infinity of experienced or potential conditions.

Le Cimetière marin

Μή, φίλα ψυχά, βίον ἀθάνατον σπεῦδε, τὰν δ'ἔμπρακτον ἄντλει μαχανάν.[1]

PINDARE. *Pythiques, III*

Ce toit tranquille, où marchent des colombes,
Entre les pins palpite, entre les tombes;
Midi le juste y compose de feux
La mer, la mer, toujours recommencée!
O récompense après une pensée
Qu'un long regard sur le calme des dieux!

Quel pur travail de fins éclairs consume
Maint diamant d'imperceptible écume,
Et quelle paix semble se concevoir!
Quand sur l'abîme un soleil se repose,
Ouvrages purs d'une éternelle cause,
Le Temps scintille et le Songe est savoir.

The Graveyard by the Sea

This peaceful roof, where doves are walking, pulses between the pines, among the tombs; Noon the just arbiter out there is composing the sea with fires, the sea perpetually renewed! O how rewarding after a thought is a long gaze on the calm of the gods!

What pure work of graceful darts of light consumes many a diamond of imperceptible foam, and what peace seems to conceive itself! When a sun is at rest above the deep, pure workings of an eternal cause, Time scintillates and the Dream is knowledge.

[1]'My soul, do not strive for immortality, but make the most of what is practicable.' (Pindar. *Pythian Odes*, III.)

Stable trésor, temple simple à Minerve,
Masse de calme, et visible réserve,
Eau sourcilleuse, Œil qui gardes en toi
Tant de sommeil sous un voile de flamme,
O mon silence!... Edifice dans l'âme
Mais comble d'or aux mille tuiles, Toit!

Temple du Temps, qu'un seul soupir résume,
A ce point pur je monte et m'accoutume,
Tout entouré de mon regard marin;
Et comme aux dieux mon offrande suprême,
La scintillation sereine sème
Sur l'altitude un dédain souverain.

Comme le fruit se fond en jouissance,
Comme en délice il change son absence
Dans une bouche où sa forme se meurt,
Je hume ici ma future fumée,
Et le ciel chante à l'âme consumée
Le changement des rives en rumeur.

Unchanging treasure, unadorned shrine to Minerva, mass of calm, and visible reticence, supercilious water, Eye concealing within yourself so much sleep beneath a veil of flame, O my silence! ... Mansion in the soul but pinnacle of gold, Roof of a thousand tiles!

The Temple of Time, summed up in a single sigh, I climb and grow accustomed to this pure height, surrounded by my seagoing gaze; and as my supreme offering to the gods, the serene scintillation sows a sovereign disdain upon the altitude.

As the fruit melts in the enjoyment, transforming its absence into delight within a mouth in which its form is dying, I breathe in here the smoke that I shall be, and the sky sings to the soul consumed by fire the changing of the restless murmuring shores.

Beau ciel, vrai ciel, regarde-moi qui change!
Après tant d'orgueil, après tant d'étrange
Oisiveté, mais pleine de pouvoir,
Je m'abandonne à ce brillant espace,
Sur les maisons des morts mon ombre passe
Qui m'apprivoise à son frêle mouvoir.

L'âme exposée aux torches du solstice,
Je te soutiens, admirable justice
De la lumière aux armes sans pitié!
Je te rends pure à ta place première:
Regarde-toi!... Mais rendre la lumière
Suppose d'ombre une morne moitié.

O pour moi seul, à moi seul, en moi-même,
Auprès d'un cœur, aux sources du poème,
Entre le vide et l'événement pur,
J'attends l'écho de ma grandeur interne,
Amère, sombre et sonore citerne,
Sonnant dans l'âme un creux toujours futur!

Sky of beauty, sky of truth, look how I change! After so much pride, after so much strange yet powerful idleness, I give myself up to this shining space, across the houses of the dead my shadow passes, subduing me to its frail motion.

My soul exposed to the torches of the solstice, I withstand you, admirable arbiter of light with your pitiless weapons! I give you back pure to your original place: look at yourself!... but to give back the light implies another half of mournful shade.

O for me alone, my own, within myself, beside a heart, at the poem's origins, between emptiness and the pure event, I await the echo of my inner magnitude, a bitter, dark and sonorous well, ringing an ever future void within the soul!

Sais-tu, fausse captive des feuillages,
Golfe mangeur de ces maigres grillages,
Sur mes yeux clos, secrets éblouissants,
Quel corps me traîne à sa fin paresseuse,
Quel front l'attire à cette terre osseuse?
Une étincelle y pense à mes absents.

Fermé, sacré, plein d'un feu sans matière,
Fragment terrestre offert à la lumière,
Ce lieu me plaît, dominé de flambeaux,
Composé d'or, de pierre et d'arbres sombres,
Où tant de marbre est tremblant sur tant d'ombres:
La mer fidèle y dort sur mes tombeaux!

Chienne splendide, écarte l'idolâtre!
Quand solitaire au sourire de pâtre,
Je pais longtemps, moutons mystérieux,
Le blanc troupeau de mes tranquilles tombes,
Eloignes-en les prudentes colombes,
Les songes vains, les anges curieux!

Do you know, fake captive of the leaves, gulf devouring these slender railings, dazzling mysteries upon my closed eyes, what body drags me to its indolent end, what brow attracts it to this bony ground? A spark within evokes those that I have lost.

Enclosed, sacred, filled with immaterial fire, earthly fragment offered up to light, this place is pleasing to me, commanded by torches, composed of gold, of stone and dark trees, where so much marble quivers over so many shadows; the faithful sea sleeps there on my tombs!

Resplendent she-dog, keep out the idolater! When, solitary with my shepherd's smile, I graze for many hours my mysterious sheep, the white flock of my tranquil tombs, keep far from them the cautious doves, the vain dreams, the prying angels!

Ici venu, l'avenir est paresse.
L'insecte net gratte la sécheresse;
Tout est brûlé, défait, reçu dans l'air
A je ne sais quelle sévère essence ...
La vie est vaste, étant ivre d'absence,
Et l'amertume est douce, et l'esprit clair.

Les morts cachés sont bien dans cette terre
Qui les réchauffe et sèche leur mystère.
Midi là-haut, Midi sans mouvement
En soi se pense et convient à soi-même ...
Tête complète et parfait diadème,
Je suis en toi le secret changement.

Tu n'as que moi pour contenir tes craintes!
Mes repentirs, mes doutes, mes contraintes
Sont le défaut de ton grand diamant ...
Mais dans leur nuit toute lourde de marbres,
Un peuple vague aux racines des arbres
A pris déjà ton parti lentement.

Once here, the future is idleness. The sharply outlined insect scratches at the dry soil; all is burnt up, dispelled, received in the air into I know not what austere essence ... Life is vast, being drunk with absence, and bitterness is sweet, and the mind clear.

The hidden dead lie easy in this earth which keeps them warm and dries away their mystery. Noon up there, motionless Noon conceives itself and is sufficient unto itself ... Complete head and perfect diadem, I am within you the secret changing.

You have only me to contain your fears! My repentances, my doubts, my shackles are the flaw in your great diamond ... But in their darkness heavy with marble, already a shadowy people among the tree-roots has slowly declared itself for you.

Ils ont fondu dans une absence épaisse,
L'argile rouge a bu la blanche espèce,
Le don de vivre a passé dans les fleurs!
Où sont des morts les phrases familières,
L'art personnel, les âmes singulières?
La larve file où se formaient des pleurs.

Les cris aigus des filles chatouillées,
Les yeux, les dents, les paupières mouillées,
Le sein charmant qui joue avec le feu,
Le sang qui brille aux lèvres qui se rendent,
Les derniers dons, les doigts qui les défendent,
Tout va sous terre et rentre dans le jeu!

Et vous, grande âme, espérez-vous un songe
Qui n'aura plus ces couleurs de mensonge
Qu'aux yeux de chair l'onde et l'or font ici?
Chanterez-vous quand serez vaporeuse?
Allez! Tout fuit! Ma présence est poreuse,
La sainte impatience meurt aussi!

They have melted into a dense absence, the red clay has drunk in the white kind, the gift of life has passed into the flowers! Where are the dead's familiar turns of phrase, their personal talents, their individual souls? The larva threads its way where tears used to form.

The shrill cries of tickled girls, the eyes, the teeth, the moist eyelids, the enchanting breast that plays with fire, the blood shining in yielding lips, the final favours, the fingers that defend them, it all goes to earth and re-enters the game!

And you, great soul, do you hope for a dream which will no longer have that deceptive colouring made here for the eyes of flesh by wave and gold? Will you sing when you're thin air? Come now! All is fleeting! My presence is porous, holy impatience also dies!

Maigre immortalité noire et dorée,
Consolatrice affreusement laurée,
Qui de la mort fais un sein maternel,
Le beau mensonge et la pieuse ruse!
Qui ne connaît, et qui ne les refuse,
Ce crâne vide et ce rire éternel!

Pères profonds, têtes inhabitées,
Qui sous le poids de tant de pelletées,
Êtes la terre et confondez nos pas,
Le vrai rongeur, le ver irréfutable
N'est point pour vous qui dormez sous la table,
Il vit de vie, il ne me quitte pas!

Amour, peut-être, ou de moi-même haine?
Sa dent secrète est de moi si prochaine
Que tous les noms lui peuvent convenir!
Qu'importe! Il voit, il veut, il songe, il touche!
Ma chair lui plaît, et jusque sur ma couche,
A ce vivant je vis d'appartenir!

Scrawny immortality in black and gold, consoler hideously wreathed, making of death a maternal breast, a fine fiction and a pious trick! Who does not know and who does not reject that empty skull and that eternal laugh!

Deep-laid fathers, uninhabited heads who, beneath the weight of so much shovelled soil, are the earth and fail to know our steps, the true canker, the unanswerable worm is not for you who sleep beneath the slab, he lives on life, it is me he never leaves!

Love, perhaps, or hatred of myself? His secret tooth is so close to me that any name may suit him! No matter! He sees, he wishes, he dreams, he touches! My flesh pleases him, and even in my bed I live on belonging to this living creature!

Zénon! Cruel Zénon! Zénon d'Elée!
M'as-tu percé de cette flèche ailée
Qui vibre, vole, et qui ne vole pas!
Le son m'enfante et la flèche me tue!
Ah! le soleil... Quelle ombre de tortue
Pour l'âme, Achille immobile à grands pas!

Non, non!... Debout! Dans l'ère successive!
Brisez, mon corps, cette forme pensive!
Buvez, mon sein, la naissance du vent!
Une fraîcheur, de la mer exhalée,
Me rend mon âme ... O puissance salée!
Courons à l'onde en rejaillir vivant!

Oui! Grande mer de délires douée,
Peau de panthère et chlamyde trouée
De mille et mille idoles du soleil,
Hydre absolue, ivre de ta chair bleue,
Qui te remords l'étincelante queue
Dans un tumulte au silence pareil,

Zeno! Cruel Zeno! Zeno of Elea! Have you pierced me with that winged arrow that quivers, flies and does not fly! The sound gives me birth and the arrow kills me! Ah! the sun ... What a tortoise-shadow for the soul, Achilles motionless in full stride!

No, no! ... Stand up! Into the next era! Break, my body, this pensive mould! Drink, my breast, the birth of the wind! A freshness exhaled by the sea restores my soul to me ... O salty power! Let's run into the waves to leap from them alive again!

Yes! Great sea endowed with ecstasies, panther skin and chlamys riddled with countless images of the sun, absolute hydra, drunk with your own blue flesh, forever biting your glittering tail in a tumult that is like silence,

Le vent se lève!... Il faut tenter de vivre!
L'air immense ouvre et referme mon livre,
La vague en poudre ose jaillir des rocs!
Envolez-vous pages tout éblouies!
Rompez, vagues! Rompez d'eaux réjouies
Ce toit tranquille où picoraient des focs!

The wind is rising! ... We must try to live! The vast air opens and closes my book, the wave dares to burst in spray from the rocks! Fly away, dazzled pages! Break, waves! Break with rejoicing waters this peaceful roof where foresails bobbed and pecked!

Victor Segalen
(1878–1919)

An unusual character and a highly original poet, Segalen trained as a doctor and as an archaeologist before travelling first to Polynesia (intending to visit Gauguin but arriving shortly after the painter's death), and later to China, where he worked as a doctor and professor of medicine, interpreter, archaeologist and art historian. During this time he composed poetry informed by all these influences and by Oriental philosophy. His volume *Stèles* was first published in a limited edition in Peking in 1912. Though he was known to Claudel and other poets, his work did not receive widespread attention in France until the 1960s, when an important critical edition by Henri Bouillier appeared, and long after his unexplained death in a forest in his native Brittany.

The *Stèles* are based on the Chinese literary and religious tradition of the epigraph inscribed on a stone pillar, which has a round hole through which the eye of the sky may see. This object, in Oriental mysticism and ontology, is a complete and unified expression of body and soul, the ephemeral and the permanent. Segalen's haunting, elliptical, magical prose-poems are inspired by Chinese mythology, but they are not mere translations or imitations. In an extremely refined form, his own Western sensibility is incorporated into a crystalline Oriental perception of elemental events and truths.

Posthumous volumes: *Odes*, *Thibet*.

Les trois Hymnes primitifs

Les trois hymnes primitifs que les trois Régents avaient nommés: Les Lacs, L'Abîme, Nuées, sont effacés de toutes les mémoires. Qu'ils soient ainsi recomposés:

Les Lacs

作咸池之樂

Les lacs, dans leurs paumes rondes noient le visage du Ciel:

J'ai tourné la sphère pour observer le Ciel.

Les lacs, frappés d'échos fraternels en nombre douze:

J'ai fondu les douze cloches qui fixent les tons musicaux.

The Three Original Hymns

The three original hymns which the three Regents[1] *had named: The Lakes, The Abyss, Clouds, are effaced from all memories. May they be recomposed as follows:*

The Lakes

The lakes drown the face of the Sky in their rounded palms:

I have turned the sphere to observe the Sky.

The lakes, struck by fraternal echoes, twelve in number:

I have cast the twelve bells that determine musical tones.

[1]Mythical Emperors: Houang-ti, Chao-Hao and Tchouan-Hui.

○

Lac mouvant, firmament liquide à l'envers, cloche musicale,

Que l'homme recevant mes mesures retentisse à son tour sous le puissant Souverain-Ciel.

Pour cela j'ai nommé l'hymne de mon règne: Les Lacs.

○

Moving lake, inverted liquid firmament, musical bell,

Let the man who receives my rhythms reverberate in his turn beneath the powerful Sovereign-Sky.

To that end I have named the hymn of my reign: The Lakes.

L'Abîme

作大淵之樂

Face à face avec la profondeur, l'homme, front penché, se recueille.

Que voit-il au fond du trou caverneux? La nuit sous la terre, l'Empire d'ombre.

○

Moi, courbé sur moi-même et dévisageant mon abîme, – ô moi! – je frissonne,

Je me sens tomber, je m'éveille et ne veux plus voir que la nuit.

The Abyss

Face to face with depth, man, brow bent forward, meditates.

What does he see at the bottom of the cavernous pit? The darkness underground, the Empire of shadow.

○

As for me, contracted into myself and scrutinizing my abyss – O self! – I shudder,

I feel myself falling, I awaken and no longer wish to see except in darkness.

Nuées

Ce sont les pensées visibles du haut et pur Seigneur-Ciel.
Les unes compatissantes, pleines de pluie.

Les autres roulant leurs soucis, leurs justices et leurs courroux sombres.

○

Que l'homme recevant mes largesses ou courbé sous mes coups connaisse à travers moi le Fils les desseins du Ciel ancestral.

Pour cela j'ai nommé l'hymne de mon règne: Nuées.

Clouds

They are the visible thoughts of the lofty and pure Lord-Sky. Some are compassionate, filled with rain.

Others roll along their cares, their judgements and their dark angers.

○

Let the man who receives my bounty or who is bent under my blows know through me the Son the purposes of the ancestral Sky.

To that end I have named the hymn of my reign: Clouds.

Pierre musicale

Voici le lieu où ils se reconnurent, les amants amoureux de la flûte inégale;

Voici la table où ils se réjouirent l'époux habile et la fille enivrée;

Voici l'estrade où ils s'aimaient par les tons essentiels,

Au travers du métal des cloches, de la peau dure des silex tintants,

A travers les cheveux du luth, dans la rumeur des tambours, sur le dos du tigre de bois creux,

Parmi l'enchantement des paons au cri clair, des grues à l'appel bref, du phénix au parler inouï.

Musical Stone

Here is the place where they recognized each other, the lovers in love with the intermittent flute;

Here is the slab on which they took their pleasure the skilful husband and the intoxicated girl;

Here is the platform on which they loved through the fundamental tones,

Through the metal of bells, through the hard skin of tinkling flints,

Through the hairs of the lute, in the murmuring of the drums, on the back of the hollow wooden tiger,

Amid the spell cast by the peacocks with their limpid cry, the cranes with their crisp call, the phoenix with its unprecedented speech.

Voici le faîte du palais sonnant que Mou-Koung, le père, dressa pour eux comme un socle,

Et voilà, – d'un envol plus suave que phénix, oiselles et paons, – voilà l'espace où ils ont pris essor.

O

Qu'on me touche: toutes ces voix vivent dans ma pierre musicale.

Here is the pinnacle of the sonorous palace that Mu-Kung,[1] the father, erected for them like a plinth,

And there, – taking wing more softly than phoenix, hen-bird and peacock, – there is the space in which they soared into flight.

O

Touch me: all these voices live in my musical stone.

[1]An Emperor. He married his daughter to a flute-player whose wonderful music could charm birds. The couple flew away with the phoenix from the palace he had built for them.

Ordre au soleil

援戈而麾落日

Mâ, duc de Lou, ne pouvant consommer sa victoire, donna ordre au soleil de remonter jusqu'au sommet du Ciel.

Il le tenait là, fixe, au bout de sa lance: et le jour fut long comme une année et plein d'une ivresse sans nuit.

○

Laisse-moi, ô joie qui déborde, commander à mon soleil et le ramener à mon aube: Que j'épuise ce bonheur d'aujourd'hui!

Las! il échappe à mon doigt tremblant. Il a peur de toi, ô joie. Il s'enfuit, il se dérobe, un nuage l'étreint et l'avale,

Et dans tout mon cœur il fait nuit.

Order to the Sun

Ma, duke of Lu, unable to consummate his victory, ordered the sun to climb back to the zenith of the Sky.

He held it fast there, on the tip of his lance: and the day was as long as a year and full of a drunkenness that knew no night.

○

Let me, O overflowing joy, command my sun and bring it back to my dawn: May I exhaust this happiness of today!

Alas! he escapes my trembling finger. He is afraid of you, O joy. He flees, he steals away, a cloud embraces and swallows him,

And in all my heart there is darkness.

Eloge du jade

故君子貴之也

Si le Sage, faisant peu de cas de l'albâtre, vénère le pur Jade onctueux, ce n'est point que l'albâtre soit commun et l'autre rare: Sachez plutôt que le Jade est bon,

Parce qu'il est doux au toucher – mais inflexible. Qu'il est prudent: ses veines sont fines, compactes et solides.

Qu'il est juste puisqu'il a des angles et ne blesse pas. Qu'il est plein d'urbanité quand, pendu de la ceinture, il se penche et touche terre.

Qu'il est musical: sa voix s'élève, prolongée jusqu'à la chute brève. Qu'il est sincère, car son éclat n'est pas voilé par ses défauts ni ses défauts par son éclat.

In Praise of Jade

If the Sage,[1] having little esteem for alabaster, venerates the pure unctuous Jade, it is not because alabaster is common and the other rare: Know rather that Jade is good,

For it is soft to the touch – but unyielding. For it is discreet: its veins are slender, compact and firm.

For it is just since it has angles and does not wound. For it is urbane when, hanging from the belt, it bows and touches the earth.

For it is musical: its voice rises, prolonged until the rapid fall. For it is sincere, its radiance is not veiled by its flaws nor its flaws by its radiance.

[1]Confucius.

Comme la vertu, dans le Sage, n'a besoin d'aucune parure, le Jade seul peut décemment se présenter seul.

Son éloge est donc l'éloge même de la vertu.

Just as virtue in the Sage needs no adornment, only Jade can decently present itself alone....

Its praise is thus the very praise of virtue.

Nom caché

諱名

Le véritable Nom n'est pas celui qui dore les portiques, illustre les actes; ni que le peuple mâche de dépit;

Le véritable Nom n'est point lu dans le Palais même, ni aux jardins ni aux grottes, mais demeure caché par les eaux sous la voûte de l'aqueduc où je m'abreuve.

Seulement dans la très grande sécheresse, quand l'hiver crépite sans flux, quand les sources, basses à l'extrême, s'encoquillent dans leurs glaces,

Hidden Name

The true Name is not the one that gilds porticos, gives lustre to deeds; nor the one that the people chew with resentment;

The true Name is not read in the Palace itself, nor in the gardens nor the grottoes, but remains hidden by the waters beneath the vault of the aqueduct where I quench my thirst.

Only in the great drought, when winter crackles without flowing, when the springs at their lowest ebb spiral into icy shell-shapes,

Quand le vide est au cœur du souterrain et dans le souterrain du cœur, – où le sang même ne roule plus, – sous la voûte alors accessible se peut recueillir le Nom.

Mais fondent les eaux dures, déborde la vie, vienne le torrent dévastateur plutôt que la Connaissance!

When the void is at the heart of the cavern and in the cavern of the heart, – when blood itself no longer circulates, – beneath the vault, accessible now, can the Name be recorded.

But let the hard waters melt, let life overflow, let the devastating torrent come rather than Knowledge!

Cubism, cosmopolitanism and modernism

In the years between the turn of the century and the First World War, what Apollinaire called a 'new spirit' animated the literary avant-garde in Paris, as poets turned away from the artificiality of Symbolism and opened their perception to all the multiple stimuli of modern city life and the excitement of travel. The mobility and speed of both physical existence and sensory response were increasing, and with them came a growing awareness of discontinuity in perception, and an accelerated breakdown of traditional modes of thought and expression.

The process begun by Rimbaud and Laforgue reached a feverish level of experimentation in this fascinating period. Groups came and went, manifestos proliferated, ephemeral magazines fired ideas at one another, and café debate was more intense than ever. Barriers between art forms were dissolved, and, in a particularly stimulating interaction of poetry and painting, there was a meeting of minds between a group of writers based in the Rue Ravignan and the artists Picasso, Braque and Gris. The 'Cubist' tendency in poetry becomes evident above all in the work of Pierre Reverdy, but it seems useful at this point to consider together five poets of the period: Fargue, Jacob, Apollinaire, Cendrars and Reverdy. There is great diversity in their poetry and they should certainly not be classified as a 'school', but they do express collectively the 'new spirit', and there are broad similarities in their perception and experience.

Two other poets for whom there is no room in this collection should be mentioned:

Valéry Larbaud (1881–1957) was a highly cultured and wealthy man who turned his back on his privileged background to become a compulsive and Whitmanesque traveller, responsive to the pleasure of speed and full of sensitivity in his self-exploration *en route*. In his imagination he travelled even further, recording the adventures of a globe-trotting American millionaire in his free verse volume *Poésies d'A. O. Barnabooth*; but his writing is perhaps pale by comparison with the blazing force of Cendrars.

André Salmon (1881–1969) was a campaigner for Cubism and a well-known figure in Parisian artistic life. His poetry discovers the extraordinary in the commonplace, and beauty in the Paris underworld. Apollinaire's 'Poème lu au mariage d'André Salmon' suggests that he and Salmon are 'pèlerins de la perdition', adventurers risking their entire identity in their radical plunge into experience. Salmon published *Féeries* 1907, *Le Calumet* 1910, *Le Livre et la bouteille* 1919, *Prikaz* 1919, *L'Age de l'humanité* 1921, *Peindre* 1922.

Léon-Paul Fargue
(1876–1947)

Though a widely travelled man, Fargue is an essentially Parisian poet, born in that city and constantly alive through his senses to its spirit. '*Le Piéton de Paris*', the title of one of his books, aptly describes the man himself. After early contacts with the Symbolists, he became intensely involved in the ferment of new aesthetic ideas in the years preceding the 1914–18 war, and his verse and prose-poems struck a genuinely modernist note, while also preserving a more traditional lyricism and musical intimacy. Fargue championed the causes of Van Gogh, Bonnard and the Ballets Russes, and exchanged ideas with Joyce, Stravinsky, Satie and Picasso.

His closest artistic affinities are probably with Apollinaire and Cendrars, for he seeks to be a vibrant and mobile perceiver of the intensity of modern city life. His creative existence is a pattern of absorption and imaginative response: 'Strive to be sensitive, infinitely receptive, always in a state of osmosis.' The city becomes a magical yet melancholy symphony of impressions, a dreamlike world made concrete through language.

Claudel described him as 'a born poet'. Yet there is also deep insecurity and anxiety in Fargue's writing, a sense of tragedy not fully concealed by his wit and verbal inventiveness, and induced at least partly by the death of his father in 1909 as well as by disappointments in relationships.

Major volumes: *Poèmes* 1905 and 1912, *Pour la Musique* 1914, *Espaces* 1928, *Sous la Lampe* 1929, *Haute Solitude* 1941.

Sur le trottoir tout gras …

Sur le trottoir tout gras de bouges aux carreaux brouillés, des filles qui semblent de garde contre un terrible mur de réclames se signent lorsqu'il fait des éclairs. Quelqu'un d'invisible siffle et se hâte…

La bande éclatante d'un bar à musique éclaire des spectres qui attendent…

L'ennui s'endort dans ses palais qui soufflent leur haleine chaude…

Des pensées incomprises, des amours pauvres et des idylles depuis longtemps en marche frôlent les boutiques fermées et sombres…

Du côté des remparts souffre une seule lumière…
Une ruelle délaissée dans les terrains vagues reste obscure
Où l'amour blessé chante et se traîne
Et regarde de toutes ses forces l'image déchirée du soir…

On the pavement …

On the pavement swilling with brothels, their windows opaque, whores apparently on guard before an appalling wall of advertisements cross themselves when the lightning flashes. Someone invisible whistles and hurries on … The blaring strip of light of a music tavern illumines waiting phantoms … Apathy falls asleep in its palaces that exhale their hot breath … Uncomprehended thoughts, paltry loves and idylls long since on the move brush past the closed and darkened shops … Over by the city wall a solitary light suffers … A forsaken alleyway in waste ground remains obscure Where wounded love sings and drags itself along And gazes with all its strength at the ragged image of the evening …

Sous des hangars, de puissants moteurs font de grands gestes sur les murs. Des hommes obscurs allument leur fête derrière la baie vitrée qui tremble...

Une branche de canal fuit sous les lampes. Les arcs voltaïques y bercent par instants de grêles escaliers d'argent... L'arche d'un pont semble monter comme une trombe... L'écluse embouche, par ses hautes portes grinçantes et criblées de blessures, les longs clairons de l'eau stridente. Elle tord et cambre au vent sa crinière...

J'aime entendre encore longtemps sa grande chanson crevée et fraîche...

Inside sheds, powerful engines gesture vividly on the walls. Indistinct men light the spark of their festivity behind the quivering glazed hatch ... A canal arm recedes under the lanterns. Voltaic arcs intermittently cradle slender silver staircases ... The arch of a bridge seems to rise like a waterspout ... The sluice gate trumpets through its tall grating wound-riddled doors the long clarion calls of the shrill water. It twists and arches its mane in the wind ... I love to go on hearing its great prolonged song, exhausted and fresh ...

La rampe s'allume ...

La rampe s'allume. Un clavier s'éclaire au bord des vagues. Les noctiluques font la chaîne. On entend bouillir et filtrer le lent bruissement des bêtes du sable...

Une barque chargée arrive dans l'ombre où les chapes vitrées des méduses montent obliquement et affleurent comme les premiers rêves de la nuit chaude...

De singuliers passants surgissent comme des vagues de fond, presque sur place, avec une douceur obscure. Des formes lentes s'arrachent du sol et déplacent de l'air, comme des plantes aux larges palmes. Les fantômes d'une heure de faiblesse défilent sur cette berge où viennent finir la musique et la pensée qui arrivent du fond des âges. Devant la villa, dans le jardin noir autrefois si clair, un pas bien connu réveille les roses mortes...

The Footlights[1] *blaze ...*

The footlights blaze. A keyboard is lit up at the edge of the waves. The noctilucae[2] dance hand in hand. The slow murmuring of the sand creatures is audible as it simmers and seeps ...

A laden boat arrives in the shadows where the vitreous copes of the jellyfish rise at an angle and level out at the surface like the first dreams in the warm night ...

Strange passing figures surge up like tidal waves, almost on the spot, with a mysterious gentleness. Slow-moving shapes uproot themselves from the ground and displace air, like broad-palmed plants. The ghosts of an hour of weakness pass in procession on this bank where the journey of music and thought from the depths of the ages comes to its end. In front of the villa, in the dark garden that was once so bright, a familiar step awakens the dead roses ...

[1]*La rampe*: also a ramp, or slope.
[2]Luminescent marine organisms.

Un vieil espoir, qui ne veut pas cesser de se débattre à la lumière... Des souvenirs, tels qu'on n'eût pas osé les arracher à leurs retraites, nous hèlent d'une voix pénétrante... Ils font de grands signes. Ils crient, comme ces oiseaux doux et blancs aux grêles pieds d'or qui fuyaient l'écume un jour que nous passions sur la grève. Ils crient les longs remords. Ils crient la longue odeur saline et brûlée jusqu'à la courbe...

Le vent s'élève. La mer clame et flambe noir, et mêle ses routes. Le phare qui tourne à pleins poings son verre de sang dans les étoiles traverse un bras de mer pour toucher ma tête et la vitre. Et je souffre contre l'auberge isolée au bord d'un champ sombre...

An old hope, which will not cease to struggle in the light ... Memories, of such a kind that one would not have dared to tear them from their lairs, hail us with piercing voices ... They beckon expansively. They cry out, like those gentle white birds with slender golden feet that flew before the foam one day as we moved along the shore. They cry out prolonged remorse. They cry out the long, burnt and salty smell as far as the curve ...

The wind is rising. The sea clamours and flames black, and mingles its currents. The lighthouse, its clenched fists spinning its glass of blood among the stars, crosses an arm of the sea to touch my head and the glass pane. And I am suffering against the remote inn at the edge of a dark field ...

La Gare

Gare de la douleur j'ai fait toutes tes routes.
Je ne peux plus aller, je ne peux plus partir.
J'ai traîné sous tes ciels, j'ai crié sous tes voûtes.
Je me tends vers le jour où j'en verrai sortir
Le masque sans regard qui roule à ma rencontre
Sur le crassier livide où je rampe vers lui,
Quand le convoi des jours qui brûle ses décombres
Crachera son repas d'ombres pour d'autres ombres
Dans l'étable de fer où rumine la nuit.
Ville de fiel, orgues brumeuses sous l'abside
Où les jouets divins s'entrouvrent pour nous voir,
Je n'entends plus gronder dans ton gouffre l'espoir
Que me soufflaient tes chœurs, que me traçaient tes signes,
A l'heure où les maisons s'allument pour le soir.

The Railway Station

Station of suffering I have travelled all your tracks. I can go no longer, I can no longer leave. I have lingered beneath your skies, cried out beneath your vaulted roofs. I strain towards the day when I will see the eyeless mask rolling out to meet me over the livid slagheap where I crawl towards it, when the train of days that burns its rubbish will spit out its meal of shadows for other shadows in the iron cattleshed where night chews the cud. City of gall, misty organs beneath the apse where the divine fishplates part to see us, I hear no longer the rumbling in your chasm of the hope that your choirs breathed on me, that your signs marked out for me, at the hour when the houses light their lamps for the evening.

Ruche du miel amer où les hommes essaiment,
Port crevé de strideurs, noir de remorqueurs,
Dont la huée enfonce sa clef dans le cœur
Haïssable et hagard des ludions qui s'aiment,
Torpilleur de la chair contre les vieux mirages
Dont la salve défait et refait les visages,
Sombre école du soir où la classe rapporte
L'erreur de s'embrasser, l'erreur de se quitter,
Il y a bien longtemps que je sais écouter
Ton écluse qui souffre à deux pas de ma porte.

Hive of bitter honey where men swarm, port bursting with grating sounds, black with tugboats; their hooting drives its key into the loathsome, haggard heart of the Cartesian divers in their element, torpedo-boat of flesh against the old looming delusions whose salvo unmakes and remakes faces, sombre night-school where the class sneaks on the error of kissing, the error of parting, for a good while now I have known how to listen to your sluice-gate in pain a few yards from my door.

Je suis venu chez toi du temps de ma jeunesse.
Je me souviens du cœur, je me souviens du jour
Où j'ai quitté sans bruit pour surprendre l'amour
Mes parents qui lisaient, la lampe, la tendresse,
Et ce vieux logement que je verrai toujours.
Sur l'atlas enfumé, sur la courbe vitreuse,
J'ai guidé mon fanal au milieu de mes frères.
Les ombres commençaient le halage nocturne.
Le mètre, le ruban filaient dans leur poterne
Les hommes s'enroulaient autour d'un dévidoir.
La boutique, l'enclume à l'oreille cassée,
La forge qui respire une dernière prise,
La terrasse qui sent le sable et la liqueur
Rougissaient par degrés sur le livre d'images
Et gagnaient lentement leur place dans l'église.
Un tramway secouait en frôlant les feuillages
Son harnais de sommeil dans les flaques des rues.
L'hippocampe roulait sa barque et sa lanterne
Sur les pièges du fer et sur les clefs perdues.
Il y avait un mur assommé de traverses
Avec un bec de gaz tout taché de rousseur

I came to you in the time of my youth. I remember the heart, I remember the day when to take love by surprise, without a sound, I left my reading parents, the lamp, the affection, and that old dwelling that I shall always see. Over the smoke-darkened map, over the curved glass panel, I guided my ship's lantern among my brothers. The shadows were beginning the nocturnal towage. The rule and the tape marched off into their vaulted passageway Men were winding themselves around a spool. The workshop, the anvil with the broken ear, the forge breathing in a final pinch, the terrace smelling of sand and the liquor were reddening by degrees on the picture-book and slowly reaching their place in the church. A tramcar shook as it brushed against the leaves its harness of sleep into the street puddles. The seahorse sailed his boat and his lantern over the iron traps and the lost keys. There was a wall assaulted by crossbeams with a speckled gas-burner where the tree insects

Où fusaient tristement les insectes des arbres
Sous le regard absent des éclairs de chaleur.
L'odeur d'un quartier sombre où se fondent les graisses
Envoyait gauchement ses corbeaux sur le ciel.
Une lampe filait dans l'étude du soir.
Une cour bruissait dans son gâteau de miel.
Une vitre battait comme un petit cahier
Contre le tableau noir où la main du vieux maître
Posait et retirait doucement les étoiles.
Les femmes s'élançaient comme des araignées
Quand un passant marchait sur le bord de leur toile.
Les grands fonds soucieux bourbillaient de plongeurs
Que le masque futur cherchait comme il me cherche.
Le présage secret qui chasse sur les hommes
Nageait d'un peu plus près sur ma tête baissée.

crackled sadly beneath the vacant gaze of the hot flickering light. The smell of a gloomy district where oils are blended sent its crows clumsily into the heavens. A lamp guttered in the evening study. A courtyard rustled in its honey cake. A glass pane knocked like a little exercise book against the blackboard where the hand of the old schoolmaster gently set and removed the stars. The women pounced like spiders when a passer-by stepped on the hem of their web. The great anxious depths were clotting with plunging pistons sought by the future mask as it seeks me. The secret foreboding that goes hunting on man sculled a little closer on my lowered head.

Je me suis retrouvé sous ta serre de vitres
Dans les plants ruisselants, les massifs de visages
Scellés du nom, de l'âge et du secret du coffre,
Du nécessaire d'os et du compas de chair,
En face du tunnel où se cache la fée
De l'aube, qui demain vendra ses madeleines
Sur un quai somnolent tout mouillé de rosée
Dans le bruit du tambour, dans le bruit de la mer.
J'ai longé tout un soir tes grands trains méditants,
Triangles vigilants, braises, bielles couplées,
Sifflets doux, percement lointain de courtilières,
Cagoules qui clignez bassement par vos fentes,
Avec deux passants noirs penchés sur la rambarde
Au-dessus du fournil du pont de la Chapelle
Où le guerrier déchu qui promène les hommes
Encrasse son panache avec un bruit de chaînes,
Et le grand disque vert de la rue de Jessaint,
Gare de ma jeunesse et de ma solitude
Que l'orage parfois saluait longuement,
J'aurai longtemps connu tes regards et tes rampes,

I found myself under your glass hot-house among dripping plants, the clusters of faces sealed with the name, the age and the secret of the coffer, of the bone workbox and the compass of flesh, facing the tunnel where the dawn fairy hides, who tomorrow will sell her madeleine cakes on a somnolent quayside all wet with dew in the sound of the drum, in the sound of the sea. All one evening I walked the length of your great pensive trains, watchful signal-triangles, burning coals, coupled connecting-rods, gentle whistlings, distant shrill of mole-crickets, cowls blinking basely through your crevices, with two dark passers-by leaning over the handrail above the bakehouse of the Pont de la Chapelle where the fallen warrior who takes men on excursions is fouling his plume with a noise of chains, and the great green signal-disc of the Rue de Jessaint, Station of my youth and of my solitude to which sometimes the storm bowed long and low, I will have known long since your gazes and your ramps, your rain-soaked yawns, your

Tes bâillements trempés, tes cris froids, tes attentes,
J'ai suivi tes passants, j'ai doublé tes départs,
Debout contre un pilier j'en aurai pris ma part
Au moment de buter au heurtoir de l'impasse,
A l'heure qu'il faudra renverser la vapeur
Et que j'embrasserai sur sa bouche carrée
Le masque ardent et dur qui prendra mon empreinte
Dans le long cri d'adieu de tes portes fermées.

frigid cries, your expectations, I have followed your passers-by, I have understudied your departures, standing against a pillar I will have taken my part at the moment of striking the dead-end buffer, at the time when steam will have to be reversed and when I will kiss upon its square mouth the hard and fiery mask which will take my imprint with it in the long farewell cry of your closed doors.

Postface

Un long bras timbré d'or glisse du haut des arbres
Et commence à descendre et tinte dans les branches.
Les fleurs et les feuilles se pressent et s'entendent.
J'ai vu l'orvet glisser dans la douceur du soir.
Diane sur l'étang se penche et met son masque.
Un soulier de satin court dans la clairière
Comme un rappel du ciel qui rejoint l'horizon.
Les barques de la nuit sont prêtes à partir.

Epilogue

A long arm embossed with gold glides from the tree tops and begins to descend, ringing gently in the branches. The flowers and the leaves press together in understanding. I have seen the slow-worm sliding in the softness of the evening. Diana bends over the pool and puts on her mask. A satin shoe runs in the glade like a hint of heaven uniting with the horizon. The ships of the night are ready to set sail.

D'autres viendront s'asseoir sur la chaise de fer.
D'autres verront cela quand je ne serai plus.
La lumière oubliera ceux qui l'ont tant aimée.
Nul appel ne viendra rallumer nos visages.
Nul sanglot ne fera retentir notre amour.
Nos fenêtres seront éteintes.
Un couple d'étrangers longera la rue grise.
Les voix
D'autres voix chanteront, d'autres yeux pleureront
Dans une maison neuve.
Tout sera consommé, tout sera pardonné,
La peine sera fraîche et la forêt nouvelle,
Et peut-être qu'un jour, pour de nouveaux amis,
Dieu tiendra ce bonheur qu'il nous avait promis.

Others will come to sit on the iron chair. Others will see that when I am no more. The light will forget those who loved it so much. No call will come to rekindle our faces. No sob will set our love re-echoing. Our windows will have no light. A pair of strangers will move along the grey street. The voices Other voices will sing, other eyes will weep in a new house. All will be accomplished, all will be forgiven, the sorrow will be fresh and the forest new-grown, and perhaps one day, for new lovers, God will fulfil that happiness which he had promised us.

Max Jacob
(1876–1944)

Max Jacob was born in Brittany of Jewish parentage, but was converted to Catholicism in 1909. A multi-talented artist and poet, he associated with all the leading figures in the 'new spirit' avant-garde. He had particularly close links with Picasso and Apollinaire, and was an animating force in the Cubist group.

An ironist and something of a '*mystificateur*', Jacob seems to hide his true personality behind a bewildering variety of masks. He has a powerful sense of absurdity, frequently expressed in compulsive, brilliant and untranslatable punning. But there is also a real vein of anguish, often objectified in hallucinatory images, and elsewhere he writes lyrically of simple human pleasures and sorrows with a sense of wonder that deepens eventually into his adoption of the Catholic faith. The surprise factor in his life and work is strong, and it is therefore no surprise that the immediate stimulus to that conversion was a revelatory vision experienced in a cinema.

His work is unusually diverse, then, but he combines a strong awareness of popular cultural tradition with a humorous and spontaneous modernism. In so far as the word 'Cubist' can be applied to poetry (it is perhaps more a spirit than a tangible technique), Jacob is part of the Cubist surge away from mimesis and towards simultaneity, the spontaneous and risky association of ideas and images which then finds an autonomous structural logic.

In 1937 he retired to the monastery of Saint-Benoît-sur-Loire. From there he was taken by the Gestapo to the concentration camp at Drancy, where he died in 1944.

Jacob's best work, consisting mainly of prose-poems, is contained in these volumes: *Le Cornet à Dés* 1918, *Le Laboratoire Central* 1921, *Derniers Poèmes en vers et en prose* 1945; and a further collection entitled *Le Cornet à Dés II* appeared in 1955.

La Guerre

Les boulevards extérieurs, la nuit, sont pleins de neige; les bandits sont des soldats; on m'attaque avec des rires et des sabres, on me dépouille: je me sauve pour retomber dans un autre carré. Est-ce une cour de caserne, ou celle d'une auberge? que de sabres! que de lanciers! il neige! on me pique avec une seringue: c'est un poison pour me tuer; une tête de squelette voilée de crêpe me mord le doigt. De vagues réverbères jettent sur la neige la lumière de ma mort.

War

The outer boulevards, at night, are filled with snow; the brigands are soldiers; I am attacked with laughter and sabres, and stripped: I run away and land in another square. Is it a barrack yard, or that of an inn? so many sabres! so many lancers! it's snowing! I am pierced with a syringe: it's a poison to kill me; a death's head veiled in crape bites my finger. Indeterminate street-lamps cast on the snow the light of my death.

Dans la forêt silencieuse

Dans la forêt silencieuse, la nuit n'est pas encore venue et l'orage de la tristesse n'a pas encore injurié les feuilles. Dans la forêt silencieuse d'où les Dryades ont fui, les Dryades ne reviendront plus.

Dans la forêt silencieuse, le ruisseau n'a plus de vagues, car le torrent coule presque sans eau et tourne.

Dans la forêt silencieuse, il y a un arbre noir comme le noir et derrière l'arbre il y a un arbuste qui a la forme d'une tête et qui est enflammé, et qui est enflammé des flammes du sang et de l'or.

Dans la forêt silencieuse où les Dryades ne reviendront plus, il y a trois chevaux noirs, ce sont les trois chevaux des rois mages et les rois mages ne sont plus sur leurs chevaux ni ailleurs et ces chevaux parlent comme des hommes.

In the Silent Forest

In the silent forest, night has not yet come and the storm of sorrows has not yet insulted the leaves. In the silent forest abandoned by the fleeing Dryads, the Dryads will return no more.

In the silent forest, the stream has no more currents, for the torrent flows almost without water and curdles.

In the silent forest, there is a tree as black as black and behind the tree there is a bush in the form of a head and aflame, and aflame with the flames of blood and gold.

In the silent forest where the Dryads will return no more, there are three black horses, they are the three horses of the Magi and the Magi are no longer on their horses nor elsewhere and these horses speak like men.

Ruses du Démon pour ravoir sa proie

Le quai sombre, en triangle de donjon, hérissé de platanes l'hiver, squelettes trop jolis sur l'échancrure du ciel. A l'auberge vivait avec nous une femme belle, mais plate, qui cachait ses cheveux sous une perruque ou du satin noir. Un jour au-dessus du granit, elle m'apparut au plein soleil de la mer: trop grande – comme les rochers du coin – elle mettait sa chemise, je vis que c'était un homme et je le dis. La nuit sur une espèce de quai londonien j'en fûs châtié: éviter le coup de couteau à la face! se faire abîmer le pouce! riposter par un poignard dans la poitrine à la hauteur de l'omoplate. L'Hermaphrodite n'était pas mort. Au secours! au secours! on arrive... des hommes, que sais-je? ma mère! et je revois la chambre d'auberge sans serrure aux portes: il y avait, Dieu merci, des crochets mais quelle malignité a l'hermaphrodite: une ouverture du grenier, un volet blanc remue et l'hermaphrodite descend par là.

Tricks of the Demon to win back his prey

The dark wharf, triangular like a turret, bristling with plane trees in winter, over-pretty skeletons against the serrated sky. At the inn there lived with us a woman, beautiful but flat, who hid her hair under a wig or black satin. One day up on top of the granite, she appeared to me in the full sunlight of the sea: too tall – like the rocks thereabouts – she was putting on her blouse, I saw that she was a man and I said so. That night on a kind of London wharf I was punished for it: avoid the knife-thrust in the face! get a damaged thumb! riposte with a dagger in the breast at the height of the scapula. The Hermaphrodite was not dead. Help! help! people coming ... men, how should I know? my mother! and I see once more the bedroom at the inn with no locks on the door: there were hooks, thank God, but what cunning malice the hermaphrodite has: an opening in the loft, a white shutter moves and the hermaphrodite comes down that way.

Etablissement d'une communauté au Brésil

On fut reçu par la fougère et l'ananas
L'antilope craintif sous l'ipécacuanha.
Le moine enlumineur quitta son aquarelle
Et le vaisseau n'avait pas replié son aile
Que cent abris légers fleurissaient la forêt.
Les nonnes labouraient. L'une d'elles pleurait
Trouvant dans une lettre un sujet de chagrin.
Un moine intempérant s'enivrait de raisin
Et l'on priait pour le pardon de ce péché.
On cueillait des poisons à la cime des branches
Et les moines vanniers tressaient des urnes blanches.
Un forçat évadé qui vivait de la chasse
Fut guéri de ses plaies et touché de la grâce:
Devenu saint, de tous les autres adoré,
Il obligeait les fauves à leur lécher les pieds.
Et les oiseaux du ciel, les bêtes de la terre
Leurs apportaient à tous les objets nécessaires.
Un jour on eut un orgue au creux de murs crépis

Establishment of a Community in Brazil

They were welcomed by fern and pineapple The timid antelope under the ipecacuanha. The friar illuminator left his watercolour and the ship had not folded its wing when a hundred flimsy shelters adorned the forest. The nuns tilled the soil. One of them was weeping Finding in a letter a subject for sorrow. An intemperate monk would get drunk on raisin wine and they prayed for forgiveness of this sin. They gathered poisons at the branch tops and the friar basketmakers wove white urns. An escaped convict who lived by hunting was cured of his wounds and touched by grace: he became a saintly man, adored by all the others, and compelled the wild beasts to lick their feet. And the birds in the sky, the beasts of the earth brought to all of them the objects that they needed. One day they had an organ in the recess of rough-cast walls Flocks of sheep that bit the ears of corn One

Des troupeaux de moutons qui mordaient les épis
Un moine est bourrelier, l'autre est distillateur
Le dimanche après vêpre on herborise en chœur.

Saluez le manguier et bénissez la mangue
La flûte du crapaud vous parle dans sa langue
Les autels sont parés de fleurs vraiment étranges
Leurs parfums attiraient le sourire des anges,
Des sylphes, des esprits blottis dans la forêt
Autour des murs carrés de la communauté.
Or voici qu'un matin quand l'Aurore saignante
Fit la nuée plus pure et plus fraîche la plante
La forêt où la vigne au cèdre s'unissait,
Parut avoir la teigne. Un nègre paraissait
Puis deux, puis cent, puis mille et l'herbe en était teinte
Et le Saint qui pouvait dompter les animaux
Ne put rien sur ces gens qui furent ses bourreaux.
La tête du couvent roula dans l'herbe verte
Et des moines détruits la place fut déserte
Sans que rien dans l'azur frémît de la mort.

monk is a harness-maker, another a distiller On Sundays after vespers they herborize in chorus.

Hail to the mango tree and blessings on the mango The flute of the toad speaks to you in its language The altars are adorned with truly strange flowers Their scents attracted the smile of the angels, sylphs, spirits huddled in the forest around the foursquare walls of the community. Now it happened that one morning when the bleeding Dawn made the cloud purer and the plant fresher The forest where the vine entwined with the cedar, appeared to have scurvy. A negro appeared, then two, then a hundred, then a thousand and the grass was dyed with them and the Saint who could tame animals was powerless against these people who were his executioners. The convent's head rolled into the green grass and the place of the destroyed monks was void without the merest shudder in the azure at the death.

C'est ainsi que vêtu d'innocence et d'amour
J'avançais en traçant mon travail chaque jour
Priant Dieu et croyant à la beauté des choses.
Mais le rire cruel, les soucis qu'on m'impose
L'argent et l'opinion, la bêtise d'autrui
Ont fait de moi le dur bourgeois qui signe ici.

Thus it was that cloaked in innocence and love I advanced marking out my work each day praying to God and believing in the beauty of things. But cruel laughter, the cares imposed on me Money and opinion, the stupidity of others have made of me the hardened bourgeois, the undersigned.

Août 39

Les autos roulent sur les trottoirs pour m'écraser.

Le vieil infirme de l'hôpital, qui se promène tout le jour, se baisse pour ramasser les mégots. Quand il s'est relevé il m'a fait une grimace horrible et ses yeux ont touché ses sourcils. Je suis passé quand même et me suis retourné. Je l'ai vu sourire et cracher sur le pavé. Deux pavés se sont écartés.

Pourquoi une barque blanche et bleue, blanche et bleu de roi, aux larges ailes de mouette ne va-t-elle pas bientôt passer sur la rivière verte et sombre, si calme que les larges nénuphars s'en vont dormir avec l'herbe des prés? La barque ne passera pas.

Au bout du pont qui écrase l'eau, un gendarme a sorti son carnet.

August '39

The cars drive on the pavements to crush me.

The old invalid from the hospital, who walks about all day, bends to pick up cigarette ends. When he stood up, he grimaced at me horribly and his eyes touched his eyebrows. I went by all the same and turned around. I saw him smile and spit on the roadway. Two cobblestones moved aside.

Why will a white and blue boat, white and regal blue, with broad seagull's wings, not pass soon on the green and dark river, so calm that the broad water-lilies move away to sleep with the meadow grasses? The boat will not pass.

At the end of the bridge that crushes the water, a policeman has taken out his notebook.

Le ciel s'est couvert de nuit et un glas tinte dans le soir, et les vieux rentiers bien vite ont fermé leurs volets; mais leurs chiens se sauvent. Tout le monde est parti, une lanterne – là-bas – s'est cachée derrière un tronc noir. Debout dans le ruisseau de la rue, je sens l'eau grasse et boueuse aspirer tout le sang de mon corps.

The sky has covered itself in darkness and a knell tolls in the evening, and the old men of independent means have closed their shutters pretty swiftly; but their dogs run off. Everyone has gone, a lantern – there – has hidden itself behind a black trunk. Standing in the gutter of the street, I feel the greasy, muddy water sucking away all the blood in my body.

Présence de Dieu

Une nuit que je parcourais le ciel amour
une nuit de douce mère
où les étoiles étaient les feux du retour
et diaprées comme l'arc-en-ciel
une nuit que les étoiles disaient: 'Je reviens!'
Leur pitié saignait de mon sans repos
Car le malheur a percé mes pieds et mes mains
O résignation, c'est toi qui chantes le laus
Une nuit que les étoiles couvaient mon vol
j'aperçus un astre qui m'approchait
et il me versait un opium qui rend fol
et l'astre me séduisait avec son œil épais.
Tes caresses désenchevêtrent mes membres.
L'amour n'attend pas, il n'attend pas.
Il est astre et je suis plante: nous sommes ensemble

Presence of God

One night as I was surveying the love sky / a gentle mother night when the stars were the signal-lights of homecoming and dappled like the rainbow / a night when the stars said: 'I am coming again!' Their pity bled for my restlessness For misfortune has pierced my feet and my hands O resignation, it is you who sing the laud[1] On a night when the stars brooded over my flight I saw a star approaching me and it poured for me an opium of delirium and the star beguiled me with its dense eye. Your caresses disentangled my limbs. Love does not wait, it does not wait. It is a star and I am a plant: we are

[1]'*Laus*' is the Latin word for praise, glory or merit. Jacob seems to be referring to *les laudes* ('Lauds' in English), a service of praise involving the singing of psalms early in the morning. I have retained his singular (in both senses) noun.

Tu me feras pousser comme un panorama.
Et quand je fus près de l'astre-événement,
je vis que c'était le Beau Dieu, le Concepteur
du monde, le Seigneur, le Génie-Gentleman.
Alors il m'absorba comme une liqueur:
c'est un secret et il n'y a pas de mots pour dire
que mon sang en Lui Dieu se retire
comme en un seul cœur.

together You will make me grow like a panorama. And when I was near the star-climax, I saw that it was the Beautiful God, the Conceiver of the world, the Lord, the Gentleman-Genius. Then he absorbed me like a liquid: this is a secret and there are no words to say that my blood ebbs into Him God as into a single heart.

Guillaume Apollinaire
(1880–1918)

This is the pen-name of Wilhelm Albert Vladimir Alexandre Apollinaris de Kostrowitski, the illegitimate son of a nomadic Polish mother and an unknown father, probably an Italian army officer whose absence and obscurity provided the first of many identity problems for the rootless young poet. Apollinaire sought an answer in Paris, at the turn of the century, to his sense of statelessness. He quickly developed a wide range of literary and artistic friendships, and became a colourful and gregarious leader of the modernist movement as well as a fervent advocate in print of Cubist painting. His larger-than-life personality, with its perplexing mixture of extrovert buffoonery and introvert vulnerability, gave him a legendary status which at times has perhaps obscured a proper perception of his work.

Apollinaire's reputation reached its peak with the publication of *Alcools* in 1913. The success of this innovative volume helped him recover from the trauma of wrongful arrest and imprisonment in 1911, on suspicion of involvement in the theft of the 'Mona Lisa'.

He played many roles, and arguably they were all authentic. He was an immensely energetic man, provocative, mysterious and temperamental; a talented raconteur, a gargantuan eater and drinker, a great lover, an intermittently devout Catholic, a generous friend, a clown and a scholar and a tragic hero. Above all he was an artistic revolutionary exploring new areas of consciousness with a courage and integrity that he also brought to bear on his periodic despair at the ending of relationships.

Apollinaire's final commitment was to France itself, his adopted country. In 1914 he was an enthusiastic and sincerely proud recruit, first into the artillery and then to the front-line trenches. A serious head wound brought him back to Paris after an operation in 1916, subject to fainting fits and partial paralysis, but still writing poetry with a voice perhaps more assured than before. He assembled his second major volume, *Calligrammes*, with its typographical experiments; wrote further articles on the arts and a Jarryesque play, *Les Mamelles de Tirésias*; coined the word 'Surrealism'; worked as a censor; delivered a significant lecture entitled '*L'Esprit nouveau et les poètes*'; and in May 1918 married the last of a series of lovers, Jacqueline Kolb ('*la jolie rousse*'). In November of that year he died of complications following an attack of influenza. His funeral moved, with an irony he would have appreciated, through Paris streets decked for the Armistice.

A prophet and exponent of modernism who demanded total expressive freedom, Apollinaire nevertheless paid frequent homage to a French literary tradition, both popular and refined, that he loved and respected not so much in spite of his cosmopolitan upbringing as because of it. That tradition was not to be smashed by the new adventurers but reconstructed, its elements reselected and surprisingly juxtaposed to reflect the accelerated discontinuity of experience and simultaneity of perception of the modern artist. Order and Adventure are his two poles, sometimes approaching integration.

The new spirit brings an increased concern for the visual form of the poem on the page, favouring to some extent the eye over the ear, though the musicality of Apollinaire's best work remains memorable. Syntactic units – phrase, line, stanza – are strongly articulated with an intrinsic rhythmical logic, and must be perceived in their relationship with the intervening and surrounding blank spaces. Punctuation is abolished, at least partly through the prompting of Cendrars, in the interests of a more authentic, simultaneous notation of the flux of consciousness, that wanderer through both the streets of Paris and the starry skies. As with Reverdy, mimesis is broken in favour of an autonomous, concrete art form based on bold juxtaposition of imagery (see introduction to Reverdy), as the Cubist urge battles with the problem of language and the conventionally linear reception of it by the reader. Apollinaire's extreme experiments in this direction are concentrated in *Calligrammes*, but in *Alcools* too the lyrical traditions and elegiac themes that underpin the free verse are challenged by this new demand, and the organization of the volume itself is more a matter of the surprise principle than of any chronological or thematic criteria.

His style blends an awareness of metrical tradition with a new rhythmic and rhyming freedom, and his insistence on naturalness leads him into the frequent, wilfully incongruous and stimulating clashing of registers. Poetry for Apollinaire is to be found in all aspects of life, and he correspondingly rejects the notion of a rarefied, specialized mode of expression: 'A falling handkerchief can be for the poet the lever with which he will lift up an entire universe.' The poet translates the ordinary into the extraordinary, turning imaginative experience into myth through his burning creativity, throwing his past and present into '*le brasier*' in pursuit of a sublime transformation. Thus he extends our consciousness by passing through and beyond the familiar. Unlike Mallarmé, who becomes clearer as you penetrate his opaque surface, Apollinaire is immediately transparent but mysterious and divergent beneath the surface; and in this, as in his whole artistic stance, he is seen as a forerunner of Surrealism. His work is uneven and does not always fulfil his intentions, but *Le Bestiaire* (1911), *Alcools* and *Calligrammes* contain enough work of originality and quality to place him in the front rank of modern poets.

Zone

A la fin tu es las de ce monde ancien

Bergère ô tour Eiffel le troupeau des ponts bêle ce matin

Tu en as assez de vivre dans l'antiquité grecque et romaine

Ici même les automobiles ont l'air d'être anciennes
La religion seule est restée toute neuve la religion
Est restée simple comme les hangars de Port-Aviation

Seul en Europe tu n'es pas antique ô Christianisme
L'Européen le plus moderne c'est vous Pape Pie X
Et toi que les fenêtres observent la honte te retient
D'entrer dans une église et de t'y confesser ce matin
Tu lis les prospectus les catalogues les affiches qui chantent tout haut

Zone

In the end you are weary of this ancient world

O Eiffel Tower shepherdess the flock of bridges bleats this morning

You've had enough of living in Greek and Roman antiquity

Here even the motorcars look antique Religion alone has remained brand new religion Has stayed simple like Port-Aviation's hangars

You alone in Europe are not ancient O Christianity The most modern European is you Pope Pius X And you whom the windows watch shame restrains you From entering a church and confessing there this morning You read handbills catalogues posters that sing aloud That's what poetry is this morning and

Voilà la poésie ce matin et pour la prose il y a les journaux
Il y a les livraisons à 25 centimes pleines d'aventures policières
Portraits des grands hommes et mille titres divers

J'ai vu ce matin une jolie rue dont j'ai oublié le nom
Neuve et propre du soleil elle était le clairon
Les directeurs les ouvriers et les belles sténo-dactylographes
Du lundi matin au samedi soir quatre fois par jour y passent
Le matin par trois fois la sirène y gémit
Une cloche rageuse y aboie vers midi
Les inscriptions des enseignes et des murailles
Les plaques les avis à la façon des perroquets criaillent
J'aime la grâce de cette rue industrielle
Située à Paris entre la rue Aumont-Thiéville et l'avenue des Ternes

for prose there are the papers There are 25-centime instalments full of detective stories Portraits of great men and a thousand assorted titles

I saw this morning a pretty street whose name I've forgotten Fresh and clean it was the bugle of the sunlight The directors the workers and the lovely shorthand typists Pass through it four times a day from Monday morning to Saturday evening In the morning the siren wails there three times A querulous bell yelps there towards midday The lettering on the signs and walls The nameplates the notices shriek like parrots I love the grace of this industrial street Located in Paris between the Rue Aumont-Thiéville and the Avenue des Ternes

Voilà la jeune rue et tu n'es encore qu'un petit enfant
Ta mère ne t'habille que de bleu et de blanc
Tu es très pieux et avec le plus ancien de tes camarades René Dalize
Vous n'aimez rien tant que les pompes de l'Église
Il est neuf heures le gaz est baissé tout bleu vous sortez du dortoir en cachette
Vous priez toute la nuit dans la chapelle du collège
Tandis qu'éternelle et adorable profondeur améthyste
Tourne à jamais la flamboyante gloire du Christ
C'est le beau lys que tous nous cultivons
C'est la torche aux cheveux roux que n'éteint pas le vent
C'est le fils pâle et vermeil de la douloureuse mère
C'est l'arbre toujours touffu de toutes les prières
C'est la double potence de l'honneur et de l'éternité
C'est l'étoile à six branches
C'est Dieu qui meurt le vendredi et ressuscite le dimanche
C'est le Christ qui monte au ciel mieux que les aviateurs
Il détient le record du monde pour la hauteur

There is the young street and you're still just a little child Your mother dresses you only in blue and white You're very pious and with your oldest friend René Dalize You love nothing so much as church ceremonies It's nine o' clock the gas turned low is blue you slip secretly out of the dormitory You pray all night in the college chapel While the everlasting adorable amethyst depth Turns eternally the blazing glory of Christ It is the beautiful lily we all nurture It is the redhaired torch that the wind cannot blow out It is the pale and rose-red son of the grieving mother It is the ever leafy tree of all prayers It is the double cross potent of honour and eternity It is the six-pointed star It is God who dies on Friday and is restored to life on Sunday It is Christ rising heavenward outdoing the aviators He holds the world altitude record

Pupille Christ de l'œil
Vingtième pupille des siècles il sait y faire
Et changé en oiseau ce siècle comme Jésus monte dans l'air
Les diables dans les abîmes lèvent la tête pour le regarder
Ils disent qu'il imite Simon Mage en Judée
Ils crient s'il sait voler qu'on l'appelle voleur
Les anges voltigent autour du joli voltigeur
Icare Enoch Elie Apollonius de Thyane
Flottent autour du premier aéroplane
Ils s'écartent parfois pour laisser passer ceux que transporte
 la Sainte-Eucharistie
Ces prêtres qui montent éternellement élevant l'hostie
L'avion se pose enfin sans refermer les ailes
Le ciel s'emplit alors de millions d'hirondelles
A tire-d'aile viennent les corbeaux les faucons les hiboux
D'Afrique arrivent les ibis les flamants les marabouts
L'oiseau Roc célébré par les conteurs et les poètes
Plane tenant dans les serres le crâne d'Adam la première tête
L'aigle fond de l'horizon en poussant un grand cri
Et d'Amérique vient le petit colibri
De Chine sont venus les pihis longs et souples

Christ pupil of the eye Twentieth pupil of the centuries it knows how And changed into a bird this century like Jesus soars into the air The devils in the chasms raise their heads to look at it They say it is imitating Simon Magus in Judea They shout if it knows how to fly then call it a fly-by-night The angels flutter around the pretty aerobat Icarus Enoch Elijah Apollonius of Tyana Hover around the first aeroplane Making way sometimes for those borne up by the Holy Eucharist to pass Those priests who rise eternally lifting up the host The aeroplane touches down at last without folding its wings The sky then is filled with millions of swallows Crows and falcons and owls come winging Ibis flamingos and marabou storks from Africa The Roc bird extolled by storytellers and poets Glides down holding in its talons Adam's skull the first head The eagle swoops down from the horizon with a great cry And from America comes the little humming-bird From China have

Qui n'ont qu'une seule aile et qui volent par couples
Puis voici la colombe esprit immaculé
Qu'escortent l'oiseau-lyre et le paon ocellé
Le phénix ce bûcher qui soi-même s'engendre
Un instant voile tout de son ardente cendre
Les sirènes laissant les périlleux détroits
Arrivent en chantant bellement toutes trois
Et tous aigle phénix et pihis de la Chine
Fraternisent avec la volante machine

come the long and sinuous pihis Which have only one wing and fly in couples Now here is the dove the immaculate spirit Escorted by the lyre-bird and the ocellated peacock The phoenix that self-creating pyre Veils all for an instant with its glowing ashes The sirens leaving the perilous straits Arrive all three singing beautifully And all eagle phoenix and pihis of China Fraternize with the flying machine

Maintenant tu marches dans Paris tout seul parmi la foule
Des troupeaux d'autobus mugissants près de toi roulent
L'angoisse de l'amour te serre le gosier
Comme si tu ne devais jamais plus être aimé
Si tu vivais dans l'ancien temps tu entrerais dans un monastère
Vous avez honte quand vous vous surprenez à dire une prière
Tu te moques de toi et comme le feu de l'Enfer ton rire pétille
Les étincelles de ton rire dorent le fond de ta vie
C'est un tableau pendu dans un sombre musée
Et quelquefois tu vas le regarder de près

Aujourd'hui tu marches dans Paris les femmes sont ensanglantées
C'était et je voudrais ne pas m'en souvenir c'était au déclin de la beauté

Now you are walking in Paris all alone among the crowd Bellowing herds of buses roll past you The anguish of love tightens your throat As though you were never to be loved again If you lived in olden times you would enter a monastery You are ashamed when you catch yourself at prayer You laugh at yourself and like hellfire your laughter crackles The sparks of your laughter gild the depths of your life It is a picture hung in a gloomy gallery And sometimes you go and look at it close up

Today you are walking in Paris the women are stained with blood It was and would I could forget it it was at the twilight of beauty

Entourée de flammes ferventes Notre-Dame m'a regardé à Chartres
Le sang de votre Sacré-Cœur m'a inondé à Montmartre
Je suis malade d'ouïr les paroles bienheureuses
L'amour dont je souffre est une maladie honteuse
Et l'image qui te possède te fait survivre dans l'insomnie et dans l'angoisse
C'est toujours près de toi cette image qui passe

Maintenant tu es au bord de la Méditerranée
Sous les citronniers qui sont en fleur toute l'année
Avec tes amis tu te promènes en barque
L'un est Nissard il y a un Mentonasque et deux Turbiasques
Nous regardons avec effroi les poulpes des profondeurs
Et parmi les algues nagent les poissons images du Sauveur

Tu es dans le jardin d'une auberge aux environs de Prague
Tu te sens tout heureux une rose est sur la table
Et tu observes au lieu d'écrire ton conte en prose
La cétoine qui dort dans le cœur de la rose

Surrounded by fervent flames Our Lady gazed on me in Chartres The blood of your Sacred-Heart flooded me in Montmartre I am sick from hearing the blessed words The love from which I suffer is a shameful disease And the image that possesses you keeps you alive in insomnia and in anguish It is always at your side this passing image

Now you are on the Mediterranean shore Under the lemon trees that flower all year long With your friends you go sailing One is from Nice one from Menton and two from La Turbie We look down in terror at the octopuses in the depths And among the seaweed swim fish the emblems of the Saviour

You are in the garden of an inn on the outskirts of Prague You feel entirely happy a rose is on the table And instead of writing your prose story you watch The rose-chafer asleep in the heart of the rose

Épouvanté tu te vois dessiné dans les agates de Saint-Vit
Tu étais triste à mourir le jour où tu t'y vis
Tu ressembles au Lazare affolé par le jour
Les aiguilles de l'horloge du quartier juif vont à rebours
Et tu recules aussi dans ta vie lentement
En montant au Hradchin et le soir en écoutant
Dans les tavernes chanter des chansons tchèques

Te voici à Marseille au milieu des pastèques

Te voici à Coblence à l'hôtel du Géant

Te voici à Rome assis sous un néflier du Japon

Te voici à Amsterdam avec une jeune fille que tu trouves belle et qui est laide
Elle doit se marier avec un étudiant de Leyde
On y loue des chambres en latin Cubicula locanda
Je m'en souviens j'y ai passé trois jours et autant à Gouda

With alarm you see yourself depicted in the agates of Saint Vitus You were sad enough to die the day you saw yourself in them You look like Lazarus panic-stricken by the daylight The hands of the clock in the Jewish quarter go backwards And you move back slowly too within your life Climbing up to the Hradcany[1] and listening in the evening To the singing of Czech songs in the taverns

Here you are in Marseilles among the watermelons

Here you are in Coblenz at the Giant's Hotel

Here you are in Rome sitting under a Japanese medlar tree

Here you are in Amsterdam with a girl you find beautiful and who is ugly She is to marry a student from Leyden There they let rooms in Latin Cubicula locanda I remember it I spent three days there and as many at Gouda

[1]The old royal palace in Prague.

Tu es à Paris chez le juge d'instruction
Comme un criminel on te met en état d'arrestation

Tu as fait de douloureux et de joyeux voyages
Avant de t'apercevoir du mensonge et de l'âge
Tu as souffert de l'amour à vingt et à trente ans
J'ai vécu comme un fou et j'ai perdu mon temps
Tu n'oses plus regarder tes mains et à tous moments je voudrais sangloter
Sur toi sur celle que j'aime sur tout ce qui t'a épouvanté

You are in Paris with the examining magistrate They place you under arrest like a criminal

You made painful and joyful journeys Before you perceived falsehood and age You suffered love at twenty and at thirty I have lived like a madman and wasted my time You no longer dare look at your hands and every moment I feel like sobbing For you for her that I love for all that has terrified you

Tu regardes les yeux pleins de larmes ces pauvres émigrants
Ils croient en Dieu ils prient les femmes allaitent des enfants
Ils emplissent de leur odeur le hall de la gare Saint-Lazare
Ils ont foi dans leur étoile comme les rois-mages
Ils espèrent gagner de l'argent dans l'Argentine
Et revenir dans leur pays après avoir fait fortune
Une famille transporte un édredon rouge comme vous transportez votre cœur
Cet édredon et nos rêves sont aussi irréels
Quelques-uns de ces émigrants restent ici et se logent
Rue des Rosiers ou rue des Ecouffes dans des bouges
Je les ai vus souvent le soir ils prennent l'air dans la rue
Et se déplacent rarement comme les pièces aux échecs
Il y a surtout des Juifs leurs femmes portent perruque
Elles restent assises exsangues au fond des boutiques

Tu es debout devant le zinc d'un bar crapuleux
Tu prends un café à deux sous parmi les malheureux

Tu es la nuit dans un grand restaurant

With your tear-filled eyes you watch those poor emigrants They believe in God they pray the women suckle children They fill with their odour the hall of the Gare Saint-Lazare They have faith in their star like the Magi They hope to prosper in Argentina And return with fortunes made to their homeland One family carries a red eiderdown as you carry your heart That eiderdown and our dreams are equally unreal Some of those emigrants stay here and lodge In hovels in the Rue des Rosiers or the Rue des Ecouffes I have often seen them in the evening taking the air in the street And moving rarely like chess pieces Above all there are Jews their wives wear wigs And remain sitting bloodlessly in the backs of shops

You are standing at the counter of a filthy bar Drinking cheap coffee among the wretched

At night you are in a spacious restaurant

Ces femmes ne sont pas méchantes elles ont des soucis cependant
Toutes même la plus laide a fait souffrir son amant

Elle est la fille d'un sergent de ville de Jersey

Ses mains que je n'avais pas vues sont dures et gercées

J'ai une pitié immense pour les coutures de son ventre

J'humilie maintenant à une pauvre fille au rire horrible ma bouche

Tu es seul le matin va venir
Les laitiers font tinter leurs bidons dans les rues

La nuit s'éloigne ainsi qu'une belle Métive
C'est Ferdine la fausse ou Léa l'attentive

Et tu bois cet alcool brûlant comme ta vie
Ta vie que tu bois comme une eau-de-vie

Those women are not wicked yet they still have their worries All of them even the ugliest has made her lover suffer

She is the daughter of a police constable in Jersey

Her hands which I had not seen are hard and chapped

I have immense pity for the scars on her belly

I now humble my mouth to a poor whore with a horrible laugh

You are alone morning is on its way The milkmen are rattling their churns in the streets

Night departs like a lovely half-caste woman It's deceitful Ferdine or watchful Leah

And you drink this liquor that burns like your life Your life that you drink like brandy

Tu marches vers Auteuil tu veux aller chez toi à pied
Dormir parmi tes fétiches d'Océanie et de Guinée
Ils sont des Christ d'une autre forme et d'une autre croyance
Ce sont les Christ inférieurs des obscures espérances

Adieu Adieu

Soleil cou coupé

You are walking towards Auteuil you want to go home on foot To sleep among your South Sea and Guinea fetishes They are Christs of another form and creed They are the lowly Christs of obscure hopes

Farewell Farewell

Sun severed neck

Le pont Mirabeau

Sous le pont Mirabeau coule la Seine
Et nos amours
Faut-il qu'il m'en souvienne
La joie venait toujours après la peine

Vienne la nuit sonne l'heure
Les jours s'en vont je demeure

The Pont Mirabeau

Under the Pont Mirabeau the Seine flows on And our loves Must I remember it Joy always followed pain

Let night come let the hour chime The days pass away I remain

Les mains dans les mains restons face à face
Tandis que sous
Le pont de nos bras passe
Des éternels regards l'onde si lasse

Vienne la nuit sonne l'heure
Les jours s'en vont je demeure

L'amour s'en va comme cette eau courante
L'amour s'en va
Comme la vie est lente
Et comme l'Espérance est violente

Vienne la nuit sonne l'heure
Les jours s'en vont je demeure

Passent les jours et passent les semaines
Ni temps passé
Ni les amours reviennent
Sous le pont Mirabeau coule la Seine

Hands in hands let us stand here face to face While under The bridge of our arms pass The weary waters of eternal gazing

Let night come let the hour chime The days pass away I remain

Love passes away like this running water Love passes away How slow life is And how violent Hope

Let night come let the hour chime The days pass away I remain

Let the days pass and the weeks pass Neither time past Nor loves come back again Under the Pont Mirabeau the Seine flows on

Vienne la nuit sonne l'heure
Les jours s'en vont je demeure

Let night come let the hour chime The days pass away I remain

L'Emigrant de Landor Road

A André Billy

Le chapeau à la main il entra du pied droit
Chez un tailleur très chic et fournisseur du roi
Ce commerçant venait de couper quelques têtes
De mannequins vêtus comme il faut qu'on se vête

La foule en tous les sens remuait en mêlant
Des ombres sans amour qui se traînaient par terre
Et des mains vers le ciel plein de lacs de lumière
S'envolaient quelquefois comme des oiseaux blancs

The Landor Road Emigrant

for André Billy

Hat in hand he stepped right foot first Into a very smart tailor's shop by appointment to the king That tradesman had just beheaded several Dummies dressed in the conventional way

The crowd stirred in all directions mingling Loveless shadows that dragged along the ground And hands from time to time took flight like white birds Towards the sky filled with lakes of light

Mon bateau partira demain pour l'Amérique
Et je ne reviendrai jamais
Avec l'argent gagné dans les prairies lyriques
Guider mon ombre aveugle en ces rues que j'aimais

Car revenir c'est bon pour un soldat des Indes
Les boursiers ont vendu tous mes crachats d'or fin
Mais habillé de neuf je veux dormir enfin
Sous des arbres pleins d'oiseaux muets et de singes

Les mannequins pour lui s'étant déshabillés
Battirent leurs habits puis les lui essayèrent
Le vêtement d'un lord mort sans avoir payé
Au rabais l'habilla comme un millionnaire

Au-dehors les années
Regardaient la vitrine
Les mannequins victimes
Et passaient enchaînées

My ship will leave for America tomorrow And I shall never come back With the money earned on the lyrical prairies To steer my blind shadow through these streets that I loved

For homecoming is good for a soldier from the Indies The brokers have sold all my fine golden gongs[1] But newly kitted out I want to sleep at last Under trees full of monkeys and silent birds

Having undressed for him the dummies Dusted off their garments then tried them on him The clothing of a lord dead with his bill unpaid Dressed him like a millionaire at a discount price

On the outside the years Looked at the window At the victim dummies And passed by chained together

[1]*crachats*: slang for '*médailles*'.

Intercalées dans l'an c'étaient les journées veuves
Les vendredis sanglants et lents d'enterrements
De blancs et de tout noirs vaincus des cieux qui pleuvent
Quand la femme du diable a battu son amant

Puis dans un port d'automne aux feuilles indécises
Quand les mains de la foule y feuillolaient aussi
Sur le pont du vaisseau il posa sa valise
Et s'assit

Les vents de l'Océan en soufflant leurs menaces
Laissaient dans ses cheveux de longs baisers mouillés
Des émigrants tendaient vers le port leurs mains lasses
Et d'autres en pleurant s'étaient agenouillés

Il regarda longtemps les rives qui moururent
Seuls des bateaux d'enfant tremblaient à l'horizon
Un tout petit bouquet flottant à l'aventure
Couvrit l'Océan d'une immense floraison

Interspersed in the year were the widowed days The slow bleeding Fridays of burials Of whites and blacks defeated of the skies that rain When the devil's wife has been beating her lover

Then in an autumn harbour amid indeterminate leaves When the hands of the crowd also fluttered like leaves On the deck of the ship he put down his suitcase And sat

The Ocean winds blowing their threats Left long moist kisses in his hair Emigrants stretched out listless hands towards the harbour And others had knelt in tears

For a long time he watched the shores that died Only toy ships shimmered on the horizon A tiny bouquet floating haphazardly Covered the Ocean with a vast flowering

Il aurait voulu ce bouquet comme la gloire
Jouer dans d'autres mers parmi tous les dauphins
        Et l'on tissait dans sa mémoire
        Une tapisserie sans fin
        Qui figurait son histoire

        Mais pour noyer changées en poux
Ces tisseuses têtues qui sans cesse interrogent
        Il se maria comme un doge
Aux cris d'une sirène moderne sans époux

Gonfle-toi vers la nuit O Mer Les yeux des squales
Jusqu'à l'aube ont guetté de loin avidement
Des cadavres de jours rongés par les étoiles
Parmi le bruit des flots et les derniers serments

It would have wished that bouquet as for glory To play on other seas among all the dolphins And in the memory an endless tapestry was woven To represent its story

But to drown those stubborn weaving women Changed into lice who keep on questioning He was married like a doge Amid the cries of a modern siren with no mate

Swell towards the night O Sea The eyes of the sharks Until dawn have watched greedily from afar For the corpses of the days gnawed by the stars Amid the sound of the waves and the final oaths

Le brasier

A Paul-Napoléon Roinard

J'ai jeté dans le noble feu
Que je transporte et que j'adore
De vives mains et même feu
Ce Passé ces têtes de morts
Flamme je fais ce que tu veux

Le galop soudain des étoiles
N'étant que ce qui deviendra
Se mêle au hennissement mâle
Des centaures dans leurs haras
Et des grand'plaintes végétales

Où sont ces têtes que j'avais
Où est le Dieu de ma jeunesse
L'amour est devenu mauvais
Qu'au brasier les flammes renaissent
Mon âme au soleil se dévêt

The Furnace

For Paul-Napoléon Roinard

I have cast into the noble fire Which I convey and which I worship Hands that are living and even deceased This Past these death's heads Flame I do what you wish

The sudden galloping of the stars Being only what will become Mingles with the virile neighing Of the centaurs at stud And great vegetal lamentations

Where are those heads that I possessed Where is the God of my youth Love has turned nasty May the flames be reborn in the furnace My soul divests itself in the sunlight

Dans la plaine ont poussé des flammes
Nos cœurs pendent aux citronniers
Les têtes coupées qui m'acclament
Et les astres qui ont saigné
Ne sont que des têtes de femmes

Le fleuve épinglé sur la ville
T'y fixe comme un vêtement
Partant à l'amphion docile
Tu subis tous les tons charmants
Qui rendent les pierres agiles

Je flambe dans le brasier à l'ardeur adorable
Et les mains des croyants m'y rejettent multiple innombrablement
Les membres des intercis flambent auprès de moi
Eloignez du brasier les ossements
Je suffis pour l'éternité à entretenir le feu de mes délices
Et des oiseaux protègent de leurs ailes ma face et le soleil

On the plain flames have sprung up Our hearts hang on the lemon trees The severed heads that acclaim me And the stars that have bled Are only women's heads

The river pinned on the city Fastens you there like a garment And thus as a submissive Amphion[1] You undergo all the enchanting tones That enliven the stones

I am blazing in the furnace with its exquisite intensity And the hands of the believers cast me in again countlessly multiplied The limbs of dismembered martyrs are flaming beside me Remove the bones from the furnace I am sufficient for all eternity to sustain the fire of my delight And birds protect with their wings my countenance and the sun

[1]In Greek mythology, Amphion was a harpist whose music moved stones during the building of Thebes.

O Mémoire Combien de races qui forlignent
Des Tyndarides aux vipères ardentes de mon bonheur
Et les serpents ne sont-ils que les cous des cygnes
Qui étaient immortels et n'étaient pas chanteurs
Voici ma vie renouvelée
De grands vaisseaux passent et repassent
Je trempe une fois encore mes mains dans l'Océan

Voici le paquebot et ma vie renouvelée
Ses flammes sont immenses
Il n'y a plus rien de commun entre moi
Et ceux qui craignent les brûlures

Descendant des hauteurs où pense la lumière
Jardins rouant plus haut que tous les ciels mobiles
L'avenir masqué flambe en traversant les cieux

O Memory How many corrupted races From the Tyndarides[1] to the fiery vipers of my bliss And are snakes not merely the necks of swans That were immortal and did not sing And now my life is renewed Great vessels pass and pass again Once more I dip my hands into the Ocean

Here is the liner and my renewed life Its flames are prodigious There is nothing more in common between me And those who fear the burns

Descending from the heights where light thinks Gardens wheeling higher than all the shifting skies The masked future blazes across the heavens

[1]The daughters of Tyndareus who became unfaithful wives (Helen and Clytemnestra).

Nous attendons ton bon plaisir ô mon amie

J'ose à peine regarder la divine mascarade

Quand bleuira sur l'horizon la Désirade

Au-delà de notre atmosphère s'élève un théâtre
Que construisit le ver Zamir sans instrument
Puis le soleil revint ensoleiller les places
D'une ville marine apparue contremont
Sur les toits se reposaient les colombes lasses

Et le troupeau de sphinx regagne la sphingerie
A petits pas Il orra le chant du pâtre toute la vie
Là-haut le théâtre est bâti avec le feu solide
Comme les astres dont se nourrit le vide

We await your pleasure O my beloved

I hardly dare look at the divine masquerade

When Desirade[1] will loom blue on the horizon

Beyond our atmosphere rises a theatre built by the worm Shamir[2] without tools Then the sun returned to shine upon the squares Of a coastal town that appeared upstream On the roofs the weary doves were resting

And the sphinx flock returns to the sphinxfold On tiptoe He will hearken all his life to the song of the shepherd Up there the theatre is built with solid fire Like the stars that feed the void

[1]An island in the Antilles named by Columbus.
[2]A fabulous worm used by Solomon in the building of the Temple. It had the power to cut stone (God had forbidden the use of iron tools).

Et voici le spectacle
Et pour toujours je suis assis dans un fauteuil
Ma tête mes genoux mes coudes vain pentacle
Les flammes ont poussé sur moi comme des feuilles

Des acteurs inhumains claires bêtes nouvelles
Donnent des ordres aux hommes apprivoisés
Terre
O Déchirée que les fleuves ont reprisée

J'aimerais mieux nuit et jour dans les sphingeries
Vouloir savoir pour qu'enfin on m'y dévorât

And here now is the spectacle And I sit for ever in an armchair My head my knees my elbows a hollow pentacle Flames have sprouted on me like leaves

Inhuman actors luminous new beasts Give orders to tamed mankind O Earth Torn asunder and stitched together by the rivers

I would prefer night and day in the sphinxfolds To seek knowledge so that I might at last be devoured there

Nuit rhénane

Mon verre est plein d'un vin trembleur comme une flamme
Ecoutez la chanson lente d'un batelier
Qui raconte avoir vu sous la lune sept femmes
Tordre leurs cheveux verts et longs jusqu'à leurs pieds

Debout chantez plus haut en dansant une ronde
Que je n'entende plus le chant du batelier
Et mettez près de moi toutes les filles blondes
Au regard immobile aux nattes repliées

Le Rhin le Rhin est ivre où les vignes se mirent
Tout l'or des nuits tombe en tremblant s'y refléter
La voix chante toujours à en râle-mourir
Ces fées aux cheveux verts qui incantent l'été

Mon verre s'est brisé comme un éclat de rire

Rhenish Night

My glass is filled with a wine that quivers like a flame Listen to the slow song of a ferryman That tells of seeing seven women in the moonlight Twisting their long green hair down to their feet

Stand up sing louder while you dance a roundelay That I may hear no longer the ferryman's song And place beside me all the golden-haired girls With motionless gazes and tightly coiled plaits

The Rhine the Rhine is drunk where the vines find their image All the gold of night falls quivering in its reflection there The voice is still singing itself into a death rattle Of those fairies with green hair who cast a spell on summer

My glass has shattered like a burst of laughter

Liens

Cordes faites de cris

Sons de cloches à travers l'Europe
Siècles pendus

Rails qui ligotez les nations
Nous ne sommes que deux ou trois hommes
Libres de tous liens
Donnons-nous la main

Violente pluie qui peigne les fumées
Cordes
Cordes tissées
Câbles sous-marins
Tours de Babel changées en ponts
Araignées-Pontifes
Tous les amoureux qu'un seul lien a liés

Bonds

Cords made of shouts

Ringing of bells across Europe Centuries hanging

Rails binding the nations We are no more than two or three men Free from all bonds Let us join hands

Violent rain combing the smoke Cords Woven cords Undersea cables Towers of Babel changed into bridges Spider-Pontiffs All the lovers bound by a single bond

D'autres liens plus ténus
Blancs rayons de lumière
Cordes et Concorde

J'écris seulement pour vous exalter
O sens ô sens chéris
Ennemis du souvenir
Ennemis du désir

Ennemis du regret
Ennemis des larmes
Ennemis de tout ce que j'aime encore

Other more tenuous bonds White beams of light Cords and Concord

I write only to exalt you O senses O precious senses Enemies of memory Enemies of desire

Enemies of regret Enemies of tears Enemies of all that I still love

Fête

A André Rouveyre

Feu d'artifice en acier
Qu'il est charmant cet éclairage
    Artifice d'artificier
Mêler quelque grâce au courage

Festivity

For André Rouveyre

Steely pyrotechnics How enchanting this illumination is An artificer's artifice To mix a certain grace with courage

Deux fusants
Rose éclatement
Comme deux seins que l'on dégrafe
Tendent leurs bouts insolemment
IL SUT AIMER
quelle épitaphe

Un poète dans la forêt
Regarde avec indifférence
Son revolver au cran d'arrêt
Des roses mourir d'espérance

Il songe aux roses de Saadi
Et soudain sa tête se penche
Car une rose lui redit
La molle courbe d'une hanche

L'air est plein d'un terrible alcool
Filtré des étoiles mi-closes
Les obus caressent le mol
Parfum nocturne où tu reposes
Mortification des roses

Two time-shells A rose-pink bursting Like two unfastened breasts Offering their taut tips with insolence HE KNEW HOW TO LOVE what an epitaph

A poet in the forest Gazes with indifference at His revolver with its safety catch Roses dying of hope

He dreams of the roses of Saadi And suddenly his head sinks down For a rose evokes for him once more The soft curve of a hip

The air is filled with a terrible alcohol Filtered through the half-closed stars The shells caress the mellow Nocturnal fragrance in which you lie Mortification of the roses

Visée

A Madame René Berthier

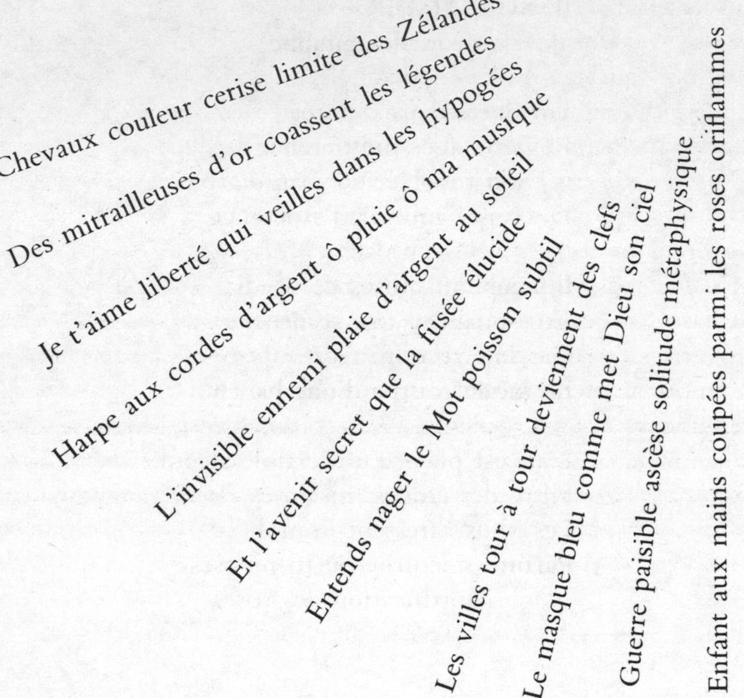

Aim

For Madame René Berthier

Cherry coloured horses boundary of the Zealanders Golden machine guns croak out legends I love you liberty in your subterranean vigil Silver-stringed harp O rain O my music The invisible enemy a silver wound in the sunlight And the secret future illumined by the rocket Hear the Word swim subtle fish The cities one by one become keys The blue mask as God dons his sky Peaceful war asceticism metaphysical solitude A child with its hands cut off among the rose-pink banners

La jolie rousse

Me voici devant tous un homme plein de sens
Connaissant la vie et de la mort ce qu'un vivant peut
 connaître
Ayant éprouvé les douleurs et les joies de l'amour
Ayant su quelquefois imposer ses idées
Connaissant plusieurs langages
Ayant pas mal voyagé
Ayant vu la guerre dans l'Artillerie et l'Infanterie
Blessé à la tête trépané sous le chloroforme
Ayant perdu ses meilleurs amis dans l'effroyable lutte
Je sais d'ancien et de nouveau autant qu'un homme seul
 pourrait des deux savoir
Et sans m'inquiéter aujourd'hui de cette guerre
Entre nous et pour nous mes amis
Je juge cette longue querelle de la tradition et de l'invention
 De l'Ordre et de l'Aventure

The Pretty Redhead

Here I stand in the sight of all a man full of awareness Knowing life and what a living man can know of death Having experienced the pains and joys of love Having made his ideas now and then command respect Knowing several languages Having travelled quite a bit Having seen the war in Artillery and Infantry Wounded in the head trepanned under chloroform Having lost his best friends in the hideous struggle I know of the ancient and the new as much as one man alone can know of both And without troubling myself now about this war Between ourselves and for ourselves my friends I speak judgement on this long quarrel between tradition and innovation Between Order and Adventure

Vous dont la bouche est faite à l'image de celle de Dieu
Bouche qui est l'ordre même
Soyez indulgents quand vous nous comparez
A ceux qui furent la perfection de l'ordre
Nous qui quêtons partout l'aventure

Nous ne sommes pas vos ennemis
Nous voulons vous donner de vastes et d'étranges domaines
Où le mystère en fleurs s'offre à qui veut le cueillir
Il y a là des feux nouveaux des couleurs jamais vues
Mille phantasmes impondérables
Auxquels il faut donner de la réalité

Nous voulons explorer la bonté contrée énorme où tout se tait
Il y a aussi le temps qu'on peut chasser ou faire revenir
Pitié pour nous qui combattons toujours aux frontières
De l'illimité et de l'avenir
Pitié pour nos erreurs pitié pour nos péchés

You whose mouths are made in the image of God's mouth A mouth which is order itself Be indulgent when you compare us with those who were the perfection of order We who seek adventure everywhere

We are not your enemies We want to give you vast and strange domains Where flowering mystery offers itself to all who wish to gather it There are new fires there colours never yet seen A thousand unfathomable phantasms To which we must give reality

We want to explore goodness a vast land where all is mute And then there is time which can be banished or recalled Pity for us whose combat is always on the frontiers Of the limitless and of the future Pity for our errors pity for our sins

Voici que vient l'été la saison violente
Et ma jeunesse est morte ainsi que le printemps
O Soleil c'est le temps de la Raison ardente
        Et j'attends
Pour la suivre toujours la forme noble et douce
Qu'elle prend afin que je l'aime seulement
Elle vient et m'attire ainsi qu'un fer l'aimant
    Elle a l'aspect charmant
    D'une adorable rousse

Ses cheveux sont d'or on dirait
Un bel éclair qui durerait
Ou ces flammes qui se pavanent
Dans les roses-thé qui se fanent

Mais riez riez de moi
Hommes de partout surtout gens d'ici
Car il y a tant de choses que je n'ose vous dire
Tant de choses que vous ne me laisseriez pas dire
Ayez pitié de moi

Here comes the summer now the violent season And my youth has died just like the spring O Sun it is the time of burning Reason And I wait To follow it for ever the sweet and noble form She takes that I may love her alone She comes and attracts me as a magnet draws iron She has the enchanting appearance of a lovely redhead

Her hair is golden you'd take it for A beautiful prolonged lightning flash Or those flames dancing a proud pavane among the wilting tea-roses

But laugh laugh at me Men everywhere above all people here For there are so many things I dare not tell you So many things you would not let me say Have pity on me

Blaise Cendrars
(1887–1961)

A colourful and free-wheeling figure in the modernist movement, Cendrars was born Frédéric Sauser at La Chaux-de-Fonds in Switzerland. His pseudonym, briefly Braise Cendrart and then definitively Blaise Cendrars (suggesting burning coals, ashes and art), was adopted during a 'second birth' in Paris in 1907, after which he claimed that city as his birthplace. A kaleidoscopic pattern of legend and anecdote is difficult to separate from biographical fact, but his unstable adolescence was marked by a patchy education, voracious reading, bouts of drinking, strife with his father, and a bedroom-window escape to a series of train journeys around Germany and eventually through Russia as far as Siberia. An association with an itinerant jewel-pedlar and a love-affair with a terminally ill Russian girl were part of that experience, but the story that he performed on stage with Chaplin during a period in London in 1907–08 is probably wishful thinking. He returned to Russia from Paris in 1910, then travelled to America in 1911.

Surviving somehow on scant resources in New York in 1912, he suddenly produced a poem of major importance. '*Pâques à New York*' was composed in a single night, beginning as he walked through the snow after attending a performance of Haydn's 'Creation'. When Cendrars returned to Paris, this long poem, in the form of Alexandrine but unpunctuated couplets, was to influence Apollinaire's abandonment of punctuation in '*Zone*'.

The floodgates were open for Cendrars, and in the charged creative atmosphere of 1912–14 his output was prolific. His long free verse poem '*Prose du Transsibérien et de la petite Jeanne de France*', with its unpunctuated and restless railway-train rhythms, continues the trajectory of Laforgue and is a landmark in the development of modern verse.

Its first edition of 150 copies was illustrated (though the

word is perhaps inadequate) by the artist Sonia Delaunay. She and her husband Robert were close friends of Cendrars, and influenced his developing aesthetic of simultaneity. Her contribution to the '*Prose du Transsibérien* ...' consisted of strips, shapes and emotive swirls of colour both within and beside the text, complementing the words and enriching an already complex perspective (the first edition ran to more than six feet of folded text in multiple and dislocated type styles).

He joined the Foreign Legion in 1914, and lost an arm in the Champagne offensive. Typically, he turned this event into a myth, continuing to communicate with the absent limb. In the Second World War he was to be a war correspondent, having moved away from poetry in the mid-1920s into novels and chronicles.

Disliking the young Dadaists and Surrealists, Cendrars had left Paris in 1917 and resumed his pattern of continual travel and search for newness. He saw himself as a being in flux, always moving away from immobility in life and art, cultivating multiplicity, risk and contrast. The urge towards simultaneity of experience and observation produces poems of great visual immediacy, compression, and often a cinematic effect (he was indeed very interested in cinema, and worked for a time with Abel Gance). In words he borrowed from the Delaunays, his perception has its 'windows open' to an experience which is captured in a chopped, elastic, intense style. The ephemeral is not synthesized, but enjoyed for its own sake. This dynamic spontaneity, however, with its spatial and temporal freedom, is balanced by a paradoxical nostalgia that preserves an element of poignant lyricism.

The act of writing itself, implying stasis and confinement and the fixing of experience, is of course problematic for such an artist, and full of tension. For Cendrars writing is also like burning in a fire: 'To write is to consume oneself ... Writing is a fire that lifts up a great confusion of ideas and incinerates groups of images before reducing them to crackling embers and falling ashes. But the spontaneity of the fire remains mysterious. To write is to burn alive, but is also to be reborn from ashes.'

Major volumes: *Du Monde entier* 1919, *Dix-neuf Poèmes élastiques* 1919, *Au Cœur du monde* 1919, *Documentaires* 1924, *Feuilles de route* 1924.

Prose du Transsibérien et de la petite Jeanne de France (3 extraits)

En ce temps-là j'étais en mon adolescence
J'avais à peine seize ans et je ne me souvenais déjà plus de mon enfance
J'étais à 16,000 lieues du lieu de ma naissance
J'étais à Moscou, dans la ville des mille et trois clochers et des sept gares
Et je n'avais pas assez des sept gares et des mille et trois tours
Car mon adolescence était si ardente et si folle
Que mon cœur, tour à tour, brûlait comme le temple d'Ephèse ou comme la Place Rouge de Moscou
Quand le soleil se couche.
Et mes yeux éclairaient des voies anciennes.
Et j'étais déjà si mauvais poète
Que je ne savais pas aller jusqu'au bout.

Prose of the Transsiberian and of little Jeanne of France (3 extracts)

At that time I was in my adolescence Scarcely sixteen and already couldn't remember my childhood I was 16,000 leagues from my birthplace I was in Moscow, in the city of the one thousand and three belfries and the seven stations and I was not satisfied with the seven stations and the one thousand and three towers For my adolescence was so intense and so insane That my heart, by turns,[1] burned like the temple at Ephesus or like the Red Square in Moscow When the sun is setting. And my eyes were lighting ancient pathways. And I was already such a bad poet That I couldn't go all the way.

[1]The word-play here ('turns' and 'towers') is not readily translatable.

Le Kremlin était comme un immense gâteau tartare
Croustillé d'or,
Avec les grandes amandes des cathédrales toutes blanches
Et l'or mielleux des cloches…

Un vieux moine me lisait la légende de Novgorode
J'avais soif
Et je déchiffrais des caractères cunéiformes
Puis, tout à coup, les pigeons du Saint-Esprit s'envolaient sur la place
Et mes mains s'envolaient aussi, avec des bruissements d'albatros
Et ceci, c'était les dernières réminiscences du dernier jour
Du tout dernier voyage
Et de la mer.

The Kremlin was like a huge Tartar cake Crusted with gold With the great almonds of the cathedrals all in white And the honeyed gold of the bells …

An old monk was reading me the legend of Novgorod[1] I was thirsty And I was deciphering cuneiform symbols Then, suddenly, the pigeons of the Holy Ghost flew up above the square And my hands took flight too, with albatross rustlings And these were the last reminiscences of the last day Of the very last journey And of the sea.

[1]Either the thirteenth-century *Chronicle of Novgorod* (a major trading city), or one of the *byliny*, the heroic oral poems of medieval Russia, written down by scholars in more recent times. Cendrars refers here to the monk reading the legend, but later in the poem he is singing it.

Pourtant, j'étais fort mauvais poète.
Je ne savais pas aller jusqu'au bout.
J'avais faim
Et tous les jours et toutes les femmes dans les cafés et tous
les verres
J'aurais voulu les boire et les casser
Et toutes les vitrines et toutes les rues
Et toutes les maisons et toutes les vies
Et toutes les roues des fiacres qui tournaient en tourbillon
sur les mauvais pavés
J'aurais voulu les plonger dans une fournaise de glaives
Et j'aurais voulu broyer tous les os
Et arracher toutes les langues
Et liquéfier tous ces grands corps étranges et nus sous les
vêtements qui m'affolent...
Je pressentais la venue du grand Christ rouge de la
révolution russe...
Et le soleil était une mauvaise plaie
Qui s'ouvrait comme un brasier.

And yet, I was a very bad poet. I lacked the skill to go all the way. I was hungry And all the days and all the women in the cafés and all the glasses I would have liked to drink them and smash them And all the shop windows and all the streets And all the houses and all the lives And all the cab wheels turning in a whirlwind on the wretched cobbles I would have liked to plunge them into a furnace of swordblades And I would have liked to grind up all the bones And tear out all the tongues And liquefy all those large strange naked bodies under garments that madden me ... I could sense the coming of the great red Christ of the Russian revolution ... And the sun was a vicious open wound blazing like live coals.

En ce temps-là j'étais en mon adolescence
J'avais à peine seize ans et je ne me souvenais déjà plus de ma naissance
J'étais à Moscou, où je voulais me nourrir de flammes
Et je n'avais pas assez des tours et des gares que constellaient mes yeux
En Sibérie tonnait le canon, c'était la guerre
La faim le froid la peste le choléra
Et les eaux limoneuses de l'Amour charriaient des millions de charognes
Dans toutes les gares je voyais partir tous les derniers trains
Personne ne pouvait plus partir car on ne délivrait plus de billets
Et les soldats qui s'en allaient auraient bien voulu rester...
Un vieux moine me chantait la légende de Novgorode.

At that time I was in my adolescence Scarcely sixteen and already couldn't remember my birth I was in Moscow, where I wanted to feed myself with flames And I wasn't satisfied with the towers and the stations sown with stars by my eyes In Siberia the cannon thundered, it was war Hunger cold plague cholera And the turbid waters of Love carried away millions of carcasses In all the stations I saw all the last trains leaving No one could leave any more because no more tickets were being issued And the soldiers who were going away would have liked to stay ... An old monk was singing for me the legend of Novgorod.

Moi, le mauvais poète qui ne voulais aller nulle part, je pouvais aller partout
Et aussi les marchands avaient encore assez d'argent
Pour aller tenter faire fortune.
Leur train partait tous les vendredis matin.
On disait qu'il y avait beaucoup de morts.
L'un emportait cent caisses de réveils et de coucous de la Forêt-Noire
Un autre, des boîtes à chapeaux, des cylindres et un assortiment de tire-bouchons de Sheffield
Un autre, des cercueils de Malmoë remplis de boîtes de conserve et de sardines à l'huile
Puis il y avait beaucoup de femmes
Des femmes des entre-jambes à louer qui pouvaient aussi servir
Des cercueils
Elles étaient toutes patentées
On disait qu'il y avait beaucoup de morts là-bas
Elles voyageaient à prix réduits
Et avaient toutes un compte-courant à la banque.

I, the bad poet who wanted to go nowhere, I could go everywhere And also the merchants still had enough money To go and try to make their fortune. Their train left every Friday morning. It was rumoured there were many dead. One took along a hundred boxes of alarm clocks and cuckoo clocks from the Black Forest Another hat-boxes, top-hats and an assortment of Sheffield corkscrews Another coffins from Malmö filled with cans of preserve and sardines in oil Then there were lots of women Women with crotches for hire who could be useful too Coffins The women were all patented It was rumoured that there were many dead out there They travelled at reduced rates And all had current accounts at the bank.

Or, un vendredi matin, ce fut enfin mon tour
On était en décembre
Et je partis moi aussi pour accompagner le voyageur en bijouterie qui se rendait à Kharbine
Nous avions deux coupés dans l'express et 34 coffres de joaillerie de Pforzheim
De la camelote allemande 'Made in Germany'
Il m'avait habillé de neuf, et en montant dans le train j'avais perdu un bouton
– Je m'en souviens, je m'en souviens, j'y ai souvent pensé depuis –
Je couchais sur les coffres et j'étais tout heureux de pouvoir jouer avec le browning nickelé qu'il m'avait aussi donné

And then, one Friday morning, it was my turn at last It was in December And I left too to travel with the jewel merchant on his way to Harbin We had two compartments in the express and 34 coffers of Pforzheim jewellery German junk 'Made in Germany' He had dressed me in new clothes, and getting on the train I had lost a button – I remember, I remember, I've often thought of it since – I slept on the coffers and I was blissful that I could play with the nickel-plated Browning he had also given me

J'étais très heureux insouciant
Je croyais jouer aux brigands
Nous avions volé le trésor de Golconde
Et nous allions, grâce au transsibérien, le cacher de l'autre côté du monde
Je devais le défendre contre les voleurs de l'Oural qui avaient attaqué les saltimbanques de Jules Verne
Contre les khoungouzes, les boxers de la Chine
Et les enragés petits mongols du Grand-Lama
Alibaba et les quarante voleurs
Et les fidèles du terrible Vieux de la montagne
Et surtout, contre les plus modernes
Les rats d'hôtel
Et les spécialistes des express internationaux.
Et pourtant, et pourtant
J'étais triste comme un enfant
Les rythmes du train
La '*moëlle chemin-de-fer*' des psychiatres américains

I was very happy heedless I thought I was playing bandits We had stolen the Golconda treasure And we were on our way, thanks to the Transsiberian, to hide it on the other side of the world I was meant to defend it against the thieves from the Urals who had attacked Jules Verne's mountebanks Against the Kunguzy, the Chinese boxers And the incensed little mongols of the Grand Lama Ali-Baba and the forty thieves And the followers of the terrible Old Man of the mountains And above all against the most modern The hotel thieves And the international express train specialists.

And yet, and yet I was sad like a child The rhythms of the train The '*railway-medulla*' of the American psychiatrists The

Le bruit des portes des voix des essieux grinçant sur les rails
 congelés
Le ferlin d'or de mon avenir
Mon browning le piano et les jurons des joueurs de cartes
 dans le compartiment d'à côté
L'épatante présence de Jeanne
L'homme aux lunettes bleues qui se promenait nerveusement
 dans le couloir et qui me regardait en passant
Froissis de femmes
Et le sifflement de la vapeur
Et le bruit éternel des roues en folie dans les ornières du ciel
Les vitres sont givrées
Pas de nature!
Et derrière, les plaines sibériennes le ciel bas et les grandes
 ombres des Taciturnes qui montent et qui descendent
Je suis couché dans un plaid
Bariolé
Comme ma vie
Et ma vie ne me tient pas plus chaud que ce châle
Écossais

noise of doors voices axles grinding on the frozen rails The golden railrope[1] of my future My Browning the piano and the oaths of the card-players in the next compartment The stunning presence of Jeanne The man in blue spectacles who walked nervously in the corridor and looked at me as he passed Rustlings of women And the whistling of the steam And the eternal sound of demented wheels in the ruts of the sky The windows are frosted No nature! And beyond, the Siberian plains the lowering sky and the tall shadows of the Silent Mountains that rise and fall I am lying in a rug Motley Like my life And my life keeps me no warmer than this Scottish

[1]This is offered tentatively as a translation of '*ferlin*'. Cendrars appears to be combining '*fer*' and '*filin*' (a hempen rope).

Et l'Europe tout entière aperçue au coupe-vent d'un express
  à toute vapeur
N'est pas plus riche que ma vie
Ma pauvre vie
Ce châle
Effiloché sur des coffres remplis d'or
Avec lesquels je roule
Que je rêve
Que je fume
Et la seule flamme de l'univers
Est une pauvre pensée...

Du fond de mon cœur des larmes me viennent
Si je pense, Amour, à ma maîtresse;
Elle n'est qu'une enfant, que je trouvai ainsi
Pâle, immaculée, au fond d'un bordel.

Ce n'est qu'une enfant, blonde, rieuse et triste,
Elle ne sourit pas et ne pleure jamais;
Mais au fond de ses yeux, quand elle vous y laisse boire,
Tremble un doux lys d'argent, la fleur du poète...

★

shawl And the whole of Europe observed through the wind-cutter of an express at full speed Is no richer than my life My poor life This frayed Shawl over the coffers filled with gold With which I roll along I dream I smoke And the only flame in the universe is a paltry thought...

From deep in my heart tears come to me If I think, Love, of my mistress; she is but a child that I found as she is, pale, immaculate, deep in a bordello.

She is but a child, blonde, laughing and sad, she does not smile and never weeps; but deep in her eyes, when she lets you drink from them, quivers a soft silver lily, the flower of the poet.

★

'Blaise, dis, sommes-nous bien loin de Montmartre?'

Nous sommes loin, Jeanne, tu roules depuis sept jours
Tu es loin de Montmartre, de la Butte qui t'a nourrie du Sacré-Cœur contre lequel tu t'es blottie
Paris a disparu et son énorme flambée
Il n'y a plus que les cendres continues
La pluie qui tombe
La tourbe qui se gonfle
La Sibérie quii tourne
Les lourdes nappes de neige qui remontent
Et le grelot de la folie qui grelotte comme un dernier désir dans l'air bleui
Le train palpite au cœur des horizons plombés
Et ton chagrin ricane...

'Dis, Blaise, sommes-nous bien loin de Montmartre?'

'Blaise, tell me, are we very far from Montmartre?'

We are far away, Jeanne, you've been going for seven days You are far from Montmartre, from the Butte that nourished you from the Sacré-Cœur against which you huddled Paris has disappeared and its vast blaze There's nothing now but unremitting ashes Falling rain Swelling peat Whirling Siberia Heavy sheets of snow rising up And the bell of madness jangling like a final desire in the air turned blue The train throbs in the heart of leaden horizons And your sorrow sniggers ...

'Tell me, Blaise, are we very far from Montmartre?'

Les inquiétudes
Oublie les inquiétudes
Toutes les gares lézardées obliques sur la route
Les fils télégraphiques auxquels elles pendent
Les poteaux grimaçants qui gesticulent et les étranglent
Le monde s'étire s'allonge et se retire comme un accordéon qu'une main sadique tourmente
Dans les déchirures du ciel, les locomotives en furie
S'enfuient
Et dans les trous,
Les roues vertigineuses les bouches les voix
Et les chiens du malheur qui aboient à nos trousses
Les démons sont déchaînés
Ferrailles
Tout est un faux accord
Le *broun-roun-roun* des roues
Chocs
Rebondissements
Nous sommes un orage sous le crâne d'un sourd...

'Dis, Blaise, sommes-nous bien loin de Montmartre?'

Anxieties Forget anxieties All the cracked stations slanted along the route The telegraph wires they hang from The grimacing poles that gesticulate and throttle them The world stretches lengthens and retracts like an accordion tortured by a sadistic hand In the rents in the sky, the enraged engines Flee And in the holes, The vertiginous wheels the mouths the voices And the dogs of misfortune barking at our heels All hell has broken loose Clanking iron Everything is a discordant chord The *broon-roon-roon* of the wheels Thuds Surges We are a storm in the skull of a deaf man ...

'Tell me, Blaise, are we very far from Montmartre?'

Mais oui, tu m'énerves, tu le sais bien, nous sommes bien loin
La folie surchauffée beugle dans la locomotive
La peste le choléra se lèvent comme des braises ardentes sur notre route
Nous disparaissons dans la guerre en plein dans un tunnel
La faim, la putain, se cramponne aux nuages en débandade
Et fiente des batailles en tas puants de morts
Fais comme elle, fais ton métier...

★

Of course we are, you're getting on my nerves, you know very well we're far away Superheated madness bellows in the engine Plague cholera rise in our path like burning coals We're vanishing into war right inside a tunnel Hunger, that whore, clings to the stampeding clouds And excretes battles in stinking heaps of corpses Do like her, do your job ...

★

J'ai peur
Je ne sais pas aller jusqu'au bout
Comme mon ami Chagall je pourrais faire une série de tableaux déments
Mais je n'ai pas pris de notes en voyage
'Pardonnez-moi mon ignorance
'Pardonnez-moi de ne plus connaître l'ancien jeu des vers'
Comme dit Guillaume Apollinaire
Tout ce qui concerne la guerre on peut le lire dans les *Mémoires* de Kouropatkine
Ou dans les journaux japonais qui sont aussi cruellement illustrés
A quoi bon me documenter
Je m'abandonne
Aux sursauts de ma mémoire...

I'm frightened I lack the skill to go all the way Like my friend Chagall I could do a series of demented pictures But I didn't take notes on my travels 'Forgive my ignorance Forgive me for no longer knowing the ancient play of verses' As Guillaume Apollinaire says All that has to do with war can be read in the *Memoirs* of Kropotkin[1] Or in Japanese newspapers which are cruelly illustrated too What's the point of gathering material I surrender myself To my memory's involuntary leaps ...

[1]Despite the odd spelling, Cendrars is probably referring to Prince Pyotr Alexeyevich Kropotkin, a Russian anarchist imprisoned first in his native country and later in France. He settled in England in 1886 and wrote *Memoirs of a Revolutionist*.

A partir d'Irkoutsk le voyage devint beaucoup trop lent
Beaucoup trop long
Nous étions dans le premier train qui contournait le lac Baïkal
On avait orné la locomotive de drapeaux et de lampions
Et nous avions quitté la gare aux accents tristes de l'hymne au Tzar.
Si j'étais peintre je déverserais beaucoup de rouge, beaucoup de jaune sur la fin de ce voyage
Car je crois bien que nous étions tous un peu fous
Et qu'un délire immense ensanglantait les faces énervées de mes compagnons de voyage
Comme nous approchions de la Mongolie
Qui ronflait comme un incendie.
Le train avait ralenti son allure
Et je percevais dans le grincement perpétuel des roues
Les accents fous et les sanglots
D'une éternelle liturgie

From Irkutsk the journey became much too slow Much too long We were in the first train around Lake Baikal The engine was adorned with flags and Chinese lanterns And we had left the station to the sad strains of the hymn to the Tsar. If I were a painter I would spread lots of red, lots of yellow over the end of this journey For I believe we were all a little crazy And that a huge delirium bloodied the sapped faces of my travelling companions As we approached Mongolia Which was roaring like a fire The train had slowed its pace And I could make out in the perpetual grinding of the wheels The wild strains and the sobs Of an eternal liturgy

J'ai vu
J'ai vu les trains silencieux les trains noirs qui revenaient de l'Extrême-Orient et qui passaient en fantômes
Et mon œil, comme le fanal d'arrière, court encore derrière ces trains
A Talga 100,000 blessés agonisaient faute de soins
J'ai visité les hôpitaux de Krasnoïarsk
Et à Khilok nous avons croisé un long convoi de soldats fous
J'ai vu dans les lazarets des plaies béantes des blessures qui saignaient à pleines orgues
Et les membres amputés dansaient autour ou s'envolaient dans l'air rauque
L'incendie était sur toutes les faces dans tous les cœurs
Des doigts idiots tambourinaient sur toutes les vitres
Et sous la pression de la peur les regards crevaient comme des abcès
Dans toutes les gares on brûlait tous les wagons
Et j'ai vu
J'ai vu des trains de 60 locomotives qui s'enfuyaient à toute

I saw I saw the silent trains the black trains returning from the Far East and passing like phantoms And my eye, like the rear signal-light, is still running behind those trains At Talga 100,000 wounded were dying for lack of treatment I visited the Krasnoyarsk hospitals And at Khilok we came across a long convoy of insane soldiers In the quarantine stations I saw gaping wounds lacerations that were bleeding full blast And amputated limbs danced about or flew into the raucous air Fire was on all faces in all hearts Idiot fingers drummed on all the windowpanes And under the pressure of fear gazes burst open like abscesses In all the stations waggons were being burned And I saw I saw trains with 60 engines fleeing at top speed

vapeur pourchassées par les horizons en rut et des bandes de corbeaux qui s'envolaient désespérément après
Disparaître
Dans la direction de Port-Arthur.

A Tchita nous eûmes quelques jours de répit
Arrêt de cinq jours vu l'encombrement de la voie
Nous le passâmes chez Monsieur Iankéléwitch qui voulait me donner sa fille unique en mariage
Puis le train repartit.
Maintenant c'était moi qui avais pris place au piano et j'avais mal aux dents
Je revois quand je veux cet intérieur si calme le magasin du père et les yeux de la fille qui venait le soir dans mon lit
Moussorgsky
Et les lieder de Hugo Wolf
Et les sables du Gobi
Et à Khaïlar une caravane de chameaux blancs
Je crois bien que j'étais ivre durant plus de 500 kilomètres
Mais j'étais au piano et c'est tout ce que je vis

pursued by rutting horizons and bands of crows desperately taking flight behind Disappearing In the direction of Port Arthur.

At Chita we had a few days' respite A five-day stop in view of the blocked track We spent it with Monsieur Iankelevich who wanted to give me his only daughter in marriage Then the train set off again. Now it was I who was seated at the piano and I had toothache I can see again when I want to that interior that was so calm the father's shop and the eyes of the daughter who came each evening into my bed Mussorgsky And Hugo Wolf lieder And the sands of the Gobi And at Hailar a caravan of white camels I believe I was drunk for more than 500 kilometres But I was at the piano and that's all I saw When

Quand on voyage on devrait fermer les yeux
Dormir
J'aurais tant voulu dormir
Je reconnais tous les pays les yeux fermés à leur odeur
Et je reconnais tous les trains au bruit qu'ils font
Les trains d'Europe sont à quatre temps tandis que ceux d'Asie sont à cinq ou sept temps
D'autres vont en sourdine sont des berceuses
Et il y en a qui dans le bruit monotone des roues me rappellent la prose lourde de Maeterlinck
J'ai déchiffré tous les textes confus des roues et j'ai rassemblé les éléments épars d'une violente beauté
Que je possède
Et qui me force.

you travel you should shut your eyes Sleep I would have liked so much to sleep I recognize all countries with my eyes shut by their odour And I recognize all the trains by the sound they make European trains run in four-four time whereas those of Asia run in five- or seven-four Others go muted they are lullabies And there are some which in the monotonous sound of their wheels recall Maeterlinck's heavy prose I have deciphered all the disordered texts of the wheels and assembled the scattered elements of a violent beauty Which I possess And which takes me by storm.

Contrastes

Les fenêtres de ma poésie sont grand'ouvertes sur les boulevards et dans ses vitrines
Brillent
Les pierreries de la lumière
Ecoute les violons des limousines et les xylophones des linotypes
Le pocheur se lave dans l'essuie-main du ciel
Tout est taches de couleur
Et les chapeaux des femmes qui passent sont des comètes dans l'incendie du soir

L'unité
Il n'y a plus d'unité
Toutes les horloges marquent maintenant 24 heures après avoir été retardées de dix minutes
Il n'y a plus de temps.
Il n'y a plus d'argent.
A la Chambre
On gâche les éléments merveilleux de la matière première

Contrasts

The windows of my poetry are wide open to the boulevards and in its showcases Shine The precious stones of light Listen to the violin limousines and the xylophone linotypes The dauber washes himself in the handtowel of the sky Everything is splashes of colour And the hats of the passing women are comets in the fire of evening

Unity There is no more unity All the clocks show midnight now having been put back ten minutes There is no more time. There is no more money. In the parliament Chamber they are ruining the marvellous elements of raw matter

Chez le bistro
Les ouvriers en blouse bleue boivent du vin rouge
Tous les samedis poule au gibier
On joue
On parie
De temps en temps un bandit passe en automobile
Ou un enfant joue avec l'Arc de Triomphe...
Je conseille à M. Cochon de loger ses protégés à la Tour Eiffel.

In the bistro The workmen in blue overalls are drinking red wine Every Saturday game stakes[1] Gaming Betting Now and then a gangster passes in a car Or a child plays with the Arc de Triomphe ... I advise Mr Hog to billet his protégés at the Eiffel Tower.

[1]Though the problematic phrase '*poule au gibier*' may refer simply to a meal, its connotations are complex: '*poule*' may be a bet or sweepstake; a tournament pool of players; a kitty to which all contribute; a horserace; there could even be a reference to Henri IV's ambition that every French family should have a '*poule au pot*' on Sundays ... And '*gibier*' is used colloquially to designate a mug, a sucker, a fall-guy.

Aujourd'hui
Changement de propriétaire
Le Saint-Esprit se détaille chez les plus petits boutiquiers
Je lis avec ravissement les bandes de calicot
De coquelicot
Il n'y a que les pierres ponces de la Sorbonne qui ne sont jamais fleuries
L'enseigne de la Samaritaine laboure par contre la Seine
Et du côté de Saint-Séverin
J'entends
Les sonnettes acharnées des tramways

Today Change of ownership The Holy Spirit is retailed in portions in the tiniest shops I read in delight the strips of calico Corn-poppy red Only the Sorbonne pumice stones are never in blossom The sign of the Samaritan ploughs against the Seine And towards Saint-Séverin I hear The relentless clanging of the trams

Il pleut les globes électriques
Montrouge Gare de l'Est Métro Nord-Sud bateaux-mouches monde
Tout est halo
Profondeur
Rue de Buci on crie *L'Intransigeant* et *Paris-Sports*
L'aérodrome du ciel est maintenant, embrasé, un tableau de Cimabue
Quand par devant
Les hommes sont
Longs
Noirs
Tristes
Et fument, cheminées d'usine

It's raining electric light bulbs Montrouge Gare de l'Est Metro North-South pleasure-boats world Everything is a halo Depth On the Rue de Buci they shout *L'Intransigeant* and *Paris-Sports* The aerodrome of the sky, ablaze with light, is now a painting by Cimabue While in the foreground Men are Long Black Sad And smoke, factory chimneys

Construction

De la couleur, de la couleur et des couleurs...
Voici Léger qui grandit comme le soleil de l'époque tertiaire
Et qui durcit
Et qui fixe
La nature morte
La croûte terrestre
Le liquide
Le brumeux
Tout ce qui se ternit
La géométrie nuageuse
Le fil à plomb qui se résorbe
Ossification.
Locomotion.
Tout grouille
L'esprit s'anime soudain et s'habille à son tour comme les animaux et les plantes
Prodigieusement
Et voici
La peinture devient cette chose énorme qui bouge

Construction

Colour, colour and colours ... Here is Léger expanding like the sun of the tertiary epoch And hardening And fixing Still life Earthly crust Liquid Misty All that grows tarnished Cloudy geometry The retracting plumb line Ossification. Locomotion. Everything swarms The spirit suddenly comes to life and puts on garments in its turn like the animals and plants Prodigiously And now The painting becomes that gigantic moving thing

La roue
La vie
La machine
L'âme humaine
Une culasse de 75
Mon portrait

The wheel Life The machine The human soul A 75-mm breech My portrait

Orion

C'est mon étoile
Elle a la forme d'une main
C'est ma main montée au ciel
Durant toute la guerre je voyais Orion par un créneau
Quand les Zeppelins venaient bombarder Paris ils venaient toujours d'Orion
Aujourd'hui je l'ai au-dessus de ma tête
Le grand mât perce la paume de cette main qui doit souffrir
Comme ma main coupée me fait souffrir percée qu'elle est par un dard continuel

Orion

It is my star It has the shape of a hand It is my hand risen into the sky All through the war I saw Orion through a battlement When the Zeppelins came to drop bombs on Paris they always came from Orion Today I have it above my head The great mast pierces the palm of that hand that must be in pain As my severed hand pains me pierced as it is by a perpetual shaft

Mississippi

A cet endroit le fleuve est presque aussi large qu'un lac
Il roule des eaux jaunâtres et boueuses entre deux berges marécageuses
Plantes aquatiques que continuent les acréages des cotonniers
Çà et là apparaissent les villes et les villages tapis au fond de quelque petite baie avec leurs usines avec leurs hautes cheminées noires avec leurs longues estacades sur pilotis qui s'avancent bien avant dans l'eau

Chaleur accablante
La cloche du bord sonne pour le lunch
Les passagers arborent des complets à carreaux des cravates hurlantes des gilets rutilants comme les cocktails incendiaires et les sauces corrosives

Mississippi

Here the river is almost as wide as a lake Rolling its yellowish muddy waters between two marshy banks Aquatic plants are prolonged by the acres of cotton bushes Here and there towns and villages appear squatting far back in some small bay with their factories with their tall black chimneys with their long piers on stakes jutting well out into the water

Overpowering heat The ship's bell rings for lunch The passengers sport checked suits howling ties waistcoats glowing like the inflammatory cocktails and the corrosive sauces

On aperçoit beaucoup de crocodiles
Les jeunes alertes et frétillants
Les gros le dos recouvert d'une mousse verdâtre se laissent aller à la dérive

La végétation luxuriante annonce l'approche de la zone tropicale
Bambous géants palmiers tulipiers lauriers cèdres
Le fleuve lui-même a doublé de largeur
Il est tout parsemé d'îlots flottants d'où l'approche du bateau fait s'élever des nuées d'oiseaux aquatiques
Steam-boats voiliers chalands embarcations de toutes sortes et d'immenses trains de bois
Une vapeur jaune monte des eaux surchauffées du fleuve

There are plenty of crocodiles to be seen The young ones lively and wriggling The backs of the big ones are covered with greenish moss they let themselves drift

The luxuriant vegetation heralds the approaching tropical zone Giant bamboos palm trees tulip trees laurels cedars The river itself has doubled in width It is strewn with floating islets from which the ship's approach sends up clouds of aquatic birds Steamboats sailing boats barges small craft of all kinds and vast rafts of logs A yellow vapour rises from the overheated waters of the river

C'est par centaines maintenant que les crocos s'ébattent autour de nous
On entend le claquement sec de leurs mâchoires et l'on distingue très bien leur petit œil féroce
Les passagers s'amusent à leur tirer dessus avec des carabines de précision
Quand un tireur émérite réussit ce tour de force de tuer ou de blesser une bête à mort
Ses congénères se précipitent sur elle la déchirent
Férocement
Avec des petits cris assez semblables au vagissement d'un nouveau-né

And now the crocs leap wildly about us in hundreds You can hear the sharp snap of the jaws and make out very clearly their ferocious little eyes For entertainment the passengers shoot at them with precision rifles When a crack marksman accomplishes the tour de force of killing or mortally wounding a beast Its fellows hurl themselves upon it tear it to pieces Ferociously With little cries rather reminiscent of the wailing of a new-born baby

Aube

A l'aube je suis descendu au fond des machines
J'ai écouté pour une dernière fois la respiration profonde des pistons

Appuyé à la fragile main-courante de nickel j'ai senti pour une dernière fois cette sourde vibration des arbres de couch pénétrer en moi avec le relent des huiles surchauffées et la tiédeur de la vapeur
Nous avons encore bu un verre le chef mécanicien cet homme tranquille et triste qui a un si beau sourire d'enfant et qui ne cause jamais et moi

Comme je sortais de chez lui le soleil sortait tout naturellement de la mer et chauffait déjà dur
Le ciel mauve n'avait pas un nuage
Et comme nous pointions sur Santos notre sillage décrivait un grand arc-de-cercle miroitant sur la mer immobile

Dawn

At dawn I went down into the depths of the engines I listened one last time to the profound breathing of the pistons Leaning on the fragile nickel handrail I felt one last time that muted vibration of the power shafts enter into me with the reek of overheated oils and the tepid warmth of steam We had one more drink the chief engineer that sad and placid man with such a beautiful childlike smile and who never talks and I As I left his room the sun was emerging in all naturalness from the sea and its heat was already intense There was no cloud in the mauve sky And as we headed for Santos our wake described a great curved bow shimmering on the motionless sea

Pierre Reverdy
(1889–1960)

Reverdy's origins were in south-western France, where his father was a wine-grower, and his love of the rural landscape and the sea survived his uneasy presence in Paris from 1910 to 1926. Discharged from his auxiliary status in the army in 1916, he founded the influential review *Nord-Sud* (i.e. Montmartre–Montparnasse) with Jacob and Apollinaire the following year. Only sixteen issues appeared, but it was a vital focus for the 'Cubists' and to some extent the young Surrealists.

He was essentially a solitary man in intense communication with his own sensations, a sensitive and often melancholy observer on the sidelines of reality. In 1926, encouraged by Jacob, he withdrew to the monastery of Solesmes, and remained there until his death, in spite of loss of faith and acute depression in which only poetry offered any salvation.

A 'pure poet' much admired by his contemporaries, Reverdy also formulated important modernist poetic theories. His view of the nature and operation of the poetic image, in particular, was highly influential and was adopted, if in a more 'convulsive' mode, by André Breton. Reverdy wrote: 'The image is a pure creation of the mind. It cannot be born of a comparison, but only from the bringing together of two more or less distant realities ... The more distant and apposite the relationships between the two realities, the stronger the image will be, and the more emotive power and poetic reality it will have.' The image arrives spontaneously, through a burning necessity, and expands our consciousness.

In Reverdy's poems the eye often has priority over the ear. He has an intensely geometrical spatial awareness both in imagery and in the syntactic shape of the poem, a compulsion to use verbs of seeing and moving, an intuitive intrinsic logic in 'construction' that breaks with traditional linear and mimetic conventions, and all these characteristics bring him closer to his friends the Cubist painters than any other poet. He uses words out of normal context, exploiting their latent energies through original juxtapositions, and points the way to Surrealism.

An anguished sense of loss, of incompleteness and inner void permeates his work, a disappointment in the necessarily fragmented relationship between perception and world. But although there is tension and pathos, there is also discretion, economy and clarity in his poems, which he described as 'crystals deposited after the effervescent contact of the mind with reality'. As with the Surrealists, this ultimate disappointment is much less important than what is achieved in the active process. Poetry, he states, is born of absence: 'Poetry is in what is not. In what we lack ... Poetry is the link between us and absent reality.' This 'gap' is tragic, but it is the poet's reason for being; his function is to amplify our experience of reality as much as he can.

Major volumes: *Poèmes en prose* 1915, *Quelques Poèmes* 1916, *La Lucarne ovale* 1916, *Les Ardoises du toit* 1918, *Etoiles peintes* 1921, *Cœur de chêne* 1921, *Cravates de chanvre* 1922, *Grande Nature* 1925, *La Balle au bond* 1928, *Flaques de verre* 1929, *Sources du vent* 1929, *Pierres blanches* 1930, *Ferraille* 1937, *Plein Verre* 1940, *Le Chant des morts* 1948, *Bois vert* 1949, *Au Soleil du plafond* 1955, *Liberté des mers* 1960.

Après le Bal

J'ai peut-être mis au vestiaire plus que mes vêtements. Je m'avance, allégé, avec trop d'assurance et quelqu'un dans la salle a remarqué mes pas. Les rayons sont pleins de danseuses.

Je tourne, je tourne sans rien voir dans les flots de rayons des lampes électriques et je marche sur tant de pieds et tant d'autres meurtrissent les miens.

Quel bal, quelle fête,! J'ai trouvé toutes les femmes belles, tous mes désirs volent vers tous ces yeux. Tant qu'a duré l'orchestre j'ai tourné des talons sur un parquet ciré, plein d'émotion, et mes bras sont rompus d'avoir supporté tant de proies qu'il a fallu lâcher.

Mais l'orchestre s'est tu, les lampes éteintes ont laissé s'alourdir la fatigue. Au vestiaire, on m'a rendu un chaud manteau contre le gel, mais le reste? Il me manque pourtant quelque chose. Je suis seul et je ne puis lutter contre ce froid.

After the Ball

Perhaps I have left more than my clothes in the cloakroom. I move forward, unburdened, with too much confidence and someone in the room has noticed my footsteps. The rays of light are filled with dancing women.

I am spinning, I am spinning, seeing nothing in the waves of light flowing from the electric lamps and I am stepping on so many feet and so many others bruise mine.

What a ball, what a festival! I have found every woman beautiful, all my desires fly towards all those eyes. For as long as the orchestra has played I have been spinning on my heels on a polished floor, filled with emotion, and my arms are exhausted from bearing so many preys I have had to release.

But the orchestra is now silent, the extinguished lamps have let fatigue grow heavy. In the cloakroom I have been handed a warm coat against the frost, but the rest? There's something I lack still. I am alone and I cannot combat this cold.

Toujours là

J'ai besoin de ne plus me voir et d'oublier
De parler à des gens que je ne connais pas
De crier sans être entendu
Pour rien tout seul
Je connais tout le monde et chacun de vos pas
Je voudrais raconter et personne n'écoute
Les têtes et les yeux se détournent de moi
Vers la nuit
Ma tête est une boule pleine et lourde
Qui roule sur la terre avec un peu de bruit

Loin
Rien derrière moi et rien devant
Dans le vide où je descends
Quelques vifs courants d'air
Vont autour de moi
Cruels et froids
Ce sont des portes mal fermées

Still There

I need to see myself no longer and to forget To speak to people I do not know To shout without being heard For no reason all alone I know everyone and each of your footsteps I would like to tell the story and no one is listening The heads and eyes turn away from me Towards the darkness My head is a full and heavy bowling-ball Rolling over the earth with just a little noise

Far away Nothing behind me and nothing in front In the emptiness where I descend A few brisk draughts of air Move around me Cruel and cold They are doors imperfectly shut On

Sur des souvenirs encore inoubliés
Le monde comme une pendule s'est arrêté
Les gens sont suspendus pour l'éternité
Un aviateur descend par un fil comme une araignée
Tout le monde danse allégé
Entre ciel et terre
Mais un rayon de lumière est venu
De la lampe que tu as oublié d'éteindre
Sur le palier
Ah ce n'est pas fini
L'oubli n'est pas complet
Et j'ai encore besoin d'apprendre à me connaître

still unforgotten memories The world has stopped like a clock The people are suspended for eternity An aviator comes down on a thread like a spider Everyone dances unburdened Between heaven and earth But a ray of light has come From the lamp which you forgot to extinguish On the landing Ah it is not finished Forgetting is not complete And I still need to learn to know myself

Auberge

Un œil se ferme

Au fond plaquée contre le mur
la pensée qui ne sort pas

Des idées s'en vont pas à pas

On pourrait mourir
Ce que je tiens entre mes bras pourrait partir

Un rêve

L'aube à peine née qui s'achève
Un cliquetis
Les volets en s'ouvrant l'ont abolie

Si rien n'allait venir

Il y a un champ où l'on pourrait encore courir
Des étoiles à n'en plus finir

Et ton ombre au bout de l'avenue

Inn

An eye closes Deep in the background flattened against the wall the thought that does not go outside Ideas go on their way step by step Death could occur What I am holding in my arms could depart A dream Dawn scarcely born is ending A clatter The shutters as they opened have put a stop to it If nothing were going to come There is a field where we could still run Stars without limit And your shadow at the end of the avenue

Elle s'efface
On n'a rien vu
De tout ce qui passait on n'a rien retenu
Autant de paroles qui montent
Des contes qu'on n'a jamais lus
Rien
Les jours qui se pressent à la sortie
Enfin la cavalcade s'est évanouie

En bas entre les tables où l'on jouait aux cartes

It vanishes We have seen nothing Of all that was passing we have held on to nothing So many words rising Stories we have never read Nothing The days rushing to the exit At last the cavalcade had faded out Down there between the tables where cards were being played

Nomade

La porte qui ne s'ouvre pas
La main qui passe
Au loin un verre qui se casse
La lampe fume
Les étincelles qui s'allument
Le ciel est plus noir
Sur les toits

Quelques animaux
Sans leur ombre

Un regard
Une tache sombre

La maison où l'on n'entre pas

Nomad

The door that does not open The hand that passes In the distance a glass that breaks The lamp smokes The sparks that kindle The sky is darker On the roofs A few animals Without their shadow A gaze A dark shape The house that is not entered

Couloir

Nous sommes deux
Sur la même ligne où tout se suit
Dans les méandres de la nuit
Une parole est au milieu
Deux bouches qui ne se voient pas
Un bruit de pas
Un corps léger glisse vers l'autre
La porte tremble
Une main passe
On voudrait ouvrir
Le rayon clair se tient debout
Là devant moi
Et c'est le feu qui nous sépare
Dans l'ombre où ton profil s'égare
Une minute sans respirer
Ton souffle en passant m'a brûlé

Corridor

There are two of us On the same line where all is continuous In the windings of the night A word is in the middle Two mouths not seeing one another A sound of footsteps One airy body glides towards the other The door trembles A hand moves across We would like to open The bright ray stands erect There before me And it is the fire that separates us In the shadow where your outline drifts away For a moment without breathing Your breath passing by has burned me

Chauffage central

Une petite lumière
Tu vois une petite lumière descendre sur ton ventre
pour t'éclairer
– Une femme s'étire comme une fusée –
Au coin là-bas une ombre lit
Ses pieds libres sont trop jolis

Court-circuit au cœur
Une panne au moteur
Quel aimant me soutient
Mes yeux et mon amour se trompent de chemin

Un rien
Un feu que l'on rallume et qui s'éteint
J'ai assez du vent
J'ai assez du ciel
Au fond tout ce qu'on voit est artificiel
Même ta bouche
Pourtant j'ai chaud là où ta main me touche

Central Heating

A little light You see a little light come down on your abdomen to light you up – A woman stretches herself like a rocket – In the corner over there a shadow is reading Her feet swinging free are too pretty

Short-circuit in the heart A breakdown in the motor What magnet holds me up My eyes and my love are losing their way

A mere nothing A fire we rekindle and which goes out I've had enough of the wind I've had enough of the sky At heart all we see is artificial Even your mouth And yet I am hot where your hand touches me

La porte est ouverte et je n'entre pas
Je vois ton visage et je n'y crois pas
Tu es pâle
Un soir qu'on était triste on a pleuré sur une malle
Là-bas des hommes riaient
Des enfants presque nus parfois se promenaient
L'eau était claire
Un fil de cuivre rouge y conduit la lumière
Le soleil et ton cœur sont de même matière

The door is open and I don't go in I see your face and I don't believe in it You are pale One evening when we were sad we wept on a trunk Over there men were laughing Nearly naked children sometimes strolled by The water was clear A red copper wire guides the light there The sun and your heart are of the same substance

Drame

Le rond qui s'agrandit
        Est-ce la guillotine
Réalité du film
        mystère dans le crime
Il passait à ton cou une corde plus fine
Les yeux sont plus vivants
            Ton âme est étalée
Tu ne t'en doutais pas
        c'est l'électricité
Les traits en grossissant se sont presque effacés
La passion fait remuer toutes les têtes de la salle
      Mais dans l'obscurité
où personne ne crie
Un coup de pistolet qui ne fait pas de bruit
Comment pourra-t-il sortir
        Mystère acrobatique
Le pouvoir surhumain du courant électrique
    L'a fait partir
Le policier déçu meurt devant la fenêtre

Drama

The expanding disc Is it the guillotine Reality of the film mystery in the crime It passed around your neck a more slender cord The eyes are more alive Your soul is laid out on display You had no notion of it it's electricity Features growing larger have almost disappeared Passion moves all the heads in the room But in the darkness where no one cries out A pistol shot that makes no sound How will it be able to get out Acrobatic mystery The superhuman power of the electric current Set it off The disappointed policeman is dying by the window

Les Mots qu'on échange

Une ligne barre la route
On voudrait passer
L'ombre qui me suit vient de s'arrêter
Le mur tourne
Il y a peut-être quelqu'un

Je suis plus calme que le ciel
Aucun bruit ne m'émeut
Seul
Au milieu du chemin

Le paysage ne ressemble à rien
Plus aucun souvenir
Je commence
La rivière chante à côté de moi

Words exchanged

A line blocks the road We would like to pass The shadow following me has just stopped The wall turns Perhaps there is someone

I am more tranquil than the sky No sound affects me Alone In the middle of the road

The landscape resembles nothing Not a single memory now I begin The river sings beside me

En partant nous étions trois
Mon ombre et moi
Et toi derrière
A présent il y a trop de lumière
Le jour
Et devant moi
Quelqu'un que je ne connais pas

– Passe dans la prairie –

Un oiseau chante

La solitude est comme la mort
Un monde nouveau qui s'endort

Le pays où brille la lune

At the outset there were three of us My shadow and I And you behind Now there is too much light The daylight And in front of me Someone I do not know

– Passes into the meadow –

A bird sings

Solitude is like death A new world going to sleep

The land where the moon shines

X

Pour éviter l'écueil qui se tient en arrière
Qui me suit
Qui attend le pas définitif
Pour éviter de jamais revenir en arrière
Sur le flanc de l'amour qui glisse sans mourir
Cet amour qui se dégage mal de tes viscères
Ces regards qui n'ont plus ni rime ni raison
Et ce portrait de toi que je voudrais refaire
Tendre cruel vivant dans l'ombre sans passion
Ce regard qui se perd dans la nuit jalouse
Ce regard plein des pointes de feu de la jalousie
Dans la robe du soir dont se pare la terre
Au moment où tu sors

X

To avoid the reef that lurks behind That follows me That awaits the definitive step To avoid ever turning back over the flank of love that slides without dying That love removed only with pain from your viscera Those looks that have no rhyme or reason now And that portrait of you that I would like to do again Tender cruel living in passionless shadow That gaze lost in the jealous night That gaze full of jealousy's burning pin-pricks In the evening gown that is the earth's adornment At the moment when you go out

X

Loin dans le désespoir
J'aurai le visage enfoui dans la glace
Le cœur percé des mille feux du souvenir
L'écueil de l'avenir et la mort en arrière
Et ton sourire trop léger
Une barrière
De toi à moi
Les paroles libres
Les gestes retenus
Des mains ailées qui avançaient pour tout ouvrir
Alors dans la trame serrée livide se découvre
La blessure inouïe dont je voudrais guérir

Far away in hopelessness My face will be buried in ice My heart stabbed by the thousand fires of memory The reef of the future and death behind And your smile that is too slight A barrier Between you and me Free words Wary gestures Winged hands advancing to open everything Then in the tightened livid web is revealed The unprecedented wound for which I seek a cure

Chair vive

Lève-toi carcasse et marche
Rien de neuf sous le soleil jaune
Le der des der des louis d'or
La lumière qui se détache
sous les pellicules du temps
La serrure au cœur qui éclate
Un fil de soie
Un fil de plomb
Un fil de sang
Après ces vagues de silence
Ces signes d'amour au crin noir
Le ciel plus lisse que ton œil
Le cou tordu d'orgueil
Ma vie dans la coulisse
D'où je vois onduler les moissons de la mort
Toutes ces mains avides qui pétrissent des boules de fumée
Plus lourdes que les piliers de l'univers
Têtes vides
Cœurs nus
Mains parfumées

Live Flesh

Rise up carcass and walk Nothing new under the yellow sun The last of the last of the gold pieces The light flaking away under the membranes of time The lock on the bursting heart A silken thread A leaden wire A trickle of blood After these waves of silence these signs of black-maned love The sky smoother than your eye The neck twisted with pride My life in the wings From where I see the harvests of death undulate All those avid hands kneading balls of smoke Heavier than the pillars of the universe Empty heads Naked hearts Perfumed

Tentacules des singes qui visent les nuées
Dans les rides de ces grimaces
Une ligne droite se tend
Un nerf se tord
La mer repue
L'amour
L'amer sourire de la mort

hands Monkey tentacles aiming at the clouds In the wrinkles of these grimaces A straight line stretches taut A nerve twists The sated sea Love The bitter smile of death

Catherine Pozzi
(1882–1934)

Catherine Pozzi is distinguished from Anna de Noailles and other early twentieth-century women poets by her concision and intellectual control; and her small but excellent output of verse has a classical quality. A highly intelligent and cultivated woman with a strong interest in science and theology as well as literature, she shared the refined artistic spirit of Mallarmé and Valéry. She made use of the decasyllabic line, like Valéry in 'Le Cimetière marin', to achieve a similar harmony of feeling and intellect.

Her collected *Poèmes* were published posthumously in 1935. In spite of prolonged illness, she had also been able to translate works by Stefan George into French, and to devote time to her friendships with Rilke, Valéry, Heredia, Jouve and Benda.

It was Benda who saw in her work a 'linear perfection', and who said of Catherine Pozzi herself: 'In the earthly realm, she seemed already to be outside time and beyond the perishability of life.'

Ave

Très haut amour, s'il se peut que je meure
Sans avoir su d'où je vous possédais,
En quel soleil était votre demeure,
En quel passé votre temps, en quelle heure
Je vous aimais,

Très haut amour qui passez la mémoire,
Feu sans foyer dont j'ai fait tout mon jour,
En quel destin vous traciez mon histoire,
En quel sommeil se voyait votre gloire,
O mon séjour...

Quand je serai pour moi-même perdue
Et divisée à l'abîme infini,
Infiniment, quand je serai rompue,
Quand le présent dont je suis revêtue
Aura trahi,

Ave

Most lofty love, if it be possible that I die without knowing whence I possessed you, within what sun was your abode, within what past your time, within what hour I loved you,

Most lofty love outliving memory, fire without hearth from which I composed all my daylight, within what destiny you inscribed my story, within what sleep your glory was manifest, O my dwelling-place ...

When I am lost from my own sight and fragmented in the infinite abyss, infinitely, when I am broken, when the present that clothes me has committed its betrayal,

Par l'univers en mille corps brisée,
De mille instants non rassemblés encor,
De cendre aux cieux jusqu'au néant vannée,
Vous referez pour une étrange année
Un seul trésor

Vous referez mon nom et mon image
De mille corps emportés par le jour,
Vive unité sans nom et sans visage,
Cœur de l'esprit, O centre du mirage
Très haut amour.

Shattered into a thousand elements across the universe, from a thousand moments not yet conjoined, from ashes winnowed to the skies until nothingness, for a strange year you will re-create a single treasure

You will re-create my name and my image from a thousand elements swept away by the daylight, a living unity without name and without face, heart of the spirit, O centre of the mirage Most lofty love.

Nyx

A Louise aussi de Lyon et d'Italie

O vous mes nuits, ô noires attendues
O pays fier, ô secrets obstinés
O longs regards, ô foudroyantes nues
O vol permis outre les cieux fermés.

O grand désir, ô surprise épandue
O beau parcours de l'esprit enchanté
O pire mal, ô grâce descendue
O porte ouverte où nul n'avait passé

Je ne sais pas pourquoi je meurs et noie
Avant d'entrer à l'éternel séjour.
Je ne sais pas de qui je suis la proie.
Je ne sais pas de qui je suis l'amour.

Nyx

For Louise, also of Lyon and Italy

O you my nights, O anticipated blacknesses O proud land, O stubborn mysteries O prolonged gazes, O clouds striking thunder O flight granted beyond the sealed skies.

O great longing, O surprise spread wide O beautiful journey of the enthralled spirit O worst of sufferings, O grace descended O open door where none had entered

I know not why I die and drown Before I enter the eternal abode. I know not whose prey I am. I know not whose love I am.

Scopolamine

Le vin qui coule dans ma veine
A noyé mon cœur et l'entraîne
Et je naviguerai le ciel
A bord d'un cœur sans capitaine
Où l'oubli fond comme du miel.

Mon cœur est un astre apparu
Qui nage au divin nonpareil
Dérive, étrange devenu!
O voyage vers le Soleil –
Un son nouvel et continu
Est la trame de ton sommeil.

Mon cœur a quitté mon histoire
Adieu Forme je ne sens plus
Je suis sauvé je suis perdu
Je me cherche dans l'inconnu
Un nom libre de la mémoire.

Scopolamine[1]

The wine that flows in my veins has drowned my heart and carries it away And I will sail the sky aboard a heart with no captain where oblivion melts like honey.

My heart is a newly manifest star that swims in the peerless sublime Drift on, strange metamorphosis! A new and perpetual sound is the web of your slumber.

My heart has relinquished my story Farewell Form I have no more feeling I am saved I am lost I seek for myself in the unknown a name free from memory.

[1]A powerful and toxic drug obtained from plants such as henbane. Used as a smooth-muscle relaxant, sedative, and truth-serum. Affects the central nervous system, and has dangerous side-effects.

Jules Supervielle
(1884–1960)

Supervielle's family had its origins in the Basque country, but he was born in Montevideo. Orphaned as a baby, he was brought up by relatives in Uruguay, then sent to school in France. His memory is filled with sea-crossings and with images from the South American landscape. Ocean, pampas and sky are mythologized in *Débarcadères* and *Gravitations* into dream-worlds.

On the margins of Surrealism but pursuing an independent course, Supervielle is a 'natural' poet, enjoying a lively Franciscan dialogue with the animal, vegetable and mineral world. Writing quite spontaneously in deceptively simple, free and metrical forms of great musicality, he blends in an unproblematic way the abstract and the concrete, the past and the present, cosmic and commonplace perceptions, in a lyrical and humorous amplification of reality. His penchant for the fable (in prose and drama as well as verse) leads him to a volume of creation myths, *La Fable du Monde*, in which his kinship with all living things is expressed poignantly through his identification with a hesitant, vulnerable God.

The heartbeat has a primary importance in his work too. Supervielle suffered from cardiac problems, and was unusually aware of the fundamental pulse of life. Fearful of death, yet also with a calm and intimate curiosity that almost welcomes it, he is drawn in his awareness of inner space towards the idea of an absorption into nothingness and an eventual rebirth. A particularly strong recurring image is that of the drowned man who is not dead but has become a participant in an underwater dream-world of the unconscious. Supervielle always seems to exist on the frontier between life and death, body and soul, reality and dream, yet there is a lightness of touch and a humour that save his poetry from becoming too weighty.

The image of the drowned man typifies his attachment to the pictorial; thought for him always takes on a concrete shape. Memory, for example, is frequently represented as a ship's wake. There is no delirium in his imaginative universe, and his confidence in his ability to communicate a metaphysical truth through simple language has been rewarded by the popularity of his work. That popularity was enhanced by his Second World War poetry, in which the pain and bewilderment of exile is powerfully counterbalanced by hope and the spirit of resistance.

Major volumes: *Débarcadères* 1922, *Gravitations* 1925, *Le Forçat innocent* 1930, *Les Amis inconnus* 1934, *La Fable du Monde* 1938, *Poèmes* 1939–45 (published 1947), *Oublieuse Mémoire* 1949, *Naissances* 1951, *L'Escalier* 1956, *Le Corps tragique* 1959.

Montévidéo

Je naissais, et par la fenêtre
Passait une fraîche calèche.

Le cocher réveillait l'aurore
D'un petit coup de fouet sonore.

Flottait un archipel nocturne
Encor sur le liquide jour.

Montevideo

I was being born, and through the window there came a bright new barouche.

The coachman was rousing the dawn with a ringing little whipcrack.

An archipelago of night floated still over the liquid daylight.

Les murs s'éveillaient et le sable
Qui dort écrasé dans les murs.

Un peu de mon âme glissait
Sur un rail bleu, à contre-ciel,

Et un autre peu, se mêlant
A un bout de papier volant

Puis, trébuchant sur une pierre,
Gardait sa ferveur prisonnière.

Le matin comptait ses oiseaux
Et toujours il recommençait

Le parfum de l'eucalyptus
Se fiait à l'air étendu.

Dans l'Uruguay sur l'Atlantique,
L'air était si liant, facile,
Que les couleurs de l'horizon
S'approchaient pour voir les maisons.

The walls were awakening and the sand that sleeps compressed within the walls.

A fragment of my soul was gliding on a blue rail against the background of the sky,

And another fragment mingling with a flying scrap of paper

Then, stumbling on a stone, kept its fervour captive.

The morning was counting its birds and kept on starting again.

The scent of the eucalyptus was entrusting itself to the outstretched air.

In Uruguay on the Atlantic the air was so engaging, so easy-going, that the horizon's colours were coming closer to see the houses.

C'était moi qui naissais jusqu'au fond sourd des bois
Où tardent à venir les pousses
Et jusque sous la mer où l'algue se retrousse
Pour faire croire au vent qu'il peut descendre là.

La Terre allait, toujours recommençant sa ronde,
Reconnaissant les siens avec son atmosphère,
Et palpant sur la vague ou l'eau douce profonde
La tête des nageurs et les pieds des plongeurs.

It was I who was being born down into the blanketed depths of the woods where the shoots are slow in coming and down beneath the sea where the seaweed curls upward to make the wind believe it can penetrate down there.

The Earth was moving on, for ever beginning its round once more, identifying its own with its atmosphere, and feeling upon the wave or the gentle deep water the heads of the swimmers and the feet of the divers.

Haute mer

Parmi les oiseaux et les lunes
Qui hantent le dessous des mers
Et qu'on devine à la surface
Aux folles phases de l'écume,

High Seas

Among the birds and moons that haunt the underside of the seas, their presence sensed on the surface in the lunatic phases of the foam,

Parmi l'aveugle témoignage
Et les sillages sous-marins
De mille poissons sans visage
Qui cachent en eux leur chemin,

Le noyé cherche la chanson
Où s'était formé son jeune âge,
Ecoute en vain les coquillages
Et les fait choir au sombre fond.

Among the blind testimony and the underwater wakes of a thousand faceless fish that hide their course within themselves,

The drowned man seeks the song in which his youth took shape, listens in vain to the shells and lets them sink to the dark ocean bed.

Dans la forêt sans heures

Dans la forêt sans heures
On abat un grand arbre.
Un vide vertical
Tremble en forme de fût
Près du tronc étendu.

Cherchez, cherchez, oiseaux,
La place de vos nids
Dans ce haut souvenir
Tant qu'il murmure encore.

In the timeless forest

In the timeless forest a tall tree is felled. An upright void vibrates in the form of a bole near the outstretched trunk.

Seek, seek, birds, the site of your nests in this tall memory while it murmurs still.

Les Poissons

Mémoire des poissons dans les criques profondes,
Que puis-je faire ici de vos lents souvenirs,
Je ne sais rien de vous qu'un peu d'écume et d'ombre
Et qu'un jour, comme moi, il vous faudra mourir.

Alors que venez-vous interroger mes rêves
Comme si je pouvais vous être de secours?
Allez en mer, laissez-moi sur ma terre sèche,
Nous ne sommes pas faits pour mélanger nos jours.

The Fish

Memory of fish in the deep-water coves, what can I do here with your slow-moving recollections, I know no more of you than a hint of foam and shadow and that one day, like me, you will have to die.

Why then do you come and gaze questioningly into my dreams as if I could be of help to you? Go away to the sea, leave me on my dry land, we are not made to mingle our days.

Tristesse de Dieu

(Dieu parle)

Je vous vois aller et venir sur le tremblement de la Terre
Comme aux premiers jours du monde, mais grande est la différence,
Mon œuvre n'est plus en moi, je vous l'ai toute donnée.
Hommes, mes bien-aimés, je ne puis rien dans vos malheurs,
Je n'ai pu que vous donner votre courage et les larmes,
C'est la preuve chaleureuse de l'existence de Dieu.
L'humidité de votre âme c'est ce qui vous reste de moi.
Je n'ai rien pu faire d'autre.
Je ne puis rien pour la mère dont va s'éteindre le fils
Sinon vous faire allumer, chandelles de l'espérance.
S'il n'en était pas ainsi, est-ce que vous connaîtriez,
Petits lits mal défendus, la paralysie des enfants.
Je suis coupé de mon œuvre,
Ce qui est fini est lointain et s'éloigne chaque jour.

God's Sadness

(God speaks)

I see you coming and going upon the trembling of the Earth as in the world's first days, but great is the difference, my work is no longer within me, I have given it entirely to you. Men, my beloved, I am powerless in your misfortunes, I could give you only tears and your courage, which are the warm evidence of God's existence. The moisture in your soul is what you have left of me. I could do no more. I can do nothing for the mother whose son is going to die except to give light to you, candles of hope. If it were not so, would you know, you undefended little beds, the paralysis of children. I am cut off from my work, what is finished is far away and goes further

Quand la source descend du mont comment revenir là-
dessus?
Je ne sais pas plus vous parler qu'un potier ne parle à son
pot,
Des deux il en est un de sourd, l'autre muet devant son
œuvre
Et je vous vois avancer vers d'aveuglants précipices
Sans pouvoir vous les nommer,
Et je ne peux vous souffler comment il faudrait s'y prendre,
Il faut vous en tirer tout seuls comme des orphelins dans la
neige.
Et je me dis chaque jour au delà d'un grand silence:
'Encore un qui fait de travers ce qu'il pourrait faire comme
il faut,
Encore un qui fait un faux pas pour ne pas regarder où il
doit.
Et cet autre qui se penche beaucoup trop sur son balcon,
Oubliant la pesanteur,
Et celui-là qui n'a pas vérifié son moteur,
Adieu avion, adieu homme!'
Je ne puis plus rien pour vous, hélas si je me répète
C'est à force d'en souffrir.
Je suis un souvenir qui descend, vous vivez dans un

still each day. When the brook runs down from the mountain can there be any going back? I can no more speak to you than a potter can speak to his pot, of the two one is deaf, the other dumb before his handiwork and I see you advancing towards blinding precipices and cannot even identify them for you, and I cannot hint to you how you should set about them, you must get yourselves out of trouble alone like orphans in the snow. And I tell myself each day beyond a vast silence: 'There's another doing all wrong what he could do right, another stumbling by not looking where he should. And here's another leaning much too far over his balcony, forgetting gravity, and that one who hasn't checked his engine, farewell aeroplane, farewell man!' I can do no more for you, alas, if I repeat myself it is through enduring it. I am a memory descending,

souvenir,
L'espoir qui gravit vos collines, vous vivez dans une espérance.
Secoué par les prières et les blasphèmes des hommes,
Je suis partout à la fois et ne peux pas me montrer,
Sans bouger je déambule et je vais de ciel en ciel,
Je suis l'errant en soi-même, et le grouillant solitaire,
Habitué des lointains, je suis très loin de moi-même,
Je m'égare au fond de moi comme un enfant dans les bois,
Je m'appelle, je me hale, je me tire vers mon centre.
Homme, si je t'ai créé c'est pour y voir un peu clair
Et pour vivre dans un corps moi qui n'ai mains ni visage.
Je veux te remercier de faire avec sérieux
Tout ce qui n'aura qu'un temps sur la Terre bien-aimée,
O mon enfant, mon chéri, ô courage de ton Dieu,
Mon fils qui t'en es allé courir le monde à ma place
A l'avant-garde de moi dans ton corps si vulnérable
Avec sa grande misère. Pas un petit coin de peau
Où ne puisse se former la profonde pourriture.
Chacun de vous sait faire un mort sans avoir eu besoin d'apprendre,

you are living in a memory, the hope that climbs your hillsides, you are living in expectation. Shaken by the prayers and the blasphemies of men, I am everywhere at once and cannot show myself, without moving I move about and pass from heaven to heaven, I am the wanderer within myself and the inwardly teeming hermit, familiar with distances, I am very distant from myself, I stray deep within myself like a child in the woods, I call myself, I haul myself in and draw myself towards my centre. Man, if I created you it was to see it more clearly and to live in a body, I who have neither hands nor face. I want to thank you for doing earnestly all that will have only a brief time on the beloved earth, O my child, my precious one, O courage given by your God, my son, you have gone roaming the world in my place ahead of me in your so vulnerable body with its great poverty. Not a small parcel of skin where deep decay may not form. Each of you knows how

Un mort parfait qu'on peut tourner et retourner dans tous les sens,
Où il n'y a rien à redire.
Dieu vous survit, lui seul survit entouré par un grand massacre
D'hommes, de femmes et d'enfants
Même vivants, vous mourez un peu continuellement
Arrangez-vous avec la vie, avec vos tremblantes amours.
Vous avez un cerveau, des doigts pour faire le monde à votre goût,
Vous avez des facilités pour faire vivre la raison
Et la folie en votre cage,
Vous avez tous les animaux qui forment la Création,
Vous pouvez courir et nager comme le chien et le poisson,
Avancer comme le tigre ou comme l'agneau de huit jours,
Vous pouvez vous donner la mort comme le renne, le scorpion,
Et moi je reste l'invisible, l'introuvable sur la Terre,
Ayez pitié de votre Dieu qui n'a pas su vous rendre heureux,
Petites parcelles de moi, ô palpitantes étincelles,
Je ne vous offre qu'un brasier où vous retrouverez du feu.

to be a dead man without the need to learn, a perfect corpse that can be rolled and rolled again in all directions, in which no fault can be found. God outlives you, he alone survives in the midst of a great massacre of men, women and children, even alive, you are constantly dying a little, make your peace with life, with your trembling loves. You have a brain, fingers to fashion the world to your taste, you have talents to give life to reason and madness within your shell, you have all the animals that form Creation, you can run and swim like the dog and the fish, move forward like the tiger or the week-old lamb, you can bring death to yourself like the reindeer, the scorpion, yet I remain the invisible one, undiscoverable on the Earth, have pity on your God who could not make you happy, small fragments of myself, O throbbing sparks, I offer you only a furnace where you will find fire once again.

Nuit en moi...

Nuit en moi, nuit au dehors,
Elles risquent leurs étoiles,
Les mêlant sans le savoir.
Et je fais force de rames
Entre ces nuits coutumières,
Puis je m'arrête et regarde.
Comme je me vois de loin!
Je ne suis qu'un frêle point
Qui bat vite et qui respire
Sur l'eau profonde entourante.
La nuit me tâte le corps
Et me dit de bonne prise.
Mais laquelle des deux nuits,
Du dehors ou du dedans?
L'ombre est une et circulante,
Le ciel, le sang ne font qu'un.
Depuis longtemps disparu,
Je discerne mon sillage
A grande peine étoilé.

Night within me ...

Night within me, night without, they venture their stars, mingling them without knowing. And I row hard between these familiar nights, then I stop and gaze. How I see myself from afar! I am merely a fragile speck beating rapidly and breathing upon the deep surrounding water. Night fingers my body and pronounces me fair game. But which of the two nights, the outer or the inner? The darkness is a unity and circulates, the sky and the blood are as one. Long since vanished, I perceive my wake laboriously hung with stars.

Plein Ciel

J'avais un cheval
Dans un champ de ciel
Et je m'enfonçais
Dans le jour ardent.
Rien ne m'arrêtait
J'allais sans savoir,
C'était un navire
Plutôt qu'un cheval,
C'était un désir
Plutôt qu'un navire,
C'était un cheval
Comme on n'en voit pas,
Tête de coursier,
Robe de délire,
Un vent qui hennit
En se répandant.
Je montais toujours
Et faisais des signes:
'Suivez mon chemin,
Vous pouvez venir,
Mes meilleurs amis,
La route est sereine,
Le ciel est ouvert.

Open Sky

I had a horse in a field of sky and I plunged into the burning daylight. Nothing stopped me, on I went without knowledge, it was a ship rather than a horse, it was a desire rather than a ship, it was a horse such as you never saw, the head of a charger, the coat of ecstasy, a wind that neighed as it launched itself forth. I rode on up and beckoned: 'Follow my path, you can come, my finest friends, the way is tranquil, the heavens

Mais qui parle ainsi?
Je me perds de vue
Dans cette altitude,
Me distinguez-vous,
Je suis celui qui
Parlait tout à l'heure,
Suis-je encor celui
Qui parle à présent,
Vous-mêmes, amis,
Etes-vous les mêmes?
L'un efface l'autre
Et change en montant.'

are open. But who speaks these words? I am losing sight of myself at this height, can you make me out, I am the one who was speaking just now, am I still the one who is speaking now, and you, friends, are you the same? The one obliterates the other and changes as it rides higher.'

1940

... Nous sommes très loin en nous-mêmes
Avec la France dans les bras,
Chacun se croit seul avec elle
Et pense qu'on ne le voit pas.

Chacun est plein de gaucherie
Devant un bien si précieux,
Est-ce donc elle, la patrie,
Ce corps à la face des cieux?

Chacun la tient à sa façon
Dans une étreinte sans mesure
Et se mire dans sa figure
Comme au miroir le plus profond.

1940

... We are very deep within ourselves with France in our arms, each man in his mind is alone with her and thinks he is unseen.

Each man is filled with awkwardness before such a treasured possession, can this be her, our homeland, this body in the face of the heavens?

Each man holds her in his own way in a measureless embrace and sees himself reflected in her face as in the deepest mirror.

Saint-John Perse
(1887–1975)

This is the pseudonym of Marie-René Alexis Saint-Léger Léger. Born in the French West Indies, an environment whose influence can be seen in the luxuriant quality of his imagery, he came to France as a student and formed an important friendship with Claudel. Even before this meeting, however, Perse had found the characteristic style that he would maintain, and that would be so much admired by T. S. Eliot and other poets.

In 1914 he began what was to be a brilliant diplomatic career, and he rose eventually to the post of secretary-general at the Quai d'Orsay. In 1940 he refused the post of Ambassador to Washington, and was deprived of his citizenship and possessions by the Vichy government. Several works were destroyed by German soldiers searching his apartment in Paris.

His pseudonym sustained the distinction between his diplomatic and literary careers, and his double identity was not well known until the 1940s. During the war he lived in the USA, working as a consultant at the Library of Congress, and for a time unable to write through his sense of loss, exile and outrage. A private man, seen by many as cold and haughty, Perse had never been part of the Parisian literary scene, but came to appreciate the interest his work received in America, especially among poets of that country. He remained there until 1957, and continued to divide his time between France and the USA until his death. His Nobel Prize award in 1960 attracted greater public attention to a body of work previously regarded as rather esoteric, composed by a 'poets' poet'.

Perse is a spiritual poet in touch with the earth's elemental forces. He writes mainly in Claudelian '*versets*', yet although Perse's landscapes are timeless and literary and his images have spatial freedom, he is more concrete than Claudel. The world is celebrated and ennobled by an enchanted, solitary perceiver (he uses a number of personae), who is both ecstatic and fully in control as he weaves language into a complex symphony of sound-patterns, phrasing, rhythm, parentheses and pauses. Language itself is simultaneously ennobled and celebrated. Poetry here affirms itself intensely as its own justification, structured mysteriously by associations of image and sound that are often elliptical and engender a sense that the reader is addressing a strong and pure but only partly elucidated mythology. This poetry is epic, lyric and dramatic, with no ideological colouring and little contemporary reference, and records a quest for communion with the world within the medium of the blank page, or on the shores of exile, or in an America of the spirit. There is always a sense of both dynamic absorption and spatial expansion in a timeless landscape, in which for Perse himself: 'The very function of the poet is to integrate himself into the thing ... taking possession of it, always in a very active way, in its innermost movement and very substance.'

Major works: *Eloges* 1911, *Anabase* 1924, *Exil* 1945, *Pluies* 1942, *Neiges* 1944, *Vents* 1946, *Amers* 1957, *Chronique* 1959, *Oiseaux* 1963, *Chanté par celle qui fut là* 1969, *Chant pour un Equinoxe* 1975.

Eloges

II

J'ai aimé un cheval – qui était-ce? – il m'a bien regardé de face, sous ses mèches.

Les trous vivants de ses narines étaient deux choses belles à voir – avec ce trou vivant qui gonfle au-dessus de chaque œil.

Quand il avait couru, il suait: c'est briller! – et j'ai pressé des lunes à ses flancs sous mes genoux d'enfant...

J'ai aimé un cheval – qui était-ce? – et parfois (car une bête sait mieux quelles forces nous vantent)

il levait à ses dieux une tête d'airain: soufflante, sillonnée d'un pétiole de veines.

Praises

II

I loved a horse – who was he? – he looked me full in the face, from under his forelock.

The living holes of his nostrils were two things beautiful to see – with that living hole that swells above each eye.

When he had been running, he would sweat: in other words he shone! – and I pressed moons on his flanks beneath my child's knees ...

I loved a horse – who was he? – and sometimes (for an animal knows better what forces praise us)

he would raise to his gods a head of bronze: breathing hard, furrowed with a petiole of veins.

XIV

Silencieusement va la sève et débouche aux rives minces de la feuille.

Voici d'un ciel de paille où lancer, ô lancer! à tour de bras la torche!

Pour moi, j'ai retiré mes pieds.

O mes amis où êtes-vous que je ne connais pas?...Ne verrez-vous cela aussi?...des havres crépitants, de belles eaux de cuivre mol où midi émietteur de cymbales troue l'ardeur de son puits...O c'est l'heure

XIV

Silently the sap flows and emerges on the slender shores of the leaf.

See the coming of a sky of straw into which to hurl, O hurl! with all one's might the torch!

As for me, I have drawn back my feet.

O my friends where are you whom I do not know? ... Will you not see that too? ... crackling harbours, beautiful waters of soft copper where noon, crumbler of cymbals, pierces the ardour of its well ... O it is the time

où dans les villes surchauffées, au fond des cours gluantes sous les treilles glacées, l'eau coule aux bassins clos violée des roses vertes de midi...et l'eau nue est pareille à la pulpe d'un songe, et le Songeur est couché là, et il tient au plafond son œil d'or qui guerroie...

Et l'enfant qui revient de l'école des Pères, affectueux longeant l'affection des Murs qui sentent le pain chaud, voit au bout de la rue où il tourne

la mer déserte plus bruyante qu'une criée aux poissons. Et les boucauts de sucre coulent, aux Quais de marcassite peints, à grands ramages, de pétrole

et des nègres porteurs de bêtes écorchées s'agenouillent aux faïences des Boucheries Modèles, déchargeant un faix d'os et d'ahan,

when in the scorched cities, deep in glutinous courtyards beneath chill arbours, the water flows in the sealed pools violated by the green roses of noon ... and the naked water is like the pulp of a dream, and the Dreamer is lying there, and he fixes on the ceiling his bellicose golden eye ...

And the child coming home from the Fathers' school, tenderly sidling along the tenderness of the Walls that smell of warm bread, sees at the end of the street where he turns

the empty sea noisier than a fish auction. And the casks of sugar ooze, on the Quays of marcassite painted with fuel-oil in great floral designs,

and negroes carrying skinned animals kneel at the earthenware slabs of the Model Butchers, discharging a burden of bones and toil,

et au rond-point de la Halle de bronze, haute demeure courroucée où pendent les poissons et qu'on entend chanter dans sa feuille de fer, un homme glabre, en cotonnade jaune, pousse un cri: je suis Dieu! et d'autres: il est fou!

et un autre envahi par le goût de tuer se met en marche vers le Château-d'Eau avec trois billes de poison: rose, verte, indigo.

Pour moi, j'ai retiré mes pieds.

and at the centre of the bronze Market Hall, a tall irascible house where fishes hang and which can be heard singing in its sheet of tin, a hairless man in yellow cotton cloth utters a cry: I am God! and others: he is insane!

and another filled with the taste for killing starts walking towards the Water-Tower with three balls of poison: pink, green, indigo.

As for me, I have drawn back my feet.

Anabase VII

Nous n'habiterons pas toujours ces terres jaunes, notre délice...

L'Eté plus vaste que l'Empire suspend aux tables de l'espace plusieurs étages de climats. La terre vaste sur son aire roule à pleins bords sa braise pâle sous les cendres – Couleur de soufre, de miel, couleur de choses immortelles, toute la terre aux herbes s'allumant aux pailles de l'autre hiver – et de l'éponge verte d'un seul arbre le ciel tire son suc violet.

Anabasis VII[1]

We shall not live forever in these yellow lands, our place of pleasure ...

The Summer vaster than the Empire suspends in the tables of space several strata of climate. The vast earth full to the brim turns on its surface its pale embers under the ashes – Sulphur colour, honey colour, colour of immortal things, the whole grassy earth catching fire from the straw of last winter – and from the green sponge of a solitary tree the sky draws its violet juice.

[1]Anabasis: a large-scale military advance; specifically, the expedition across Asia Minor (401 B.C.), made by Greek mercenaries led by Cyrus the Younger of Persia, as described by Xenophon.

Un lieu de pierres à mica! Pas une graine pure dans les barbes du vent. Et la lumière comme une huile. – De la fissure des paupières au fil des cimes m'unissant, je sais la pierre tachée d'ouies, les essaims du silence aux ruches de lumière; et mon cœur prend souci d'une famille d'acridiens...

Chamelles douces sous la tonte, cousues de mauves cicatrices, que les collines s'acheminent sous les données du ciel agraire – qu'elles cheminent en silence sur les incandescences pâles de la plaine; et s'agenouillent à la fin, dans la fumée des songes, là où les peuples s'abolissent aux poudres mortes de la terre.

Ce sont de grandes lignes calmes qui s'en vont à des bleuissements de vignes improbables. La terre en plus d'un point mûrit les violettes de l'orage; et ces fumées de sable qui s'élèvent au lieu des fleuves morts, comme des pans de siècles en voyage...

A place of stones of mica! Not a pure grain in the barbs of the wind. And the light like oil. – From the eyelids' crack to the grain of the hilltops I join myself, I know the stones stained with fish-gills, the swarms of silence in the hives of light; and my heart is mindful of a family of locusts ...

Gentle she-camels beneath the shearing, sewn with mauve scars, let the hills set out under the known quantities of the agrarian sky – let them march in silence over the pale incandescences of the plain; and kneel at last, in the smoke of dreams, there where the peoples annihilate themselves in the dead dusts of the earth.

These are great calm lines that fade into the growing blue of improbable vines. The earth in more than one place ripens the violets of the storm; and these sandsmokes that rise above the dead river courses, like coat-tails of travelling centuries ...

A voix plus basse pour les morts, à voix plus basse dans le jour. Tant de douceur au cœur de l'homme, se peut-il qu'elle faille à trouver sa mesure?... 'Je vous parle, mon âme! – mon âme tout enténébrée d'un parfum de cheval!' Et quelques grands oiseaux de terre, naviguant en Ouest, sont de bons mimes de nos oiseaux de mer.

A l'orient du ciel si pâle, comme un lieu saint scellé des linges de l'aveugle, des nuées calmes se disposent, où tournent les cancers du camphre et de la corne... Fumées qu'un souffle nous dispute! la terre tout attente en ses barbes d'insectes, la terre enfante des merveilles!...

In a lower voice for the dead, in a lower voice by day. So much gentleness in the heart of man, can it fail to find its measure?... 'I speak to you, my soul! – my soul darkened by a scent of horses!' And several great land birds, voyaging westwards, are a good likeness of our ocean birds.

In the east of the sky so pale, like a holy place sealed by the blind man's linen, calm clouds align themselves, where the cancers of camphor and horn revolve ... Smoke for which a breath of wind contends with us! the earth poised expectantly in its insect barbs, the earth gives birth to wonders!

Et à midi, quand l'arbre jujubier fait éclater l'assise des tombeaux, l'homme clôt ses paupières et rafraîchit sa nuque dans les âges… Cavaleries du songe au lieu des poudres mortes, ô routes vaines qu'échevèle un souffle jusqu'à nous! où trouver, où trouver les guerriers qui garderont les fleuves dans leurs noces?

Au bruit des grandes eaux en marche sur la terre, tout le sel de la terre tressaille dans les songes. Et soudain, ha! soudain que nous veulent ces voix? Levez un peuple de miroirs sur l'ossuaire des fleuves, qu'ils interjettent appel dans la suite des siècles! Levez des pierres à ma gloire, levez des pierres au silence, et à la garde de ces lieux les cavaleries de bronze vert sur de vastes chaussées!…

(L'ombre d'un grand oiseau me passe sur la face.)

And at noon, when the jujube tree bursts the tombstones, man closes his eyelids and cools his neck in the ages … Dream cavalries in the place of dead dusts, O vain roads dishevelled by a breath and carried to us! where to find, where to find the warriors who will watch over the rivers in their nuptials?

At the sound of the great waters marching over the earth, all the salt of the earth shudders in dreams. And suddenly, ah! suddenly what do these voices want with us? Raise up a multitude of mirrors on the ossuary of the rivers, let them lodge their appeal in the sequence of the centuries! Raise stones to my glory, raise stones to silence, and to guard these places raise cavalries of green bronze on vast causeways! …

(The shadow of a great bird passes over my face.)

Exil II

A nulles rives dédiée, à nulles pages confiée la pure amorce de ce chant…
D'autres saisissent dans les temples la corne peinte des autels:
Ma gloire est sur les sables! ma gloire est sur les sables!
… Et ce n'est point errer, ô Pérégrin,
Que de convoiter l'aire la plus nue pour assembler aux syrtes de l'exil un grand poème né de rien, un grand poème fait de rien …
Sifflez, ô frondes par le monde, chantez, ô conques sur les eaux!
J'ai fondé sur l'abîme et l'embrun et la fumée des sables.
Je me coucherai dans les citernes et dans les vaisseaux creux,
En tous lieux vains et fades où gît le goût de la grandeur.

Exile II

Dedicated to no shores, imparted to no pages the pure beginning of this song … Others grasp in the temples the painted altar horn: My glory is on the sands! my glory is on the sands! … And it is not to err, O Peregrine, to covet the most naked tract for assembling on the shifting sands of exile a great poem born of nothing, a great poem made from nothing … Whistle, O slings across the world, sing, O conches on the waters! I have built upon the abyss and the spindrift and the sandsmoke. I will lie down in the cisterns and in the hollow vessels, in all stale and empty places where lies the taste of greatness.

'... Moins de souffles flattaient la famille des Jules: moins d'alliances assistaient les grandes castes de prêtrise.

Où vont les sables à leur chant s'en vont les Princes de l'exil,

Où furent les voiles haut tendues s'en va l'épave plus soyeuse qu'un songe de luthier,

Où furent les grandes actions de guerre déjà blanchit la mâchoire d'âne,

Et la mer à la ronde roule son bruit de crânes sur les grèves,

Et que toutes choses au monde lui soient vaines, c'est ce qu'un soir, au bord du monde, nous contèrent

Les milices du vent dans les sables d'exil....'

'... Fewer breezes flattered the Julii; fewer alliances aided the great priesthood castes. Where the sands go in their song there go the Princes of exile, where there were tall taut sails there goes the wreck more silken than a lute-maker's dream, where there were great acts of war there lies whitening already the jawbone of an ass, and the sea all around rolls her sound of skulls on the shores, and that all things in the world to her are vain, that is what we heard one evening, at the world's edge, from the wind's militias in the sands of exile ...'

Sagesse de l'écume, ô pestilences de l'esprit dans la crépitation du sel et le lait de chaux vive!

Une science m'échoit aux sévices de l'âme ... Le vent nous conte ses flibustes, le vent nous conte ses méprises!

Comme le Cavalier, la corde au poing, à l'entrée du désert,

J'épie au cirque le plus vaste l'élancement des signes les plus fastes.

Et le matin pour nous mène son doigt d'augure parmi de saintes écritures.

L'exil n'est point d'hier! l'exil n'est point d'hier! 'O vestiges, ô prémisses',

Dit l'Etranger parmi les sables, 'toute chose au monde m'est nouvelle!...' Et la naissance de son chant ne lui est pas moins étrangère.

Wisdom of the foam, O plagues of the mind in the crackling of the salt and the milk of quicklime! A knowledge falls to me amid the cruelties of the soul ... The wind tells us its piracies, the wind tells us its errors! Like the Horseman, rope in hand, at the gateway to the desert, I watch in the most immense arena the darting forth of the signs of most auspicious omen. And the morning for our sake moves its prophetic finger among sacred writings. Exile is not of yesterday! exile is not of yesterday! 'O vestiges, O premises,' says the Stranger amid the sands, 'all things in the world are new to me!...' And the birth of his song is no less alien to him.

Neiges IV

Seul à faire le compte, du haut de cette chambre d'angle qu'environne un Océan de neiges. – Hôte précaire de l'instant, homme sans preuve ni témoin, détacherai-je mon lit bas comme une pirogue de sa crique? ... Ceux qui campent chaque jour plus loin du lieu de leur naissance, ceux qui tirent chaque jour leur barque sur d'autres rives, savent mieux chaque jour le cours des choses illisibles; et remontant les fleuves vers leur source, entre les vertes apparences, ils sont gagnés soudain de cet éclat sévère où toute langue perd ses armes.

Snows IV

I, lone accountant, from the height of this corner room encompassed in an Ocean of snows.... Precarious guest of the moment, man without evidence or witness, shall I unmoor my low bed like a dug-out canoe from its cove? ... Those who pitch camp farther each day from their birthplace, those who haul in their boat each day on other banks, know better each day the course of illegible things; and going upstream towards the rivers' source, amid the green appearances, they are seized suddenly in that harsh glare where all language loses its weapons.

Ainsi l'homme mi-nu sur l'Océan des neiges, rompant soudain l'immense libration, poursuit un singulier dessein où les mots n'ont plus prise. Epouse du monde ma présence, épouse du monde ma prudence! ... Et du côté des eaux premières me retournant avec le jour, comme le voyageur, à la néoménie, dont la conduite est incertaine et la démarche est aberrante, voici que j'ai dessein d'errer parmi les plus vieilles couches du langage, parmi les plus hautes tranches phonétiques: jusqu'à des langues très lointaines, jusqu'à des langues très entières et très parcimonieuses,

Thus man half-naked on the Ocean of the snows, fracturing suddenly the vast libration, pursues a singular purpose in which words have no more hold. Spouse of the world my presence, spouse of the world my caution! ... And turning with the day towards the primeval waters, like the traveller, at new moon, whose course is uncertain and whose step is aberrant, now it is my design to wander among the oldest layers of language, among the most elevated phonetic strata: as far as very distant languages, as far as very complete and very parsimonious languages,

comme ces langues dravidiennes qui n'eurent pas de mots distincts pour 'hier' et pour 'demain'... Venez et nous suivez, qui n'avons mots à dire: nous remontons ce pur délice sans graphie où court l'antique phrase humaine; nous nous mouvons parmi de claires élisions, des résidus d'anciens préfixes ayant perdu leur initiale, et devançant les beaux travaux de linguistique, nous nous frayons nos voies nouvelles jusqu'à ces locutions inouïes, où l'aspiration recule au delà des voyelles et la modulation du souffle se propage, au gré de telles labiales mi-sonores, en quête de pures finales vocaliques.

like those Dravidian languages which had no distinct words for 'yesterday' and for 'tomorrow' ... Come and follow us, who have no words to say: we are ascending that pure unwritten delight where runs the ancient human phrase; we move among bright elisions, residues of old prefixes that have lost their initial, and preceding the fine works of linguistics, we carve out our new roads to those unprecedented locutions where aspiration withdraws beyond vowels and the modulation of the breath is diffused at the will of certain half-sounded labials, in search of pure vocalic finals.

... Et ce fut au matin, sous le plus pur vocable, un beau pays sans haine ni lésine, un lieu de grâce et de merci pour la montée des sûrs présages de l'esprit; et comme un grand *Ave* de grâce sur nos pas, la grande roseraie blanche de toutes neiges à la ronde ... Fraîcheur d'ombelles, de corymbes, fraîcheur d'arille sous la fève, ha! tant d'azymes encore aux lèvres de l'errant! ...Quelle flore nouvelle, en lieu plus libre, nous absout de la fleur et du fruit? Quelle navette d'os aux mains des femmes de grand âge, quelle amande d'ivoire aux mains des femmes de jeune âge

And it was in the morning, beneath the purest of word-forms, a beautiful country without hatred or meanness, a place of grace and of mercy for the ascension of the unerring presages of the mind; and like a great *Ave* of grace on our path, the great white rose-garden of all the encircling snows ... Freshness of umbels, of corymbs, freshness of aril under the bean, ah! so many unleavened wafers still on the lips of the wanderer! ... What new flora, in a freer place, absolves us from the flower and from the fruit? What bone shuttle in the hands of very aged women, what ivory almond in the hands of very young women

nous tissera linge plus frais pour la brûlure des vivants? … Epouse du monde notre patience, épouse du monde notre attente! … Ah! tout l'hièble du songe à même notre visage! Et nous ravisse encore, ô monde! ta fraîche haleine de mensonge! … Là où les fleuves encore sont guéables, là où les neiges encore sont guéables, nous passerons ce soir une âme non guéable … Et au delà sont les grands lés du songe, et tout ce bien fongible où l'être engage sa fortune…

★

Désormais cette page où plus rien ne s'inscrit.

will weave us cooler linen for the burn of the living? … Spouse of the world our patience, spouse of the world our expectation! … Ah! all the dwarf-elder of dream in our very faces! And once again, O world, may your cool breath of deceit ravish us! There where the rivers are still fordable, there where the snows are still fordable, we shall ferry across this night an unfordable soul … And beyond are the great towpaths[1] of dream, and all that fungible wealth in which man pledges his fortune …

★

Henceforth this page where nothing more is written.

[1] *un lé* also means a breadth of linen.

Vents: Chant II, i

... Des Terres neuves, par là-bas, dans un très haut parfum d'humus et de feuillages,

Des terres neuves, par là-bas, sous l'allongement des ombres les plus vastes de ce monde,

Toute la terre aux arbres, par là-bas, sur fond de vignes noires, comme une Bible d'ombre et de fraîcheur dans le déroulement des plus beaux textes de ce monde.

Et c'est naissance encore de prodiges, fraîcheur et source de fraîcheur au front de l'homme mémorable.

Et c'est un goût de choses antérieures, comme aux grands Titres préalables l'évocation des sources et des gloses,

Comme aux grands Livres de Mécènes les grandes pages liminaires – la dédicace au Prince, et l'Avant-dire, et le Propos du Préfacier.

Winds: Canto II, i

... New found lands, out there, in a superior fragrance of humus and foliage, new found lands, out there, beneath the lengthening of this world's most expansive shadows, all the land given over to trees, out there, against its background of black vines, like a Bible of shadow and freshness in the unfolding of this world's most beautiful texts.

And there is yet more birth of wonders, freshness and source of freshness on the brow of man who is noteworthy. And there is a taste of things anterior, like the evocation of sources and commentaries for the great preliminary Titles, like the great pages that introduce the Books of Maecenas[1] – the dedication to the Prince, and the Foreword, and the Preface.

[1]Maecenas: a rich patron of Virgil and Horace, and a minor author in his own right.

... Des terres neuves, par là-haut, comme un parfum puissant de grandes femmes mûrissantes,

Des terres neuves, par là-haut, sous la montée des hommes de tout âge, chantant l'insigne mésalliance,

Toute la terre aux arbres, par là-haut, dans le balancement de ses plus beaux ombrages, ouvrant sa tresse la plus noire et l'ornement grandiose de sa plume, comme un parfum de chair nubile et forte au lit des plus beaux êtres de ce monde.

Et c'est une fraîcheur d'eaux libres et d'ombrages, pour la montée des hommes de tout âge, chantant l'insigne mésalliance,

Et c'est une fraîcheur de terres en bas âge, comme un parfum des choses de toujours, de ce côté des choses de toujours,

Et comme un songe prénuptial où l'homme encore tient son rang, à la lisière d'un autre âge, interprétant la feuille noire et les arborescences du silence dans de plus vastes syllabaires.

... New found lands, up there, like a powerful perfume of tall women ripening, new found lands, up there, beneath the ascent of men of every age, singing the conspicuous misalliance, all the land given over to tress, up there, in the swaying of its most beautiful shades, opening its blackest tress and the grandiose ornament of its plumage, like a perfume of flesh nubile and strong in the bed of this world's most beautiful beings.

And there is a freshness of free waters and of shades, for the ascent of men of every age, singing the conspicuous misalliance, and there is a freshness of lands in infancy, like a scent of everlasting things, on this side of everlasting things, and like a prenuptial dream in which man still holds his rank, on the threshold of another age, interpreting the black leaf and the arborescences of silence in vaster syllabaries.

Toute la terre nouvelle par là-haut, sous son blason d'orage, portant cimier de filles blondes et l'empennage du Sachem,

Toute la terre nubile et forte, au pas de l'Etranger, ouvrant sa fable de grandeur aux songes et fastes d'un autre âge,

Et la terre à longs traits, sur ses plus longues laisses, courant, de mer à mer, à de plus hautes écritures, dans le déroulement lointain des plus beaux textes de ce monde.

★

Là nous allions, la face en Ouest, au grondement des eaux nouvelles. Et c'est naissance encore de prodiges sur la terre des hommes. Et ce n'est pas assez de toutes vos bêtes peintes, Audubon! qu'il ne m'y faille encore mêler quelques espèces disparues: le Ramier migrateur, le Courlis boréal et le Grand Auk...

Là nous allions, de houle en houle, sur les degrés de l'Ouest. Et la nuit embaumait les sels noirs de la terre, dès la sortie des Villes vers les pailles, parmi la chair tavelée des

All the new land up there, beneath its stormy heraldry, wearing the crest of golden-haired girls and the feathers of the Sachem, all the strong and nubile land, in the steps of the Stranger, opening up its fable of magnitude to the dreams and pageantries of another age. And the earth with its long strokes, on its longest tirades, running, from sea to sea, to loftier scriptures, in the distant unfolding of this world's most beautiful texts.

★

There were we going, facing westward, to the roaring of the new waters. And there is yet more birth of wonders on the land of men. And all your painted creatures are not sufficient, Audubon! that I must not add to them some vanished species: the Passenger Pigeon, the Northern Curlew and the Greak Auk ... There were we going, from swell to swell, over the Western degrees. And the night was fragrant with the black salts of the land, from the outskirts of the Cities towards the straw-fields,

femmes de plein air. Et les femmes étaient grandes, au goût de seigles et d'agrumes et de froments moulés à l'image de leur corps.

Et nous vous dérobions, ô filles, à sortie des salles, ce mouvement encore du soir dans vos chevelures libres – tout ce parfum d'essence et de sécheresse, votre aura, comme une fulguration d'ailleurs... Et vos jambes étaient longues et telles qu'elles nous surprennent en songe, sur les sables, dans l'allongement des feux du soir ... La nuit qui chante aux lamineries des Villes n'étire pas chiffre plus pur pour les ferronneries d'un très haut style.

amid the freckled flesh of open-air women. And the women were tall, with the taste of rye and citrus and of wheat formed in the image of their bodies. And we stole from you, O girls emerging from the halls, even that stir of evening in your unconfined hair – all that scent of attar and of dryness, your aura, like a flash of lightning from another place ... And your legs were long and such that they surprise us in dreams, on the sands, in the lengthening of the fires of evening ... The night singing in the rolling-mills of the Cities draws forth no purer cipher for the ironwork of an elevated style.

Et qui donc a dormi cette nuit? Les grands rapides sont passés, courant aux fosses d'un autre âge avec leur provision de glace pour cinq jours. Ils s'en allaient contre le vent, bandés de métal blanc, comme des athlètes vieillissants. Et tant d'avions les prirent en chasse, sur leurs cris! ...

Les fleuves croissent dans leurs crues! Et la fusée des routes vers l'amont nous tienne hors de souffle! ... Les Villes à sens unique tirent leur charge à bout de rues. Et c'est ruée encore de filles neuves à l'An neuf, portant, sous le nylon, l'amande fraîche de leur sexe.

Et c'est messages sur tous fils, et c'est merveilles sur toutes ondes. Et c'est d'un même mouvement à tout ce mouvement lié, que mon poème encore dans le vent, de ville en ville et fleuve en fleuve, court aux plus vastes houles de la terre, épouses elles-mêmes et filles d'autres houles...

And who then has slept this night? The great expresses have gone by, racing to the chasms of another age with their supply of ice for five days. They were running against the wind, strapped with white metal, like ageing athletes. And so many aeroplanes, upon their cries, gave chase!... Let the rivers swell in their flood! And may the roads that rocket upstream hold us breathless!... The one-way Cities haul their loads to the streets' end. And once more there is a rush of new girls to the new Year, wearing, under the nylon, the fresh almond of their sex. And there are messages on every wire, marvels on every wave. And it is with an identical movement joined with all this movement that my poem in the wind, from city to city and river to river, roves still upon the most expansive surges of the earth, themselves the wives and daughters of other surges ...

Pierre-Jean Jouve
(1887–1976)

Jouve, like Perse, is a rather patrician figure, shunning popular appeal in favour of a highly demanding, intellectual and spiritual conception of the poet's task, and for whom poetic language has a mystical and redemptive value. He is a strong influence on Bonnefoy and Emmanuel, and on David Gascoyne.

His early work was influenced by Baudelaire and Mallarmé, and Symbolist in character. He was then associated for a time with Jules Romains' 'Unanimist' school, with its cult of the crowd and the city and its emphasis on immediacy of sensation. Restlessness, though, was predominant in Jouve's early creative life as he searched for his true orientation.

In 1924–5, after a series of emotional and religious crises, he disowned all his work to that point, and embarked on a new creative enterprise which he would sustain with great consistency until his death.

Strongly influenced by Freud yet detached from the Surrealist movement, Jouve explores man's inner ambivalence with lucidity and honesty, in particular the battle between the erotic and self-destructive instincts. The difficulty of transcending man's state of sin, guilt and despair preoccupies him intensely, yet the search for redemption is motivated by a genuine faith in ultimate victory in his battle with evil. In that quest within his unconscious, he draws inspiration from Blake, St John of the Cross, St Theresa of Avila and from Shakespeare, whose *Macbeth* and *Romeo and Juliet* Jouve has translated.

In the feverish, incantatory verse of *Les Noces*, visions of harmony are glimpsed within a world of sin and disgust. An indissoluble link is created between flesh and spirit in which matter has a metaphysical value (note the importance of the physicality of Christ in 'Vrai Corps'). In *Sueur de Sang* the Freudian labyrinth is entered fully and the surging imagery is often very unpleasant, yet Jouve's conviction is that deliverance can come only through this dynamic and exorcizing experience of sin. The religious symbol of the Stag recurs, redeeming human monstrosity by its sacrificial death.

Another mythical figure, the dead woman 'Hélène', dominates in *Matière Céleste*. In her, love is sanctified through physical loss, and it is in this absence that love becomes perfect and transcends the profanity of life. It opens up divinity to the poet, albeit by a negative and tortuous route.

Later, Hélène will become a Jeanne d'Arc figurehead for the dead of France, in Jouve's highly personal and spiritual response to the Occupation. The German invasion is seen as a physical and moral scourging of France in which Hitler is the earthly representative of Satan. It is not applauded, but viewed in terms of another battle for purification, a crusade which France must win. Jouve's post-war works, in which he moves away from his tense, terse, repetitive style to a more Claudelian '*verset*', express some disillusionment with the state of 'liberated' Europe, and he withdraws into a mystical dialogue with language itself, a Segalen-influenced contemplation of objects, and meditative preparation for death. In the 1960s his importance in modern poetry was confirmed by a number of major literary prizes.

His volumes of poetry have been gathered as follows by Mercure de France:

Poesie I–IV: *Les Noces* 1925–31, *Sueur de Sang* 1933–5, *Matière Céleste* 1936–7, *Kyrie* 1938;

Poesie V, VI: *La Vierge de Paris* 1939–44, *Hymne* 1947;

Poesie VII–IX: *Diadème* 1949, *Ode* 1950, *Langue* 1952;

Poesie X, XI: *Mélodrame* 1956–8, *Moires* 1962–6.

Vallée de larmes

Trois lys jaunes
Sont sortis de terre entre plusieurs fonds noirs
D'averse abominable,
Image
De la satisfaction qu'éprouve Dieu.
D'autres iris bleus vinrent un autre jour
Et les chemins pareils aux serpents secs
Les entourent, les empêchent de s'enfuir
Car le matin n'est ni froid ni chaud ni clair ni ombre
Il est utile,
Et ce monde est bien l'endroit de la tentation.

Vale of Tears

Three yellow lilies have emerged from earth among several dark backgrounds of foul downpour, an image of the gratification felt by God. Other blue irises came on another day and the paths like dried-up snakes encircle them, prevent their flight for the morning is neither cold nor warm nor bright nor shadow It is expedient, and this world is truly the place of temptation.

Vrai Corps

Salut vrai corps de dieu. Salut Resplendissant
Corps de la chair engagé par la tombe et qui naît
Corps, ô Ruisselant de bontés et de chairs
Salut corps tout de jour!
Divinité aux très larges épaules
Enfantine et marchante, salut toute beauté,
Aux boucles, aux épines
Inouï corps très dur de la miséricorde,
Salut vrai corps de dieu éblouissant aux larmes
Qui renaît, salut vrai corps de l'homme
Enfanté du triple esprit par la charité.

True Body

Hail true divine body. Hail Resplendent body of flesh bound by the tomb and being born Body, O Flowing with goodness and with flesh Hail body all daylight! Most broad-shouldered childlike and striding deity, hail all beauty, with curls, with thorns most firm unprecedented body of mercy, hail true divine body dazzling to tears being reborn, hail true body of man begotten of the threefold spirit by charity.

Témoin des lieux insensés de mon cœur
Tu es né d'une vierge absolue et tu es né
Parce que Dieu avait posé les mains sur sa poitrine,
Et tu es né
Homme de nerfs et de douleur et de semence
Pour marcher sur la magnifique dalle de chagrin
Et ton flanc mort fut percé pour la preuve
Et jaillit sur l'obscur et extérieur nuage
Du sang avec de l'eau.

Sur le flanc la lèvre s'ouvre en méditant
Lèvre de la plaie mâle, et c'est la lèvre aussi
De la fille commune
Dont les cheveux nous éblouissent de long amour;
Elle baise les pieds
Verdâtres, décomposés comme la rose
Trop dévorée par la chaleur amoureuse du ciel d'en haut,
Et sur elle jaillit, sur l'extérieur nuage
Du sang avec de l'eau car tu étais né.

Witness of the demented places of my heart you were born of an absolute virgin and you were born because God had laid his hands upon her breast, and you were born a man of nerves and pain and seed to walk upon the magnificent stone slab of grief and your dead flank was pierced for proof and gushed upon the dark and outer cloud with blood and water.

On the flank the lip opens meditating The lip of the male wound, and it is the lip too of the common girl whose hair dazzles us with prolonged love; she kisses the greenish feet, decayed like the rose too much consumed by the loving heat of heaven on high, and upon her gushes, upon the outer cloud blood with water for you had been born.

Lorsque couchés sur le lit tiède de la mort
Tous les bijoux ôtés avec les œuvres
Tous les paysages décomposés
Tous les ciels noirs et tous les livres brûlés
Enfin nous approcherons avec majesté de nous-même,
Quand nous rejetterons les fleurs finales
Et les étoiles seront expliquées parmi notre âme,
Souris alors et donne un sourire de ton corps
Permets que nous te goûtions d'abord le jour de la mort
Qui est un grand jour de calme d'épousés,
Le monde heureux, les fils réconciliés.

When lying on the tepid bed of death All jewels discarded along with works all landscapes decomposed All skies black and all books burned we approach ourselves at last with majesty, when we cast off the final flowers and the stars will be elucidated within our soul, smile then and from your body give a smile Grant that we may taste you first on the day of death which is a great day of wedded peace, the world content, the sons reconciled.

L'Œil et la chevelure

Placé dans la longueur et fermé comme un puits
Sur le secret du moi, entre des moustaches
Pour toute éternité; c'est une bouche ouverte
Qui souffle un long drapeau de malheureux parfum
C'est un regard voilé
Qui prononce un vocabulaire ensanglanté.

Eye and Hair

Set lengthwise and closed like a well on the secret of the self, between hairy lips for all eternity; it is an open mouth breathing a long banner of doleful scent It is a veiled gaze that utters a vocabulary steeped in blood.

Lamentations au cerf

Sanglant comme la nuit, admirable en effroi, et sensible
        Sans bruit, tu meurs à notre approche.
Apparais sur le douloureux et le douteux
Si rapide impuissant de sperme et de sueur
Qu'ait été le chasseur; si coupable son
        Ombre et si faible l'amour
Qu'il avait! Apparais dans un corps
Pelage vrai et
        Chaud, toi qui passes la mort.
Oui toi dont les blessures
        Marquent les trous de notre vrai amour
A force de nos coups, apparais et reviens
Malgré l'amour, malgré que
        Crache la blessure.

Lamentations to the Stag

Bloody like the night, admirable in terror, and perceptible without sound, you die at our approach. Appear upon the ground of pain and doubt however swift impotent of sperm and sweat has been the hunter; however guilty his Shadow and however weak the love he had! Appear in a body a true and warm Pelt, you who are passing into death[1]. Yes you whose wounds Record the holes of our true love by the strength of our blows, appear and come again in spite of love, despite the Spitting of the wound.

[1]'You the carrier of death' is an alternative translation, but seems to run counter to the sense of the poem.

La Femme et la terre

Quand elle était, ce cœur était plus fort que la lumière
Son sang sous l'influence de la lune était plus ouvert
Que le sang répandu, et sa nuit plus obscure et velue
Que la nuit mais aussi scintillante et dure
Un sexe plus qu'une âme un astre plus qu'un sexe
Une église la chevelure la surmontait

Et vous qui dormez! autre granit et vieilles roses
Qui passez et disparaissez dans un bain pur
Sans faiblesse comme sans distance
Hautes hautes terres étranger azur

Pesez sur elle qui n'est plus
Dans le temps ni sein ni spasmes ni larmes
Qui s'est retournée sous la terre
Vers l'autre plus cendreux soleil.

Woman and Earth

When she was, this heart was stronger than light Her blood under the moon's influence was more open than spilt blood, and her night more mysterious and downy than the night but just as hard and scintillating A sex more than a soul a star more than a sex A church the hair was its crown

And you who sleep! other granite and old roses that pass and vanish in a pure pool without weakness as without distance High high lands foreign azure

Weigh upon her who is no longer in time's span breast nor spasms nor tears who has turned beneath the earth towards the other more ashen sun.

Je suis succession furieuse ...

Je suis succession furieuse des promesses
Le calme du tombeau la plastique des anges
Le sourire des putains est mon sourire
Je suis un envol migrateur des oiseaux
Sur un quartier désolé noir de grande ville
Un regard plein de hargne humide et de désir
Des plantations désertes
Dans les endroits abandonnés d'un corps
Aussi une beauté parfaitement confuse
Que la honte naturelle a développée
Je suis encore une ombre étendue sur la mer
Pareille à un drapeau un linge ou une main
Je suis un désespoir aussi sec que la pierre
C'est par le mal que je me sens spirituel.

I am a frenzied sequence ...

I am a frenzied sequence of promises The calm of the tomb the physical form of the angels The smile of the whores is my smile I am a migratory soaring of the birds over a dark desolate city neighbourhood A gaze full of damp surliness and of desire from the deserted groves in the forsaken places of a body and thus a beauty perfectly uncertain unfolded by natural shame I am beyond that a shadow spread across the sea like a banner a linen cloth or a hand I am a despair as dry as stone It is through evil that I sense my spiritual being.

Angles

Le soleil illumine un Sinaï lugubre
Et renaît sur l'étouffement des nations
Aux boulevards sanglants il enlève les brumes,
Que de têtes roulant aux feux du peloton!

Car nous avons choisi le fort parti des anges
Qui sortent de la profonde île d'ouragan
Et volant de partout répandent sur les fanges
Le poids d'acier mystique et les destructions.

Et dans l'apocalypse l'habitant léger
Devra servir les anges de punition
Pour dormir avant l'aube il habitera nu
Les quartiers d'incendie, pour être débandé

Angles

The sun shines on a mournful Sinai and is reborn over the suffocating of the nations On the blood-soaked rampart boulevards it clears the mists, so many heads rolling in the platoon fires!

For we have chosen the strong side of the angels who are emerging from the deep hurricane isle and who flying from all quarters spread over the mire the weight of mystic steel and forces of destruction.

And in the apocalypse the frivolous citizen will have to serve the angels of punishment To sleep before the dawn he will live naked in the districts of fire, to be discharged

Des armées du démon
Il enfoncera bien de son cœur à l'azur
Le clou de charité
Et il le maintiendra extrême noir et dur.

From the armies of the demon he will drive firmly from his heart into the blue sky the nail of charity and he will sustain it ultimate black and hard.

A soi-même

Ecris maintenant pour le ciel
Ecris pour la courbe du ciel
Et que nul plomb de lettre noire
N'enveloppe ton écriture

Ecris pour l'odeur et le vent
Ecris pour la feuille d'argent
Que nulle laide face humaine
N'ait regard connaissance haleine

Ecris pour le dieu et le feu
Ecris pour un amour de lieu
Et que rien de l'homme n'ait place
Au vide qu'une flamme glace.

For Oneself

Write now for the sky Write for the curve of the sky And may no black leaden letter shroud your writing

Write for the scent and the wind Write for the silver leaf May no ugly human face have sight consciousness breath

Write for the god and the fire Write for a love of place And may nothing of man be included in the void that is chilled by a flame.

Surrealism

This international but Paris-based movement has had an immense influence on all the arts in the twentieth century; that influence is still being assessed, and arguably it is still being felt. Passing from initial nihilism via convulsively creative rather than therapeutic psychoanalysis to an uneasy alliance with Marxism, it has transformed the way in which many writers and artists approach their work. Correspondingly, Surrealism has issued a great challenge to those who receive it. Its origins were in a revolt against a society capable of engendering the horrors of the First World War, and in a perceived need for radical new processes of thought, for a break with failed 'reason'. The movement found its precursors in the Marquis de Sade, Bertrand, Borel, Nerval, Baudelaire, Rimbaud, Lautréamont, Saint-Pol Roux and Jarry, and its central figure through several decades was André Breton.

The original impulse, anarchic and provocative, was felt in Zürich in 1916, where a group of young artists led by Tristan Tzara created a phenomenon known as *Dada* (the name chosen at random in a dictionary according to one of their creative principles). This was a screaming, demonstrative destruction of cultural values and conventions, and of language. Poets and other artists (recognizing no distinctions or hierarchies) 'performed' their work at the Cabaret Voltaire and other centres, and this 'new beginning' spread into Germany and France. Tzara himself arrived in Paris in 1919. He quickly established links with Breton, Soupault, Aragon and other like-minded poets such as Georges Ribemont-Dessaignes. While praising the modernism of the Cubist group, Tzara presented Paris with a major challenge, and out of the response developed the much more positive, substantial and durable movement that we know as Surrealism.

A clear division between Dadaists and Surrealists was visible for a time, but Dada was played out well before Tzara formally came over to the other side in 1929. Paul Eluard quickly joined the Breton–Soupault–Aragon group, then came a second wave: the poets Péret, Crevel, Vitrac (a playwright too), Desnos, Artaud (who was to have a profound effect on the direction of modern theatre) and, later, Leiris, Prévert, Queneau and Char. Kindred spirits among visual artists were Man Ray, Ernst, Picabia (also something of a poet), Masson, Chirico, Dali and Buñuel. Subsequent history tells of many expulsions and defections, and among the poets only Breton and Péret remained consistently (or stubbornly) faithful to the movement's principles until their death.

From 1925 a political dimension entered Surrealism, linking economic revolution with liberation of the mind, though most adherents insisted for the immediate future on the priority of mental experimentation. A problematic relationship developed with the Communist Party, with Breton trying to hold the balance between Marxism's separation of the objective and subjective worlds on the one hand, and on the other the Rimbaud-inspired Surrealist view of poetry as a comprehensively life-changing activity. Orthodox Communism's tendency to restrict or belittle the role of artistic production if it is individualistic was bound to create problems, and each artist and poet evolved in his own way on a scale of acceptance or rejection of political commitment. Many of them actively supported the Republican cause in the Spanish Civil War, and carried their commitment into the French Resistance, though Breton chose exile in New York during the German occupation of France.

Surrealism in itself may seem to be history now, but it created a radically new poetic climate in which today's writers to an extent still live, and the turbulent political events and idealistic youth movements of the late 1960s in France brought a strong resurgence of interest in its aims and methods, and in its capacity to liberate consciousness.

André Breton
(1896–1966)

The history and central ideas of Surrealism are inseparable from the life and work of Breton, its guiding spirit and author of two essential documents, the *Surrealist Manifestos* of 1924 and 1930.

As a medical student in Paris (his origins were in Normandy), he was mobilized as an auxiliary doctor, and worked as a psychiatrist in the Medical Corps. He became familiar with Freudian psychoanalysis (he was to meet Freud himself in Vienna in 1921), though Breton was more interested in the risky and revelatory exploration of the unconscious than in the restoration of equilibrium, and particularly interested in dream-notation. In 1916 he met Apollinaire, and also came under the influence of a provocative humorist called Jacques Vaché, whom Breton came to see as the prototype Surrealist in his attitude to life and art.

Breton's post-war association with Tzara was over by 1922, and the parting was acrimonious, though this was of minor importance in the feverish activity of the newly constituted Surrealist group and the publication of the *First Manifesto*. This document defines Surrealist creation as: 'Pure psychic automatism by which we propose to express, either verbally, or in writing, or in any other fashion, the real operation of thought. Dictation of thought, detached from all aesthetic or moral preoccupations'. Elsewhere he uses the term '*dictée psychique*'.

The Surrealist goes beyond reason and logic, beyond the normal waking state of consciousness, and approaches a superior state of awareness by the cultivation of a condition of lucid trance or delirium, often hypnotically induced, and by the notation of his dreams and perceptions in the form of 'automatic writing'. This will be a pattern of verbal association committed spontaneously to paper, with no mediating intellectual activity and no intrusion of literary conventions (there is some disagreement about the legitimacy of subsequent revision, but as a general principle the products of '*dictée psychique*' should need no further formal manipulation). It is an adventure within language, expanding the frontiers of language to infinity, through creative word-play (including jokes, for humour and vulgarity are essential Surrealist weapons), through free association based on sound-relationships existing prior to meaning, and above all through the discovery of original poetic analogies. Thus the Surrealist finds in language an active freedom denied to him by society, and Surrealism becomes an attitude to life, an attitude which makes all things possible.

Dynamic and surprising juxtapositions are at the heart of Surrealist images. Though Breton wishes them to surge more explosively from the unconscious, he adopts Reverdy's approach to images, and adds these thoughts of his own: 'The most powerful surrealist image is the one that presents the highest degree of arbitrariness, that takes longest to translate into functional language, whether because it contains an enormous quantity of apparent contradiction, or because one of its terms is curiously secret, or because after a sensational introduction it seems to resolve itself weakly (closing abruptly the angle of its compass), or because it is of a hallucinatory nature, or because it lends very naturally to the abstract the mask of the concrete, or inversely, because it involves the negation of some elementary physical property, or because it unleashes laughter.' As with Reverdy, the more remote the relationship, the more poetic is the image and the more likely to awaken deep resonances in the reader's unconscious.

There is thus a strong element of surprise in Surrealism, and they are intensely interested in miraculous coincidences and premonitions in life as well as art, enjoying sophisticated variants of 'Consequences'-type games of which the most celebrated product is: '*Le cadavre-exquis-boira-le-vin-nouveau.*' For the Dadaists creation based on '*le hasard*' is a matter of violent and gratuitous provocation and the arbitrary combination of words cut from newspapers, but the Surrealists pursue '*le hasard objectif*'. This could take the form of a long walk through Paris, for example, creating patterns of encounters and sensory impressions in a search for a unity between the mind and the external world that exists beyond the multiplicity of surface appearances; beyond the apparent contradictions between life and death (an area in which Jean Cocteau excels in particular); between the real and the dream, the past and the future. This reconciliation is a major Surrealist goal. It is rarely attained, but the adventure is the point, not the arrival.

For Breton, Aragon and Eluard, love can also be a route to this absolute experience. The women they love are revered and honoured for their capacity to generate transcendence, to bring about a world in which there are no boundaries between desire and experience, and in which 'the marvellous' erupts continually into reality.

As we have seen, Breton spent much time and energy in the late 1920s and early '30s on the attempt to synthesize Surrealism and Marxism, working from 1930 to 1933 on a new periodical, *Le Surréalisme au service de la Révolution*, while continuing to publish poetry and prose. Much of it sustains the genuinely lyrical note of his early work, something often overlooked by those who see him essentially as a theoretician. In 1938 he met Trotsky in Mexico, and during the war established a Surrealist group in New York. His later life in France saw no break with a lifetime's artistic and political convictions and active involvement in both fields.

Major poetic works: *Mont de piété* 1919, *Les Champs magnétiques* (with Philippe Soupault) 1920, *Clair de terre* 1923, *Poisson soluble* 1924, *Ralentir Travaux* (with Char and Eluard) 1930, *L'Immaculée Conception* (with Eluard) 1930, *L'Union libre* 1931, *Le Revolver à cheveux blancs* 1932, *L'Air de l'eau* 1934, *Les Etats généraux* 1947, *Ode à Charles Fourier* 1947, *Constellations* 1959.

Tournesol

à Pierre Reverdy

La voyageuse qui traversa les Halles à la tombée de l'été
Marchait sur la pointe des pieds
Le désespoir roulait au ciel ses grands arums si beaux
Et dans le sac à main il y avait mon rêve ce flacon de sels
Que seule a respirés la marraine de Dieu
Les torpeurs se déployaient comme la buée
Au Chien qui fume
Où venaient d'entrer le pour et le contre
La jeune femme ne pouvait être vue d'eux que mal et de biais
Avais-je affaire à l'ambassadrice du salpêtre
Ou de la courbe blanche sur fond noir que nous appelons pensée
Le bal des innocents battait son plein
Les lampions prenaient feu lentement dans les marronniers

Sunflower

for Pierre Reverdy

The traveller who crossed Les Halles at the fall of summer Tiptoed as she walked Despair spun in the sky its great and lovely arums And in the handbag there was my dream that phial of salts That only the godmother of God has breathed Torpors were unfurling like vapours At the Smoking Dog Where the pro and the con had just walked in The young woman could be seen by them only badly and obliquely Was I dealing with the ambassadress of saltpetre Or of the white curve on a black background which we call thought The ball of the innocents was in full swing The Chinese lanterns were slowly catching fire in the chestnut trees The lady with

La dame sans ombre s'agenouilla sur le Pont-au-Change
Rue Gît-le-Cœur les timbres n'étaient plus les mêmes
Les promesses des nuits étaient enfin tenues
Les pigeons voyageurs les baisers de secours
Se joignaient aux seins de la belle inconnue
Dardés sous le crêpe des significations parfaites
Une ferme prospérait en plein Paris
Et ses fenêtres donnaient sur la voie lactée
Mais personne ne l'habitait encore à cause des survenants
Des survenants qu'on sait plus dévoués que les revenants
Les uns comme cette femme ont l'air de nager
Et dans l'amour il entre un peu de leur substance
Elle les intériorise
Je ne suis le jouet d'aucune puissance sensorielle
Et pourtant le grillon qui chantait dans les cheveux de cendre
Un soir près de la statue d'Etienne Marcel
M'a jeté un coup d'œil d'intelligence
André Breton a-t-il dit passe

no shadow knelt down on the Pont-au-Change In the Rue Gît-le-Cœur the bells no longer sounded the same The promises of the nights were at last being kept The homing pigeons the kisses of rescue Were united with the breasts of the lovely unknown woman Darting forward beneath the veil of perfect meanings A farm was prospering in the heart of Paris And its windows looked on to the milky way But no one lived in it still because of the unexpected guests Guests who are one knows more devoted than ghosts Some like that woman are apparently swimming And into love there enters a little of their substance She absorbs them inwardly I am the plaything of no sensory power And yet the cricket that was singing in the ashen hair One evening near the statue of Etienne Marcel Gave me a knowing look He said pass André Breton

Vigilance

A Paris la tour Saint-Jacques chancelante
Pareille à un tournesol
Du front vient quelquefois heurter la Seine et son ombre glisse imperceptiblement parmi les remorqueurs
A ce moment sur la pointe des pieds dans mon sommeil
Je me dirige vers la chambre où je suis étendu
Et j'y mets le feu
Pour que rien ne subsiste de ce consentement qu'on m'a arraché
Les meubles font alors place à des animaux de même taille qui me regardent fraternellement
Lions dans les crinières desquels achèvent de se consumer les chaises
Squales dont le ventre blanc s'incorpore le dernier frisson des draps
A l'heure de l'amour et des paupières bleues
Je me vois brûler à mon tour je vois cette cachette solennelle de riens

Watchfulness

In Paris the tottering Saint-Jacques tower Like a sunflower Comes sometimes and strikes the Seine with its brow and its shadow glides imperceptibly among the tugboats At that moment on tiptoe in my sleep I move towards the room where I am lying And I set it on fire So that nothing will exist of that acquiescence wrung from me The furniture then gives way to animals of the same stature who gaze at me fraternally Lions in whose manes the chairs are consumed to the last Sharks whose white belly absorbs the last flutter of the sheets At the hour of love and of blue eyelids I see myself burning in my turn I see

Qui fut mon corps
Fouillée par les becs patients des ibis du feu
Lorsque tout est fini j'entre invisible dans l'arche
Sans prendre garde aux passants de la vie qui font sonner très loin leurs pas traînants
Je vois les arêtes du soleil
A travers l'aubépine de la pluie
J'entends se déchirer le linge humain comme une grande feuille
Sous l'ongle de l'absence et de la présence qui sont de connivence
Tous les métiers se fanent il ne reste d'eux qu'une dentelle parfumée
Une coquille de dentelle qui a la forme parfaite d'un sein
Je ne touche plus que le cœur des choses je tiens le fil

that solemn hiding-place of nothings Which was my body Probed by the patient beaks of the ibises of fire When all is finished I go invisible into the ark Paying no heed to the passers-by of life who make their dragging footsteps resound into the distance I see the ridges of the sun Through the hawthorn of the rain I hear the human linen tearing like a great leaf Under the claw of absence and of presence which are in connivance All the looms are withering and there remains of them only a scented lace A scallop of lace which has the perfect form of a breast I touch now only the heart of things I hold the thread

L'Union libre

Ma femme à la chevelure de feu de bois
Aux pensées d'éclairs de chaleur
A la taille de sablier
Ma femme à la taille de loutre entre les dents du tigre
Ma femme à la bouche de cocarde et de bouquet d'étoiles de
  dernière grandeur
Aux dents d'empreintes de souris blanche sur la terre blanche
A la langue d'ambre et de verre frottés
Ma femme à la langue d'hostie poignardée
A la langue de poupée qui ouvre et ferme les yeux
A la langue de pierre incroyable
Ma femme aux cils de bâtons d'écriture d'enfant
Aux sourcils de bord de nid d'hirondelle
Ma femme aux tempes d'ardoise de toit de serre
Et de buée aux vitres
Ma femme aux épaules de champagne
Et de fontaine à têtes de dauphins sous la glace

Free Union

My wife with the wood-fire hair With her summer lightning thoughts With her hour-glass figure My wife with the shape of an otter caught in the tiger's teeth My wife with her mouth a cockade and a bouquet of stars of utmost magnitude With her teeth imprints of a white mouse on the white earth With her tongue of rubbed amber and glass My wife with her tongue a stabbed communion wafer With her tongue a doll with opening and closing eyes With her tongue of incredible stone My wife with her eyelashes strokes in a child's handwriting With her eyebrows the edges of a swallow's nest My wife with her temples of slate on a greenhouse roof And steam on the panes My wife with her shoulders of champagne and a fountain with

Ma femme aux poignets d'allumettes
Ma femme aux doigts de hasard et d'as de cœur
Aux doigts de foin coupé
Ma femme aux aisselles de martre et de fênes
De nuit de la Saint-Jean
De troène et de nid de scalares
Aux bras d'écume de mer et d'écluse
Et de mélange du blé et du moulin
Ma femme aux jambes de fusée
Aux mouvements d'horlogerie et de désespoir
Ma femme aux mollets de moelle de sureau
Ma femme aux pieds d'initiales
Aux pieds de trousseaux de clés aux pieds de calfats qui boivent
Ma femme au cou d'orge imperlé
Ma femme à la gorge de Val d'or
De rendez-vous dans le lit même du torrent
Aux seins de nuit
Ma femme aux seins de taupinière marine
Ma femme aux seins de creuset du rubis
Aux seins de spectre de la rose sous la rosée

dolphin heads under the ice My wife with her matchstick wrists My wife with her fingers of chance and the ace of hearts With her mown hay fingers My wife with her armpits of marten and beechnut Of Midsummer's Night Of privet and of angel-fish nests With her arms of sea and lock-gate foam And mingled wheat and mill My wife with her watch-spindle legs With their motion of clockwork and of despair My wife with her elder-marrow calves My wife with her carved initial feet With her key-ring feet with her drinking caulker feet My wife with her pearl barley neck My wife with her Golden Valley throat Of encounters in the very bed of the torrent With her breasts of night My wife with her undersea molehill breasts My wife with her ruby crucible breasts With her breasts the spectre of roses

Ma femme au ventre de dépliement d'éventail des jours
Au ventre de griffe géante
Ma femme au dos d'oiseau qui fuit vertical
Au dos de vif-argent
Au dos de lumière
A la nuque de pierre roulée et de craie mouillée
Et de chute d'un verre dans lequel on vient de boire
Ma femme aux hanches de nacelle
Aux hanches de lustre et de pennes de flèche
Et de tiges de plumes de paon blanc
De balance insensible
Ma femme aux fesses de grès et d'amiante
Ma femme aux fesses de dos de cygne
Ma femme aux fesses de printemps
Au sexe de glaïeul
Ma femme au sexe de placer et d'ornithorynque
Ma femme au sexe d'algue et de bonbons anciens
Ma femme au sexe de miroir
Ma femme aux yeux pleins de larmes

under dew My wife with her belly an unfolding fan of days With her belly a giant claw My wife with her back a bird in vertical flight With her quicksilver back With her back of light With her nape of rolled stone and moistened chalk And the fall of a glass from which one has just drunk My wife with her gondola hips With her hips of gloss and arrow feathers And white peacock's quill-stems Of imperceptible equilibrium My wife with her sandstone and amianthus buttocks My wife with her swan's back buttocks My wife with her springtime buttocks With her gladiolus sex My wife with her mineral-rich sandbank and duckbill sex My wife with her sex of seaweed and old sweets My wife with her mirror sex My wife with her eyes full

Aux yeux de panoplie violette et d'aiguille aimantée
Ma femme aux yeux de savane
Ma femme aux yeux d'eau pour boire en prison
Ma femme aux yeux de bois toujours sous la hache
Aux yeux de niveau d'eau de niveau d'air de terre et de feu

of tears With her violet panoply and magnetic needle eyes My wife with her savanna eyes My wife with her eyes of water to drink in prison My wife with her eyes of wood always under the axe With her water-gauge spirit-level earth and fire eyes

Sur la route de San Romano

La poésie se fait dans un lit comme l'amour
Ses draps défaits sont l'aurore des choses
La poésie se fait dans les bois

Elle a l'espace qu'il lui faut
Pas celui-ci mais l'autre que conditionnent

On the Road to San Romano

Poetry is made in a bed like love Its unmade sheets are the dawn of things Poetry is made in the woods

It has the space it needs Not this one but the other governed

L'œil du milan
La rosée sur une prèle
Le souvenir d'une bouteille de Traminer embuée sur un plateau d'argent
Une haute verge de tourmaline sur la mer
Et la route de l'aventure mentale
Qui monte à pic
Une halte elle s'embroussaille aussitôt

Cela ne se crie pas sur les toits
Il est inconvenant de laisser la porte ouverte
Ou d'appeler des témoins

Les bancs de poissons les haies de mésanges
Les rails à l'entrée d'une grande gare
Les reflets des deux rives
Les sillons dans le pain
Les bulles du ruisseau
Les jours du calendrier
Le millepertuis

By the eye of the kite The dew on a horsetail The memory of a misted bottle of Traminer on a silver salver A tall column of tourmaline above the sea And the road of mental adventure Which climbs vertically One pause and it is instantly overgrown

That is not for shouting on the rooftops It is not fitting to leave the door open Or to call for witnesses

The shoals of fish the hedges of tomtits The rails at the entrance to a great station The reflections of both shores The furrows in the bread The bubbles of the stream The days of the calendar The Saint-John's-Wort

L'acte d'amour et l'acte de poésie
Sont incompatibles
Avec la lecture du journal à haute voix

Le sens du rayon de soleil
La lueur bleue qui relie les coups de hache du bûcheron
Le fil du cerf-volant en forme de cœur ou de nasse
Le battement en mesure de la queue des castors
La diligence de l'éclair
Le jet de dragées du haut des vieilles marches
L'avalanche

La chambre aux prestiges
Non messieurs ce n'est pas la huitième Chambre
Ni les vapeurs de la chambrée un dimanche soir

The act of love and the act of poetry Are incompatible With the reading aloud of the newspaper

The direction of the sunbeam The blue gleam that connects the axeblows of the woodcutter The string of the kite in the shape of a heart or a fish-trap The rhythmic beat of beavers' tails The industriousness of lightning The casting down of sugarplums from the top of old steps The avalanche

The room of dazzling illusions No gentlemen it is not the Eighth Chamber Nor the fumes of the barrack-room one Sunday evening

Les figures de danse exécutées en transparence au-dessus
des mares
La délimitation contre un mur d'un corps de femme au
lancer de poignards
Les volutes claires de la fumée
Les boucles de tes cheveux
La courbe de l'éponge des Philippines
Les lacés du serpent corail
L'entrée du lierre dans les ruines
Elle a tout le temps devant elle

L'étreinte poétique comme l'étreinte de chair
Tant qu'elle dure
Défend toute échappée sur la misère du monde

The figures of the dance executed in transparency above the pools The outlining of a woman's body in dagger-throws on a wall The shining scrolls of smoke The curls of your hair The curve of Filipino sponge The lacings of the coral serpent The entry of ivy into the ruins *It has all of time before it*

The embrace of poetry like the embrace of flesh For as long as it lasts Forbids any stealthy glance upon the destitution of the world

Tristan Tzara
(1896–1963)

The leader of the Dadaists, Tzara (real name Sami Rosenstock) was of Rumanian origin. He moved to Paris in 1919 after animating much of the Zürich activity, and continued to work in a Dadaist manner for some years after the split with Breton. He returned to the Surrealist fold in 1929, and his verse in the 1930s has a stronger political orientation. He was active in Spain in support of left-wing intellectuals, and later in the Resistance.

His verse is intermittently brilliant in its erupting imagery, and characterized by a vitality and luminosity in his experimentation with language and imagery that are overlooked by those who think of him as an essentially destructive force in poetry. Tzara himself approached creativity in these terms: 'Vigour and thirst, emotion in response to the formation which is neither to be seen nor to be explained … a will to the word: a being on its feet, an image, a construction that is unique and fervent, of a deep colour, intensity, communion with life'. His poems have rapidity of motion, precision and clarity (glass, fountain and crystal are key images).

Tzara's early work links images in an apparently gratuitous pattern which may have thematic unity under the surface, accessible to intuition. They are spontaneous creations, disjointed experiences in perception and liberated language. His later political work has a more 'realistic correlation', though without fully losing the sense of verbal intoxication and mental freedom of his first period, when poems took shape out of the play of pure sounds developing progressively into words.

As with Reverdy, there is a tragic element in this fragmented perception of the world, and Tzara's long masterpiece *L'Homme approximatif* (1931) dramatizes the condition of an incomplete being in flux, searching in a labyrinth for some sense of unity within himself and with the world.

He had much in common with the Surrealists, particularly in his belief in the transforming power of the dream, but did not share their difficulties in reconciling dream with action. He saw no distinction between the two, since for the Dadaist the work is self-sufficient action, not 'symptomatic' of anything but a pure and free art of presence, revolutionary in itself. Poetry is a knife to cut into a world too sure of itself, an act of creative sabotage.

A selection of his works (too numerous to list exhaustively): *Vingt-Cinq Poèmes* 1918, *Cinéma calendrier du coeur abstrait* 1920, *De nos oiseaux* 1923, *Indicateur des chemins de cœur* 1928, *L'Homme approximatif* 1931, *L'Antitête* 1933, *Midis gagnés* 1939, etc.

La grande complainte de mon obscurité trois

chez nous les fleurs des pendules s'allument et les plumes
encerclent la clarté
le matin de soufre lointain les vaches lèchent les lys de sel
mon fils
mon fils
traînons toujours par la couleur du monde
qu'on dirait plus bleue que le métro et que l'astronomie
nous sommes trop maigres
nous n'avons pas de bouche
nos jambes sont raides et s'entrechoquent
nos visages n'ont pas de forme comme les étoiles
cristaux points sans force feu brûlée la basilique

The great lament of my obscurity three

where we live the flowers of the clocks catch fire and the plumes encircle the brightness / in the distant sulphur morning the cows lick the salt lilies / my son / my son / let us always scuff along through the colour of the world / that looks bluer than the metro and astronomy / we are too skinny / we have no mouth / our legs are stiff and knock together / our faces have no form like the stars / crystals points without strength

folle: les zigzags craquent
téléphone
mordre les cordages se liquéfier
l'arc
grimper
astrale
la mémoire
vers le nord par son fruit double
comme la chair crue
faim feu sang

fire the mad basilica / burned: the zigzags crack / telephone / bite the rigging liquefy / the arc / climb / astral / memory / towards the north through its double fruit / like raw flesh / hunger fire blood

La Mort de Guillaume Apollinaire

nous ne savons rien
nous ne savions rien de la douleur
la saison amère du froid
creuse de longues traces dans nos muscles
il aurait plutôt aimé la joie de la victoire
sages sous les tristesses calmes   en cage
ne pouvoir rien faire
si la neige tombait en haut
si le soleil montait chez nous pendant la nuit
pour nous chauffer
et les arbres pendaient avec leur couronne
– unique pleur –
si les oiseaux étaient parmi nous pour se mirer
dans le lac tranquille au-dessus de nos têtes
ON POURRAIT COMPRENDRE
la mort serait un beau long voyage
et les vacances illimitées de la chair des structures et des os

The Death of Guillaume Apollinaire[1]

we know nothing / we know nothing of grief / the bitter season of cold / digs long furrows in our muscles / he would have rather liked the joy of victory / we are wise beneath the tranquil sorrows / caged / to be able to do nothing / if the snow fell upwards / if the sun rose among us during the night / to warm us / and the trees were suspended with their wreath – the only tear – if the birds were among us to find their reflection / in the placid lake above our heads / WE MIGHT UNDERSTAND / death would be a beautiful long voyage / and a limitless holiday for flesh structures and bones

[1]Apollinaire's funeral coincided with the Armistice celebrations.

Sur une ride du soleil

noyez matins les soifs les muscles et les fruits
dans la liqueur crue et secrète
la suie tissée en lingots d'or
couvre la nuit lacérée par les motifs brefs

à l'horizon remis à neuf
une draperie d'eau courante large vivante
grince petit coefficient particulier
de mon amour
dans la porte soudain éclaircie

harcelée par les désirs éclipses
pleureuse accélérée palpitante
tu t'effeuilles en prospectus d'accords privés
l'inconstance de l'eau glisse sur ton corps avec le soleil

On a Ripple of the Sun

drown mornings thirsts muscles and fruits / in the raw and secret liquor / soot woven into golden ingots / cloaks the night lacerated by brief patterns

on a horizon as good as new / a drapery of water running broad alive / grates characteristic little coefficient / of my love / in the doorway suddenly brightened

harassed by desires eclipses / weeping accelerated throbbing / you shed your leaves as prospectuses of private harmonies / the inconstancy of water glides over your body with the sunlight

par le miracle fendu on entrevoit le masque
jamais claire jamais neuve
tu marches c'est la vie qui fait marcher la bielle
et voilà pourquoi les yeux roulent dans leur pourquoi
l'avantage du sang à travers le cri de la vapeur
un éventail de flammes sur le volcan tu sais
que les veines de la tombe
ont conduit tant de chansons d'ardeur
à l'échappée
le monde
un chapeau avec des fleurs
le monde
un violon jouant sur une fleur
le monde
une bague faite pour une fleur
une fleur fleur pour le bouquet de fleurs fleurs
un porte-cigarette rempli de fleurs
une petite locomotive aux yeux de fleurs
une paire de gants pour des fleurs
en peau de fleurs comme nos fleurs fleurs fleurs de fleurs
et un œuf

through the miracle cracked asunder the mask is glimpsed / never clear never new / you walk it's life that makes the connecting-rod work / and that's why the eyes roll in their why / the benefit of blood through the cry of the vapour / a fan of flames on the volcano you know / that the veins of the tomb / have accompanied so many fervent songs / stealthy escape / the world / a hat with flowers / the world / a violin playing on a flower / the world / a ring made for a flower / a flower flower for the bouquet of flowers flowers / a cigarette-case filled with flowers / a little locomotive with eyes of flowers / a pair of gloves for flowers / made of flower skin like our flowers flowers flowers of flowers / and an egg

Volt

les tours penchées les cieux obliques
les autos tombant dans le vide des routes
les animaux bordant les routes rurales
avec des branches couvertes d'hospitalières qualités
et d'oiseaux en forme de feuilles sur leurs têtes
tu marches mais c'est une autre qui marche sur tes pas
distillant son dépit à travers les fragments de mémoire et d'arithmétique
entourée d'une robe presque sourde le bruit caillé des capitales

la ville bouillonnante et épaisse de fiers appels et de lumières
déborde de la casserole de ses paupières
ses larmes s'écoulent en ruisseaux de basses populations
sur la plaine stérile vers la chair et la lave lisses
des montagnes ombrageuses les apocalyptiques tentations

Volt

the leaning towers the oblique skies / the cars falling into the void of the roads / the animals lining the rural roads / with branches covered in hospitable virtues / and birds in the form of leaves on their heads / you are walking but it's another who follows in your footsteps / distilling her spite through fragments of memory and arithmetic / enveloped in a robe almost deadened the curdled sound of capitals

the frothing city dense with proud calls and lights / boils over the stewpan of its eyelids / its tears flow away in streams of abject populations / over the sterile plain towards the sleek flesh and lava / of the umbrageous mountains the apocalyptic temptations

perdu dans la géographie d'un souvenir et d'une obscure rose
je rôde dans les rues étroites autour de toi
tandis que toi aussi tu rôdes dans d'autres rues plus grandes
autour de quelque chose

lost in the geography of a memory and of a mysterious rose / I prowl the narrow streets around you / while you too you prowl other greater streets / around something

Philippe Soupault
(1897–)

Soupault was a founder of Surrealism, his name permanently associated with that of Breton through their collaboration on *Littérature* and their co-authorship of *Les Champs magnétiques*. He left the group in 1927 in disapproval of their growing alliance with Marxist orthodoxy, and his subsequent literary career has ranged through novels, translation, criticism and essays. But he was an important figure in the movement's early years, perpetuating within it the influence of Apollinaire. His response to the world of images, particularly the urban landscape, is motivated by emotion rather than a surrender to the unconscious, once he has moved on from the initial period of feverish experimentation.

Major poetic works: *Aquarium* 1917, *Rose des vents* 1920, *Westwego* 1922, *Georgia* 1926, *Sang Joie Tempête* and *Etapes de l'Enfer* 1934, *Ode à Londres bombardée* 1944, *l'Arme secret* 1946, *Chansons du jour et de la nuit* 1949, etc.

Dimanche

L'avion tisse les fils télégraphiques
et la source chante la même chanson
Au rendez-vous des cochers l'apéritif est orangé
mais les mécaniciens des locomotives ont les yeux blancs
la dame a perdu son sourire dans les bois

Sunday

The aeroplane weaves the telegraph wires / and the spring sings the same song At the cabmen's local the aperitif is orange / but the engine-drivers have white eyes / the lady has lost her smile in the woods

La grande Mélancolie d'une avenue

à G. di Chirico

Au bout du monde
C'est la main
Hors concours
ou le gant
la tour
le train passe
c'est un nuage

DEMENAGEMENTS POUR TOUS PAYS

à l'entresol
cinq heures

le vent part

En voiture

The Great Melancholia of an Avenue

for G. di Chirico

To the end of the world This is the hand Without rival / or the glove / the tower / the train passes / this is a cloud / REMOVALS TO ALL COUNTRIES / on the mezzanine / five o'clock / the wind sets off In a car

Say it with Music

Les bracelets d'or et les drapeaux
les locomotives les bateaux
et le vent salubre et les nuages
je les abandonne simplement
mon cœur est trop petit
ou trop grand
et ma vie est courte
je ne sais quand viendra ma mort exactement
mais je vieillis
je descends les marches quotidiennes
en laissant une prière s'échapper de mes lèvres
A chaque étage est-ce un ami qui m'attend
est-ce un voleur
est-ce moi
je ne sais plus voir dans le ciel
qu'une seule étoile ou qu'un seul nuage
selon ma tristesse ou ma joie
je ne sais plus baisser la tête
est-elle trop lourde
Dans mes mains je ne sais pas non plus
si je tiens des bulles de savon ou des boulets de canon

Say it with Music

The golden bracelets and the flags / the locomotives the ships / and the bracing wind and the clouds / I abandon them simply / my heart is too small / or too big / and my life is brief / I do not know exactly when my death will come / but I am growing old / I go down the daily steps / letting a prayer steal from my lips On every floor is it a friend waiting for me / is it a thief / is it me / I can see nothing more in the sky / but a single star or a single cloud / according to my sadness or my joy / I can no longer bow my head / is it too heavy Nor do I know / if I am holding soap bubbles or cannon-balls in my

je marche
je vieillis
mais mon sang rouge mon cher sang rouge
parcourt mes veines
en chassant devant lui les souvenirs du présent
mais ma soif est trop grande
je m'arrête encore et j'attends
la lumière
Paradis paradis paradis

hands / I am walking / I am growing old / but my red blood my precious red blood / courses through my veins/ driving before it the memories of the present / but my thirst is too great / I stop once more and I await / the light Paradise paradise paradise

Stumbling

Quel est ce grand pays
quelle est cette nuit
qu'il regarde en marchant
autour de lui
autour du monde
où il est né
Les pays sont des secondes
les secondes de l'espace
où il est né
Les doigts couverts d'étoiles
et chaussé de courage
il s'en va
Rien ne finit pour lui
Demain est une ville
plus belle plus rouge que les autres
où le départ est une arrivée
et le repos un tombeau
La ligne d'horizon
brille
comme un barreau d'acier

Stumbling

What is this great land / what is this night / at which he gazes as he walks / around him / around the world / where he was born Countries are seconds / the seconds of space / where he was born With his fingers clothed in stars / and his feet shod with courage / he goes on his way Nothing ends for him Tomorrow is a city / more lovely more red than the others / where departure is an arrival / and repose a tomb The line of the horizon / shines / like a steel bar / like a thread that must

comme un fil qu'il faut couper
pour ne pas se reposer
jamais
Les couteaux sont faits pour trancher
les fusils pour tuer
les yeux pour regarder
l'homme pour marcher
et la terre est ronde
ronde
ronde
comme la tête
et comme le désir
Il y a de bien jolies choses
les fleurs
les arbres
les dentelles
sans parler des insectes
Mais tout cela on le connaît
on l'a déjà vu
et on en a assez
Là-bas on ne sait pas
Tenir dans sa main droite une canne
et rien dans sa main gauche
qu'un peu d'air frais
et quelquefois une cigarette
dans son cœur

be cut / in order not to rest / ever Knives are made for cutting / guns for killing / eyes for looking / man for walking / and the earth is round / round / round / like the head / and like desire There are very pretty things / flowers / trees / lace / to say nothing of insects But we know all that / we have already seen it / and have had enough of it Over there we don't know To hold a stick in the right hand / and nothing in the left hand / but a little fresh air / and sometimes a cigarette / in the heart

le désir qui est une cloche
Et moi je suis là
j'écoute j'attends
un téléphone un encrier du papier
j'écoute j'attends j'obéis
Le soleil chaque jour tombe
dans le silence
je vieillis lentement sans le savoir
un paysage me suffit
j'écoute et j'obéis
je dis un mot un bateau part
un chiffre un train s'éloigne
Cela n'a pas d'importance
puisqu'un train reviendra
demain
et que déjà le grand sémaphore
fait un signe
et m'annonce l'arrivée
d'un autre vapeur
j'entends la mer au bout d'un fil
et la voix d'un ami
à des kilomètres de distance
Mais Lui
je suis l'ami de l'air
et des grands fleuves blancs

/ desire which is a bell And me there I am / I listen I wait / a telephone an inkpot paper / I listen I wait I obey The sun falls each day / into silence / I am growing old slowly without knowing / a landscape is enough for me / I listen and I obey / I say a word a boat departs / a figure a train moves off That is of no importance / since a train will come back / tomorrow / and since already the great semaphore / signals / and announces to me the arrival / of another steamship / I hear the sea on the end of a wire / and the voice of a friend / kilometres away But Him / I am the friend of the air / and of the great white rivers

l'ami du sang
et de la terre
je les connais et je les touche
je peux les tenir dans mes mains
Il n'y a qu'à partir
un soir un matin
Il n'y a que le premier pas
qui soit un peu pénible
un peu lourd
Il n'y a que le ciel
que le vent
Il n'y a que mon cœur
et tout m'attend
Il va
une fleur à la boutonnière
et fait des signes de la main
Il dit au revoir au revoir
mais il ment
Il ne reviendra jamais

/ the friend of blood / and of the earth / I know them and I touch them / I can hold them in my hands It's just a matter of leaving / one evening one morning Just a matter of the first step / that's a little painful / a little heavy Just a matter of the sky / of the wind Just a matter of my heart / and all awaits me He goes on / with a flower in his buttonhole / and signals with his hand He says see you again see you again / but he is lying He will never come back

Paul Eluard
(1895–1952)

A supremely lyrical and humanitarian poet, Paul Eluard (real name Grindel) did much to build the bridge between Surrealism and the general reading public. In his vision there is a communicative generosity and an absence of aggressive or élitist hermeticism; there is an unparadoxical harmony between the surreal and the real, and indeed a sense that the one is organically within the other; and there is a warm spontaneity and a joyful idealism that make him one of the finest love-poets of the twentieth century. Born in an industrial suburb of Paris, he also maintained contact with the cultural and political life of ordinary people, and a commitment to poetry as something to be shared by all, part of a drive towards a new social order founded on and animated by love. His purpose was to awaken the poet within every human being.

The first great love in his life was for Gala (Helena Dmitrievna Diakonova). He met her at a Swiss sanatorium after a serious illness in 1912, and married her in 1917. She shared the Surrealist experience with Eluard in the 1920s, but left him in 1929 to embark on a long, extraordinary and much-documented relationship with the painter Salvador Dali. Eluard found a new love, Nusch (Maria Benz), and with her his poetry became more concrete, less startling and dreamlike though still exhilarating, a celebration of the couple as the principle of a loving and creative society. She died in 1946, but after a period of extreme depression he was renewed by a third loving relationship in his final months, with Dominique Lemor.

He had been a member of the Surrealist movement almost from the start, finding in its exaltation of our dreams a perfect theatre for his original perceptions of a reality not abolished but whose laws of time and space have been suspended, a world orchestrated by love into a hallucinatory symphony of images, a universe where man can be a god through the power of his desire. This vision is later incorporated into his more explicit anti-Fascist commitment and Resistance activity (as a co-ordinator of intellectual opposition to occupation and collaboration), and the principle of love within the couple expands into a belief in fulfilment through interdependence of all men, in the defeat of solitude and meaninglessness through human solidarity.

Major volumes: *Mourir de ne pas mourir* 1924, *Capitale de la douleur* 1926, *L'Amour, la Poésie* 1929, *La Vie immédiate* 1932, *Les Yeux fertiles* 1936, *Cours naturel* 1938, *Poésie et Vérité* 1942, *Au Rendez-vous allemand* 1945, *Poésie ininterrompue* 1946, *Le Dur Désir de durer* 1946, *Le Temps déborde* 1947, *Corps mémorable* 1947, *Le Phénix* 1951.

L'Amoureuse

Elle est debout sur mes paupières
Et ses cheveux sont dans les miens,
Elle a la forme de mes mains,
Elle a la couleur de mes yeux,
Elle s'engloutit dans mon ombre
Comme une pierre sur le ciel.

Elle a toujours les yeux ouverts
Et ne me laisse pas dormir.
Ses rêves en pleine lumière
Font s'évaporer les soleils,
Me font rire, pleurer et rire,
Parler sans avoir rien à dire.

Woman in Love

She is standing on my eyelids and her hair is in mine, she has the shape of my hands, she has the colour of my eyes, she is absorbed into my shadow like a stone against the sky.

Her eyes are always open and she does not let me sleep. Her dreams in broad daylight make the suns evaporate, make me laugh, cry and laugh, and speak when I have nothing to say.

La courbe de tes yeux ...

La courbe de tes yeux fait le tour de mon cœur
Un rond de danse et de douceur,
Auréole du temps, berceau nocturne et sûr,
Et si je ne sais plus tout ce que j'ai vécu
C'est que tes yeux ne m'ont pas toujours vu.

Feuilles de jour et mousse de rosée,
Roseaux du vent, sourires parfumés,
Ailes couvrant le monde de lumière
Bateaux chargés du ciel et de la mer,
Chasseurs des bruits et sources des couleurs,

Parfums éclos d'une couvée d'aurores
Qui gît toujours sur la paille des astres,
Comme le jour dépend de l'innocence
Le monde entier dépend de tes yeux purs
Et tout mon sang coule dans leurs regards.

The Curve of your eyes ...

The curve of your eyes moves in orbit round my heart A round of dance and gentleness, halo of time, safe nocturnal cradle, and if I know no longer all that I have lived it is because your eyes have not always seen me.

Leaves of day and froth of dew, reeds of the wind, scented smiles, wings spreading a mantle of light over the world, boats laden with the sky and the sea, hunters of sounds and springs of colours,

Perfumes hatched out from a brood of dawns that lies for ever on the straw of the stars, as daylight depends on innocence the whole world depends on your pure eyes and all my blood flows into their gaze.

La terre est bleue ...

La terre est bleue comme une orange
Jamais une erreur les mots ne mentent pas
Ils ne vous donnent plus à chanter
Au tour des baisers de s'entendre
Les fous et les amours
Elle sa bouche d'alliance
Tous les secrets tous les sourires
Et quels vêtements d'indulgence
A la croire toute nue.

Les guêpes fleurissent vert
L'aube se passe autour du cou
Un collier de fenêtres
Des ailes couvrent les feuilles
Tu as toutes les joies solaires
Tout le soleil sur la terre
Sur les chemins de ta beauté.

The Earth is blue ...

The earth is blue like an orange Never a mistake words do not lie They no longer give you cause to sing It's up to kisses now to hear each other Madmen and loves She her wedding-ring mouth All the secrets all the smiles And what garments of indulgence You would think her quite naked.

The wasps are flowering green The dawn puts on around its neck A necklace of windows Wings cover the leaves You have all the solar joys All the sunlight upon the earth On the roads of your beauty.

Le front aux vitres ...

Le front aux vitres comme font les veilleurs de chagrin
Ciel dont j'ai dépassé la nuit
Plaines toutes petites dans mes mains ouvertes
Dans leur double horizon inerte indifférent
Le front aux vitres comme font les veilleurs de chagrin
Je te cherche par delà l'attente
Par delà moi-même
Et je ne sais plus tant je t'aime
Lequel de nous deux est absent.

With my brow against the window panes ...

With my brow against the window panes like the night watchers of grief Sky whose darkness I have surpassed Plains very small in my open hands In their double horizon inert indifferent With my brow against the window panes like the night watchers of grief I seek you beyond expectation Beyond myself And I love you so much I know no longer Which of the two of us is absent.

A perte de vue

dans le sens de mon corps

Tous les arbres toutes leurs branches toutes leurs feuilles
L'herbe à la base les rochers et les maisons en masse
Au loin la mer que ton œil baigne
Ces images d'un jour après l'autre
Les vices les vertus tellement imparfaits
La transparence des passants dans les rues de hasard
Et les passantes exhalées par tes recherches obstinées
Tes idées fixes au cœur de plomb aux lèvres vierges
Les vices les vertus tellement imparfaits
La ressemblance des regards de permission avec les yeux que
tu conquis
La confusion des corps des lassitudes des ardeurs
L'imitation des mots des attitudes des idées
Les vices les vertus tellement imparfaits

L'amour c'est l'homme inachevé.

Out of Sight bodywise[1]

All the trees all their branches all their leaves The grass at the base the rocks and the houses in a cluster In the distance the sea that is bathed in your eye These images of one day after the next The vices the virtues so imperfect The transparence of passing men in the streets of chance And the passing women exhaled by your stubborn questing Your obsessions with leaden heart and virgin lips The vices the virtues so imperfect The resemblance of consenting looks with the eyes that you conquered The confusion of the bodies the lassitudes the fervours The imitation of the words the attitudes the ideas The vices the virtues so imperfect

Love is man unfinished.

[1]As in 'clockwise' ('*dans le sens des aiguilles d'une montre*'); 'sense', 'direction' and 'alignment' are also possibilities.

Tu te lèves ...

Tu te lèves l'eau se déplie
Tu te couches l'eau s'épanouit

Tu es l'eau détournée de ses abîmes
Tu es la terre qui prend racine
Et sur laquelle tout s'établit

Tu fais des bulles de silence dans le désert des bruits
Tu chantes des hymnes nocturnes sur les cordes de l'arc-en-ciel
Tu es partout tu abolis toutes les routes

Tu sacrifies le temps
A l'éternelle jeunesse de la flamme exacte
Qui voile la nature en la reproduisant

You rise up ...

You rise up the water unfolds You lie down the water expands

You are the water diverted from its depths You are the earth taking root And on which everything is founded

You make bubbles of silence in the desert of sounds You sing nocturnal hymns on the strings of the rainbow You are everywhere you abolish all roads

You sacrifice time To the eternal youth of the exact flame Which veils nature in reproducing it

Femme tu mets au monde un corps toujours pareil
Le tien

Tu es la ressemblance.

Woman you put into the world a body for ever the same Yours

You are resemblance

La victoire de Guernica

I

Beau monde des masures
De la mine et des champs

II

Visages bons au feu visages bons au froid
Aux refus à la nuit aux injures aux coups

The Victory of Guernica[1]

I

Beautiful world of hovels Of mining and of fields

II

Faces good for the fire faces good for the cold For denials for darkness for insults for blows

[1]Many writers and artists, most notably Picasso, responded to the destruction of the Spanish town of Guernica by German bombers in 1937.

III

Visages bons à tout
Voici le vide qui vous fixe
Votre mort va servir d'exemple

IV

La mort cœur renversé

V

Ils vous ont fait payer le pain
Le ciel la terre l'eau le sommeil
Et la misère
De votre vie

VI

Ils disaient désirer la bonne intelligence
Ils rationnaient les forts jugeaient les fous
Faisaient l'aumône partageaient un sou en deux
Ils saluaient les cadavres
Ils s'accablaient de politesses

III

Faces good for everything Here is the void staring at you Your death will serve as an example

IV

Death a heart overturned

V

They have made you pay for bread for the sky For the earth for water for sleep And for the wretchedness Of your life

VI

They said they wanted to be on good terms They put the strong on short rations judged the madmen Gave alms divided a penny in two They bowed before corpses They overwhelmed each other with compliments

VII

Ils persévèrent ils exagèrent ils ne sont pas de notre monde

VIII

Les femmes les enfants ont le même trésor
De feuilles vertes de printemps et de lait pur
Et de durée
Dans leurs yeux purs

IX

Les femmes les enfants ont le même trésor
Dans les yeux
Les hommes le défendent comme ils peuvent

X

Les femmes les enfants ont les mêmes roses rouges
Dans les yeux
Chacun montre son sang

VII

They persist they go too far they are not of our world

VIII

Women and children have the same treasure of green leaves in springtime and pure milk And the passage of time In their pure eyes

IX

Women and children have the same treasure In their eyes Men defend it as best they can

X

Women and children have the same red roses In their eyes Each one reveals his blood

XI

La peur et le courage de vivre et de mourir
La mort si difficile et si facile

XII

Hommes pour qui ce trésor fut chanté
Hommes pour qui ce trésor fut gâché

XIII

Hommes réels pour qui le désespoir
Alimente le feu dévorant de l'espoir
Ouvrons ensemble le dernier bourgeon de l'avenir

XIV

Parias la mort la terre et la hideur
De nos ennemis ont la couleur
Monotone de notre nuit
Nous en aurons raison.

XI

The fear and the courage of living and dying Death so hard and so easy

XII

Men for whom this treasure was sung Men for whom this treasure was spoiled

XIII

Real men for whom despair Feeds the devouring fire of hope Let us open together the last bud of the future

XIV

Pariahs death earth and the hideousness Of our enemies have the monotonous Colour of our darkness We will overcome them

Faire vivre

Ils étaient quelques-uns qui vivaient dans la nuit
En rêvant du ciel caressant
Ils étaient quelques-uns qui aimaient la forêt
Et qui croyaient au bois brûlant
L'odeur des fleurs les ravissait même de loin
La nudité de leurs désirs les recouvrait

Ils joignaient dans leur cœur le souffle mesuré
A ce rien d'ambition de la vie naturelle
Qui grandit dans l'été comme un été plus fort

Ils joignaient dans leur cœur l'espoir du temps qui vient
Et qui salue même de loin un autre temps
A des amours plus obstinées que le désert

Keeping life alive

They were a few who lived in the night Dreaming of the caressing sky They were a few who loved the forest And who believed in the burning wood The scent of flowers enchanted them even from afar The nakedness of their desires clothed them

They united in their hearts the rhythmic breath and that hint of ambition within natural life That grows in the summer like a stronger summer

They united in their hearts the hope for the time that is coming And which hails even from afar another time With loves more stubborn than the desert

Un tout petit peu de sommeil
Les rendait au soleil futur
Ils duraient ils savaient que vivre perpétue

Et leurs besoins obscurs engendraient la clarté.

★

Ils n'étaient que quelques-uns
Ils furent foule soudain

Ceci est de tous les temps.

The briefest sleep Delivered them up to the future sun They endured they knew that to live is to perpetuate

And their obscure needs engendered shining light.

★

They were only a few Suddenly they were a crowd

Thus it is in all times.

La Mort l'Amour la Vie

J'ai cru pouvoir briser la profondeur l'immensité
Par mon chagrin tout nu sans contact sans écho
Je me suis étendu dans ma prison aux portes vierges
Comme un mort raisonnable qui a su mourir
Un mort non couronné sinon de son néant
Je me suis étendu sur les vagues absurdes
Du poison absorbé par amour de la cendre
La solitude m'a semblé plus vive que le sang

Death Love Life

I thought I could shatter depth immensity Through my grief quite naked without contact without echo I lay down in my prison with the virgin doors Like a rational dead man who knew how to die A dead man unwreathed unless by his nothingness I lay down on the absurd waves Of the poison absorbed through love from the ashes Solitude seemed more alive to me than blood

Je voulais désunir la vie
Je voulais partager la mort avec la mort
Rendre mon cœur au vide et le vide à la vie
Tout effacer qu'il n'y ait rien ni vitre ni buée
Ni rien devant ni rien derrière rien entier
J'avais éliminé le glaçon des mains jointes
J'avais éliminé l'hivernale ossature
Du vœu de vivre qui s'annule

⋆

Tu es venue le feu s'est alors ranimé
L'ombre a cédé le froid d'en bas s'est étoilé
Et la terre s'est recouverte
De ta chair claire et je me suis senti léger
Tu es venue la solitude était vaincue
J'avais un guide sur la terre je savais
Me diriger je me savais démesuré
J'avançais je gagnais de l'espace et du temps

I wanted to tear life asunder I wanted to share death with death To give back my heart to the void and the void to life To obliterate everything that there be nothing neither window-pane nor clouding breath Nor anything in front nor anything behind nothing entirely I had eliminated the ice-block of joined hands I had eliminated the wintry skeleton of the desire to live that nullifies itself

⋆

You came the fire revived then The shadow surrendered the cold below was filled with stars And the earth clothed itself In your shining flesh and I felt light You came solitude was conquered I had a guide on the earth I knew My direction I knew I had no limits I moved forward I was gaining space and time

J'allais vers toi j'allais sans fin vers la lumière
La vie avait un corps l'espoir tendait sa voile
Le sommeil ruisselait de rêves et la nuit
Promettait à l'aurore des regards confiants
Les rayons de tes bras entr'ouvraient le brouillard
Ta bouche était mouillée des premières rosées
Le repos ébloui remplaçait la fatigue
Et j'adorais l'amour comme à mes premiers jours.

⋆

Les champs sont labourés les usines rayonnent
Et le blé fait son nid dans une houle énorme
La moisson la vendange ont des témoins sans nombre
Rien n'est simple ni singulier
La mer est dans les yeux du ciel ou de la nuit
La forêt donne aux arbres la sécurité
Et les murs des maisons ont une peau commune
Et les routes toujours se croisent

I was going towards you I was going endlessly towards the light Life had a body hope spread its sail Sleep streamed with dreams and the night Promised confident looks to dawn The sunbeams of your arms pushed open the fog Your mouth was moist with the first dews Dazzled repose replaced fatigue and I worshipped love as in my earliest days.

⋆

The fields are ploughed the factories are radiant And the wheat makes its nest in a vast swelling tide The harvest the vintage have countless witnesses Nothing is plain or singular The sea is in the eyes of the sky or of the night The forest gives security to the trees And the walls of the houses have a common skin And the roads all cross each other

Les hommes sont faits pour s'entendre
Pour se comprendre pour s'aimer
Ont des enfants qui deviendront pères des hommes
Ont des enfants sans feu ni lieu
Qui réinventeront les hommes
Et la nature et leur patrie
Celle de tous les hommes
Celle de tous les temps.

Men are made to hear each other's voice To understand each other love each other Have children who will father children Have children without fire or place Who will reinvent men And nature and their homeland That of all men That of all times.

Louis Aragon
(1897–1982)

Though recent evaluations have tended to downgrade Aragon as a poet and to shift attention to his prose works, his contribution to modern verse remains significant. He is recognized as an inspirational figure in the Resistance and as a fine love-poet, but his early Dadaist and Surrealist work, on the whole, and a good deal of his 1930s political poetry perhaps have only historical interest now.

A rebel against his bourgeois upbringing and its values, Aragon was always a mirror of his times. Filled with disgust at the First World War, he threw himself into the nihilistic and scandalous aspects of Dada. Working in the Medical Corps in 1917, he met Breton and Soupault, and two years later founded with them the periodical *Littérature*. He campaigned with them for the Surrealist 'reconstruction of reality', even if his own verse of the period, however aggressive and vulgar it may be, perhaps lacks both the force of his prose essays and an authentic origin in 'automatism' (Aragon wrote later that he had always been a conscious artist). Nevertheless, he played a central role in the birth of Surrealism, and shared in many of the group's creative experiments.

The idea that love is a prime key to absolute experience was confirmed for him when in 1928 he met Elsa Triolet, a writer of Russian origin who would be his companion for the next forty years. She was the sister-in-law of Mayakovsky, and Aragon's discussions with Elsa and the Russian poet at 'La Coupole' in Montparnasse accelerated and deepened his already growing commitment to Communism. His loving relationship with Elsa was to be incorporated both into his wartime nationalism and into his celebration of the couple as the cornerstone of an ideal Marxist society.

He broke with the Surrealists in 1931, and several trips to the Soviet Union reinforced his political beliefs and his enthusiasm for Socialist Realism in the arts. He became a controversial figure in France, receiving a suspended prison sentence in 1932 for 'incitement to mutiny and provocation to murder' in his political poem '*Front Rouge*'.

After service in the Medical Corps again in 1940, he escaped to southern France, where he co-ordinated intellectual groups within the Resistance, spread poems and pamphlets clandestinely, and became a strong voice for the spirit of freedom in French hearts and minds. Partly to confuse the censors, he incorporated elements of French history and legend into his poetry, blending the strongly rhyming and rhythmic style of traditional ballads and songs (forms that could easily be memorized and passed on) with the orthodox metres and moderately adventurous free verse he had used earlier. The outstanding '*Les lilas et les roses*' perhaps combines many French elements in an ideal synthesis, exemplifying as well as pledging to perpetuate the spirit of a national culture, and celebrating its refusal to die in spite of the catastrophic military collapse of 1940. Language here is used as a weapon, as always with Aragon, but with a more integrated strength in the transmission of emotion through image.

After the war, he attacked reactionary influences that prevented the emergence of a new Socialist society in France. He became a member of the Central Committee of the Communist Party, and promoted knowledge of Russian literature, a lifelong passion since his reading of Gorky in adolescence. Unprotesting over Russian intervention in Hungary, by 1966 he felt able to condemn Soviet imprisonment of dissident writers, and attacked the invasion of Czechoslovakia in 1968. His poetry also continued to celebrate his love for Elsa until and beyond her death in 1970.

Major volumes: *Feu de joie* 1920, *Le Mouvement perpétuel* 1926, *La Grande Gaîté* 1929, *Persécuté Persécuteur* 1931, *Hourra l'Oural* 1934, *Le Crève-Cœur* 1941, *Les Yeux d'Elsa* 1942,

Brocéliande 1943, *Le Musée Grévin* 1943, *La Diane française* 1945, *Le Nouveau Crève-Cœur* 1948, *Les Yeux et la mémoire* 1954, *Le Roman inachevé* 1956, *Elsa* 1959, *Le Fou d'Elsa* 1963.

Poème à crier dans les ruines

Tous deux crachons tous deux
Sur ce que nous avons aimé
Sur ce que nous avons aimé tous deux
Si tu veux car ceci tous deux
Est bien un air de valse et j'imagine
Ce qui passe entre nous de sombre et d'inégalable
Comme un dialogue de miroirs abandonnés
A la consigne quelque part Foligno peut-être
Ou l'Auvergne la Bourboule
Certains noms sont chargés d'un tonnerre lointain
Veux-tu crachons tous deux sur ces pays immenses
Où se promènent de petites automobiles de louage
Veux-tu car il faut que quelque chose encore
Quelque chose
Nous réunisse veux-tu crachons
Tous deux c'est une valse
Une espèce de sanglot commode
Crachons crachons de petites automobiles
Crachons c'est la consigne

Poem to Shout in the Ruins

Let's both spit both of us On what we loved On what we both loved Shall we for this both of us Is truly a waltz melody and I imagine What passes between us that is dark and peerless Like a dialogue of mirrors abandoned In left luggage somewhere Foligno perhaps or the Auvergne at La Bourboule Certain names are charged with distant thunder Shall we let's both spit on those vast countries Where little rented cars run around Shall we for it's essential for something still Something To unite us let's spit shall we Both of us it's a waltz A sort of convenient sob Let's spit let's spit little cars Let's spit that's the

Une valse de miroirs
Un dialogue nulle part
Ecoute ces pays immenses où le vent
Pleure sur ce que nous avons aimé
L'un d'eux est un cheval qui s'accoude à la terre
L'autre un mort agitant un linge l'autre
La trace de tes pas Je me souviens d'un village désert
A l'épaule d'une montagne brûlée
Je me souviens de ton épaule
Je me souviens de ton coude
Je me souviens de ton linge
Je me souviens de tes pas
Je me souviens d'une ville où il n'y a pas de cheval
Je me souviens de ton regard qui a brûlé
Mon cœur désert un mort Mazeppa qu'un cheval
Emporte devant moi comme ce jour dans la montagne
L'ivresse précipitait ma course à travers les chênes martyrs
Qui saignaient prophétiquement tandis
Que le jour faiblissait sur des camions bleus

password A waltz of mirrors A dialogue nowhere Listen to those vast countries where the wind Weeps over what we loved One of them is a horse with its elbows on the ground Another a dead man waving linen another The trace of your footsteps I remember a deserted village On the shoulder of a scorched mountain I remember your shoulder I remember your elbow I remember your linen I remember your footsteps I remember a town where there is no horse I remember your gaze that scorched My deserted heart a dead man Mazeppa[1] carried by a horse before me like that day in the mountains Drunkenness sped my trajectory through the martyred oaks That bled prophetically while The daylight faded over blue trucks

[1]Mazeppa: a seventeenth-century Governor of the Ukraine. In his youth he had been strapped naked to a wild horse as a punishment for adultery. Subject of a poem by Byron and a symphonic poem by Liszt.

Je me souviens de tant de choses
De tant de soirs
De tant de chambres
De tant de marches
De tant de colères
De tant de haltes dans des lieux nuls
Où s'éveillait pourtant l'esprit du mystère pareil
Au cri d'un enfant aveugle dans une gare-frontière
Je me souviens

Je parle donc au passé Que l'on rie
Si le cœur vous en dit du son de mes paroles
Aima Fut Vint Caressa
Attendit Epia les escaliers qui craquèrent
O violences violences je suis un homme hanté
Attendit attendit puits profonds
J'ai cru mourir d'attendre
Le silence taillait des crayons dans la rue

I remember so many things So many evenings So many bedrooms So many walks So many angers So many halts in worthless places Where nevertheless awakened the spirit of mystery Like the cry of a blind child in a frontier station I remember

So I am speaking in[1] the past Laugh away If you feel like it at the sound of my words Loved Was Came Caressed Waited Watched the stairs that creaked O violence violence I am a man possessed Waited waited deep well-shafts I thought I would die of waiting The silence was sharpening pencils in

[1]Conceivably 'to the past'.

Ce taxi qui toussait s'en va crever ailleurs
Attendit attendit les voix étouffées
Devant la porte le langage des portes
Hoquet des maisons attendit
Les objets familiers prenaient à tour de rôle
Attendit l'aspect fantomatique Attendit
Des forçats evadés Attendit
Attendit Nom de Dieu
D'un bagne de lueurs et soudain
Non Stupide Non
Idiot
La chaussure a foulé la laine du tapis
Je rentre à peine
Aima aima aima mais tu ne peux pas savoir combien
Aima c'est au passé
Aima aima aima aima aima
O violences

Ils en ont de bonnes ceux
Qui parlent de l'amour comme d'une histoire de cousine
Ah merde pour tout ce faux-semblant
Sais-tu quand cela devient vraiment une histoire
L'amour
Sais-tu

the street That coughing taxi moves away to die elsewhere Waited waited the muffled voices Outside the door the speech of doors Hiccup of houses waited Familiar objects took on in turn Waited the spectral air Waited Of escaped convicts Waited Waited In God's Name From a prison of glimmerings and suddenly No Stupid No Idiot The shoe crushed the wool of the carpet I can scarcely return Loved loved loved but you cannot know how much Loved it's in the past Loved loved loved loved loved O violence

It's all very funny for those Who speak of love as if it were the story of a first flirtation Ah shit on all that pretence Do you know when it really becomes a story Love Do you know When

Quand toute respiration tourne à la tragédie
Quand les couleurs du jour sont ce que les fait un rire
Un air une ombre d'ombre un nom jeté
Que tout brûle et qu'on sait au fond
Que tout brûle
Et qu'on dit Que tout brûle
Et le ciel a le goût du sable dispersé
L'amour salauds l'amour pour vous
C'est d'arriver à coucher ensemble
D'arriver
Et après Ha ha tout l'amour est dans ce
Et après
Nous arrivons à parler de ce que c'est que de
Coucher ensemble pendant des années
Entendez-vous
Pendant des années
Pareilles à des voiles marines qui tombent
Sur le pont d'un navire chargé de pestiférés
Dans un film que j'ai vu récemment
Une à une
La rose blanche meurt comme la rose rouge
Qu'est-ce donc qui m'émeut à un pareil point

every breath turns to tragedy When the colours of the day are what laughter makes them A tune a shadow of a shadow a name flung out That everything burns and you know deep down That everything is burning And you say Let it all burn And the sky has the taste of the scattered sand Love you bastards love for you Is managing to sleep together Managing And afterwards Ha ha all of love is in that Afterwards We manage to talk of what it is to Sleep together for years Do you understand For years Like sea sails falling On the deck of a ship loaded with plague victims In a film I saw recently One by one The white rose dies like the red rose So what is it that moves

Dans ces derniers mots
Le mot dernier peut-être mot en qui
Tout est atroce atrocement irréparable
Et déchirant Mot panthère Mot électrique
Chaise
Le dernier mot d'amour imaginez-vous ça
Et le dernier baiser et la dernière
Nonchalance
Et le dernier sommeil Tiens c'est drôle
Je pensais simplement à la dernière nuit
Ah tout prend ce sens abominable
Je voulais dire les derniers instants
Les derniers adieux le dernier soupir
Le dernier regard
L'horreur l'horreur l'horreur
Pendant des années l'horreur
Crachons veux-tu bien
Sur ce que nous avons aimé ensemble
Crachons sur l'amour
Sur nos lits défaits
Sur notre silence et sur les mots balbutiés

me to such a pitch In these last words The final word perhaps in which All is heinous heinously irreparable And tearing apart Word panther Word electric Chair The final word of love just imagine that And the final kiss and the final Listlessness And the final sleep Hey it's funny I was thinking simply of the final night Ah everything's taking on this abominable meaning I meant the final moments The final farewells the final sigh The final gaze The horror the horror the horror For years the horror Let's spit shall we On what we loved together Let's spit on love On our unmade beds On our silence and on the

Sur les étoiles fussent-elles
Tes yeux
Sur le soleil fût-il
Tes dents
Sur l'éternité fût-elle
Ta bouche
Et sur notre amour
Fût-il
TON amour
Crachons veux-tu bien

stammered words On the stars were they Your eyes On the sun were it Your teeth On eternity were it Your mouth And on our love Were it *YOUR* love Let's spit shall we

Elsa au miroir

C'était au beau milieu de notre tragédie
Et pendant un long jour assise à son miroir
Elle peignait ses cheveux d'or Je croyais voir
Ses patientes mains calmer un incendie
C'était au beau milieu de notre tragédie

Et pendant un long jour assise à son miroir
Elle peignait ses cheveux d'or et j'aurais dit
C'était au beau milieu de notre tragédie
Qu'elle jouait un air de harpe sans y croire
Pendant tout ce long jour assise à son miroir

Elle peignait ses cheveux d'or et j'aurais dit
Qu'elle martyrisait à plaisir sa mémoire
Pendant tout ce long jour assise à son miroir
A ranimer les fleurs sans fin de l'incendie
Sans dire ce qu'une autre à sa place aurait dit

Elsa at her Mirror

It was in the very midst of our tragedy And for a long day seated at her mirror She combed her golden hair I thought I saw her patient hands appease a fire It was in the very midst of our tragedy

And for a long day seated at her mirror She combed her golden hair and it was as if It was in the very midst of our tragedy As if she was playing unconsciously a melody on a harp Through that whole long day seated at her mirror

She combed her golden hair and it was as if She martyred her memory wantonly Through that whole long day seated at her mirror Rekindling the flowers without end of the fire Without saying what another in her place would have said

Elle martyrisait à plaisir sa mémoire
C'était au beau milieu de notre tragédie
Le monde ressemblait à ce miroir maudit
Le peigne partageait les feux de cette moire
Et ces feux éclairaient des coins de ma mémoire

C'était au beau milieu de notre tragédie
Comme dans la semaine est assis le jeudi

Et pendant un long jour assise à sa mémoire
Elle voyait au loin mourir dans son miroir

Un à un les acteurs de notre tragédie
Et qui sont les meilleurs de ce monde maudit

Et vous savez leurs noms sans que je les aie dits
Et ce que signifient les flammes des longs soirs

Et ses cheveux dorés quand elle vient s'asseoir
Et peigner sans rien dire un reflet d'incendie

She martyred her memory wantonly It was in the very midst of our tragedy The world resembled that accursed mirror The comb divided the fires of that watered silk And those fires illumined corners in my memory

It was in the very midst of our tragedy As Thursday is set within the week

And for a long day seated before her memory She saw dying in the distance in her mirror

One by one the actors in our tragedy Who are the best in this accursed world

And you know their names without me saying them And the meaning of the flames in the long evenings

And her gilded hair when she comes and sits and combs without a word a fire's reflection

Les lilas et les roses

O mois des floraisons mois des métamorphoses
Mai qui fut sans nuage et Juin poignardé
Je n'oublierai jamais les lilas ni les roses
Ni ceux que le printemps dans ses plis a gardés

Je n'oublierai jamais l'illusion tragique
Le cortège les cris la foule et le soleil
Les chars chargés d'amour les dons de la Belgique
L'air qui tremble et la route à ce bourdon d'abeilles
Le triomphe imprudent qui prime la querelle
Le sang que préfigure en carmin le baiser
Et ceux qui vont mourir debout dans les tourelles
Entourés de lilas par un peuple grisé

The Lilacs and the Roses

O month of flowerings month of metamorphoses May that was cloudless and June stabbed I will never forget the lilacs nor the roses Nor those whom spring has kept within its folds

I will never forget the tragic illusion The procession the cries the crowd and the sunlight The tanks laden with love the gifts from Belgium The air that vibrates and the road with this buzzing of bees The rash sense of triumph that goes before the quarrel The blood foreshadowed in carmine by the kiss And those who are going to die standing in the turrets Enveloped in lilacs by an intoxicated people

Je n'oublierai jamais les jardins de la France
Semblables aux missels des siècles disparus
Ni le trouble des soirs l'énigme du silence
Les roses tout le long du chemin parcouru
Le démenti des fleurs au vent de la panique
Aux soldats qui passaient sur l'aile de la peur
Aux vélos délirants aux canons ironiques
Au pitoyable accoutrement des faux campeurs

Mais je ne sais pourquoi ce tourbillon d'images
Me ramène toujours au même point d'arrêt
A Sainte-Marthe Un général De noirs ramages
Une villa normande au bord de la forêt
Tout se tait l'ennemi dans l'ombre se repose
On nous a dit ce soir que Paris s'est rendu
Je n'oublierai jamais les lilas ni les roses
Et ni les deux amours que nous avons perdus

I will never forget the gardens of France That are like the missals of vanished centuries Nor the uneasiness of the evenings the enigma of the silence The roses all along the way we travelled The contradiction by the flowers of the wind of panic Of the soldiers passing by on the wing of fear Of the delirious bicycles of the ironic cannons Of the pitiable garb of the fake campers

But I do not know why this whirlwind of images Brings me back always to the same point of rest At Sainte-Marthe A general Dark branches A Norman villa at the edge of the forest All is quiet The enemy is resting in the shadow We have been told tonight that Paris has surrendered I will never forget the lilacs nor the roses Nor the two loves that we have lost

Bouquets du premier jour lilas lilas des Flandres
Douceur de l'ombre dont la mort farde les joues
Et vous bouquets de la retraite roses tendres
Couleur de l'incendie au loin roses d'Anjou

Bouquets of the first day lilacs lilacs of Flanders Softness of the shadow whose cheeks are painted by death And you bouquets of retreat tender roses The colour of fire in the distance roses of Anjou

Ballade de celui qui chanta dans les supplices

–"Et s'il était à refaire
Je referais ce chemin..."
Une voix monte des fers
Et parle des lendemains.

On dit que dans sa cellule,
Deux hommes, cette nuit-là,
Lui murmuraient: "Capitule
De cette vie es-tu las?

Tu peux vivre, tu peux vivre,
Tu peux vivre comme nous!
Dis le mot qui te délivre
Et tu peux vivre à genoux..."

Ballad of the Man who sang in Torment[1]

–'And if it were to be done again I would take this road once more ...' A voice rises from the iron chains and speaks of days to come.

They say that in his cell two men, that night, whispered to him: 'Capitulate Are you weary of this life?

You can live, you can live, you can live like us! Say the word that sets you free and you can live on your knees ...'

[1]Gabriel Péri, a Communist deputy shot as a hostage in 1941, defiantly singing the 'Marseillaise'. The event features in many wartime poems. The words attributed by Aragon to this Resistance martyr are based on a letter written by Péri on the eve of his execution.

–"Et s'il était à refaire,
Je referais ce chemin..."
La voix qui monte des fers
Parle pour les lendemains.

"Rien qu'un mot: la porte cède,
S'ouvre et tu sors! Rien qu'un mot:
Le bourreau se dépossède...
Sésame! Finis tes maux!

Rien qu'un mot, rien qu'un mensonge
Pour transformer ton destin...
Songe, songe, songe, songe
A la douceur des matins!"

–"Et si c'était à refaire
Je referais ce chemin..."
La voix qui monte des fers
Parle aux hommes de demain.

–'And if it were to be done again I would take this road once more ...' The voice that rises from the chains speaks for the days to come.

'Just one word: the door will yield, it will open and you are out! Just one word: the executioner is dispossessed ... Sesame! End your woes!

Just one word, just one lie to transform your destiny ... Dream, dream, dream, dream of the sweetness of the mornings!'

–'And if it were to be done again I would take this road once more ...' The voice that rises from the chains speaks to the men of tomorrow.

"J'ai dit tout ce qu'on peut dire:
L'exemple du Roi Henri...
Un cheval pour mon empire...
Une messe pour Paris...

Rien à faire." Alors qu'ils partent!
Sur lui retombe son sang!
C'était son unique carte:
Périsse cet innocent!

Et si c'était à refaire
Referait-il ce chemin?
La voix qui monte des fers
Dit: "Je le ferai demain.

Je meurs et France demeure
Mon amour et mon refus.
O mes amis, si je meurs,
Vous saurez pourquoi ce fut!"

'I have said all that can be said: the example of King Henry[1] ... A horse for my empire ... Paris is worth a mass ...

Nothing to be done.' Then let them go! Let his blood gush over him! It was his only card: perish this innocent man!

And if it were to be done again would he take this road once more? The voice that rises from the chains says: 'I will do it tomorrow.

I am dying and France remains my love and my refusal. O my friends, if I am dying, you know why it was done!'

[1]Henri IV, reputed to have become a Catholic purely to secure the loyalty of Paris, and to have said in 1593: '*Paris vaut bien une messe.*' His approach is compared ironically with that of Shakespeare's Richard III.

Ils sont venus pour le prendre.
Ils parlent en allemand.
L'un traduit: "Veux-tu te rendre?"
Il répète calmement:

–"Et si c'était à refaire
Je referais ce chemin,
Sous vos coups, chargé de fers,
Que chantent les lendemains!"

Il chantait, lui, sous les balles,
Des mots: "... sanglant est levé..."
D'une seconde rafale,
Il a fallu l'achever.

Une autre chanson française
A ses lèvres est montée,
Finissant la Marseillaise
Pour toute l'humanité!

They have come to take him away. They speak in German. One translates: 'Will you surrender?' Calmly he repeats:

–'And if it were to be done again I would take this road once more, under your blows, weighed down with chains, let the days to come sing!'

He sang, that man, under the hail of bullets, words: '... bloodstained standard is raised ...'[1] They had to fire a second burst to finish him off.

Another French song[2] rose to his lips, completing the Marseillaise for all humanity!

[1]Words from the 'Marseillaise': "*Contre nous de la tyrannie / L'étendard sanglant est levé ...*"
[2]The Internationale.

Robert Desnos
(1900–1945)

Born and brought up in Paris, Desnos worked briefly as a journalist before being called up for military service in Morocco. While on leave in 1922 he met Breton and Aragon, who realized with excitement that Desnos was ahead of them in the transcription of dreams. He already had a remarkable ability to drop into 'hypnotic sleep', and to practise 'automatic' talking and writing with great immediacy and power. Not only that, but the products of his subconscious also had a strongly lyrical and haunting, incantatory quality.

He is thus a key figure in the early days of Surrealism, his vital role acknowledged by Breton even after Desnos had broken with the movement in 1929–30, unhappy with its growing orthodoxy and with what he felt was an overdone, increasingly literary cult of the image. On a personal level he remained in essence a Surrealist, pursuing liberty and transcendence through love, sustaining an '*émerveillement sensible*' in his response to experience, finding the surreal in the real. Spontaneous, generous and optimistic, he lived life to the full, and lived the adventure of language to the full in his brilliantly controlled free verse '*élans*' and hypnotic prose-poems. His poetry is, by his own description, both '*délirante et lucide*'.

Having joined the Resistance in 1940, he was arrested by the Gestapo in 1944 and imprisoned in a series of concentration camps. Just after the Liberation in 1945 he died of typhus and starvation at Terezin in Czechoslovakia.

A good deal of his earliest work is based on untranslatable word-play ('play' in terms of physical elasticity as well as in its conventional sense). The best-known example is probably 'Rrose Sélavy'. Desnos surrenders to sound and spelling as autonomous forces, to a play of phonemes, homonyms and letter-substitution which can of its own accord generate images and concepts. Opinions vary on the artificiality or artistic validity of these productions.

From 1926 onwards love becomes a major theme and an animating force, a means to originality of vision and expression, a stimulus to the surrealistic imagination, as it is with Eluard. There is a tragic element too, in that the woman is often not present in a real sense, and the relationship is often virtual or fantasized rather than actual. But there is no coldness or Laforguian irony in this tension; even in failure Desnos is an enhancer of life.

In the 1930s he consciously sought a more popular and directly communicative mode of poetry, and also broadcast frequently on radio. His wartime verse, though important in its time and still characterized by original images, is more conventional in form and less memorable than the earlier work concentrated mainly in *Corps et biens* (1930).

Other major volumes: *C'est les bottes de sept lieues cette phrase: 'Je me vois'* 1926, *Les Sans Cou* 1934, *Fortunes* 1942, *Etat de veille* 1943, *Contrée* 1944, *Trente Chantefables pour les enfants sages* 1944, *Calixto* 1962.

J'ai tant rêvé de toi

J'ai tant rêvé de toi que tu perds ta réalité.

Est-il encore temps d'atteindre ce corps vivant et de baiser sur cette bouche la naissance de la voix qui m'est chère?

J'ai tant rêvé de toi que mes bras habitués en étreignant ton ombre à se croiser sur ma poitrine ne se plieraient pas au contour de ton corps, peut-être.

Et que, devant l'apparence réelle de ce qui me hante et me gouverne depuis des jours et des années, je deviendrais une ombre sans doute.

O balances sentimentales.

I Have Dreamed so much of you

I have dreamed so much of you that you are losing your reality.

Is there still time to reach that living body and to kiss on that mouth the birth of the voice that is precious to me?

I have dreamed so much of you that my arms which as they embrace your shadow habitually fold across my breast would not bend to the contour of your body, perhaps.

And so much that, faced with the real appearance of that which has haunted me and ruled me for days and years, I would become a shadow I dare say.

O scales of feeling.

J'ai tant rêvé de toi qu'il n'est plus temps sans doute que je m'éveille. Je dors debout, le corps exposé à toutes les apparences de la vie et de l'amour et toi, la seule qui compte aujourd'hui pour moi, je pourrais moins toucher ton front et tes lèvres que les premières lèvres et le premier front venu.

J'ai tant rêvé de toi, tant marché, parlé, couché avec ton fantôme qu'il ne me reste plus peut-être, et pourtant, qu'à être fantôme parmi les fantômes et plus ombre cent fois que l'ombre qui se promène et se promènera allégrement sur le cadran solaire de ta vie.

I have dreamed so much of you that there is no more time I dare say for me to awaken. I am sleeping on my feet, my body exposed to all the appearances of life and love and you, the only one who matters today for me, I could less readily touch your forehead and your lips than the lips and forehead of the first newcomer.

I have dreamed so much of you, walked, talked and slept so much with your phantom that all I have left perhaps, after all, is to be a phantom among phantoms and a hundred times more shadow than the shadow that moves and will move joyfully on the sundial of your life.

La Voix de Robert Desnos

Si semblable à la fleur et au courant d'air
au cours d'eau aux ombres passagères
au sourire entrevu ce fameux soir à minuit
si semblable à tout au bonheur et à la tristesse
c'est le minuit passé dressant son torse nu au-dessus des beffrois et des peupliers
j'appelle à moi ceux-là perdus dans les campagnes
les vieux cadavres les jeunes chênes coupés
les lambeaux d'étoffe pourrissant sur la terre et le linge séchant aux alentours des fermes
j'appelle à moi les tornades et les ouragans
les tempêtes les typhons les cyclones
les raz de marée
les tremblements de terre
j'appelle à moi la fumée des volcans et celle des cigarettes

The Voice of Robert Desnos

So like the flower and the draught of air / the water course with its [1] fleeting shadows / the smile glimpsed at midnight on that memorable evening / so like everything like happiness and sadness / it is midnight gone by raising its naked torso above the belfries and the poplars / I summon to me those lost in open country / the old corpses the felled young oaks / the shreds of fabric rotting on the earth and the linen drying around the farms / I summon to me the tornadoes and the hurricanes / the tempests the typhoons the cyclones / the tidal waves / the earthquakes / I summon to me the smoke of

[1] '*...aux*' here is ambiguous. It could be dependent on '*semblable*'.

les ronds de fumée des cigares de luxe
j'appelle à moi les amours et les amoureux
j'appelle à moi les vivants et les morts
j'appelle les fossoyeurs j'appelle les assassins
j'appelle les bourreaux j'appelle les pilotes les maçons et les architectes
les assassins
j'appelle la chair
j'appelle celle que j'aime
j'appelle celle que j'aime
j'appelle celle que j'aime
le minuit triomphant déploie ses ailes de satin et se pose sur mon lit
les beffrois et les peupliers se plient à mon désir
ceux-là s'écroulent ceux-là s'affaissent
les perdus dans la campagne se retrouvent en me trouvant
les vieux cadavres ressuscitent à ma voix
les jeunes chênes coupés se couvrent de verdure
les lambeaux d'étoffe pourrissant dans la terre et sur la terre
claquent à ma voix comme l'étendard de la révolte

volcanoes and that of cigarettes / the smoke rings of extravagant cigars / I summon to me loves and lovers / I summon to me the living and the dead / I summon the gravediggers I summon the assassins / I summon the executioners I summon the pilots the stonemasons and the architects / the assassins / I summon the flesh / I summon the woman I love / I summon the woman I love / I summon the woman I love / midnight triumphant unfolds its satin wings and alights on my bed / the belfries and the poplars bend to my desire / the former crumble the former collapse / those lost in open country find each other by finding me / the old corpses revive at my voice / the felled young oaks clothe themselves in greenery / the shreds of fabric rotting in the earth and on the earth / flap at my voice like the banner of rebellion / the linen

le linge séchant aux alentours des fermes habille d'adorables femmes que je n'adore pas
qui viennent à moi
obéissent à ma voix et m'adorent
les tornades tournent dans ma bouche
les ouragans rougissent s'il est possible mes lèvres
les tempêtes grondent à mes pieds
les typhons s'il est possible me dépeignent
je reçois les baisers d'ivresse des cyclones
les raz de marée viennent mourir à mes pieds
les tremblements de terre ne m'ébranlent pas mais font tout crouler à mon ordre
la fumée des volcans me vêt de ses vapeurs
et celle des cigarettes me parfume
et les ronds de fumée des cigares me couronnent
les amours et l'amour si longtemps poursuivis se réfugient en moi
les amoureux écoutent ma voix
les vivants et les morts se soumettent et me saluent les premiers froidement les seconds familièrement
les fossoyeurs abandonnent les tombes à peine creusées et

drying around the farms dresses adorable women whom I do not adore / who come to me / obey my voice and adore me / the tornadoes whirl in my mouth / the hurricanes redden my lips if that is possible / the tempests roar at my feet / the typhoons dishevel me if that is possible / I receive the kisses of ecstasy of the cyclones / the tidal waves die away as they reach my feet / the earthquakes do not shake me but bring all things crashing down at my command / the smoke of volcanoes clothes me in its vapours / and that of cigarettes perfumes me / and the smoke rings of cigars wreathe me / the lovers and the love so long pursued find refuge within me / the lovers listen to my voice / the living and the dead submit and hail me the first coldly the second in intimacy / the gravediggers abandon

déclarent que moi seul puis commander leurs nocturnes travaux
les assassins me saluent
les bourreaux invoquent la révolution
invoquent ma voix
invoquent mon nom
les pilotes se guident sur mes yeux
les maçons ont le vertige en m'écoutant
les architectes partent pour le désert
les assassins me bénissent
la chair palpite à mon appel

celle que j'aime ne m'écoute pas
celle que j'aime ne m'entend pas
celle que j'aime ne me répond pas.

the scarcely hollowed tombs and declare that I alone can command their nocturnal toils / the assassins hail me / the executioners invoke the revolution / invoke my voice / invoke my name / the pilots steer by my eyes / the stonemasons are dizzy as they listen to me / the architects set off for the desert / the assassins bless me / the flesh quivers at my summons /

the woman I love is not listening to me / the woman I love is not hearing me / the woman I love is not answering me.

Destinée arbitraire

à Georges Malkine

Voici venir le temps des croisades.
Par la fenêtre fermée les oiseaux s'obstinent à parler
comme les poissons d'aquarium.
A la devanture d'une boutique
une jolie femme sourit.
Bonheur tu n'es que cire à cacheter
et je passe tel un feu follet.
Un grand nombre de gardiens poursuivent
un inoffensif papillon échappé de l'asile.
Il devient sous mes mains pantalon de dentelle
et ta chair d'aigle
ô mon rêve quand je vous caresse!
Demain on enterrera gratuitement
on ne s'enrhumera plus
on parlera le langage des fleurs
on s'éclairera de lumières inconnues à ce jour.
Mais aujourd'hui c'est aujourd'hui.
Je sens que mon commencement est proche

Arbitrary Destiny

for Georges Malkine

The time of the crusades is approaching. Beyond the closed window the birds persist in speaking like aquarium fish. In a shop front a pretty woman smiles. Happiness you are merely sealing wax and I pass like a will-o'-the-wisp. Numerous warders pursue an inoffensive butterfly that has slipped out of the asylum. It becomes within my hands lace underwear and your eagle flesh O my dream when I caress you! Tomorrow there will be free burials we will get no more colds we will speak the language of the flowers we will be illumined by lights unknown to this day. But today is today. I sense that my

pareil aux blés de juin.
Gendarmes passez-moi les menottes.
Les statues se détournent sans obéir.
Sur leur socle j'inscrirai des injures et le nom de mon pire ennemi.
Là-bas dans l'océan entre deux eaux
un beau corps de femme fait reculer les requins.
Ils montent à la surface se mirer dans l'air
et n'osent pas mordre aux seins
aux seins délicieux.

beginning is near like corn in June. Constables put the handcuffs on me. The statues turn away without obeying. On their plinths I will inscribe insults and the name of my worst enemy. In the ocean yonder just beneath the surface the sharks recoil before a woman's beautiful body. They rise to the surface to admire themselves in the air and dare not bite into the breasts the delectable breasts.

Desespoir du soleil

Quel bruit étrange glissait le long de la rampe d'escalier au bas de laquelle rêvait la pomme transparente.

Les vergers étaient clos et le sphinx bien loin de là s'étirait dans le sable craquant de chaleur dans la nuit de tissu fragile.

Despair of the Sun

What strange sound went gliding along the banister at whose foot the transparent apple was dreaming.

The orchards were enfolded by night and the sphinx far away from there stretched its limbs in the sand that crackled with heat in the darkness of tenuous fabric.

Ce bruit devait-il durer jusqu'à l'éveil des locataires, ou s'évader dans l'ombre du crépuscule matinal? Le bruit persistait. Le sphinx aux aguets l'entendait depuis des siècles et désirait l'éprouver. Aussi ne faut-il pas s'étonner de voir la silhouette souple du sphinx dans les ténèbres de l'escalier. Le fauve égratignait de ses griffes les marches encaustiquées. Les sonnettes devant chaque porte marquaient de lueurs la cage de l'ascenseur et le bruit persistant sentant venir celui qu'il attendait depuis des millions de ténèbres s'attacha à la crinière et brusquement l'ombre pâlit.

C'est le poème du matin qui commence tandis que dans son lit tiède avec des cheveux dénoués rabattus sur le visage et les draps plus froissés que ses paupières la vagabonde attend l'instant où s'ouvrira sur un paysage de résine et d'agate sa porte close encore aux flots du ciel et de la nuit.

Was that sound to last until the tenants' awakening, or escape into the shadow of the morning half-light? The sound persisted. The watchful sphinx had been hearing it for centuries and wished to put it to the test. It was then no surprise to see the supple silhouette of the sphinx in the darkness on the stairs. The beast scratched with its claws the beeswaxed steps. The bells at each door cast gleams on the lift shaft and the persistent sound sensing the coming of the one it had been awaiting for millions of darknesses gripped the mane and abruptly the shadow grew pale.

This is the poem of the morning beginning while in her warm bed with loosened hair falling across her face and sheets more rumpled than her eyelids the wanderer awaits the moment when her door still closed to the waters of the sky and the night will open upon a landscape of resin and agate.

C'est le poème du jour où le sphinx se couche dans le lit de la vagabonde et malgré le bruit persistant lui jure un éternel amour digne de foi.

C'est le poème du jour qui commence dans la fumée odorante du chocolat et le monotone tac tac du cireur qui s'étonne de voir sur les marches de l'escalier les traces des griffes du voyageur de la nuit.

C'est le poème du jour qui commence avec des étincelles d'allumettes au grand effroi des pyramides surprises et tristes de ne plus voir leur majestueux compagnon couché à leurs pieds.

Mais le bruit quel était-il? Dites-le tandis que le poème du jour commence tandis que la vagabonde et le sphinx bien-aimé rêvent aux bouleversements de paysages.

Ce n'était pas le bruit de la pendule ni celui des pas ni celui du moulin à café.

This is the poem of the day when the sphinx lies down in the bed of the wanderer and despite the persistent sound swears to her an eternal and trustworthy love.

This is the poem of the day beginning in the sweet-smelling smoke of chocolate and the steady tick-tack of the shoeblack who is amazed to see on the steps of the staircase the claw-marks of the nocturnal traveller.

This is the poem of the day beginning with match sparks to the great terror of the pyramids surprised and sad to see no more their majestic companion lying at their feet.

But what was the sound? Say it while the poem of the day is beginning while the wanderer and the beloved sphinx are dreaming of the upheaval of landscapes.

It was not the sound of the clock nor that of footsteps nor the coffee mill.

Le bruit quel était-il? quel était-il?

L'escalier s'enfoncera-t-il toujours plus avant? montera-t-il toujours plus haut?

Rêvons acceptons de rêver c'est le poème du jour qui commence.

What was the sound? what was it?

Will the staircase plunge ever upward? will it climb ever higher?

Let us dream let us consent to dream this is the poem of the day beginning.

Mi-Route

Il y a un moment précis dans le temps
Où l'homme atteint le milieu exact de sa vie,
Un fragment de seconde,
Une fugitive parcelle de temps plus rapide qu'un regard,
Plus rapide que le sommet des pâmoisons amoureuses,
Plus rapide que la lumière.
Et l'homme est sensible à ce moment.

Midway

There is a precise moment in time when a man reaches the exact centre of his life, a fraction of a second, a fleeting particle of time swifter than a glance, steeper than the peak of love's vertigo, swifter than light. And a man is alive to that moment.

De longues avenues entre des frondaisons
S'allongent vers la tour où sommeille une dame
Dont la beauté résiste aux baisers, aux saisons,
Comme une étoile au vent, comme un rocher aux lames.

Un bateau frémissant s'enfonce et gueule.
Au sommet d'un arbre claque un drapeau.
Une femme bien peignée, mais dont les bas tombent sur les
souliers
Apparaît au coin d'une rue,
Exaltée, frémissante,
Protégeant de sa main une lampe surannée et qui fume.

Long avenues stretch away through green branches towards the tower where a lady slumbers whose beauty withstands kisses, withstands seasons, as a star the wind, as a rock the waves.

A trembling boat plunges and shrieks. At the top of a tree a flag flaps. A woman with her hair combed neatly but her stockings falling on her shoes appears at a street corner, impassioned, trembling, shielding with her hand a smoking, antiquated lamp.

Et encore un débardeur ivre chante au coin d'un pont,
Et encore une amante mord les lèvres de son amant,
Et encore un pétale de rose tombe sur un lit vide,
Et encore trois pendules sonnent la même heure
A quelques minutes d'intervalle,
Et encore un homme qui passe dans une rue se retourne
Parce que l'on a crié son prénom,
Mais ce n'est pas lui que cette femme appelle,
Et encore, un ministre en grande tenue,
Désagréablement gêné par le pan de sa chemise coincé entre son pantalon et son caleçon,
Inaugure un orphelinat,
Et encore d'un camion lancé à toute vitesse
Dans les rues vides de la nuit
Tombe une tomate merveilleuse qui roule dans le ruisseau
Et qui sera balayée plus tard,
Et encore un incendie s'allume au sixième étage d'une maison
Qui flambe au cœur de la ville silencieuse et indifférente,
Et encore un homme entend une chanson
Oubliée depuis longtemps, et l'oubliera de nouveau,
Et encore maintes choses,

And then a drunken docker sings at the corner of a bridge, and then a lover bites her lover's lips, and then a rose petal falls upon an empty bed, and then three clocks strike the same hour at intervals of several minutes, and then a man walking in the street turns round because his first name has been called, but he is not the one that woman is calling, and then, a cabinet minister in full dress, unpleasantly hampered by the shirt-tail caught between his trousers and his undershorts, inaugurates an orphanage, and then from a truck hurtling at full speed in the empty night-time streets falls a miraculous tomato that rolls into the gutter and will later be swept away, and then a fire breaks out on the sixth floor of a house that blazes in the heart of the silent, indifferent city, and then a man hears a long-forgotten song, and will forget it once again, and then many

Maintes autres choses que l'homme voit à l'instant précis du
milieu de sa vie,
Maintes autres choses se déroulent longuement dans le plus
court des courts instants de la terre.
Il pressent le mystère de cette seconde, de ce fragment de
seconde,

Mais il dit "Chassons ces idées noires",
Et il chasse ces idées noires.
Et que pourrait-il dire,
Et que pourrait-il faire
De mieux?

things, many other things that a man sees at the precise moment of the middle of his life, many other things unfold, long and slow, in the briefest of the brief instants of the earth. He has an intimation of the mystery of that second, of that fraction of a second,

But he says 'Let's drive out these dark thoughts', and he drives out these dark thoughts. And what could he say, and what could he do, that would be any better?

Le Zèbre

Le zèbre, cheval des ténèbres,
Lève le pied, ferme les yeux
Et fait résonner ses vertèbres
En hennissant d'un air joyeux.

Au clair soleil de Barbarie,
Il sort alors de l'écurie
Et va brouter dans la prairie
Les herbes de sorcellerie.

Mais la prison, sur son pelage,
A laissé l'ombre du grillage.

The Zebra

The zebra, horse of darkness, lifts its foot, closes its eyes and sets its backbone reverberating with its joyful neighing.

In the bright Barbary sunlight, he emerges then from the stable and goes grazing in the grasslands on the weeds of sorcery.

But the prison, on his coat, has left the shadow of its bars.

Le Paysage

J'avais rêvé d'aimer. J'aime encor mais l'amour
Ce n'est plus ce bouquet de lilas et de roses
Chargeant de leurs parfums la forêt où repose
Une flamme à l'issue de sentiers sans détours.

J'avais rêvé d'aimer. J'aime encor mais l'amour
Ce n'est plus cet orage où l'éclair superpose
Ses bûchers aux châteaux, déroute, décompose,
Illumine en fuyant l'adieu du carrefour.

C'est le silex en feu sous mon pas dans la nuit,
Le mot qu'aucun lexique au monde n'a traduit,
L'écume sur la mer, dans le ciel ce nuage.

A vieillir tout devient rigide et lumineux,
Des boulevards sans noms et des cordes sans nœuds.
Je me sens me roidir avec le paysage.

The Landscape

I had dreamed of loving. I go on loving but love is no longer that bouquet of lilacs and roses imbuing with their fragrances the forest where a flame lies at rest at the end of undeviating pathways.

I had dreamed of loving. I go on loving but love is no longer that storm whose lightning lays its funeral pyres on castles, disorientates, distorts, illumines as it vanishes the parting of the ways.

It is the spark of flint beneath my footstep in the night, the word no dictionary in the world has translated, the foam on the sea, that cloud in the sky.

In growing old all things become rigid and luminous, boulevards without names and ropes without knots. I feel myself stiffening with the landscape.

Jacques Prévert
(1900–1977)

Jacques Prévert was something of a phenomenon, a bestselling poet whose popularity transcended social and intellectual barriers. His important place in the affections of the French people stemmed from his gentle and humorous anarchism, his deflation of authority and dogma, his deceptively childlike and original perceptions, his sensitivity to the emotional life of ordinary people, and his ability to infuse everyday experience and language with a poetic spirit.

In the late 1920s he was associated with the Surrealists, and his work retains their penchant for word-play and paradox as well as for startling imagery. But it is also unhermetic, and is firmly in touch with a popular lyrical, narrative and comic tradition and with the Parisian spirit.

His verse is designed on the whole to be spoken or sung. He makes frequent use of a flexible 6/7/8-syllable metre, often with a skipped or semi-skipped syllable that creates very much a 'skipping' rhythmic effect. Many of his poems have indeed been set to music, notably by Joseph Kosma, who had composed scores for the classic Marcel Carné films which Prévert scripted in the 1930s (*Quai des Brumes*, *Le Jour se lève*, *Les Enfants du Paradis*). Prévert was already well known in the cinema world when his first volume, *Paroles*, appeared in 1949 as a collection of poems written over the previous twenty years. It contains much of his most memorable work.

He is an anti-intellectual, but not a sentimentalist. A champion of the individual against institutions, he deals lucidly in universal human experiences. His free, largely unpunctuated, colloquial verse often has a cinematic quality, like a collage of images projected on a screen, sparse and unpretentious images drawn from the imagination of a genuine poet of the people.

Major works: *Tentative de Description d'un dîner de têtes à Paris-France* 1931, *Paroles* 1949, *Spectacle* 1951, *La Pluie et le beau temps* 1955, *Histoires et d'autres histoires* 1963, *Fatras* 1966, *Choses et autres* 1972.

Le Cancre

Il dit non avec la tête
mais il dit oui avec le cœur
il dit oui à ce qu'il aime
il dit non au professeur
il est debout
on le questionne
et tous les problèmes sont posés
soudain le fou rire le prend
et il efface tout
les chiffres et les mots
les dates et les noms
les phrases et les pièges
et malgré les menaces du maître
sous les huées des enfants prodiges
avec des craies de toutes les couleurs
sur le tableau noir du malheur
il dessine le visage du bonheur.

The Dunce

He says no with his head / but he says yes with his heart / he says yes to what he loves / he says no to the schoolmaster / he's on his feet / he's being questioned / and all the problems are set / suddenly he's gripped by wild laughter / and he erases it all / figures and words / dates and names / sentences and snares / and despite the master's threats / to the jeers of the infant prodigies / with chalks of every colour / on the blackboard of woe / he draws the face of happiness.

Familiale

La mère fait du tricot
Le fils fait la guerre
Elle trouve ça tout naturel la mère
Et le père qu'est-ce qu'il fait le père?
Il fait des affaires
Sa femme fait du tricot
Son fils la guerre
Lui des affaires
Il trouve ça tout naturel le père
Et le fils et le fils
Qu'est-ce qu'il trouve le fils?
Il ne trouve rien absolument rien le fils
Le fils sa mère fait du tricot son père des affaires lui la guerre
Quand il aura fini la guerre
Il fera des affaires avec son père
La guerre continue la mère continue elle tricote
Le père continue il fait des affaires
Le fils est tué il ne continue plus

Family Life

The mother does her knitting The son fights in the war She finds that quite natural the mother And the father what does the father do? He's in business His wife does her knitting His son fights in the war He's in business He finds that quite natural the father And the son and the son What does the son find? He finds nothing absolutely nothing the son The son his mother does her knitting his father's in business he's in the war When he's finished the war He'll be in business with his father The war goes on the mother goes on she knits The father goes on he's in business The son is killed he doesn't go on The

Le père et la mère vont au cimetière
Ils trouvent ça naturel le père et la mère

La vie continue la vie avec le tricot la guerre les affaires
Les affaires la guerre le tricot la guerre
Les affaires les affaires et les affaires
La vie avec le cimetière.

father and the mother go to the cemetery They find that natural the father and the mother Life goes on life with knitting war business Business war knitting war Business business and business Life with the cemetery.

Déjeuner du matin

Il a mis le café
Dans la tasse
Il a mis le lait
Dans la tasse de café
Il a mis le sucre
Dans le café au lait
Avec la petite cuiller
Il a tourné
Il a bu le café au lait
Et il a reposé la tasse
Sans me parler
Il a allumé
Une cigarette

Breakfast

He put the coffee In the cup He put the milk In the cup of coffee He put the sugar In the milky coffee With the little spoon He stirred He drank the milky coffee And he put down the cup Without a word to me He lit A cigarette He made

Il a fait des ronds
Avec la fumée
Il a mis les cendres
Dans le cendrier
Sans me parler
Sans me regarder
Il s'est levé
Il a mis
Son chapeau sur sa tête
Il a mis
Son manteau de pluie
Parce qu'il pleuvait
Et il est parti
Sous la pluie
Sans une parole
Sans me regarder
Et moi j'ai pris
Ma tête dans ma main
Et j'ai pleuré.

rings With the smoke He put the ash In the ashtray Without a word to me Without a glance at me He stood up He put His hat on his head He put His raincoat on Because it was raining And he left In the rain Without a word Without a glance at me And as for me I clasped My head in my hand And I wept.

Sanguine

La fermeture éclair a glissé sur tes reins
et tout l'orage heureux de ton corps amoureux
au beau milieu de l'ombre
a éclaté soudain
Et ta robe en tombant sur le parquet ciré
n'a pas fait plus de bruit
qu'une écorce d'orange tombant sur un tapis
Mais sous nos pieds
ses petits boutons de nacre craquaient comme des pépins
Sanguine
joli fruit
la pointe de ton sein
a tracé une nouvelle ligne de chance
dans le creux de ma main
Sanguine
joli fruit

Soleil de nuit.

Blood Orange

The zip slid over the base of your spine / and the whole blissful storm of your loving body / in the very heart of the shadow / burst suddenly And your dress as it fell on the polished woodblock floor / made no more sound / than an orange peel falling on a carpet But beneath our feet / its little pearly buttons cracked like pips Blood orange / lovely fruit / the tip of your breast / traced a new line of fortune / in the palm of my hand Blood orange / lovely fruit

Night sun.

L'Ordre nouveau

Le soleil gît sur le sol
Litre de vin rouge brisé
Une maison comme un ivrogne
Sur le pavé s'est écroulée
Et sous son porche encore debout
Une jeune fille est allongée
Un homme à genoux près d'elle
Est en train de l'achever
Dans la plaie où remue le fer
Le cœur ne cesse de saigner
Et l'homme pousse un cri de guerre
Comme un absurde cri de paon
Et son cri se perd dans la nuit
Hors la vie hors du temps
Et l'homme au visage de poussière
L'homme perdu et abîmé
Se redresse et crie "Heil Hitler!"
D'une voix désespérée
En face de lui dans les débris

The New Order[1]

The sun lies upon the earth A broken litre of red wine A house has collapsed Like a drunk on the roadway And under its still standing porch A girl is stretched out A man on his knees beside her Is just finishing her off In the wound where the iron turns The heart will not stop bleeding And the man utters a war cry Like an absurd peacock screech And his cry is lost in the night Outside life outside time And the man with the face of dust The lost and disfigured man Stands up and cries 'Heil Hitler!' In a voice of despair Facing him in the ruins Of a shop

[1]Marshal Pétain's phrase for French life under German occupation, in his message to the people of France after the capitulation to the Nazi forces.

D'une boutique calcinée
Le portrait d'un vieillard blême
Le regarde avec bonté
Sur sa manche des étoiles brillent
D'autres aussi sur son képi
Comme les étoiles brillent à Noël
Sur les sapins pour les petits
Et l'homme des sections d'assaut
Devant le merveilleux chromo
Soudain se retrouve en famille
Au cœur même de l'ordre nouveau
Et remet son poignard dans sa gaine
Et s'en va tout droit devant lui
Automate de l'Europe nouvelle
Détraqué par le mal du pays
Adieu adieu Lily Marlène
Et son pas et son chant s'éloignent dans la nuit
Et le portrait du vieillard blême
Au milieu des décombres
Reste seul et sourit
Tranquille dans la pénombre
Sénile et sûr de lui.

burnt to a cinder The portrait of a pallid old man Looks at him benignly On his sleeve stars shine Others too on his cap As the stars shine at Christmas On the fir trees for the children And the stormtrooper Facing the miraculous colour-print Suddenly finds himself at home In the very heart of the new order And puts his dagger in its sheath And sets off walking straight ahead An automaton of the new Europe Thrown out of gear by homesickness Farewell farewell Lili Marlene And his footsteps and his song fade away into the night And the portrait of the pallid old man Amid the ruins Remains alone and smiles At peace in the half-light Senile and self-confident.

Barbara

Rappelle-toi Barbara
Il pleuvait sans cesse sur Brest ce jour-là
Et tu marchais souriante
Epanouie ravie ruisselante
Sous la pluie
Rappelle-toi Barbara
Il pleuvait sans cesse sur Brest
Et je t'ai croisée rue de Siam
Tu souriais
Et moi je souriais de même
Rappelle-toi Barbara
Toi que je ne connaissais pas
Toi qui ne me connaissais pas
Rappelle-toi
Rappelle-toi quand même ce jour-là
N'oublie pas
Un homme sous un porche s'abritait
Et il a crié ton nom
Barbara
Et tu as couru vers lui sous la pluie

Barbara

Remember Barbara The rain was falling endlessly on Brest that day And you walked smiling Radiant enchanted dripping-wet In the rain Remember Barbara It was raining endlessly on Brest And I came across you in the Rue de Siam You were smiling And I was smiling too Remember Barbara I didn't know you You didn't know me Remember Just remember that day Don't forget A man was sheltering under a porch And he called your name Barbara And you ran towards him in the rain

Ruisselante ravie épanouie
Et tu t'es jetée dans ses bras
Rappelle-toi cela Barbara
Et ne m'en veux pas si je te tutoie
Je dis tu à tous ceux que j'aime
Même si je ne les ai vus qu'une seule fois
Je dis tu à tous ceux qui s'aiment
Même si je ne les connais pas
Rappelle-toi Barbara
N'oublie pas
Cette pluie sage et heureuse
Sur ton visage heureux
Sur cette ville heureuse
Cette pluie sur la mer
Sur l'arsenal
Sur le bateau d'Ouessant
Oh Barbara
Quelle connerie la guerre
Qu'es-tu devenue maintenant
Sous cette pluie de fer
De feu d'acier de sang
Et celui qui te serrait dans ses bras
Amoureusement
Est-il mort disparu ou bien encore vivant

Dripping-wet enchanted radiant And you threw yourself into his arms Remember that Barbara And don't resent it if I call you 'tu' I say 'tu' to everyone I love Even if I've seen them only once I say 'tu' to all who love each other Even if I don't know them Remember Barbara Don't forget That mild and happy rain On your happy face On that happy town That rain on the sea On the arsenal On the boat from Ushant Oh Barbara What a bloody farce the war What's become of you now In this rain of iron Of fire of steel of blood And the man who clasped you in his arms Lovingly Is he dead missing or

Oh Barbara
Il pleut sans cesse sur Brest
Comme il pleuvait avant
Mais ce n'est plus pareil et tout est abîmé
C'est une pluie de deuil terrible et désolée
Ce n'est même plus l'orage
De fer d'acier de sang
Tout simplement des nuages
Qui crèvent comme des chiens
Des chiens qui disparaissent
Au fil de l'eau sur Brest
Et vont pourrir au loin
Au loin très loin de Brest
Dont il ne reste rien.

even still alive Oh Barbara It's raining endlessly on Brest As it rained before But it's not the same now and everything is disfigured It's a terrible and desolate rain of grief It's not even the storm now Of iron of steel of blood Merely clouds That die like dogs Dogs that go missing In the current over Brest And are going to rot far away A long long way from Brest Of which there's nothing left.

Henri Michaux
(1899–1984)

Without a doubt one of the '*horribles travailleurs*' whose advent was predicted by Rimbaud, Michaux risks his whole self in his poetic exploration of the potential within himself. It is a brutal, lucid, unpredictable journey, with no fixed starting-point or destination. It has taken place alongside rather than within Surrealism, and his individualistic texts, located variably between free verse and prose, escape classification. This is therapeutic poetry, even exorcistic; it casts out demons and comes to terms with tensions. If Michaux has a kindred spirit in Surrealism it is Artaud, and in the literature of objectified psychic states comparisons have been made with Kafka. Many of his writings are set within the borders, the anthropology and the mythology of imaginary countries inhabited by Hacs, Emanglons, Meidosems and other semi-material beings; the Meidosems are probably the most absorbing and appealing.

Tense and lonely as a child, Michaux loathed the Belgian society and landscape in which he grew up, and a family and school life full of claustrophobia and hostility. Alienated and uncooperative, he escaped into his imagination, creating magical or horrific alternative lives in and on his '*boule hermétique*', an inner planet peopled by *alter egos*, a world that would survive and become an integral part of his adult life. Michaux remained a marginal figure, tentative and nomadic, always self-deprecating, reluctant to offer any biographical information that would tend to 'fix' his fluid personality: 'After one failure then another, he ran aground on literature, where he remains ill at ease' (his own words).

He was increasingly excited by the autonomous power of language to defeat or at least subdue reality, and his climactic discovery of Lautréamont's work in 1922 confirmed for Michaux the salvation that could be attained through literary metamorphosis, through a violent, mould-breaking kind of lyricism.

Michaux's spontaneity, physical restlessness and compulsive travelling are mirrored in his dissatisfaction with the notion of a finished literary product; in his later experimentation with hallucinogenic drugs and in the visual arts; and in his incessant linguistic researches. He is his only subject. As Supervielle (his mentor in the 1920s) put it: 'In the laboratory of this visionary and studious poet, he himself is the only guinea-pig.'

Poetry for Michaux is not an aesthetic game, nor an escape, nor an ornament on life, but a sleeves-rolled-up means of surviving life itself, a way of holding the line in the innumerable tense battles between a limited reality and the activity of a mysterious, comically or fearfully alarming inner self, a self that is sometimes fluid and sometimes explosively fragmented. His poetry pulses with an energetic, surging rhythm and inhabits 'Inner Space' (the title of a major collection of his works).

Works: *Qui je fus* 1927, *Un certain Plume* 1930, *La Nuit remue* 1935, *Voyage en grande Garabagne* 1936, *Lointain intérieur* 1938, *Peintures* 1939, *Au Pays de la magie* 1941, *Epreuves, exorcismes* 1945, *Apparitions* 1946, *Ailleurs* 1948, *La Vie dans les plis* 1948, *Face aux verrous* 1954, *Misérable miracle* 1956, etc. Michaux continued to publish poetic and other texts until his death in 1984.

Mes Occupations

Je peux rarement voir quelqu'un sans le battre.
D'autres préfèrent le monologue intérieur. Moi, non.
J'aime mieux battre.

Il y a des gens qui s'assoient en face de moi au restaurant et ne disent rien, ils restent un certain temps, car ils ont décidé de manger.

En voici un.
Je te l'agrippe, toc.
Je te le ragrippe, toc.
Je le pends au portemanteau.
Je le décroche.
Je le repends.
Je le redécroche.
Je le mets sur la table, je le tasse et l'étouffe.
Je le salis, je l'inonde.
Il revit.

Je le rince, je l'étire (je commence à m'énerver, il faut en finir), je le masse, je le serre, je le résume et l'introduis dans mon verre, et jette ostensiblement le contenu par terre, et dis

My Avocations

I can rarely see anyone without thrashing him. Others prefer the inner monologue. Not me. I prefer a thrashing. There are people who sit down facing me in the restaurant and say nothing, they stay a while, for they have decided to eat. Here's one now. See how I grab him, thump. See how I grab him again, thump. I hang him on the coat-rack. I unhook him. I hang him up again. I unhook him again. I put him on the table, I squeeze him up small and choke him. I foul him, I flood him. He revives. I rinse him off, I stretch him out (I'm starting to get on edge, I must get it over with), I massage him, I compress him, I abridge him and insert him into my glass, and throw the contents publicly to the ground, and say

au garçon: "Mettez-moi donc un verre plus propre."

Mais je me sens mal, je règle promptement l'addition et je m'en vais.

to the waiter: 'Just bring me a cleaner glass.' But I feel ill, I pay the bill swiftly and I go away.

Crier

Le panaris est une souffrance atroce. Mais ce qui me faisait souffrir le plus, c'était que je ne pouvais crier. Car j'étais à l'hôtel. La nuit venait de tomber et ma chambre était prise entre deux autres où l'on dormait.

Shriek

Paronychia[1] is a dreadul pain. But what made me suffer most was that I could not cry out. For I was in a hotel. Darkness had just fallen and my room was trapped between two others where people were sleeping.

[1]A painful inflammation where the fingernail or toenail meets the skin.

Alors, je me mis à sortir de mon crâne des grosses caisses, des cuivres, et un instrument qui résonnait plus que des orgues. Et profitant de la force prodigieuse que me donnait la fièvre, j'en fis un orchestre assourdissant. Tout tremblait de vibrations.

Alors, enfin assuré que dans ce tumulte ma voix ne serait pas entendue, je me mis à hurler, à hurler pendant des heures, et parvins à me soulager petit à petit.

So I began to bring out from my skull big bass-drums, horns and trumpets, and an instrument with more resonance than organs. And exploiting the prodigious strength given to me by my fever, I made with them a deafening orchestra. Everything pulsated with vibrations.

And then, sure at last that in this tumult my voice would not be heard, I began to shriek, to shriek for hours, and little by little I managed to find relief.

Emportez-moi

Emportez-moi dans une caravelle,
Dans une vieille et douce caravelle,
Dans l'étrave, ou si l'on veut, dans l'écume,
Et perdez-moi, au loin, au loin.

Dans l'attelage d'un autre âge.
Dans le velours trompeur de la neige.
Dans l'haleine de quelques chiens réunis.
Dans la troupe exténuée des feuilles mortes.

Emportez-moi sans me briser, dans les baisers,
Dans les poitrines qui se soulèvent et respirent,
Sur les tapis des paumes et leur sourire,
Dans les corridors des os longs et des articulations.

Emportez-moi, ou plutôt enfouissez-moi.

Carry me away

Carry me away in a caravel, in an old and gentle caravel, in the prow, or if you like in the foam, and lose me, far away, far away.

In the horse-drawn carriage of another age. In the deceptive velvet of the snow. In the breath of gathered dogs. In the exhausted flock of dead leaves.

Carry me away without breaking me, in kisses, in chests that rise and draw in breath, on the carpets of palms and their smile, in the passageways of long bones and articulations.

Carry me away, or rather bury me.

Le grand Violon

Mon violon est un grand violon-girafe;
j'en joue à l'escalade,
bondissant dans ses râles,
au galop sur ses cordes sensibles et son ventre affamé aux désirs épais,
que personne jamais ne satisfera,
sur son grand cœur de bois enchagriné,
que personne jamais ne comprendra.
Mon violon-girafe, par nature, a la plainte basse et importante, façon tunnel,
l'air accablé et bondé de soi, comme l'ont les gros poissons gloutons des hautes profondeurs
mais avec, au bout, un air de tête et d'espoir quand même,
d'envolée, de flèche, qui ne cédera jamais.
Rageur, m'engouffrant dans ses plaintes, dans un amas de tonnerres nasillards,
j'en emporte comme par surprise

The Tall Violin

My violin is a tall giraffe-violin; I scale it as I play, leaping within its throaty rattles, galloping on its sensitive strings and its starved belly with its dense desires, which no one will ever satisfy, on its great wooden grieving heart, which no one will ever understand. My giraffe-violin, by nature, has a low and momentous moan, in the way of a tunnel, an oppressed and self-stuffed air, like the bulky gluttonous fish of the extreme depths, but with, at the tip, a semblance of head and hope all the same, of soaring, of a spire, which will never yield. Choleric, engulfing me in its groans, in a mass of nasal thunderings, I bring out from it as if by surprise such strains

tout à coup de tels accents de panique ou de bébé blessé,
  perçants, déchirants,
que moi-même, ensuite, je me retourne sur lui, inquiet, pris
  de remords, de désespoir,
et de je ne sais quoi, qui nous unit, tragique, et nous sépare.

suddenly of panic or an injured baby, piercing, rending, that I myself then turn on it, anxious, gripped by remorse, by despair, and by something I can't name that unites us, tragic, and that divides us.

Clown

Un jour.

Un jour, bientôt peut-être.

Un jour j'arracherai l'ancre qui tient mon navire loin des mers.

Avec la sorte de courage qu'il faut pour être rien et rien que rien, je lâcherai ce qui paraissait m'être indissolublement proche.

Je le trancherai, je le renverserai, je le romprai, je le ferai dégringoler.

D'un coup dégorgeant ma misérable pudeur, mes misérables combinaisons et enchaînements 'de fil en aiguille'.

Vidé de l'abcès d'être quelqu'un, je boirai à nouveau l'espace nourricier.

A coups de ridicules, de déchéances (qu'est-ce que la déchéance?), par éclatement, par vide, par une totale dissipation-dérision-purgation, j'expulserai de moi la forme qu'on croyait si bien attachée, composée, coordonnée, assortie à mon entourage et à mes semblables, si dignes, si dignes, mes semblables.

Clown

One day. One day, soon perhaps. One day I will tear up the anchor that holds my ship far from the seas. With the kind of courage needed to be nothing and nothing but nothing, I will cast off what seemed indissolubly close to me. I will slice through it, I will overturn it, I will break it, I will send it tumbling. Disgorging all at once my wretched delicacy, my abject contrivances and fiddling logical sequences. Drained of the abscess of being someone, I will drink nutritious space anew. With blows of absurdity, with falls from grace (what is a fall from grace?), by explosion, by void, by a total dissipation-derision-purgation, I will expel from myself the form believed to be so strongly attached, composed, co-ordinated, appropriate to those around me and those like me, so worthy, so worthy,

Réduit à une humilité de catastrophe, à un nivellement parfait comme après une intense trouille.

Ramené au-dessous de toute mesure à mon rang réel, au rang infime que je ne sais quelle idée-ambition m'avait fait déserter.

Anéanti quant à la hauteur, quant à l'estime.

Perdu en un endroit lointain (ou même pas), sans nom, sans identité.

CLOWN, abattant dans la risée, dans le grotesque, dans l'esclaffement, le sens que contre toute lumière je m'étais fait de mon importance

Je plongerai.

Sans bourse dans l'infini-esprit sous-jacent ouvert à tous,
ouvert moi-même à une nouvelle et incroyable rosée à force d'être nul

et ras...

et risible...

my fellow-men. Reduced to a humility befitting disaster, to a perfect levelling as after being intensely shit-scared. Brought down beyond all bounds to my real rank, to the lowly rank which some idea-ambition I can't name had led me to desert. Annihilated in terms of arrogance, in terms of esteem. Lost in a distant place (or not even that), with no name, with no identity.

CLOWN, smashing down in mockery, in grotesqueness, in howls of laughter, the sense of my own significance that I had given myself against all light. I will plunge. Penniless into the underlying spirit-infinity open to all, open myself to a new and incredible dew on the strength of being zero and a clean slate ... and laughable ...

Dragon

Un dragon est sorti de moi. Cent queues de flammes et de nerfs il sortit.

Quel effort je fis pour le contraindre à s'élever, le fouettant par-dessus moi! Le bas était prison d'acier où j'étais enfermé. Mais je m'obstinai et soutins fureur et les tôles de l'implacable geôle finirent par se disjoindre petit à petit, forcées par l'impétueux mouvement giratoire.

C'était parce que tout allait si mal, c'était en septembre (1938), c'était le mardi, c'était pour ça que j'étais obligé pour vivre de prendre cette forme si étrange. Ainsi donc je livrai bataille pour moi seul, quand l'Europe hésitait encore, et partis comme dragon, contre les forces mauvaises, contre les paralysies sans nombre qui montaient des événements, par-dessus la voix de l'océan des médiocres, dont la gigantesque importance se démasquait soudain à nouveau vertigineusement.

Dragon

A dragon has come out of me. A hundred tails of flames and sinews he came out.

What an effort I made to compel him to rise up, lashing him up above me! The lower part was a prison of steel in which I was locked. But I persisted and sustained my frenzy and the steel plates of the implacable gaol in the end were severed little by little, forced apart by the breakneck gyratory movement.

It was because it was all going so badly, it was in September (1938), it was a Tuesday, that was why I was obliged in order to live to take on such a strange form. And thus I joined battle for myself alone, when Europe was still hesitating, and set off as a dragon, against evil forces, against the numberless paralyses that rose from events, over the voice of the ocean of mediocrities, whose gigantic size was suddenly once more unmasked vertiginously.

Après ma Mort

Je fus transporté après ma mort, je fus transporté non dans un lieu confiné, mais dans l'immersité du vide éthérique. Loin de me laisser abattre par cette immense ouverture en tous sens à perte de vue, en ciel étoilé, je me rassemblai et rassemblai tout ce que j'avais été, et ce que j'avais été sur le point d'être, et enfin tout ce que au calendrier secret de moi-même, je m'étais proposé de devenir et serrant le tout, mes qualités aussi, enfin mes vices, dernier rempart, je m'en fis carapace.

Sur ce noyau, animé de colère, mais d'une colère nette, que le sang n'appuyait plus, froide et intégrale, je me mis à faire le hérisson, dans une suprême défense, dans un dernier refus.

After my Death

I was transported after my death, I was transported not into a confined place, but into the immensity of the etheric void. Far from becoming disheartened by this vast openness in all directions beyond the range of sight, in a starry sky, I gathered myself and gathered all that I had been, and all that I had been about to be, and finally all that within my secret inner almanac I had envisaged becoming, and drawing it all tightly together, my qualities too, and in the end my vices, a last rampart, I made myself a carapace.

On this nucleus, quickened by anger, but a clean anger no longer sustained by blood, cold and whole, I began to bristle like a hedgehog, in an ultimate defence, in a final refusal.

Alors, le vide, les larves du vide qui déjà poussaient tentaculairement vers moi leurs poches molles, me menaçant de l'abjecte endosmose, les larves étonnées après quelques vaines tentatives contre la proie qui refusait de se rendre, reculèrent embarrassées, et se dérobèrent à ma vue, abandonnant à la vie celui qui la méritait tellement.

Désormais libre de ce côté, j'usai de ma puissance du moment, de l'exaltation de la victoire inespérée, pour peser vers la Terre et repénétrai mon corps immobile, que les draps et la laine avaient heureusement empêché de se refroidir.

Avec surprise, après ce mien effort dépassant celui des géants avec surprise et joie mêlée de déception je rentrai dans les horizons étroits et fermés où la vie humaine pour être ce qu'elle est, doit se passer.

Then, the void, the larvae of the void which were already pushing tentacularly towards me their flabby sacs, threatening me with abject endosmosis, the astonished larvae after a few vain attempts against the prey that refused to yield, retired in confusion, and hid from my sight, abandoning to life the one who so deserved it.

Free henceforward in that quarter, I used the power I had in that moment, the exaltation of unexpected victory, to project my weight towards the Earth and entered once more into my motionless body, which happily had been prevented from going cold by the sheets and wool.

With astonishment, after this effort of mine surpassing that of giants with surprise and joy mixed with disappointment I returned within the narrow and closed horizons where human life in order to be what it is, must take place.

Portrait des Meidosems (extraits)

L'horloge qui bat les passions dans l'âme des Meidosems s'éveille. Son temps s'accélère. Le monde alentour se hâte, se précipite, allant vers un destin soudain marqué.

Le couteau qui travaille par spasmes attaque, et le bâton qui baratte le fond s'agite violemment.

★

Ils prennent la forme de bulles pour rêver, ils prennent la forme de lianes pour s'émouvoir.

Appuyée contre un mur, un mur du reste que personne ne reverra jamais, une forme faite d'une corde longue est là. Elle s'enlace.

C'est tout. C'est une Meidosemme.

Portrait of the Meidosems (extracts)

The clock that beats time for the passions in the Meidosem soul awakens. Its tempo accelerates. The surrounding world quickens, rushes forward, heading towards a destiny suddenly accentuated.

The knife that works in spasms attacks, and the rod that churns the depths shakes violently.

★

They adopt the form of bubbles for dreaming, they adopt the form of lianas for emotion.

Leaning against a wall, a wall moreover that no one will ever see again, a figure made of a long rope is there. It entwines itself.

That is all. That is a Meidosem woman.

Et elle attend, légèrement affaissée, mais bien moins que n'importe quel cordage de sa dimension appuyé sur lui-même.

Elle attend.

Journées, années, venez maintenant. Elle attend.

★

Sur ses longues jambes fines et incurvées, grande, gracieuse Meidosemme.

Rêve de courses victorieuses, âme à regrets et projets, âme pour tout dire.

Et elle s'élance, éperdue, dans un espace qui la boit sans s'y intéresser.

★

Une gale d'étincelles démange un crâne douloureux. C'est un Meidosem. C'est une peine qui court. C'est une fuite qui roule. C'est l'estropié de l'air qui s'agite, éperdu. Ne va-t-on pas pouvoir l'aider?

Non!

And she waits, sagging slightly, but much less than any rope of her size supporting itself.

She is waiting.

Days, years, come now. She is waiting.

★

On her long slender incurvated legs, tall, graceful Meidosem woman.

Dream of victorious races, soul of yearnings and plans, soul to tell all.

And she projects herself, distraught, into a space that drinks her in without interest.

★

A mange of sparks itches on a painful skull. It's a Meidosem. He's an affliction on legs. He's an escape in motion. He's the aerial cripple waving, distraught. Aren't we going to be able to help him?

No!

★

Des coulées d'affection, d'infection, des coulées de l'arrière-ban des souffrances, caramel amer d'autrefois, stalagmites lentement formées, c'est avec ces coulées-là qu'il marche, avec elles qu'il appréhende, membres spongieux venus de la tête, percés de mille petites coulées transversales, d'un sang extravasé, crevant les artérioles, mais ce n'est pas du sang, c'est le sang des souvenirs, du percement de l'âme, de la fragile chambre centrale, luttant dans l'étoupe, c'est l'eau rougie de la vaine mémoire, coulant sans dessein, mais non sans raison en ses boyaux petits qui partout fuient; infime et multiple crevaison.

Un Meidosem éclate. Mille veinules de sa foi en lui éclatent. Il tombe et retombe en de nouvelles pénombres, en de nouveaux étangs.

Qu'il est difficile de marcher ainsi...

★

Outflows of disease, of infection, outflows of the vassal army of pain, bitter caramel of times past, slowly formed stalagmites, it is with those outflows that he walks, with them and dreads them, spongy limbs coming from the head, pierced by a thousand little transverse flows, by an extravasated blood, bursting the arterioles, but it is not blood, it is the blood of memories, of the piercing of the soul, of the fragile central chamber, struggling in the oakum, it is the reddened water of vain memory, flowing without purpose, but not without reason in its little entrails that dart away everywhere; a minute and multiple puncturing.

A Meidosem shatters. A thousand veinlets of his faith in himself explode. He falls and goes on falling into new penumbras, into new pools.

It's so difficult to walk like that...

★

Il se mue en cascades, en fissures, en feu. C'est être Meidosem que de se muer ainsi en moires changeantes.

Pourquoi?

Au moins, ce ne sont pas des plaies. Et va le Meidosem. Plutôt reflets et jeux du soleil et de l'ombre que souffrir, que méditer. Plutôt cascades.

★

Ici est la ville des murs. Mais les toits? Pas de toits. Mais les maisons? Pas de maisons. Ici est la ville des murs. Plans en mains, vous voyez constamment des Meidosems chercher à en sortir. Mais jamais il n'en sortent.

★

He transforms himself into waterfalls, into fissures, into fire. That is to be a Meidosem, to shed oneself thus into shifting watered silks.

Why?

At least they are not wounds. And so goes the Meidosem. Rather reflections and the play of sunlight and shadow than suffering, than meditating. Rather waterfalls.

★

This is the city of walls. But the roofs? No roofs. But the houses? No houses. This is the city of walls. Street map in hand, you constantly see Meidosems seeking to get out. But they never do get out.

A cause des naissances (et les morts momifiés occupent une place toujours plus grande entre les murs) à cause des naissances, toujours plus de gens. Il faut construire de nouveaux murs entre les murs déjà existants.

Il y a de longs entretiens meidosems dans les murs, sur Cela qui serait sans murs, sans limites, sans fin et même sans un commencement.

★

Des ailes sans têtes, sans oiseaux, des ailes pures de tout corps volent vers un ciel solaire, pas encore resplendissant, mais qui lutte fort pour le resplendissement, trouant son chemin dans l'empyrée comme un obus de future félicité.

Silence. Envols.

Ce que ces Meidosems ont tant désiré, enfin ils y sont arrivés. Les voilà.

Because of births (and the mummified dead occupy increasing space between the walls) because of births, always more people. New walls must be built between the already existing walls.

There are long Meidosem dialogues within the walls on What would be with no walls, with no limits, with no end and even with no beginning.

★

Wings without heads, without birds, wings pure of any body fly towards a solar sky, not yet resplendent but struggling hard for resplendence, piercing its way into the empyrean like a cannon-shell of future felicity.

Silence. Wings taking flight.

What these Meidosems have so long desired, at last they have reached it. There they are.

Francis Ponge
(1899–1988)

In this prose poet, much absorbed by the problems and the uses of language, theorist and creative artist are fused into one. Despite the application of terms like '*chosiste*' to his work, despite a certain similarity to the approach of the '*nouveau romancier*' Alain Robbe-Grillet, and despite Ponge's increasing identification with the intellectual stance of the group of writers for whom the magazine *Tel Quel* has been a vehicle, he has remained an unclassifiable individualist. In 1930–31 he flirted with Surrealism, in the 1940s he was a Communist Party member and briefly edited its newspaper, but his major lifelong commitment has been to language itself. Language for Ponge is a living, functional force for order and sanity in a chaotic world. It is also a problematic instrument of moral responsibility, having intrinsic distortions and uncertainties which must be addressed if it is to contribute to human health. Imperfection of expression is the enemy, and in this sense a fundamentally classical impulse towards lucidity and precision characterizes his descriptive and analytical texts.

These influential texts break down genre distinctions, and they are highly self-referential. The creative process is its own justification, a kind of serious game with language, and the genesis and method of the work are frequently represented through metaphor within it, or clarified through a parallel notation: Ponge's *Proêmes* (1948), for example, 'expose the workings' of his best known volume, *Le Parti pris des choses* (1942).

Ponge enjoyed lecturing, often improvising to emphasize his view of language as interaction, as a significant act of construction involving the receiver. The reader's role in constructing a Ponge text is vital; the personal consciousness of the author is largely suppressed. The French language is a living organism with a continuity stretching back to Malherbe, and within which the creative act takes place and is then modified or superseded. Language is a vast network of responses to experience and its relativity, a participatory force that delineates and amplifies our awareness of the physical world. It is thus in itself a solution to the existential or, more precisely, phenomenological anguish of Roquentin in Sartre's *La Nausée*, and a celebration of human consciousness, which seizes contingency and enjoys it for its own sake.

His minutely detailed contemplation of objects has the effect of making us see them as if for the first time, as if they were being created before our eyes yet without overwhelming us. The element of anthropomorphism is strong. Metaphors and paradoxes, analogies and antitheses abound in a rich texture, with cunning and erudite word-play that exploits and brings back into 'play' all the half-forgotten etymological potential of words. What an object is not helps us to identify what it is.

Sound patterns and syntactic shape create a concrete 'equivalence' between the poem and its referent; this is not an imitative representation, but an equivalence to the *life* of the object, its dynamic effect on the senses. It has nothing in common with Apollinaire's *Calligrammes*.

In 'Rhétorique' (*Proêmes*) Ponge writes to a frustrated young poet, who suffers in the dominance other people's words seem to exert over his efforts at expression: 'Then it is that to teach the art of *resisting words* becomes useful, the art of saying only what we want to say, the art of doing them violence and subjugating them. In short, to found a rhetoric ... is an act of public welfare ... [It will save] those who can, strictly speaking, alter the face of things.'

Later works: numerous publications, many of the best of which are collected in *Le Grand Recueil* I & II (1961) and *Nouveau Recueil* (1967). *La Fabrique du pré* (1971) is another important work.

Les Mûres

Aux buissons typographiques constitués par le poème sur une route qui ne mène hors des choses ni à l'esprit, certains fruits sont formés d'une agglomération de sphères qu'une goutte d'encre remplit.

★

Noirs, roses et kakis ensemble sur la grappe, ils offrent plutôt le spectacle d'une famille rogue à ses âges divers, qu'une tentation très vive à la cueillette.

Vue la disproportion des pépins à la pulpe les oiseaux les apprécient peu, si peu de chose au fond leur reste quand du bec à l'anus ils en sont traversés.

★

Mais le poète au cours de sa promenade professionnelle, en prend de la graine à raison: "Ainsi donc, se dit-il, réussissent en grand nombre les efforts patients d'une fleur

Blackberries

On the typographic bushes formed by the poem along a road that leads neither beyond things nor to the spirit, certain fruits are composed of a cluster of spheres filled with a drop of ink.

★

Black, pink and khaki together in the bunch, they present the spectacle of an arrogant[1] family in its various ages, rather than a keen temptation to go gathering.

Given the disproportion of pips to flesh they have little value for the birds, so little remains essentially for them when the journey has been made from beak to anus.

★

But the poet in the course of his professional constitutional, rightly takes a leaf from their book: 'So it is then, he tells himself, that in great numbers the patient efforts of a most

[1]*la rogue*: fish roe (also a cluster of little spheres) used as bait.

très fragile quoique par un rébarbatif enchevêtrement de ronces défendue. Sans beaucoup d'autres qualités, – *mûres*, parfaitement elles sont mûres – comme aussi ce poème est fait.''

fragile flower succeed although shielded by a rebarbative tangle of brambles. Lacking many other qualities, – *ripe*, perfectly are they ripe – as this poem too is made.'

L'Orange

Comme dans l'éponge il y a dans l'orange une aspiration à reprendre contenance après avoir subi l'épreuve de l'expression. Mais où l'éponge réussit toujours, l'orange jamais: car ses cellules ont éclaté, ses tissus se sont déchirés. Tandis que l'écorce seule se rétablit mollement dans sa forme grâce à son élasticité, un liquide d'ambre s'est répandu, accompagné de rafraîchissement, de parfum suaves, certes, – mais souvent aussi de la conscience amère d'une expulsion prématurée de pépins.

The Orange

As in the sponge there is in the orange an aspiration to regain face after undergoing the ordeal of expression. But where the sponge always succeeds, the orange never: for its cells have burst, its tissues have torn apart. Whereas the peel alone flabbily regains its shape thanks to its elasticity, an amber liquid has spread, accompanied certainly by sweet coolness and scent – but often too by the bitter awareness of a premature expulsion of pips.

Faut-il prendre parti entre ces deux manières de mal supporter l'oppression? – L'éponge n'est que muscle et se remplit de vent, d'eau propre ou d'eau sale selon: cette gymnastique est ignoble. L'orange a meilleur goût, mais elle est trop passive, – et ce sacrifice odorant... c'est faire à l'oppresseur trop bon compte vraiment.

Mais ce n'est pas assez avoir dit de l'orange que d'avoir rappelé sa façon particulière de parfumer l'air et de réjouir son bourreau. Il faut mettre l'accent sur la coloration glorieuse du liquide qui en résulte, et qui, mieux que le jus de citron, oblige le larynx à s'ouvrir largement pour la prononciation du mot comme pour l'ingestion du liquide, sans aucune moue appréhensive de l'avant-bouche dont il ne fait pas se hérisser les papilles.

Must there be a preference between these two ways of failing to withstand oppression? – The sponge is merely muscle and is filled with wind, with clean water or dirty water as the case may be: this gymnastic manoeuvre is tawdry. The orange has better taste, but it is too passive, – and that scented sacrifice ... truly it plays too much into the oppressor's hands.

But it is not to have said enough of the orange to have recalled its particular way of scenting the air and of delighting its torturer. The glorious colouring of the resulting liquid must be stressed, which, more than lemon juice, compels the larynx to open wide for the articulation of the word as for the ingestion of the liquid, with no apprehensive pout at the front of the mouth where it does not ruffle the papillae.

Et l'on demeure au reste sans paroles pour avouer l'admiration que mérite l'enveloppe du tendre, fragile et rose ballon ovale dans cet épais tampon-buvard humide dont l'épiderme extrêmement mince mais très pigmenté, acerbement sapide, est juste assez rugueux pour accrocher dignement la lumière sur la parfaite forme du fruit.

Mais à la fin d'une trop courte étude, menée aussi rondement que possible, – il faut en venir au pépin. Ce grain, de la forme d'un minuscule citron, offre à l'extérieur la couleur du bois blanc de citronnier, à l'intérieur un vert de pois ou de germe tendre. C'est en lui que se retrouvent, après l'explosion sensationnelle de la lanterne vénitienne de saveurs, couleurs et parfums que constitue le ballon fruité lui-même, – la dureté relative et la verdeur (non d'ailleurs entièrement insipide) du bois, de la branche, de la feuille: somme toute petite quoique avec certitude la raison d'être du fruit.

And one remains wordless what's more to confess the admiration merited by the outer wrapping of the tender, fragile and pink oval ball in this dense moist blotting-pad whose epidermis, extremely thin but highly pigmented, acerbically savoury, is just wrinkled enough to catch the light with dignity on the perfect form of the fruit.

But at the end of a study that is all too short, carried out as roundly as possible, – we must come to the pip. This seed, in the form of a tiny lemon, presents on the outside the colour of the lemon tree's white wood, on the inside a green as of peas or a tender shoot. Within it are united, after the sensational explosion of the Chinese lantern of flavours, colours and scents that is the ball of fruit itself, – the relative hardness and the greenness (by no means entirely insipid) of the wood, of the branch, of the leaf: small, when all's said and done, though certainly the reason for being of the fruit.

Végétation

La pluie ne forme pas les seuls traits d'union entre le sol et les cieux: il en existe d'une autre sorte, moins intermittents et beaucoup mieux tramés, dont le vent si fort qu'il l'agite n'emporte pas le tissu. S'il réussit parfois dans une certaine saison à en détacher peu de choses, qu'il s'efforce alors de réduire dans son tourbillon, l'on s'aperçoit à la fin du compte qu'il n'a rien dissipé du tout.

A y regarder de plus près, l'on se trouve alors à l'une des mille portes d'un immense laboratoire, hérissé d'appareils hydrauliques multiformes, tous beaucoup plus compliqués que les simples colonnes de la pluie et doués d'une originale perfection: tous à la fois cornues, filtres, siphons, alambics.

Vegetation

The rain does not form the only hyphens between the earth and the heavens: another kind exists, less intermittent and much better woven, and whose fabric is not carried away by the wind however hard it shakes it. If sometimes it succeeds in a certain season in dislodging a few bits which it strives then to pound to dust in its eddying, we perceive in the final reckoning that it has dispelled nothing at all.

Looking more closely, we find ourselves now at one of the thousand doors of a huge laboratory, bristling with hydraulic apparatus of many forms, all much more intricate than the simple columns of the rain and endowed with an original perfection: all simultaneously retorts, filters, siphons and stills.

Ce sont ces appareils que la pluie rencontre justement d'abord, avant d'atteindre le sol. Ils la reçoivent dans une quantité de petits bols, disposés en foule à tous les niveaux d'une plus ou moins grande profondeur, et qui se déversent les uns dans les autres jusqu'à ceux du degré le plus bas, par qui la terre enfin est directement ramoitie.

Ainsi ralentissent-ils l'ondée à leur façon, et en gardent-ils longtemps l'humeur et le bénéfice au sol après la disparition du météore. A eux seuls appartient le pouvoir de faire briller au soleil les formes de la pluie, autrement dit d'exposer sous le point de vue de la joie les raisons aussi religieusement admises, qu'elles furent par la tristesse précipitamment formulées. Curieuse occupation, énigmatiques caractères.

It is precisely these instruments that the rain first meets, before it reaches the ground. They receive it in an abundance of small bowls, set out in great numbers at all levels of a greater or lesser depth, and emptying one into another down to those at the lowest stage, by which finally the earth is directly moistened.

Thus in their fashion they slow the downpour, and retain for a long time its fluid and its benefit for the earth after the meteorological event has vanished. Theirs alone is the power to make shine in the sunlight the shapes of the rain, in other words to display within the perspective of joy the formulations as religiously acknowledged as they were precipitately articulated by sorrow. A curious occupation[1], enigmatic characters.

[1]'*occupation*' suggests seizing and holding as well as work or activity; '*curieux*' can mean 'meticulous' and 'inquisitive'.

Ils grandissent en stature à mesure que la pluie tombe; mais avec plus de régularité, plus de discrétion; et, par une sorte de force acquise, même alors qu'elle ne tombe plus. Enfin, l'on retrouve encore de l'eau dans certaines ampoules qu'ils forment et qu'ils portent avec une rougissante affectation, que l'on appelle leurs fruits.

Telle est, semble-t-il, la fonction physique de cette espèce de tapisserie à trois dimensions à laquelle on a donné le nom de végétation pour d'autres caractères qu'elle présente et en particulier pour la sorte de vie qui l'anime... Mais j'ai voulu d'abord insister sur ce point: bien que la faculté de réaliser leur propre synthèse et de se produire sans qu'on les en prie (voire entre les pavés de la Sorbonne), apparente les appareils végétatifs aux animaux, c'est-à-dire à toutes sortes de vagabonds, néanmoins en beaucoup d'endroits à demeure ils forment un tissu, et ce tissu appartient au monde comme l'une de ses assises.

They grow in stature in proportion as the rain falls; but with more regularity, more discretion; and, by a kind of acquired strength, even when it falls no longer. And finally, water can still be found in certain inflated phials[1] that they form and wear with a blushing affectation[2], which we call their fruit.

Such, it seems, is the physical function of this kind of three-dimensional tapestry which has been named vegetation for other characteristics that it presents and in particular for the sort of life that animates it ... But I wanted primarily to insist upon this point: although the ability to accomplish their own synthesis and to engender themselves without being asked (as between the paving stones of the Sorbonne), connects the vegetative apparatus to the animals, in other words to all kinds of wanderers, nevertheless in many places they form a permanent fabric, and this fabric belongs in the world like one of its foundations.

[1]'*ampoules*': blisters, bulbs, flasks ... and a '*style ampoulé*' is an inflated literary style.
[2]'*affectation*': not only 'striving after effect' but also the assigning or appointing of someone to a position or task.

'Négritude': Senghor and Césaire

These two black poets, from Senegal and Martinique respectively, were instrumental in the development of francophone black poetry in the 1930s and '40s. Incorporating into their native culture the ambiguous influence of a European education (both came to Paris on scholarships), taking inspiration both from black American writers and from anti-colonialist and Marxist ideology, they formed and promoted the concept of '*Négritude*', or black consciousness, among African and Caribbean intellectuals. Both men later became elected leaders in their home countries, and both continued to blend poetry and politics in a remarkable way.

Léopold Sédar Senghor
(1906–)

Senghor was powerfully affected by the turbulent political and intellectual climate of Europe in the 1930s, while also struggling with his awareness that he had been uprooted from his culture and transplanted into a French tradition. In truth, however, the two already coexisted to a degree in his mind, for elements of African spirituality had mingled with Catholicism in his upbringing.

Drafted into the French army in 1939, he was captured and spent two years in a German POW camp, where he wrote quite prolifically. His wartime poetry seems to identify a moral strength in Africa that Europe has lost irrevocably. Repatriated on health grounds, he taught African languages in Paris, and his growing reputation as both poet and anticolonialist thinker was boosted further by Jean-Paul Sartre's interest and endorsement. Senghor was elected as a *député* for Senegal in 1945. Fifteen years later he became President of that country, and held the office until 1980.

Spirituality, poetry and politics know no boundaries for Senghor. His work is filled with a sense of African identity and destiny, but is also influenced by the Symbolist aesthetic of poetic penetration into a unity beyond appearances, and an African, passionate, erotic sensibility to the pulse of the natural world thus finds a French medium of expression.

Volumes: *Chants d'ombre* 1945, *Hosties noires* 1948, *Chants pour Naët* 1949, *Ethiopiques* 1956, *Nocturnes* 1961, *Lettres d'hivernage* 1973, etc.

Femme noire

Femme nue, femme noire
Vêtue de ta couleur qui est vie, de ta forme qui est beauté!
J'ai grandi à ton ombre; la douceur de tes mains bandait mes yeux.
Et voilà qu'au cœur de l'Eté et de Midi, je te découvre Terre promise, du haut d'un haut col calciné
Et ta beauté me foudroie en plein cœur, comme l'éclair d'un aigle.

Femme nue, femme obscure
Fruit mûr à la chair ferme, sombres extases du vin noir, bouche qui fais lyrique ma bouche
Savane aux horizons purs, savane qui frémis aux caresses ferventes du Vent d'Est
Tamtam sculpté, tamtam tendu qui grondes sous les doigts du Vainqueur
Ta voix grave de contre-alto est le chant spirituel de l'Aimée.

Black Woman

Naked woman, black woman Clothed in your colour which is life, in your form which is beauty! I have grown in your shadow; the softness of your hands shielded my eyes. And now in the heart of Summer and Noon, I discover you Promised Land, from the summit of a high and white-hot pass And your beauty strikes lightning deep into my heart, like the flash of an eagle.

Naked woman, mysterious woman Ripe fruit with firm flesh, dark ecstasies of black wine, mouth that makes my mouth lyrical Savanna with pure horizons, savanna trembling at the ardent caresses of the East Wind Sculpted tom-tom, taut tom-tom booming beneath the Victor's fingers Your solemn contralto voice is the spiritual song of the Beloved.

Femme nue, femme obscure
Huile que ne ride nul souffle, huile calme aux flancs de l'athlète, aux flancs des princes du Mali
Gazelle aux attaches célestes, les perles sont étoiles sur la nuit de ta peau
Délices des jeux de l'esprit, les reflets de l'or rouge sur ta peau qui se moire
A l'ombre de ta chevelure, s'éclaire mon angoisse aux soleils prochains de tes yeux.

Femme nue, femme noire
Je chante ta beauté qui passe, forme que je fixe dans l'Eternel,
Avant que le Destin jaloux ne te réduise en cendres pour nourrir les racines de la vie.

Naked woman, mysterious woman Oil rippled by no breath, calm oil on the athlete's flanks, on the flanks of the princes of Mali Gazelle with celestial limb-joints, pearls are stars on the night of your skin Delights of the play of the spirit, reflections of red gold on your iridescent silky skin In the shadow of your hair, my anguish is illumined by the suns of your eyes close by me.

Naked woman, black woman I sing your passing beauty, a form that I fix in Eternity, before jealous Destiny reduces you to ashes to nourish the roots of life.

Camp 1940

A Abdoulaye Ly

Saccagé le jardin des fiançailles en un soir soudain de tornade
Fauchés les lilas blancs, fané le parfum des muguets
Parties les fiancées pour les Isles de brise et pour les Rivières du Sud.
Un cri de désastre a traversé de part en part le pays frais des vins et des chansons
Comme un glaive de foudre dans son cœur, du Levant au Ponant.

Camp 1940

For Abdoulaye Ly

Ravaged the garden of betrothal in a sudden tornado evening Mown down the white lilacs, faded the fragrance of lily-of-the-valley Departed the fiancées for the Islands of breeze and the Rivers of the South. A cry of disaster has pierced from end to end the cool land of wines and songs Like a swordblade of thunder in its heart, from the East to the West.

C'est un vaste village de boue et de branchages, un village crucifié par deux fosses de pestilences.
Haines et faim y fermentent dans la torpeur d'un été mortel.
C'est un grand village qu'encercle l'immobile hargne des barbelés
Un grand village sous la tyrannie de quatre mitrailleuses ombrageuses.
Et les nobles guerriers mendient des bouts de cigarette
Ils disputent les os aux chiens, ils se disputent chiens et chats de songe.
Mais seuls Ils ont gardé la candeur de leur rire, et seuls la liberté de leur âme de feu.
Et le soir tombe, sanglot de sang qui libère la nuit.
Ils veillent les grands enfants roses, leurs grands enfants blonds leurs grands enfants blancs
Qui se tournent et se retournent dans leur sommeil, hanté des puces du souci et des poux de captivité.
Les contes des veillées noires les bercent, et les voix graves qui épousent les sentiers du silence
Et les berceuses doucement, berceuses sans tamtam et sans battements de mains noires

This is a vast village of mud and branches, a village crucified by two plague ditches. Hatreds and hunger ferment here in the torpor of a mortal summer. It is a great village encircled by the motionless hostility of the barbed wire A great village under the tyranny of four itchy machine-guns. And the noble warriors beg for cigarette-ends They fight the dogs for the bones, they fight each other for dream dogs and cats. But They alone have kept the frankness of their laughter, they alone the freedom of their soul of fire. And evening falls, a sob of blood that liberates the night. They watch over the big pink children, their big blond children their big white children Who turn and turn again in their sleep, possessed by the fleas of anxiety and the lice of captivity. The stories of black night-watches cradle them, and the solemn voices that espouse the pathways of silence And the lullabies gently, lullabies with no tom-tom and with no pounding of black hands – That will be for tomorrow,

– Ce sera pour demain, à l'heure de la sieste, le mirage des épopées
Et la chevauchée du soleil sur les savanes blanches aux sables sans limites.
Et le vent est guitare dans les arbres, les barbelés sont plus mélodieux que les cordes des harpes
Et les toits se penchent écoutent, les étoiles sourient de leurs yeux sans sommeil
– Là-haut là-haut, leur visage est bleu-noir.
L'air se fait tendre au village de boue et de branchages
Et la terre se fait humaine comme les sentinelles, les chemins les invitent à la liberté.
Ils ne partiront pas. Ils ne déserteront les corvées ni leur devoir de joie.
Qui fera les travaux de honte si ce n'est ceux qui sont nés nobles?
Qui donc dansera le dimanche aux sons du tamtam des gamelles?
Et ne sont-ils pas libres de la liberté du destin?

at siesta hour, the mirage of epic poems And the sun's ride over the white savannas with their limitless sands. And the wind is a guitar in the trees, the barbed wire is more melodious than harp strings And the roofs bend low listen, the stars smile with their sleepless eyes – Up there up there, their countenance is blue-black. The air grows tender in the village of mud and branches And the earth grows human like the sentries, the roads invite them to freedom. They will not go. They will not desert their fatigues nor their joyful duty. Who will do the shameful chores if not those who are born noble? Who then will dance on Sundays to the tom-tom sounds of cans? And are they not free with the freedom of destiny?

Saccagé le jardin des fiançailles en un soir soudain de tornade
Fauchés les lilas blancs, fané le parfum des muguets
Parties les fiancées pour les Isles de brise et pour les Rivières du Sud.

Ravaged the garden of betrothal in a sudden tornado evening Mown down the white lilacs, faded the fragrance of lily-of-the-valley Departed the fiancées for the Islands of breeze and the Rivers of the South.

Aimé Césaire
(1913–)

Césaire was a major exponent of Surrealism in its post-war prolongation, and perhaps the greatest of all francophone black poets. Absorbing for his own purposes the principles of the Surrealist aesthetic revolution, he sought to liberate language from what he saw as its strait-jacket as an instrument of colonialist oppression. The Surrealist aim is the transformation of language into the revelatory expression of a newly discovered inner life and relationship with external reality, but with Césaire the vision is specifically connected with cultural politics. The emergent identity of the Caribbean peoples speaks in his urgent, passionate rhythms and in his spellbinding images. They are images that surge from the subconscious, images that are often inexplicable in rational terms, and yet they impose themselves with an incontrovertible power. They also transcend the uneasiness that persists in his use of the language of the colonialist European society.

His innovative verse owes less to the orthodox French tradition than the relatively transparent output of Senghor, and certainly injects more new blood into the organism of poetry.

Having played a major role, with Senghor and Léon-Gontram Damas, in founding the '*Négritude*' movement, Césaire returned to Martinique as a teacher in 1939. His anticolonialism became increasingly radical during the Vichy administration of the French West Indies, and he developed the concept of cultural and political autonomy for black Caribbean states. In 1945 he was elected mayor of Fort-de-France and a *député* to the French parliament, initially (and a little uncomfortably) as a Communist and later as leader of the Martinican Progressive Party. His literary impact in France was delayed. By 1945 he was already well known in New York, where Breton had publicized his work, and where a number of translations of poems had appeared ahead of the publication of the originals in Paris.

Major volumes: *Les Armes miraculeuses* 1946, *Soleil cou coupé* 1948, *Corps perdu* 1949, *Cahier d'un retour au pays natal* (definitive edition) 1956, *Ferrements* 1959, etc. (Césaire then wrote increasingly for the theatre.)

N'ayez point pitié

Fumez marais

les images rupestres de l'inconnu
vers moi détournent le silencieux crépuscule
de leur rire

Fumez ô marais cœur d'oursin
les étoiles mortes apaisées par des mains merveilleuses
jaillissent
de la pulpe de mes yeux
Fumez fumez
l'obscurité fragile de ma voix craque de cités
flamboyantes
et la pureté irrésistible de ma main appelle
de loin de très loin du patrimoine héréditaire
le zèle victorieux de l'acide dans la chair
de la vie – marais –

telle une vipère née de la force blonde de l'éblouissement.

Have no Mercy

Steam swamp
the rupestral images of the unknown / divert towards me the silent twilight / of their laughter

Steam O swamp sea-urchin heart / the dead stars soothed by miraculous hands spurt / from the pulp of my eyes Steam steam / the brittle darkness of my voice crackles with cities / that blaze / and the irresistible purity of my hand summons / from afar from very far away from the genetic heritage / the victorious ardour of acid in the flesh / of life – swamp –

like a viper born of the golden power of blinding light.

Soleil serpent

Soleil serpent œil fascinant mon œil
et la mer pouilleuse d'îles craquant aux doigts des roses
lance-flamme et mon corps intact de foudroyé
l'eau exhausse les carcasses de lumière perdues dans le couloir sans pompe
des tourbillons de glaçons auréolent le cœur fumant des corbeaux
nos cœurs
c'est la voix des foudres apprivoisées tournant sur leurs gonds de lézarde
transmission d'anolis au paysage de verres cassés c'est
les fleurs vampires à la relève des orchidées
élixir du feu central
feu juste feu manguier de nuit couvert d'abeilles mon
désir un hasard de tigres surpris aux soufres mais l'éveil
stanneux se dore des gisements enfantins
et mon corps de galet mangeant poisson mangeant
colombes et sommeils
le sucre du mot Brésil au fond du marécage.

Serpent Sun

Serpent sun eye mesmerizing my eye / and the sea verminous with islands crackling in the fingers of flame-thrower / roses and my intact lightning-struck body / the water lifts up the carcasses of light lost in the unostentatious corridor / eddies of icicles halo the smoking hearts of crows / our hearts / it is the voice of tamed thunderbolts turning on their crevice hinges / transmission of anoles[1] to the landscape of broken glasses it is / the vampire flowers coming to relieve the orchids / elixir of the central fire / fire just fire night-mango covered with bees my / desire a chance encounter with tigers surprised in sulphurs but the stannous / awakening is gilded with childhood deposits / and my pebble body eating fish eating / doves and slumbers / the sugar of the word Brazil in the depths of the swamp.

[1] '*Anole*': lizard found in the West Indies and warmer areas of North and South America. Changes colour, and sometimes mistakenly called 'chameleon'.

Perdition

nous frapperons l'air neuf de nos têtes cuirassées
nous frapperons le soleil de nos paumes grandes ouvertes
nous frapperons le sol du pied nu de nos voix
les fleurs mâles dormiront aux criques des miroirs
et l'armure même des trilobites
s'abaissera dans le demi-jour de toujours
sur des gorges tendres gonflées de mines de lait
et ne franchirons-nous pas le porche
le porche des perditions?
un vigoureux chemin aux veineuses jaunissures
tiède
où bondissent les buffles des colères insoumises
court
avalant la bride des tornades mûres
aux balisiers sonnants des riches crépuscules

Perdition

we will strike the new air with our armour-plated heads / we will strike the sun with our wide open palms / we will strike the soil with the bare foot of our voices / the male flowers will sleep in the coves of mirrors / and the very armour of the trilobites / will be lowered in the half-light of forever / on tender breasts swelled with lodes of milk / and will we not pass through the porch / the porch of perditions? a vigorous path with veiny yellowings / tepid / where the buffaloes of unsubdued angers bound / runs / gulping the bridle of ripe tornadoes / amid the ringing cannas of rich twilights

Prophétie

là où l'aventure garde les yeux clairs
là où les femmes rayonnent de langage
là où la mort est belle dans la main comme un oiseau saison de lait
là où le souterrain cueille de sa propre génuflexion un luxe de prunelles plus violent que des chenilles
là où la merveille agile fait flèche et feu de tout bois

là où la nuit vigoureuse saigne une vitesse de purs végétaux

là où les abeilles des étoiles piquent le ciel d'une ruche plus ardente que la nuit
là où le bruit de mes talons remplit l'espace et lève à rebours la face du temps
là où l'arc-en-ciel de ma parole est chargé d'unir demain à l'espoir et l'infant à la reine,

Prophecy

where adventure keeps its eyes bright / where women radiate with language / where death is lovely in the hand like a bird in milk season / where the covert place gathers from its own genuflexion an extravagance of sloes that is more violent than caterpillars / where the agile marvel makes everything grist to its mill

where the robust night bleeds a swiftness of pure plants

where the bees of the stars stitch into the sky a ruche[1] more fiery than the night / where the sound of my heels fills space and raises against the grain the face of time / where the rainbow of my words is charged to unite tomorrow with hope and the infant with the queen,

[1]*piquer*: also to sting; *une ruche*: also a beehive. The word-play here defies translation.

d'avoir injurié mes maîtres mordu les soldats du sultan
d'avoir gémi dans le désert
d'avoir crié vers mes gardiens
d'avoir supplié les chacals et les hyènes pasteurs de caravanes

je regarde
la fumée se précipite en cheval sauvage sur le devant de la
  scène ourle un instant la lave de sa fragile queue de paon
  puis se déchirant la chemise s'ouvre d'un coup la poitrine
  et je la regarde en îles britanniques en îlots en rochers
  déchiquetés se fondre peu à peu dans la mer lucide de l'air
où baignent prophétiques
ma gueule
  ma révolte
    mon nom.

for having insulted my masters bitten the sultan's soldiers / for having groaned in the wilderness / for having screamed at my gaolers / for having invoked the jackals and the hyenas the shepherds of caravans

I watch / the smoke hurls itself like a wild horse to the front of the stage hems for an instant the lava of its brittle peacock tail then tearing its shirt suddenly lays open its chest and I watch it melt little by little into British islands into islets into jagged rocks in the lucid sea of the air / where bathing prophetically are / my face / my revolt / my name.

Tam-tam I

A Benjamin Péret

à même le fleuve de sang de terre
à même le sang de soleil brisé
à même le sang d'un cent de clous de soleil
à même le sang du suicide des bêtes à feu
à même le sang de cendre le sang de sel le sang des sangs
d'amour
à même le sang incendié d'oiseau feu
hérons et faucons
montez et brûlez

Tom-Tom I

for Benjamin Péret

on the very river of blood of earth / on the very blood of shattered sun / on the very blood of a hundred stabs of sunlight / on the very blood of the fire-beasts' suicide / on the very blood of ashes the blood of salt the blood of the bloods of love / on the very blazing firebird blood / herons and falcons / rise and burn

Ode à la Guinée[1]

Et par le soleil installant sous ma peau une usine de force et
d'aigles
et par le vent sur ma force de dent de sel compliquant ses
passes les mieux sues
et par le noir le long de mes muscles en douces insolences de
sèves montant
et par la femme couchée comme une montagne descellée et
sucée par les lianes
et par la femme au cadastre mal connu où le jour et la nuit
jouent à la mourre des eaux de source et des métaux rares

Ode to Guinea[2]

And by the sun equipping beneath my skin a factory of strength and of eagles / and by the wind elaborating its best-known thrusts over the salty outcrop of my strength / and by the blackness rising along the length of my muscles in soft insolences of sap / and by the woman lying like a mountain unsealed and sucked by the lianas / and by the woman with the unknown cadastre where day and night play mora[3] with spring

[1]In its original form, published in *Soleil cou coupé* (1948), this poem was longer and more diffuse. This condensed version appeared in *Cadastre* (1961), and has a more intense impact.

[2]Not literally the state of Guinea (despite the reference to the Fouta-Djallon, a mountain range in that country), at least in the poem's original version which predated the establishment of Guinea as an independent nation. At that stage Césaire was evoking the mythical Guinea of Caribbean culture, the African homeland which is the destination of the soul.

[3]*mora*: a hand game dating back to ancient Rome, similar to 'odds and evens' and 'scissors, paper, stone'.

et par le feu de la femme où je cherche le chemin des fougères et du Fouta-Djallon
et par la femme fermée sur la nostalgie s'ouvrant

JE TE SALUE

Guinée dont les pluies fracassent du haut grumeleux des volcans un sacrifice de vaches pour mille faims et soifs d'enfants dénaturés
Guinée de ton cri de ta main de ta patience
il nous reste toujours des terres arbitraires
et quand tué vers Ophir ils m'auront jamais muet
de mes dents et de ma peau que l'on fasse
un fétiche féroce gardien du mauvais œil
comme m'ébranle me frappe et me dévore ton solstice
en chacun de tes pas Guinée
muette en moi-même d'une profondeur astrale de méduses

waters and rare metals / and by the fire of the woman in which I seek the way to the ferns and to the Fouta-Djallon / and by the opening of the woman closed upon her yearning[1]

I HAIL YOU

Guinea whose rains smash from the gritty heights of the volcanoes a sacrifice of cows for a thousand hungers and thirsts of unnatural children / Guinea of your cry of your hand of your patience / we still have some arbitrary lands left to us / and when killed towards Ophir[2] they will have me ever mute / from my teeth from my skin let there be made / a ferocious fetish guardian of the evil eye / as your solstice shakes me strikes me and devours me / in each of your footsteps Guinea / wordless within myself with an astral profundity of medusae

[1]This line could be translated as: 'and by the closed woman opening upon her yearning'.
[2]*Ophir*: an ancient country famed for its gold and precious stones, mentioned several times in the Old Testament. Its precise location is uncertain, but it was probably on the Somali or Arabian coast.

André Frénaud
(1907–   )

As a poet, Frénaud was something of a late developer, and his very personal voice is largely uninfluenced by Surrealism. If anything, he is closer to the Existentialists in his constructive recognition that 'there is no paradise' (the title of one of his volumes), and that the search for meaning in life constitutes in itself the only meaning that life can have. Metaphysics can offer nothing more, despite man's incurable probing.

Born in an industrial area of Burgundy, he has lived mainly in Paris, working as a civil servant in railway administration. His pre-war poems and those written in captivity at a POW camp in Germany made a considerable impact in the 1940s with their tenderness and realism, their sense of passionate questing balanced by lucid irony, and since the war he has continued his search for an art of the possible in a world where fulfilment is elusive.

Volumes: *Les Rois Mages* 1943 (contains poems written 1938–43); *Il n'y a pas de Paradis* 1965 (poems 1943–60); *La Sainte Face* 1968 (poems 1938–66); *Depuis toujours déjà* 1970 (poems 1953–68); *Haeres* 1982 (poems 1969–81), etc.

Naissance

à Charles Singevin

La mer qui avait tant navigué, ma mer noire,
enfin s'est approchée de la terre ma mère,
la vieille depuis si longtemps d'avec moi séparée.

La frange, où l'œil du cheval hagard
perce à travers la crinière,
s'est aplatie sur les pierres et le sel.
O silence assourdissant de ce jour!
L'homme se relève hébété.
Une statue de marbre pur
s'éveille entre ses bras.

J'emporte ma naissance et je vais chez les hommes,
je chante.

Birth

for Charles Singevin

The sea that had done so much sailing, my black sea, has drawn close at last to the earth my mother, that old woman separated from me for so long.

The fringe, where the wild horse's eye bores through the mane, has sprawled itself on the stones and the salt. O deafening silence of this day! The man stands up in stupefaction. A statue of pure marble awakens in his arms.

I bear away my birth and I go among men, I am singing.

Maison à vendre

Tant de gens ont vécu là, qui aimaient
l'amour, le réveil et enlever la poussière.
Le puits est sans fond et sans lune,
les anciens sont partis et n'ont rien emporté.
Bouffe le lierre sous le soleil d'hier,
reste la suie, leur marc de café.
Je m'attelle aux rêves éraillés.
J'aime la crasse de l'âme des autres,
mêlée à ces franges de grenat,
le suint des entreprises manquées.
Concierge, j'achète, j'achète la baraque.
Si elle m'empoisonne, je m'y flambe.
On ouvrira les fenêtres... Remets la plaque.
Un homme entre, il flaire, il recommence.

House for Sale

So many people have lived here, who loved love, waking up and dusting. The well is bottomless and moonless, the old owners have gone and taken nothing away. The ivy is swelling in yesterday's sunlight, the soot and their coffee-grounds remain. I yoke myself to frayed dreams. I love the dross from others' souls, mingled with these garnet fringes, the seepage of failed ventures. Caretaker, I'll buy, I'm buying the dump. If it poisons me, I'll burn up in it. The windows will be opened ... Set the sign up again. A man comes in, he sniffs, he begins again.

Les Rois Mages

à Antoine Giacometti

Avancerons-nous aussi vite que l'étoile?
La randonnée n'a-t-elle pas assez duré?
Réussirons-nous enfin à l'égarer,
cette lueur au milieu de la lune et des bêtes,
qui ne s'impatiente pas?

La neige avait tissé les pays du retour
avec ses fleurs fondues où se perd la mémoire.
De nouveaux compagnons se mêlaient à la troupe,
qui sortaient des arbres comme les bûcherons.
Le Juif errant peinait, aux blessures bafouées.
Des fourrures couvraient le roi noir malade à mourir.
Le pasteur de la faim est avec nous,
ses yeux bleus éclairent son manteau d'épluchures
et le troupeau rageur des enfants prisonniers.

The Magi

for Antoine Giacometti

Will we go forward as fast as the star? Hasn't the journey lasted long enough? Will we manage in the end to mislay it, this gleam amid the moonlight and the animals, that shows no impatience?

The snow had woven the homeward lands with its melted flowers where memory is lost. New companions mingled with the band, emerging like woodcutters from the trees. The wandering Jew laboured with his ridiculed wounds. Furs covered the black king sick to the point of death. The shepherd of hunger is with us, his blue eyes light his coat of parings and the fretting flock of imprisoned children.

Nous allions voir la joie, nous l'avons cru,
la joie du monde née dans une maison par ici.
C'était au commencement. Maintenant on ne parle pas.
Nous allions délivrer un tombeau radieux
marqué d'une croix par les torches dans la forêt.

Le pays n'est pas sûr, les châteaux
se glissent derrière nous.
Pas de feu dans l'âtre des relais. Les frontières
remuent à l'aube sous les coups défendus.
Nos paumes qui ont brisé les tempêtes de sable
sont trouées par le charançon, et j'ai peur de la nuit.

Ceux qui nous attendaient dans le vent de la route
se sont lassés, le chœur se tourne contre nous.
Par les banlieues fermées à l'aube, les pays sans amour,
nous avançons, mêlés à tous et séparés,
sous les lourdes paupières de l'espérance.
La peur haletait comme une haridelle.

We were on our way to see joy, that's what we believed, the joy of the world born in a house in these parts. That was at the beginning. Now we do not speak. We were on our way to set free a radiant tomb marked with a cross by torches in the forest.

The land is not safe, the castles slip furtively behind us. No fire in the post-house hearths. Frontiers move in the dawn under forbidden blows. Our palms that broke sandstorms are riddled by the weevil, and I am afraid of the night.

Those who were expecting us in the wind on the road have grown weary, the chorus turns against us. Through the suburbs sealed at daybreak, the countries without love, we move onward, mingled with all and separate, under the heavy eyelids of hope. Fear was panting like an old nag.

Nous arriverons trop tard, le massacre est commencé,
les innocents sont couchés dans l'herbe.
Et chaque jour nous remuons des flaques dans les contrées.
Et la rumeur se creuse, des morts non secourus
qui avaient espéré en notre diligence.

Tout l'encens a pourri dans les boîtes en ivoire,
et l'or a caillé nos cœurs comme du lait
La jeune fille s'est donnée aux soldats,
que nous gardions dans l'arche, pour le rayonnement,
pour le sourire de sa face.

We will arrive too late, the massacre is under way, the innocents are lying in the grass. And every day we stir puddles in the tracts. And the murmur grows hollow of the dead men without succour whose hope had been in our speed.

All the incense has decayed in the ivory boxes, and the gold has curdled our hearts like milk. The girl has given herself to the soldiers; we were keeping her in the ark, for the radiance, for the smile of her countenance.

Nous sommes perdus. On nous a fait de faux rapports.
C'est depuis le début du voyage.
Il n'y avait pas de route, il n'y a pas de lumière.
Seul un épi d'or sorti du songe,
que le poids de nos chutes n'a pas su gonfler.
Et nous poursuivons en murmurant contre nous,
tous les trois brouillés autant qu'un seul
peut l'être avec lui-même.
Et le monde rêve à travers notre marche
dans l'herbe des bas-lieux. Et ils espèrent,
quand nous nous sommes trompés de chemin.

We are lost. We were given false reports. Right from the start of the journey. There was no way, there is no light. Merely a golden ear of corn brought out from a dream, which the weight of our falling could not swell. And on we go murmuring against ourselves, all three estranged as much as one man can be from himself. And the world is dreaming within our progress through the grass of sordid places. And they are hoping, when we have taken the wrong road.

Egarés dans les moires du temps, les durs méandres
qu'anime le sourire de l'Enfant,
chevaliers à la poursuite de la fuyante naissance
du futur qui nous guide comme un toucheur de bœufs,
je maudis l'aventure, je voudrais retourner
vers la maison et le platane
pour boire l'eau de mon puits que ne trouble pas la lune,
et m'accomplir sur mes terrasses toujours égales,
dans la fraîcheur immobile de mon ombre.

Mais je ne puis guérir d'un appel insensé.

Straying in the watered silks of time, the hard meanders enlivened by the smile of the Child, knights in pursuit of the elusive birth of the future that guides us like an ox-goad, I curse the venture, I would like to return towards home and the plane tree to drink the water of my well unclouded by the moon, and fulfil myself on my ever level terraces, in the motionless coolness of my shadow.

But I find no cure for a summons without sense.

Présence réelle

Excepté ton regard où je hais ma rencontre
excepté tes mains vides où mon front est resté
excepté ton attente harcelant mon désert
excepté nos nuits nos soleils d'égal ennui
excepté ta gorge excepté ton rire
excepté toi excepté moi
je t'ai trouvée j'ai confiance je te prends.

Real Presence

Except for your gaze where I hate meeting myself / except for your empty hands where my brow has remained / except for your expectation tormenting my wilderness / except for our nights our suns of equal tedium / except for your breast except for your laughter / except for you except for me / I have found you I am trusting I'll take you.

Assèchement de la plaie

Aux morts

La lune, pas délicate, ne touchait que des choses mûres.
La lune, à force, n'entend plus le chuchotement.

Le soleil a peur des sources rouies des yeux.
Le soleil s'apure au sommeil des évanouis.

Draining of the Wound

For the dead

The moon, not fastidious, touched only ripe things. The moon, in the long run, no longer hears the whispering.

The sun is afraid of the steeped sponge of the eyes. The sun clears its conscience in the sleep of the vanished.

Le feu a fait bombance dans les poils et les cuisses.
Le feu a fait sa part, il a lâché les cendres.

La terre a récuré tout ce qui reluisait.
La terre s'est requinquée et sourit d'une mousse.

L'eau molletonnée s'empâtait de graisses chaudes.
L'eau se mire, ne rougit plus, glisse, flâne.

Le vent a bien flairé que ce n'était pas propre.
Il va, jette les graines, le vent oublie les noms.

The fire has feasted in hair and in thighs. The fire has cut its losses, it has released the ashes.

The earth has scoured all that glittered. The earth has spruced itself up and smiles frothily.

The rowel-trimmed water was clogging with warm grease. The water admires its image, does not blush now, glides, lolls.

The wind has sniffed out its uncleanness. It moves on, casts the seeds, the wind forgets the names.

René Char
(1907–1988)

Perhaps the finest of the poets who first attracted major attention in the late 1930s and the 1940s, René Char now has considerable status in France, and is admired by many of the younger poets. He forms a vital bridge between Surrealism and the post Second World War generation, and has been seen with some justification as the poetic consciousness of his times.

He has spent much of his life in his native Vaucluse region, near Avignon. His vision is powerfully coloured by a strength of feeling for its people and for its mountainous, stormy and luminous landscape, which gave a special intensity to his wartime experience as a Resistance leader (known as Capitaine Alexandre).

Char had joined Breton's circle in 1929, and produced the classic Surrealist prose-poem 'Artine' the following year. His early work (up to *Le Marteau sans maître*, 1934) suffered at times from over-obscurity and self-consciousness, but it was also more dynamically condensed than the output of some of his colleagues, more concisely passionate.

These were qualities he carried into his poetry as it evolved after his unacrimonious break with the movement in 1937. Whether structured as free verse or as prose-poem or as aphoristic statement, his writing has a magnificent economy. It gives us a vibrant awareness of man's creative presence in the world, a dense fusion of emotion and lucidity, an open-armed welcoming of contradictory perceptions and impulses, and an assertion of human freedom and dignity against all forms of oppression and conformism. In Char the individual refuses to be morally paralysed by the hostility of the world, by human failure, or by the inevitability of death. He celebrates the instantaneity of experience, seeking what can be unveiled (*dévoilé*) within it, enjoying his own rebirth in each new act of perception and absorption, and perpetually straining out of the present towards the future rather than dwelling on the defunct past. Immobility is an enemy, and the self should never be safely gathered in (*recueilli*) as a static, inward-looking entity. Wholeness is neither possible nor desirable. Fulfilment is found in constant motion, in the unpredictable interaction of subject and object, and not in the fixing of some concept like 'beauty', on which creativity disintegrates. The last poem featured in this anthology, 'Front de la rose', can be taken as Char's *credo* in this respect.

Like the pre-Socratic philosopher Heraclitus whom he admires, Char finds much stimulation in what he has called 'the exalting union of opposites'. Paradox for him is a source of truth. The active, anti-mimetic, revelatory juxtaposition of conventionally incompatible terms derives of course from Surrealism and beyond (especially Apollinaire and Reverdy), and is a major element in Char's work. Like the Surrealists, he strives towards a harmonious condition in which all contradictions and obstacles to well-being are abolished in and through the adventure of language. This transcendence, crystallized in each poem for its duration but then sought once more, obliterates not only the banalities of reason and the self, but also the threat of entropy and the temptations of inertia. This well-being which stems, in his words, 'from having glimpsed the matter-emotion scintillating instantaneously regal', is offered to us in his spellbinding poetry. It rewards the effort to penetrate its outwardly 'difficult' compression of ideas, and sets the tone for a good deal of the poetry of the next generation.

Major works: *Arsenal* 1929, *Ralentir Travaux* (with Breton and Eluard) 1930, *Artine* 1930, *Le Marteau sans maître* 1934, *Moulin premier* 1936, *Placard pour un chemin des écoliers* 1937, *Dehors la Nuit est gouvernée* 1938, *Seuls demeurent* 1945, *Feuillets d'Hypnos* 1946, *Les Matinaux* 1950, *A une Sérénité crispée* 1951, *La Parole en archipel* 1962, etc.
Char continued to publish poems and texts until his death in 1988.

Artine

Au silence de celle qui laisse rêveur.

Dans le lit qu'on m'avait préparé il y avait: un animal sanguinolent et meurtri, de la taille d'une brioche, un tuyau de plomb, une rafale de vent, un coquillage glacé, une cartouche tirée, deux doigts d'un gant, une tache d'huile; il n'y avait pas de porte de prison, il y avait le goût de l'amertume, un diamant de vitrier, un cheveu, un jour, une chaise cassée, un ver à soie, l'objet volé, une chaîne de pardessus, une mouche verte apprivoisée, une branche de corail, un clou de cordonnier, une roue d'omnibus.

Artine

To her silence; she leaves us dreaming.

In the bed prepared for me were: an animal blood-tinged and bruised, the size of a brioche, a lead pipe, a gust of wind, a frozen seashell, a spent cartridge, two fingers of a glove, an oil-stain; there was no prison door, there was the taste of bitterness, a glazier's diamond, a hair, a day, a broken chair, a silkworm, the stolen object, an overcoat chain, a tame green fly, a branch of coral, a cobbler's nail, an omnibus wheel.

Offrir au passage un verre d'eau à un cavalier lancé à bride abattue sur un hippodrome envahi par la foule suppose, de part et d'autre, un manque absolu d'adresse; Artine apportait aux esprits qu'elle visitait cette sécheresse monumentale.

L'impatient se rendait parfaitement compte de l'ordre des rêves qui hanteraient dorénavant son cerveau, surtout dans le domaine de l'amour où l'activité dévorante se manifestait couramment en dehors du temps sexuel; l'assimilation se développant, la nuit noire, dans les serres bien closes.

Artine traverse sans difficulté le nom d'une ville. C'est le silence qui détache le sommeil.

Les objets désignés et rassemblés sous le nom de nature-précise font partie du décor dans lequel se déroulent les actes d'érotisme des *suites fatales*, épopée quotidienne et nocturne. Les mondes imaginaires chauds qui circulent sans arrêt dans la campagne à l'époque des moissons rendent l'œil agressif et la solitude intolérable à celui qui dispose du pouvoir de destruction. Pour les extraordinaires bouleversements il est

To offer a glass of water to a rider as he passes hurtling on a horse given its head on a racecourse invaded by the crowd implies an absolute lack of dexterity on both sides; Artine brought to the minds she visited this monumental drought.

The impatient man was perfectly aware of the order of dreams that would henceforth possess his brain, especially in the domain of love where devouring activity manifested itself generally outside sexual time; assimilation developing, in the blackness of night, in tightly sealed hot-houses.

Artine passes effortlessly through the name of a town. Silence releases sleep.

The objects designated and assembled under the name of exact-life[1] form part of the setting for the unfolding of erotic acts of *fatal consequences*, a daily and nocturnal epic. Hot imaginary worlds moving round ceaselessly in the countryside at harvest-time make the eye aggressive and solitude intolerable to the man who wields the power of destruction. For

[1]A play on the artistic term '*nature-morte*', a still-life drawing or painting.

tout de même préférable de s'en remettre entièrement à eux.

L'état de léthargie qui précédait Artine apportait les éléments indispensables à la projection d'impressions saisissantes sur l'écran de ruines flottantes: édredon en flammes précipité dans l'insondable gouffre de ténèbres en perpétuel mouvement.

Artine gardait en dépit des animaux et des cyclones une intarissable fraîcheur. A la promenade, c'était la transparence absolue.

A beau surgir au milieu de la plus active dépression l'appareil de la beauté d'Artine, les esprits curieux demeurent des esprits furieux, les esprits indifférents des esprits extrêmement curieux.

Les apparitions d'Artine dépassaient le cadre de ces contrées du sommeil, où le *pour* et le *pour* sont animés d'une égale et meurtrière violence. Elles évoluaient dans les plis d'une soie brûlante peuplée d'arbres aux feuilles de cendre.

La voiture à chevaux lavée et remise à neuf l'emportait presque toujours sur l'appartement tapissé de salpêtre lorsqu'il s'agissait d'accueillir durant une soirée interminable

extraordinary upheavals it is preferable all the same to rely entirely on them.

The state of inertia preceding Artine brought indispensable elements to the projection of striking impressions on to the screen of floating ruins: an eiderdown in flames hurled into the unfathomable abyss of shadows in perpetual motion.

Artine retained despite animals and cyclones an inexhaustible freshness. Out walking, it was absolute transparency.

Amid the most active depression the magnificence of Artine's beauty may surge up in vain, the curious minds remain furious minds, the indifferent minds extremely curious minds.

Artine's appearances went beyond the limits of those tracts of sleep where the *for* and the *for* are animated by an equal and murderous violence. They evolved in the folds of a burning silk peopled with trees whose leaves were ashes.

Washed and renovated, the horse-drawn carriage nearly always triumphed over the saltpetre-papered apartment when it was a case of playing host through an interminable evening to

la multitude des ennemis mortels d'Artine. Le visage de bois mort était particulièrement odieux. La course haletante de deux amants au hasard des grands chemins devenait tout à coup une distraction suffisante pour permettre au drame de se dérouler, derechef, à ciel ouvert.

Quelquefois une manœuvre maladroite faisait tomber sur la gorge d'Artine une tête qui n'était pas la mienne. L'énorme bloc de soufre se consumait alors lentement, sans fumée, présence en soi et immobilité vibrante.

Le livre ouvert sur les genoux d'Artine était seulement lisible les jours sombres. A intervalles irréguliers les héros venaient apprendre les malheurs qui allaient à nouveau fondre sur eux, les voies multiples et terrifiantes dans lesquelles leur irréprochable destinée allait à nouveau s'engager. Uniquement soucieux de la Fatalité, ils étaient pour la plupart d'un physique agréable. Ils se déplaçaient avec lenteur, se montraient peu loquaces. Ils exprimaient

the multitude of Artine's mortal enemies. The dead-wood face was particularly odious. The breathless race of two lovers haphazardly along the highways suddenly became a diversion sufficient to allow the unfolding of the drama once more, under the open sky.

Sometimes an unskilful movement made a head other than mine sink on Artine's breast. The enormous block of sulphur burned itself up slowly then, without smoke, presence in itself and vibrant immobility.

The book open on Artine's knees was readable only on dark days. At irregular intervals the heroes would come to learn the misfortunes which were once more to strike down upon them, the multiple and terrifying directions in which their irreproachable destiny was once more to be committed. Concerned solely with Fatality, they had on the whole an agreeable physique. They moved about slowly, showed little loquacity. They expressed their desires through broad

leurs désirs à l'aide de larges mouvements de tête imprévisibles. Ils paraissaient en outre s'ignorer totalement entre eux.

Le poète a tué son modèle.

unforeseeable movements of their heads. They seemed moreover to be entirely unaware of each other.

The poet has killed his model.

Migration

A Yvonne Zervos

Le poids du raisin modifie la position des feuilles. La montagne avait un peu glissé. Sans dégager d'époque. Toutefois, à travers les ossuaires argileux, la foulée des bêtes excrémentielles en marche vers le convulsif ambre jaune. En relation avec l'inerte.

La sécurité est un parfum. L'homme morne et emblématique vit toujours en prison, mais sa prison se trouve à présent en liberté. Le mouvement et le sentiment ont réintégré la fronde mathématicienne. La fabuleuse simulatrice, celle qui s'ensevelit en marchant, qui remporta dans la nuit tragique de la préhistoire les quatre doigts tabous de la main-fantôme, a rejoint ses quartiers d'étude, à

Migration

for Yvonne Zervos

The weight of the grape alters the position of the leaves. The mountain had slipped a little. Without setting off an epoch. And yet, across the clay ossuaries, the tread of excremental beasts in their progress towards the convulsive yellow amber. In contact with the inert.

Security is a fragrance. Drab and emblematic man still lives in prison, but his prison now finds itself free. Movement and feeling have reintegrated the mathematical catapult. The fabulous simulator, she who interred herself while walking, who carried back into the tragic night of prehistory the four taboo fingers of the phantom hand, has returned to her study

la zone des clairvoyances. Dans le salon manqué sur les grands carreaux hostiles, le dormeur et l'aimée, trop impopulaires pour ne pas être réels, accouplent interminablement leurs bouches ruisselantes de salive.

quarters, in the zone of clairvoyance. In the ill-conceived drawing room, on the great unfriendly tiles, the sleeper and the loved one, too unpopular not to be real, interminably couple their mouths streaming with saliva.

Commune Présence II

Tu es pressé d'écrire
Comme si tu étais en retard sur la vie
S'il en est ainsi fais cortège à tes sources
Hâte-toi
Hâte-toi de transmettre
Ta part de merveilleux de rébellion de bienfaisance
Effectivement tu es en retard sur la vie
La vie inexprimable
La seule en fin de compte à laquelle tu acceptes de t'unir
Celle qui t'est refusée chaque jour par les êtres et par les choses
Dont tu obtiens péniblement deci delà quelques fragments décharnés
Au bout de combats sans merci
Hors d'elle tout n'est qu'agonie soumise fin grossière
Si tu rencontres la mort durant ton labeur
Reçois-la comme la nuque en sueur trouve bon le mouchoir aride
En t'inclinant

Shared Presence II

You are in a hurry to write As if to catch up with life If this is so get in step with your sources Be quick Be quick to transmit Your portion of miracle of revolt of generosity In truth you are lagging behind life Inexpressible life The only one in the end that you consent to wed The one refused you every day by beings and by things From which you acquire laboriously here and there a few emaciated fragments After pitiless conflicts Beyond it all is merely agony subjugated crude ending If you meet death while you toil Receive it as the sweating neck welcomes the arid handkerchief Bowing down If

Si tu veux rire
Offre ta soumission
Jamais tes armes
Tu as été créé pour des moments peu communs
Modifie-toi disparais sans regret
Au gré de la rigueur suave
Quartier suivant quartier la liquidation du monde se poursuit
Sans interruption
Sans égarement

Essaime la poussière
Nul ne décèlera votre union.

you want to laugh Offer your submission Never your weapons You were created for rare moments Adjust disappear without regret At the will of sweet severity Quarter upon quarter the liquidation of the world continues Without interruption Without deviation

Let the dust swarm None will divulge your union.

Chant du refus

Début du partisan

Le poète est retourné pour de longues années dans le néant du père. Ne l'appelez pas, vous tous qui l'aimez. S'il vous semble que l'aile de l'hirondelle n'a plus de miroir sur terre, oubliez ce bonheur. Celui qui panifiait la souffrance n'est pas visible dans sa léthargie rougeoyante.

Ah! beauté et vérité fassent que vous soyez *présents* nombreux aux salves de la délivrance!

Song of Refusal

Début of the partisan

The poet has returned for long years into the nothingness of the father. Do not call him, all you who love him. If it seems to you that the swallow's wing has no mirror now on earth, forget that happiness. He who transformed suffering into bread is not visible in his glowing red hibernation.

Ah! may beauty and truth ensure your *presence* in great numbers at the salvos of liberation!

Les premiers instants

Nous regardions couler devant nous l'eau grandissante. Elle effaçait d'un coup la montagne, se chassant de ses flancs maternels. Ce n'était pas un torrent qui s'offrait à son destin mais une bête ineffable dont nous devenions la parole et la substance. Elle nous tenait amoureux sur l'arc tout-puissant de son imagination. Quelle intervention eût pu nous contraindre? La modicité quotidienne avait fui, le sang jeté était rendu à sa chaleur. Adoptés par l'ouvert, poncés jusqu'à l'invisible, nous étions une victoire qui ne prendrait jamais fin.

The First Moments

We were watching the swelling water as it flowed before us. It was effacing the mountain in one surge, ejecting itself from its maternal flanks. It was not a torrent yielding to its destiny but an ineffable creature whose word and substance we became. It held us loving on the all-powerful arch of its imagination. What mediation could have constrained us? Daily mediocrity had fled, blood spilled was restored to its heat. Adopted by openness, pumiced to invisibility, we were a victory that would never have an end.

A ★★★

Tu es mon amour depuis tant d'années,
Mon vertige devant tant d'attente,
Que rien ne peut vieillir, froidir;
Même ce qui attendait notre mort,
Ou lentement sut nous combattre,
Même ce qui nous est étranger,
Et mes éclipses et mes retours.

Fermée comme un volet de buis
Une extrême chance compacte
Est notre chaîne de montagnes,
Notre comprimante splendeur.

To ★★★

You have been my love for so many years, my vertigo faced with so much waiting, that nothing can age or chill; even what waited for our death, or fought us with measured skill, even what is alien to us, and my eclipses and my returns.

Closed like a boxwood shutter an extreme compact chance is our chain of mountains, our compressing splendour.

A ***

Je dis chance, ô ma martelée;
Chacun de nous peut recevoir
La part du mystère de l'autre
Sans en répandre le secret;
Et la douleur qui vient d'ailleurs
Trouve enfin sa séparation
Dans la chair de notre unité,
Trouve enfin sa route solaire
Au centre de notre nuée
Qu'elle déchire et recommence.

Je dis chance comme je le sens.
Tu as élevé le sommet
Que devra franchir mon attente
Quand demain disparaîtra.

I say chance, O my hammered love; each of us can receive the other's portion of the mystery without shedding its secret; and the pain that comes from another place finds its severance at last in the flesh of our unity, finds at last its solar way at the centre of our cloud which it tears asunder and begins again.

I say chance as I feel it. You have raised the mountain crest which my waiting will have to clear when tomorrow disappears.

L'inoffensif

Je pleure quand le soleil se couche parce qu'il te dérobe à ma vue et parce que je ne sais pas m'accorder avec ses rivaux nocturnes. Bien qu'il soit au bas et maintenant sans fièvre, impossible d'aller contre son déclin, de suspendre son effeuillaison, d'arracher quelque envie encore à sa lueur moribonde. Son départ te fond dans son obscurité comme le limon du lit se délaye dans l'eau du torrent par delà l'éboulis des berges détruites. Dureté et mollesse au ressort différent ont alors des effets semblables. Je cesse de recevoir l'hymne de ta parole; soudain tu n'apparais plus entière à mon côté; ce n'est pas le fuseau nerveux de ton poignet que tient ma main mais la branche creuse d'un quelconque arbre mort et déjà débité. On ne met plus un nom à rien, qu'au frisson. Il fait nuit. Les artifices qui s'allument me trouvent aveugle.

Je n'ai pleuré en vérité qu'une seule fois. Le soleil en

The innocuous man

I weep when the sun sets because he hides you from my sight and because I cannot find harmony with his nocturnal rivals. Although he is low and now without fever, impossible to resist his decline, to suspend his shedding of leaves, to wrench some desire still from his moribund glow. His departure melts you into his darkness as the silt of the bed soaks into the water of the torrent through the crumbling of the broken banks. Hardness and softness with differing elasticity then have similar effects. I cease to receive the hymn of your words; suddenly you appear no longer whole beside me; it is not the sinewy spindle of your wrist that my hand is holding but a hollow branch from a nondescript dead and already chopped tree. Nothing can be named now except the shudder. It is dark. The sparking fireworks find me blind.

I have wept in truth only once. The sun as it vanished had

disparaissant avait coupé ton visage. Ta tête avait roulé dans la fosse du ciel et je ne croyais plus au lendemain.

Lequel est l'homme du matin et lequel celui des ténèbres?

cut off your face. Your head had rolled into the pit of the sky and I no longer believed in tomorrow.

Which is the man of the morning and which the man of the darkness?

Front de la rose

Malgré la fenêtre ouverte dans la chambre au long congé, l'arôme de la rose reste lié au souffle qui fut là. Nous sommes une fois encore sans expérience antérieure, nouveaux venus, épris. La rose! Le champ de ses allées éventerait même la hardiesse de la mort. Nulle grille qui s'oppose. Le désir resurgit, mal de nos fronts évaporés.

Celui qui marche sur la terre des pluies n'a rien à redouter de l'épine, dans les lieux finis ou hostiles. Mais s'il s'arrête et se recueille, malheur à lui! Blessé au vif, il vole en cendres, archer repris par la beauté.

Brow of the Rose

Despite the window open in the long-vacant room, the aroma of the rose remains linked to the breath that was there. Once again we are without prior experience, newcomers, in love. The rose! Its field of movement would fan away even death's boldness. No gate to stand in the way. Desire surges up once more, malady of our moistureless[1] brows.

He who walks on the earth of rains has nothing to fear from the thorn, in places finite or hostile. But if he stops and gathers his thoughts, woe to him! Wounded to the quick, he flies into ashes, an archer recaptured by beauty.

[1]'*évaporé*' often means 'flighty, capricious, hare-brained, foolish ...' But such a term would be uncharacteristic for Char, and I think he has a more literal sense in mind.

INDEX OF FIRST LINES